Plan B Omnibus

a mystery and crime anthology

Darusha Wehm, editor

Plan B Omnibus
a mystery and crime anthology

Edited by Darusha Wehm

Published by in potentia press

ISBN 978-0-9917831-5-1

© 2014 Darusha Wehm

cover illustration by Meriel Jane Waissman

http://www.plan-b-magazine.com

Table of Contents

Table of Contents

> It's not their first choice: the events that precipitate a crime story, a mystery tale or a suspense yarn. Sure, there are a few career criminals around, but even their stories are the ones where it all goes pear-shaped and they need to try something else. The perfectly-executed scheme where nothing goes wrong doesn't make for an interesting story. We want to read about those times when criminals and hapless civilians are forced to resort to Plan B.

This was how I introduced *Plan B: Volume I*, the first anthology from Plan B Magazine. Two years and fifty-two stories later, it's still a good way to describe the tales you'll find here.

When I started Plan B Magazine, I wanted to showcase voices that possibly weren't being heard in other mystery magazines—perspectives, times and parts of the world that maybe weren't what people first think of when they think of crime stories. I also wanted to bring the best of North America and UK to a wider audience. In this omnibus volume of all the stories run on Plan B from Volumes One through Four, you'll find a wide mix of stories from light-hearted romps to harrowing realism, from the mean streets of LA to the kava-bars of Vanuatu.

I hope to continue to bring Plan B's unique mix of stories and by supporting the magazine through your purchase of this anthology, you'll help give these tales their voice.

Thank you. And enjoy the ride.

Darusha Wehm, editor
Plan B Magazine

The first Plan B story is a tale of felonies, fishermen and foodies, not for the faint of heart. Of course, the faint of heart wouldn't be here in the first place.

The Way to a Man's Heart
by Gary Cahill

DIVER JOE SLIPPED and slithered and stumbled through the pre-dawn dank, between the lobster pots. Less than an hour to sunrise, running way late, riding the edge the way binge drinking makes you—sure, one more, plenty of time. Until the clock runs out.

Rockport had been a dry town forever; archetypical, right down to the de rigueur liquor store just across the city line, decked out like a Christmas tree; winking, beckoning. In time, the law moved on to allow serving legal hooch with a proper dinner, and a looser attitude prevailed, in general, about getting gassed now and then. But touristy galleries, shops, and charm kept the place a heavy duty anachronism up the road on Cape Ann from wilder and hard-worn Gloucester, the historic fish town famous for courageous captains, storms of the century, and an indulgent undercover world of vice that would stroke-out most modern Americans. The natives learned to put on a happy face for visitors, but beneath the veneer in underground Gloucester the fleet's always in—without the spiffy uniforms. Along the entire Cape, like anywhere, human weakness and desire proffered piles of criminal cash, and Diver Joe was off to retrieve a to-the-gills green-stuffed duffel bag from the bottom of Rockport Harbor.

Mask, foot fins, small scuba tank and a cord-drawn navy blue ditty bag—Joe quick-changed at the edge of T-Wharf, his street clothes left on the rocks above the tide line. He submerged and moved away and down and aimed for the breakwater. At its outer reaches the harbor was no more than twenty-five feet deep, way less in close. The duffel was guaranteed waterproof to thirty, easy enough to find among the buoys he'd mapped in memory. Chuckling over maybe being arrested for drunk diving; seriously hoping the sun and the local watermen didn't rise too soon. Lobstering was permitted an hour before and after daylight, so a zippy in-and-out for Joe was paramount.

But staring into the business end of a pump action bird gun off the stern of an outboard-motored utility boat was unexpected. As was the kid behind the gunman with the fishing gaff, a tool somewhere between meat hook and harpoon. Behind the shotgun was Sammy Calley, mid-fifties, sea-weathered well past that, denim pants and jacket over a snap-up lumberjack, with his son, Gorton's-fisherman-yellow slickered Davey, holding the whale gutter like a bayoneted rifle. Already balding at twenty, there was a great darkness behind Davey's eyes and no fear or regret in seeing dead things in front of them. Sammy kicked over a rope so Diver Joe didn't need to keep treading.

"Diving's illegal in Rockport Harbor, and plenty other places 'round here, 'cept sometimes if you're working on a boat," sounded Sammy's New England-*achusetts* twang, accent ludicrously over the top, hard-angled arrogance amplified by having the upper hand. It played like a north of Boston reading of *Deliverance*, or *Cool Hand Luke*. "You weren't planning a little nightshift dirty work on my lobster boat, were ya? More than enough trouble catching those bottom bugs and tryin' to sell 'em to city markets when nobody's got the proper money anymore. Barely make a fuckin' dime, and you're down there messing me up, yankin' my boat out from under me? Sabotage? That it?" Joe knew this guy didn't believe that. Salty'd seen the bag, if not while cruising the harbor then obviously now, tethered to Joe's midsection.

Diver Joe started to tell him, making more sense than either Calley could grasp.

"Listen, you know I wasn't screwing with anybody's boat. There's the bag. I had to do it and not be seen, it's going somewh—"

"Whoa, whoa, nothing's going nowhere, and ... what's your name again, there, Flipper?"

"Joe. You've seen me around."

"Yep, yes, Joe the Diver, up from Florida early in the summer. Tanned and blonde. Made yourself useful around town, I know, fittin' in real nice. What's in the bag, Diver Joe? And what a bag, my, my. Where d'ya get something so rough and ready?"

Joe, trying to keep it civil, "Northwest somewhere ... Oregon, maybe? Made for mountaineering, for some reason waterproof to 10 meters, 10 yards, whatever." Grinning. "I don't know how many fathoms."

Sammy didn't crack a smile. Apparently not a laughing matter.

Insistent. "What's in the bag, Joe?" Quick, Davey with a half-lunge, Sammy's left hand holding back his kid. "Show us what's inside the bag, or Davey's gonna show us what's inside you."

Joe was still in the water, the bag on the deck, waiting to be flayed, but Davey seemed to admire the thing as he opened the seals and the zippers and freed well into six figures, banded grands and five-Cs and on down, piles of it.

The hoarse awed whisper was Sammy's. "How much?"

"Three hundred thousand, a little over. Don't know exactly."

It looked like six billion.

Diver Joe knew where this was going, tried to head it off with the truth.

"Listen, this is not local. It's about Rhode Island, you know what I mean? Providence? Familiar with what goes on in Providence all these years? With who's waiting for this?" Joe watched the money going back into the bag, gun barrel at the bridge of his nose. Careful.

"*Listen to me*, this is the real deal. I was planted here for this. We dunked it to cool it off, and now it's—"

"We, huh?" The bag held too much to allow Sammy to think straight. "Who's we? An army's comin' to bail you out, escort all this to the bigwigs in the million dollar suits, am I right? Please, you're all alone here."

"Not for long. Up from Connecticut and New York, tonight. They're both in on this, and we're responsible, *severely* responsible, for getting this to—"

"Both? Both? There's gonna be only *two* of them trying to ride this out of here?"

The gun shook in his hands. "Break my back when the money's good, now I'm breakin' it when the money's for shit, and if you think this God-sent whorin', gamblin', drug money's leavin' my hands with only *two* of *anybody*—"

"Either one's always been enough, from what I hear. We're meeting on Bearskin Neck after everything shuts down tonight. Wise up. Just let it go, or bring me over there with the duffel and arrange something, work it out. Nobody in charge ever wants a mess, any attention. They might settle with you. Within reason."

Joe didn't sense any recognition of reality, much less reason, with the Calley family. He tried to not sound desperate. "You take this, you run, they'll find you. These guys, some other guys, doesn't matter, they'll get you and your son." Worth a shot mentioning the kid.

"Oh, I guess we'll need to meet the tough guys over on the Neck. But I don't think Diver Joe Makes Three is going to happen."

A train out of New York, running on the New Haven line, stopped at Norwalk and passengers stepped off, one with an illegit name for a bastard boy. Mom called him Johnny Ray after her favorite '50s cloudy-eyed balladeer, and the Connell thing was pasted on, JonRay knew, to obscure his parentage. No father ever around that he could remember, but he'd always been treated with deference in the city, respect he assumed reflected some serious wiseguy's tryst leading to his appearance on Earth. Having no idea if he was Italian enough to ever be a made man, or full on Irish, or even just a little Azorean, he chose to honor a roughhewn appreciation for street food and big flavor by identifying himself as "Gourmandish", eating his way, *con brio*, through the local cuisines everywhere he was "assigned", as they called it—barely gaining a pound, loving every bite. JonRay was looking for a starchy lump named Glen.

Not his real name either, but a mutation of Geraldo Leonardo Simone, everyone hoping for his sake the Geraldo part wasn't after the TV talk show guy, but knowing better. Glen had the Town Car, found JonRay, and they got started, heading to a rendezvous at Rockport, Massachusetts. It was early afternoon, and JonRay was stoked.

Ready.

Set.

Although a faithful trencherman, he'd skipped breakfast.

Go.

"Oh, man, before we leave town, Swanky Franks, whadaya say? Couple o' dogs, real vampire killers, then hit the road, got plenty of time, and they're—"

"We just got in the car and you're talkin' about hot dogs? Vampire killers? What the hell ... *what?*"

JonRay, perplexed. "Garlic, in droves. Swanky's is not just some hot dog dump. In fact, Connecticut's kind of a happy hot dog hunting ground. Blackie's in Cheshire, Rawley's, I mean Paul freakin' Newman ate at Rawley's, oh, and Super Duper Weenie, exit 25, off Route 95—"

"Four fuckin' hot dog joints in 30 seconds? This how it's gonna go? You know, I heard about you. They *warned* me. Look, I'm in with you and Florida blondie on a delivery ..." He waited. Dramatically. "... but without all this one from column 'A' shit," and he waited again on his leftover 1960s' laugh line. Hadn't been funny then.

JonRay's mood was dampened. A little. He hoped side-splittin' Glen didn't have a million of 'em.

"Well, listen, you can't deny the pizza, some of the greatest in the world is in New Haven. Man, since the '30s, Pepe's and Sally's, the Spot, and Modern, there's a Pepe's right here in Fairfield now, and what's that other new one over—"

Glen was adrift, trying to understand, a renegade among Italians, being what used to be called a "meat and potatoes man"; way past well-done and boiled plain, respectively.

"Jesus. Bread dough with whatever you got sittin' around put on top, right? Basically? It's all spiced up and you get it with burned edges sometimes and—" Oh my God, Glen, please, already JonRay could hardly take any more.

What a dope.

There must be something. Ice cream? I scream, you scream ... forget it. White Farms,—ooooh, White Farms—right where they were headed; their black raspberry would be lost on this guy. Doughnuts; Coffee An' in Westport versus New York's Doughnut Plant? In the city Mark's got the edge with organic ingredi... forget it. Aaaah, ace in the hole, seafood. Fried clams, even better on Cape Ann than Cape Cod, oysters, those sweet, tiny Maine shrimp, so many places ... forget it. This guy's benchmark for fried fish was that finned scaly cardboard at the local deli every Friday, just like Mom used to buy when she thought the Church was still forcing it down your throat. Christ almighty already. Just deadhead to Rockport, leave Glen to his white bread double mayo on a buttered dinner roll or whatever, and see if anybody at the luncheonette ever found the old recipe for that butter-creamy clam chowder. Best ever, anywhere. Two years ago a waitress promised she'd look.

And the lobster place on Bearskin Neck, Moore's. Oh, man. Then just sit back, wait out the twilight, the evening, the last straggling tourists, meet with Joe and his duffel bag and baby that money all the way into Big Daddy's arms, back down in Providence.

That is, meet with Joe up past the strudel place, and just sublime it is, stall a little bit leaving town until it opens early in the morning, grab a white bakery boxful for the road. Hey, never know when you'll be by here again. Golden opportunity. Really shouldn't pass it up.

Glen showed concern for his teammate. "Ah, sorry. Jesus Christ. And I should come up with another God to swear on."

JonRay was not in the mood anymore. "How's Yahweh? Ganesha? Shiva?"

"What?"

"Oh, just swear, go ahead. Christ. That's right. Christ."

"See? See what I mean? JonRay, I think I'll just call you 'Hungry' the rest of the trip. No, you know what? 'HungRay', what with your name and all. Yeaaah."

JonRay was hoping Glen got his own filthy joke, though it seemed unlikely. He tried.

"Whoa, come on, the ladies love me, but you're embarrassing me here. I know lesser men envy *real* men, but... "

Glen stared ahead, looked left, checked the rearview, merged left, looked straight ahead again.

Just driving. Not a word.

Hopeless. You know what?

Forget it.

The phone call was less than comforting; an hour late, gruff, grumbling, and not Diver Joe on the other end. Joe was sick, no, couldn't talk, but he had a carry bag he needed delivered to some friends, in town for the salt air and stunning sunsets. Just trying to do the right thing, be on the Neck after it shuts down.

Click.

What the hell.

The brevity left more time to pointlessly triple check their loaded 9s, and dwell a little on the rocking sundown they'd just witnessed. People paid a lot to bed-and-breakfast near Pigeon Cove and watch the day drop off a granite coastline into open water. Worth every penny, thought JonRay.

"Worth every dime," said Glen.

Close enough.

Heavy, thick, warm for October, fog and mist and dew points giving after-midnight Bearskin Neck the movie look of East London, Whitechapel—home of the Ripper. Soles sucking up wetness, kissing the dark with every step toward land's end, where the breakwater jutted out to confront the open Atlantic invading the stony harbor. Jon-Ray to the left, Glen the right, guns pocketed, walked toward the traffic turnaround where the stores and restaurants stopped and the road fell away on each side to popweed, sea moss, and water lapping at the angled rocks. Some days you could watch terns and gulls dump clams and crabs over the edge to crack open the shells. Smart little bastards.

Davey got the drop on JonRay, junior pointing a javelin with a sickle on the side, apparently designed to scare you to death before you bled out, just to be sure. Glen faced the more understandable bird gun in the hands of a jean-clad human weathervane, shifting the barrel back and forth in front of him, guarding the duffel bag behind him. For now it's hands up. They'd move for their hardware soon enough.

JonRay called out to Sammy Calley across the street. "How come no Joe on the phone? Something wrong with his throat?" And looking dead ahead at the blade and the kid, saw Davey's buried eyes twinkle, like stars in blackest outer space. "Listen, you caught Joe hauling the bag, you know what's up. You certainly know this is not gonna buy the beach house in ... Manila, or wherever." Jeez, that was smooth, why not Baghdad? Or that acid dump town in China, make it truly appealing, you dunce? "This is going to some importan—"

"Yeah, I heard it. *Heard ... it ... allow.*" Sammy aiming higher, closer to Glen with the gun. He called over to JonRay.

"Gonna be a finder's fee for my services here, know what I mean? Too much luck to turn my back on, so let's figure how to explain Joe Cousteau's actions. Some money's gonna be gone and we're gonna blame Diver Joe. Say he snatched it, took off, now here's me and my boy to follow through best we can, doin' the right thing. Certainly don't want no trouble down in Providence, no way. We'll bring a good bit back." Yeah, keep it honest. Like us.

Glen was itching. "You and your boy. Who are you guys anyway, John Wayne and Captain Ahab?"

"I'm Sammy, he's Davey, and let's keep it straight, you mouthy scumbag. We're gonna wash this filthy money off your hands. You and Dirty Harry over there."

"What, I'm Dirty Harry?" A major compliment. "Then you know how this is gonna turn out."

And Glen. "Wow, Sam and Dave, the Bluefish Brothers, the *Lemon Sole* Men, you guys know that shrimp boat song?" Sammy moved first.

And before Glen had his automatic anywhere near out and aimed, Sammy flipped his shotgun barrel back into a two-hand grip and bashed the hardwood stock into the left of Glen's face, cheek shattered, teeth knocked loose, the greasy-phlegm flow of a garbled wounded night bird screech drooling to the pavement, and as Glen did a soft-shoe stagger toward the edge, Sammy wound up and launched another huge whack and crack that caught Glen leaning and dancing and sent him over. He hit bottom on the back of his neck, driving his head face first into his chest. He was broken dead on the rocks before the giant awful sound stopped reverbing around the harbor, bouncing from stone to wharf to water.

There had not been the alarming report of a scattergun, breaking the hush of night in this sleepy place. And with little notice taken, it all soon faded, to nothing.

Davey was ready. He followed Dad's orders. "Get down there and get him in the boat, take him out." A speed-jacked monkey-Davey clamber scrambled down to Glen, yanked him over into a motored skiff, puttered toward the break, and used his fishing gaff, over and over, to open up wide and make certain Glen would not come bobbing to the surface if the little arm-and-leg anchors broke loose.

JonRay walked toward Sammy, looked over. "Lotta sharks around here I suppose?"

"If they can really smell only one drop of blood in a million drops of water? Guess we're gonna find out."

"So, what's the plan here, Clyde, or is it Dillinger? I'm way late making this phone call and any respectable mobster anywhere will kill you over ten grand and a missed call, much less a sack like this. And by the way, much less means what, exactly? How much you taking?"

"Listen, John." Well, at least he almost got the name right. "Mind your own goddamn business here, and how much is *none of* your business."

"I need to know all the particulars, jack-off. I need to make them believe you told me a square story when we got up here and you said Joe took off with fistfuls of cash and Glen got ... well, what about Glen? Where is he? Settle down to do some farmin'? The new harbormaster, is he? Found a good hearted woman and decided to—"

"*Stop it* ... stop it. I get it. I'm shakin', OK?" And he was. "If I still smoked I'd be doin' 'em all right now."

JonRay smiled. You want to smoke I'll cram twenty down your throat and torch 'em.

Maybe later. .

"Sammy? You know what a dung heap you and Davey the Knife stepped in? Up to your eyes, and now you've got to crawl out. I'm calling. Now. And don't be leaning in over the phone, 'cause if they smell something fishy ... ah, sorry." Oh, screw sorry. Hey Sammy, first-time crime, aren't you glad you got your feet wet?

That one's for funnyman Glen.

"How much you takin', Sammy?"

Mr. Del would answer. DellaVerde. Perhaps you haven't heard of him, for although he cuts a striking figure it is a low profile. That famous logo with the marionette on strings, unseen hands manipulating the action? DellaVerde gets the puppeteer the gig. Books the room. Waters down the whiskey.

Owns the club.

And turns out the lights.

Won't ever see a cell. Left standing, while the rest take the fall.

He rarely gets personally involved. But he was right there to accept the phone from Andy.

"Mr. Connell, is it? We've met before, you remember."

"Yes, Mr. Del, a beautiful seafood dinner on Federal Hill, the old neighborhood."

To the point, darkly. "And does familiarity truly breed contempt,

Mr. Connell? How long need I wait for your call? How long do I wait for *anyone's* call, other than too long? But I know *you*, and I know of you from ... others. This is not your way. Shall I assume something's *changed* with the original plan?"

JonRay, looking at Sammy, nodding, smiling, "*Yes*, that's *right*. Ah, nothing's as it was. That was a long time ago."

Mr. Del tried the obvious. "How many? Two?"

"Well, yes, but he is shorter." Added a little laughter.

"One, then. All right, give me the new story. Then tell him I said the meet is at the laborers' union hall, upstairs, quiet, out of the way, but you turn me down, very respectfully, *very gently* Mr. Connell, tell him you're looking after his safety, and we'll agree on a homey tavern near the water, good pizza, we're adding on a room or two, and we'll talk in the work area. How long, Mr. Connell?"

"We're leaving right away." He worked in their names. "Mr. Sam Calley and his son Dave came upon this mess and when me and Glen Simone arrived—"

"You said only one other."

"Yes, only Mr. Calley."

"And Mr. Simone is making this trip?"

"No, sir."

Three beats, exhaled. "Is Joe making this trip?"

JonRay thought, man, don't give it away to Sammy, and said, "Noooo, sir. No."

Low breathing, steady, maintaining, then careful directions to the tavern/pizza joint/construction site.

Halting.

"Tell him ... what I told you."

Terse.

"Bring the bag. And bring the bagman."

JonRay drove the Town Car, Sammy and JonRay's 9 riding shotgun, silent all the way save for Sammy rehearsing his speech. JonRay made it clear he'd put the lobsterman in the middle, and let him claw his way out. Sammy had it down; lay it off on Diver Joe making a run for it with a big cut, JonRay and Glen stumbling in, the Calleys trying to set it right. Oh, with Davey staying home tonight, always work to do, it's so hard these days, and Glen hunting for Joe, because, well, all that missing money. The tavern was easy to find, even in the dark, a light left on in the building proper, others burning in the unfinished annex to the side. Tires on the gravel drive announced their arrival.

"Sammy."

"What?"

"No gun."

He left it, and they stepped in through split plastic sheeting.

The room was prepped for company with a cobbled plywood desk, two empty visitors' chairs in front, one left, one center, and another throning DellaVerde, still enough shiny slate hair to sweep back nicely, top streaked, sides nearly solid cream with a silver current running; so complex for what's really just black and white. Charcoal suit, burgundy vest, eyeballing JonRay all the way. JonRay had seen this set-up before, and stepped lively to the left-side chair as Mr. Del waved at him to sit. The rest of the place was a work in progress; raw wood, saw horses, Sheetrock and, JonRay noticed, a couple too many drop cloths. Mr. Del nodded and Sammy edged up to the table with the duffel.

"Just a moment, Mr. Calley. Andy, please, a nice red. Nothing too fancy, *da tavola*, you know, but not like that piss in a basket. Something easy, no pressure. Sometimes a table wine is all you need, yes, Mr. Calley?"

The bottle arrived, with three glasses. JonRay couldn't see the label; might be from France, Italy, Chile, or New Jersey for that matter. Mr. Del raised a hand to hold off opening it just yet.

"The bag, and your story, Mr. Calley."

"Call me Sammy, please."

Mr. Del looked at him. Not moving. Until he opened the duffel, and Andy started counting.

"I caught the other one bringing this up out of the harbor, it's illegal to dive there, and I stopped him. It's illegal. And me and my son, we got him over to T-Wharf and saw what he had, and he said he was takin' off with what was comin' to him and all, before two others, this gentleman John right here, and—"

"Yes, Mr. Calley, where is Glen? He knows he should be here. He's important in this."

"Hunting down that Joe, I think, must've took ... *taken* off on his trail. Joe told me what this all was, and who the two gentlemen coming to Rockport were, and—"

"So Joe didn't take it all, he left the rest for you, to buy your silence if you could get away with it? Is that right?" Mr. Del's hands were steepled in front of his chin. "But you knew what you were getting into if you tried that. And so we have here how much, Andy?"

Sammy sat down in the centered chair, uninvited. Mr. Del's hands went to the table, fingers splayed. He stared.

And Andy, not quite done, said "Almost there, Mr. Del, but around two hundred, little over."

DellaVerde's face reddened, then darkened, as an internal clock rolled back to a time when he was less refined and reasoned, more coarse and wild.

Andy backed off.

"So, Joe doesn't take it all, and simply dust you and your son, but covers his traitorous behavior by leaving the large end with you, and you bring that in to get yourself out from under because it's more than what's missing?"

A wave, rolling, deep blue, sad.

Louder.

"You think any of our people would run with that much, with New York and Connecticut in with us? With the long history of our connections up and down the seaboard, Mr. Calley? Does it seem to you that anyone would do that?" DellaVerde relaxed, settled, lowered his shoulders. He called Andy to open the wine, rose up from his chair, knees flexed, reached to read the label. Calley was sheet white and wide-eyed. Andy, experienced, played it halfway.

"So, Joe did this, yes? Joe." Three beats, a breath. "I brought him up," choking, struggling to continue, "... *ahh* ... brought him *here*, from Florida. He worked for us. For me. And now you're telling me *Joe* did this," all the way out of the chair now. Pained, welling. "Me like a father to him, my nephew, my beautiful sister's son, did *this* to me?" Three unseen guys with guns would make sure Sammy went nowhere, but he wasn't moving. DellaVerde flexed his knees again, still reading the label.

His hand slid up to the neck and the bottle, like a tennis racket, mashed Sammy Calley's head, knocked him to his right, broke him open, bleeding, snotting, crying onto an incredibly well-placed drop cloth. Location, location.

JonRay was impressed. And the wine was obviously from New Jersey.

"JonRay, where's Glen?"

Sammy's wimpering was already annoying.

"Gone. He's over, Mr. Del."

"And Joe."

"I don't know. We never saw him or heard from him. The kid had that look and the tools, though. That's a little rough I said that. I'm sorry."

"That's all right. Mr. Calley will most certainly tell me before he dies. Some people will go up to Rockport to find Joe and finish off the Calleys." Sammy wailed and DellaVerde would have kicked that yapper shut but for his fine Italian shoes. Someone else provided a heel to the teeth, and JonRay finally saw the three guys in the shadows. Waiting. Ah, well ....

"Quite a mess we have, Mr. Connell," said Mr. Del, calming. "Often these failures are wiped from memory from the top down; make just a bit *more* mess, break out the hoses and wash *everything* away. You know that, don't you? And here you are."

"Yes, I know how ... it usually goes."

"Well this is ..." backhanding the air, "*unusual*, particularly because it's not going to end that way. I appreciate all you've done. Thank you for bringing the lobsterman to me. We'll declaw and split and gut him before we boil him. Although you'll certainly tell me steaming in sea water is the only way. Your reputation precedes you."

"Yes, sir, Mr. Del. Thank you. I hope ... thank you." Stopped sweating, started breathing again.

"Here's a key card, a new hotel up around the way, toward the city center. A small suite, nice, not the Ritz. I'll be sending over a beautiful red clam pie, garlic, fresh basil, charred edge, somewhere between Pepe's and what you get in Trenton, just fabulous. And three or four of those Boston lagers? Or would you prefer an unassuming red? Not this wine on the table; *I'm* drinking this. And I'm still going to need the bottle." Indeed. With his good fortune, JonRay had forgotten

Sammy, leaking on the plastic, facedown on the floor. "My driver will have the Town Car, and when you're ready tomorrow, whatever time, he'll take you back to New York. And don't worry, there'll be no one-way detour deep into the woods. You're going home. I'll call ahead, let everyone know of your ... triumph over circumstance."

Nothing caps a skin-of-your-teeth, nail-biting adventure like ...

Dessert.

And JonRay knew just where to go.

"Lee," whose name was Lido, actually, "whadaya say, sweet tooth's got me. Listen, off 95, exit 24, Route 58 up to Bethel, like, fifteen, twenty miles. Oh my God, Dr. Mike's. Ever been? Last stop on the ice cream jubilee train, my man. What? *Jubilee Train*; great song. By Dave Alvin? With the Blasters? It's like a rockin' *People Get Ready*, the train to paradise. Oh, come on, don't be like Glen. Pain in the ass, he was. I mean it's terrible what happened to him. No great loss to the culinary world. Yes! All right, Lee, I'm buyin'. Any flavor you want, but you must add a scoop of the mystical Chocolate Lace, *say hallelu-jah*, and ..." it was almost too good to be true, "*they make their own whipped cream*, put it in a cup to take it with you. This is great for us, to not pass this up. You really don't know if you'll ever be by here again." And quit jabbering.

He almost lost it, and put his head against the cool window. Yeah, you really don't.

The south of France, a beautiful woman, obsession, murder. What more could a man want from a quick jaunt across the Channel?

A Week Abroad
by Tom Ward

HE RAISED THE cup to his lips and took a sip of the rich coffee. He held the cup there a moment and looked at her over the rim, like a spy looking over the top of a newspaper. She sat a few tables along, half hidden in the shade of the parasol. Where the sun hit her it lit her up like dynamite. He lowered the cup. That's right, she was dynamite. He looked over again, trying to only move his eyes, not his head too. No one wants to look like they're staring. She was beautiful; anyone could see what all the fuss was about. The way her bare shoulder caught the sun, her skin like powdered snow on a mountain top. Her red dress tight around her breasts and her cream silk scarf tied firmly around her neck. Like a bow on a gift. Hair like black lace flowed down her back. He couldn't see its length now as she sat facing him, but he knew it reached to just above the curve of her hips. A mouth to die for, he could just about make out red lipstick on the tip of the cigarette she held nonchalantly in her left hand, the smoke drifting with no rush, penetrated by the bright sun's rays like a mist around her, an aura of mystery. Or danger.

He saw all of this from the corner of his eyes. He saw more than this. The white tulip brooch she wore on her dress. The black high heels she wore, now hidden under her table. No more than four inches. She was roughly five eight herself, so no more than six foot with the heels. He lifted the cup from the shiny ring of coffee in his saucer and took another sip. It looked like some would drip from the bottom of the cup so he took a napkin and wiped it and then wiped the saucer. Three times. Clockwise motion.

A dog barked in the square and some pigeons flew up from the fountain, the flap of their wings mingling with the trickle of the clear water. It had an almost green tint to it. Not a polluted green, a nice green. He liked it. Colours were important to him. He enjoyed all sorts of details that most people did not notice. The dog had left the square, disappeared down the third alley way. He was pleased; animals annoyed him. Never work with children or animals. The only distraction now was the little yappy dog the two women next to him had. It was a Chihuahua and the two women yapped along with it. They had come over with it in one of their designer handbags. He hated to imagine the mess it left in there. He thought about this now, and wiped his hands on his trousers under the table.

She had loved it when the women had sat down beside her, the Chihuahua poking its face out of the handbag, yelping and scrambling to escape. She had moved her chair closer and commenced stroking the foul little animal as she asked the women it's name, breed and price.

The two new women droned on for minutes in response, obstructing his view. They were old money and tasteless. She knew what was in good taste. He imagined she was being polite about the dog. The worst thing was the women let it wander all over. They had no control, no discipline. He felt it now, sniffing against his shoe. His freshly polished shoe. He could imagine its wet nose dripping onto his foot and gave the dog a quick jab in the ribs with his toe. It yelped and went scurrying back to the women at the next table. They looked shocked and stared over at him with big frowning brows. He smiled across at them and held his gaze until they looked away and began muttering to the dog, 'Ah ma Cherie!'

He ignored them now and took another sip of his coffee. It was strong, better than anything he'd had in England. He finished the cup but kept it held to his lips so that he could watch her over the rim. A waiter came out of the café and over to her table. He could not hear what was being said but knew it was in French. She smiled at the waiter as he poured her more coffee, and she stretched her legs out under the table. The yappy dog ran over and licked her heels but she didn't seem to notice. He would have liked to kill the dog. The waiter went back inside and he put his cup down and looked out over the square. It was empty apart from a few couples walking in the sun. He could hear the dog yapping again and he ground his teeth. He was getting annoyed. He had to remind himself about this. Breathe in. One, two. He felt his pulse slow down and ran a hand through his blond hair, making sure it was still slicked back. He could feel a slight sweat on his brow. For God's sake, this was no good, if she saw him looking nervous...He took his handkerchief from his breast pocket and dabbed the corners of his forehead before placing it back in the pocket. He straightened his narrow tie.

A different waiter came out of the café carrying a tray with cakes and coffee for the two women next to him. It was the blond waiter. He worked Mondays, Tuesdays, Wednesdays and Saturdays, and today was a Wednesday. The other one worked every day and the skinny one was not here. He only worked Friday to Monday. She knew them all. She had been a regular here each day for the past two weeks. Normally between twelve and two. Before those two weeks she had been in the town a month. He knew all this but it was the first time he'd been to the café and he had only been in the town a week.

The women cooed next to him as the waiter placed their cakes on the table. One of them touched the waiter's arm and the other laughed. The waiter smiled at them. It was disgusting and he had to grip his knee under the table to control himself. The waiter finished at the table and turned to go back inside. He called out to him,

'*Monsieur, café s'il vous plaît.*' The waiter nodded, '*Oui*' then went back into the cafe. He'd had to turn in his seat to call to the waiter, and now something dug into his ribs. He could not reach inside his jacket to move it, so he sat back in the chair and ignored the discomfort.

Her cigarette smoke drifted across to him and he inhaled it deeply without trying to look like he was doing so. It tasted sweet. The coffee was sweet as well. Everything was too sweet. The women next to him with their sweet tooth. He checked his watch, it was almost two; she would be leaving soon, back to her hotel. He glanced over at her. She seemed to be in no rush. She leant back leisurely in her chair and smoked her cigarette, letting the smoke escape through her red lips. The lips were like a wound and he thought of his own wound, the scar across his left cheek. It was not yet fully healed and always turned a bright red in the sun. He wondered if she had noticed it. If she had noticed him. It would be better if not.

'*Monsieur, votre café.*' It was the waiter. He placed the new cup on the table and took up the old one.

'*Merci*'. The waiter smiled, his blond hair shining in the sun, 'Ah, you are English, *non?*' He said nothing.

'I have seen you admiring the woman over there.' He rolled his eyes to indicate the direction and then winked.

'Yes, she is very beautiful, she comes here every day.' The waiter continued. 'They say she is famous. Perhaps she will give you an autograph; she is English too, non?'

He took a sip of the coffee then put down the cup. He gave the waiter his smile. The same one he had given the women.

'Is she? I can't say I know who she is. I'm not sure she is famous at all, I hadn't really noticed her until just now.' He saw the waiter looking confused and added,

'But yes, she is rather beautiful, I suppose.' The waiter smiled and nodded.

'*Oui monsieur, très belle!*' He smiled back and after a few seconds the waiter nodded, '*Monsieur,*' and went back inside.

She stood up now and stubbed out her cigarette on her saucer. He checked his watch. It was two p.m. exactly. The women called over to her and she came over and kissed them goodbye, not quite touching their cheeks. Air kisses. Then she tucked her slender legs under her, her dress riding slightly up her thighs as she bent down to lift the dog up and kiss it goodbye. He could almost have been sick. He drank the rest of his cup of coffee in one go, ignoring the heat and watched her as she walked past him and across the square. She hadn't looked at him. He took out his wallet and placed a twenty euro note under his saucer then took out his sunglasses from his inside jacket pocket. He put them on and brushed his hair back then counted to ten before rising and following her across the square.

She was the other side of the fountain now and about to turn down the second alley. He was in no rush to catch her. The idea was to keep some distance. Besides, he could hear the rhythmic click of her heels on the cobbled street. He matched her pace and followed along behind her, watching the two curves of her behind move as she walked. Now they were into the alley and she turned a corner. It did not matter if she got away; he knew which was her hotel.

He was certain it was her. He had watched her for a week without her realising. The first time he saw her he had checked her against the photograph he carried in his wallet and was sure. He should have burnt the picture after that but he couldn't bring him himself to do it; he was lonely at nights in this town where he knew no one. He remembered when the fat man had given him the picture. He had sat in the office somewhere in London. It was night time outside but the fat man had called him in. 'Urgent business'. His office was dark and the lights were dim. The deep green of the leather made the chair seem uncomfortable. It was all too formal. The fat man had sat back behind his desk and offered him a whisky. He didn't drink. A haze of cigar smoke filled the room and the taste had stung his throat. It was a bitter taste, not like the sweetness of her cigarette. The fat man had forgotten about it once he had started talking and the stub lay smouldering in a gold ash tray. Suddenly he had become all business. He'd leant forward over the desk and stopped stroking his yellow and black tie. He had been biting his nails. The fat of his cheeks wobbled as he spoke and continued moving a split second after his jaw had stopped. The fat man had explained everything and then raised his eyebrows as if inviting questions but he had none. It was simple enough. He reached into a drawer in his desk and took out a small photograph which he slid across the desk.

'Recognise her?'

'No.' He answered.

'You're perfect for this.' The fat man laughed.

He had looked at the picture for a second before slipping it into his inside pocket. She was beautiful; there was no doubt about it, but money was more beautiful to him. The fat man spoke again,

'You have ten days. This needs to be done.' He nodded and rose to leave.

'Ten days.' The fat man repeated. He smiled at him, left the office as silently as a wisp of smoke, and stepped out into the wet London night.

He continued after her, occasionally losing sight of her, but always hearing the click-click-click of her heels. They walked through winding alleyways but neither of them were lost. He had rehearsed this walk many times over the past week. They came to her hotel, a five-star palace with golden lions outside and a red carpet lining the steps up to the door. She walked slowly up the steps with practiced grace and the doorman bowed as he opened the door for her. She smiled and touched him lightly on the shoulder. He saw this and tried not to clench his fist. He took off his sunglasses and put them in his left jacket pocket as he walked up the steps. The doorman was still trying to stop himself smiling as he nodded, '*Monsieur*'. He slipped a fifty euro note into the doorman's pocket as he passed. The doorman thanked him with a straight face.

She wasn't too far ahead of him now, he could see her at the desk as the Concierge handed her the room key. She held it in such a way that he could only make out one of the numbers on the tag. It didn't matter; he knew exactly which room she was in. There was no need to sit in the lobby and pretend to be occupied whilst he watched the numbers change above the elevator. He made sure he was out of her field of vision as the elevator arrived and she stepped in and turned to face outwards. Then the golden doors closed and the first few numbers lit up one by one and she headed to her floor.

He took the stairs. Slowly. He had no need to rush. Let her get settled in her room. Let her get halfway through pouring a drink or drawing a bath. It wouldn't do to be seen hurrying up the stairs either. Not in a place like this and not in any place he'd worked. It dug into his ribs again as he walked but it was just something you had to deal with. Six floors. Four more to go. He was making good time. Quick, but not too quick. He wasn't sweating; he was too fit for that.

After the ground floor the stairs had been sectioned off from the corridor of each floor and a door led out at the top of each flight. He reached the sixth floor. Six Oh Seven. He stood a moment at the door and listened. He could hear no one. It was silent above him and below him. He took off his shoes and placed them neatly beside the door. He quietly slid it open and stepped out into the sixth floor corridor.

He checked his appearance in a wall length mirror and straightened his tie. His hair was all right for now. He was just a business man heading to his room.

Six Oh Seven was around a bend and he padded quietly across the carpet in his socks and stopped at the corner. He could still hear nothing but he waited a few minutes. The last thing he wanted was a maid to come bustling out of a room and surprise everyone. Or an American family on their holidays. When they got scared they were worse than an alarm. No one was around. He was certain. It was the middle of the day and most people would be out visiting the town. He took a last look around the corner and then leant back against the wall.

He always kept a pair of leather gloves in his trouser pockets and he took them out now. They were the only thing he had in there, other than a wallet which contained only one hundred euros cash and the photograph. He slipped the gloves on and stretched his fingers out in them to make sure they slid fully into place. Still no sound. It was time to earn his money. He reached his right hand into the left side of his jacket and brought his Beretta pistol out of its holster. A different man might have remarked on the multinational aspect of the whole affair. An English man in France with an Italian pistol. He didn't have time for such thoughts. His mind was clear as an empty glass vase. He pulled back the slide and checked the round in the chamber. Still no noise in the corridor. He kept a silencer in his holster and took this out now and screwed it slowly onto the pistol, using his thumb and forefinger. Three turns. Clockwise motion. He held the pistol in his left hand and undid his jacket buttons so that his jacket swung open. He checked the safety was still on and tucked the pistol into his waistband.

Still no noise. He looked quickly back down the corridor and then around the corner and saw no one. It was time. He walked around the corner and quickly moved over to the light switch. He flicked it and the lights went out, leaving the corridor in darkness except for the lights of the emergency signs and the elevator lights. He padded slowly up to her door, sticking to the wall. Six Oh Seven. He ran a gloved hand through his hair and put his ear to the door. There was no light coming from under the door, she must have been in the bathroom. He stood for a whole minute with his ear against the door and his mouth open to reduce cavity noise and enable him to hear what was going on in the room rather than his own breathing. There was no one moving inside. He could get in and come up on her quietly and catch her unawares. It was a shame really, all that beauty going to waste. They told him she was talented too. Maybe if she hadn't expanded her talents into the fat man's area of expertise she would've lived to become an icon. He brushed his hair back. Never mind.

He took the pistol out and took off the safety. He knelt now beside the door and laid the pistol next to him, at a right angle to the door and within arm's reach. He reached into his side jacket pocket and took out a thin piece of metal wire which he inserted into the lock with the steady hand of a surgeon. Still no sound from inside. His total concentration was on the task at hand now as he made subtle movements with the wire, slightly to the left, a little bit up. He worked for thirty seconds until there was a soft click and the lock was open. Now he had to act fast. He placed the wire back in his pocket and picked up the pistol, making certain the safety was off. No sound from inside.

His gloved left hand turned the door knob slowly as he pushed the door open with his right shoulder. He stepped into the room and raised his right hand holding the pistol, gently kicking the door shut with his heel as he did so. The room was dark and he quickly scanned each corner whilst he still stood in the doorway. She wasn't there. The sound of running water came from the bathroom and light shone into the room from the doorway to the left. He took a step towards it, treading slowly in his socks. His focus was on the door and a hundred different scenarios played through his mind in a split second as he prepared himself to burst through into the bathroom.

He took another step towards the door and the sound of running water and suddenly there was a new noise, a sort of 'phish' sound that seemed to come from inside the room. It was followed immediately by another. He wondered where it had come from. It was a sound he knew well but he was confused as to where it had come from without him making it. She was in the bathroom, surely. He turned on his heel to scan the room again but felt unsteady and his knee twisted under him. His pistol dropped to the floor with a soft thud as it landed on the deep carpet. He took a step towards the wardrobe, feeling weaker now. Suddenly his knees buckled and he knelt in the carpet. The carpet was deep and white but there were flecks of red, little drops as through someone had flicked a brush dripped in red paint across the room.

A soft cough escaped his mouth and as he held up a gloved hand he was surprised to see the same red shining on his black leather glove. He couldn't kneel anymore and fell backwards to lie on the carpet, his long legs tucked under him. He could smell her now, a soft perfume that he'd never smelt. It was strange he hadn't smelt it; he had been so well prepared. Everything was fully researched. It was all in the details. All in the preparation. He hadn't let himself become distracted. The smell got stronger and he knew it was her smell as it was mixed with a sweet cigarette odour. He pushed himself up on one elbow but a 'phish' knocked him back down. The carpet was wet. Funny. What kind of hotel was this? His breathing was heavy now and it felt like something was bubbling in his chest. He tried to look what the problem was but could only move his head to the side. A pair of black heels stepped from behind a dress screen and as he moved his eyes he could see they led up to a pair of slender legs. They approached slowly over the carpet and he could make out the hem of a red dress.

She was stood next to him now. The perfume overwhelmed him. It became a part of him. It was inside him and seemed to bleed out of him. He breathed deeply but couldn't quite catch his breath. A shiny black high heel touched his head and rolled it back so that he was looking straight up. He couldn't see the ceiling; his vision was blocked by a red dress that reached almost as far as he could see. Two red cushions seemed to be floating in the darkness where the dress ended. They seemed to smile down at him and he smiled back weakly. His first genuine smile in a long time. Something black blocked his vision, something cylindrical and cold looking. He tried to stretch his neck to see around it, to see her but he couldn't move it. He let out a last rasping breath and looked into the barrel of her gun. A millisecond later a last 'phish' sound echoed softly around the room whilst his brains seeped into the carpet like the slow spread of split red wine.

The morning after the night before. Sometimes you'll do just about anything to make the day more bearable, and sometimes you should have just stayed in bed.

The High Road
by Sarah M. Chen

AS JAY STAGGERED to the bathroom to take a piss, the last thing he was thinking of was his pickup truck. Why should he? It was, well who the hell knew what time it was, but it was daytime and Jay had just woken up. So obviously his first thought was smoking a bowl. It was always his first thought, but this morning he was feeling particularly crappy. His head felt like somebody hammered a nail into it and his tongue was stuck to the roof of his mouth. Some weed should do the trick, set him right.

His second thought as he splashed water onto his face and stared at his bloodshot eyes in the mirror was that he should go right back to bed, sleep the hangover off. He had no business doing anything today.

Jay's third thought, and this was an important one, was what the hell happened last night at Ken and Claudia's? He had a vague recollection of Jell-O shots and licking Jell-O off his fingers, or at least someone's fingers, and sucking down shots of Jaeger with some crazy guy named Bob or Rob who just moved to Hermosa Beach. God, the thought of it made Jay's head spin and not in a good way.

Marco, Jay's roommate, and his girlfriend Chelsea were going at it behind Marco's closed door which wasn't making Jay's hangover any better. Did they have to be so loud all the time? Jay pounded on Marco's door as he shuffled by on his way to the kitchen.

"Go away," Marco yelled from the other side of the door. "I'm busy."

"Yeah, no shit," Jay yelled back. "The whole fucking neighborhood can hear you." He heard Marco mumble something inaudible followed by Chelsea's high-pitched squeal.

That's it. I can't get through this day without some weed, Jay thought. Not with these two clowns here. I just want to smoke a bowl and pass out with the blankets over my head.

It wouldn't have been so bad if Gina hadn't just dumped him. Saying she wanted someone more stable. What the hell did she want, an old fart in his forties who sat in a cubicle all day? Sure, Jay was just a bartender at Hennessey's, but it's not like he was going to do that forever. He had plans, big plans to be, well to be something that made a lot of money.

In the kitchen, Jay poured himself a glass of water and sucked it down. The green glowing numbers of the microwave clock read twelve-thirty. He noticed discarded wrappings from El Tarasco scattered on the counter top. Hardened cheese and beans were stuck to a plate in the sink. Jay's stomach churned as he leaned against the counter, staring at it. Was that from last night? Did he eat that?

Jay shook his head and decided he didn't want to know. He plodded back to his room, trying to ignore Marco's headboard pounding against the wall, and dug around the pockets of his jeans from last night. No weed. Jay scanned his room and noticed his hoodie draped across the chair. He vaguely remembered flinging it off last night before passing out in his bed. Jay checked both pockets and this time came up with a lighter. That was a start.

Maybe he'd left the baggie of pot in his truck. Kicking aside dirty jeans and button-down work shirts, Jay found a reasonably clean pair of surfer shorts. He pulled them on and added a T-shirt that reeked of cigarette smoke. He must have worn it last night. He burped, tasting onions and hot peppers. Guess he really did eat El Tarasco after the party.

Grabbing his keys and sunglasses, he stepped outside and was immediately assaulted by the sunlight. Jay slapped on his shades and trudged down the apartment building walkway in his flip flops, keys jangling in his hand. It was another picture perfect day in Hermosa Beach. The marine layer had cleared by now, unveiling a cloudless blue sky and a view of Abe's Liquor down the street. A lone bird chirped a steady beat that pierced Jay's brain like an ice pick.

He plodded down the stairs and exited his apartment building, wincing as the blue metal gate clanged shut behind him. Jay headed in the general direction of Abe's Liquor, thinking a Gatorade sounded good until he realized he only had a dollar in his shorts pocket.

By the time he arrived at Abe's, he also realized something else. His truck wasn't there. He always parked on the residential street in front of Abe's, just before the metered parking on Pier Avenue.

What the hell? Jay stood in front of Abe's and looked around. Families and couples headed down to the beach for lunch or some sun. Kids barreled down the street on skateboards. Cars slowly cruised by, looking for parking at the scarce metered spots. But no silver pickup.

Christ, where was it? Jay traced his steps back, staring at each parked car so he wouldn't miss it. When he arrived at his apartment building, he paused. He could either turn left and head down the narrow one-way street or keep going towards the basketball courts. He chose the latter.

By the time he arrived at the courts, Jay was feeling a twinge of anxiety. He had to have simply missed it, right? There was no way he'd park this far down. He turned back around and headed towards his apartment building, feeling like a doofus even though nobody was paying any attention to him. Still no truck. He turned down the one-way street at the corner of his building and stopped when he reached Monterey Avenue. He wouldn't park this far. He might as well have walked home from the party.

Jay toyed with that idea as he headed back to his building. Did he walk home last night? Nah, there's no way he'd walk, the party was like ten blocks away. Plus he picked up El Tarasco, right? He wouldn't have done that on foot. No, he definitely drove home. Jay was sure of that. Obviously, wasn't the wisest choice since he was clearly too messed up to remember anything.

Jay arrived back at his building, and panic was setting in. Okay, relax, Jay, relax. He took a deep breath, smelling the salt air, and exhaled slowly. No problem, it will all work out. Yeah, yeah, okay. He just needed to get his mind clear. Figure out what to do next.

What to do next was score some weed, Jay thought. Once he did that, then he could get his head on straight. Maybe call the cops, report his truck stolen. His Toyota wasn't exactly brand new, hell it had almost a hundred thousand miles, but she looked good for her age. And he'd just bought a new bed liner. Some jerk stole his previous one so this time, he went all out and purchased a heavy-duty bed liner that fit securely in the bed and on the sides. Now the entire goddamn truck was gone.

Only problem now was that Jay had no way of getting to his dealer's place without his truck. The guy lived all the way up in Hollywood which might as well be another planet. Cab fare would cost him an entire weekend of tips. And Jay wasn't even going to begin to try and tackle public transportation in L.A.

What he needed now was a place to score some weed that was walking distance. That pretty much meant it had to be a dealer who was a few blocks away, anything further than that and he'd need a ride. Shit, he didn't even have a bike.

The only person who came to mind was Bee. His real name was something Vietnamese that Jay couldn't pronounce so everyone just called him Bee. He never had very good weed but was usually good for a dime bag.

He headed to Bee's place, a couple blocks south and then a few blocks west towards the ocean. It was a small rundown duplex that was a termite's dream but at least it was three blocks from the Strand. Hermosa Beach was an eclectic mix of wealthy singles and not-so-wealthy surfers and artists which resulted in some odd-looking neighborhoods. Bee's place looked like a tree house that had fallen in between a palatial home under construction and one that was literally a glass fortress with lion statues in the front yard.

Jay knocked on Bee's door and waited. He could hear music inside so knew Bee was home. He pounded louder. Jay turned the doorknob and it was unlocked so he walked in.

Bee wasn't sitting in his usual spot on the couch in front of the big screen television. Some movie was playing with the sound muted. Wu-Tang Clan's "Cash Rules Everything Around Me" bumped loudly from the Bose speakers. It reeked of cigarette smoke and an ashtray lying on the stained carpet was overflowing with butts.

"Bee!" Jay turned down the hallway, towards the bedroom and stuck his head in. The sheets were in a tangled ball and the comforter was lying on the floor. A black lace bra was draped across a chair.

He was about to start scrounging around for Bee's stash when the music out in the living room stopped and someone yelled, "Hey." Jay walked out of the bedroom to see Bee standing in front of the doorway, beanie on his head, holding a plastic bag with what looked like a soda inside. He was smiling, then when he saw Jay his smile disappeared and he tensed up.

"Dude, you left the door wide open." Bee held his hands up in a 'what the hell?' gesture.

"Yeah, well you left it unlocked. You gotta be more careful. Anyone could just walk in."

Bee made a noise out of the side of his mouth and shut the door. He pulled the bottle out of the plastic bag. Gatorade. "You look like shit, man." He took a swig and stared at Jay. "What you doing here?"

The edge in Bee's voice threw Jay off. "I just wanted to know if you got a dime bag. I'll hit you back later."

"Nah, man, I'm tapped out." Bee capped the Gatorade and set it down on the coffee table. Then he snatched a pack of cigarettes off the table, stuck one in his mouth.

Jay knew Bee was lying. He always had weed. "Not even a quick bong hit?"

Bee lit the cigarette and smoke blew out of his mouth when he asked, "Why you coming here anyway? What about your boy, what's-his-name? Gonzo?"

"Mondo."

"Yeah, him." Bee pointed his cigarette at Jay. "Why don't you go see him?"

Jay shrugged. "I was nearby. Just need something to tide me over."

Bee's eyes narrowed until they were little slits. "What you really want?"

Jay decided to just come out with it. "Look, I don't have a ride at the moment. How 'bout you take me to Mondo's? I'm good for an ounce once we get there. The guy owes me."

"All the way up in Hollywood? Past Sunset?"

"Yeah."

"I'm busy, man. Got things to do." He gestured to the disheveled living room as if that proved how busy he was. "Take the bus or something."

Jay snorted. "Yeah, right. I wanna get there sometime this year." He had an idea. "How 'bout I borrow your car then? I'll bring it right back."

Bee hesitated, then said, "I can't."

"What do you mean you can't?"

"I just can't, okay?" Jay watched as Bee started cleaning the living room, but it seemed like he was just picking stuff up and putting it on the floor in another spot. He added, "Someone's using it."

"Who?"

"A friend."

"What friend?"

Bee said nothing.

"When are they bringing it back?" Jay demanded. He heard someone open the front door behind him and whirled around to see Gina standing in the doorway looking all sun-kissed and smiling. As soon as she saw Jay, she scowled.

"What are you doing here?" she asked. She was wearing jean shorts and a pink bikini top. A tote bag with what looked like a beach towel inside was slung across one shoulder.

"What are you doing here?" Jay asked. God, she looked hot. Jay felt a stirring in his surfer shorts which only made him feel worse.

They stared at each other for a beat and then with flared nostrils, Gina strutted by Jay towards Bee. She dumped her tote bag by the couch and threw the car keys onto the coffee table. Bee put his arm around Gina's tanned shoulders.

"You're fucking kidding me, right?" Jay looked from Bee to Gina, back to Bee. "This is the guy you dump me for?" The image of the black lace bra in Bee's room flashed through his head. It blurred his vision for a second and he struggled to regain focus. "A low life drug dealer?"

"Hey," Bee began, but Gina flicked him on the head, and he shut up. Clearly, she'd already dug her claws into him, Jay thought. Poor schmuck.

"Bee's got more going for him than you have in your pinkie finger," she spat.

Jay shook his head. "That doesn't even make sense."

Gina harrumphed and crossed her arms, giving Jay her best red lipstick pout.

"I'm outta here," Jay grumbled. He shot Gina one last glare and then pointed his finger at Bee. "The bitch ain't worth it, dude."

Jay heard Gina cursing as the door slammed shut behind him. That didn't go the way I planned, Jay thought. All he wanted was some weed and now he had visions of Gina's bra in Bee's room.

Jay plodded along in his flip flops, away from the beach towards Pacific Coast Highway, the most congested street in Hermosa Beach that became Sepulveda Blvd. once you hit Manhattan Beach to the north. By the time he reached the local 7/11 on Pacific Coast Highway, he was thirsty and his head was killing him. But he wasn't getting much with a buck.

Jay debated about returning to his apartment to pick up his wallet but figured he probably didn't have much money in there either. He could at least get a drink at home. Flustered with indecision, he sat down on the end of a bench to go over his choices.

He heard muttering nearby and turned to see a homeless guy, or what looked like a homeless guy, sitting on the other end of the bench. His back was turned to Jay and he was sitting next to a shopping cart piled with plastic bags filled with God knows what.

Jay realized he was sitting at a bus stop. Maybe it was fate. The sign on the post showed a picture of a bus with illegible writing underneath. Jay got up to check it out, trying not to stand too close to Crazy Bag Man, his smell forcing Jay to breathe through his mouth. He scanned the sign for any mention of Hollywood, but it looked like the only route this bus took was to Long Beach. Wait a minute. Inglewood, Lawndale, Hawthorne, LAX. Jay realized numerous bus routes stopped here and it was like trying to decipher the menu at that stupid French restaurant Gina made him go to on their last date.

"Goddamn it," Jay muttered. There was no way he was going to figure this out. Just then a bus pulled up, creaking and groaning, and the doors swung open. Jay waited until a few people disembarked, brushing past him, before he poked his head in to see a fat black lady sitting at the wheel. She turned to Jay with a look that made him flinch. Man, what was she so angry about?

"You coming on?" she demanded.

"Uh, I don't know." God, this woman made him nervous, giving him flashbacks of Mr. Burndell calling on him in seventh grade math class. "Where does this go?"

"The airport."

"Uh, I—I just want to go to Hollywood."

"Well, I don't go to Hollywood. You can take this to LAX and then a shuttle to the Metro Station on Aviation. Then take the Green Line to the Blue Line."

This was much more complicated than Jay could have ever imagined. "The what to the what?"

"Mister, you coming on or not?" She was clearly finished with helping Jay.

Jay decided to hell with it and stepped onto the bus. "I—I have a dollar, is that enough?"

"It's one fifty."

Jay scrounged around in his surfer shorts knowing full well he didn't have anything else and shrugged. "All I got is a buck."

"Then I suggest you find fifty cents or step off."

"Come on, can't you cut me a break here?"

"If you don't have one fifty, you need to please step off."

Jay glanced at the few people sitting in the bus who looked either pissed or bored.

"Mister, I need to ask you to please step off."

"Fine, fine, I'm stepping off. Jesus." Jay exited the bus, and the doors almost clipped him in the ass before they sealed shut with a hiss. He whirled around to cuss her out but the bus was already pulling away.

"You spare a quarter?"

Jay turned to see the homeless guy looking at him. Only it wasn't a guy but a very ugly woman. Or was it a guy? Jay tried not to stare at the sunburned face covered in some kind of crust peeking out of a curtain of stringy hair. He almost gagged as the ripe smell wafted into his nostrils.

"A quarter?" the person repeated.

"Uh, sorry," Jay mumbled and turned away, heading north on Pacific Coast Highway. Maybe he should just go home. Call it a day and admit failure. Navigating through Los Angeles was just way too complicated without a car. You had to have a PhD just to read the bus signs.

Jay pressed the walk button at the crosswalk and waited, feeling sorry for himself. The green walk signal flashed and Jay was about to step off the curb to cross when he heard a horn honk and someone yelling. Jay turned to see a white limousine careening towards him. It screeched to a stop at the curb. The passenger window rolled down and a guy inside called out, "Jay."

Jay walked over to the limo and stooped down to see a skinny white guy wearing a suit and tie smiling at him. "What's up, Jay? How's it hanging?"

It took Jay a second and then it hit him. The crazy guy he did shots with last night, Rob. Or Bob. "Hey, man, what's up?"

"Last night was epic, right? Totally epic." The guy was grinning from ear to ear.

"Uh, yeah. Epic." Jay nodded, taking in the limo. It was a white Hummer limousine with the words 'Mr. Kash,' along with a phone number, scrolled across the tinted windows. "You own this thing?"

"Yup. Well, no. I drive for a company."

"Let me guess, Mr. Kash?"

"Yup. But gonna start my own limo service soon."

"Uh-huh." Jay nodded, scrambling to piece together what they talked about last night. Something about moving here recently. Kind of a drifter. "Sure."

"So what are you up to, Jay? Out for a stroll?" The guy had a manic energy that was unnerving. And the way he kept saying Jay's name. It made him uncomfortable.

"Uh, well, yeah. Trying to—"Then it dawned on him what a stroke of luck this was. "Trying to get up to Hollywood, man."

"Yeah? Well, hop right in, Jay." The passenger door swung open, beckoning him. "Got a pickup at LAX but after that we're golden."

"Cool." Jay folded his body into the limo passenger seat, air conditioning blasting him, and looked over at his ticket to Hollywood. "Thanks, man." He turned the vent away, already feeling goose bumps on his arms.

"No problem, Jay. No problem at all." The limo veered into traffic, and Jay gripped the handle above him. Rob or Bob seemed keyed up on something, he was all jittery. "So what's in Hollywood? Some sweet piece of ass? Getting some action, huh, Jay, huh?" He nudged Jay with his bony elbow, poking him in the side. The limo swerved to the right and Jay heard a horn honk behind them.

"Uh, not exactly." Jay didn't want to tell this guy he was scoring some weed. Then he'd have to share it. "Just visiting a friend." He glanced out his window to see a guy in a Prius flipping them the bird.

"Gotcha, gotcha." He tapped his steering wheel with both hands like it was a drum although there was no music on. "So what, you were gonna walk to Hollywood?" He cackled like it was the funniest joke in the world.

"Uh, no, I was—"Jay didn't feel like explaining anything to this whack job. "Taking a walk."

"Uh-huh, uh-huh." The guy floored it and they plowed through a red light.

Jay looked over at his driver. He was bouncing all over the place and sweating. Man, he was on some serious crank or something. Jay wondered if they would even make it to LAX, let alone Hollywood.

The limo veered left and Jay gripped the handle again. He realized he hadn't even put his seatbelt on so immediately buckled himself in.

"Where you going, dude?" Jay turned to his driver. "LAX is that way." He pointed in the other direction. "We're going back to Hermosa now."

"Yeah, yeah, I know." The guy was speeding down Pier Avenue like there were no crosswalks or pedestrians.

"Watch out," Jay cried, pointing at a blonde guy biking across a crosswalk, maneuvering carefully with a surfboard under his arm. Rob or Bob whizzed by the surfer, narrowly missing him, until Jay heard a thwack at the driver's side front of the limo.

"Holy shit, I think you clipped his board." Jay spun around to see the surfer, still managing to hang onto the surfboard, plow into a parked car, and topple to the ground.

"Gotta make a stop first, Jay. Will take two seconds."

"What? I thought you had to pick up some people at LAX?"

"Yeah, yeah, I'll get to them. No worries, Jay. It's all good in the hood." They turned down a one-way alley and Jay was jostled around as the guy flew across the uneven pavement at fifty miles an hour.

Jay was about to tell the guy he wanted out. No weed was worth this much. Then suddenly they screeched to a stop, almost skidding into the garage door of a rundown duplex. He turned to Jay and said, "Wait here. Some business I got to take care of."

"What?" Jay stared into those crank-crazed eyes. The guy was totally off his rocker.

Crazy Rob or Bob said nothing and ran back to the spacious passenger area of the limo. Jay turned around to see him rummaging underneath the seats, coming up with a backpack.

"What are you doing?"

He watched Rob or Bob bound up the stairs two at a time with the backpack, knocking on the front door of the top apartment. He danced around the landing like he had to take a piss. Finally, the door opened and some big Mexican guy with a shaved head beckoned Rob or Bob inside. They both disappeared into the apartment.

Christ, what the hell was he doing? Jay realized he was bouncing his knee up and down and tried to remain calm. God, now he felt like he was on crank too. He thought his heart was going to explode out of his chest, he was so keyed up. What was in that backpack? Drugs? Cash? Was this idiot doing a drug deal right now? Jay looked around nervously to see if anyone was watching them, like cops. A white Hummer limo with the words 'Mr. Kash' wasn't exactly discreet.

Jay noticed the nutcase didn't even take the keys, they were still in the ignition. He was about to slide over to the driver's side and ditch Rob or Bob, but the apartment door flew open and Rob or Bob stepped out onto the landing. He waved to Jay and then a shot rang out. Rob or Bob jerked, then crumpled to the ground.

"Oh shit, oh shit." Jay was frozen with terror unable to take his eyes off Rob or Bob's inert body.

He heard angry voices, something like "stupid, get him inside," and then the same Mexican guy with the shaved head stepped out. He reached down and gripped underneath Rob or Bob's arms, dragging him across the landing and disappeared inside. Then another Mexican guy, this one with tattoos all over his neck and arms and wearing a wifebeater, stepped out onto the landing, looking around.

Jay sucked in his breath and was just about to shrink down in his seat, but it was too late. The guy saw him. He and Jay locked eyes, and Jay's heart surged up to his throat. He was screwed.

Things happened really quickly after that, and Jay had never moved so fast in his life. While the tattooed guy was shouting, Jay scrambled over to the driver's seat and turned the engine over. Jay looked up and saw the big Mexican guy, followed by two of his buddies, charging down the stairs towards him. One of them had a gun.

With shaking hands, Jay shifted the limo into drive and hit the gas, barreling down the alley. Shots rang out and Jay heard pinging sounds behind him. Then glass shattered, and he figured they hit the back window.

Jay cornered the limo onto Hermosa Avenue, the main drag for bars and restaurants, fishtailing like crazy. Goddamn this thing was a monster. Jay felt the limo skidding to the left and cranked the wheel hard to the right. He overcompensated and with sick horror, realized he was heading straight for a cab that was pulling away from the curb. Jay slammed on the brakes, but it was too late and he plowed right into the driver's side of the cab.

Jay stumbled out of the limo, dazed and disoriented. It felt like he was in a dream, a really bad dream. Sirens were going off in the distance and he wondered if someone reported the gunshots. Where were those Mexican dudes? Jay scanned the growing crowd of onlookers but didn't see them. The cab driver was already out of the cab, yelling and pointing.

"Stop right there, put your hands up."

Jay turned to see that two cop cars had formed a V behind the limo, blocking traffic. One cop, a burly blonde guy, had a megaphone and was shouting orders.

"I said put your hands up, face the limo, and spread your legs."

Were they shouting at him? Jay complied and another cop, a stocky Asian guy, frisked him.

"Okay, hands behind your back."

Jay obeyed and felt the cold metal handcuffs snap on each wrist.

"Hey, wait a minute—"he began, turning around.

"I said, face the limo." The cop shoved him against the car, and Jay nearly did a face plant.

"You got it wrong, man." He tried again, this time facing the limo. "The Mexican dudes are who you want. They killed Rob or Bob."

"This guy has ruined me. Look at my cab." The cabbie was walking back and forth, throwing his hands around, but nobody was paying any attention to him.

The cop grabbed Jay by the shoulder and roughly spun him around. "Let's go, dipshit." Another cop, a female, started reading him his rights.

"What am I being arrested for?" Jay demanded as the Asian cop marched him past the limo.

"That's the guy."

Jay stopped and turned to see the surfer who Rob or Bob almost ran over pointing at him.

"That wasn't me," Jay pleaded. "It was Rob or Bob."

"Uh-huh. Rob or Bob. Right." The cop shoved Jay towards the cop car and he stumbled. "Move it, asshole."

"Hey, I didn't do anything wrong."

"We have several reports of a white Hummer limo with the words 'Mr. Kash' on it driving like a maniac all over Hermosa Beach."

"Look, it wasn't me."

"You telling me there's another white Hummer limo with the words 'Mr. Kash' on it driving around like a maniac?"

"No, I—"

"Get in there, doofus." Jay was shoved into the back of the cop car and the door slammed shut.

The Asian cop climbed in the front and the female cop joined him. The siren went on and they reversed until they were in the middle of the intersection of Hermosa Avenue and Pier Avenue. Then they veered left, heading east on Pier Avenue towards the police station.

Jay tried again. "Look, this is just a misunderstanding. That limo isn't mine."

The female cop turned around. "So now we can add stolen vehicle to the charges."

"No. Jesus, that's not what I meant." Jay gave up and sank back into the seat. The car smelled like puke. He gazed out the window as they sped past Abe's Liquor towards the police station which was three blocks up. As they approached the station, slowing to turn into the City Hall parking lot, Jay spotted his truck at a meter, a ticket tucked underneath his windshield wiper.

"Hey, there's my truck." Jay sat up, craning his head around as they cruised by it. He would have pointed if he didn't have his hands cuffed behind his back. "I found my truck." Even the bed liner was intact.

"Congratulations," the female cop said.

Jay leaned back, smiling. At least the day wasn't a total disaster.

A high-profile murder case. A hot-shot cop on the rise. The wrong kind of killer.

Interview Room C
by Josh MacLeod

"IT'S STRANGE. Sitting here is all strange. I suppose I should say I never thought I would get caught, but everyone who says that is caught. Still, I would have thought Internal Affairs would have more important things to do: I gave the press what they wanted. I was already a hero before that case. I suppose sleeping with Shapiro's wife started your investigation, eh? No, no, don't bother to answer. It's not as if you people investigate yourselves.

"Am I bitter? Of course I'm bitter. Three *years* on the Dangerfield case. I'd like to say it was my crowning achievement but I'd be lying. It was good work. Solid police. Mr. Dangerfield, a real-estate tycoon with more enemies than God, found dead by his wife. Everyone's alibi checked out. Hers, the kids, his lover, her lover, their kids. No one was squeaky clean, everyone had a motive, but he was alone in the house.

"The Mayor was involved, friend of Mr. Dangerfield's from way back. Shit got political: we never looked too deep into why. Not that the Mayor had him killed, nothing like that. He pressed the department for answers but manpower shrunk as other cases demanded resources. Usual drill, same old BS. Told the Mayor if he wanted it solved faster we should have more funding. The Captain was down right sarcastic to me about that one.

"The break was horrible. Routine triple-check and we got a break from some suit who was finally home when we came to call. She'd seen the butler two blocks from the mansion not long before the killing despite him having the night off. Alibi was a couple of friends who swore blind he'd been there. You have any idea what that was *like*? Spend months on a case you'd banked on getting you up past Detective, have the entire thing stall for even longer, and then you find out the butler did it?

"The fucking butler. I could have spit nails. I confronted him with the evidence, he admitted everything. Like they do. Words spilling out of him like pus from a wound, going on about how he'd been treated like shit, as if Dangerfield didn't treat everyone like shit. I cut him off with, 'No.' He said, 'What?' And I said: 'No. I am not telling the mayor the butler did it.' He didn't understand, so I explained. I said: 'We need a better killer than that.' I understand his phone recorded it, some fancy modern camera shit that fell out of his pocket when I shot him.

"Three times, to the chest, body wrapped in carpet, into his car, left it on the train tracks to be destroyed by a train. Didn't know about the phone. I guess it fell out in the driveway. I must have kicked it into the bushes. I made it into a suicide that he tried to hide as murder so his wife would get the life insurance. Then I tossed a case together about Dangerfield's second ex-wife using the butler's friends to help break her alibi.

"I didn't have money to bribe them with. I had a gun and threats. You know how that works. But you're IA, so I suppose not. You only see it when it fails. I imagine it was Rictor—he seemed the brightest of a dull bunch—who figured that if I was in jail it meant I couldn't do anything to him. As though no one has friends or is owed favours. I should have spelled that out, then.

"My mistakes? I just said it. Rictor. Not the phone: someone would have found and played it. You'll find some file somewhere about it, buried in some hard-copy cabinet someone has lost the key to. We have a few of those. But the mayor was spinning glib and everything coming up roses, a movie made about the killing. You know the type: the lone Detective slogging through the streets, damsel in the wings, beautiful but deadly. So the truth got buried. Leastways until you people dug it up.

"The movie tanked. You probably know that, but the actor they had was five-foot-nothing, a pissant of an excuse of a Detective, even for IA. If the real story came out, it would probably do better. Not make the department look good, but you knew that going into this. Heh. You people know shit. See, the mystery isn't why the butler did it. Not even that the Detective—me, in case you need to take notes—killed him. It's why I was never charged. The phone would have been recovered during the last sweep of the property; cell phones don't magically turn up three years later, so everyone will scream conspiracy and ask questions you'd rather they didn't about the why of this investigation.

"And then it'll go to court, with jurors raised by CSI bullshit who will be convinced you'd have been able to find proof of what I did at the scene of a three-year old case. You know anything you found would likely not hold water. I know it, but they aren't about to believe that. The department covering for me, though, that they'll believe. And tossing me out to dry because of Shapiro, too.

"You think you can throw mud around and none of it stick to you? Even I couldn't do that in my prime. So go get the Captain and he and I can talk. I'm a good press draw still. The Mayor likes me. This comes out, what do you think happens to our funding? You get the Captain, you mention the butler, and the Mayor, and what I did for this department. You do that and we'll just see what happens next."

What happens when the balance of power in a prison is
turned upside down? Warning: gritty, realistic and disturbing.

Hostage
by Tekla Dennison Miller

THE PORTER'S MOP hissed as it glided across the linoleum floor and
slapped against the cellblock's moldings. His muscles flexed with each
push and pull working in concert with the constant *swish, swish*. The
methodic rhythm interrupted the early Sunday morning quiet. A
prisoner rolled over on his bunk. A toilet flushed. Officer Sherwood
took a routine count. Her rubber-soled shoes squeaked as she made
her way down the gallery.

When Sherwood approached cell 103, the door swung open. Suddenly, a hand thrust out, grabbed her arm and yanked her through the
opening. The officer's count board crashed to the floor. The cell door
banged shut. A thundering noise rumbled through the second tier of
the prison block.

"He's got her," the porter yelled. "Baker's got Officer Sherwood in
his cell."

Jill Sherwood raised her head and stared into the angry eyes of a
prisoner, Paul Baker.

Baker twisted Jill's right arm as he pointed a piece of pipe at her
face and laughed. He used her arm as a lever to throw Jill onto his
bunk.

Sprawled across the cement bed, Jill watched, paralyzed, as Baker
piled the mattress against the door and quickly tied one end of a
sheet to the door handle. The other end had already been secured to
what was left of the radiator, preventing the door from swinging open
onto the cell block's walkway. Baker created a formidable barricade
with his meager cell furnishings.

Baker turned to Jill. "You don't move unless I tell you. And you
don't talk to nobody but me . . . or I'll kill you." Spit flew from his
mouth.

Jill pulled herself up and rested her back against the soiled gray
cell wall, clammy from the summer's humidity. Her mouth formed
silent words when Baker gripped a fistful of her hair, and pulled her
head toward him. "Did ya hear me?" he screamed. He tugged her hair

again. "Answer me when I talk to you."

Jill winced and nodded. An involuntary gasp forced its way from deep inside her.

Baker let go of her hair. He threw his head back and laughed. But his laughter abruptly stopped as he jabbed Jill's ribs with the pipe he'd been holding. "This ain't personal," he said. "It's not between you and me. It's me and them mothafuckas." He tilted his head toward the door. "Including your pig husband, the great Lieutenant Billy Sherwood."

Jill crumpled from the blow. But the pipe didn't break her skin. The homemade weapon appeared to be from the cell radiator, pieces of which were strewn across the floor. What radiator could withstand Baker's rage?

"Call the captain for help," Officer Williams, ordered as he banged at the cell door. "Baker, let her go, man," he yelled. "Don't be stupid." Williams' body thumped against the cell door in an attempt to dislodge it.

Jill glimpsed the outline of the officer's head as it jerked back and forth across the narrow door window. *What took him so long to get here?*

Jill heard the other block officer, Clarence Thompson, shout, "Forget it, Williams. It's too late. Baker's got the door tied shut."

The image of Thompson trying to wrench Williams away from the cell door formed in Jill's mind. She wanted to shout, *Don't leave me, Williams!* Yet Baker's threat hung in the air. He would kill her if she disobeyed his order not to talk to anyone but him.

Baker's lips curled back, exposing his teeth like a mad dog. "I ain't lettin her go. And I ain't talkin to nobody but The Man. So get The Man here, Williams."

The Man. Baker meant the prison's hostage negotiator. Jill had been an officer less than six months at Century State Prison and now she found herself the victim in the second hostage taking. In the first one, Baker also took a woman officer hostage. He played out that scenario just long enough to make everyone feel anxious about his threats. Baker had little to lose. He'd been sentenced to life for murder.

Jill's entire body trembled. Would she die at Baker's hand? Jill knew Baker should've been transferred from the prison after the first incident. She shouldn't be facing him like this. How many times would prison officials let Baker have his way? What chance did she have to get out of his cell alive?

Jill slid her body across Baker's bunk, to try and get as far from him as possible. She held her breath so she didn't react to the pain in her ribs where the pipe hit. When she reached the corner, she laid her head back and watched Baker.

Without warning Jill's breathing quickened. She pressed her hand across her mouth to quiet the noise so she didn't incite Baker. She couldn't stop the sounds and her body gave into convulsive motions.

Jill consoled herself with thoughts about the last time Baker took a hostage. He let the officer go within an hour and walked calmly from his cell. It was a terrifying hour, but nobody got hurt. Maybe her situation would turn out the same. She could survive an hour.

WHACK!

Jill bolted upright. The impact of the pipe banging against the cinder block wall vibrated through her body like thousands of needle pricks. Baker hadn't had a weapon the last time.

WHACK!

Baker paced the cell—ten deliberate steps in each direction. Each time he reached Jill he slammed the pipe against the wall just above her head. Each time the piercing sound pulsated through her body. Each time it drove her deeper into a human ball rolled into the far-thest corner of the bunk. Vomit rose into her throat. She swallowed it back. Jill clasped her hands behind her head and pulled forward with all the strength she had. But it didn't shut out the sound of the pipe slamming into the wall. If she buried her face between her thighs, and pressed them against her chest, and pressed her upper arms against her ears, would the tormenting sound of the pipe go away?

WHACK!

Though tucked deep into herself, she couldn't block out that sound or pretend Baker had disappeared. What if he missed the wall? *Think of positive things. You'll get through. Don't do anything to provoke him. What did they say in training? If you make it through the first twenty minutes, you probably won't be killed.*

WHACK!

How long had she been in his cell?

Baker walked faster.

All sorts of thoughts rushed through Jill's mind. She knew when she took the job the inmates at that prison were the most dangerous in the state. And she was told about Baker the first day. He raped and murdered more than one woman. Why hadn't she listened to her husband and asked for a transfer from that joint?

Jill lifted her head just enough to see Baker raise the pipe over her. It was too late to think about what she should've done. Like a turtle, she retracted her head and shuddered. She just didn't want Baker to kill her.

WHACK!

She could hardly breathe. The cell was too damn hot. But Baker didn't deserve even those meager surroundings. If the bunk wasn't cement, he'd tear it up like he did the radiator and use the pieces for weapons.

Williams and Thompson were still at the cell door. They talked in low voices. Williams ordered Thompson to call the shift commander to see what kept the negotiator. But Thompson didn't leave. Instead he whined, "We're in big fuckin trouble. She's a rookie and the only woman on duty in this block."

Thompson walked back and forth. "I'm suppose to make the eight a.m. round, Williams, not her."

The footsteps stopped. Jill wanted to call out, *You got that right, Thompson.* You're always supposed to be doing something that I end up doing.

"When Baker grabbed her, she was doing my job, man," Thompson confessed "What do ya think the warden's gonna say 'bout that?"

WHACK!

Both stopped talking as the pipe's thwack resonated. Jill flinched at the sudden interruption fearing the worst. She could almost see the two officers facing each other, heads tilted toward the cell door to hear what might come next. When nothing happened, Williams continued, "That's not the only thing that's gonna piss the warden off, Thompson. Nobody noticed that Baker's cell door was unlocked."

Williams and Thompson were silent for a few moments. Then Williams spoke again. "But that's not the problem right now. It's saving her," he scolded Thompson. "So hustle your ass and call the shift commander. I'll stay here until help arrives."

The cell block became unusually quiet. Water dripped from the faucet and hit the cell's sink in a perfect cadence--drip, drip, drip. Then the prisoners started yelling. Their voices sounded like a musical round as they shouted one after the other.

"The Man's here, Baker."

"Baker, The Man's here."

"Tell 'em whatcha want—to get outta this mothafuckin hole."

"Hey Baker, take me with ya."

Jill peeked through the narrow cell door window directly across from her. Tony Dodge's blank face filled the window as he stared into the cell. The Man. The negotiator. His eyes darted from one corner of the room to another. He appeared to be sizing up the situation. Although he was one of the prison psychiatrists, Jill had little respect for him. In the past he seemed to spend more of his time boasting about the books he'd published than with the prisoners on his caseload.

"It took you long enough to get here," Williams chided.

But Dodge wasn't the type to throw on last night's clothes even in an emergency—he must be ready, look good, in case he might be interviewed for the evening news.

Nevertheless, his arrival calmed Jill. She reminded herself he did negotiate the three previous hostage situations, including the last one with Baker. All of them were brought to successful conclusions though a couple of officers suffered minor injuries.

The last time Baker took a hostage it was also on a Sunday when there were fewer officers and administrators on duty. For the past several months, he'd been quiet. No trouble. His compliant behavior convinced everyone he'd changed and just wanted to do his time. So the officers became too lax, too trusting, and stupid.

Jill also reminded herself that if she got out of the cell alive, she'd never do Thompson's or anyone else's job. She'd never cover their asses again.

The cell block quieted once more and Baker stopped pacing. Yet the sound of the pipe slamming against the wall still echoed in Jill's aching head.

The prisoners on the block stopped their taunting, no doubt to eavesdrop on Dodge. He spoke to someone out of Jill's range of vision. "Baker appears more agitated this time," he reported. "And unlike the last time, he has a weapon."

Jill imagined Dodge pushing his fingers through his raven hair as he talked. What did he mean Baker was more agitated? Her body felt stiff from sitting on the hard, damp cement surface. Yet her spine felt as though it was massaged by a hundred fingers made of ice. *Agitated, agitated, agitated*, repeated over and over in her head. Her heart beat so hard she saw her chest move with its rhythm.

Suddenly Jill remembered something else from training. Never use the same negotiator if the hostage taker was the same or if they knew each other, because the hostage taker would know what to expect. He'd have the advantage.

The sound from Jill's hammering heart pounded its way into her head and roared into her ears. She clutched her knees to her chest, tighter than she had earlier. She lowered her head onto her knees and rocked. *This can't be happening.*

The other prisoners on the block resumed their taunts.

"Hey Dodge. Think you're gonna save that honky's ass?"

"Baker, get us all outta here with you."

"Big man Dodge. Let's see ya open the door."

The sound of their voices reverberated down the block into a deafening explosion of words making it difficult for Dodge to talk with Baker. Usually the prisoners were removed from the area during a hostage incident. But not this time. There was no way that group of killers and rapists could be herded from their cells without a lot of problems. Maybe even a riot. The time was right for a riot. They were all hyped up.

Opportunity. That's what it was all about. Prisoners are opportunists. They look for the right time to make their moves. Was Baker waiting for Jill to walk by his cell that morning? He'd had a fight with her husband earlier that week when he searched Baker's area. Was she the pay back?

Jill chastised herself for taking Thompson's count for him. He'd been a lazy bastard from the start. As a fish—a new officer, and a woman trying to prove she could do the job, Jill did more than her share. Yet what would that prove if Baker killed her?

Jill lifted her head heavy with sweat. She breathed in the thick summer air pushing through the window hinged slightly open. Baker paced the cell again, taking long measured strides as he twisted the pipe in his hand. When he reached the door window he shouted at Dodge, "Hey man, whatcha got for me this time? A ride out of this joint to the Feds like I asked the last time? You can do it. You're my friend ain't ya, Dodge?"

WHACK! Baker slammed the pipe against the cell door.

Jill pressed her fingers into her temples and rubbed. She sneaked a look at her watch. The second hour had begun. She was no closer to getting out.

Jill noticed her wet clothes. Or perhaps just her pants. When had it happened? Did Baker know about her wet pants?

Baker came at Jill, slamming the pipe into the palm of his hand. He was right. They should've transferred him after the last hostage thing—like they were supposed to.

Funny, Jill hadn't noticed before that moment that Baker had no shirt on. A patchwork of scars covered his chest. Most of them looked like knife wounds. The milky scar tissue glowed in what little sunlight squeezed between the bars covering the gritty outside cell window.

Baker leaned his glistening, muscular body toward Jill. He pointed the pipe at her head. Jill recoiled. She thought he would hit her for sure that time. Instead he asked in a deep controlled voice, "Whatcha rubbing your head for? Want some aspirin?"

Jill nodded as her mouth formed the soundless word yes.

Baker walked to the cell door window and negotiated with Dodge. They agreed that Baker would give up some of the radiator parts in exchange for aspirins. It seemed to make no difference that the aspirins would go to Jill. Dodge unlocked the cell door slot where officers usually delivered Baker's food tray. The grating sound of the metal door slot opening echoed down the block. Jill placed her hands over her ear to cutoff the jarring noise which she had never noticed before.

The officers would give no food to Baker that day.

Dodge and Baker exchanged items.

After the exchange Dodge watched Baker give the aspirins and a paper cup filled with water to Jill. When she finished, Baker took the cup and nabbed a few squares of toilet paper from a roll sitting on the floor next to the stainless steel toilet. He turned back to Jill and wiped the tears from her face.

"It's them." He gestured with his thumb at the door. "But ya gotta be my bargaining chip for a little while longer. OK?"

Jill closed her eyes and nodded. Still she could see Baker's wicked glare.

When Baker wiped away her tears again, Jill opened her eyes. She studied Baker. She believed the deep creases she'd seen earlier in his face had melted away. Could Baker really care about what happened to her? Or could it be just another game so Baker got what he wanted?

Jill didn't care. She only wanted to live.

Jill rested her hands on her chest hoping that gesture would stop her pounding heart. Her eyes followed Baker as he trod across the cell. His scars gleamed. Perhaps what had been said about Baker wasn't true. Perhaps he'd been a victim himself. He was just twenty years old, a kid only a few years younger than Jill. Yet his face often looked like an old man's, especially when he became anxious. His rage nurtured the hate that flooded his mind and etched the meanness on his face. Jill shared a cell with that Baker.

Dodge's face, still framed by the cell door window, appeared less tense, almost victorious, since Baker gave him parts of the radiator. Hope filled Jill. Maybe it would end peacefully. She shook her head. Baker seemed determined. When Baker reached Dodge he stared him down with eyes filled with contempt and superiority. Dodge shuffled his feet and shifted his head away from the window. He no longer looked pleased with himself.

Jill had to force her eyes to remain open. She couldn't let the exhaustion overcome her. She had to stay alert. But it was so damn hot. How did the prisoners stand that heat all day? No wonder they walked around in their undershorts. No wonder their tempers flared. The heat can do that to anyone. Jill had to ignore all that. She had to be vigilant.

A light breeze forced its way into the cell between the bars covering the outside window just above the bunk. The window's hinged six-inch opening allowed in needed air, and didn't pose a security problem. Or so the officers had been told. Jill scooted closer to the vent to gain full benefit from the cool breeze. It helped settle her nausea.

Almost the entire prison came in view from the window, though its dirty coating distorted the scene. Jill imagined what it would be like as a segregated prisoner like Baker. He no doubt spent endless hours staring through the unforgiving bars. He had no identity, no other choices.

Jill halted her reverie when she heard Baker at the door, mumbling something to Dodge. She ignored the conversation and gazed at the identical two-story brick-buildings that surrounded a college-like quad. It all seemed out of place. Her mind wandered back to her thoughts about being a prisoner. She'd keep a constant and envious vigil over the animated prison compound: officers scurried along the flower-lined sidewalk; general population inmates went to work, chow hall or sick call; nurses headed to the segregation cell blocks to distribute medicine and listen to prisoners complain; teachers rushed to get to classes on time; psychologists, carrying an armload of files, raced to counseling sessions. As a prisoner, the only other world Jill would know came through the narrow window in the cell door as she strained to see who walked the block.

Baker's voice increased to a shout which drew Jill's attention to him. "You're an asshole, Dodge," he screamed. "I can't let you have this." He waved the pipe above his head. "Unless you can give me a ride outta here, you understand?"

Any hope Jill had felt earlier had been erased. She decided her own imagination would be her only salvation. So she turned back to the window. Jill watched the continuous rounds of officers patrolling the yard. She heard the steady chatter from their hand-held radios. Could the conversation be about her locked in Baker's cell? She couldn't make out any words. Instead, Baker's booming voice came at her like a challenge. "Where's your big-shot husband now?"

Jill wondered too. She imagined him pacing the prison's waiting room or harassing the warden for answers. Jill's eyes followed the twelve-foot electrified double chain link fence topped with razor ribbon as though she searched for her husband. Instead she saw an officer in the gun tower across the quad. The stern-looking watchman kept an automatic rifle at his fingertips. On normal days he waited to break up a yard fight or stopped an escaping prisoner from scaling the fence. On normal days he raised binoculars to his eyes and surveyed the grounds. On normal days, he often looked disappointed when he couldn't fire off a round.

On normal days.

The leaves on the trees that bordered the prison shivered against a radiant, blue sky. Though a comforting vista the officers' tactical movements on the compound aroused thoughts of looming danger. Jill then considered the flowers along the sidewalks. They seemed silly, twisted and colorless to her at that moment. Did the tower officer ever notice the flowers and question them?

Hour number three had come and gone. Baker paced like a caged circus lion. Cage. Cell. No difference. The walls seemed to press in on Jill, crowding out the air. Though prisoners called a cell their house, the only living things that could be at home in them were the cockroaches and the occasional transient rat. Who could survive in such a dungeon? Who could remain gentle, forgiving? The system made Baker an animal.

Baker left the door window. He talked to Jill as he walked back and forth, back and forth. "You know, the last time I took a hostage I tried to get outta here for protection. The officers here like to play with me. Abuse me."

He stopped and stared at Jill. His eyes accused her. "They mess with my time outta my house and do things like trip me so I fall."

Baker stabbed the pipe into the air punctuating each phrase. "And sometimes they just beat me for kicks." Stab, stab.

He walked again, faster, faster. "But nobody hears what I'm sayin." Stab. "I'm always the bad guy." Stab.

Baker suddenly stopped in the center of the cell and cocked his head like a dog. He listened to the other prisoners' warnings. The lines in his face deepened with each alarming prediction forecasted by his block mates.

"Baker. The SWAT Team's here."

Baker's eyes widened. He looked like a wild animal caught in a trap as the quick footsteps of heavy boots progressed down the gallery walk.

"They're comin' to get ya, Baker."

Baker rubbed his head in a frenzied motion. Drool seeped from the corner of his mouth.

"Your ass is cooked this time, Baker. Game's up."

WHACK!

Baker bashed the pipe against the cell door. His hand quaked from the vibration. "Dodge!" he shouted. "I don't want no cops in here. Just you. Keep them outta here, and I'll come out at noon."

Dodge didn't answer.

"Dodge! D' ya hear me?"

What seemed like several minutes ticked before Dodge responded. "Okay, Baker," he conceded. "You have twenty minutes . . . 'til noon. But after that, it's out of my hands. The SWAT Team will take over."

Baker turned toward Jill. The angry lines in his face diminished, even though nothing had really been promised. Jill wanted to believe it was a good sign. Maybe Baker had tired of the game. Or maybe he feared the SWAT Team would come in and he'd get hurt or even killed. Maybe he thought the game had gone too far that time.

Suddenly Baker's mouth formed an unbalanced smile. His eyes turned to ice. He moved like a robot as he covered the cell door window with a blanket.

Jill couldn't see Tony Dodge anymore.

And no one could see her.

Baker broke his promise. They all broke their promises.

Jill rummaged through her training. If she made it beyond the first twenty minutes—*I'll be all right, I'll be all right, I'll be all right.* The mantra kept rhythm with her increased heart beat.

Baker circled his large sweaty hands around Jill's ankles. He pulled her so that her back flattened against the cement bunk. He pressed the pipe against her chest using his left hand, while he ripped her slacks and panties off with his other hand.

Jill couldn't breathe. *You don't have to do this Baker.*

I'm on your side.

I can help you.

I'm not one of them.

Though the words formed in Jill's head, her pleas went soundless. Only gasps forced their way out as Baker's body bumped heavily into her, smashing Jill into the hard bed.

Baker's eyes never looked away from Jill.

Tears stung Jill's cheeks as they flowed down to the bunk. She turned her head so she didn't see Baker's bloodthirsty stare. Her tears formed small dark circles on the cement. She wondered if Baker planned to kill her.

Baker's heaviness pushed into Jill in one final moment of conquest. Then he lifted his body off hers. He put the pipe down on the floor and pulled up his white prison issued undershorts. He walked to the cell door. He methodically moved the mattress and untied the sheets. He opened the door and sauntered out of the cell onto the block at exactly noon.

State Police officers in impeccable blue fatigue-like uniforms surrounded Baker. They cuffed his hands behind him. One officer stood to each side and each clenched one of Baker's arms. A third officer stepped behind Baker as the three led him away to the unacknowledged cheers of his block mates.

Jill prayed that it all had been a bad dream. But when she pulled herself up, the pain that shot down her back into her groin told her otherwise. She leaned against the dank wall. Her thighs seemed glued together from the poison that had spewed from Baker. She stared at her underpants and uniform slacks heaped on the floor. How could that tainted pile have ever held any authority?

Alone in the cell. No one—not Dodge, not Thompson, not Williams—peered through the open door. It was as though Jill didn't exist.

Then, from the other end of the block, a male voice commanded, "Someone get the hostage and debrief her."

Jill snatched one of the sheets from the floor, wrapped it around her, and waited.

A big city private eye is visiting home in the hopes of getting a few days away from crime. But crime can be found anywhere, even the college football field in a small town. Unfortunately.

Trouble's Bruin
by Laird Long

THE STADIUM ROCKED with the frenetic cheers of the home crowd. I had been told that the locals took their football seriously, but this was seriously loco. The band pounded out an all-too-familiar tattoo just as the noise level in the stadium threatened to dip below the ear-splitting threshold. The band was making sure that the surrounding ten miles of countryside knew it was football day at the old college campus, and why weren't you there? Cheerleaders, toilet paper, and confetti whizzed through the air like friendly shrapnel as the Solano Community College Bruins scored yet another touchdown. SCCB 52, College of the Redwoods Corsairs 10. It almost made me wistful for the parity that permeated the pro game. A quartet of bare-chested, brown and yellow-slathered college boys jostled me as they head-slapped each other in pigskin ecstasy. The watered-down coke in my paper-thin 'souvenir' cup made like Angel Falls over top of the head of the College president two rows down.

"That's the signal to go!" I screamed at my sister.

"I'm not hungry!" she bellowed back.

The Solano Community College's educational leader toweled his pink-skinned head off with some tissues his wife handed him. His myopic eyes tracked my way, so I stared down at the gridiron and took a sip from my empty cup. A cannon faintly exploded in one of the checkered end zones and the crowd went ballistic. End of the third quarter.

Jenny grabbed my arm. "Look!" she screamed, and pointed.

I looked. The Bruins mascot, Bruno the Bruin, an actual, live flea-covered black bear, specially bred to manufacture hoopla on a football sideline, was ever-so-gently mauling the College of the Redwoods Corsairs' mascot—Pete the pirate. The poor bugger in the black tights and plumed hat was getting a heavy dose of bear breath, and he didn't look any too keen about it. The crowd, however, lapped it up like a sundae in a miniature football helmet. Twenty thousand week-end warriors erupted in one gigantic belly laugh as Bruno ripped the pirate's puffy shirt to pieces, sending the half-naked buccaneer rock-eting across the field like a towel swabby at the fishermen's Y who's just discovered that he's cleaning out Davy Jones' locker. Pete hit the player's tunnel doing thirty, with Bruno and his handler in hot pur-suit. I implored my sister to do the same, but sensitive persuasion was as lost in the deafening cacophony as a pacifist at an NRA conven-tion.

"Good God, Charles, did you see this?"

I swirled some orange juice around in my mouth, trying to rinse out the whiskey smell. Some pulp caught in the drainpipe of my mouth and I gagged. I spat the juice back into the glass; if I'd wanted an orange, I would have eaten one.

"Did you hear me?" Jenny tried again. She was asking a lot of questions for a Sunday morning. "Take a look at this."

I slowly shuffled out of the kitchen, into the living room, and flopped down on the futon. I stared at the TV from between my knees. I was wearing pajama bottoms and a growth of beard. "What?"

Jenny pointed at the TV screen and pushed up the volume. The cadaver-faced news anchor with the head of starched hair said: "Again, to repeat our top story: Solano Community College's beloved mascot, Bruno, has been put down. He had mauled, and fatally in-jured, football cheerleader Marcie Piper during the fourth quarter of yesterday's football game, a sixty-nine to fourteen victory for the home team over the Yuba College 49'ers. Ms. Piper died of her inju-ries at the Health Sciences Centre early last night. The four year old bear was given a lethal injection at one o'clock this morning. He had been made an honorary faculty member only six weeks ago. Piper's funeral service will be held at two p.m., Monday afternoon. A memo-rial service for Bruno, who ends his tenure with an eighteen and four record, will be held at Student Hall later this week."

Jenny clicked off the TV and swiveled around on the legless couch to stare at me. Water bubbled at the bottom of her baby-blues. "That poor bear," she said.

I picked at the orange peel wriggling around between my lowers.

"Bear? What about the cheerleader? She must've been groped like a supermodel riding a rush-hour subway."

Jenny sniffled and nodded her head. She's a good kid, but her undying love for the furrier of God's creatures sometimes blinds her to the needs of the upright, two-legged population. "Weren't you friends with Piper's brother?" I asked.

She blew her nose. "Yes, we went out briefly. I should give him a phone call, you're right." She reached for the cordless phone sitting on the coffee table.

"Give him my condolences." I fought my way off the futon.

"Where are you going?"

"You don't have any extra-pulp beer do you?"

Jenny frowned. "No, just regular beer."

"That's where I'm going."

"Dang it, Mr. Sydney, I'm tellin' ya, there's somethin' fishy about the whole thing!"

"Easy, big boy."

Joshua Piper stopped pacing the room and the pictures stopped rattling on the walls. He sank back down into a chair. Parts of him spilled over the sides. He was built like a M1-A1 Abrams battle tank, but without the subtlety. He stood six foot six and weighed three hundred and forty pounds. He had a sun-blasted face and a yellow crew-cut you could clean your golf cleats on. His right eye was slightly bigger than his left, and his eyebrows were the color of wheat chaff. He was from some state in the northern part of the country where they grow sugar beets, mosquitoes, and O-linemen. He was the starting center for the Bruins football team. He was the late Marcie Piper's brother.

"It just don't seem right, is all. Dang it!" He pounded a meaty fist into a meaty hand and the foundation of the house sagged. "You know, I heard some rumors 'bout Marcie and that Klassenmeyer dude!" He looked at me with his clear, blue eyes and I knew that if I looked back long enough I would see the prairie sky.

I didn't. "Coroner said accident, police said accident, Harold Klassenmeyer, Bruno's handler, said accident, half a football stadium of drunken witnesses said accident. I think your sister's death was an accident, Joshua. Bruno went wild and attacked your sister. Maybe he didn't mean to kill her, but she died." I smiled sympathetically. It took a lot of energy. "The sooner you accept it, the better. You have any other brothers or sisters?"

"Sure, I got three brothers and five other sisters."

"There you go."

Jenny poked me in the ribs with a pointy elbow. "But surely you can at least look into it a bit, Charles," she suggested. "You are a private investigator, after all. Don't you have some responsibility in a situation like this?" She smiled nervously at Joshua and his face lit up like Paul Bunyan's jack-o-lantern.

I swiveled my head around and gave Jenny an icy stare. "Yes, I am a private investigator. A private investigator that is leaving for Los Angeles in four hours. My holiday in beautiful but troubled Suisun City is over, and I have cases waiting for me back at the office." I said it slow enough so that everyone could understand the logic. "And I have zero responsibility to anyone unless I'm getting paid, so-"

"I'll pay ya!" Joshua blurted.

"Sure, but-"

"Where'd you get the money?" Jenny interrupted. "When we were dating, when you were taking me to all the best buffets in town, I always had to pick up the cheque."

Joshua blushed. His big, red ears stuck out like handles. "I know, I know," he conceded. "But I got an alumni sponsor now." He shrugged off the chair and stood up. "We'll pay your goin' rate, Mr. Charles."

"Sydney."

"Then it's a deal," he said, and pumped my arm like the handle of a deep-water well.

I borrowed Jenny's Sunbird and drove out to the Klassenmeyer animal sanctuary and petting zoo. It was little more than a hobby farm with kennels, but the kids seemed to get a kick out of it. There were a couple of busloads of them on a field trip from some local school, and they were doing their level-best to put the fear of humans into a flock of Canada geese. A woman I took to be Mrs. Klassenmeyer was giving her gums a work-out, lecturing our nation's future on the finer points of migratory waterfowl, so I cornered an idle farmhand named

Vance Jeeter. He was slopping around in the pig enclosure. He was a tall, thin drink of dirty water, with a haircut from the Jack Dempsey era. He was wearing overalls and a sleeveless undershirt. He gave me a sour look before pointing me in the direction of the male of the Klassenmeyer species. I found him in the tool shed.

"Quite the set-up you've got here, Mr. Klassenmeyer," I said by way of salutation.

He threw a sewer snake down onto a chewed-up wooden counter and looked at me.

"I'll know where to come if the weatherman forecasts forty days and forty nights of rain," I joked.

"That one never gets stale," he responded. He had a slight German accent. He spat on the dirt floor of the shed and I could see that he was going with smokeless tobacco these days. Couldn't tell the brand though.

He was a big, rough-hewn guy, with features not unlike a grizzly bear. He had a thick, brown beard, long, brown hair, small eyes, a long nose, and big, hairy, red hands with plenty of grease and sod under the uncut nails. He could have used the giant mitts to catch salmon from the stream that flowed across the open field out back.

I grinned. "Yeah, you sure have a lot of animals," I pressed on. "Minus one bear, of course."

He stiffened. "You heard about that, huh?"

"That's what I'm here to talk to you about, Harold. I-"

"I told the cops everything." His teeth flashed white and sharp-looking. "I don't know you from nothing." He turned away, started re-arranging his tool collection.

A duck waddled by in front of me, then a rabbit hopped through on the right-of-way. I realized that if I stood there much longer, Bambi, Thumper, and the rest of the forest animals would come marching along to the tune of *Seventy-Six Trombones*. I was tempted to jam my way into the tool shed to force some hospitality, but it was dark in there, and there were a lot of sharp objects lying about. "Joshua Piper hired me to look into the death of his sister. I'm a private investigator from Los Angeles. Joshua's not so sure the mauling was an accident."

Klassenmeyer dropped a chisel and didn't bother picking it up.

When he glanced at me, there was fear in his beady eyes. He was obviously a guy who only talked gruff.

I poured it on. "He's a big boy, Harold. None too bright and plenty mad. He's got it in his jarhead that maybe you and Marcie were a little more than just Bruin boosters."

No response. He fiddled with his beard.

"He thinks that maybe you took advantage of his innocent, high-plains sister and then tried to cover things up before the Missus dropped the hammer." I was grasping for straws, but sometimes a straw can give you just enough air to go on breathing when you're in over your head. "I've tried to calm him down, but–"

"Get out," Klassenmeyer rasped.

"I can talk to your wife."

A disgusted look creased his prematurely weathered face. "You do that. She won't tell you nothing."

And that told me something. It told me that Mrs. Klassenmeyer knew about the rumors, and so Harold really didn't have anything to hide from her.

Mrs. Klassenmeyer was standing on the porch of the big, white farmhouse as I trudged down the dirt drive to Jenny's car. She was a tall, gaunt woman with a face as sharp and frigid as the brow of an iceberg. She didn't bother wearing any make-up. She yelled something I didn't hear clearly and a massive sow detached itself from where it had been jawing with Vance Jeeter and charged me. I barely out-legged the enraged ham on the hoof to the car without losing a calf muscle. Mrs. Klassenmeyer and the pig regarded me coolly as I waved and drove away. Vance Jeeter was doubled over with laughter, desperately trying to hold his guts in.

Jenny answered the doorbell when it rang. Then she yelled: "Charles!"

I put down the paper, not very upset at the idea of shelving the story I had been reading about Mrs. Olsen's coffee shop expansion—from three tables to four. It was the hardest news item in the local rag. I went to the back door. Two policemen were standing there. "Hi," I said.

"Charles Sidney?" the short one asked. He sported a pushed-in nose that he hadn't cultivated from gardening. His partner was a tall, soft, goofy-looking character who had his eyes glued to Jenny's chest.

"Yeah."

"I'm Officer Gordy, and this is Officer Siemens." He gestured at his partner. Siemens wagged his head, but not his eyes. "We want to ask you some questions."

"What about?"

"Harold Klassenmeyer killed himself last night. You were out to see him yesterday afternoon."

I swallowed hard and nodded. "Come in," I said. "But maybe your buddy can park his eyeballs on the back porch. I don't think he's going to find any clues in my sister's t-shirt."

Gordy grinned and glanced back at Siemens. Siemens looked at me and smiled.

We adjourned to the living room. Siemens sat down and stared at Jenny's legs. They were packaged for display in a pair of white short-shorts. Gordy provided the details as his partner stocked up on eye candy: Klassenmeyer had hung himself in the barn around eleven the previous night; he had left a confessional letter stating that he had been sleeping with Marcie Piper, had impregnated her, had panicked, and had used Bruno as a sharp-toothed weapon when Marcie had insisted that he divorce his wife and marry her. The letter said that Bruno was only supposed to scare her off, not kill her off.

I shook my head in honest wonderment. "How'd he get Bruno to attack the girl?" Even as I asked it, the vision of a panicked pirate floated up behind my eyes.

Gordy wiped his nose with the back of his freckled hand. "Code word. The Klassenmeyers train dogs for the police department, and guard dogs for a couple of security companies. I guess other animals can be taught to attack on cue."

An angry sow stared back at me from the pooled reflections of my mind. "Amazing," I said. "There ought to be a law."

"There is," Gordy replied. He spoke in the dreary, dry monotone of a public policy professor. "What did you go to see Klassenmeyer about?"

Siemens looked up. "Yeah, what'd you want with him?"

He said it a little too belligerently for my liking, so I got up on my hind paws and growled. "I had a date with one of his mallards."

Siemens smirked. "Yeah? Which one?"

"The one that dumped you."

Gordy smiled. "Easy, Sydney, we aren't accusing you of anything. Just doing our job."

"Okay," I said, and told him my story.

Siemens told me that the Piper death was a closed case and that maybe I should shove for smogtown. I told him to put his eyeballs back where they belonged—in his navel.

Joshua and his alumni boosters were paying me until the end of the week, so until the end of the week I would work. I had little to go on other than the brief impression I had of Harold Klassenmeyer. He hadn't looked or acted like someone who would use a bear to attack a defenseless girl. In fact, he hadn't looked like he had the ruthlessness to castrate a goldfish.

I drove over to the campus residences on College Drive and looked for some witnesses to the Piper pawing - cheerleaders. A girl named Kindra Cummings provided some useful information. Her roommate directed me to the football stadium, where I found Kindra keeping track of player movements; mainly in the back field.

"You've got really deep eyes, Charles. Like, you know, there's a whole bunch more layers to you, but you only show the world the top layer."

"That's the way I got it figured too, Kindra. I'm like an onion—you go too deep and I'm only going to leave you crying."

"Wow!"

"You're a cosmetology major, right?"

"Hey, how'd you know? You're like a real Shylock Holmes aren't you?"

"I'm brain-heavy, all right," I responded. "Actually, your roommate told me."

Kindra giggled. She was the kind of class spirit any jock could score a touchdown with. There just wouldn't be any point-after, that's all. She had a pleasant, vacuous face, long, blonde hair, and a toned, athletic body. You could have parked a football between her breasts.

"Was Mr. Klassenmeyer really struggling to hold Bruno back before he broke free and attacked Marcie?" I asked. I had to ask it a second time, because the first time she was waving to one of the tight ends on the practice field. I gently steered her out of the sun and into one of the tunnels.

"Yeah, like he was really holding on. A death grip, you know. But, you know, the leash just snapped."

"Does Mrs. Klassenmeyer attend home games?"

"Huh? Hey, there's Bobby-Joe Bola! Hi, Bobby-Joe!" She waved. Bobby-Joe made a 'call me' sign with his hand.

I waved my hand in front of Kindra's face.

"Huh? Oh yeah, she was in the first row, right behind the home players' bench. Like she always is, you know."

"Within earshot?"

Kindra's face screwed up with concentration. It wasn't a good look for her. "Yeah, I think so. You can see how close the stands are to the benches. And we were, like, right behind the Bruins' bench at the time. Mrs. Klassenmeyer could sure use some make-up, you know. She should, like, let me take a crack at her face."

"I bet your hands could work miracles."

Kindra smiled. She looked at me meaningfully, and then made the none-too-subtle gesture of smoothing down her t-shirt and caressing her mammoth bumpers at the same time. "You maybe wanta get something to eat? Or, like, go back to my room to, you know, finish up your questions? I think you could learn a lot more from me, Charles."

I smiled back at her. "I bet I could," I replied, "but I don't think your roommate wants to be disturbed. She was studying."

"Cindi? She'll help you out too, if you want. We both will. You know?"

I shook my head. "No, I don't. I never went to college."

I walked over to the campus library and did a little research—on hardcopy and on the internet. I read all about animal training; training animals to obey and to attack, and the different levels of attack. The library technician-in-training probably thought I was setting up a militia compound somewhere in the California backwoods or, worse yet, a religious retreat. I told her that I was doing an article for Dog Fancy magazine: dog meets man, man trains dog to hate, dog attacks girl, dog and man are put to sleep. Her hand floated over the panic alarm as I spoke.

The next day, Sunday, I drove outside city limits to the Jeeter residence. It was a short drive. Jeeter didn't have an address, as such, but Jenny knew where he lived and had given me instructions. He lived three miles down a dry, dusty road that had more potholes in it than teahead commune on the moon. Jenny's car rattled and shimmied all the way, but the robot-craftsmanship held together. I finally came to a clearing in a clump of pine trees. I shuddered to a stop twenty yards in front of Jeeter's plywood playground. Tree stumps, rusted car shells, and other assorted garbage littered the yard. Jeeter's tiny shanty was that color of faded grey barns get right before they fall down.

I banged on the screen door, and a minute later he appeared. He was holding a beer in one hand and a cigarette in the other. He was swaddled in a pair of dirty, blue sweatpants, and a stained, San Francisco 49'ers sweatshirt. He was any ordinary guy enjoying his Sunday morning before the NFL kicked off.

"Hi ya, Vance, mind if I-"

"Get lost, rent-a-cop!"

I tore the screen door open and dragged Jeeter out into the light of day. There was no point in beating about the bush with this guy—the mind games of the cold-call interrogation would be lost on a man of Jeeter's obvious rustic simplicity. He was one of God's children, and I got Old Testament on him. I slugged him in the gut with a short, sharp uppercut. He keeled over and started spewing a Budweiser product all over his geraniums.

He looked up at me with road-kill eyes. "What'd you hit me for?"

"I needed some exercise. Still do."

"Yeah, so what'd you want?"

"Answers."

He crawled over to a tree stump and sat down. He squinted into the sun. " 'Bout the Klassenmeyers?"

" 'Bout the Klassenmeyers."

He picked his beer can up off the ground and downed what was left. "What's it worth to you?" He grinned.

I could have bitch-slapped his ears off for the information, but I'm a capitalist at heart. I handed him five twenties. When he counted it twice and started drooling, I knew I had given him about three twenties too much. But he told me almost everything I needed to know. It must get lonely when your only neighbors are chop-shops and grow operations, because he chatted up a veritable storm. As his diatribe wound down, I was providing fewer and fewer questions and he was providing more and more answers. I began to get worried that he was going to get sunburned sitting out in that hot sun for so long, so I had him wrap it up. I put my finger down and he tied the knot. He wanted to give me a tour of his pond out back, where he grew frogs for research labs and educational institutions, but I said no thanks. We shook hands and I pointed the car's nose in the general direction of the Klassenmeyer farm.

It was a beautiful day—sunny, warm, breathless; the kind of day where the last thing you want to do is confront a couple of angry farm animals. I powered down the windows as I drove along the dirt road to the Klassenmeyers. I parked the car, exchanged steely glances with a couple of pigs and headed for the tool shed to pick up a leash I had noticed hanging on the wall when I had been there last time. I broke the lock with my bolt cutters and found the leash. I walked over to the pig pen, spoke the few words that Vance Jeeter had taught me, and looped the leash over the bristly neck of the sow that had given me the bum's rush a couple of days previous. Greta was her name. I picked the lock on the front door of the house and Greta and I strolled in. The horses in the corral let loose with some angry whinnying when the pig and I busted through the front door. I think the rough translation was: 'No animal must ever live in a house...'.

The time was 11:20 a.m., and, thanks to Jeeter, I knew that the abruptly-widowed Mrs. Klassenmeyer would be home from church at exactly 11:45 a.m. Even though her husband hadn't been planted and sodded over yet, she wasn't going to miss out on her usual Sunday service. She was a creature of habit, like a bear or a pig. Greta and I helped ourselves to some cherry pie that was sitting idle in the cafeteria-sized refrigerator in the kitchen. Greta's lips were soon as red as an Amish kid with a Sears bra sale flyer.

At precisely 11:45 we heard a car pull up alongside the house. Someone slammed a car door, walked briskly across the front porch, and then stopped dead at the open front door. She didn't balk for long, however. Mrs. Klassenmeyer pulled open the screen door and yelled: "Who's there!?"

I let the echo go to sleep before I replied. "Just me and my friend," I said.

She gave a clipped-off scream, then stumbled through the door. Her face turned whiter than the chalky cliffs of Dover when she gandered Greta and me lounging about on her plastic-wrapped couch. Greta grunted a greeting.

"Isn't she a ham?" I said, patting Greta's flank. I pointed to the open door. "Bacon enter, I'm afraid."

I pointed at the frozen Klassenmeyer and tapped Greta on the hindquarters. "Argot!" I yelled.

The pig bounded off the couch, flew around the coffee table, and lunged at Klassenmeyer's legs. Her mouth snapped air as I held tight with the leash. It wasn't easy. The leash sang with tension like the guy wires on the Edmund Fitzgerald. Mrs. Klassenmeyer slammed backwards against the wall, then slumped down into a fetal ball on the floor. She had found that it was a hell of a lot tougher being on the other end of the leash.

"Okay, okay, you know! Please don't let her hurt me!"

I didn't know a whole lot, but I had my suspicions. As Greta angrily snapped at her Sunday shoes, Helga Klassenmeyer spilled what was left of her guts. She told me about training Bruno, Greta, and other animals, to obey commands via code words; about her finding out about her husband's pompom poking and Marcie's unplanned pregnancy; about her righteous, matrimonial rage; about her putting too thin a leash on a three hundred pound bear; about her screaming out an attack code word during the football game; about her pounding relentlessly on her grieving husband after Marcie's death, until he was swept under by a roiling sea of guilt, leaving a half-bogus, half-truthful suicide note behind as a legacy to his poor decision-making.

The pig and I listened impatiently. She was hungry and I was angry. I pulled her tail and gave her the stand down code word: 'sarno'. She promptly ceased her menacing masticating and I rewarded her with another piece of pie. I telephoned Officer Gordy at the police station. He wasn't in, he was working a Bruins charity car wash, but eventually two men in a patrol car arrived and carted Mrs. Klassenmeyer off. She was desperately trying to regain her dignity, but the odds weren't good.

"Yeah?"

"Is that any way to greet a potential wealthy client?"

"You're not a potential client and you're not wealthy - you're my sister. What's up?" I asked. I was in a hurry. I was double-parked in a tinted-window, rented van across the street from the Sheridan Motel, a love shack on Hollywood Boulevard, and my jealous client's husband was about to enter Room 202. I had it on good authority that something warm and soft was waiting for him inside the cheesy cracker box, and that something wasn't the Pillsbury doughboy. I shifted the cell to my other ear. "Well?"

"Oh, I just wanted to let you know that your friend Helga Klassenmeyer is dead."

"Wow! They've finally streamlined the death sentence appeal process. All those letters to my state legislator paid off."

The door to Room 202 suddenly opened and something naked latched on to my man like a carp on a crayfish. He glanced around in embarrassment, pushed the bottle-blonde with the pillow chest inside, and slammed the door shut.

"How and when did she die?"

"She killed herself a day after they let her out on bail."

I slipped an infra-red digital camera into my jacket pocket and eased out of the van. "She felt a little guilty, I guess." I jogged across the busy street, padded up some concrete stairs, and set up shop under the window of the conjugal cubicle. The night manager, fifty bucks, and a couple of metal clasps on the curtain rod made sure that the drapes didn't quite close all the way. Leaning against the grungy, paper-thin, stucco wall, I could hear bedsprings squealing out a throaty number. I peeked in the dirty window and eyeballed the oldest tango performed on a cotton dance floor known to man and woman. "How'd she do it?" I whispered into the phone.

"The police found her in the reptile house," Jenny replied. "At the

Klassenmeyer animal sanctuary, you know." She paused dramatically.

The man in the skin-tight suit let out a roar that would have shaken the monkeys out of a monkey-puzzle tree.

"She had a python wrapped around her neck."

My man gave a porcine grunt and collapsed onto his cushiony playmate. I wobbled my head in amazement. "'The coward sneaks to death, the brave live on'," I quoted, then pocketed the cell phone and started snapping pictures.

When a job seems to be easy money, maybe what you were
hired for isn't exactly why you're there.

Three Times a Killer
by Michael Haynes

I WAS SITTING at a bar, drinking another Black Label, when the man
came up to me. I should have known he was bad news, a fellow like
that with his nice suit, in a low-rent bar like the one I was in that day.
Maybe it was the beer, maybe it was that I was still basically a kid,
only twenty years old, but I didn't twig to it.

"I hear you're looking for work, Lawrence," he said, lowering himself gently onto the stool next to mine.

I took another swallow, cool-like, before answering. "If the pay's
right, sure."

The suit nodded and pulled an envelope from his pocket. "I've got
a problem, see. Girl trouble."

He grinned at me like we understood each other. I would have just
as soon punched that smarmy grin off his face, but I needed money
and there wasn't no use biting the hand. I grinned back at him.

"My secretary's threatening to tell my wife about... about our affair. If I don't pay her off. And I can get the money but, you know, not
all at once."

It wasn't hot in the bar, but the man in the suit pulled out a handkerchief and wiped some sweat from his forehead.

"I need to get her out of town. My secretary, I mean. Somewhere
that she can't go to my wife until I pull everything together to pay her
off."

I rolled the bottle of beer between my hands, letting the beads of
water soak into my skin. "And she's not interested in clearing out,
right?"

He nodded. "But I've got a vacation place, way out of town. Just a
cabin, really, but if someone could take her there and make sure she
stayed put for, oh, a week I suppose. Then it would all be right as
rain."

A week of sitting around keeping an eye on a girl didn't sound like
tough work. I asked him what he was paying and the figure he threw
out got my attention.

"I'm just watchin' this girl, right? Not getting rid of her or nothing?"

The handkerchief again, dabbing at his hairline. "Right, just watching her and, for God's sake, making sure she doesn't get to a telephone."

He handed me the envelope and I peeled it open. Leopards stared up at me from a bunch of 200 rand notes. There was also a small photo of a woman, maybe in her thirties, blonde hair. Not particularly attractive, or at least not my type. She looked hard, and I wondered what a doughy suit had that would interest her.

"That's half," he said. "You'll get the other three thousand at the end of the job. There's also a map to the cabin."

The man glanced around the room. His expression gave me the sense that he was just now really getting a feel for the place he'd strolled into with three thousand rand.

"You do have access to a car, don't you?"

I flashed the man another grin and tucked away the envelope he'd given me. "As long as folks are still out there driving on the streets of Durban, I'll have access to all the cars I need."

Marvin, an old school buddy, was behind the wheel of the car I'd boosted overnight. He drove slowly through a neighbourhood with tree-lined streets.

"She comes through here every day, the man said. Early-like, running." I was jabbering, adrenaline pumping through my veins, eyes checking out every angle looking for the girl, looking for signs of the police, too.

Marvin grunted and just kept driving.

A few minutes later, I caught sight of the woman through the dawn haze. I pointed her out to Marvin. He pulled up to a stop alongside her and before she knew what was happening, I'd thrown the door open and gotten my arms around her waist. I felt the soles of her running shoes bash my shins. She drew breath for one loud yell as we tumbled into the back seat of the car.

"Go! Go!"

Marvin took off but not so fast that we peeled out or revved the engine. I crawled over the woman and got the door slammed shut.

We were off.

She was thrashing around and yelling and though I hadn't intended to hurt her, I reached out and smacked her hard across the face. The hit silenced her for a moment and by the time she was thinking about starting up a new ruckus, I had my gun out and pointed in her direction.

Sweat gathered at my temples and I felt my stomach flipping around. Stealing cars and a bit of petty theft doesn't usually require gunplay and though there was no chance I'd have let this girl know that—or Marvin, for that matter—I'd never actually aimed a gun at a person before that moment.

"Best for us all," I told her, "if you stay quiet."

She looked at the muzzle of the gun, looked up in my eyes, and I'd swear that she knew. But she licked her lips, nodded, and fell silent. The three of us stayed that way on the road out of town, west through the Drakensberg Mountains, and on out to the cabin tucked back on a dirt road, north of Ladysmith.

Several hours later, Marvin turned off onto that narrow road, the last turn on our map. For the first time since leaving home that morning, I started to relax. There wouldn't be any police back here. The hard work was over; now we just had to sit tight and keep our eye on the lady until the suit had her money and then everyone could go off their own ways.

"This place looks familiar, I bet," I said to the woman.

Her brow furrowed and she didn't answer me, except by shaking her head.

"What, lover boy never brought you out here for holiday? Told his wife that he had a business meeting?"

The woman's tongue flicked out, licked her lower lip. She took in a deep breath, let it out, and then spoke. "I don't know what the hell you're talking about."

I laughed, but it pissed me off that the first thing she said to me proper was a lie. "Sure you don't, love. And we're all just chums out here for a drive."

She opened her mouth to say something else. The car hit a bump just as she did and jolted us around in the back seat. Something flashed in her eyes and I could tell she was thinking about going for my piece. I braced myself against the door and lifted the gun up, pointed it at her again, holding it with both hands.

For a half-second, she still looked like she was going to try for it. But she shook her head a tiny bit and slumped back against her own side of the car. Slowly, my heart went back to its normal pace.

We went over a few more bumps in the road and I was about to ask Marvin if he could maybe try to not shake the car apart before we got to the cabin when we came around a bend and there it was. The car jerked to a halt several metres from the front door.

"Right. Home again, home again." I opened my door, grabbed our captive's arm, and led her and Marvin inside.

"How much are you taking him for?" I asked the girl as I shuffled a deck of cards. The light coming in through the windows was fading fast as the late-June sun sank in the sky. I offered Marvin a cut. He waved his hand at the cards and I dealt them out.

The girl didn't say anything. I glanced over her way before picking up my hand.

"I asked you a question, you know. Answering is polite."

"So is letting people go about their morning exercise without plucking them off the road."

I ran a hand through my hair and gave her a little grin. "I guess that's fair." I turned back to the game. I had a pair of aces and crap besides. Marvin threw away two cards, so I dealt him a couple and took three for myself. I didn't get any help from the deck.

Marvin tossed a fiver on the table. I thought about it for a second, shrugged, and tossed my cards down.

While he picked up the deck and began to shuffle I stood up and walked over to where the girl sat in a big overstuffed chair.

"Look, we're all just trying to get paid here, right? And since your boss man may be a few days coming through with the money, what's the harm in being at least halfway friendly?"

She looked up at me. "I wasn't kidding, you know. In the car. I don't have the first bloody clue what you're going on about. I've got no boyfriend and my boss is a woman. And no, I'm not having an affair with her, either."

I took her in. If she was feeding me a line, then she was good at it.

I ran my hand over my scruffy beard and thought for a moment. Then I dug out the photo I'd been given and tossed it over to her.

She glanced at it, frowned, and looked up at me.

"That is you, right?"

"Of course it is."

I let out a breath I hadn't realized I'd been holding. "Good. It would've been embarrassing if I'd snatched the wrong person."

I saw the sneer flit across her face before she could suppress it. "Who gave this to you?" she asked quickly, flicking a corner of the picture with a fingernail.

I laughed, a sharp little sound. "Well, now that's a good question. Fellow said he was your boyfriend. Told me that you were sticking it to him, threatening to go to his wife if he didn't pay you off."

"And, what, he hired you to bring me out here and...?"

"Keep an eye on you until he had your money."

A little glimmer of fear showed up in her eyes. "This man. What did he look like?"

I described the fellow. Bald head, nervous eyes, glasses, suit.

"Shit!" She jumped up from the chair. "Look, I think it would be a really good idea if we got out of here. Right now."

Marvin had set the deck of cards down on the table and he was eyeing us intently. "Why's that?" he asked.

"That man your buddy described? He is my boss, sort of. Not directly, I mean. But he's the president of our company."

"And?"

She swallowed hard. "And if he's gone to the trouble of getting me out here, he must know that I've found out about his embezzling and that I was going to go to the cops." She darted around the room, shaking her head. "I'd thought I would dig up a bit more from the accounts, make sure the case was rock-solid, that no one could turn it back and say that I'd been involved or something, you know? Shit."

I felt a lump form in my guts. If she was telling the truth, then the suit wasn't going to be looking to get her paid off and out of town. He'd be looking for something much more permanent.

Marvin turned toward me. "This on the level?"

How the fuck should I know? I ran my hand over my face, thought hard. I didn't have a name for the person who'd hired me, didn't even have a name for the woman we'd grabbed. It had seemed like an easy job. Maybe too damned easy.

I went to the window and glanced out. It was already so dark that I couldn't see more than a dozen metres from the cabin. I didn't hear anything, but what did that mean? Anyone could've been out there.

I turned back and saw that Marvin was standing up, getting his gear together.

"I'm with her," he said. "Let's get out of here."

I walked over by him and lowered my voice. "What if she's playing us?"

He glanced at her, looked back at me. "I don't think so, Lawrence."

"So what, then?"

Marvin scratched his head and sighed. "We'll figure that out, right?"

I crossed the room and took the woman by her arm. Marvin got to the door first and pulled it open. A bang greeted him and a bullet zinged through the room.

He swore and slammed the door shut.

"Give me the girl!" he yelled.

I hesitated briefly. "Look," he said. "We give her to them and they've got no reason to worry about us, right? I ain't got no evidence of anything."

"No, you'd just be a witness to murder."

He shook his head. "Do you have a better plan?"

Marvin yanked the girl out of my grasp. She bucked against his hold but he dragged her up to the front door.

He slid it open just a crack. "I've got the woman and I'm sending her out. My buddy and me will stay in here until you're gone."

No voice answered him and after several heartbeats he opened the door a bit wider. As he did so, the woman kicked her heel up, catching him between the legs. Marvin's gun clattered to the ground and both he and the woman fell, knocking the door wide open. From outside came a second shot and then a third. Marvin cried out and the woman scuttled away from the door.

I headed for the back of the cabin, where it butted up against a bunch of trees. The girl was alongside me and stopped my hand when

I went to grab for the handle of the back door. I saw she held Marvin's pistol in her other hand. Right, then.

She indicated the open window off to one side of the room. A quick glance outside confirmed what she suspected. There was a man waiting on the other side of the back door, ready to shoot whoever came through it. Meanwhile, voices were growing louder at the front.

I took a deep breath, said a little prayer, leaned out the window and took two shots. The man at the back door crumpled to the ground. For a fraction of a second, I thought about what I had just done, but the girl hissed "Come on!" and I put everything out of my mind except survival.

She burst through the door and I followed. We went around a corner, keeping low, listening for the other people. I heard at least two inside the cabin.

At the front of the cabin I scanned the area. If there was anyone out there, the darkness had them well-covered.

"Make a run for the car?" I asked the woman in a whisper.

She nodded. I counted three with my fingers and then we both sprinted across the open ground. She got to the car first. A shot rang out just as her fingers touched the door handle. She screamed and dropped to the ground, Marvin's gun bouncing beneath the car. Bright red blood stood out against the car door's beige paint.

I turned, saw the shooter, and pulled my trigger. The bullet caught him in the shoulder. He fell in the grassy lawn and my second shot stilled him forever.

In the echoes of the gunshots, nearly everything went still. Only whimpers from the woman I'd kidnapped that morning reached my ears. I knew there was another person out there looking for me. But now I was the one who could camp outside, watching for someone to come through the door.

I crouched down behind the car, letting its bulk shield most of my body. The stillness dragged out long enough that I began to wonder if maybe I'd been mistaken. If everyone but me and the woman was dead or gone.

Then, from inside, a voice: "Don't shoot, Lawrence. You and I can still get out of this with what we want."

The suit from the Durban bar stepped slowly into the frame made by the open doorway. He held his hands up, his gun loose in his right hand. I kept my own weapon steady on him.

"You don't really want any part of this, do you, Lawrence?" He took a couple of slow steps forward, toward the cabin's porch. "I checked up on you, after all. You're not a violent fellow."

My heart thudded and it felt like I could sense my pulse in my neck, in my arms, in every inch of my body. I thought about the man at the back door, the man sprawled out here in the front yard. Not a violent fellow?

The suit had gotten to the front of the porch and was about to lower his foot onto the first step when I fired. My bullet caught him square and he tumbled down the front stairs. I waited, holding my breath, watching to see if he moved again. His left arm moved once and I got ready to take another shot. But then he got still and stayed that way.

A breeze I hadn't noticed rustled the leaves of the trees around us. In the distance an animal howled. The wounded woman sobbed.

I stayed crouched there, three times a killer. From somewhere a few tears gathered in the corners of my eyes. I didn't bother to wipe them away.

I stood at last, tucked my gun into my pants, and went around to where the woman leaned against one of the car's rear tires.

"They're all dead," I told her.

She nodded, her face pale in the dim early evening moonlight.

I bent down and inspected her wound. The bullet had passed through her left hand; it was a bloody mess and I figured she was in shock.

"Come on," I told her. "Let's get out of here. I'll drop you off at a hospital, they can get that patched up for you."

She didn't answer me. I reached out for her good hand with one of mine and after a brief hesitation, she took it and pulled herself up.

I got in the car, turned the engine over, and circled the car around the lawn. We went down the bumpy dirt road at a crawl in the dark; when I got to the main road I wanted to floor it, to burn off some of the nervous energy in a burst of speed. But I kept it to the limit.

The girl dozed off and on during the drive.

At one point, she woke and in a painfully clear voice asked, "What happens now?"

I waited a few seconds, hoping she'd drop back off to sleep. But I felt her eyes on me and couldn't avoid the question.

"Like I said back there, I'll drop you off at a hospital. Then I'll be on my way." I shrugged. "And we can both pretend like this never happened."

I chanced a peek over at her. She nodded drowsily. "Never happened..."

"Exactly right," I lied.

Jealousy—the catalyst for many a crime story. Usually the characters are all human, though.

Polly Wants...

by Kou K. Nelson

"GOOD MORNING, POLLY," the lady said as she walked into the room.

She flung open the drapes, illuminating the small office.

"Good morning," the parrot said, bobbing its grey head, shuffling its feet back and forth on her perch.

"Polly want an apple?" the lady asked.

She opened the cage and offered the bird a slice of apple as the bird stepped into the door frame.

"Apple," the bird said, reaching for the fruit, but nipping the woman's finger.

The fruit fell to the floor.

"Bad bird," the lady scolded, sucking her finger as she retrieved the apple.

"Cracker," the bird squawked and retreated into the cage.

"Silly bird," the lady said. "No crackers in the morning."

"Cracker," the bird mumbled and shuffled to the end of its perch, pressing itself against the wrought iron bars.

The bird's pupils grew and shrank and it shook its head repeatedly. The woman frowned and stepped back from the cage.

"Fucking bird," the man muttered from the doorway behind her.

"What's that?" she asked, turning around.

The man was thin, unshaven.

"You care more about that fucking bird than you do me," he said. "Have you made the coffee yet?"

"No," she admitted reluctantly.

He shrugged.

"Alright. Alright," she said, leaving the room.

"Pretty bird," the parrot said, shuffling towards towards the cage door.

The man lunged at the cage, startling the parrot, making it screech and beat its wings. The man cackled.

"What's going on in there?" the lady called from another room.

The man glanced down the hallway.

"Bad bird," the parrot said.

"Shut the fuck up, or I'll make you shut up," the man growled before leaving.

"Cracker," the bird said, ruffling its feathers.

The parrot stood on its perch by the window.

"Pretty bird. Grape." *Whistle, cluck.* "Good morning." *Cluck,cluck, whistle.*

The lady walked into the room. "How are you doing, Polly?"

The parrot sidled across the perch to be closer to the lady. *Whistle.* "Pretty bird. How are you doing, Polly?"

The lady laughed. "I'm doing fine, thank you."

She opened the drawer of her desk and the parrot cocked its head.

"Ready to work?" the lady asked.

"Work!" the parrot squawked, then made clicking sounds, rolling a bit of something in its beak.

"Good, Polly," the lady said and pulled out a plastic box. "Ready?" she asked as she opened it.

The bird teetered on the very end of the perch.

"Bad bird," the lady said. "No peeking," she laughed again.

"Bad bird," the parrot said and repeated the woman's laugh.

The bird stepped back.

The woman held up an object. "What color is this?"

"Green," the parrot said.

"Good, Polly," the woman replied with a smile and held out a small slice of orange.

The bird took the orange with its beak, and ate while the woman typed something and then scrounged around in the box. She held up another object.

"What shape is this?" she asked.

The parrot turned its left eye to it and scratched its head with its foot. "Square," it said.

"Good, Polly," the woman said and this time held out two things. "Strawberry or banana?" she asked.

"Berry," the bird said and took the strawberry from the woman.

The lady typed some more.

"Want some tunes?" she asked before turning on the music.

The bird clucked and whistled, bobbed, and wove its head. It made some new noises: *POP! Bapapapapapap! SHRIEEEEEEEEEK! POP! BANG!*

The woman turned around, her eyes large. "When did you learn that?" she asked, drawing her face closer to the bird and furrowing her brow. "Jared!" she called down the hall. "Jared! Have you been playing that stupid video game again?"

"What?" the man's voice called back.

The woman stood and went to the doorway. The parrot quieted and cocked its head.

"Didn't I ask you not to play that horrid game?" the woman demanded. "It's violent and now Polly's imitating gunfire and screams."

Polly made the new sounds again and the woman frowned at it.

"What?" the man asked again as he walked up to the doorway.

The bird sidled closer to the window, clucking and grumbling softly.

"That video game - -" the lady began.

"I told you, I gave *Guns of Glory* to Sid," the man said to the lady, although he glanced at the parrot.

"Bad bird," the parrot said and the man narrowed his eyes at it.

"Well, Polly's making sounds from it and she wasn't doing it last week," the lady explained.

The man shrugged. "So the bird makes some noise. Maybe this is just the first time you heard it."

"She understands," the lady said.

She returned to her desk and held up two objects from the box. The bird slowly returned to the center of its perch.

"Which one's purple, Polly?" the lady asked.

"Purple," the bird said, using its beak to tug on the purple key.

"Voila," the woman said to the man.

The man folded his arms across his chest. "It's just associating words to specific objects," he said. "It's not like it knows what those words mean."

"Isn't that how language begins?" the woman asked.

The bird shuffled impatiently on its perch. "Pretty bird," the parrot said.

"Yes, you're a pretty bird, Polly," the woman sighed, turning back to the bird. "Banana or strawberry?"

The man raised a finger at the bird.

"Cracker," the bird said.

"Fucking pigeon," the man muttered as he left. "I'll get you."

The room flashed blue and red. The parrot flapped its wings, uncomfortable in the dark. Two men carried lights on large sticks.

"Any word from the neighbors?" the taller man in black said to the other man in black.

The bird cocked its head as the light outside caught on the shiny objects, like mirrors on the men's chests. Something else shiny dangled from their waists.

"Nobody heard anything," the shorter man said. "The back window's busted, but this room's the only one trashed."

Both men shined their lights onto the scattered paper and the lady on the floor. Her eyes didn't shine in the light.

"What's going on here?" the unshaven man said as he came rushing into the room then stopped abruptly. "Oh, shit ..."

The parrot squawked and beat its wings wildly, stirring up paper and other detritus.

"Hey! Hey! Hey!" the men in black cried out at the bird. "Settle down, now!"

The bird stopped beating its wings and let them droop while it panted and eyed the man.

"I'm her boyfriend, officers," the man said motioning to the lady, then buried his hands in his hair. "Oh, shit. Ohshitohshitohshit."

"Cracker," the bird said.

The man dropped his hands and glared at the parrot. He waved his arms at it, making it flap its wings again. "Fuck you," he said.

"Enough, o.k.?" the shorter man said, placing himself between the bird and the unshaven man.

The man nodded and ran a hand through his hair again. The taller man in black pulled out a pen and paper from his pocket.

"Where were you before you came here?" the taller man said.

"At school," the man unshaven man replied, then glanced at the woman and wiped his mouth. "Oh, shit, she's dead, isn't she?"

"Seems like it," the tall man muttered as he wrote.

The parrot tilted its head and looked at the figure on the floor. "I'll get you," the parrot said, imitating the man's voice.

"What's that?" the shorter man in black said, looking at the unshaven man first and then the bird.

"Fucking parrot," the unshaven man said with a shrug and nervous laugh.

"So, you were at school?" the other man in black continued.

"Yeah, the university. I - -"

"Shut the fuck up, or I'll make you shut up," the bird said using the man's voice again.

The men in black looked at the bird and frowned.

"It's just a bird," the unshaven man said.

The bird used the new noises, the ones the lady didn't like, the banging and popping and shrieking.

"Is that gunshot the bird's doing?" the shorter man in black asked his companion.

"Sounds like it," the taller man in black said and shined his light on the red splotch on the lady's chest.

The men in black looked at the other man.

"Bad bird," the parrot clucked and shook its head. "Bad bird."

"It's just a fucking bird," the unshaven man said to the men in black, his voice higher-pitched.

"I'll get you," the bird said in the man's voice then started to squawk and beat its wings once more.

"Holy crap," the shorter man in black gasped, his mouth dropping open. "Do you think that parrot is actually trying to tell us something?"

The unshaven man's eyes grew wide. "It's a *bird*! A fucking bird, goddammit!"

"Shut the fuck up, or I'll make you shut up," the bird screamed in the man's voice. "I'll get you! I'll get you!"

The men in black exchanged glances.

"You're going to have to come with us, sir," the taller one said, putting the shiny objects that dangled from his waist onto the unshaven man's wrists.

They made a clicking sound which the parrot copied.

"Are you kidding me?" the unshaven man said in dismay. "You're arresting me because of what a *bird* said?"

"Well, you *are* the boyfriend," the shorter man acknowledged. "So that would make you a person of interest anyway."

"You believe that bird?" the man said as they dragged him out of the room. "You *believe* a fucking pigeon?"

"Cracker," the parrot said and imitated the lady's laugh.

Simple jobs have a way of becoming more complicated, but that's why they pay you the big bucks, isn't it?

Hazard Pay
by Nick Andreychuk

THE STENCH OF stale urine made me want to vomit into the piss-warm beer I was drinking from a dirty glass. I tried to ignore it because I'd picked the stool at the end of the bar, close to the stinking washrooms, for a reason—I wanted to listen to the conversation next to me.

Normally, I sat at the other end of the bar, near the cash register, so that I could flirt with the waitresses when they placed their drink orders. But no time for that tonight, just official P.I. business, as my partner Diggs used to call it. I'd been tailing the man sitting beside me for the last few weeks. I couldn't believe my luck when he led me right to one of my favorite downtown haunts, Sauce & Brews. S&B's notorious for selling the cheapest hot wings in Buffalo—and considering that Buffalo is world-famous for its deep-fried chicken wings, that's saying something. The place was as dark as a cavern though, so I figured the low utility bill probably balanced out any money lost on wing sales.

Actually, I really couldn't have *asked* the guy, Laslo, to have his meeting at a better location. I mean, if he'd gone to some ritzy place like Chez Nous, I would've stuck out like a Leafs fan at a Sabres game, and he might have paid me more attention. But since I received a big "hey" from the bartender and friendly nods from several regulars, I blended right in with the S&B crowd.

Laslo didn't even glance at me when I sat next to him. Of course, watching the entrance occupied his full attention anyway. Laslo looked about forty, with wispy black hair and more than a little gray. With his beer gut and haggard features, he would've fit right in at S&B. Only his three-piece suit stood out.

Just as the bartender placed a second shot of tequila and a beer chaser in front of me, a man in an expensive suit walked in, his bald head barely clearing the doorframe. He stopped and scanned the dark room, looking for Laslo. Either that, or he'd come in to ask directions to Chez Nous.

Sure enough, the suit walked directly to the empty stool next to Laslo. He looked around nervously when he sat. I ignored him, and pretended to be transfixed by the TV mounted on the corner wall of the well-stocked bar. The Sabres were playing—and winning—so most eyes in the place were on the game anyway.

After the new guy had relaxed a little with the help of a martini, I cocked my ear towards them, being careful not to make eye contact.

"...don't understand why we can't just do it here," Laslo said.

"It's not private enough," the other man replied.

"I like crowds. Nothing personal, but I'm not going out back with you. I've got the sample in my hand—do you want it or not?"

"Very well—give it to me."

Then, so fast and inconspicuously that I would have missed it if I hadn't looked over just then, Laslo slipped Baldy an envelope.

"Okay, Conway, so when do I get my million?"

I nearly spit out my brew. *Million?* That was a lot of dough. I'd have to talk to my client about upping my fee.

"*Never* mention my name, nor discuss the amount in a public place." I'd already returned my gaze to the TV screen, but I didn't have to look at Conway to sense his irritation. "Now," he said, "*if* this program performs the way you say it will—with no loopholes, a virtually *impenetrable* firewall—and *if* you deliver the entire, unencrypted program, *then* you will be appropriately rewarded."

"Rewarded how?"

"When ,u give me the program, I'll give you the access code for an off-shore bank account."

"Okay. So, where and when do we meet next?"

Just then, a familiar, greasy teenager slunk past us into the men's washroom. I'd actually been hoping to run into this punk for the last few days, but the timing couldn't have been worse. The washroom door had stuck slightly open, but it squeaked loudly as the teenager pulled on it to get inside.

"Sounds good to me," Laslo said.

Damn. I'd missed Conway's answer.

Frustrated, I stood and headed into the can. The giant cat-litter stench worsened considerably inside, wreaking havoc on my nostrils. The source of the smell was obvious. S&B didn't have urinals like most civilized places. Instead, some genius had thought it would be manly to have a long trough instead—like the ones I've seen in the barracks of old war forts. You could only fit three guys comfortably across, and often there were five or six guys pushing to get in—not exactly my idea of male bonding. At this moment, however, the washroom's only occupant was the sleazeball I'd followed in.

A sleazeball drug-dealer who went by the street name K-Z, whatever that stood for. I'd heard his name from my twelve-year-old nephew, Jake Diggs. He's not my nephew by blood, but he calls me uncle and his father's the closest thing I ever had to a brother. And ever since his father died, Jake's looked up to me like a big brother. When I'd seen him last, he'd been all shook up because one of his friends had gotten a "bad rush" from some crap K-Z had sold him. K-Z regularly pushed to kids. It made my stomach turn. I'd been hoping to have a few words with him ever since. And tonight was my lucky night. K-Z's luck, on the other hand, was about to take a turn for the worse.

He looked up as I walked in, then looked away as he zipped up and stepped away from the trough.

"*Yo,*" I said. "Aren't you K-Z?"

He turned toward me. "Yeah. What's it to you?"

I pulled out a picture of my nephew, which I happened to be carrying for this specific purpose, and showed it to him. "You recognize this kid?"

"I see a lot of losers like this...I don't know...perhaps you could give me somethin' *more*, to jog my memory?" K-Z held out his hand expectantly.

"Sure thing," I said. I reached into my pocket and pulled out a roll of coins. Ten bucks worth of quarters, but I had no intention of greasing his palm. I wrapped my fingers around the roll, and drove my fist into his kidneys.

He doubled over, coughing.

I gave him a minute to recover, then shoved the picture under his face and repeated my question.

He spat on it.

I grabbed the front of K-Z's shirt, wiped off the spit, put the picture away, then drove my weighted fist into his left shoulder-blade.

He screamed in pain as he fell to his knees. Then he pulled a knife from his jacket pocket. I'd expected him to be carrying, so I was ready for it. As he jabbed the knife toward me, I grabbed his forearm and smashed his wrist onto the edge of the trough. I heard a bone snap and the knife flew into the yellow-stained back wall of the communal urinal. It slid down and landed with a small splash.

"I'm gonna mess you up!" K-Z wailed.

"No, what you're going to do is stay the hell away from the kid in the picture. Better yet, find a new neighborhood, 'cause if I ever see you again, I'm going to kill you."

"Fuck you."

I backhanded him hard across the face.

K-Z spat a wad of blood onto my shoes. "I said, *fuck you!*"

"All that blow's gone to your head, 'cause you're one stupid shithead." I returned the coins to my pocket, grabbed him by the back of his belt, and shoved him headfirst over the edge of the trough. "Now, do I make you fish out your knife with your teeth, or are you going to get the hell out of Buffalo?"

With his nose inches away from so much piss and puke and God-knows-what-else, K-Z suddenly became more cooperative. "Sure, boss—whatever you say, man. Just let me up!"

I pulled him up and flung him backward toward one of the stalls. He stumbled as he knocked into the toilet. Its seat was up, so K-Z fell ass-first into the unflushed bowl.

I left him there to contemplate his future.

When I returned to the bar, the stools next to mine were empty. No worries though, I figured that the main exchange wouldn't be going down until at least the next day. Besides, I knew where Laslo lived. I considered ordering some wings and watching the rest of the hockey game, but I figured I should make sure Laslo had gone home and then check in with my client. Plus, I didn't feel like being in the middle of the scene K-Z was sure to make when he came out of the can.

Sure enough, when I pulled up in front of Laslo's low-rise apartment, I could see him through the window. Watching TV alone.

After sitting in my car and watching him for more than an hour, I decided that Laslo had settled in for the night. I took out my cell-phone and called my client. I gave him a full report, except that I left out the part about how I technically didn't follow Laslo home. Oh, and I also left out the buyer's name—just in case I needed leverage later. When I told him about the million-dollar price tag, my client flipped out.

I held the phone an inch away from my ear as he shouted, "A million! We're talking about a program that's going to revolutionize the electronic security of any and all computer systems online or off. That idiot's going to make me lose *billions*! And for what? A lousy million!"

I figured that then would be as good a time as any to mention that I wanted him to triple my daily pay for me to continue.

"I'll give you *ten times* as much—*if* you stop the exchange from taking place."

"He's at home right now. Why don't you just come over here and demand that he return the program?"

"Because he probably has backup copies—he's the one who developed the program in the first place. He thinks he owns it, but he knew when he signed on with us that everything developed at Disctech is Disctech property. No, the only way is to stop the exchange."

"Even if I do, what's to say he won't find another buyer?"

"You're right. I'm going to kill that bastard!" He paused, then asked, "Do you carry a gun?"

"Why? Are you expecting the exchange to get violent? I told you when you hired me that I don't do volatile situations anymore. Not after what happened to my partner—" Diggs had been killed in the crossfire when a love triangle went bad.

"Shit happens."

"Hey, show some respect! You could only hope to be *half* the man he—."

"Look, I didn't mean anything by it—"

"I'm not risking my hide for what you're paying me, even at three or ten times the usual rate."

"Would you let me finish? Look, Laslo's not the violent type. Before he pulled this stunt, I didn't think he had any backbone at all. I don't expect the exchange to get violent. What I was *trying* to say is that I want you to take care of this problem *permanently*."

"Hold it, I don't do that type of thing." Well, maybe a drug-dealer or a rapist, but a white-collar criminal? No way. What kind of lowlife did he take me for?

"I'll give you a *million*."

I almost reconsidered. Almost. I'd promised Diggs on his death-bed that I'd look out for his kid, and I figured that putting Jake through college would be a big step toward insuring his future. But college tuition isn't a good enough reason for murder. "No way," I said. "I'll tell you what. For that kind of money, I'll rough him up, give him a good scare, but I ain't no cold-blooded killer." I really didn't want to put a beating on Laslo either since I had no beef with him, but a mil is...well, it's a damn good incentive is what it is.

"There's too much at stake here. He has to be stopped. If you won't take care of this, I'll—"

A car door slammed in front of me and I missed the end of my client's rant. I'd been so intent on the phone conversation—and, admittedly, more than a little distracted by the thought of getting my hands on a million bucks—that I'd looked away from Laslo's window. I'd purposely parked behind his car earlier, and now I watched it speed off down the street.

"Shit, he's leaving."

"Follow him! What the hell do I pay you for?"

"Well, you're not paying me to whack him, and I'm not budging until we're clear on that."

"Fine. Just stop the transaction, and I'll reward you handsomely."

"I'm glad we agree. I'll call you later."

I turned off the phone, and took off after Laslo. His car's disgusting bright purple paintjob made it easy to spot. Laslo led me right back to Sauce & Brews. Shit. He'd be suspicious if he saw me walking in there again. I had to get in ahead of him, so he'd think that I'd never left.

I parked a few cars back from his, and ran to catch up to him.

He was about to pass a middle-aged woman talking on a public telephone. I had to think fast, so I'm not too proud of what I did.

The woman's back was to us. I stepped over to her left side, stretched my arm around her back, and squeezed her right breast.

She screamed and turned to Laslo as he walked past on her right. He heard her outcry and turned toward her.

The woman swung the handset at him and balled him out for being a pervert.

He didn't even notice as I slipped past them and entered S&B.

The place was still packed, but the stools near the washroom were empty again. I quickly returned to my previous spot and ordered another beer.

Laslo looked a little frazzled when he came in a minute later. Apparently my presence didn't surprise him, because he barely glanced at me, even though he was walking right toward me. He approached the stool he'd been sitting in before, but then walked right on by. To my surprise, he went straight out the back door. So much for refusing to do the exchange out back.

Damn. Now I needed an excuse for going out there.

I hurried over to a regular who I knew to be a chain-smoker and asked him for a butt. He obliged without hesitation, but gave me a quizzical look as he handed me the cigarette. I just shrugged. Fortunately, the game had him too distracted for him to consider asking me when I'd taken up smoking.

I walked out the back door, and stopped dead in my tracks.

Laslo lay on the ground, blood streaming from his chest. I didn't see anyone around, so I crouched down and checked for a pulse. I found a weak beat. *Better than nothing.*

I took off Laslo's tie to use as a makeshift bandage. With his entire shirt soaked in blood, it took me a moment to find the small wound. *A bullet hole?* Who the hell shot him? My client? But he didn't know where we were. Did he?

"Ain't this my lucky day." Someone had stepped out from behind a dumpster.

It was K-Z. And he had a gun.

"You bastard," I said. "What'd you shoot him for? Tired of killing people slowly with your chemicals?"

"Hey, man, it's his own fault. I was in the middle of a transaction—yeah, that's right, *bitch*, I'm still conducting business in your neighborhood...*no one* tells me where I can operate. So, anyway, this putz," K-Z gestured at Laslo with his gun, "comes bursting into the middle of my deal. He startled me, so I popped him." K-Z shrugged, then scowled. "Scared off my customer too, so he deserves what he got."

I had a feeling that K-Z planned to pop me too, so I wanted to keep him talking until I could figure a way out. Regrettably, the only things that came to my mind were antagonistic. I noticed that K-Z's right wrist sported a poorly wrapped tensor bandage—the kind you'd find in a cheap first aid kit. "I'm surprised you were able to shoot straight with your left hand," I said.

"Fuck you. I'm ambidextrous."

"*Woo*, big word—did you learn that before you flunked out of kindergarten?"

K-Z stepped toward me, his gun pointed at my head.

"I've had enough of your lip," he said. "You won't be able to shoot your mouth off once I *shoot your mouth off*..."

His finger tightened on the trigger.

I jumped up, pulling out my roll of coins as I did so, and threw the coins as hard as I could at his head.

He ducked, and I leapt for the door.

He fired and my gut burst into flames. The blow knocked me off my feet. I looked up and saw him walking toward me. He held the gun out at arm's length, ready to finish me off.

Suddenly, the door swung open.

"Oh my Lord!" a familiar voice screamed.

K-Z fired once more—the bullet grazed the pavement inches from my head—then he ran off into the night.

The next day, the article in the paper referred to Conway and me simply as "bar patrons"—our names were never mentioned. And the article stated that Laslo lost his life for his wallet, which the police had later found in K-Z's possession.

My nephew came to visit me in the hospital, and he brought me some beef jerky. He didn't think I'd want the girly flowers or chocolates his mom had wanted to buy. What a kid. He asked me if he could do anything to help me get better, and I told him to go to college.

"But uncle," he said, "I don't have to think about that for years."

I looked him hard in the eyes, and said, "It's never too early to think about your future."

When Jake left, his mother hung back. She touched my hand gently. "It's good of you to want Jakey to go to college," she said. "But I don't think I'll be able to afford it."

"Jake's going to college," I said. "And that's a promise."

She didn't argue, just told me to get well, and followed after little Jake Diggs.

Later that day, my client came to visit me as well. He informed me that the police had told him that they hadn't found any computer disks in Laslo's possession. He assumed that K-Z had stolen it as well. I didn't disagree. I handed him the private investigation report I had done on Laslo—the report that didn't include Conway's name. I felt I owed more of a debt to the man who'd saved my life than I did to my client. Besides, I don't particularly like smarmy businessmen who try to coerce me into offing their disloyal employees.

My client didn't bring flowers, but he did bring my paycheck. He wasn't too happy with my report, but he paid me anyway—the last day at triple my original fee. Of course, he never realized just how *much* he actually paid me. After all, that bullet nearly ended my life, and I'd forewarned him about the high price for risking my life, so I didn't feel guilty when I forgot to mention that I'd found a certain disk in Laslo's pocket. I figured I was owed a little hazard pay...

A former police officer finds a boatload of trouble while looking for a woman who goes missing after a row around the lake.

The Woman Who Rowed Away
by Tom Swoffer

I WAS SITTING on the deck of my family-inherited summer cottage, nursing my third seven-seven and watching the late afternoon sun setting like a dark purple bruise over the lake, when I first spotted her. Though nearly a hundred yards away, that lustrous yellow bikini instantly caught my attention. Even from this distance I could tell how spectacularly she filled it out.

I had come up here from the city to forget about signing my final divorce papers this morning. After twelve years of marriage Liz and I had lost all faith in each other's fidelity. In response, she'd left me: my share of our joint account- fifteen grand in cash, which I intended to blow a fair share of drowning my anger and frustration, while still owing almost twelve on my car; an assortment of odds and ends- mostly junk except for the collection of rare coins my grandfather had bequeathed me, and now would most likely serve as my pension someday; and this run down old cottage she'd rarely visited. What I wanted was to get drunk and watch the sun drop off the horizon, just like the direction my life now seemed headed.

Why couldn't my neighbor in sunny yellow be seventy years old, like the Uptons, who lived down the road? Why was she parading around on her deck, her light-brown hair glowing like warm honey, reminding me of the one thing I would miss with my wife- notwithstanding her willingness to share it with others: screwing each other silly on a sultry summer day.

The body certainly was mesmerizing, but what about her face? Against my better judgment, I got the binoculars that sat on the kitchen window sill. Focusing them on her was like watching a flower bloom. Her lips, soft and supple, held an enigmatic smile; one of those classically eloquent noses you wanted to kiss the tip of; and eyes clear and deep as a mid-summer's day sky—a face that could easily inspire desirable dreams in both poets and fools. She sat down gracefully, extending her long, firm legs along the lounge chair, while her ample breasts gently rose and fell like a hypnotist's watch rhythmically rising and falling before my longing gaze.

Reluctantly, I pulled the binoculars away before she noticed me ogling her like some horny teenager. Though her attention seemed drawn to something across the horizon of the lake. I wondered if she even noticed my presence, so obviously lost in personal thoughts of her own.

The next morning I was awoken by a quick series of sharp knocks. I looked over at the clock on the nightstand: nine-thirty. Pushing myself out of bed, the hangover hammering my defenseless brain like some sadistic pile-driving maniac, I stumbled out to the front door. Two men, wearing cleanly pressed off-the-rack suits stood there, badges in hand and routine questions in their eyes.

"Sorry if we woke you," one of them said, watching me leaning precariously against the door jamb in my shorts, bare feet and bloodshot eyes. "Just asking everyone if they'd seen Rachel Hall out on the lake this morning."

"Sorry, I don't know who Rachel Hall is."

My answer seemed to get the other police officer's attention. "She lived next door to you?"

That perked my attention. "Something wrong?"

"That's what we're trying to find out. We found her kayak floating upside down on the lake this morning."

I felt like he'd sucker-punched me in the gut. "I saw her out on her deck last evening. Guess I slept in this morning."

"Sorry to have woken you," the first officer said, and they both turned and headed for their car parked at the end of my driveway. Before the one officer got into the passenger side he looked back at me with a hint of suspicion in his eyes.

If they had detected any signs of guilt, however, it'd been because I didn't want to mention what I'd been doing with my binoculars. Feeling even more disheartened than I'd felt yesterday, I made some strong, dark coffee then sprawled on a deck chair and let the morning sun broil last night's booze out of me. I looked over at Rachel Hall's cottage and sensed an eerie emptiness there. I remembered her gazing out over the lake and it was then that I saw the police boat. Two men were leaning over the side, apparently looking for something in the water. I brought out my binoculars again to get a better look.

About the time I had them focused a diver popped out of the water. I could tell by the expression on all their faces that they were disappointed over something. I didn't need to read lips to know they were searching for her body.

An image of a woman materialized: tangled in weeds at the bottom of the lake, fish swimming through her flowing honey-brown hair. What a waste. And for a moment I thought: Why couldn't it have been the cheating bitch I'd married?

I continued watching the police boat drag its net slowly back and forth, back and forth near where her kayak had been pulled ashore. Time stopped—it could have been an hour, it could have been an eternity of loss and regret, until I heard another knock on my front door.

I felt a sudden chill slide down my spine; then realized the police had no reason to notify me if they found her body.

The Uptons, the elderly couple who lived down the road, were standing at my door. The old man smiling patiently at his wife as she gazed forlornly at what survived of the shrubbery in front of the cottage.

"Hello," the old man said, "it's been a long time since we've seen you up here, Tony."

"It's nice to see you again, Mr. Upton. Mrs. Upton."

The old lady took one more look at the shrubbery before her dim eyes turned towards me. "It's such a shame no one's been able to care for your place in such a long time."

My mother had stopped coming up here after my father died, and my sister and both brothers had their own family weekend getaways. "Well, I think I may be coming up here more often now," I told her. Yard work had never really been my thing, but I suppose it could take my mind off all the negative crap I'd been forced to swim in lately.

"Liz didn't come with you?" Mrs. Upton asked, though I sensed she already knew the answer.

"She's kind of moved on," I mumbled.

The old man placed an arm tenderly across his wife's shoulders and asked, "Can we talk to you for a few minutes, son?"

"Of course," I automatically replied. I'd known these people since

I was nine years old, and had always respected their kindness and wisdom towards me and my family. I offered them the couch and asked if I could make another pot of coffee.

"Oh no," Mrs. Upton quickly answered. "We had our breakfast long ago."

I sat down opposite them. It was plain in their anxious faces they wanted to ask me something so I tried to make myself as open as possible.

"I suppose you heard about Rachel?" the old man finally asked after silently consulting with his wife as to who would start. "She was our niece."

"My sister and her husband died just before Rachel graduated from high school," Mrs. Upton added. "She's been very independent since then."

"The police were here earlier. I'm afraid I didn't get a chance to meet her," I said.

Fighting back tears, Mrs. Upton stated, "Deep down, she's a good person, Tony. Maybe she could be a little too wild at times, but she's still young. It's that husband she married..." she concluded, no longer able to fight off her tears.

"The police asked us if Rachel seemed depressed," Mr. Upton confided, watching me to be sure I understood the implications of that.

"Why would they ask you a question like that?" I snapped, ready to jump up and go punch the idiot who'd asked them such a question.

"Because the lake was so calm this morning. And I'd told them how she was an excellent swimmer..."

"Rachel was on the crew team that year she went to college," Mrs. Upton interjected.

"She rowed around the lake every morning since she'd come up here," Mr. Upton explained. "All the way around."

"She was in excellent shape," Mrs. Upton smiled proudly through her teary eyes.

I hoped she didn't notice me blush as her remark reminded me of what I'd been doing with my binoculars yesterday. "What can I do to help?"

"You were a policeman for a while, weren't you?" Mr. Upton asked;

and both of them looked towards me pleadingly. "We don't usually like to pry, but..."

"Go talk to that husband of hers," Mrs. Upton demanded, her eyes dry and angry now. "Rachel told me all about his fooling around. She admitted she only married him for his money."

"Suppose she was getting ready to divorce him. That's what she told me she was up here for," Mr. Upton finished.

I recalled that look Rachel had as she gazed towards the setting sun: serene and reflective, yet also a look of finality, similar to Liz's the day I walked out of the house for the last time. "I'll do what I can," I promised them.

After they left I thought about making myself a drink, noticed the clock hadn't reached noon yet, so poured some juice into a tall, ice filled glass and went back out to the deck. With a name, she now seemed more real; not just some anonymous stranger in a yellow bikini; not to mention that face, as it had suddenly focused in my binoculars.

I scanned the lake, hoping against cruel common sense I'd see her swimming gracefully towards me, like Gene Tierney in that old movie, Leave Her To Heaven.

But I couldn't ignore the police boat still drifting on the other side of the lake. I'd been a cop for three years, close to promotion to detective bureau, when I'd married Liz. Six months into our marriage she insisted I quit the force and go work for her father's company, supervising routine security, before he'd closed his manufacturing plant. Except for an incident with one disgruntled maintenance man, the job had been as boring and duplicitous as our marriage eventually became.

I really didn't expect to learn anything talking to Rachel's husband, I just wanted to see how he was taking his wife's disappearance. Hall owned a construction company, and when I called his office his secretary directed me out to Black Diamond, an old mining town about an hour out of Seattle, about to surrender whatever dignity it may once have had to the rapaciousness of suburbanization and his sprawling housing development.

A number of cookie-cutter housing shells dotted a freshly logged hillside with a shabby single-wide trailer at the entrance, marked with a cheap, generic Office sign out front. I parked between one of those behemoth extended-cab pickups and a tiny red convertible sports car.

A young peroxide-blonde, wearing a halter-top and jeans that looked sprayed on her curvaceous body, sat cross-legged on a couch, lazily skimming through a fashion magazine. She barely glanced at me as I entered.. A thick man sat at a desk back in a dark corner. He wore a short sleeve shirt with the name Bruno sewn over the pocket, which showed off not only his assortment of tattoos but also his muscle-bound bulk. He had a shaved head, gold earrings that glittered dully in the shaded light, and black wrap-around sunglasses on his forehead which emphasized his tough demeanor. "Can I help you?" he barked at me, without any hint of actually following through with that idea.

I tried making my strained smile friendly despite not feeling any friendly vibes around me. "I'd like to talk to Mr. Hall for just a moment. I promise I won't take up too much of his time."

"What about?"

"I'm staying up on Lake Walker, next door to Mrs. Hall's cottage."

The blonde lowered her magazine and stared at me.

"Yeah?" he snapped, giving the blonde a warning glance before leaning back and crossing his thick arms.

"I'm gonna go," the blonde said, jumping off the couch.

"You mind your own business," Bruno snarled, sliding his sunglasses down.

"Why don't you just mind your own damn business, Bruno," the blonde spat, strutting out of the trailer with a challenging look on her nervous face. Bruno watched her leave; even through the sunglasses I could feel the venom in his eyes.

I realized if I had any chance at seeing Hall, I'd need to break through Bruno's hostility. "Really I'm here for the Uptons, Mrs. Hall's aunt and uncle. They're quite upset about what's happened. I guess they just wanted me to find out if Mr. Hall could help them. Maybe any information about why Mrs. Hall could have had an accident."

"What do you think Hall could tell them? He wasn't there," Bruno said, as we both listened to the sports car start up and roar off, blowing a spray of gravel against the trailer.

"Maybe if I could just have a few minutes of his time. I realize he must be very busy..."

"Yeah, he is. Like I told you, he wasn't anywhere near there. Why would he know anything."

"Certainly he's concerned about her disappearance, though?"

Bruno sat up, grabbing the edge of the desk with his meaty hands. "You ain't no cop, so why don't you mind your own business."

I could tell by the way he was ready to spring at me our conversation was finished. "Well, thanks for your time," I said, turning and walking out the door. Half expecting Bruno wrapped around my neck before I reached the safety of my car.

I stopped at the liquor store to pick up another jug of whiskey; all I wanted to do was get good and drunk. Before getting out of my car, though, I thought about Rachel Hall. She seemed like a goddess on a pedestal to me now, and she'd died before I'd ever gotten the chance to actually meet her. I knew she was going to haunt my dreams for awhile.

I pounded the steering wheel. "No," I said firmly to myself. I wasn't going to give up this easily. Tomorrow I'd go to Hall's house and talk to him face to face. I owed it to the Uptons and Rachel, and maybe even to myself.

Next morning I expected them to answer the door with wary expectation, but instead was greeted by Mr. Upton's stunned face. "You hear the news?" he asked as he drew me into their neat little cottage.

Mrs. Upton was sitting at the kitchen table, looking equally stunned and lost. I figured the police must have found Rachel's body.

"I slept late," I told them. I hadn't followed the news reports since I'd come to Lake Walker. The world seemed to be spinning down the toilet; and now it'd become too personal.

Before I could tell them about my plans to confront Hall, the old man said: "They found Darrell Hall dead this morning."

I felt as stunned as they looked. "Accident?" I asked, though I sensed the answer already.

Mrs. Upton continued staring across the table, reminding me of Rachel's eyes—though hers had been decisive; the old lady's looked like she'd just been told life had officially been called off because of irrevocable darkness. "No, somebody slit his throat while he was sleeping," she said, a painful resignation in her voice as she forced out the uncomfortably accurate word slit.

"Was he alone?"

"Some girl was there; claims she was passed out drunk and didn't see anything. Police are holding her and some man who was living in their guest house though," Mr. Upton offered.

I thought about Bruno. Would he be jealous over a bimbo like that?

They both looked at me with confused eyes. "They think it was a burglary. The police are investigating."

Which one of them said that I'd forgotten by the time I made my way back home. I don't think they even cared what I'd learned, or not learned yesterday. They just sat at the table, numb. Without Darrell Hall to blame, they were faced with the bitter fact that there may never be any explanation why their beloved niece had disappeared.

Long past midnight I found myself staring out at the moon-dappled lake, wondering how I was going to put my own life back together. Trying out easily dismissed options born of desperation and grasping-at-straws hopelessness when something caught my eye. For a moment I thought it was just a mirage, and then I saw it again—a dim light sweeping around inside Rachel's cottage. Then I noticed the canoe tied to the dock below her deck. I hadn't seen it earlier.

My immediate thought: dumb kids, taking advantage of a tragedy to burglarize the place.

Damn it, maybe I couldn't help the Uptons find closure, but at least I could help protect the property.

I grabbed my flashlight and before slipping out the front door I debated whether to take the old shotgun hung across the fireplace. Then I realized I didn't know where the shells were, or even if it still worked after so many years. There was a baseball bat leaning next to the door so I grabbed that.

Cautiously, I crept down the lane towards the cottage, loose gravel scrunching under my sneakers sounding loud in the still night air. When I made it to the front door I could see the light was now steady at the rear of the cottage.

I could try the front door, but was uncertain whether it would be unlocked, or worse, creak when I opened it. I had to make my way around to the back, and confront whoever was in there directly.

Luckily for me, the path next to the cottage had been paved, so the only sounds were crickets and the lapping of the lake against the dock. I didn't hear any voices or footsteps inside. Creeping up the steps on to the deck I tip-toed lightly over to the door. By then I'd figured there was only one person inside.

Gambling I was right, and hoping some luck was due to come my way, I slowly twisted the knob. I should've been in Vegas, because the door swung open without a squeak.

On the kitchen table a gym bag sat wide open between two flickering candles. Someone's dim silhouette stood at the table, hands and wrists clearly lit by the light, methodically pushing bundles of cash and jewelry into the bag.

The hands suddenly stopped as I came through the door. I snapped on my flashlight with my right hand, my left firmly gripping the bat.

Her startled eyes looked wild in the harsh light, but that only seemed to make her even more alluring. I felt frozen, stunned, as if a dream had miraculously come to life. "You're her."

She could easily have picked up a gun and blown me dead. "Who the hell are you?"

"My name's Tony Denton. I'm your next door neighbor. Saw a light in here and came to investigate. Everyone thinks you're dead." The words rolled out as if from an automaton.

She saw me staring at the gym bag. "Yeah," she snapped, "it's money. And none of this is any of your concern. You've accomplished your mission, superhero, now please go back home and forget you ever saw me."

"What should I tell the Uptons? They've been worried sick about you. Even asked me to try and talk to your husband." I stopped. A shadow of panic slashed across her face when I mentioned her husband. "You know he's dead?"

"So I heard. Whatever made you think Darrell would talk to you? He has trouble with communication issues, in case you didn't notice," she said, clutching the gym bag protectively.

"Tell you the truth, I never got past Bruno."

"What did he say?" She seemed eager to hear my response.

"He definitely doesn't have communication issues. He told me to get lost, loud and clear," I confessed. "Nobody seemed too worried about you, except for the Uptons."

She momentarily relaxed her defenses. "I'm sorry about Aunt Marilyn and Uncle John. But I think they'd rather believe their own explanation than face the truth."

I knew it was time for me to leave, but that image of her parading around in that yellow bikini wouldn't let me go. "I realize this truth of yours isn't any of my business..."

"A superhero; and a wise man," she broke in. "As complex as you seem to be, I still don't see any need for you to hang around. I'll contact my aunt and uncle later."

I took one more glance at the gym bag and when I looked up her eyes glared at me with an icy intensity. Since she now considered me a wise man I figured I'd offer up what I knew; or at least assumed I knew. "Why did you kill him?"

She continued staring at me, and I felt like a deer being watched by a cougar. Then she relaxed her grip on the gym bag and gave me a quick, faint smile; like a blowtorch melting the icy atmosphere in the room. "Sure, why not. I guess I'm going to have to trust you. Or else kill you, too."

She closed the gym bag, appraising me for a moment. "Darrell's company was going broke. In case you haven't noticed, not many people can afford to buy a new house right now. Drowning in debt can twist you into a lot of knots. Darrell was already a spoiled little punk, had inherited the company from his daddy. Only time he ever touched a hammer was one night when he was drunk and waved one at me."

"I never touched my wife," I interjected.

"Oh," she laughed, "you're a goddamn eunuch, too?"

Her laugh made me blush, but at least I'd gotten her to laugh. Certainly a positive step in the right direction. "My problem was she was more than willing to touch any guy who pleased her."

"Who cares about that crap, anymore? I didn't kill Darrell just because he could be a cheating, sadistic bastard sometimes. Show me someone broke and frustrated who isn't. But when some money comes along—a lot of money," she glanced affectionately towards the gym bag, " it can motivate you to do some desperate things."

"You said he was broke?"

"Until a few weeks ago he was. Then he found some people willing to loan him money. And it was cash, not another bank loan. Not that any bank would loan him money right now anyway.

"Bruno came with the money; I guess you could call him a guard dog. A mongrel dog, at that," she spat bitterly. "When he started acting like I was just collateral that was the final straw. I knew where Darrell kept the money- two hundred and fifty thousand dollars, all untraceable cash," she finished, resting her hand on the gym bag while smiling like a cat who'd just stolen the cream.

"They're probably gonna have to let Bruno out in seventy-two hours. Don't you think he'll put two and two together and come looking for you?"

That wiped the smile off her face. "That's why I need to leave. Now."

"The reason the Uptons asked me to talk to your husband is because I was once a cop," I told her. Her eyes went wide, and for a second I caught myself wondering what the hell I was getting myself into. After all, she'd just slit her husband's throat; could I have ever gone that far with Liz? But that yellow bikini's radiance still wouldn't let go of me. "Sounds like you need a guard dog, too?"

For the first time she studied me seriously and not just as some annoying intruder. "I still don't really know who you are," she said, then smiled coyly, "except you like to watch people with your binoculars."

Now she really got me blushing.

"Like what you saw?"

I returned her smile with my own oh-shucks version that made her laugh some more.

She examined me for a long moment. I knew if I tried to say one word it might easily enough be the wrong one. Finally she exhaled, looking at the full gym bag then back towards me. "You think you can handle Bruno more successfully next time; if he ever does manage to find me?"

Her use of the word "me" didn't fly over my head. She was willing to use me, but how much would she need me? I realized my future depended on my ability to remain important in her life—I couldn't afford to screw it up like I'd done with my marriage. This felt like "till death do us part," for real. "I want to start over, too. Maybe we've just met—but I feel we're at the same crossroad in our lives."

She petted the gym bag like an old friend. "I guess we'll find that out soon enough. Only other people I can trust is my aunt and uncle."

"Think Bruno might bother them?" I asked.

She sighed, looked at me. "I already texted the relatives. Aunt Marilyn will be hosting my memorial the day Bruno gets out of jail." I could tell from the tone in her voice she was trying to convince herself this was enough to protect them.

"Maybe I can leave a threatening message on his phone. Don't try to find us. Might make him by-pass the Uptons altogether."

I managed to make her smile more relaxed. "Good old Aunt Marilyn and Uncle John. They're so attached to their own secure little life on this lake. Money don't mean much to them at their age." She looked around her cottage. "Speaking of which. We both stand to lose some abandoning these properties."

"Well, sometimes property can be nothing but an anchor strapped to your ass when you feel it's time to fly," I offered. "Afraid I can't match your quarter mil, but I do have a few things I can add to the pot."

"You're gonna be my guard dog, remember?" she grinned deviously, though she didn't put much emphasis into it.

"Of course," I answered, not even trying to sound convincing.

She reached behind the gym bag, pulled out a small automatic handgun and slipped it inside the bag. "Be careful," she said, "you've convinced me that doing this solo's too risky. But for right now you're only a probationary guard dog."

Then she looked at the baseball bat I'd been holding. "What did you expect to do with that. Challenge any intruder you found to a baseball game?"

I tapped the bat lightly on my other hand a few times and said: "I'm a superhero, remember?"

She scrutinized me up and down one last time before zipping up the gym bag. "I wonder what the hell I'm getting myself into," she said, before looking out the window with that same assured expression she'd had while studying the horizon. "All right," she finally said, "get what you need and meet me at the boat. We have to be across the lake before dawn."

"You're gonna wait for me, aren't you?" The last time I'd committed myself to a woman hadn't gone so well and I just couldn't hold back from asking.

She turned towards me with that enigmatic smile: "I guess you'll just have to trust me."

When you're in the spy business it pays to remember that you're never off the job, even at a party.

The Uninvited Spook
by C.D. Reimer

HE ADJUSTED THE parabolic microphone to aim at the apartment building across the street. The angle wasn't perfect for this type of surveillance since he had to hide in the shadows of an air conditioning unit under a clear night sky with a rising full moon. With advanced notice, he could've gotten a room a few floors below with a better line of sight than this.

With the small binoculars hanging around his neck, he surveyed the apartment at the southwest corner of the building and thirteen stories above downtown. The kitchen window on the south side was brightly illuminated to reveal two women—one older, one younger—fussing over something coming out of the oven. He turned up the volume for his headphones.

"Hey, Gracie," a woman voice said, not visible from the window. "Where's your husband?"

"George should be here any minute," the older woman said, putting a tray of appetizers into the oven. "Unless he got stuck in traffic or caught up with work."

Indeed, he mused, *where's George tonight?*

The west side of the apartment was where the darkened bedroom windows were located. Satisfied that no one occupied those rooms, he readjusted that parabolic microphone to the balcony on the southwest corner, with glass doors looking into the living room. Three old men in business suits stood together at the railing, paying more attention to their drinks than either the traffic below or the night skies above.

"Do you think George should retire?" the man on the left said. "Seventy-five is too old even for the civil service and it's very unlikely that the next administration will appoint him to anything important."

"Of course not," the man on the right said. "The Agency should assign him a desk job to push paperwork like the rest of us, and let him choke to death on a Philly steak sandwich during his lunch break."

"That's being cruel," the middle man said. Before the right man could respond, he turned towards the balcony doors and shouted: "Where's your husband?"

"He'll be dead if he doesn't show up soon," Gracie shouted back, sounding close but far away. She wasn't visible in either the kitchen or living room windows. "Retirement will be the least of his problems."

He chuckled. Gracie could always be counted to ride the tail end of a conversation.

"I think—" the middle man started.

"Let's not go there," the right man jumped in. "A thinking spook is always bad for the spy business."

The left man choked on his drink trying to laugh.

"Thinking is bad for *you*," the middle man retorted. "No, I was thinking that we should have George assigned as the station chief in Moscow."

Moscow?

"Moscow!" the right man said, spilling his drink. "What the hell for?"

The middle man held up his hand. "He's the last of the old school Kremlinologists still working. If the Russian spies were returning to the KGB playbook of spies assassinating spies in Europe, and pushing for another Cold War with the United States, a veteran spymaster like him would be perfect. His appointment would create a stir in the intelligence community since he's so well known. While everyone watches him, we can insert a younger agent to run the show behind his back."

"The perfect figurehead," the left man mused. "Good idea."

He snorted. *What are these idiots thinking?*

Then he noticed the curtain twitching in the rear bedroom window. Pointing his binoculars in that direction, he saw the brief opening and closing of the bedroom door against a brightly lit hallway. He frowned.

"Exactly," the middle man chimed in. "He's more paranoid than the Russians are themselves."

The old men laughed.

Idiots.

The right man spoke over his shoulder to the balcony doors. "I don't suppose Gracie would care to live in Moscow again?"

"Oh, hell no," she replied, still sounding very close and far away, and not visible from any window. "You can't have a decent fight with your husband without half the wives of the Politburo finding out first. The eighties were the pits."

He smiled as the old men chuckled. The eighties were the pits. When had serving in Moscow ever been a good thing?

Scanning all the windows again, he still couldn't see Gracie. The other women—including the one he heard but hadn't seen be-fore—gathered up trays of food to take out of the kitchen. The old men went back inside as the women cried out that the food was ready. The headphones buzzed with small talk of food, grandkids and real estate prices.

He leaned back against the air conditioning unit to ponder what he heard so far this evening. What's an old spook supposed to do at the end of his career? It's a question that had bothered him for years. Neither a desk job nor a figurehead position sounded appealing. Short of dying in the field or writing a kiss-and-tell memoir, there's never been a good alternative for an old spook.

With the headphones on he didn't hear the rooftop door open with a loud click behind him. He did feel the business end of a semi-automatic gun nestled itself behind his right ear, and he held still as a shadow loomed over him. His headphones were jerked off his head and thrown against the parabolic microphone.

"What's wrong with you?" Gracie asked in a tight whisper. He looked over his shoulder. It was just the two of them on the roof, with a gentle breeze and moonlight reflecting off of her Glock 23. He'd given it to her as an anniversary present a few years ago. "You were supposed to be home an hour ago."

He pushed the gun away from with one gloved finger. "There are spooks in our apartment."

"The only friends you have are spooks, honey," she said, with-drawing the gun. "It's supposed to be a *surprise* birthday party for you."

"Why didn't you tell me?"

"It was meant to be a surprise."

"So?"

"What part of surprise don't you understand?"

"You didn't tell me."

"God!" she screamed at the night sky, scaring some nearby roosting birds into flight. "My mother was right that I should've never married a spook—especially a paranoid Kremlinologist. You and your stupid games."

"Honey—"

"I don't want to hear it. Pack up your equipment and come home. You better have a good excuse for being late when you show up. I'm not covering for you."

"I was spying on the roof, listening to my traitorous friends talk shop, and my beloved wife of thirty years pulls a gun on me."

"That'll work," she said, pocketing her gun. "Except no one will believe that you're a pistol-whipped husband."

He chortled. "How about shooting me in the leg so I can stagger in to tell a wild story?"

"Don't tempt me." She turned around and left, letting the rooftop door slam behind her.

He smiled and looked back through the binoculars. Now it was time to play the spooks at their own game with a suave entrance and witty party conversation based on the intelligence he gathered. This was going to be the best "surprise" birthday party he had in years.

That moment that his face I see,
I know the man that must hear me:
To him my tale I teach.
- Samuel Taylor Coleridge

But Not Forgotten
by Martin Roy Hill

I DIDN'T SET out to kill Frank Adams because I wanted his money. There was little enough of that left in the family to bicker over, let alone kill for. Besides, I already had gotten everything I could ever want or need from Frank. My wife. His friendship. His respect. I owed Frank Adams more than I could ever repay. And so I decided to kill him.

That Saturday we set out for the marina as we had done each weekend for more than a year, ever since we had placed Frank in the home. No, *placed* is much too a delicate word. We were forced to lock him away like a crazy aunt.

Strange, though. He was never troublesome on those day trips. The disease that ate at his brain was responsible for the frequent moods swings—one moment a disruptive child, the next an abusive bully—that made caring for him impossible for his wife and daughter. But those swings never occurred when we were together. Perhaps what was left of his dignity held his moods in check around me. Or maybe his long love for the sea, what he could remember of it, soothed him somehow. Then again, it may simply have been because age had shrunk him, and the man who once stood eye-to-eye with my six-foot frame now stood small and frail before me.

On our day trips, I drove him to the commercial basin on the point where the fishing boats and charter yachts moored. We stayed away from the private marinas, where we might run into people Frank knew. And we never went to the yacht club anymore. Bobbie, his daughter and my wife, and Nance, his wife of nearly 50 years, didn't want Frank's friends to see him that way. "They should remember him as the man he was," Nance insisted.

The man he was. Frank Adams, naval war hero, successful businessman, renowned yachtsman. Now the man who was Frank Adams was a pathetic soul ravaged by a mysterious dementia that slowly robbed him of his memories and his dignity. The Navy officer whose actions saved dozens of his shipmates after their destroyer sank at Leyte Gulf, the businessman who built a successful marine insurance company from scratch, the sailor who twice won the Transpac yacht race from Los Angeles to Hawaii—once by sailing through a hurricane—all of this had been taken from him by this devastating illness.

In time, the doctors told us, he wouldn't remember any of us—not his wife, not his daughter, not me. The illness had already turned his rich, commanding baritone voice timid and halting. Soon, he would lose the ability to speak altogether. Eventually, the illness would destroy so much of his brain it wouldn't be able to continue the simplest life functions and he would die.

Frank fidgeted in his seat. He pulled his glasses from his pocket, put them on, took them off, put them back in his pocket. He cleared his throat. "Where're we going, Mark?" he asked, his voice a harsh, hoarse whisper.

"The marina, Frank. To see the boats."

"Oh."

"Like we do each weekend, Frank."

"I see."

He didn't, of course. We had the same conversation each weekend. The illness seemed to steal the memory of each trip even before the day was done.

"Ah, Mark, I really don't know if we should," Frank said. "Maybe we should head back now. I have a lot of stuff to do."

"Stuff, Frank?"

"Work," he said. "I've got a lot of work at the office to do. There are a lot of people waiting for this big proposal, and I have to spearhead the thing..."

I let Frank ramble. There was no work, no office. Frank seemed blissfully unaware the business he had built was no longer his. That was good. When the cost of his care forced us to sell, the disease had not progressed enough to spare Frank the heartbreak. Now, it was as if the event had never occurred. Now the nursing home was Frank's office, and its staff his employees.

"It's the weekend, Frank," I said. "You don't work on the weekend. It's our time to go to the marina. Like we do every weekend."

"Sure, I know that, but...."

The sentence hung suspended, unfinished. Frank fussed nervously with his glasses again, putting them on, taking them off. He'd lost track of what he was saying.

Frank was fidgeting with his glasses the first time I met him. Bobbie had brought me home to meet the family, and Frank was in his study poring over charts for the Transpac. He placed the glasses on his nose to trace a rhumbline with his finger, then removed them and chewed on their ear tips as he contemplated the course line. Frank was locked in his thoughts, oblivious to us standing in the den until Bobbie called his name. Embarrassed, he seemed uncertain what to do with his glasses as Bobbie introduced us.

Despite his initial embarrassment, Frank and I took an instant liking to each. We'd both been naval officers—Frank on a destroyer in the Pacific, me on Swift boats in Vietnam—and we both loved sailing.

We spent that evening reviewing his charts and telling war stories. That's when I first heard about the battle of Samar Island, where Frank's tincan went down after helping fend off a Japanese attack on the Leyte Gulf landing forces. Most of the crew made it off the ship, but half of those died in the water waiting for rescue, some from exposure, some from shark attacks. Frank was awarded the Navy Cross for his role in keeping the few survivors alive.

That was also the first time I learned of Frank's ambivalence to his own survival. "We lost a lot of good men," he told me. "Why I survived and they didn't...." He shook his head. "I've never felt right about that, Mark."

I didn't think much of the remark at the time. Most of us who have been to war and lost friends feel a certain uneasiness about our own survival. Survivor's guilt, they call it. It wasn't until several years later, after we had won Frank's second Transpac victory, that I understood the depth of his remorse.

The race got underway from Los Angeles with full knowledge there was a tropical storm brewing near Hawaii. But after plotting the storm's course, the weather service assured us it was blowing to the southwest, well away from the course we'd have to sail. They were wrong.

Halfway through our crossing, the storm reared and grew to full hurricane force. It also reversed course, blowing straight in front of the racing fleet. Most of the boats turned back. Frank was among the few skippers willing to challenge the ocean's fury.

Frank lashed himself down in the racing yacht's cockpit, and stayed there for nearly 48 hours guiding us through the storm. Looking at the pitiful man sitting next me as we drove to the marina, it was hard to remember him as he was then, strapped to the helm, wrapped in a yellow slicker, bellowing into the wind verses from *The Rime of the Ancient Mariner*, the same poem he had recited to keep his men calm, awake and alive after the sinking of their ship.

When the storm passed, we found ourselves so far ahead of the remaining racers we knew we had already won. The crew began celebrating before we even made port. All except Frank, who stayed alone at the helm, quietly dealing with his own demons.

"I'm sorry, Mark," he said as I slipped into the cockpit beside him.

"Sorry, hell, Frank," I said. "We won."

Frank's gaze was held on the sea. He shook his head. "I put you and the others at risk," he said. "I shouldn't have done that. I wasn't thinking about anyone but myself."

"We *won*, Frank. You've always said sometimes you gotta take chances to win."

"I shouldn't have risked you, Mark," he said. "Or the others."

"We didn't try to stop you, Frank," I said. "You gotta take chances."

"I wasn't thinking of winning, Mark. I thought maybe....." Frank looked at me, but his stare was dark and distant. "I was hoping—I wanted the sea to take me back, the way it should have done. To set the record straight."

"What are you talking about, Frank? What record?"

"Samar," he said. He turned his gaze back to the sea and didn't say anything more.

No one really knew just when the illness set in. Frank had always been a little distracted. We passed it off as simple absentmindedness whenever he left his briefcase on a plane or misplaced a document. But when he began repeatedly missing important meetings, we started to suspect his memory gaps were more than simple forgetfulness. The night Frank got lost driving home from his office, we knew there was something more seriously wrong with him.

From that point on, we simply watched as he deteriorated into the hapless man he now was. It was a damning, wrenching experience, watching a man for whom the mind and physical prowess was everything shrink into a confused and frightened animal. There were still occasional moments of clarity, when the old Frank Adams seemed to struggle through to the surface, but they grew fewer with each passing month. In each of our souls we secretly wished his body would give out before his brain finally did. A sudden heart attack, a stroke, something that would take him quickly and spare him this growing indignity. We never actually spoke about this, but we could read it in each others' eyes whenever Frank left the room.

The illness not only took away the man Frank Adams was, it took all he had earned and built over the years. Frank's business was gone, as well as his beloved racing sloop, both sold to pay for Frank's special care. Nance and Frank's house was put on the block, and the money from that was gone as well.

The savings and investments Frank and Nance had built up went before everything else. For that matter, so had the savings Bobbie and I had put away. All that was left was Frank's retirement funds, and they were perilously low. Nance moved in with us to conserve that money for Frank's care, but it was only a matter of time before that, too, was drained.

It was on one of our weekends at the docks that the idea of killing Frank first came to me. We stopped to admire a yawl tied up to the charter docks. She was a vintage craft, with teak decks and trim, the type of boat that draws the attention of even the driest landlubber. Frank stopped to admire the boat each time we came to the marina. Each time it was like he saw her for the first time.

"I know this boat," Frank said.

"Of course, you do, Frank," I said. "We were here last weekend, remember?"

Frank looked at me like I was crazy.

"No.....No, I don't, Mark. That may be, but I don't think so." His face brightened. "You know where I know her from? I served on her during the war. In the Pacific!"

"No, Frank," I said. "You were on a destroyer, remember? The destroyer went down at Leyte Gulf. Remember?"

Frank started shaking his head. "Leyte Gulf? Went down? I don't think so. This is my destroyer. I remember standing watch there at the helm...."

Frank let the sentence hang unfinished. His face twisted in anguish. Tears swelled in his eyes.

"Samar," he said. "Not Leyte. Samar. Oh, God, please don't let me forget them, too."

He rested his head on the cool metal railing bordering the docks, his sobs barely heard over the screech and cry of the dock's chafing gear and rubber fenders. When he finished, he looked out at the bay and pounded the railing.

"God, I hate this," he said, his voice a harsh whisper whipped by the wind. "I wish God had just let me die out there."

Frank walked a few yards, wiping his eyes dry with his sleeve. Then he stopped and stooped down. He turned back to me, holding in his hand a short length of ordinary braided rope.

"What's this doing here, Mark? This is from my boat. I recognize it. But what's it doing here? I keep my boat at the yacht club."

Frank turned one way, then the other, looking for a boat that was no longer his. He had already forgotten his anguish. He spotted the yawl and dropped the rope.

"Hey, Mark," he said. "Look at her. She's a beaut, isn't she....?

From that moment on, my plan began to evolve. Its details came to me slowly, in small bits as if I were daydreaming. In that reverie, I easily became convinced of the truth in what we all thought but never spoke of: that Frank Adams would be better off dead. I reasoned he was no longer truly alive, that he was simply the flesh and blood remains of a man who once was; a walking skeleton with no mind, no memories, no joy and no soul. I told myself that if I were so afflicted, I would prefer death than being stripped of all control over my bodily functions, to having my legacy robbed from my family, to be driven into a state of financial despair and forced into county care where I would simply be an unthinking piece of dying flesh. It was easy for me to see the simple truth in all this, for I still believed I had my own powers of reasoning.

It took me a week to steel my resolve, another to execute my plans. I called on Frank early that Saturday, knowing it would be my last chance to spend time with him. As we neared the marina, I told him I had a surprise for him.

"What do you mean, Mark? What kind of surprise? Can I see it?"

"Not yet, Frank," I said. "When we get to the docks."

I parked, and we walked straight to the charter wharf, where Frank once again discovered the yawl he so admired.

"My she's yar, isn't she, Mark?"

"Yes, she is, Frank," I said. "Remember my surprise?"

"Surprise?"

"I told you I had a surprise for you."

Frank looked puzzled. "I guess so," he said.

"Well, this is it," I said. "We're going out on that yawl."

Frank's eyes brighten, and just as quickly clouded. "I don't know, Mark. I—ah—may not have the time. I have to get back to the office, you know."

"Now, Frank, I've discussed this with Nance and Bobbie, and they think it's swell. So do the people at the office. You need some time off. They all agreed to that."

I had, indeed, discussed the outing with Nance and Bobbie, and with the people at the nursing home. They all agreed the trip would be good for Frank. They didn't know, of course, I wouldn't be bringing him back.

Frank fell quiet and studied the yawl with a doubtful stare. I wondered what strange convolutions of thought went on in his depredated brain. Had the lure of the sea I had counted on been taken from him? Did some fear tear at him? Did some ancient instinct warn him of unknown danger? I began to think he would back out of the cruise. I almost hoped he would.

But there was no more need to convince Frank.

"Well, then, okay! Let's go!" he shouted, and sprinted across the brow like a young boy on an adventure.

I had signed the charter papers the day before, and I wasted no time taking the boat out of the slip. Frank insisted on helping, letting go the mooring lines and, after we'd motored into the channel, helping to set the sails. I was amazed at how adeptly Frank handled the sheets and halyards, as if he suffered no diminished capacity at all.

The illness destroying his brain seemed to have missed this, and I wondered if it was by simple chance or because Frank somehow fought to preserve this last part of himself.

After we cleared the channel buoys, I turned the helm over to Frank. He had no problem keeping the compass steady on our course while I studied the weather. The sky was overcast and the wind blew hard. Froth curled the top of the waves. The sea spray was cold. A man in the water wouldn't wait long before hypothermia set in.

While Frank steered, I slipped into the engine compartment and worked the throttle until the auxiliary motor flooded. This was my plan. When Frank "accidentally" fell aboard, I would be unable to start the motor. A boat under sail blows at the mercy of the wind and sea. Without the auxiliary motor, it would be impossible to bring the yawl around in time to save Frank.

That, at least, would be my story.

I finished with the motor, and went forward to fetch sodas and sandwiches the charter company had stored aboard for us. As I returned aft, I heard Frank's voice. I thought he was talking to himself, carrying on one of his long, droning conversations as he frequently did when by himself.

I was wrong.

Frank stood at the helm, his back stiff and straight, both hands gripping the wheel, the wind whipping up his thinning gray hair and flapping the loose ends of his jacket. His voice was deep and rich, his articulation without fault. I marveled at the sight and listened to his words.

"God save thee, ancient Mariner! From the fiends that plague thee thus!"

The Rime of the Ancient Mariner. How, I wondered, had he regained his full voice? Where in his afflicted brain did he store those words?

I placed the sandwiches and drinks next to Frank and checked our course. The lubber line was dead on due west. I popped open one of the sodas and sat back listening to Frank's recital.

"That reminds me of the hurricane," I said, after he finished. "Remember the hurricane, Frank?"

"What hurricane?" he asked.

"The one we sailed through going to Hawaii. During the Transpac.

Remember?"

Frank furrowed his brow, then shook his head. "Was I there?"

"You were there, Frank," I assured him. "That was your second Transpac win, remember?"

"'Fraid I don't, Mark. I don't think I've been to Hawaii—except during the war. Oh—" Frank snapped his fingers. "You mean Halsey's Typhoon, don't you? I remember that. Sure I do."

Frank was in a hospital in Pearl Harbor recovering from the injuries he received at Leyte Gulf when Bull Halsey's fleet encountered the typhoon. I let the subject drop, and tried another.

"Tell me about the war, Frank," I asked. "About Leyte Gulf—Samar, that is."

Frank looked puzzled at first, then anxious, his mind unable to recognize the words.

"I don't know, Mark, about that," he said. "I know I was there once—"

It struck me that the illness plaguing Frank's brain had finally stripped away the ghosts that haunted him all these years, and that thought hit me like a blow. What I was doing, what I had planned was all predicated on Frank's desire to return to the sea, to even the score he had always felt was necessary to rid him of the guilt he endured for having survived while others did not. I had convinced myself I was doing Frank a favor, fulfilling his last wish. Without his memories of the war, without its ghosts, what I was planning to do seemed too much like—well, like murder.

"The war, Frank, the war," I said, surprised at the urgency in my voice. "You know, when your destroyer was sunk by the Japanese. You were in the water a long time. There were sharks."

"Oh, that," Frank said. He sat down, his body sagging again. "Of course, I remember that. Nothing can make me forget that, Mark."

I felt my heart start beating again.

"Tell me about it, then, Frank. About the battle."

Frank searched the fragments of his memory, then slowly put the story together. "We were—where were we?—off Samar Island, that's it. North of the landing at Lady—no, Ley-tee Gulf. That was it.

"The Japs came down on us from...the north?" I nodded my concurrence, and Frank looked pleased. "They wanted the landing fleet and the little carriers we were guarding. Old—what was his name? Seems I just had it." He looked at me apologetically. "I'm sorry, Mark. I just don't remember things anymore."

"That's okay, Frank. Do you mean the captain?"

"No, though he was a fine man. That was...the typhoon!" Frank snapped his fingers as he grasped the memory.

"Bull Halsey?"

"That's it. Halsey was supposed to be up there to the north to block them, but he went off chasing a Jap ghost fleet. Left us there damn naked with all these Japs coming at us."

"What'd the Japanese have, Frank. What kind of ships?"

"Oh, God, I don't know. All kinds." Frank patted the yawl's gunwale and smiled broadly. "Not like this little lady. Isn't she a beaut, Mark? We could've used her there, I tell you."

"There were battleships, weren't there, Frank? And cruisers?"

Frank set his eyes on the horizon. He squinted as if he seemed to see it all again.

"Oh, God, yes. Battlewagons—the biggest the Japs had, the...the..."

"The Yamato."

"That's right, of course. What you said. How could I forget? They had cruisers, too. And tincans, lots of them. We watched their pagoda masts come over the horizon, then next thing shell splashes were coming up all around us."

"Then what?"

"Well, let's see. Captain—Captain? I can't remember his name now. A great guy. Best tincan skipper in the Navy. I bet he made admiral. You met him, didn't you?"

"No," I said. "He died there at Samar, Frank. When the ship went down. Remember?"

Frank became distracted by his sandwich. He picked it up, sniffed it, then took the pieces of bread apart to examine the makings.

"Who made these, Mark? Did you make these?"

"No, the charter company did, Frank. Something wrong?"

"No, they're fine. Just fine." He took a bite and set the sandwich down. He picked up the soda and studied the can while he chewed.

"What did the captain do, Frank?"

"Captain?"

"Your skipper on the tincan. At Samar."

"Oh, that. He ordered us to attack."

"The Japanese fleet? By yourselves?"

"There were—oh, four or five other tincans, but we were the closest to the Japs. So we laid a smokescreen and then made a torpedo attack. Got us a cruiser, too."

"Then what, Frank?"

Frank thought a moment. He took his glasses from his pocket and put them on, then took them off, looked at them, and put them away.

"Oh, I don't know. Something. You know."

"Is that when your ship started getting hit?"

Frank nodded, and fumbled with the glasses in his pocket.

"Yeah. I guess so. You were there."

"No, I wasn't there, Frank. I wasn't even born yet. You were there. Remember?"

"Of course, I remember. It was like...like someone picked us up and threw us into a wall. But we kept going. I remember. Yeah. The other tincans came and made their attacks, and the skipper said we should follow them in and give them cover fire." Frank chuckled and shook his head. "Cover fire with our puny five-inch guns.

"The exec said, 'Just give the word, captain.' And the skipper said, 'The word is given.' And we went back in at the Japs."

"But you turned them back."

"Yeah, somehow. I don't understand it. 'Course, we were goners by then. The ship was taking hits from all sides and going under and the skipper gave the word to abandon her. He never made it off the ship, the skipper. I remember now. A good man. I just wish I could remember his name...."

"Evans," I said. "Ernest Evans. Remember? He got the Medal of Honor."

Frank nodded, but he was thinking of something else.

"Damndest thing, though," he said. "After we were in the water, a Jap tincan came by. We thought they were going to machine-gun us, but the Jap skipper...he saluted us. Can you imagine that? He *saluted* us. I shouted out, 'Look at that, boys. He's saluting us.' Everyone thought I was shell-shocked or something 'til they looked up and saw him, too."

"What happened after that, Frank?"

Frank had a distant look on his face, as if watching something deep in the past.

"Then the Japs—the Japs just went away. Everyone just went away and forgot about us for two days and two nights. Everyone except the sharks."

Tears swelled in Frank's eyes and streaked across his face, blown by the wind. He picked up his sandwich, then set it down without a bite. He began humming something but it wasn't a tune. The words began trickling from his mouth, low and soft.

"Her lips were red, her looks were free/Her locks were yellow as gold," he recited. "Her skin was white as leprosy/The Night-mare LIFE-IN-DEATH was she/Who thicks man's blood with cold."

"You recited that poem to keep your men calm in the water, didn't you, Frank?"

Frank shook his head.

"Sure you did," I said. "It was in your citation. The one for the Navy Cross. It said you kept the survivors from panicking and kept their spirits up by reciting that poem."

"I don't remember it that way," Frank said.

"You don't remember reciting the poem?"

"I remember," Frank said. "I remember it like...yesterday. It's all I can remember. It just didn't happened like that, like they say in that piece of paper."

Frank fumbled with his glasses again, putting them on, taking them off. He finally put them away, and wiped the tears from his face with his coat sleeve. Then he looked at me, and for the first time in what seemed ages I saw the clarity in his eyes that I had come to expect from Frank Adams.

"I kept reciting that poem to keep *myself* from panicking," he finally said. "I was so scared, Mark. The only way I could keep from screaming myself mad was to recite that stupid poem I had to memorize in high school.

"There were a lot better men than me in that water, Mark. A lot braver. When I made it and they didn't, it—it just didn't seem right. I swore right then I had to make something out my life. I owed them that much at least, not to waste the life they gave me."

Frank slipped his glasses into his pocket.

"Now it's all gone. Everything. I know it is, Mark." Frank tapped his head. "In the few moments I have like this, I know it is. I've let you and Nance and Bobbie down. I've let those men down. And now, I can't even remember their names or faces anymore. It's not fair." Frank put his face in his hands. "It's never been fair."

I moved next to Frank and placed my arm around his shoulders. The wheel was loose and began to spin. The boat slipped off a wave and rolled steeply to starboard. I looked past him, and watched the waves frothing. One quick shove, and it would be over.

"You did all by right them, Frank," I said. "You've done all right by everyone."

I braced a foot against the port bulkhead as the yawl took the reverse roll. Frank's weight leaned heavily against me. He wasn't bracing himself against the movement of the boat. He was as limp as rag doll, almost as if he knew what I had in mind and was making it easier.

The deck straightened, and Frank's weight lightened. I kept the pressure against him, waiting for the roll to starboard. The bow pitched up on the next wave, and slipped off to the right again. The deck began to list in the same direction. I pressed my weight against Frank's.

Frank patted my leg. "Thank you, Mark," he said. "I've always loved you like a son."

The soda cans tumbled with a clatter as the deck began its steep roll. The remains of our sandwiches followed the cans. The boom swung wildly above our heads as the boat swung off course.

Just one quick shove. One quick push and it all would be over. Frank's pain and despair. Our emotional and financial drain. Everyone would be better off.

But I just couldn't do it.

No matter how sick his brain might be, this was still Frank Adams, the man I had grown to love and respect. A man who still had much more to give than he took. A hero in my eyes and everyone else's, if not in his own.

I grabbed the stuffed collar of Frank's lifejacket and pulled hard to the left. The deck flattened out. I took the wheel and swung the bow back into the sea. The roll lessened. I set the autopilot and sat back.

Frank looked at me sadly.

"I love you, too, Frank," I said. "We all do."

Frank said nothing.

"Listen, we'll just let the autopilot drive her for a while. I'll go below and get some more sodas and sandwiches. But you keep an eye out for traffic, okay?"

Frank nodded, but remained silent.

Everything in the cabin not lashed down had crashed to the floor and slid around. I picked it all up. The wind blew harder now, singing a low mournful tune as it whipped through the halyards and strained the canvas. I thought I heard voices above deck.

I carried the sodas and sandwiches up the short ladder to the aft well. Frank was no longer at the helm. I looked to starboard, then port, but I didn't see him. Then I heard his voice behind me.

"Don't just stand there," he shouted. "The skipper's ordered us over the side. She's going down."

Frank was 'midships, one hand holding the starboard guy wire, one foot on the gunwale. He was hunched over, as if ducking shrapnel.

"Frank, what you are talking about?"

"The ship's going under. The captain's ordered her abandoned."

"The captain?"

"He just came by with the bosun," Frank shouted. He stepped up to the gunwale and teetered there. "They went up the air castle."

I dropped the food and rushed across the deck and caught Frank's lifejacket and pulled him in. He struggled, then stopped. His eyes were pleading but perfectly clear.

"Please, don't stop me, Mark," he said. "Please."

I studied his face, but could find no reason to stop him.

Frank straightened to attention. "Just give the word, captain," he said.

"The word," I whispered, "is given."

My grip slackened. Frank patted my shoulder, then slipped into the sea. He disappeared beneath the waves for a moment, then surfaced and turned to me.

"Thank you, Mark," he shouted. Then he saluted. I returned

the salute.

"You see that, boys?" Frank shouted. "That Jap officer just saluted us, by God."

A wave splashed across Frank's face, then a second and a third. I watched as he drifted farther from the boat. He began to disappear between the troughs, but I could still hear his voice.

"Come on, boys. Keep together. Don't spread out. Keep together now."

I lost him in the sea. I tuned the radio to the emergency channel, and made my Mayday call. The wind blew past my ears, and carried with it was Frank's rich baritone voice. I could just make out the opening lines to *The Rime of the Ancient Mariner*.

They say the apple doesn't fall far from the tree, and it's especially true in a storm.

The Little Outlaw
by Mike Miner

MARY WAS SUPPOSED to be asleep. She was upstairs, in her room, in
her bed, but the sound of thunder, like a bowling ball being dropped
on the roof, was keeping her up.

The little man in the radio was reading the news. Johnny Pesky
went four for five with five RBI's as the Red Sox beat up on the Detroit Tigers at Briggs stadium thirteen to three, every Boston player
had gotten a hit including the pitchers. The storm now smacking the
state was expected to last until morning. A dazzle of light followed by
a crackling punch of noise seemed to agree. Mary shivered. According
to local police, the main branch of the Rockville Bank had been
robbed, the suspects remained at large. She knew there wasn't really a
little man in the radio, but her mother used to tell her that when she
was younger, that there was a little man in a suit or a tiny woman
singing a song. Now Mary was ten and realized you couldn't believe
everything you heard, but these tiny people were stuck in her head.

The little man kept talking. The bridge on Route 74 was flooded.
The National Weather Service advised that folks stay home if at all
possible. Over fifty percent of Connecticut homes were without
power. Then the little man put on some music. T-Bone Walker and
his new song, *Stormy Monday*. She pictured a miniature T-Bone
Walker strumming a toy guitar inside their wooden Crosley radio and
was just drifting off as he moaned, *Tuesdays are just as bad*, when the
power went out.

Downstairs, Hank said, "Goddammit." Hank was Mary's mother's
husband. Not her father. He was a man of few words. *Goddammit* was
one of them. He preferred to communicate with nods and grunts but
he was kind and honest and in daylight hours, almost always tending
to the farm. But no matter how hard he worked, the bank seemed
forever poised to take it away. This rain would not help the corn crop.

The sound of Mary's mother, Linda, searching for matches and
lighting candles. Mary heard footsteps coming up the stairs, the familiar creaks as her mother made her way into her room and left a lit

candle there. Mary pretended to be asleep.

It felt like the house was inside a dragon's mouth, its wheezing breath made the candle's flame dance. The power flickered and fragments of the little man's voice could suddenly be heard: *A daring raid by at least two men.* Static. Silence. *Police are currently searching for suspects, but the storm is doing much to hamper their efforts.*

The windows, right on cue, lit up day bright and a terrible clap shook the house. Then there was another light but this one moved through Mary's windows, growing, making shadows against the wall. Headlights.

Mary listened closer and could just make out, through the wind, the hum of an engine.

We repeat, the little man had one more thing to tell them, *these suspects are considered armed and extremely dangerous.* Then nothing.

"Hank, someone's in the driveway," her mother said.

"What?"

"A car."

"Well, goddammit."

Mary heard a drawer being opened, the sound of a pistol chamber snapping open, being checked. She threw the covers off and snuck to her bedroom window, bare toes on wood. She pulled back her curtain.

Headlights were all she could see until another lightning flash revealed a big, black car, wide and shaped like a bullet. Then the night swallowed it again.

"Who is it?" Mary's mother asked.

"A black Cadillac."

In the hallway now, the slapping rain hid the sound of Mary's creaking footsteps, down the stairs; she stopped just outside the doorway to the kitchen, peeked around the wall.

Hank had the door open to the outside, a large revolver in his hand.

"Well, who is it?"

"Son of a bitch," Hank said.

"What?"

The sound of car doors slamming. The noise of men muttering, grunting.

"Hank, what is happening?"

"We've got company."

"Who?"

"Well, it's dark but it sure looks like your bank robbing ex-boyfriend."

A thunderclap exactly timed with Mary's gasp.

The door loose on its hinges slapped open, the sound of the storm loud, two men in dark trenchcoats, dripping with rain, their feet squished and squeaked on the wood floor.

"Patrick?" Mary's mother said.

Mary examined the two men. One of them was taller than the kitchen door and almost as wide. A huge square head with a fat jaw and tiny marbles for eyes. His expression reminded Mary of the Donovans' German Shepherd. She would not have been surprised if the man had started growling.

The other one turned at her mother's voice. Patrick. He pushed a wet mop of red hair out of his face. He was thin, with a narrow face and devilish eyes. A small grin appeared when he looked at her mother.

"Linda, me lass," an Irish brogue, "we are terribly sorry to trouble you on such a night as this. This is my partner, James."

James nodded slightly.

"What do you want?" Hank said.

"Ah, this must be Henry. You look as sturdy as I imagined you, sir."

The words sounded like a song in Patrick's voice.

"Might I bother you for a chair, lass?"

Mary's mother dragged a chair out from under the table.

Patrick winced as he moved to the chair and let out a breath when he sat. Mary saw him look at the blood on his hand. But the grin stayed on his face.

"To your question, Mr. Henry," he looked up, "A roof, a dry floor."

"Patrick, what happened?" her mother asked.

"A scratch."

"A bullet," James said.

"Henry, might I add, we're in a position to reward your generosity handsomely."

Hank's face changed at that.

Even in the dead of night with nothing but candlelight to see by, this was no palace. Everything was tired, mismatched, second hand. Mary looked at her nightgown, lent from a cousin, two sizes too big.

"What did you have in mind?" Hank asked.

"Talk about numbers later, Hank. Patrick, you're bleeding and you need mending."

Patrick's grin faltered slightly. "I never did get far arguing with you, girl."

"Can you stand?"

"Ay."

Mary's mother grabbed a candle and led Patrick out of the room.

"Rest assured, Henry," Patrick called behind him, "'tis a seller's market."

Then Mary was in front of Patrick in the doorway. His eyes went big and his grin grew wider.

"The famous Mary, I presume. Lovely as your mother. Did we wake you, lass?"

"Who are you?"

Patrick chuckled, her mother stiffened.

"Patrick O' Malley, at you service, Miss."

"Mary," her mother said, "Get a bowl of hot water and some towels."

"Why?"

"Just do it, child, and bring it to the guest room."

Nothing was said in the kitchen as Mary gathered her mother's supplies. Both men stood and watched her as though awaiting instructions. Several times, Mary snuck a peek at the hulking James. A gleam in his eye, in his smile, that she did not like. What big teeth he had.

In the guest room, Patrick had his shirt off and Mary's mother was probing with her fingers. Seeing the puckered wound made Mary's stomach buzz, her head spin, she needed to sit down. Patrick sucked in some air.

"Still in there," her mother said.

"To be sure."

"Needs to come out."

"To be sure."

"Here's your water, mom."

Mary's mother took the bowl and a towel and began to clean the wound. Mary looked away.

"Thank you, Mary. Off to bed with you."

"But mom..."

"Not tonight, Mary. Please."

Mary left. But did not go far, and returned to listen just outside the door.

"She has your eyes," Patrick said.

"And your everything else. A little outlaw in the making. Always figuring the angles."

"This was how you wanted things as I recall. A sturdy man, a solid home for your daughter."

"I don't recall the subject of you arriving unannounced in the middle of the night."

Patrick made a noise of discomfort. "Well I thought that was understood."

"Damn you, Patrick O' Malley. Damn your wit and your charm and your smile, damn it all to hell."

Mary had never heard her mother use language so foul.

"Don't you dare laugh at me."

"Don't make me laugh. It hurts."

They spoke quietly, sounding like snakes hissing. Mary could just make out their words. She was confused by her mother's tone which seemed full of affection even though the words were angry. Mary had once had her mouth washed out with soap for saying, "Dammit," after skinning her knee, a word she'd overheard Hank use a thousand times.

"How is sturdy and solid Henry working out for you?"

"Stop smiling before I knock your teeth out. You know why I did it."

"She seems a lovely girl."

"Just shut up. I'm going to mend you. You're going to stay the night. In the morning, you and your flunky will leave. Forever."

"That's what you want?"

"Don't say anything else."

"How about a kiss then?"

The last sentence spoken so low, blood pounded so loud, Mary doubted her ears. So she leaned around the wall and peeked in.

Patrick's hands were running through her mother's hair. Running everywhere. Mary's mind twirled. She pulled her head back, stood flat against the wall, tried to breathe quietly. The sounds of lips touching and heavy breathing, a storm of kisses.

"Patrick O' Malley you are a bank robbing son of a bitch."

"And I never stopped loving you, angel."

"You are leaving in the morning. Forever."

"Come with me."

Mary's world was a much different place than the one she had gone to bed in. Her mother had become a stranger.

"We need more water."

Mary bolted as quickly and quietly as she knew how, running like a cat up to her room. Into her bed.

She had planned on slipping back down to do some more eaves-dropping, but her sheets wrapped around her and the night seemed full of bedtime stories for her, things she'd never known, if she would just listen. And sleep.

The storm continued its tale, whispering and shouting it. The rain pelted the house. But among the sounds, a wooden creak from the doorway to her room. Mary's eyes fluttered open as lightning flashed, revealing a large silhouette—James.

Then dark. Blackness. Mary's ears and eyes strained. Her body locked, she perspired with the effort. The night outside, a funhouse of noises. More flashes, but no James in the doorway. Yet she could smell him, the scent of a strange person, cheap aftershave.

Another flash and here he was, on his knees, face to face with Mary.

"Are you scared?"

She wanted to scream so badly.

"Are you scared of the storm?"

His breath was gasoline. In the barely lit room his eyes looked black.

"It's okay," he said. "Take my hand."

She stayed immobile under the sheets, her hands squeezed her legs.

Another flash. Another crack. She flinched.

James leaned his massive head closer. "It's just a storm, Mary." He stroked her hair. "Now take my hand." His voice turned hard and flat.

She tried to hold the tears back. James gently rubbed the corner of her eye. With the storm, would anyone hear if she screamed?

"Mary, don't upset your Uncle James."

He pulled the covers back revealing her too big nightgown, lightning illuminated the faded pink roses on it.

Mary shivered and closed her eyes and shivered.

She wondered what Patrick and her mother were doing down the hall. Wondered where Hank was.

Flash. Crack. Much louder, right on top of the house, like it was in the room. And James was on top of her, so heavy and sweaty and stinking and she screamed and twisted and punched and hissed, "Damn you, damn you, damn you."

But James said nothing. Did nothing. Didn't even breathe.

Hank pulled James off of her and the big man crumbled like a brick wall to the floor.

Mary gasped, wondering absently when was the last time she had taken a breath.

She was in Hank's arms. Hank. The smell of him, pipe smoke and Old Spice aftershave and sweat from a day in the fields, smelled like home.

"Okay," he said.

He picked her up, grabbed a blanket and carried her to the couch in the family room.

"Don't leave," she said.

"Okay."

He must have left at some point, because when she woke up, Hank was gone.

Was it a dream?

She was still on the couch. She crept upstairs. Mom asleep in her bed. No Hank. Patrick snoring softly in the guest bed.

Mary eyed the door to her room for a while before opening it. No James. Her bed was made. She rubbed her eyes. She went to her bedroom window and looked down at the driveway. No rain. No black car.

In the early daylight the night before seemed impossible.

She sniffed the air in her room. She sniffed again. Gunpowder.

She looked at the floor. Drops of blood.

Downstairs she put on a coat and shoes. Still chilly outside. Everything was wet. She thought she could hear the sound of Hank's tractor a ways off, in the north field the other side of the hill.

She found the car in the barn, still slightly wet from last night's rain. She looked inside. Saw more blood. Saw the bags in the backseat.

When Mary went back inside, Patrick was in the kitchen listening to a tiny Billie Holiday sing *Stormy Weather* from inside the radio. He had a cup of coffee in front of him. He nodded to her.

"Been an age since I had a cup of coffee in someone's kitchen." He took a sip. "Would you care for one?"

She grinned. Shook her head.

Patrick shrugged. Took another sip.

"Are you my father?"

He seemed to ponder the flavor of the coffee, looked deep into his mug, decided he liked it, then looked at Mary. "Yes, lass."

She nodded, not quite sure what to do with this information.

"Must be confusing for you. All of this. You look quite a bit like me mum, you know, your grandmother."

Mary's eyes widened.

"A lovely woman. That's where you get your green eyes from."

Mary pictured someone taking a woman's eyes out, handing them to her mother, her mother placing them into Mary's face.

The little man in the radio started talking about the robbery again.

Police in Tolland County are conducting a house by house search. Road blocks are in place. Expect delays on the roads.

Patrick sighed. "They'll be along soon, I imagine. Tell me, Mary, have you seen my friend, James?"

After a moment, Mary shook her head.

Patrick nodded. "Odd."

"Do you love my mother?"

"I do. I always did."

"Are you taking her with you?"

Patrick tried his smile but saw that he needed more for the likes of Mary. He needed an answer, maybe even the truth, "If she'll come."

"What about me?"

"The lam is no place for a little girl. Your mother knew that, we both did. That's why things are the way they are."

"Because you're a robber?"

Patrick shrugged.

"What was the first thing you ever stole?"

He smiled. A genuine smile, not meant to charm. "A kiss from your mum."

Mary giggled.

"I've been stealing things ever since."

"Why?"

Patrick seemed to consider this. "Nobody ever asked me that before." He scratched his chin. "Why did the chicken cross the road?"

"To get to the other side."

"Why did Mr. Everest climb that mountain?"

Mary didn't know.

"Because it's there," Patrick pointed to Mary's ear. "And I want it here." Patrick touched her ear lobe and produced a silver dollar in his hand. "Like magic."

"Robbing's not like magic," Mary said.

"Sure it is," Patrick said. "Just another trick."

"But that doesn't explain why you do it."

Patrick smiled at his daughter.

"Why do you rob banks?"

"Because I'm good at it, my dear." He twirled the coin in his fingers and made it vanish. "I'm good at making money disappear."

"How's your stomach?"

Patrick grimaced. "Sore."

"Maybe you're not as good as you think."

Patrick looked ready to speak but then he heard the sound of Hank's tractor. Hank parked it near the barn and turned off the engine. He walked in the kitchen door, looked at Patrick.

"Cops. A few miles up the road."

"How long?" Patrick asked.

"If they're coming straight here, five minutes."

"I'm obliged," Patrick said. "Henry, is James about?"

Hank stared at his hands as he rubbed the calloused palms together. "He overstepped his bounds."

"Did he now?"

Hank said nothing.

"And was the resolution a permanent sort of thing?"

Hank had nothing but a hard look for Patrick.

Mary heard her mother's steps on the stairs. She walked into the kitchen with a bag in her hand and tears in her eyes.

Mary didn't know if her mother had already told Hank. He didn't look surprised. "You better go if you're going," Hank said looking at nobody, then walked outside.

Patrick stood then bent and kissed Mary on the head. "Farewell, angel."

Mary and her mother slowly met each other's eyes.

"Take me with you, Mommy."

She shook her head. "I can't."

"Then stay."

Tears gushed. "I can't."

Mary looked around at their threadbare lives. How could her mother ever have chosen this?

"Kiss me, Mary. Give us a hug."

She remembered Patrick and her mother the night before. The way they kissed and hugged, like they were the last two people alive. She stood and went to her mother and hugged her, smelled her perfume. Her mother smothered her with kisses. "Don't forget me, Mary. Don't hate me. Hank will take good care of you."

"I know, Mommy."

Mary was surprised that she wasn't crying. Just like Hank, she had seen this coming.

She watched her mother run to the barn as Patrick drove the sleek, black sedan toward her. In her mother went. Long after they'd driven away, Mary watched the end of the driveway.

From somewhere, the sound of sirens.

Hank came into the kitchen and turned up the radio.

The little man told them about the chase. The chase for Patrick O' Malley through four states. The police would lose them, then find them again. Mary and Hank sat in the kitchen listening. Hank lit candles and made dinner, and let Mary stay up past her bedtime until she fell asleep at the table. Then Hank must have carried her to bed.

In the morning, she woke and found him with a cup of coffee still listening to the little man who explained that the chase had come to an end.

Mary found her mother's mug and poured herself a cup, sipped the hot, bitter taste.

Patrick O' Malley's black Cadillac had skidded over a bridge embankment. They'd come back through Connecticut and run into the flooded bridge on Route 74. Hank moved to turn the radio off but Mary stopped him.

"That was a fine automobile," Hank said.

Divers had found three bodies. James Keegan, a known associate of O' Malley's had been found with a bullet in his back in the trunk of the car. Also the body of Patrick O' Malley and an as-yet unidentified woman. The divers continued to search for the estimated one hundred thousand dollars stolen from the main branch of the Rockville Bank.

They won't find it, Mary knew.

"The hell were they doing coming back this way?" Hank wondered aloud.

"The money," Mary said.

It took seven potato sacks to hold all of the loot. A long time to finish moving it. She remembered the smell of the bills, a dirty smell, she hated it and wondered if she would ever stop smelling it.

Piles and piles of money but she didn't want any of it. All she wanted was for her mother to come back. To show her parents she was a good thief too, an outlaw, like her dad.

Appearances can, and will, be deceiving.

Shadows
by E. J. Togneri

IN THE YEAR 2012, hiring a PI was a luxury purchase, the kind most people had cut back on, an unintentional deferral for cheating husbands and insurance fraudsters. So on that gloomy November day, I welcomed new client Catherine Sigerman to my dimly lit New Brunswick office. A paying gig would give me a break from my own case and cash to probe the shadows.

As soon as Catherine caught sight of me, her green eyes flickered, her shoulders tensed, the hand on her black shoulder bag tightened. I knew the pattern well. When her gaze dropped to my wheelchair, I used the moment to examine her in turn. A redhead with freckles powdered over, in her mid-thirties, a devotee of step aerobics. When she looked at me again, her smile lifted one corner of her mouth. Now polite, blank eyes assured me they had not noticed anything out of the ordinary, or if perchance they had, it was of no consequence; it simply didn't exist. It would never be mentioned; she would swear she had never even looked.

"Mr. McLean?" she asked. A half-grimace replaced the half-smile. Her next words couldn't get past her lips.

I leaned on my elbows and swung my body closer to the desk. "Did you bring the letter?" I asked, motioning her to a chair. Working as a PI had taught me that jumping right into clients' problems interrupted their cogitation of mine. I extracted my pen from between the yellow pages of a legal pad and flipped past the list of names I had painstakingly accumulated over the years.

"I . . . I . . . " Her gaze darted to the window where a fall shower drilled the poor souls in line at the check cashing store across the street from my office, and then back to an inch above my head. Catherine sighed, slid a white envelope from the side pocket of her purse, and tapped it against her wrist. "It isn't so much the letter. It's what's inside."

With one hand, I slid open my side drawer and pulled out a pair of latex gloves from an open box. After I snapped them on, I said,

"Please sit, while I have a look."

She handed me the envelope and finally lowered herself onto one of the faded gray chairs that flanked my desk.

The New Brunswick, New Jersey Post Office had cancelled the stamp and postmarked the letter October 24. Both the send to and return addresses were the same, and indicated the location of the house in an area where million dollar homes sprang up faster than the brush they'd replaced. The addresses were on preprinted labels, the kind charities sent petitioning a substantial contribution for your name and address next to a stuffed teddy bear or some other innocuous symbol. The letter itself contained a bit of melodramatic dialogue that could easily have come from a reality show that purported to reveal an investigation's inside story. *Stay away from Dornish or you'll be sorry* was printed in Arial font on pink paper, sans punctuation.

I glanced at Catherine. "Dornish?"

"One of my boyfriends." She blushed. "You may have heard of him. The diet guru? The Mineral Diet. Nutrition and Chelation. He's a doctor."

"Tell me about your relationship with him."

That brought her dimples out of hiding. "We've been dating for about eight months. I'm divorced. Three years. First time I've been serious with anyone since then."

"Who would have a problem with that?"

She hesitated. "He's also got an ex. Mine's in California and he left me, so probably not him. The other guy I'm dating, Robert Prince, isn't very happy about the competition." She shrugged like she had a lot of practice not caring if guys were happy.

"Anybody else you're close to?"

"My mother, but she's in Florida. Not too understanding, I don't tell her much. My daughter, seventeen, but going on twelve." She shook her head.

"I'll fingerprint the envelope and letter, of course. Anyone else beside you handle them?"

"I don't think so. What about the contents?"

I peered inside the envelope at a brownish powdery substance containing small metal bits. "Hard to say. I'll drop it at the lab. They'll direct bill you."

"Just like a pap smear." Catherine made a face, then shuddered. "I always hate waiting to find out if I've got another year." She bowed her head and came up dabbing at the outer corner of her eye. A tear glistened down one cheek. "Do you think I'm in danger?"

I trotted out the platitudes my aunt had used on me when I was six and the doctors said I would never walk again. They still didn't work.

Doctor Dornish's office wasn't too far from, mine just a mile, but on the good side of the tracks. My office nestled among a bevy of pawn-broker shops, not massive Robert Wood Johnson Hospital buildings.

I watched patients come and go as I waited until ten minutes before the appointment I'd arranged. I flung my car door open, dragged the wheelchair from behind my seat. With one hand, I snapped it open. After setting the brake and plopping the cushion on, I gripped one arm of the chair, pulled myself closer, and grabbed the other side. Powering myself up, as if on parallel bars, I jungle-gymed into the chair. I locked the car, which produced a beep, and spun my way through the parking garage and finally to the Center's entrance and the right floor. When I reached his office, I stopped at the desk to announce myself.

Five minutes later, the receptionist showed me into Doctor Dornish's office. The place was empty save for blue carpeting and custom office furniture; the most prominent piece, a large cherry desk. Medical articles lay pressed under the glass that covered its surface. Several plastic stands held brochures touting the values of minerals in the diet, cleansing the colon, and specialized nutrition for the aging body. While waiting, I flipped through these, noting the lack of copper sources in my diet and deciding my colon was doing just fine on its own.

After I replaced the last brochure, Dornish breezed in with long, fast strides and a patient's file, playing busy doctor to the hilt. He wore his white lab coat unbuttoned to show off his tall, lean body; more likely the result of good genes than mineral supplements. I figured the nurse had mentioned me in detail as he already had blank eyes beneath his heavy brows and kept his gaze on my shoulders and above, a feat managed even while seating himself. "Ms. Sigerman told me about the letter," he said. "Jealous acts like these are quite beyond my understanding."

"Have you received a similar communication?" I asked.

"Me? They wouldn't dare." He twirled a pen between his fingers as we spoke.

"Any idea who they are?"

"My compliments on your brevity. Most people don't bother getting to the point. You're an unusual man." His gaze drifted downward slightly, but he caught himself and stared back into my eyes.

"So you don't take the threat seriously?"

"I'm not sure what to make of it. Perhaps my rival . . . or someone is acting childishly, almost adolescent, if you get my drift. Anyway, Ms. Sigerman has you to do the investigating. We're meeting for dinner. I'll be sure to tell her how thorough you are." He stood, then lifted a brow toward my barely-filled trousers. "I work wonders with marginal chronic deficiencies and connective tissue. Stop at the desk to make an appointment on your way out." The doctor hurried away, sliding his pen into his lab coat pocket.

What'd you know? The bullet lodged in my spine was good for something after all, my daily quota of metals. The hell with supplements. I rolled out of the office without a backward glance.

Kim Sigerman, the daughter, looked nothing like Catherine. A long ponytail gathered black strands of hair high on her head. She wore low-rise black jeans with a pink tee that skimmed her waist. She carried an overfilled book bag in front of her as she stepped off the school bus. If anyone had cautioned her to beware of strangers, the warning must not have included those in wheelchairs because she came straight over. I had parked my car around the corner and sat under a maple that had rained its leaves into the gutter and planned on clogging the sewer.

"You're Raymond McLean, the P.I., right?" she asked, not bothering with polite eyes.

"Right."

"Mom is so freaked out."

"About?"

"That creepy letter." Kim's forehead wrinkled as if doubts crept in about my intelligence.

"That's why I'm here," I reassured her.

"So?"

"What can you tell me?"

She dropped her book bag to the ground. "I got home first on Friday and brought the mail in. I thought the letter looked a little strange with those labels, you know, but then who knows with junk mail. Ninety percent of what we get. No spam filters on snailmail." She laughed and her star earrings fluttered. "Mom didn't open it until the weekend."

"When did she tell you about it?"

Her forehead wrinkled again, this time in thought. "Saturday evening. I thought she should call the cops. That would have been way cool, but she said no."

"Any idea who sent it?"

"Boring-nish. That's what I call him. Mr. Nutrition!"

"Why would he warn against himself?"

"Reverse psychology. You know you always want what you're not supposed to have. I think he's trying to get Momsy to settle down to one man."

"So put one over on Robert Prince."

She nodded. "Exactly and Mom too."

"There's got to be more to it."

"You are pretty smart. You know my dad died, right?"

"I thought your parents were divorced."

"Widowed the first time." Kim looked at the time on her cell phone. "Hey, can we grab a burger, and I'll tell you all about my trust fund and the so-called investment opportunity of a lifetime? We're probably having sprouts for dinner, and I'm starving."

"Let me guess, The Cheesecake Factory at the mall?"

She smiled and swung the book bag back on her shoulder. "There's hope for you yet."

They were waiting for me outside my apartment building. Two men, one bulky, one thin, dressed in suits in spite of the unusually warm evening air. The badge holders on their belts gave them away. They approached me when I started up the ramp by the entrance.

The thin one smelled like peppermint, as if he'd just sucked on a couple of Tic Tacs before getting in my face.

"You seem to like trouble," he said, positioning himself right in front of me.

My hands gripped the handrims hard, turning my knuckles white and flexing the biceps I spent hours working out every night.

"Oh, look. Ray's got muscles," the bulky guy said, leaning on the rail, his size double-e's stretched out. "You need some help there, Benny?"

Benny held his face inches from mine. "You want to strut your stuff, wise guy? You think you could take an able-bodied man?"

"I don't think," the bulky man said, "that he could take another gimp."

I stared into his eyes, holding myself back from launching the first punch. If they could get me to hit them, they would retaliate more than in kind, and the law was on their side.

Benny retreated a few inches. "Scott, he breathed on me. His breath smells like shit."

"Now, why'd you want to go and do something like that?" Scott asked. "You son of a bitch."

"You guys own the air?" I asked. "Oh, right. That's where you get your brains."

Benny's hand snapped out to slap me, but I caught it by the wrist. "Let me hypothesize. You came all the way out of your jurisdiction to give me a message from the Councilor, right?"

Scott laughed. "Don't answer that."

"Stop bothering his partners." Benny said.

"And?" I asked.

"No and," Scott said and yawned. "Just stop it."

I released Benny's hand. "Wiley's the one who should stop it."

"Take the warning," he said, then glared at me and walked away.

Before Scott could move, I pushed hard on the handrims, steering a bit to the right.

"Oww! Geez. You ran over my toe," he cried.

I raced up the ramp, stopped at the door, and twirled around. "Don't come back," I said. "Or I'll have to call the *Home News* and give them an exclusive on corrupt cops."

"We're giving you a pass on account of you being of the cloth yourself, your father and all," Scott called, as he limped to the dark sedan.

"Get smart, wise guy." Benny called, rubbing his wrist.

As I locked the door behind me, I heard the car doors slam and the motor start.

I woke the next morning to my phone playing the eerie tones of *Close Encounters of the Third Kind*. My shoulders, elbows, and wrists ached so I knew I was still alive.

Catherine waited for me to say hello and ask what she wanted before she burst into tears.

"It's another letter," she said between sobs. "And I think I know who sent it."

Despite my demands, I couldn't get anything more from her. I decided to drop by after I picked up the lab results.

In her neighborhood, the homes were the kind you could get lost in, single families the size of apartment buildings, big enough for three generations to share quarters, but most likely inhabited by a solitary couple with one-point-five children, every one of them with their own private ballroom-sized bathroom. Crystal chandeliers sparkled through massive windows above the front doors. White was a popular color for the siding and the people inside.

I used my hand controls to park in front of a creamy vanilla mansion, my tan Ford, a wart blemishing its outline. I pulled out my wheelchair, set it up, and then spun my way to the massive front door.

Catherine answered it and burst into fresh tears at the sight of me. She bent over and buried her face into my shoulder. Her coppery curls tickled my face and smelled of jasmine like she'd bathed in a rainforest. Lost in her scent and touch, I gripped the handrims of my chair to keep my arms from wrapping themselves around her. "Come into my parlor," she finally said.

I did my best fly imitation, tough going because my wheels kept sinking into the thick beige carpet. She dropped onto a silk-covered chaise and leaned back on a half dozen accent pillows that cost more than I earned in a week.

"Do you have the lab results?" she asked.

"Right here." I pulled out the large envelope at my side and fanned out the report pages. "Okay, chili powder, cinnamon, black pepper, vetivert, galangal, and iron filings. Mean anything to you?"

"I think so," she whispered. "You can stop investigating." She pointed to a table positioned behind her sofa where a pack of pink paper lay.

I pushed closer for a look and rubbed a sheet between two fingers. "Right weight and color. Where did you find it?"

"By Kim's computer." She grimaced. "There's more. The labels, too."

"Hmmm, how about the recipe ingredients?"

"I wasn't completely honest with you detective." Catherine held her head high and met my eyes. "My daughter is a practicing Wiccan."

"So you're saying the recipe is associated with witchcraft."

"I have no doubt it's one of her spells. She's confused and possibly suicidal."

"What brings you to that conclusion?"

She retrieved an envelope from under one of the silk cushions. "Read it."

In addition to the letter, the envelope held a melted mass of blue and black wax. Words on the letter spelled out "Dump Dornish or someone will die."

"Are you sure it's your daughter, Ms. Sigerman? Surely, Robert Prince or Dr. Dornish have had access to your home and the labels."

She sighed. "Of course, but they don't practice witchcraft."

"I had a good rapport with Kim. Let me talk to her and see what's going on."

Eyes teary, she nodded and attempted a smile. "I don't want to charge her."

"Of course not. I'm going to take this." I held up the new letter. "I'll see myself out."

I rode to East Brunswick library. Access was a charm. The front door jerked open after I pressed the handicap panel. Bookcases lined wide aisles that held pine-veneered tables and computers with Internet access. I could get to the periodicals, references, and movies fine. The stacks were tight, but a friendly librarian would help. Problem was, I wasn't feeling too friendly. I leaned on my hands and shifted on my cushion. No sense getting a pressure sore.

I pushed my chair to the computer reserved for catalog searches and typed in "Wicca." The answer was in the stacks, of course. I squeezed into the proper aisle and reached with the tips of my fingers to pull down a book. Two more fell with it and crashed onto my lap, one of the few times not having feeling was a boon.

Within an hour, I had the information I needed, but decided to check the newspaper archives to see what I could find about Kim's father, Gary Kewes. The owner of a local pharmacy and a proponent of homeopathic medicine, he had succumbed to a heart attack. From the obituary, I gleaned he had waited to marry until he established his business. Catherine had formerly owned a herbarium, growing and drying herbs for therapeutic purposes, and that was how they met.

As I put back the archive, I let my hand rest on the fiche file dated twenty years earlier and considered rereading the newspaper's rendition of my past. A librarian stared at me, looking as if she wanted to be helpful. I pulled away, wheeling my chair out of the building and back to my car.

Once back in New Brunswick, I called Kim and left a message for her to meet me at Menlo Park Mall after school. I dusted both letters and envelopes for prints. The envelopes were hopeless, the letters less so. I matched prints from the first and second letters, but found only one set on the second.

Before Catherine pulled me off the case, I wanted to talk to Robert Prince. He worked at one of the local drug firms in their IT department, one that hadn't been outsourced to India yet. He agreed to take an afternoon coffee break with me in the cafeteria of his building.

To kill time before heading there, I called more people who had business dealings with Wiley from the list I'd made. I was up to the K's: Kaan, Kaplan, Kerry . . . One said Wiley had given him a scholarship, another that he had helped him with a case before the school board. Neither had any information about political corruption. The third had signed a nondisclosure agreement and said he did not want to get involved in politics. I dated and noted their responses more as a way to stay sane than in support of my investigation. At two o'clock,

I headed over to meet Mr. Prince, arriving at the building exactly on time.

I endured the polite eyes of the receptionist and security guard until Robert appeared. Based on the effusive welcome the receptionist gave him, women found him attractive, even though his hair had receded slightly. I guessed the thickness of his mustache made up for it. He obviously dressed to match his eyes as he wore a pale green jacket the same exact shade. Coffee was free to employees and Robert served me, mixing in the two sugars I requested and insisting on carrying both cups to a table near a window. The view was of the parking lot and red brick buildings, but it gave him somewhere else to look.

"I'm sorry, but I don't know anything about the letters," he said, staring into his cup, then out the window.

"How about Dr. Dornish?" I asked.

"A quack, a popular quack." Robert rolled his eyes. "Catherine's overly impressed with his theories."

"Do you think he would send the letters as a kind of reverse psychology?"

Robert shrugged. "I think he's capable of it."

"What do you think of Kim?"

"As culprit or daughter? I don't know. She's in a bit of a dream world, but basically a good kid." Robert took a slug of coffee.

"She mentioned a trust fund?"

"I wouldn't know about that."

"What about Catherine? Your relationship with her."

"We've been dating ever since her ex left. Did she tell you he used to work here in accounting?" He shot a glance at me. "I guess not. Could never understand why he'd leave her."

"Why did he quit the company?" I asked.

"Didn't want to go along with the corporate program."

Odds on that meant tweaking financial reports before they went to the shareholders. "You're still dating Catherine?"

"We're on for Saturday, a banquet at Charter Oak."

"Can I ask you what you do in IT?"

"VP and Chief Information Officer."

That explained why he hadn't been outsourced.

Shoppers crowded Menlo Park Mall. A short woman with large shopping bags in both hands bounced one into me as she passed. When she realized what she'd done, her mouth flew open and her face paled. I backed out of the stream of people heading toward the Macy's preholiday sale.

Kim showed up twenty minutes late, dressed all in black.

"McLean, my man, don't you know enough not to go to the mall on a sale day?"

"Burger?" I asked.

She shook her head slowly, a Ray Charles kind of shake. Her eyes were too bright. "I'm on a diet."

"What else are you on?"

She giggled. "Are you detecting on me now?"

"Do you write anonymous letters, Kim? Do you think that's funny?"

"No! I'm not like that."

"What are you like? Are you a witch?"

She leaned close to my ear and whispered, "I can do magick."

Her earrings swung in my face, not stars as I had thought, their five points formed pentagrams. She smelled of lavender and liquor.

I drove her home.

"That's a cool car," she said. "It's almost like magic how it drives."

I nodded.

"Thanks for not giving me a lecture," Kim said and paused at the door of that oversized house. "What's your mother like?"

"Thoughtful and quiet." I didn't mention the dead part.

"Mine's mixed up." She opened the door. "Mom, I'm home!"

Catherine came running into the foyer, breathless, but elegantly dressed and made up like an actress playing a mother. She glanced at me. "You see why I need your help." She grabbed her daughter's hand. "Darling, I was so worried."

Kim pulled her hand away. "I'm late, no big deal."

"We need to talk, Kimmie. You don't like Dr. Dornish, do you?"

"No. He's a phony."

"And you have magical powers. You can cast spells. Make me fall out of love with him." Catherine sounded like an attorney leading a hostile witness. "Didn't you tell me that?"

"Mom, he just wants my trust fund. I can help you."

"With a spell?"

"Yes."

Catherine threw me a triumphant glance. "My poor darling," she said, drawing Kim close. "I understand what you did. You can tell us."

"I swear, I didn't write those letters." Tears streaked down Kim's face.

"Your mother knows exactly who wrote those letters," I said and stared at Catherine.

She gazed at me warily, forgetting all about polite eyes. "I'm afraid my daughter is having a breakdown as you've just witnessed. I'll need to call the doctor. You'll excuse us, I'm sure."

"No way."

"Then I'll have to call the police."

"Do as you like, but you're not declaring this child incompetent so you can take over her trust fund."

Kim's eyes widened and she broke away from her mother's grip.

"Your mother wrote those letters, Kim."

"Darling, don't listen to this poor excuse for a man."

"Think about it. She looked at your *Book of Shadows*, that's your spell book, isn't it?"

Kim nodded.

"She found a spell for falling out of love, brewed it up and put it in a letter. Then she looked for a private eye, one she thought would be so hungry for some cash, she could lead him by the nose through her little plan. That's why she came to my office on the seedy side of New Brunswick. She tells me she found the stationary by your computer, gets you to handle the letter before she gives it to me except she messed up and didn't get your prints on the second one."

Catherine dove straight at me. She slapped my face and tried to claw my eyes. "Shut up!" she screamed.

I grabbed her wrists and held her.

Squirming, Catherine appealed to her daughter. "Kim, my money's gone, honey, paying for this house. Buying you the best of every-thing," she cried. "Our only chance was Dr. Dornish."

"Why didn't you tell me?" Kim asked. "Why did you have to try and trick me? You're as bad as Dornish. No, worse." Her cheeks turned red.

Catherine sagged against me. Tears flowed down her face. "You don't understand. Nobody understands."

I pushed her away.

I understood treachery too well. My father had put his oar in with Peter Wiley and when it went bad, came home and killed me. That's what I told 9-1-1 when I called, "My daddy shot my mommy, then he killed me too."

But all that was history, and I had shadows to probe.

The gift that keeps on giving sometimes gives you a little
more than you bargained for.

Pongo's Lucky Day
by Craig Faustus Buck

PONGO SMITH'S ADRENALINE could have burst a fire hose. The cash
wouldn't stop gushing. He had to keep pulling bills from the slot to
make room for the ATM to feed new ones. Then his sluggish brain
kicked in. *This is too good to be true.* He felt a blast of fear as cold as the
snow-packed slopes that surrounded the Indian casino. He knew the
eye in the sky was watching so he took a deep breath and tried to appear relaxed, hoping whatever video feed he was on wasn't being
monitored. But he couldn't resist looking around to make sure he
wasn't being watched by anyone else. He didn't see anyone looking his
way. No widened eyes, no suddenly averted gazes.

Pongo tightened the drawcord hem of his Billabong Snowboard
jacket to seal it around his narrow waist, then zipped it halfway up
and jammed the mess of hundred-dollar bills inside against his stomach. Two of the Benjamins escaped, fluttering to the floor. Pongo
snapped them up with the speed of a frog's tongue.

Was he on some sort of hidden camera reality show? Was he an
unwitting sucker in a money laundering scam, headed for a mugging
as soon as he hit the casino parking lot? Or was this simply a de-
mented ATM?

He'd only had two hundred-eighty-seven bucks to his name when
he'd tried the first withdrawal. And he'd only requested a hundred.
But the damned thing had seemed to spit out a C-note for every dollar he'd requested. *That comes to ... uh ...* took him a while to slog
through the zeros. *Ten grand!*

Pongo was ecstatic. He reinserted his ATM card and punched in
his PIN to try another withdrawal. He should only have a hundred-
eighty-seven bucks in his account if the ATM had recorded the previous transaction as he'd entered it. Or negative ten grand if it had
recorded how much it had actually spat out. But his account still read
two-eighty-seven. The ten grand had not registered at all. Pongo's
adrenaline began to spike anew.

He requested two hundred dollars this time. His finger trembled when he hit the submit button. He had a powerful urge to look around again but he was afraid of attracting the attention of Casino security, so he bit down on his tongue to force calm.

Even before this runaway ATM, he'd been nervous at the Inn of the Mountain Gods because he'd checked in with a Mastercard that had a better-than-even chance of being confiscated. Any day now, his account was destined to be tossed into the slavering maw of a collection agency.

And collectors made Pongo sick to his stomach. His old man— forced by a low IQ and a piss-poor education to take whatever shitty job he could find—had been a collector. Every night, over dinner, he would regale the family with tales of his day's work and inevitably reduce them all to tears. Pongo's father had eventually escaped collections by hanging himself with a phone cord. Pongo often wondered if his own life was headed down the same path. He, too, had neither finished high school nor been expected to.

The ATM's rhythmic money count shook him from his reverie. The slot door clacked open and bills quickly stacked. Pongo had to move fast to keep them from jamming the narrow mouth of the machine. He couldn't believe this was happening to him. In all of his twenty-four years, he'd never won so much as a free ringtone, yet here he was, stuffing another two hundred hundreds inside his jacket. Before ejecting his card he checked his balance again. Still two eighty-seven.

What the hell, he'd go for the max. He reinserted the lame-duck Mastercard and requested the maximum withdrawal of six hundred dollars. Despite having nowhere near six hundred dollars in his account, the withdrawal was approved and the machine started counting. The process seemed to take for blessed ever and Pongo hoped it would never end. He steeled himself to collect the bills and did his best to block the cash slot from view as he raked the six hundred Cs into his belly-stash. Ninety grand coughed up by one ATM in less than ten minutes! What are the odds?

Pongo silently thanked God for His bounty. Or gods, as the case may be, seeing as how he was in Mescalero Apache territory. These Indians had to be Trump-rich to build this ginormous ski resort. And now, somehow, Pongo was sharing the wealth, as if he'd been inducted into the tribe. He felt like doing an Apache victory dance.

Pongo sensed eyes on his back. He turned to see two good-looking babes laughing at him, like the girls used to in high school. He'd always hated that but at least in high school they'd had reason; he'd been a doofus. These girls didn't even know him. It finally occurred to him that the cash in his jacket was making him look like the Pillsbury Doughboy. Burning with embarrassment, he slunk off to his room to disgorge the booty. Now that he was rich he'd make sure no girl ever ridiculed him again.

He got out of the elevator on the third floor and scanned the corridor. It looked disturbingly long and narrow, as if he were peering down the floral-wallpapered throat of a boa constrictor. Pongo held his breath and speed-walked to his room. On the way, he passed a housekeeping cart and swiped a half-dozen pillowcases.

His hands shook as he ran his keycard through the lock. The light blinked red. He wiped his brow with his forearm and it came away wet. He tried the key again and again it flashed red. He looked around for a place to stash the money in case he had to call Security to get into his room.

Unless Security already knew. Maybe they'd disabled his lock to trap him in the hall. He looked up and down the corridor to form an escape plan. In either direction, there was nothing but a long string of locked doors. He was boxed in. No escape. Fear gripped him, the tension making his muscles ache like a bad flu.

He excitement just fed his rising panic as he swiped the lock again and again like a maniac. Red. Red. Red. Red. He wiped his brow again and his forearm came away drenched. The sweat splattered his jacket and dripped across his hand into the key slot. He wondered if the sweat of his brow would change his luck as he lowered the card for what felt like the hundredth swipe. Red.

Pongo tried to think, but his brain was blinking red as well. He stared at the door. Three fifty-five. Series. By twos. His room was a series. Three five five wasn't. Shit! He moved to three five seven and tried his key card. Green! Tonight's lucky color! He felt like someone had pricked his tension balloon with a pin.

He opened the door and entered his room. He'd gotten away with it! He felt like throwing open the windows and taking a huge breath of fresh air only the windows didn't open so he settled for a lungful of A/C.

Pongo hung out the *Do Not Disturb* sign before closing the door and securing the night latch. The belly of his jacket bulged like he was nine months' pregnant.

He uncinched his waist cord and let the cash flow out of him onto the bed, as if he were giving birth to it. He had to push piles of money toward the head of the bed to make room for it all. The result was like a high pile of autumn leaves except prettier. The last thing of beauty he'd seen on that bed had been the Rasta chick with the round ass from Milwaukee who he'd picked up on the slopes after acing the semis to qualify for yesterday's finals. He was surprised to find himself thinking about her at a moment like this. She was just a trophy lay, after all. But she'd been full of surprises.

Still, no matter how great the sex had been it was no way as orgasmic as a haystack of money. Pongo was back in the present, having a mental climax. In a seizure of joy, he dove on top of the green pile. He almost puked from the sour, sickly smell of the cash. Pongo jumped off the bed, brushing hundreds off his body like they were leeches. He envisioned these bills being passed through thousands of filthy hands: meat packers, fish gutters, morgue attendants, sump pumpers, peep show janitors, open-sored junkies, yuck. He flashed on his Sunday school teacher condemning "filthy lucre" when he was a kid. He finally understood what it meant.

He went into the bathroom and tried to scrub the smell off his face.

When he returned, he considered the pile of money. It was physically repulsive but so what? Is that any reason not to love it?

Grabbing a pillowcase, he started stuffing it with cash. He glanced at his scarred, worn Sector Nine snowboard leaning against the wall. So 2007. He could finally replace the old jalopy with that four-hundred-dollar K2 he'd been drooling over for six months.

After the third pillowcase, Pongo went into the bathroom and stared into the Apache basket-weave-framed mirror. The last time he'd looked he'd seen crystal-blue eyes that had lost their luster. He'd thought the blond ponytail looked juvenile and the whole effect was generally depressing and unattractive.

But that was before the miracle. Now he looked aglow with the aura of wealth. His eyes were on fire, blue fire, like the bottom of a gas flame. He thought his ponytail made him look like a younger Ben Franklin, except with a stoner grin and a smaller nose. He smiled at the thought of his image on a hundred-dollar bill.

It didn't surprise him that he looked better now than he had before. The last time he'd checked a mirror, namely about an hour earlier, he'd been homeless, having run out on his landlord owing fifteen-hundred bucks' back rent. He'd been loveless, having finally proposed to his girlfriend of two years only to be ridiculed for even dreaming she'd ever marry a dumb loser like him. Then she'd moved in that night with a chef she'd been fucking, as if running a Spam Sushi food truck made him such a hot shit genius.

Pongo had been unemployed with no immediate prospects for work and no skills beyond snowboarding and passable surfing. He'd tried pro snowboarding but just wasn't born with the requisite aerial chops. And the academic world—snowboard instructing—was small and competitive. It took years to claw your way to the top for that brass ring of eighteen bucks an hour. With only two hundred eighty-seven dollars in the bank, he'd been moments away from the gutter.

But now he had enough money to cure all of his woes. He could pay off the landlord, quit looking for work and buy a new girlfriend. As far as Pongo was concerned, his troubles were over.

Especially if he did just one more run.

He threw on his jacket and headed downstairs. He felt like he was on top of things for the first time in his life, or maybe second if you count that time he landed his first triple flip. Sadly, his only triple flip. If he'd landed one yesterday he might have taken the bronze instead of the bruise. But fuck it! He could buy a triple flip now. His future was hanging a Uey.

By the end of the night he'd emptied three ATMs and had somewhere in the neighborhood—using a good GPS—of a million dollars in hundred dollar bills, now piled high on the king-size bed despite the eight pillowcases he'd already stuffed. How the hell was he going to get this cash out of here?

He whipped out his iPhone to Google the weight of a million dollars. If he hadn't been in a hurry, he would have figured it out on paper, just for the fun of it. He was proud of the fact that he'd never once failed algebra, not even a quiz. And he'd gone all the way from Algebra I through II. He leaned on this achievement to prop up his ego whenever someone questioned his IQ, which was annoyingly frequent. He couldn't understand why. When dope dealers accidentally tried to rip him off because they couldn't do the multiplication, it was his knack for math that set them straight. But his so-called friends still called him Dumbo instead of Pongo. Maybe now that he had some cash, he could buy the respect he deserved.

His research revealed that a million in hundreds only weighs twenty-two pounds, so he was good on weight, but volume was another matter. If the bills are crisp and new and machine-packed, they'd still take up four cubic feet. Pongo figured he'd have to add at least one more cubic foot to make up for crinkled bills and sloppy packing since he had the feeling he didn't have time to stack it all neatly before someone figured out it was missing. He doubted he could stuff that much in the trunk of his car, even if it were empty.

This was a problem because he wanted to get the hell off the Reservation. It was crawling with greedy drunks who'd gladly kill for that pile of money, be they Apaches, professional gamblers, tourists or tribal cops. Pongo imagined a tomahawk splitting his skull and peeling his scalp.

No. He couldn't afford any downer thoughts right now. He threw his hands over his ears and started humming *Achy Breaky Heart*—his favorite song when he was fifteen. Drown out the negativity, just like that Rasta chick taught him. She definitely had something going on. Maybe he should call her again.

He forced himself to think about his soon-to-be new K2 Happy Hour snowboard and new Subaru WRX and a rented chopper to take him and his friends to the ends of the earth. He'd pop the cherries of virgin mountains, lay tracks where man has never laid before. Maybe bring the Rasta chick along for the ride.

Knock! Knock!

The sound echoed through the room like a shotgun blast. His eyes swung to the door, which was shaped like the entrance to a wigwam, and his stomach suddenly felt like it was being sucked into his intestines. He'd flown off hundred-foot dead-drop cliffs with nothing more than a fat stick between him and death but he'd never felt fear like this. He imagined the corridor lined with tribal cops in flak jackets, automatic weapons drawn. Did they know he was in the room? Or were they just searching for him in the most likely places?

Pongo started shaking like a fly hitting a web. He quietly tipped an overstuffed club chair, pulled his precious Swiss Army Snowboard knife from his pocket, and sliced through the thin fabric beneath the chair. Pulling out a few large wads of stuffing, he replaced them with a pillowcase full of cash. If the cops or security or whoever the hell they were took the rest, he might still get away with the one or two hundred grand in the chair. That would be enough for him to move on.

Another knock and then a voice said, "Hello?"

It was a surprising voice, not the Apache hotel dick ex-commando cigar-riven voice he'd expected. It was a woman's voice, and it was sultry.

He set the chair back upright and hid the excess stuffing under the mattress. Then he threw the blanket over the pile on the bed.

She knocked again. "I know you're in there."

"What do you want?" he asked in a quavering voice, as if he'd just heard her for the first time.

"You, baby. It's your lucky day."

He squinted through the spyhole and his heart popped a rivet. It was the redhead MILF he'd tried to pick up in the bar last night. She'd claimed she was too tired to party, which he'd taken as a reaction to his miserable showing in the finals. But she'd scribbled his room number on a napkin anyway, just in case she changed her mind, she'd said. And here she was, decked out in a black cocktail dress that showed off some world-class cleavage, though he assumed it was engineered by some serious underwire, considering how she had to be fifteen, twenty years older than he. Not that he had a problem with that. Older chicks were kinky. They liked to do stuff younger chicks found gross, the kind of stuff Pongo had only seen in pornos but couldn't get out of his mind. Maybe that ATM was just the beginning. Maybe this *was* his lucky day.

He felt a stiffy coming on and reached toward the door but then paranoia stepped in. What if the cops were using this chick to lure him out of his room so they could get the drop on him? Could they arrest him? Had he done anything illegal? This gave him pause. After all, he wasn't stealing anything, the machine was broken. It was like finding money in the street. Wasn't it finders keepers?

"This isn't a good time," he said in a voice that he hoped would sound hostile but just came out loud

"I thought you wanted to party? You're not going to make me beg for it, are you?" Jesus! She was offering it up on a platter.

The thought struck him that she was coming on pretty strong. Could she be a hooker? She was certainly hot enough. What if she was trolling for work? Did he care? He was rolling in disposable income. His newfound luck was making him horny and now the solution to that problem had landed on his doorstep.

He considered the risk. At her age, she wasn't going to pack much of a punch. And she couldn't weigh more than one-ten. He was an athlete with a good forty pounds on this cougar. He could take her with one hand tied behind his back if he had to. Why not have some fun and send her home happy? He checked the bed to double-check that the money was covered, then he tossed his backpack on top of it to make the other bed their logical destination.

Pongo broke into a lascivious grin and opened the door to wave her in. The woman sashayed into the room like a sex goddess and kicked the door closed behind her with her high heel.

"That's better," she said and put her hands on his chest. Her touch was electric. He reached around to grab her ass and she shoved him hard, sending him sprawling backwards onto the floor.

"What the…"

"Shut up!" she said.

He liked the way she said it, like she was playing dominatrix. The image of her wearing a strap-on flashed through his mind. He'd never tried that before and wasn't sure he wanted to. But this chick made him feel like he was about to go places he'd never been.

Then she yanked the bedding off the cash, sending his backpack flying, and wolf-whistled at the sight of the pile.

Reality finally kicked him in the ass: this babe had no interest in him; she was after the money. How the hell had she found out?

"I'm calling security," he said.

"Bullshit." She grabbed a handful of cash and tossed it in the air, just to watch it fall.

"Don't touch that!" He picked up the phone. "I'm counting to three."

"Do I look like a six-year-old? I saw you take the money. I want my half."

"No way. I don't even know you."

"So what?"

"So I don't just up and give money to strangers."

"Fine." She pulled a stiletto from her purse and snapped it open. "I'll take it all."

Pongo was hypnotized by the blade gleamed under the overhead light. It was long and sharp and a lot more lethal than his snowboard knife. His knife featured built-in tools to adjust his bindings, not to draw blood. The thought of sticking it into a person repelled him. Yet she looked like she wouldn't give it a second thought. She oozed danger like no woman he'd ever met. He was scared shitless, but that just stoked his hormones, like carving the edge of a thousand-foot cliff. This chick was sizzling, even if she *was* trying to rip him off.

"You're not going to shiv me with that blade so what's the point?"

"The point is, you're not worth a nickel to me so why would I let you stand between me and all that money when I can just kill you? It's simple logic."

"That is faulty logic, dude. Totally faulty. There's plenty here for both of us. We just have to figure out a fair split, that's all."

"The one who walks out alive gets it all. That sounds like a fair split to me."

"Man, you really need to chill. That kind of thinking can get you killed on a mountain like this. And what's with the stiletto, by the way. That is *so* West Side Story." He couldn't resist the reference; he'd been a Jet in his middle school production with a stiletto that sprang a plastic comb instead of a blade.

Hers was no toy. She extended the blade just inches from him his eyes, sprinkling light from the faux crystal ceiling lamp onto his face. She slowly circumnavigated his head, tracing a circle in the air with the tip of the knife.

"Stilettos are weapons for rhinestone cowgirls, is that what you mean?"

"Something like that, yeah."

"You sexist pig. You want to see what it feels like to be sliced open by a wussy blade? Is that how you're gonna guard your precious cash? By trying to demean my womanhood?"

It was beginning to dawn on Pongo that this chick may not be a reasonable person. Hookers were not notorious for their emotional stability. Maybe logic wasn't his best bet.

"I was just trying to be friendly, okay?" he said. "I didn't mean to offend your precious little stiletto. Didn't even know it had feelings. Bottom line: you're not going to use it on me and we both know it."

When she didn't respond Pongo started to sweat. "Right?" he asked.

She coughed out a laugh and he pounced for the knife, imagining the pain of it slicing his fingers off. But he caught her by surprise and she jumped back, dropping the knife on the floor. He swept it up victoriously.

"Who's got the knife now, bitch?" he said.

"You do," she said, pulling a gun from her purse. The feeling that she was a dangerous woman returned in rolling waves of nausea. This was the first gun barrel he'd ever looked down, and the experience was not cool.

"You are dealing some extremely serious blows to your hotness," he said.

"I'm glad to hear it. A girl hates to use her service revolver on an admirer."

The words echoed around in the winding canyons of his brain. Service revolver? "You're a cop?" he asked incredulously.

"I'd tell you but I'd have to kill you. Yes, I'm a cop. Whoops."

"Cops don't just go around killing people."

"For a million dollars?" She lowered her voice to a sexy purr. "I can be a very dirty cop."

He didn't appreciate the joke. "You need my help," he said.

"You don't seem to understand. You know I'm a cop. I can't take that money and let you live. It's that simple."

"It's, like, way far from simple. How are you going to get all that cash out of here? You can't exactly stuff it in your little hooker purse."

"Getting the money out of here is a solution, not a problem.," she said. "I'm in hock to some very ugly people. At least I was until you came along."

She thumbed off the safety on her revolver and clicked back the hammer.

Sweat poured off him now, despite the frigid air conditioning.

"Take the money," he said. "Leave me a couple grand walking money and I'm out of here like we never met. I swear to God. You'll be home free: no clean up, no noise, no worry about getting caught, no electric chair."

"They haven't used the chair in decades," she said.

"Whatever. You're taking a big chance shooting me. It's totally unnecessary."

"I don't see it as being all that risky. See, I work security here when I'm off-duty. I was at my post when I saw you palm a hundred dollar chip off the blackjack table. So I tailed you to your room. I checked with the front desk to ID you—they'll verify that—then I knocked on your door. You invited me in, then turned on me with that girly stiletto in your hand. I had to shoot in self-defense. It was me or you."

He looked down at the stiletto and wondered if it was smarter to toss it aside or hold onto it. He decided to wipe it with his shirt to clean off his prints.

"Don't bother," she said. "I'll just put them back after you're dead."

"You still have to get the money out of here. That'll be a lot easier with two of us."

"I work undercover. I can become whatever I want to in pursuit of my job and right now I suspect drug dealing in our offsite laundry. Poof, I'm the delivery guy. I'll just waltz out of here with that money in a canvas laundry bin."

"How are you going to do that if someone reports gunfire? They'll be here in seconds."

She pulled a suppressor from her purse.

"You anticipate my every need, don't you? You might have been a pretty good fuck."

His hopes rallied. "You could still find out," he said.

She laughed so hard, she couldn't screw the suppressor on straight. "Is your dick as big as your ego? Because your brain isn't even close."

Fury blew through him like a gas explosion. "Fuck you! I passed Algebra!"

His words flew out by reflex, as did the knife. Her gun fired, launching the suppressor across the room. Pongo watched it bounce off the floor and lodge in the ceiling. It took him a moment to realize she'd been skewered by the stiletto, whose handle now protruded from her glorious cleavage. She dropped the gun. Her face was frozen in shock and he saw the gleam drain from her eyes as she collapsed onto the bed. Her blood started seeping onto the money making it look as horrid as it smelled.

He heard running footsteps in the hall, someone shouting about shots fired. He was trapped. Pongo stared at the gruesome corpse on the pile of filthy lucre. He'd just killed a cop. He did the math: at worst he'd spend the rest of his life in a maximum security penitentiary being serially raped. If he was lucky, they'd put him to death instead. Somehow, the best thing that ever happened to him had morphed into a total catastrophe.

His eye fell on the gun. As if in a trance he reached for it. It would be so easy to just put it in his mouth and carve his last trail.

"Security! Open up!" This time the voice met his expectations. Doom was pounding on his door.

Pongo looked out the window and saw the white snow on the rooftop below. So pure. So innocent. He lifted the gun and and closed his eyes, thinking *luck don't fail me now*. Then he fired.

When Security came through the door they saw a shattered window and, beyond it, a lone figure on an old Sector Nine taking big air off the roof, doing a triple flip into the parking lot. And, damn, if he didn't stick a perfect landing.

A searing portrait of hatred and regret.

Flames
by Robert Guffey

AS THE 19ᵀᴴ of April dissolved into the 20th, Samuel crept into an alley permeated by the stench of week-old garbage. Piles of rotting food, broken wine bottles, torn magazines, and a horde of other useless objects had spilled out of a large blue bin standing against a graffiti-stained brick wall. A stray black cat leaped out of the refuse and darted in front of his path. Christ, just what he needed.

Samuel knelt down in front of the church's back door. The lock was primitive; it would be easy. He reached into his belt and removed two pencil-thin lock picks made of hand-finished clock spring steel. He eased them into the lock. After a mere flick of the wrist the tumbler snapped aside.

Samuel returned the picks to his belt. He pushed the door inward, stepped inside. The room was dark, but not indiscernible. It was a kitchen. Lori's detailed blueprints of the church had indicated as much. According to the plans, a door leading to the basement was located on the left.

The plans were correct. Exactly ten feet to his left stood a plain wooden door. He turned the knob and found it to be unlocked. Lori had told him that the pastor locked every door, including this one, night after night. Odd. Perhaps the pastor was in the basement. If so, he was going to receive quite a shock in a few moments. He patted the concealed gun strapped to his side, drew reassurance from its presence.

Samuel opened the door slowly, using the knob to lift the door up just enough to prevent it from creaking. The door pressed against something lying on the floor: a small blue lump. Samuel knelt down to examine it. He was surprised to see that it was a raggedy white doll with yellow yarn for hair, two red circles for cheeks, black buttons for eyes, a fluffy denim dress for clothing. It appeared to have been sewn by hand. What was it doing on the kitchen floor?

Since he had no way of knowing, and couldn't care less even if he did, Samuel slid the doll across the linoleum floor with his foot. He opened the door the rest of the way, withdrew a powerful flashlight from his belt, slipped through the doorway. He shone the light from side to side, found himself on a landing just above a flight of wooden stairs. The beam illuminated only Samuel's immediate surroundings. The bottom of the stairs was obscured by darkness.

Samuel descended the stairs, attempting to place his boots on the far edges of each step to soften the creaking. If the pastor was indeed here, he would have to be hiding in the dark. Samuel found this unlikely. Perhaps the old man had just forgotten to lock the basement door this one unfortunate night. Unfortunate for the pastor, at least.

Twenty-four steps later Samuel reached the bottom of the stairs. Placing his feet on the concrete floor, he swung the beam of light from one side of the basement to the other. Piles of cardboard boxes connected by silken spider webs lined the walls. To his right were the circle of wooden barrels Lori had told him about. Behind the barrels, in the corner of the room, stood the boiler. Samuel approached it.

He set the tool box beside the boiler, then slipped the flashlight between his teeth. He crouched down and lifted the lid from the tool box. Inside sat a dry cell, an alarm clock, a single stick of phosphorous, and seven sticks of dynamite. Though the alarm clock was already set for two o'clock, he had not yet connected the electrical wires. He wasn't too keen on kissing the material plane goodbye due to some jackass turning on his cell phone too close to his toolbox. He would have to trail the wires from the blasting cap to the dry cell, then from the dry cell to the hammer of the bell as well as the bell itself.

He was in the midst of doing exactly this when he heard the rustling behind him. In one swift motion Samuel released the wires, pulled the revolver from his belt, and spun around. He saw someone emerging from beneath the stairs. A black man. From his soiled clothes and haggard appearance, he was obviously used to sleeping on the streets. He seemed to be in his late 40s, though he could've been younger. Samuel knew all too well how the streets could age you beyond recognition. The man had the distinctive, roadmap face of a professional alcoholic. His eyes were filled with fear. Upon seeing the gun his arms shot into the air.

"Who the fuck are you?" Samuel said.

"I ain't nobody," the man said, his voice trembling. "Hey, listen, man, I ain't seen shit, okay? Just let me go and I won't say nothin'. I don't want no trouble. I was just lookin' for a place to sleep. I had no idea this was your squat."

"How'd you get in here?"

The man pointed up at the basement window, which was open a crack. Samuel cursed himself. A fine housebreaker I am, he thought. I could've come in through the fuckin' window.

"I just wanted some sleep," the man repeated.

"Shut up." The smart move would've been to shoot him, but Samuel wasn't feeling all that smart today. He was just feeling tired. Tired of everything. He whipped out the handcuffs from the breast pocket of his repairman's uniform and began walking toward the man.

"Hey, wh-what're you doin'?" the man said, backing away toward the stairs.

"Don't move one more inch," Samuel said as softly as possible. The man obeyed. Samuel slapped one end of the handcuffs around the man's left wrist, then connected the other end to the railing of the stairway. The man began whimpering like a little baby. Samuel didn't like that, he didn't like that at all. He wished he had something to stuff in the man's mouth,—even a handkerchief would do—but he hadn't prepared for this possibility. Nothing ever went smoothly for him.

He leaned into the man's pockmarked face and pressed his gun against his cracked lips. "Listen to me very carefully. I've got a job to do and I need to concentrate. It'll be very dangerous for both you and me if I *can not* concentrate. I don't want to hear a peep out of you. If I feel my concentration slipping I'm liable to turn around and plant a bullet in your face, you got that? Just nod if you understand." The man nodded, his mouth just barely touching the barrel of the gun. "Thank you for your cooperation, sir." He pulled the gun away from the man's face, then glanced at his wrist watch. Ten to one.

He turned his back on the man, kneeled in front of the toolbox. He began connecting the wire to the blasting cap. Despite Samuel's warning, the man continued to whimper. Perhaps he didn't even know he was doing it. Samuel managed to block out all the sounds surrounding him. A delicate, dangerous procedure like this commanded his entire attention. He took a deep breath before twisting the wire around the nodes of the dry cell. From the dry cell he connected it to the bell of the alarm clock.

While tying the wire around the hammer of the bell, he heard the creaking behind him. He glanced over his shoulder. The man was trying to squeeze his wrist through the handcuff.

"God damn you," Samuel said, trying not to lose his cool. "Sit the fuck down." He had to say it twice before the idiot paid him any attention. At last the man sank down to the dusty floor and drew his knees to his chest, his left arm still dangling above his head. Samuel closed his eyes for a moment, trying to regain his focus. He pushed the man out of his mind again, continued trailing the wire from the alarm clock back to the blasting cap, completed the three-way connection. He slid the toolbox behind the boiler, destroying an intricate pattern of spider webs that had no doubt hung there for a very long time. He shined his light on a small dark creature scurrying across his boot—an ugly, mottled brown spider. His first instinct was to step on it, but he held back. After all, what would be the point?

Samuel started back up the stairs, not even glancing at the handcuffed man.

"Hey, where're you goin'?" the man said. "You're not gonna just leave me down here, are you? I'm tellin' you, I didn't see a thing, man. I don't care about what you got down here. I don't *care*. I just wanted a place to sleep. I just wanted—" His words segued into heavy sobs.

Near the top of the stairs, Samuel turned around and said, "Heads up." The man glanced upwards just in time to see the keys flying towards his head. He tried to catch them, but they bounced off his fingertips and landed somewhere in the darkness surrounding him. Samuel couldn't waste any more time. He silently wished the man luck, then locked the basement door behind him. Why make it easy? Besides, there was always the window.

Samuel retraced his steps. He padded across the kitchen floor, listened carefully, but could hear no sounds emerging from the adjoining rooms. As he closed the back door of the church, Samuel heard Trimble's crackling voice through his ear piece; the only sign of life in the area was now a mangy-looking black cat, he was told. Good, good. Samuel jogged down the alley, out onto the sidewalk, and across the street toward the van. Trimble swung open the doors for him as he approached. The teenager was bubbling over with excitement, but knew better than to utter a word.

Samuel shut the doors behind him, then began slipping out of his uniform. Trimble peered into his surveillance periscope, which was disguised as a roof vent. Making sure everything was in order one last time, no doubt. The kid's exuberance disgusted Samuel. Fifteen years before, Samuel had been just like him.

"What do you see?" Samuel said. He hoped the nervousness in his voice was not obvious.

"Looks like some nigger tearing past the church," Trimble said. "He's going north on Avalon. You think he might've seen something?"

So he escaped. Samuel felt relieved, though he couldn't say why. Only a year ago he would've shot the man without a second thought. "I doubt it," he said. "Let's just go." He threw his uniform into a cardboard box beside the swivel chair.

"I could put Lori on his tail."

"I said forget it." Samuel glanced at his watch. One o'clock on the dot. "Just tell her to go back to the motel. We'll meet her there."

Samuel locked the doors of the truck, then climbed into the driver's seat. He drove out of there at a safe, sane pace. No reason to draw attention to themselves.

Well, looks like another routine work day has come to a close, he thought, not without sarcasm.

Samuel and Trimble were too wired to go to sleep when they arrived back at the motel room, an insect-ridden dump called The Detroit Motor Inn off Sunset and Pico in Hollywood. At 3:40 Trimble switched on the radio. He searched the dial for an all-news station. At last he found KNX 1070 AM. A continuous stream of late-breaking news poured out of the announcer's mouth, everything from traffic jams to natural disasters. No news on the church, not yet.

At 3:51 Lori strolled into the motel room as if she'd just returned from a mild sorority party. She was a pretty young blonde who looked like she should be jumping up and down in a cheerleader's outfit at a high school football game rather than coordinating mass bombings. Rumor had it she was fucking one of the Generals.

Lori plopped down on Trimble's bed and told them she had stayed behind to record the conflagration from a distance. Through a hand-held night vision viewer, the explosion had looked like a magnificent firework display in honor of the Fourth of July. There were a lot of respectable businessmen and "philanthropists" who would pay loads of cash for such a video. She seemed to think it would become as much in demand as the video of the July '77 Son of Sam shootings; she'd heard a copy had gone for $30,000 during a private auction only a few months before. To celebrate, she withdrew a bottle of champagne from a brown paper bag, courtesy of the Generals themselves. She poured three glasses.

At 4:05 the announcer informed them that the St. John African Methodist Church had been engulfed by flames. Even now the fire department was attempting to control the spread of the fire. The announcer was not yet certain whether or not there had been any fatalities, or if this fire was connected to the wave of church burnings that had swept across the country in recent months. Samuel, Trimble and Lori clinked their glasses together and toasted this most special day, so long in planning.

At 5:00 they learned that there had been five fatalities connected to the fire, including a fireman who was shot by a local resident as he climbed a ladder toward the second floor of the church. Lori laughed at that last bit of news. The bottle of champagne was almost empty. As he grew more and more drunk, Trimble kept mumbling about how proud his dad was going to be. Outside, the sun was just beginning to rise.

By 5:10 Trimble was fucking Lori in the squeaky bed as Samuel sat on the carpet, in the dark, his ear pressed up against the radio's speaker as if he could draw more information from it by squeezing its metal casing. His stomach was upset, his chest tight, his forehead clammy and warm. Something was wrong, he knew it.

At seven minutes after the hour the announcer returned with an update. The firemen had removed four charred corpses from the blackened rubble. Apparently the bodies were those of the Reverend Robert L. Cather and a local homeless family that the pastor had been allowing to sleep in the church for the past three months. The family included an adult Caucasian male, an adult Caucasian female, and their eight-year-old daughter. Their names were not yet known.

Samuel switched off the radio, closed his eyes, opened the door slowly, using the knob to lift the door up just enough to prevent it from creaking. The door pressed against something lying on the floor: a small blue lump. Samuel knelt down to examine it. He was surprised to see that it was a raggedy white doll with yellow yarn for hair, two red circles for cheeks, black buttons for eyes, a fluffy denim dress for clothing. It appeared to have been sewn by hand. He remembered kicking the doll across the kitchen floor, discarding it like a piece of trash.

Behind him, Lori and Trimble were sound asleep. Samuel switched off the radio and turned on the television. The lead story on the Channel Five news was the church burning. The station played a video depicting the bodies being pulled out of the rubble. On a stretcher lay a small body, a blackened hand sticking out from beneath the sheet.

By the top of the hour they had attained a photo of the family. The little girl's name was Celia Shepard. She was eight and half years old. The station overlapped her face with live video of what little was left of the St. John Church, while a newscaster reported the details of Shepard's life.

Samuel switched off the television and stared at the fibers in the carpet for a very long time. Diffuse, gray light peeked in through the closed curtains. Because the curtains were blue they cast an ethereal glow upon every object in the room. He felt like he was half-dead, floating in a limbo of his own creation; if he didn't leave soon he thought he might sink into the confusion within his own mind, never to re-emerge. A vertiginous sensation swept over him.

He rose to his feet, burst out of that tomb-world, shut the door behind him. He leaned against the door, closed his eyes, breathed in the cool morning air. He remained there for a moment, trying to re-gain his equilibrium. A distant rumbling assaulted his ears; he imagined it was the sound of Sisyphus's rock rolling down the hill for the millionth time. He opened his eyes and saw that it was a delivery man pushing a dolly of boxes through the parking lot. The delivery man walked past Samuel.

"Good morning," Samuel said. He just wanted to hear someone

else's voice.

The delivery man glared at him with contempt, then continued walking. The look in his eyes said it all: *child-killer*. The delivery man paused outside the check-out window. He asked the clerk to open the door to the office. As the clerk did so, he seemed to throw a nervous glance toward Samuel. After the delivery man rolled the dolly inside, the clerk locked the door behind him. Would they discuss Samuel within the safety of the office? Would they decide to call the police based merely on the guilt etched into Samuel's face? Worse yet, would they contact his superiors and warn them that they had a weakling in their midst, a "useless eater?"

Samuel pushed himself away from the door, cut through the parking lot, and rounded the motel. He and Trimble had left the van a few blocks away just to be safe. He patted his pockets and was glad to find that he hadn't left the keys back in that limbo. He almost got hit by a car while crossing the street. He barely noticed. If he got hit by a car, he got hit by a car. What did it matter? What did anything matter?

He climbed into the driver's seat of the van, slipped his hands around the steering wheel. He lowered his head back against the vinyl seat and closed his eyes once more. His grip on the wheel tightened progressively as if he were in danger of floating away. At first he saw only darkness behind his eyes, darkness populated by green rods and floating red circles. The rods and circles were then disrupted by a rift in the darkness through which light poured in and revealed a naked black boy, only about eight years old, his body covered by a criss-crossing roadmap of thin bloody streaks as if he'd been whipped by a metal wire over and over again. (Yes, Samuel had seen this boy during his initiation, oh so long ago. *How ... oh God, how could I ...?*) The boy glanced up. Through his empty eye sockets one could see tiny human beings trapped within the walls of his skull, lodged up to their bare waists, their bony arms stretching outward in a desperate attempt to touch the freedom that lay beyond the boy's eyes. Samuel peered closer. Inside the eyes of one of these trapped men he could see something else: a white woman in her late twenties locked in a small room filled with smoke, her face etched with panic as she slammed her fists through a window, trying so hard to save the small child clutching at her leg. Inside her eyes Samuel could see something else:

a small body lying on a stretcher, covered almost entirely by a white sheet that failed to hide the girl's charred hand. And something else ... a raggedy white doll with yellow yarn for hair ... a delivery man with a contemptuous glare in his eyes ... a night clerk with an accusation upon his lips ... a pair of giddy teenagers overbrimming with too much death.

Samuel's eyes snapped open.

He stared at himself in the rearview mirror, recalled the oath he had been forced to utter during his initiation:

"Let me bear witness to you, my brothers, that should an enemy of our CAUSE—whether he be from within or from without—bring hurt to you, I will chase him to the ends of the earth and remove his head from his body."

The reflection in the mirror was quite different from the boy who uttered those words fifteen years ago. But in other ways, it was exactly the same. He sat and stared at that reflection for a very long time, unmoving.

Then he looked into those gray eyes and said, "Fuck off."

He slipped the keys into the ignition and drove away as fast as possible. He didn't know where he was going, didn't need to, not yet. However, he thought he might welcome the opportunity to lose his head along the way.

He drove aimlessly for awhile, not thinking of anything at all. He punched the button on the CD player. Chaotic music blared out of the speakers: one of Trimble's favorite bands, RAHOWA. According to Trimble the name was derived from the first two letters of the phrase RAcial HOly WAr. The disc began in the middle of a weird tune called "Sick City," a cover of an old Charlie Manson song, one of the many he recorded before being railroaded into prison. "... to say sick city so long farewell/And die."

Samuel slammed his fist into the off button. The music wasn't making him feel any better. He drove in silence for a long time and was surprised, two hours later, when he found himself parked right across the street from the smoldering remains of the St. John African Methodist Church. He realized he'd been sitting there for awhile. The sun had fully risen and was beating down hard on the shimmering black asphalt and the rats that scampered about amidst the rubble that jutted up out of the ground where the holy building had once stood. A holy building. A Holy War. Samuel began to giggle. He couldn't stop himself. It was like having a bad case of the hiccups.

After a few minutes he got himself under control. He squinted through the glare, searching for any trace of the milling crowds that inevitably lingered around fresh disaster sites, but other than one or two dark faces passing by the open windows in the tenement buildings surrounding the street, the block appeared to be deserted.

As if an outside force were in control of his body, he found himself leaving the van and strolling toward the remains of the church. He paused in front of the empty space that the large double doors had once occupied. The police had ringed the area with a wide band of yellow ribbon (*yellow yarn for hair*), like the kind used to commemorate the first Gulf War.

A war. Racial Holy War.

Samuel felt the giggles returning. Oh God, he thought, what the hell am I going to do? This was a question he asked himself perhaps a hundred times over the course of the next twenty minutes while just standing there, staring....

He didn't notice them, not through the intermittent giggles and glaring white sunlight and his own confusion. He only spotted them through his peripheral vision when they were already within thirty feet of him: a group of young black men, perhaps as many as a dozen, flanked by a familiar face, the homeless man whose life Samuel had spared. He looked frightened. "He's the one," he said, pointing at Samuel.

The young man at the head of the group nodded solemnly and told him to go. The homeless man scampered away.

Samuel patted his jacket, remembering now that he'd left his gun in the van. He spun around and started walking toward it. Too late. Six of the men placed themselves between him and the van. The others strolled up behind him. Samuel stared into the leader's cool brown eyes.

"I... I don't want any trouble," Samuel said. His head was on fire. Sweat beads dripped into his eyes. So hard to see in this glare....

The leader smiled without humor.

Samuel felt nauseous. He needed to urinate bad. He tried to say, "I can tell you who was behind the fire." But for some reason it was difficult to form words.

He glanced up slowly. A few dark faces peered down at him, peeking out from behind the surrounding tenement windows. Waiting to see what would happen.

He could feel the hatred closing in around him as a scattershot series of images sliced through his mind: a black cat in a doorway, an empty bottle of champagne, a bed creaking beneath the weight of two indistinct bodies fucking each other in the lengthening shadows of sunrise.

White flesh charred black with fire.

A church burning to the ground, filtered red.

Yellow yarn, curling in upon itself like the legs of a wounded spider, as it blackens, disintegrates, and disappears.

Sometimes, even superheroes need to call 911.

Faster Than a Speeding Bullet
by Sally Carpenter

SUPERMAN LAY FACE down in the alley next to a Dumpster, a circle of dried blood staining his red cape. Detective Harbison gazed down at the body and decided that regular bullets could take down the Man of Steel just as well as kryptonite.

"Poor Markie!" The Latina standing beside him dug her plump fingers into her skirt pocket and pulled out a tissue. "He's a good customer. He says, 'Imelda makes the best coffee in town.' Markie comes in my diner when he takes a break from work." The alley where they stood was just behind the tiny restaurant.

"His work?" If Harbison wasn't investigating a murder, he'd make jokes about what sort of work a man clad in blue tights and red briefs might do.

"Si, over there." She gestured toward Hollywood Boulevard. "He's very good with the children. They love him." Imelda wiped her eyes with the tissue. "This neighborhood is so bad. Last week a thief steal money from my diner, now this. The police, they do nothing to make it safe."

Imelda went on to say she found Markie early that morning as she opened her shop for breakfast. The night before, when she tossed the day's trash into the Dumpster, the alley was empty of bodies. Then she burst out crying and the interview was over.

The street had no nightclubs and the stores closed early after the tourist trade eased off, so the uniforms would have a tough time finding witnesses. Harbison didn't like the escalation of crime along this street. The past week the local shops had suffered a rash of break-ins. The burglar left no fingerprints and the grainy videotapes from cheap surveillance cameras only showed a figure dressed in black clothes and a dark hood. Maybe Superman had caught the burglar in the act and the thief overpowered him.

In the stifling August heat, Harbison walked west along Hollywood Boulevard, the most famous tourist trap of L.A. The detective felt sorry for the mob of sweating tourists who spent their savings and hard-earned vacation time in search of glamour and celebrities. What they found in Hollywood were seedy apartment buildings, tattoo parlors, tacky souvenir shops and overpriced restaurants. In an effort to squeeze every nickel from the hapless visitors, even the McDonald's had pay toilets. And the stars were either shooting films in Canada or residing behind gated driveways in the more well-heeled sections of town.

Harbison ignored the loud-mouthed street hustlers selling maps of the stars' homes or handing out free tickets to sitcom screenings. He stopped in front of Grauman's Chinese Theatre where he figured Markie worked. The concrete patio embedded with the hand- and footprints of movie stars was a prime location where tourists, hungry for any kind of Hollywood fantasy, had their pictures taken with costumed performers.

Today, a quartet of icons was working. The Hulk made a muscle for some youngsters. A Michael Jackson impersonator, sporting a rhinestone glove, moonwalked while a couple recorded him with a camcorder. Two nubile 20-something women, both attired in tight T-shirts and short shorts, posed on either side of Darth Vader as a third friend snapped a photo. Vader had his arms around the women's waists, pinching and rubbing. Harbison couldn't see Vader's face beneath the helmet, but he reckoned the man was leering.

Spider-man was unoccupied at the moment so Harbison tapped the man's shoulder from behind. Spidey spun around and crouched in a defensive pose, arms out at his side.

"Excuse me, Mr. Spider-man." Harbison couldn't believe he was talking to a cartoon character. Police academy had not prepared him for this.

"Stop in the name of the law!" The webbed hood muffled the man's voice. "Are you the Green Goblin?"

"No, I *am* the law." Harbison palmed his badge and discreetly showed it to the webslinger as not to alarm the passers-by. He leaned close to where his figured Spidy's ears would be under the hood and spoke softly. "Detective Harbison, LAPD."

Spidey's head jerked up in what the detective assumed was a gesture of astonishment. He hated that mask. Part of his work involved reading reactions and expressions, and he couldn't do that with the man's face covered. "I'm conducting an investigation. Can we go somewhere private and talk?"

Spider-man nodded, motioned for Harbison to follow and led him two blocks away to a store that sold postcards with photos of L.A. smog and imitation Academy Awards made of cheap plastic covered with gold foil. Despite the shabby decor, at least the store had a working air conditioner, much to Harbison's relief. The men entered a storage room in the back where Spider-man snapped on a wall switch and closed the door behind them. Harbison's hand moved toward the gun in the shoulder holster beneath his linen jacket. Was this an ambush?

But Spidey only sank into a frayed lawn chair in a corner. "It's my brother's shop. I come in here to eat lunch and change clothes. I don't ride the bus dressed like this. Can I get you something to drink?" The web slinger removed a cold can of Coke from a small refrigerator.

"No thanks, I'm good."

Spidey's chair was the only one in the room and Harbison preferred not to sit on the large cardboard boxes that filled the room. The wall crawler pulled off the hood and wiped his sweaty forehead with the back of his hand. He popped open the can and drank. The man had droopy eyelids, a crooked nose, warts and bushy eyebrows. Hardly the distinguished face of a superhero.

"What's your name? I can't call you Spider-man."

"Let me introduce myself." He unzipped the black vinyl pouch attached to a thin belt. The man removed a card laminated in plastic and handed it to Harbison. The photo ID was for Victor Lieberman of Canoga Park, a street performer registered with the city of Santa Monica.

"The card lets me work at the Third Street Promenade. I split my time between Hollywood and there. At night I hire out for private parties. Those Spider-man movies with Tobey Maguire were the best thing for my business."

"Do you have to register to work in Hollywood?"

"No, and that's a shame. That means any creep can put on a Halloween costume and rip off the guests. And they do, too. They overcharge for tips. They're obnoxious to get attention. They give the rest of us a bad name. Me, I take my work seriously. I'm the face of Hollywood. I give the guests good memories. I don't want them bad mouthing L.A. 'cause some idiot in a mask jerked them around."

"Do you know the man who played Superman? Markham Bennington?"

"Markie? Sure, everybody knows Markie."

"Did he rip off the tourists?"

"No way. He's one of the best. Takes real skill to handle the guests, especially when they're hot and tired. Even the cranks walk away from Supes with a smile. Why do you ask? Is he in some kind of trouble? Did someone lodge a complaint?"

"He's dead. Murdered last night."

Victor dropped his Coke can. "Markie? Dead? I can't believe that. Not Markie. How?"

"Someone shot him in an alley. Did Mr. Bennington get along with the other performers? Did he step on anyone's turf?"

"No, Markie isn't . . . wasn't territorial. Shared the sidewalk with everyone. That's the kind of guy he was."

"What can you tell me about the other performers?"

"Nothing. I don't know names, just their characters. I only see them in costume. And I don't let anyone see me without the mask." He held up the hood. "I love people. I do. I'd be a knockout as a retail clerk or wait staff. But what manager would hire a guy with a puss like this?" Victor laughed. "When I put on the mask, I'm not the kid who got teased and kicked around 'cause his face made people puke. I'm *Spider-man*. People respect me. Tell me where I can find a better job than that." Victor picked up the soda can and tossed it into a blue recycling bin and then used a rag to mop up the spilled drink. "Unless you have more questions, I gotta go. I don't earn any money sitting in here."

Harbison thanked Victor for his time. Before he returned Victor's ID card he jotted down the address and phone number in a memo book. Spider-man masked himself and headed for the store's unisex restroom while Harbison brought the Michael Jackson impersonator to the storage room for questioning.

On the street the man resembled the famed singer so much, right down to the high-pitched voice, that Harbison expected the performer to jump on a table and start singing "Billie Jean." Instead, in the privacy of the storage room, the performer pulled off his glove, scratched his scalp, and shattered the illusion by speaking in a gravely baritone.

"I'm Tim Bukowlski. Grew up on the streets in South Central and now I work on the streets in Hollywood. Worked for a while as a session singer, made decent money, but that wasn't for me. Now I'm my own boss and do the music I like. I'm not just an anonymous voice in the background. So what can I do for you, detective?" Harbison told him about Markie's death. "Damn! What kind of louse would want to hurt Superman?"

"That's what I'm trying to find out. Did Mr. Bennington ever fight with a tourist?"

"Hell, no. Some of the tourists get demanding, you know, wanted Markie to do stupid stuff for them, but hey, nobody's gonna kill a guy over that."

"What about the store owners along the street?"

"They couldn't live without us. We make the tourists happy, and happy people spend money. I've seen lots of Supermen but Markie, he was the boss. Didn't have to pad out his suit like some of them do."

"Did the other performers have a grudge against Markie? Maybe he made more tips than they did?"

Tim shrugged. "Who knows? These actors, they come and go. The young kids think it's an easy job, work a couple of days and quit. Or they're hired for a commercial, they're gone. Most of them don't stick around long enough to work up a grudge."

"What about two on the street now? The Hulk and Darth Vader? Do you know them?"

"Hulk, yeah, he's been around a year or so. He's all right. The other guy, he's new. Don't know him at all. He doesn't talk to anyone. Showed up a week ago, I think."

A week ago—that's when the burglaries started along Hollywood Boulevard.

Tim continued. "Come to think of it, last night when we got off work, Markie left with Darth Vader. The helmet dude was in our faces all day, yelling at the tourists, pushing people around. Markie said he wanted buy the guy a cup of coffee and talk to him, get the nutcase to straighten out before he started throwing punches. Fights ruin everybody's business."

So Vader might have been the last person who saw Markie alive. And Markie probably took Vader to Imelda's Diner for that cup of joe. But Vader wouldn't kill Markie for scolding him—would he?

Outside in the heat and the blinding sunlight, Harbison returned to the Chinese Theater where Darth Vader was trying to drum up business by waving his light saber, although he seemed to scare people more than entice them. Harbison figured that with the helmet on, nobody could identify him. The gloved hands left no fingerprints. What a perfect disguise for a criminal.

Harbison showed his badge. "Excuse me, sir, LAPD."

Vader swung the saber hard at the cop. Harbison raised his hand to deflect the wand and screamed as the weapon smashed into his arm.

The prop must have had an iron pipe inside it.

The detective assumed the saber was only a cheap plastic toy from a department store, but this guy meant business. Vader lashed out again and Harbison ducked. The deadly saber cleared his head by inches. Vader turned and ran.

"Stop! Police!"

Harbison reached for the gun under his jacket—using his left hand because his shooting arm was injured—but stopped. He couldn't risk a stray bullet striking a bystander. He cradled the broken arm against his chest and, blinking back tears of pain, pursued the suspect. He shouted for someone to stop Vader, but the tourists only stood and gawked as if the chase was merely a promotion for a new action film.

Even with the heavy costume and limited vision of the helmet, Vader easily threaded his way through the crowd. Harbison followed, his shoes slapping down hard on the Walk of Fame stars embedded in the sidewalk. He bumped the pedestrians aside with his shoulder, ignoring their curses. He felt dizzy and forced himself to keep moving. If the pain in his arm didn't stop him, the heat would.

A traffic light turned red, a walk light signaled "go," and Vader dashed into the crosswalk. Harbison knew he'd never reach the crossing before Vader was safely on other side. But at the intersection the driver of an SUV, having waited impatiently for the oncoming traffic to clear, made a left turn on the red light. The SUV's front bumper knocked Vader to the pavement.

The driver pulled over, stopped and got out of the vehicle. He was more interested in the negligible damage to his bumper than in the health of the accident victim. Harbison caught up and, in between gasps of air as he tried to catch his breath, ordered the bystanders to move Vader onto the sidewalk, out of the traffic. Juggling his cell phone with one hand, he called for an ambulance and backup. Then the cop knelt beside Vader and pulled off the helmet. The man was unconscious but alive. At least Harbison was safe from another whack with the lead pipe.

Children clustered around, staring first at the defrocked Vader and then at Harbison. The detective smiled. "You see, kids, this is what happens when you go over to the Dark Side."

At the hospital, the uniformed cops removed the guy's gloves and ran his prints. The department had a warrant out for the man, Ed Tasser, on suspicion of burglary for some mom-and-pop stores in the San Fernando Valley. With the Darth Vader disguise, he easily hid from the cops in plain sight. Markie probably learned the thief's identity over the cup of coffee and that's why Tasser silenced him.

A doctor set Harbison's broken arm in a cast. "How did you hurt yourself, detective?"

"I was chasing Darth Vader along the Walk of Fame. Last night he murdered Superman."

The doctor smiled and nodded as if that statement made complete sense.

Harbison shook his head and muttered, "Only in Hollywood."

Disasters bring out the best in people—but that's not all they bring.

Government Assistance
by M. A. B. Lee

SCAM IS SUCH an unpleasant word, all phlegmy and in the throat. I prefer to think of my work as art, performance art, if you will. I have been doing it for many years and have developed a level of skill one can only call expert, if I do say so myself.

My presence in Florida at the time of the hurricane was entirely fortuitous. I came down to these sunny climes on the spur of the moment, to escape the chill of the approaching northern winter, and because a stroke of bad luck had brought me to the attention of the Danbury Police Department. It was merely a fluke. It is, after all, impossible to plan for everything. Some might say I out-stayed my play, but it was a calculated risk, and, as always I was prepared. I disappeared quietly and completely, leaving nothing behind but a handful of unsharpened pencils.

I had been in Steinhatchee for two weeks when Hurricane Inez formed up in the Caribbean. Truth be told, the hurricane was a godsend for me. I was bored with fishing and reading and even the weekly poker games with my fellow lodgers, which I played straight for the novelty of it. So as Inez worked her erratic way up along the east coast of the state, I prepared, and when she swung back out to sea, I thanked my landlady, paid my bill, and headed out of town.

Several hours later I was driving down the interstate on the east coast of Florida, an area damaged, but not devastated, by the storm. To my mind, it is a region singularly lacking in appeal, made up largely of tract housing developments and strip malls lined up along the interstate. But from the point of view of my work, it was ideal. Working this particular play, I never visit two houses in the same area, and the highway would allow me to easily jump from neighborhood to neighborhood. This particular performance is simple and straightforward.

"Good morning," I begin, having chosen a house where some downed trees or a collapsed pool enclosure indicates some minor damage. "My name is Frank Johnson and I am from the Federal

Emergency Management Agency. I am here to assess your eligibility for the SALA program." A little stiffness in the speech, I have found, adds to the verisimilitude of being a bureaucrat. The clipboard thick with forms and the plastic pocket protector full of pens also help.

"SALA is the Storm Assistance Living Allowance program," I explain when the homeowner looks blank. "The program provides emergency funds for meals and hotels and even to board pets if the home is unlivable due to hurricane damage."

I name a generous per diem and explain the process: I inspect the house and determine it is unlivable. Then I fill out the form, sign it and give it to the homeowner. All the homeowner has to do is take it to the FEMA trailer, which is always parked at an address some distance from them, and they will receive cash for eight weeks of living expenses. I emphasize the word "cash". By this time I am in the house, standing or sitting in the living room.

I look around and say, "However, fortunately for you, it doesn't appear that your house has suffered extensive damage, so I am not sure you would qualify."

The next part is the true art of the matter. I must lead the homeowner to make the offer. Oh yes, the offer must come from the homeowner. Complaints to the police are greatly minimized when it was the homeowner himself who suggested the bribe. I have already introduced the homeowner to the possibility of getting money for nothing, now I show him how simple it is.

"Of course, there are no hard and fast rules as to what makes a house unlivable. It is completely up to the inspector," I say, "and I am allowed a great deal of discretion."

At this point most homeowners put two and two together and make an offer. I never take less than one hundred dollars, and I'm happy to take more. I give them the form, signed by me, attesting to the fact that their house is unlivable due to storm damage, and they give me the cash. Then they drive off to wherever I have told them the FEMA mobile office is, and I leave the neighborhood before they discover the ruse.

Now it is true that not every homeowner sees my visit as an opportunity for apparently getting something for nothing. But it goes quickly if they don't, so I maximize my time with the "paying" audience. And that day, things were going delightfully. The roll of bills in my pocket was not inconsiderable.

I decided to visit one final house then drive down to Miami, which is a particularly fertile area for people with my skills. I was in an older development with a number of tall trees and I drove slowly to avoid downed limbs. I stopped in front of a well-kept house at the end of a cul-de-sac. A large oak had fallen over and clipped the edge of the garage roof and now blocked the drive, but that was the only observable damage. As I exited the car, I heard sharp crack coming from the back of the house. Another tree giving way, I thought, and wondered if it might have caused real damage to the home. I decided to chance it and rang the bell.

After a short delay, the door was opened by a woman. She was no longer young but certainly not old, with thick black hair pulled away from a pale oval face and dark blue eyes. She looked at me nervously, then peered beyond me, as if expecting someone else.

"Good afternoon," I gave my best smile and pulled out my identification. "I'm Frank Johnson from FEMA. That's the Federal Emergency Management Agency. I'm here in your neighborhood to see if we can be of assistance. We have a new program called SALA. It provides funds to people who have to leave their homes because of storm damage. I am inspecting homes in your neighborhood to determine how much damage they have sustained and whether the owners are eligible for this program."

For a moment she said nothing, then she smiled and said, "Oh please, come in. I'm Mrs. Williams. But you can call me Ester."

She gestured for me to sit down on the sofa and she took a chair opposite. Although she was doing a good job of hiding it, I sensed that she was still tense. Most people wouldn't have noticed, but I am very good at reading people. It is a necessary skill if one is to be successful in my business. It is difficult to keep the attention of an audience so distracted, and I considered making a graceful, if unprofitable, exit. But I looked again into her dark blue eyes and decided to continue. Not that I am open to temptations of the flesh while I am working. I simply decided a distracted audience would make the play a greater challenge, and I am not one to walk away from a challenge.

I went over the details of the program carefully and concluded by saying, "And it is quite easy to obtain this cash payment. The FEMA trailer is parked at the Cross Corners Shopping Center. That's only a fifteen minute drive."

By the time I finished she was somewhat more at ease.

"But, do you think our house has been damaged badly enough to qualify for this program?" she asked.

I heard the 'our' and presumed there was a husband in the picture somewhere. I found myself happy that he wasn't here now.

Ordinarily at this point I would introduce the homeowner to the idea that I was the sole judge of whether or not there they qualified for the program. But a successful professional is always ready to modify the script as conditions dictate. I felt she needed more time to calm down and focus on the opportunity I was about to present to her. So I decided to go more slowly.

"Let's inspect the damage and see what I can do," I answered.

"Yes, of course," she said, rising. She led me out the front door and we walked slowly around the house. I made notes as we went. The fallen oak had done more damage than I originally thought to the garage roof. In the back, a large tree limb had fallen and broken a section of fence. The brick patio which bordered the entire length of the house was strewn with branches but undamaged, and the sliding glass doors that led into the house were intact. I wondered about the tree I had heard fall and where it might be.

"There's no damage at the other end of the house," Ester said, and took my arm and led me through the kitchen door back to the living room. Now as we sat down, she sat next to me on the sofa.

I looked through my notes, then said, "Of course there isn't any hard and fast rule about what damage makes a house unlivable. It's left to the inspector to decide. But it would be difficult for me to say the amount of damage you suffered would qualify you for the program."

"Yes, I know. We were very lucky." Ester looked at me, tried to smile, then began crying.

This was an unusual situation. I've had many home owners get angry when I announce that they were not eligible for the money, but I've never had one cry.

"Please," I said. "Don't be upset. Perhaps there's something I can do."

I pressed my handkerchief into her hands. They were warm and soft.

"I am so sorry," she began, dabbing her eyes. "It's not you, I'm just upset, about...well it's just...no, never mind. I can't burden a stranger, it's not your concern."

"No," I protested. "Please, if I can help in any way."

She cast her eyes down. I could tell there was an element of performance here. She was using what might be called her "feminine wiles" to convince me to assist her, but what else did she have? I silently applauded her. She was very effective and would have done well in my business.

"Would you help?" she began uncertainly. "I'm so scared, you see. It's Derek, my husband. I want to leave him, but I'm afraid. I told him I wanted a divorce and he threatened me. And now he's out looking for gasoline for the generator, and I could leave, but that tree is blocking the garage door. I just want to get away." She began crying again.

"My dear, dear Ester." I said. "Please, let me drive you somewhere safe, a friend's house perhaps."

"Oh, would you, Frank? We can leave before he gets back. He's dangerous, you know. I'm so scared."

"Don't worry now." I reached over and squeezed her hand. "I'm here. I can protect you."

"Thank you," she said. "Thank you so much. Just give me a few minutes to throw some things in a suitcase, all right? You won't leave, will you?"

"No, of course not. I give you my word. We will walk out of here together."

She went down the hall and opened a door on the right. She came out a few minutes later.

"Oh Frank, look what I found in his dresser." She was holding out a small gun. "I didn't even know he had it."

I took the gun from her.

"Well, he doesn't have it anymore." I said. "Go get ready and we'll leave." Before she returned to the bedroom, she turned and gave me a grateful smile.

I put the safety on and stuck in the gun in my pocket. I wondered what sort of fellow this Derek was. A brute no doubt, Ester would be lucky to get away from him. I looked at the bedroom door impatiently. It would be best to leave before he got back. I wasn't afraid, but I didn't want a scene, and I certainly didn't want to draw the gun unless it was absolutely necessary. I hoped her friend's house was at some distance. It would give us a chance to talk. We could go somewhere for coffee, perhaps. Maybe I would even tell her about myself, I was convinced she would appreciate my skill.

A siren in the distance interrupted my daydream. I was reminded that many types of official emergency workers would be around now. I wanted to be out of the neighborhood before it was discovered that I was not one of them.

"Ester," I called. "Ester, are you ready?" I went to the bedroom door. Outside I heard a car pull into the driveway and a car door slam. We could go out the patio door to avoid confronting Derek. I stuck my hand in my pocket and held the gun. Knocking gently, I pushed open the bedroom door.

Ester was nowhere to be seen and the door that led to the patio was open. The room was in total disarray. Someone had rifled through the closet leaving clothes and shoes scattered everywhere. All the drawers of the dresser were opened and a jewelry box was spilled onto the floor. The dressing table mirror had been removed revealing the door to a wall safe. And in the corner next to the bed lay the body of a middle-aged man wearing jeans and a sweatshirt. He was lying face up with a small dark hole in the middle of his forehead and a pool of blood around his head. I had barely taken this all in when I heard someone behind me.

"Hands up!"

I turned and faced two policemen, guns drawn.

I raised my hands and said, "Please, I work for the government." When faced with the unexpected I always keep the play going.

"Yeah sure, mister." one of the cops said. "Turn around and put your hands on your head."

In an instant I was in handcuffs and one of the cops was checking my pockets. He withdrew the FEMA identification, read it, and handed it to his partner. I thought for a moment things would work out, but then he withdrew the roll of money. It was a large roll.

"So how many places did you have to break into to get this wad?"

Then he found the gun.

"It's been fired recently," he told his partner after sniffing the barrel. "Poor bastard. Did he walk in while you were trying to get into the safe?"

"No," I protested. "I didn't shoot anyone. Ask Ester, she gave me the gun. It was her husband's."

"Well, I don't know who Ester is," began the policeman. "Mrs. Sarah Willson, wife of this here deceased, didn't say anything about any Ester. She said she was checking the neighbor's house for damage when she heard the shot. She ran back and found the room ransacked and her husband on the floor. So she got out of there quick and called us."

The other policeman chimed in. "Let's just go outside and see what Mrs. Willson has to say." He pushed me out the door.

Outside, Ester, or Sarah, stood next to the patrol car.

"Ester, tell these men I'm here to help." They looked at her.

"Who is he? Did he kill my Jack?" Her voice rose to an hysterical pitch. "Why is he calling me Ester?"

I could only admire her performance.

Even in the shadow of war, the friendship of children is the most effective melting pot.

Ninety Miles, A Million Miles
by Gary Cahill

AT SEVEN YEARS old I was already more of a soldier than they would ever be. A better secret agent. A real stand-up guy, even. Like, Aunt Maeve would start smoking and reaching for a bottle in her handbag, and I loved her, so you're not hearing it from me. My neighbor from across the street was inside his front door with some man when I was on the sidewalk. Mr. Fessente told me he had to teach that man a lesson was all, and no need to tell anybody, OK? The man left looking sick and afraid, and that was good enough to lock that up in my memory vault. My friend Hermie from Cuba told me it was his father who got so mad about the news on TV and drank too much and that was why his dog Moochie got out the door and down the stairs and hit by the car right in front on their block. He limped now, but he was fine. Moochie, I mean. And I would hold onto that secret, too. I knew what Hermie was talking about with his dad.

I misheard most of the invective the first time around, not speaking the language, but Mr. Montero would get broken-record drunk and then unleash the needle-skip-repeat over-and-over screeching assonant violence of the hell-black bottom soul-dredging in his voice—well, I became a quick study in the phonics version of Cuban epithets, like pop singers do with lyrics in German and Japanese and Mexican Spanish without ever crossing a border, or even eating the food.

If Enrique was home, he'd be in the other room, door closed to little effect in stanching the oily spew, and at a ripe-aged fourteen have a few pops and share the mighty curses with his father Orlando and the uncle and the union hall roughnecks, all truck drivers and waterfront dock guys, who dragged themselves away from an open bar tab at the shot-and-a-beer joint around the corner over to the Montero apartment for even more free beers from Orlando's *"mi frigi es su frigi"*, and tumblers of cheap rum, and a sacramental communal loaf of balled-up Wonder Bread, each slice rolled and molded around salted butter and white sugar centers. No; it was not an attempt at a poor man's candy truffle. It was, in its useless excess, somehow very American.

Like a trailer truck air horn, "... *poner su mierda en mi polla!*"

"What's your dad saying, Hermie?"

Enrique's little half-brother told me about "your shit", and this time, for once, we didn't laugh at the wildly vicious "my dick". We barely understood it, what it meant, really, both of us still plowing through the third grade.

Blaring like an ocean liner powering through the harbor, *"Voy a cagar en la boca de su madre!"*

Herm had taught me a few things during recess at school. I knew "boca" and "madre", and after the first blast's translation I could guess a couple things he wanted to do in somebody's mother's mouth.

Laughing and growling leaked from the door jamb, while slapping glasses and bottles clacked in ominous toasts to some agreeable vileness.

"Jesus, Herm. Who are they talking about?"

"The man on the TV, President John."

"President John?"

"Sorry, I don't pay that much attention. What is it? *Kenny?*"

"No. Kennedy."

"Yes, right, they say, *fucking Kennedy*."

His mother was all over him. *"Herminio*, no, don't you be like that, don't say those things. Do not talk like that, about the president, about anyone. Nothing is so simple to just swear at it."

Could have fooled me.

The Cubans had started showing up in big numbers the year before, in 1961, my parents explaining that freedom to do the things we did every day was not a priority of a new government run by someone named Fidel Castro. Not that the guy he replaced had been any party, either, my dad said. There was a lot of *U.S.A.* drum-beating around town about this, that it showed just how great the United States was, with so many people coming here to live with us. I hadn't formulated any major complaints myself. So I figured people coming from other countries, *"refugees"* I was told they were called, would be more than happy to be here and join right along in being *"Americans"*, as I was told *we* were called, until I got the idea that northeast New Jersey was sort of a waiting room for the return flights to Cuba, once the deal with this Castro person was straightened out. Which seemed to pretty much be killing him and anyone close to him and not being too concerned who took over, according to the Cuban families in my neighborhood, most definitely including the Monteros, meaning the men of the house, Orlando and Enrique. By the start of the school year back in September '61, a lot of the Spanish and English spoken by the new neighbors, most of the adults, anyway, centered around the words *la Playa Girón, Bahía de Cochinos, Fidel al infierno*, and *U.S. invasion, Bay of Pigs, hero prisoners of war*, and, in the most sainted tones of all, *Brigada Asalto 2506*, with the numeral *vente cinco cero seis* given, like Sinatra reading a lyric, the rich rubato care and respect it apparently deserved.

Oh, and, of course, *fucking Kennedy*.

Late October the next year me and Hermie and everybody else spent two weeks slumping off to elementary school, looking at the sky over us and over the river to New York City, expecting that on one of these crisp autumn days, one of the blue-pretty sunshiny mornings that in our minds' eyes got darker hour by hour, we were going to be blown up and burned and our ashes dissolved like salt in boiling water, our insignificance subsumed into giant atomic bomb blasts, like we'd seen on TV destroying whole islands in the ocean and in pictures in magazines of cities in Japan, exploding on us for some reason we wouldn't even be able to understand fifty years later. Russian rockets in Cuba, American rockets aimed at everybody, missile launching sites we drove by on the way to visit my dad's friends or go to the shore, or to the forests and parks up north, or to Long Island, seemed like everywhere, fenced in with warnings about law and trespassing and shooting, all of it making us think we were going to die, soon, whatever dying really was, as we pushed toward our ninth birthdays.

I've heard about the "duck-and-cover" exercises they performed in schools with classroom desks and chairs shielding kids from nuclear holocaust, but we enacted the equally legendary *controlled exit to the brick and concrete hallways*, where, in strictly enforced life-saving ascending size order, as we marched and then squat-sat, we lined up along the wall with hands clasped over our bowed heads to protect us from the broken glass, the jeweled radioactive shards our keepers expected to be flying at sound-speed and letting our blood flow after the blinding million-billion-degree fireball blasted out the windows; the death of a thousand cuts versus the sun exploding.

Yes, we were taught to fear the windows breaking.

And as I recall, it was Jimmy Daley who spoke for us all when he cracked, "Breaking glass? What about the *melting* glass?" Jimmy managed to get in "and melting bricks, even" along with a howling "nothing left but glowing dust" as they hauled him away toward the principal's office, keeping him low to the floor to minimize the kicking. His kicking, not theirs. I hoped they'd bring him around to the nurse's office, since they were whacking him like it was Catholic school. I guess practicing for war is hell, too.

And when after two weeks it was all over, and we were certainly, just like that, going to shift right back to normal little kid life, the Montero men were weirder than ever, like they *wanted* a war. Maybe not the war we almost got, but some kind of war. Perhaps they were unclear on the details. But they expected something to happen that didn't, and the execration and threats and fury redoubled and amplified.

"What about Enrique? Listen to him," said Hermie, sniffling, embarrassed.

"He's ..." as she waved her hands overhead, "... older, in with his father and the rest, they brought him along on these things, it's something done, *finito*, too late to fix, I don't know."

But she did know, about her stepson Enrique. Who was always *only* Enrique to her; not Kiko, not Kiki, no terms of endearment offered or expected from her mouth, and absolutely no mention, ever, of his abandoning birth mother Silvia, who saw something or suffered something back in Havana in the '50s, and ditched Mr. Montero, and broke Enrique's heart, but didn't outrun the cold steel retribution enacted by her husband, with his co-killer brothers and *amigos*, who all wound up with blood and so much more of her on their hands. A big enough pile of *dinero* ensured no witnesses to pack them off to the slammer, and when one day brother José Montero got shivery-shaky from guilt and cold feet, the next day he just wasn't around, at all, anymore. The lie on Silvia was she'd been stepping out, got in over her head with the wrong crowd—it was easy with all the hotel bars and American-run casinos and drugs. Or, you know, something, wink-wink, even *worse*. Like that.

Now living among the New Jerseyans, the Monteros weren't Irish or Italian or German or something else that had taken root. The family drama hadn't played out *here*, for God's sake. And it just faded. It wasn't even back story, just myth. Was it because they were *other people, not like us, they have their ways*? I wonder how being creamily porcelained Swedish would have played out.

And the knife that found its way into Silvia found memorial residence in an ornate jewelry box in Enrique's room, along with a psyche-scarring lesson that stuck to the walls around him and enveloped a wounded boy's mind; a lesson on the fate of traitors.

But Idoya, Hermie's loving mom, kept her arms wrapped around him. "Not you, Herminio, *mi amado*, not like this. This is a new country, a new place for us, to stay, to live, to move on from what was behind. To not just live in America, to be real Americans. I don't know if I'd want to go back."

I always thought New Jersey winters might change her mind.

She cried, sitting with us, for a long time, sobbed hard thinking back about being a descended Iberian Basque, her features a cast of Moorish darkness generating a sneering unwelcoming racism among the more lilied European Cubans, no matter which horrible despot, from Fulgencio Batista to Fidel, was running things. And meanwhile the party in the other room never paused, never broke. They never even heard her.

She hadn't known about Silvia until she'd birthed her son. She would not be deserting "my darling, *mi hijo, Herminio*", for anything. I would start to come by for after-school homework and sometimes lunch on Saturdays, and be with her and Hermie, while Enrique and his father and the others were drifting into something else.

Not that Mr. Montero didn't clearly love "*mi Idoya*" as well as he could. Often on those Saturdays, the apartment lighted by his burn for her, I would hear his sing-song love-talk counterpoint weaving its way through my recall of the damning curses and vengeance oaths of the nights before. I watched as he stroked the lightest of caresses along her blushing cheeks and brow, and lifted my face to his and her mingled sweat, a musky-sweet luring distraction I didn't understand. *"Querida,"* he'd say slyly, each time. *"Dulce. Adoncia."* And, each time, he'd tumble out *"amor"*, and *"mi vida"*, and *"todo mi corazón"*, and then she'd stop him, right there, each time, to remind him he'd already left nearly all of his heart and soul behind *"en Habana, en Cooba"*, as they pronounced them, and his own tears would come as he hid in the other room.

I wondered if he cried because he was sorry she believed it or because it was true.

Or because the dream of returning to his beloved island was slipping away.

Slipping away, until late December, when the President made a fifty-three million dollar deal to get those captured heroes of *Brigada Asalto 2506*, the Bay of Pigs invaders, freed from their prisons in Cuba, and sent to Miami. Mr. Montero and his *wanna-be* soldier son now substantially softened their rhetoric, and the two of them planned to drive down along with Uncle—*Tío*—Tito to Florida to be there for the big celebration in the Orange Bowl football stadium to welcome these men home, to America. Although I was still confused about them calling *here* home when they'd tried to start their own war in another country, and I guess take it over. I was eight, after all, and Hermie wasn't all that interested, so we were a little sketchy on the details. Hermie did tell me his dad and brother and uncle planned to be away for a while, through New Year's, that they were going to be seeing some important men from the *Brigada* and other groups about helping to make Cuba free again.

Somehow, someday. Any way.

"Hermie, where's your dad?"

I was afraid he'd deserted them, or been kicked out, and what that might mean if the stories about Silvia back in Cuba were true.

It was well on into March, and I hadn't seen much of him since he'd driven back from Florida with Enrique and *Tío* Tito, all of them having turned a page on the President. The *Brigada* leaders had presented Kennedy with their battle flag, hidden away during the terrible time in Cuban jails, and he had reciprocated by emotionally vowing to hand it back in a "free Cuba". Many dark-hearted and serious veterans were not buying it; once bitten and all that. But Orlando and Tito wanted in on whatever it took to oust the *Fidelistas*.

"He's in training now, to be a soldier, it's his new job, he sends money to *mamá* every week, and he says they'll be going in to win Cuba back. He talks to 'Rique a lot on the phone, from Louisiana and Texas, 'in the field' he calls it but I think its like woods or a swamp, and right by a *real* base near Fort Benning in Georgia. He says he's going to Guatemala or Nicarag... "

Enrique bolted from the other room straight toward us, covered the floor like Groucho in two giant steps, smoke from the ears and daggers from the eyes, and just in the nick pulled back on a two-shoulder shove that would have flown Hermie's ass off the wooden chair and onto the floor and instead cuffed him across the back of his neck and on the crown of his head, and knocked him woozy. Enrique forced a chuckle to lighten it up. He would not have a career in the theater.

"Hey, Hermie, *Herminio*," pointedly, "easy there. Family business, family business. You answer too many questions. And you, *hombrecito* ...," as he shook his head and "tsk, tsk"-ed me. No career in the movies, either. He knew his father called me *hombrecito*. Maybe he thought he was taking his place. "And perhaps you ask too many."

I told him, "Your father is always nice to me, you and *Tío* Tito and everybody taught me to play soccer at that big VFW park by the river where he brings us, Hermie shows me how he paints those nature pictures with his watercolors. You're all fans of baseball and I got you going with the Yankees. He's my friend, like you guys. I asked one question because I don't see him. Sorry. Did he join the army? Is it secret? That brigade you always talked about?"

Enrique's face was blank. His jaw slid back, forth and back. He leaned over to cut me in, share the inside story, as much as he could. "OK. It's not the army. But it is pretty secret, for now. Let's not talk about it too much, *sí*?"

"OK. *Sí, señor*. The secret is mine. I mean, ours." I smiled.

And he really needed to practice that vacant chuckle.

April changed everything. And in the Montero house, everything old was new again. The screaming. The majestic cursing. The swearing allegiance to violence and retribution. I was there the night Orlando and Tito came back from ... wherever. They'd picked up the bar gang, after quite a few at the tavern on the corner, and shanghaied Enrique on the way into their bedroom meeting hall across from me and Hermie at the kitchen table, ignoring us and Idoya, off to making some choices.

Hermie translated.

"*Macosa!*" Punk!

"*Cobarde!*" Weakling! Coward! Quitter!

"*Pendejo!*" ??? Silence.

"Not in front of my mother," he said.

Orlando and Tito were out of their khakis and cammo, and out of a job. Whatever *operaciones* and *actividades* and *aventuras* being planned in the military trade had been scrapped; all the money spent, and all the plotting and training, for naught.

"They are *never* going to invade! They are *never* going to take it back! They pulled the plug!"

"What does he mean 'take it back'?" I said. Hermie tried to wave me off, too late. "I didn't know we owned Cuba."

"You little bastard." A little of the drink was talking, but most of it was Mr. Montero for real, staring past my eyes like he wanted in behind to rip them out. "What the hell is this place you live, the United States? America comes to Cuba, you *reinvent* the place with the guns and the gambling, then the oil companies and the army and the spies and *la Mafia* run everything, and I'm on the right side of all that. And then they all get run out by some back-stabbing fuckers who turn *comunistas*, and that stands? Stays that way? No, no, it *will not stand*, something will give." He turned toward the hall to head downstairs and drink the night away. "If I can't have Cuba," musing, conspiring with himself, "I will have the man in the middle. You play us for fools, so shame on you. And fool us again? Shame on us, for believing in you. But three is the charm, yes? The lucky charm. Luck of the Irish?" He passed the doorjamb and dropped an octave to a dripping mutter. "If we can't get home, we should get Kennedy."

Mr. Fessente, from across the street, seemed a nice fellow, but so did Mr. Montero. So I made sure to keep our secret about that man inside his front door. We all got to see him a lot in the neighborhood, usually on his porch, scanning the street, smoking cigarettes, waving and calling hello and watching as we went home or back to the schoolyard to play. A bigger man than most of our dads, round from neck to waist, not bouncy fat but hard, and looked like he could move on his feet when he sort of danced down his front steps and zipped along the sidewalk a couple blocks to the corner to confer with Paulie the street sweeper, a yippy little fellow with a too-high-shaved haircut and what we thought of as a squirrelly voice. It seemed a strange pairing, until we sort of heard around that you could bet money you gave to Paulie on all the sports games and you could go to him if you won, but you had to speak to Mr. Fessente if you lost. Especially if you had been given credit or were late paying, when he would waste no time coming to see *you*.

Mr. Fessente had some job with the different union halls that put a lot of townies to work on the waterfront and on the trucks and trains, so he was popular, it seemed. People didn't really say anything bad about him. I don't remember ever hearing a crack or a joke, even. And soon Mr. Montero was talking to him a lot, about working, I guess, but it was like they knew each other or had something going on. I thought maybe they played cards, or Mr. Montero expressed an interest in the unions and wanted to be involved in what they were doing. I'd see him get into Mr. Fessente's car, a gigantic brand new '63 Oldsmobile 98, and Hermie told me they'd take off for the Teamsters union building next town over, which had something to do with trucks and shipping and loaning money for big building projects around the country, and talk big plans with important people from all over. Soon, Mr. Montero started driving himself, in his not gigantic but pretty snappy brand new '63 Chevy Impala. I made sure not to say anything in front of Enrique so he didn't find out his brother was talking to me about "family business" again.

Hermie kept up the chatter, though.

"*Papá*'s been down to New Orleans, other places too, and says he'll be traveling more in the fall, for some work with people with big money, and thinks he'll have prospects for a good job after Thanksgiving. He's making money now after the army work stopped, but he says it looks really good for him later on." His dad had brought him a menu from a great restaurant called Antoine's, and we read the listings of all sorts of wonderful-sounding food with strange and exciting Frenchified names. We looked forward to what we'd see from Mr. Montero in November. He said he'd be moving around the country, following very important government people, checking security and safety measures, part of a back-up team in case there was trouble finishing the job. When he said that last thing, he seemed to think it was a little bit funny, for some reason.

Hermie got officially stamped and cancelled travel postcards as mementos when his *papá* came home for Thanksgiving. They were from Chicago on November 2nd, a New York City hotel on the 8th and 14th— Hermie wondered why his dad was staying in a hotel just across the river from home, must have been for work—Tampa and Miami on the 18th, Dallas, Texas on the 21st, and another one from Dallas on November 22nd . And Hermie wondered about the need for the second one from Dallas, like it was a commemorative for what happened there. One day he would figure it out, collect *that* secret to *his* innermost place, and lock it away for good.

Soon, Orlando Montero found the fear biding its time, lost hold of himself, spent the next three and a half years in a drunken, downward drift, being paid regularly through the mail, for what no one knew, less and less often venturing outside, until out of nowhere some friend of Mr. Fessente called one day, told him something or other about coming in to one of the union halls for a high level meeting. Some people swore up and down they saw him there, and yeah, they'd say, oh, that's right, yes, I remember now, he left early, after some hotheaded talk, in a big hurry. They found him in the Impala, driver's door open, covered with white powder the cops said was cocaine and heroin, shot with a big gun in each shoulder and each knee, his chest hacked and blade-opened with a machete, or from the looks of it maybe a broadsword. Touristy postcards from big American cities were tossed on the passenger seat, and one from Texas shoved so far into his mouth it jammed past his tonsils down his throat.

Mr. Fessente gave a lot of money to Idoya for the funeral, and then after that, for a long time, piled on enough to keep Hermie in art lessons for his painting all through high school and college, and enough for Idoya to keep herself well until, years later, she died.

He also looked into Enrique's eyes at the cemetery, and gave him a job. A hair-trigger temper guaranteed he wouldn't last long and soon be out on his own or in the ground, but like his father, Enrique learned to exact his lust for revenge on targets in view, marks he could reach out and touch—like "freeing Cuba" by running guns and drugs, and bombing local social clubs and concert halls—and never realize he'd all but given up on ninety miles south of Florida.

And these days, fifty years later for Christ's sake, me and my city kid concrete-battered knees can hit the old neighborhood, longing for a proper *café con leche,* and hobble up the street into the crusty old bowels of all that murderous fetid prideful shit, righteous though they claim it be.

One night a newer, happier-mileage model of some half-sized 4X4 SUV thing rolled up, slowed, and kept going when the driver saw me, staring at the back end of his car. He'd found the right address I think, but discretion and valor and all that sent him on along. I held a hard look on him, all the way into the cover of dark, the white paint job back-dropping a souvenir fake Florida license plate above the legit New York tag; "Key West" it read, "90 Miles to Cuba".

Oh, come on, Juan.

It might as well be between the moon and Mars.

There was one day after school a couple weeks after Halloween, a year before the storms of November '63, and learning about guns in the streets. I don't know why my head calls up that one afternoon, falling as it did between Cuba and Dallas, but I can wipe dry my eyes and see it clear—after class we left the schoolyard and I looked out across the roofs of houses and the big Palisades cliff and over the rail yards and the old shipping piers, across the Hudson past Hell's Kitchen and the West Side, and up and up to the top of the mighty Empire State Building, coolest thing in the world, as we all walked home.

I'm going to take a couple grand and give it to Hermie and have him paint it; not his vision, but mine, from my memory. From my mind's eye to his hands, we'll take our childhood back, and right next to my window that opens to a view of the real thing, I'll hang it on my wall. *Our* Empire State'll be getting *us* back. And there it'll stay, just like I remember it.

Human beings have the remarkable ability to adapt to just about anything.

Inured
by Stephen D. Rogers

THE FERRY TO Martha's Vineyard was mostly empty up here on the rooftop level, the sky gray and the wind sharp, the smell of the open water different than that found on the beaches of Cape Cod.

Almost all of the other passengers were seated comfortably inside, many taking advantage of the snack bar or the free wireless. On my way up I'd passed both families too excited to sit still and business people more than happy to sit back and let someone else do the driving for a while.

Me, I stood at the rail, watching the wake stir up the gray-green seas, and tried to ignore the voice coming over the loudspeaker.

"Will the owner of a silver Audi with New Jersey plates please report to the freight deck to disengage your alarm?"

This was the fourth announcement in fifteen minutes. Maybe the car was a rental, and the driver hadn't noticed the plates, didn't know an Audi from a Chevy. Or maybe the driver was simply deaf. Could deaf people get a license to drive?

The announcements had been insistent enough that I'd almost gone down to the freight deck myself, and my car was parked back in the lot at Woods Hole.

The woman I meant to interview worked at a bed and breakfast within easy walking distance of the dock. Leaving my car on the mainland was cheaper than transporting it, and the fresh air would do me good.

A grunt as a heavy man joined me, favoring his right knee. "Can't say I care for how those stairs gave as I climbed them."

"Yeah." Unlike the inside stairs, they bowed for some reason. Of course I'd acclimated and then forgotten the fact by the time I reached the top.

The stranger's hand pressed his baseball cap onto his head to keep it from going overboard. "There's the island already."

"It looks closer than it is."

"I remember when journey this would take hours. At least it

seemed that way when I was younger." He frowned. "Those kids down below, plugged into their electronics, they have no sense of adventure. We always enjoyed the trip over almost as much as being on the island. Watching for whales."

"I haven't seen so much as a gull today."

He joined me at the rail. "The kids are missing this to blow up mutants or chat with their friends back home. 'What are you doing?' 'Nothing. What are you doing?' 'Nothing.'" He shook his head. "And they're not."

I nodded.

He held out his hand. "Frank Harris, from Cherry Hill."

"Dan Stone." I shook his meaty fist. "You drive a silver Audi?"

"Finest piece of machinery I've ever owned."

"I think your alarm might be going off."

"That's the rumor." Frank pointed the visor of his cap towards our destination. "Are you visiting Martha's Vineyard or returning?"

"Just going over for the day."

"You must be a local then."

"I live in Wicket—"

"I remember passing through Wicket." Frank punched me on the shoulder. "We'd stop for clams and beach toys, my father itching to get back on the road, get to where he was going. This was before they tacked 25 onto the end of 495. Now people never have to leave the highway."

The speaker came alive with another call for the owner of a silver Audi with New Jersey plates, the "please" noticeably less heartfelt. Frank appeared oblivious.

"Don't you want to check that?"

Frank shrugged. "Somebody bumped against my car. What am I going to do, swab for DNA?"

"You could turn off the alarm."

He grunted, looking out over the rail. "The noise will keep anybody else from wandering too close. I had the battery checked before I left Jersey, so it'll last until we dock."

I glanced at my watch. "There's probably people trying to work down there."

"That's not my problem."

"It is if they get so aggravated that they key your car."

Frank clapped me on the back. "You make a good point, my friend. Hey, if I don't see you, enjoy the island."

"You too." As Frank made his way down the stairs, I went back to examining our wake, searching for patterns in the white foam. Such a human trait, that. Searching for patterns, for answers, for reasons.

It kept me solvent, anyway.

Kimberly Owens disappeared without a trace three years ago. The night her boyfriend proposed to her, she waited until he was asleep and then packed her bags, taking off without leaving so much as a note behind.

My client was the boyfriend, Nathaniel Fisher, a marine biologist working at the Woods Hole Oceanographic Institute.

After two years, he still didn't understand what went wrong and he needed closure. Or maybe his new fiancée needed the closure, since she was the one paying for my time.

They'd come to me last summer offering a set amount of money. I countersigned the agreement and said I wouldn't need a quarter of their deposit, that I'd probably locate Miss Owens by the end of the week. Given the databases I subscribed to as a licensed investigator, I actually expected to find Kimberly the next day.

That was a little over fifty-two weeks ago.

Nathaniel and Hannah still hadn't married, their lives on hold as they waited patiently for me to produce results. Of course by now, they'd probably given up any hope of that, simply going through the motions until the money ran dry.

I wondered how their love had weathered the never-ending investigation, the promises I'd made in good faith, the leads that led nowhere. I wondered if their relationship would survive my final—yet incomplete—report. Whether I would.

"Will the owner of a silver Audi...."

Had Frank changed his mind about checking, or was he still on his way down to the freight deck?

I tracked a pair of gulls across the leaden sky.

After that first meeting, I never saw Hannah again, and could only guess at her motivation, needing to know what fault Kimberly had found in the man she still thought perfect.

Nathaniel was the client I saw on a weekly and then a monthly basis as my updates became redundant. When I called him this morning, I wasn't even sure he recognized my voice, but then he'd been at work, and probably busy.

All of Kimberly Owens's ties were on the Cape. She'd been born and raised on the peninsula, acting as though off-Cape could hold no attraction. After graduating from Cape Cod Community College, she worked and lived in the various Mid Cape towns until she met Nathaniel. Three months later, she'd moved all the way to Standish, where the canal and the mainland beyond were clearly visible through Nathaniel's floor-to-ceiling windows.

Starting the night Kimberly slipped out of his front door, she had not once touched any of the databases I monitor, not in the two years before I'd been hired, and not in the year since.

Such a thing should not have been possible.

Not if she was alive.

Nathaniel was a marine biologist. He knew all about ocean scavengers. Why then hire me?

The voice came over the loudspeaker again. "Vehicle owners should report to the freight deck as we prepare to dock at Oak Bluffs."

I patted my back pocket to make sure the free tourist map hadn't blown away, and fifteen minutes later I was climbing Ocean Ave towards the Seabreeze Inn.

After my initial investigation stalled, I'd asked Nathaniel for a list of Kimberly's known email accounts, screen names, and online identities. Off the clock I still routinely ran searches, looking for likely hits.

Last week, one KimmyDimmy243—once Kimberly's login at an online bookseller—had posted a comment at a community dedicated to the discussion of inns.

During a discussion on negative experiences with staff, Kimmy-Dimmy243 had defended Caitlan (Seabreeze Inn, Oaks Bluff, Martha's Vineyard) who'd once gone above and beyond the call of maid duty, at least for her.

While Nathaniel had claimed on the phone this morning that Kimberly never indicated the slightest desire to visit the islands, a person could easily change that much in three years. Besides, how many people would purposely select KimmyDimmy243 as a public identifier?

For one thing, it was long.

The Seabreeze Inn boasted a wrap-around porch, sprinkled with groupings of chairs that looked out over the Atlantic, her breezes tickling the many wooden and metal wind chimes that hung from exposed beams.

I marched inside and dinged the bell that was centered on the counter.

A hand-lettered sign informed me that Oak Bluffs was formerly known as Cottage City, a fact that might come in handy if I ran into my friend from the ferry and needed to make conversation. Since Martha's Vineyard was even smaller the Cape, there was a good chance I wouldn't be able to avoid seeing Frank, not unless he stayed in his car.

A forty-something woman with black hair pinned up into a bun came through the doorway behind the counter. "Welcome to Seabreeze. I'm Elizabeth, the innkeeper."

"Actually, I'm looking for one of your employees. Caitlan?"

The woman somehow smiled without her skin moving. "Caitlan only works here in the mornings. Right now you might find her at the Flying Horses."

"Thanks so much." I paused, gambled that inside that Elizabeth was a Liz. Or even a Beth. "Perhaps you might recognize this woman."

Elizabeth examined Kimberly's face before shaking her head. "I'm afraid not. Is she in some type of trouble?"

"I'm just helping a mutual friend locate her, since I'm here." I accepted the picture back from Elizabeth's outstretched hand. "Apparently, Kimberly recently stayed at the Seabreeze."

"Not in the last ten years." Her tone left no room for dispute.

"Are you sure?"

"Yes."

Apparently her skin wasn't the only thing about her that was immobile. "We might be talking as long as three years ago."

Elizabeth frowned, seemingly unhappy that I would doubt her. "I have an extraordinary memory for faces. I never forget them. If that woman ever stayed at the Seabreeze, she'd be up here." Elizabeth tapped the side of her head.

"Maybe you were on vacation."

"If I took vacations, that would be possible, but I don't." Elizabeth moved the bell a quarter-inch to the left. "I'm afraid your mutual friend misled you."

"Wouldn't be the first time."

She crossed her arms. "So what does this Kimberly person have to do with my employee?"

"My friend said Kimberly mentioned Caitlan."

"And this happened three years ago?"

"Yes." I'd never felt comfortable lying to people, and sometimes that manifested in a reluctance to break away until I'd outweighed the falsehoods with truths. "Maybe there's another Seabreeze on the island. Another Caitlan."

"That is extremely unlikely."

I shrugged. "So many things are."

"Enjoy your visit." With that, Elizabeth turned away.

Apparently, I was dismissed.

According to my free map, the Flying Horses Carousel was located at the foot of Circuit Avenue. Head back down Ocean, cross over to Kennebec, and then over to Circuit. That's if I trusted a map intended for entertainment purposes only.

The stroll was pleasant enough anyway, with vacationers tossing Frisbees in Ocean Park for the amusement of those sitting on gingerbread porches, toasting another perfect day.

I walked between the two groups and tried not to get sucked into the illusion that time had no meaning here, that all was as it should be, and would be ever more. Until the week was up and everybody went back to their normal lives.

Kennebec—only one block away—belonged to the locals who fed the dream, and the vendors who delivered to the rear of the stores fronted on Circuit.

The Cape was probably no different but I'd grown inured.

As I passed the public restrooms, I saw a long-skirted woman with one hand poised over her open mouth before I noticed the homeless man. He was lying at her feet, nestled against the legs of a park bench.

She spoke without looking at me. "My husband has gone for the police."

The man was gray. His clothes, his hair, his skin. The gray of dust and decay.

I heard the crackle of the officer's radio before he came around the corner and cleared the area by asking us to move on. I passed another officer striding towards the scene as I exited out onto Circuit.

The day's earlier clouds had parted to allow the sunshine through, and this commercial stretch was protected from the sharp winds I'd experienced on the ferry ride over, but I still felt a chill that I hadn't before.

Sighting a coffee shop, I went in and ordered a large to go. Made small talk as I waited and paid. Glanced at posters about something or other.

A man was dead.

Out on the sidewalk again, I faltered. Caitlan could wait a little longer before she blew my case wide open.

I hadn't seen evidence that the man's death was anything more than unattended, but of course his passing would be investigated to determine whether someone was to blame.

The way he lay there, fetal, looking as though he'd died of exposure. Here? Today?

I sipped my coffee, hoping it wasn't still too hot.

Oak Bluffs wasn't Boston, or even Wicket. This was the Vineyard, a resort community for the refined. And yet, a weather-beaten homeless man had walked among them. Died.

Who was he? Where had he come from? What reversal of fortune had left him a gaunt figure, unshaven, and bound in rags?

Maybe Kimberly, too, had taken to the streets. Perhaps Nathaniel's proposal had broken her somehow, and she never managed to pull herself back together. Was she crouched in a doorway? Hollowed by drugs? Buried as Jane Doe?

Three young girls in matching yellow smocks skipped by me, all singing the same song, if not in harmony. Following behind, their father carried two beach chairs, and their mother the sand toys. A family out enjoying a wonderful day together.

I tossed my coffee cup into a nearby trashcan and headed down-hill, slowing only when I reached the end of the road.

Across the street, the open doors of the Flying Horses Carousel enlivened the atmosphere with carnival music, the flashing lights of arcade games, and the joyful sounds of children at play.

Unless Caitlan was one of the teenage boys monitoring the carou-sel, she was the employee sitting behind the cash register, which would make talking to the twenty-something easier. She couldn't es-cape, but she'd feel protected.

I stood in line, waiting for a couple with one child to decide whether to buy six single tickets or a group of eight, and then asked whether she was Caitlan.

"Do I know you?"

"I'm looking for someone you once helped. She was a guest at the Seabreeze Inn." I handed Caitlan the picture.

Caitlan froze, and then over-reached when she tried to feign non-chalance. "I never saw her before."

"She said otherwise."

"She's lying."

"Why would she do that?" I wondered how many times a shift the employees had to hear the carousel music replayed, imagining the song would pale after the first hundred repetitions.

"Who are you?"

"My name's Dan Stone. I'm a private investigator."

"Big deal."

As the carousel song ended, I could hear the arcade games through the open door on my left. "I've been hired to track down Kimberly. Your name came up during my investigation."

"Whip-de-do."

I leaned against the counter. "So tell me about the woman you helped without ever meeting."

Caitlan glared at me. I held her gaze. There was nowhere for her to go.

"Kim wasn't really a guest."

"How so?"

Shaking her head, Caitlan gave off a growl. "I would get in so much trouble if Elizabeth learned what I did."

"I'm sorry." The innkeeper struck me as someone who would follow up. "Elizabeth knows why I came to see you."

Caitlan swore, and then winced, looking around at the nearest little kids. She then took a deep breath before continuing. "She's going to fire me. I just know it."

"What happened with Kim?"

Someone tapped me on the shoulder. "Excuse me. Are you in line?"

"No." I moved aside to allow the group access to Caitlan, and turned to watch the operation. As the carousel spun, the people riding on the outside horses grabbed rings from a long wooden arm.

Some of the riders were quick enough to score two or three rings before their horses galloped past.

There was another arm for the inside riders, although I only caught glimpses of it during the brief periods when it wasn't blocked by either row of horses.

The employee inside the carousel lifted a microphone. "The brass rings are in the chutes."

The smell of popcorn told me the group from the counter was coming closer, and then they passed me for the picket-fence maze leading to the ride. I returned to my interview, suddenly hungry.

Caitlan had shifted, now sitting on her hands. "Why do you want to know about Kim?"

"My client wants to make she's all right. Three years ago Kimberly—Kim—just up and disappeared without a word to anybody."

"She's an adult, and this is a free country. She didn't break any laws, did she?"

That depended on whether she'd defaulted on any outstanding debts. "When was the last time you heard from Kim?"

"That's none of your business."

I shrugged. "Since I'm being paid to ask these questions, it literally is my business. Kim left people behind. They're concerned about her."

"If Kim wanted them to know where she was, they'd know."

"Perhaps she's not able to communicate with them." I flashed back to the dead homeless man.

Caitlan was just about to respond when a man stepped in front of me. "I want four brass rings."

"What color would you like?"

"Brass color." He was a bit brassy himself, loud and flashy, demanding attention.

"No, the ribbons." Caitlan pointed to the display over her shoulder where large brass rings hung from ribbons of various colors.

"What difference does it make? Just give me four red ribbons. No, one of them doesn't like red." He ran his fingers through his hair, twice. "Make it two red and two blue. Wait. I just know that someone's going to scream when there's no green. Make it one of each color."

"We have six colors."

"Just pick four. I'm in a rush."

After he completed his transaction and stormed away, I stepped back up to the counter. "Maybe I could buy you a coffee or something after work."

"Once I leave here, I punch in at Zapotec, and I'm closing tonight."

I opened my arms as far as I could without bumping anybody. "Help me help Kim."

"I don't think she needs your help."

"That would be great. Really, I'd be thrilled to learn that Kim is leading a vibrant and happy life here in Oak Bluffs. I'll deliver my message, wish her well, and purchase my return ticket to Woods Hole."

"What's your message?"

"When was the last time you saw her?"

Caitlan mashed her lips together. We went for subtle lipstick shades here in New England. "What did you tell Elizabeth?"

I moved to allow people access to the arcade room. "That I was looking for you. Then I showed her the picture of Kim and said she'd stayed at Seabreeze."

"You didn't."

"I've always found that truth is the best policy." And if Caitlan wanted to take that as a hint, I wouldn't complain. "Elizabeth is going to fire me because of you. Seabreeze is my year-round job. You don't realize what that means."

"I'm sorry."

Caitlan leaned forward, her face flushed. "With two words, Elizabeth could keep anybody else from hiring me. I'll never survive." Another flash of the homeless man.

"Asking questions is how I do my job."

She mimicked me, "'How I do my job.' That's easy for you to say. You have one. You know how many hours I work here? How many hours I spend waiting on tables? I can't survive the winter on that kind of money."

A group of kids approached the counter, herded by two women kept busy counting heads. I stepped away to stare at a plaque.

The carousel was built by the Charles W. Dare Company in 1876and brought here eight years later.

More fodder for Frank when and if I ran into him.

The group of kids now being herded into the maze, I went back to the counter.

"Listen, Caitlan, the sooner you answer my questions, the sooner I'm out of your hair." I glanced up at the one-way mirror. "Your boss might be wondering what we've been talking about for so long."

She stood. "And later, are you going to come over to the restaurant and harass me there?"

"When did you last see Kim?"

"She stayed one night. That's it. One night. It must have been three years ago. Then she left. That's it. That's all I know."

It would be easy to consider Caitlan's statement a setback, but this was the first indication that my client hadn't killed and buried Kimberly the night she supposedly disappeared. Which was a good thing.

Besides, of course that wasn't all Caitlan knew.

"What did the two of you talk about?"

She rolled her eyes. "Kim was only here one night."

"Kim must have said something."

"Her parents. She was furious with them. Probably still is if she never got in touch."

"What about Nathaniel, her boyfriend?"

"I don't remember her mentioning a Nathaniel."

The brass rings were in the chutes. What were the odds that I was going to be able to grab one today? "Did she talk about being engaged?"

"Not unless she was engaged to her parents."

"What did she say about them?" Her parents hadn't indicated any significant problems.

"You've got to be kidding. This was two winters ago."

Six months after Kimberly disappeared. Had she not left the Cape until then? Where had she hidden? I'd interviewed her family, friends, and coworkers, most of them at least twice.

Three teenage girls stepped in to purchase as many eight-packs, giggling the entire transaction. Racy times ahead.

As soon as they joined the others waiting a turn, I stepped back into the fray. "Why would Elizabeth fire you?"

Caitlan threw her hands up into the air. "Kim came over that day, just because. She walked off the ferry, headed straight to Zapotec for a margarita. One became more than one and she missed the last ferry back."

"You snuck her into the Seabreeze."

"It was just for one night, and the place was half empty." Caitlan leaned forward. "Elizabeth never knew. Elizabeth can never know."

My stomach felt as though I'd gobbled a dozen large popcorns. "She's going to ask you about Kimberly."

"Kimberly didn't have enough money for a room. I was living at home, and no way could she have stayed there. It was winter."

"You did what you thought was right." I paused a beat, letting Caitlan process my statement. "You work here, an inn, a restaurant. You're conditioned to help people."

"I couldn't just let her freeze to death."

I nodded. "And you figured out both how to sneak her in and keep her presence a secret. That must not have been easy."

"I told Kim no lights, no running water." Caitlan half smiled. "Anyway, I'm the maid. Resetting a room as if no one has ever been there is my job."

"You took a big gamble."

Caitlan continued to talk as she helped the next customer. "Kim had been at Zapotec for hours, and we chatted for a lot of them. It was slow that night. Kim, she was just one of those people you know you can trust."

Until she disappears in the middle of the night. "Did you see her board the ferry?"

"I was busy straightening the room." Caitlan shrugged.

"Thanks for all your help." I double-tapped the counter. "And good luck."

I spent the next three hours walking Oak Bluffs, showing Kimberly's picture to anybody who wasn't a tourist, but nobody remembered ever seeing the woman I'd been entrusted to find.

"Hey, my friend."

"Frank." I clapped his arm. "Get your car off the ferry all right?"

"I think mine was the last vehicle they let disembark." He waved his ice cream cone, white with brown chunks. "Except for the garbage truck in front of me."

Despite his sour face, I found it hard to believe someone would be transporting garbage onto the island. "Well, you're here now."

Frank nodded before taking a bite of his ice cream. "This place never changes. Exactly the same as when I was a kid."

"Is that good?"

"You bet. I'll walk with you a while. Keep you company. No man's an island, they say, even on an island." He stopped. "What's with that?"

I turned to see the public bathrooms. The park bench was now covered with cut flowers. Above was pinned a handwritten message, unreadable at this distance. "Looks like a memorial."

"I've heard taking a dump described as a religious experience, but I've never heard of anybody actually building a shrine."

I faced Frank, keeping my tone neutral. "Even in paradise, people die."

"You can bet they don't advertise the fact." Frank took another bite of his ice cream. "Enjoying your visit?"

"I am, actually." I wasn't any closer to finding Kimberly, but at least I knew she was alive.

Even more important, so was I.

It doesn't take much to fan the flames.

Embers
by Michael Haynes

SUNDAY AFTERNOON, THE end of Dad's and my weekend together, was fading fast. If he didn't have me to Mom's by six there'd be hell to pay. Dad was sitting in a chair, eyes closed. I started gathering up things, throwing them in the trunk of the car.

I tossed some water on the center of our fire and turned away. A moment later, I was yanked back by the collar of my shirt.

"What did you just do, Jackson?" My father had leaned over and his face was close to mine. The alcohol on his breath that meant I'd be the one in charge of getting us back on time was sharp in my nostrils.

"I put out the fire, dad. We're leaving, right?"

He shoved me away and I fell to the ground.

"You did not put out the fire!" He grabbed a bucket and stormed off toward the creek. A few minutes later he lugged it back, full of water and dumped it on the ashes, flooding the firepit.

"*I* put out the fire. *You* might as well have just pissed on it." He shook his head. "Remember, you can never be too sure that you've gotten all the embers out. Even if they're not glowing and you can't see 'em, they can still catch a fire."

Beth's eyes were hot on me as the silence stretched out in the wake of her question. It must've only been a few seconds but it felt much longer.

"Enough about my woes," she had said. "What about you? Are you happily married?"

My tongue worked behind my teeth and in my clenched left hand my thumb teased at the rim of my wedding band, worn smooth after twenty-some years. I thought about the bowling ball out in the car; it had been an anniversary present last year. I should have been using it right then, knocking down pins with the guys from work instead of sitting in a bar with an old flame.

"No," I lied. She hid the flash of excitement well; I only caught it for a half-second on her face, but it told me everything I needed to know.

I took a swallow of my beer and reached for the cigarette she'd left in the ashtray.

"I thought you'd quit years ago. Back when we were still—"

I cut her off with a shrug and said, "Things change." She was right, though. I had quit. Stayed quit, too. Right up until that moment.

When we left that night we parted with a quick hug, like two people at a class reunion who knew each other just well enough that it would be awkward not to hug but not so well that the hug itself wasn't awkward, too.

By the fourth Thursday night that I'd skipped bowling to have drinks with Beth, we were leaving the bar after a couple of quick ones and heading back to her apartment.

Beth and I met in high school and ended up at the same college together. Through those years we were in a constant roundabout of breaking up and making up and breaking up again. No matter what had been said or what other relationship one of us fell into, days or weeks or months later one of us would call the other and then we'd be right back in the thick of it.

Until the last time. Catching me in bed with her big sister had seemed well and truly like the last straw for her and, being honest with myself, I think that was half of why I did it. Even if I did wear the bruises from Beth's fists for a week afterward.

For years I'd thought about just how lucky I was that I hadn't met Carol, the woman who found enough good in me to marry, until several months after that last break-up. Because if I'd met her before I'd burned those bridges well and truly with Beth, I know I would've ended up breaking Carol's heart back then.

Looking back now, I know we would have all been better off for that. Because those bridges weren't burned quite as well as I'd imagined.

"Jackson?" A voice, instantly recognizable, cut across the lobby of the theater. Beth's voice. I hadn't heard it in decades but still a jolt ran through me at the sound. "Jackson Ellis?"

I turned and when I saw her it was like stepping back through time. Maybe there was a bit of silver starting to show in her hair, a few wrinkles around the eyes that hadn't been there back in the old days, but I felt a second jolt run through me as I took in her smile, her body.

"Beth."

She smiled. "Wow! You recognize me?"

How could I have not recognized her? I nodded.

"Impressive. It's only been, what, twenty-two years?"

Twenty-three.

"What are you doing here?" I asked, the words feeling foolish even as they materialized.

And, of course, she rolled her eyes at me. "Going to see a movie, duh!"

She laughed and I laughed, too. "No, I meant... *Here*. Kansas City here. The last I'd heard you were out east."

"Keeping tabs on me?"

"Well, you know. You hear things."

"Right. So, had you heard that my dad died?"

I remembered now, too, how she somehow always could make me feel like I'd found the worst possible thing to have said. "No. I'm sorry for your loss."

"Thank you." She brushed a loose strand of hair away from her face. "Six months ago. Bobby was supposed to take over the garage but he's..." She waved a hand and I could fill in the blanks. Unreliable. A drunk. Probably a crook, to boot. "So I came home. I just got a new place. You should come see it one day."

Carol came over then, back from a post-screening run to the restroom. I introduced the two of them to each other and couldn't miss the flickers of hostility on both ends of the handshake.

"We're already going to be later than we told the sitter, Jack," Carol said, putting her arm around my waist and using it to urge me toward the door.

Beth smiled brightly and waved as I walked away.

"Who was that?" Carol asked on the ride home.

"A school friend. Beth James."

The car was silent for a moment or two. "I don't remember you mentioning her."

"Well, I probably had a bunch of friends who've never come up. This is the first time I've seen her since college."

I thought briefly that Carol was going to press for more information, but neither of us said another word the rest of the ride home.

And here I was on another Thursday night at Beth's apartment with my bowling ball sitting idle in my back seat. I wondered—not for the first time—when it would all come crashing down. When Carol would ask Fred or Alan or Marshall about how the league was going and they'd mention how much they missed my 186 average. She would ask what they meant and everyone would look puzzled. And there wouldn't be any hope of a good explanation.

Whenever I thought about this, I felt a tiny bit sick. I remembered growing up in two houses and didn't want that happening to our kids. I'd tell myself that Beth and I just had to be extra-careful and remember what lies we'd told which people, not be seen together in public—we'd long stopped bothering with meeting at the nearby bar. There wasn't any reason we would necessarily get caught. But then, it would only take once.

I put it out of my mind, wrapped my naked body around Beth's, and lost myself in her smell, her feel, her taste.

An hour later, the alarm on my phone rang. Time to be going. I climbed out of Beth's arms, out of her bed.

"Do we really have to wait another week?" she asked.

"Carol will wonder if I change my routines."

"What about some Saturday morning when she's going to those antique malls?"

"You mean when I watch the kids?" The exchange, of course, for Thursday night bowling.

"You could find someone else to watch them one time." She rolled around on the bed and reached out for me. Her hands on my bare skin were electrifying.

"And Lydia or Frank would mention spending the day with Aunt Jamie or whoever and then where would we be?"

She pouted but didn't push any further. No one said having an affair was easy.

I spent a minute under a freezing cold shower to wash off anything that might give me away.

"Next Thursday," I promised with one last kiss as I finished dressing. She nodded and smiled. I hurried to my car.

The string of numbers on the screen when my phone rang didn't even look like a real phone number. I'd been called in to work to resolve a crisis with the quarterly numbers. No fun for me and Carol was pissed about missing her time away from the kids which meant that the rest of the weekend would suck. I almost let the call roll to voice mail but picked it up near the end of the ringtone.

"Is this Jackson Ellis?"

The voice was unfamiliar and oddly formal; something about it instantly put me on edge. I took a second before answering "Yes."

The man said his name was Sturgis, that he was with the police department and could I please meet him down at the hospital.

"Is something wrong?" I asked.

"It would be best if we talked here," he said. "Do you need an officer to give you a ride, sir?"

My mouth felt dry. I swallowed and said that I could drive myself. "I'll be there in twenty minutes," I said before we hung up. I noticed that he hadn't told me to hurry and tried to imagine that meant the best rather than the worst.

But it was bad. As bad as it could have been. There had been a car accident and not only had Carol not survived but Frank was dead, also. Lydia was in surgery. Six hours later, they came to tell me that my entire family was gone.

I went home, numb. I thought about calling Beth, bitterly realizing that there wasn't any point in feeling guilty about being with her any longer. But the thought made me feel nauseous and I crawled into bed fully dressed. Amazingly, I fell straight into a deep slumber.

"You understand that you're here voluntarily, Mister Ellis?"

"Of course."

The detective flicked the switch on a recorder and recited his name, mine, the date and time. A thin manila folder sat in front of him.

"Mister Ellis, had your wife's car been repaired recently?"

My breath caught. I tried to remember, had it been? "No," I said after a minute.

"Right. Any reason to think someone would want to hurt her?"

"What are you suggesting, Detective—"

"Just answer the question, please, sir."

"No! No one would want to hurt her. She's... she was... a kindergarten teacher for God's sake."

He nodded, not seeming surprised by the answer.

"What's this about?"

"Are you sure you don't know, sir?"

Something awakened deep in my brain, some hint of understanding, but I pushed it down. "No, Detective, I don't know and I'd very much like to understand!"

He fingered the folder, slowly opened it and looked at the papers inside. He gnawed his lower lip for several seconds.

"What it says here, Mister Ellis, is that your wife's brakes didn't fail by chance." He looked up at me. "Someone wanted those brakes to go bad."

I couldn't take my eyes off his. My mind raced to the only logical place for it to go in this situation; the only person who might have wanted to see something happen to Carol. The only person I knew who worked in a garage.

"Do you have any idea how this might have happened?"

I tried to say "no" but the word wouldn't come out. Tears gathered in my eyes. I was shaking my head without even realizing I was doing it. The detective took that for an answer, closed the folder and nodded.

"You'll let us know if you think of anything later?"

I croaked out a "yes."

The detective stood and reminded me that he was sorry for my loss. "We'll let you know if we have any news," he said. "Or any more questions."

I sat in the dark, smoking a cigarette, watching the embers at the end of it flare into brightness and fade back again.

I'd never smoked in my house before.

The doorbell rang once and then a second time a minute later; I answered that second ring.

I opened the door and saw Beth standing there. My stomach lurched and before I could tell her to get the hell away from me she pushed past me and came inside.

The air outside was cold. I shut the door.

Beth's face was red but not just from the chill. Her eyes were red, too, and tear tracks zig-zagged across her skin.

We stood there silently and I took the last puff from my cigarette. Finally, with a voice that felt just barely hanging together she said, "You weren't answering your phone."

I nodded.

"Jackson, I—"

Hearing my name come from her wrenched me from my paralysis.

"No!" The word echoed through the empty house. "No. Whatever you came here to say, don't say it." I turned back toward the door. "In fact, you can just get yourself right out of here and hope that I don't get past my guilt enough to tell the police what the hell happened."

Her hand touched my shoulder and before I knew what was going on I pivoted and struck out at her with a clenched hand. She stumbled back and fell on her ass on the carpeted floor.

"I swear I thought it would just be her!" Her voice was pleading.

Words tumbled through my brain, wanting to ask if that would have made it right, to ask what made her think I would want that anyway. But none of them came out, just a scream.

I fell on her and for half a second I saw in her eyes that she thought this was the start of forgiveness, of reconciliation, of a future together. And then my hands were around her throat. And I was squeezing.

There is a preacher here. Non-denominational, they tell me. My choice whether I speak with him or not between now and the time when I go for that final stroll.

I won't talk to him; he would try to offer forgiveness and a chance for eternal life. I never believed in that before, why would I start now?

No. That's not quite true. I do want to believe now. But only so I can get what the hell I deserve.

They say blood is thicker than water, but some friendships
are made of thicker stuff still.

Grave Designs
by Mike O'Reilly

THERE IS NO surer sign of damnation than the need to pay a priest
for a eulogy.

He whispered the prayers.

His hand was trembling and his eyes were black hollows burrowed
into his skull. A three-day growth filled the hollows of his cheeks.

Johnny's corpse had looked healthier before they closed the lid.

The priest finished and folded a once-purple stole into the pocket
of his coat and turned away without saying a word.

There wasn't much more to say. Johnny wasn't a good man, but he
was my mate.

My name is Ignatius Kelly, though nobody but my mother ever
calls me that. She had a thing for popes.

Everyone else calls me Mick.

I was a cop, now I'm not.

Johnny wasn't much of anything. But for one thing, he would have
been nothing at all.

In 1971, in a southeast asian paddy field, Johnny had picked me up
like a rag doll and carried me, unconscious and bleeding, 300 metres
to a medic and salvation. He was shot twice in that 300 metres but he
never dropped me and it wasn't until he placed me softly on the
ground next to the medic that he collapsed to the ground himself.

The war changed both of us, Johnny most of all. He picked up a
bottle as soon as he came home and never put it down. He survived
on charity and petty crime until the day he died.

There are some things you never forget and some debts you can
never repay. He carried a card in his wallet with my name and number
on it. Never went anywhere without it. I had lost count the times I
had answered early morning phone calls to drive him home from a
hospital or drunk tank, sweating bullets and smelling of cheap booze
and self destruction.

I knew what he was and I loved him, despite himself.

They found the card in an otherwise empty wallet. A police officer woke me early on a Tuesday morning and told me he was dead.

They had found Johnny in his car at Point Erin. The police report read suicide. There was a 9 mm handgun in his right hand, the barrel in his mouth and a hole the size of a tennis ball in the back of his head. There was no sign of a struggle and he had a gut full of booze and benzos.

I didn't believe it. Johnny was terrified of death. He'd no more eat a gun than I'd walk on water.

Johnny had a brother, long since lost to him. A victim, like so many others, of Johnny's excesses. He was a corporate lawyer with more money than Croesus. He sounded like a creep to me, but family is family. It only seemed fair to drop in and let him know of his brother's resting place. And since I had forked out for the plot and fifty bucks for the priest, maybe I could make good some of my losses.

His brother's place was a two-story glass palace. It was flanked by hundred-year-old villas that could have been covers from House & Garden. It looked like a hooker at a tea party.

The door was a solid slab of black laminate that looked as inviting as the gates of hades. There was a doorbell, but this was definitely a door that needed to be pounded.

A blonde woman opened the door. I suppose I shouldn't have been surprised. She was thirty, maybe a well tended forty, and definitely built for speed. She had live wire eyes and a drink in her right hand. She didn't speak, just tilted her head slightly and smiled.

It was a full beam, high wattage, punch you in the groin, sort of smile.

"I'm looking for Tony," I said.

She turned from the door and yelled. "Tony."

Face like a goddess, voice like a banshee.

Tony looked like a Devonport lawyer. He would have been a few years younger than me. Maybe fifty, but without the scars. He wore a pink shirt, open at the neck. He was tanned to a dull leather and had spent as much time on the treadmill as he had on a sun bed. He was holding a drink so cold he was at risk of frostbite.

I guess I looked like I was going to make a sales pitch for Jesus.

He looked at me and wrinkled his nose.

"Can I help you?" he said, with no indication that he had any intent to.

"My name's Mick, I was a friend of your brothers." I held out my hand.

He looked at it for a moment before reaching out and shaking it.

"I haven't seen my brother in a long time."

"He's dead."

"How did he die?" He leaned against the doorframe.

"He was shot. The cops seem to think it was suicide."

"He was always troubled."

"He had his off days." I looked past him, down the marble floor of the entryway. I took a step across the threshold. It was rude, but I was getting sick of the great outdoors. He thought about closing the door, but in the end his manners got the better of him and he allowed me in.

The place was no better inside than out. The entry way was a grey marble, and opened up into a living room that looked like a designers revenge. The woman was sitting on a white leather couch. She was wearing a silk skirt, the colour of fresh cream, that made her almost blend into the furniture. The skirt rode up her thighs as she crossed her legs and she made a production number out of smoothing it back to a PG rating.

I sat down in one of the armchairs opposite. The air hissed out of the cushions as the chair moulded around me. It was the ugliest piece off furniture I had seen in a long time, but damn it was comfortable. All I needed was the remote and a good view of the telly and I could have moved in.

"So, what is it we can do for you? Mr?"

"Mick. Just Mick." I stroked the leather of the armchair. "You see, the cops called me when they found him. Since he had fuck all, I paid for the service and the plot. I thought you might, you know, like to know where to pay your respects."

Tony smirked, and I swear to god and all his angels, he winked at me.

"Kylie, would you get me my cheque book? It's on the ..."

"I know where it is," she said.

I bet she did.

" I was just wondering, when was the last time you saw Johnny?" I said.

"It would have been Christmas. He came over looking for money."

"You didn't invest?"

"Mick," he sat in the armchair nearest mine, all of a sudden familiar. "One reason I have money is by not giving it away to alcoholic criminals. I gave him a piece of turkey and a Christmas cracker."

"Fair enough."

Kylie returned with the cheque book. It was in a leather case that looked like it cost more than my car. He took a fountain pen from his shirt.

"How much was it you said you were out of pocket?'

"I hadn't." I stood and held out my hand. "If you were looking to pay your respects, he's in the cemetery off Karangahake road. Shouldn't be hard to find."

Turns out I didn't need the money that much after all.

He didn't stand.

"Kylie can show you to the door." He unfolded the newspaper on his lap and began to read.

Kylie took her time walking the few feet to the door. I didn't complain. The view was worth it.

She opened the door and I stepped through. Her hand brushed my shoulder. I turned and she reached into her blouse, pulling a small scrap of paper from the strap of her bra. She pressed it into my hand and closed the door before I could speak.

I didn't open it until I sat behind the wheel of my car..

The note was written in purple ink and full of girlish curves. It had a phone number. Hers, I hoped.

I rang the number later that night. She picked up after one ring. Her voice was muffled.

"Hello."

"It's Mick."

"Meet me at Melodies, in Takapuna. Give me twenty minutes. Ok?"

"Make it thirty."

She hung up.

Even with thirty minutes the drive from my place to Takapuna was going to be tight. Given more time I would have dressed for the occasion, but she would have to take me as I was, rough edges and all.

I was late.

She beat me there, sitting in a booth at the back, already sipping from a tall glass. The glass was filled with ice and frosted with condensation. It was pretty quiet for a Thursday night. Another couple were whispering to each other in a dark corner and a well-dressed man sat at the bar nursing a bottle of beer and a paper.

I sat in the booth, opposite her.

She just looked up and smiled, before sipping from her drink.

"Would you like a drink?"

I shook my head.

"Suit yourself." She waved to the waiter. He nodded and dropped off another drink, beside the one she had only half finished.

I watched her sip the drink for a while. It could have been the booze, but she seemed at ease. If she was afraid of being caught out on the town, she wasn't showing it. After a while, impatience got the better of me.

"So, you wanted to chat?"

She stopped sipping for a moment. Dabbed at her lips with a napkin.

"I thought you might like to talk about Johnny"

I didn't say anything.

"You were friends?" She said. I nodded. "I liked Johnny. He seemed nice."

"He was a good mate."

There was a pause as she sipped from her drink again.

"Tony is full of shit," she said, finally.

"I liked him. I was thinking of inviting him to my book club. Do you reckon he'd be keen?"

She laughed. It was like a cool breeze on a hot day.

"Tony and Johnny were together three weeks ago. They came in late. Tony thought I was asleep. I don't sleep much. I hadn't taken my pills yet." She hunched down close to the table, whispering. I had to bend down in order to hear her, bringing me even closer to her lips.

"They were arguing. Tony was shouting."

"What were they fighting about?"

"I don't know, they were arguing about red pills."

It didn't sound like Johnny. He never had much to do with drugs.

"How did it end?"

"They were both angry. I heard Tony yelling at Johnny, 'Just fucking do it' and slamming the door. Next time I heard Johnny's name it was from you."

I waved at the waiter and ordered a black coffee. I wasn't sure I could afford it, but there was always the hope she would pick up the tab.

"I didn't even know Tony had a brother. The first time I met him was about two months ago."

"I don't suppose he was that keen on people finding out his family history."

She canted her head to one side, and looked at me.

"You don't know much about your husband, do you love? How long have you been married?"

"Two years," she sipped from her drink, her eyes hard above the glass. "And don't call me love."

Her voice suddenly as grey as steel.

"I'm sorry."

"Apology accepted. I really must be going."

We stood together. I stepped out from the booth to help her put on her coat.

She turned and shrugged her shoulders into the coat.

"I really did like Johnny," she said. She leaned closer and kissed me. I could taste the gin on her lips. "Call me again."

She turned in a swirl of hair and perfume.

I sat back down at the booth. The coffee had gone cold.

The waiter came and asked if I wanted a refill. I said no. He stood silently beside me for a moment. It took me that long to realise she hadn't paid.

I couldn't sleep.

Assuming Kylie wasn't full of shit. It made no sense.

Red pills. Johnny was a thief, admittedly not a very good one, but he was no drug dealer. I didn't think he had the guts for it.

And why would Tony make contact with Johnny when they had been estranged for so long? He didn't seem the type to become suddenly sentimental.

The light of the new day had started to leak around the edges of my blinds when it dawned on me.

It was in the paper. A week or so before a hiker had found a decomposing body in dense bush on the Coromandel.

I thought I still had the story in one of the stacks of old papers that littered my floor. It took me twenty minutes of searching before I found it. The article was buried on the inside front page. There it was, Red Hills. The body belonged to a drug dealer, Mark Tuki. He was small time but had some big time gang connections. His big brother was Colin 'Horse' Tuki, and there was nothing small about him. The Disciples Motorcycle Club owned the drug trade in the upper North Island and Colin Tuki owned the Disciples.

Police had identified Mark through fingerprints. He had been struck once from behind before having his face battered by a rock 'til it resembled a pudding. Police hadn't found much in the way of forensics, but given the victim I suspected they weren't looking that hard either.

All it took was a phone call.

I called Colin Tuki.

Not directly.

We moved in different social circles.

I called a friend, he called someone else, who called someone else, and I got a call just after lunch.

The voice over the phone didn't give a name. If I wanted to talk to 'Horse,' I would have to be at a construction site in Mangere Bridge, at midnight. He hung up before I could ask any more questions.

Meeting a gang member, still grieving for the untimely death of his brother, in a deserted building site, after dark, sounded like a pretty good way of getting killed to me, but I needed to know if there was some connection.

I kept telling myself, if it was a dead trail, there was no harm done. I would walk away. Forget Tony, forget Kylie and leave Johnny's memory dead and buried.

I still didn't know what I was going to do if his brother was connected to his death.

The rest of the day went slowly. It was too hot and humid to sleep and my guts were doing lazy somersaults every time I thought about heading into Mangere.

It would take me half an hour to drive to the spot. I set off early, getting there about half an hour early. I drove down the gravel access road to the site. The road opened out onto a roughly rectangular vehicle park. It was ringed with front end loaders and graders. A white truck was parked in front of a dusty white portacom. A single light shone above its door. I sat at the entrance to the yard for a while before gently edging my car towards the portacom. I made it halfway across before I was pinned in headlights. There were four of them, one in each corner of the yard. Their lights, burning on high beam, blinded me. I stopped the car, opened the door and took a step into the open, shielding my eyes, straining to see anything against the glare.

The only way out of the yard was the way I had driven in. I turned and saw a fifth vehicle pull in behind me, blocking my exit. It had its lights off. Its engine idled. The driver tweaked the gas and the engine roared. I flinched, stumbling back into my car. Satisfied that he had scared seven shades of shit out of me, he turned off the engine and it sat softly ticking as it cooled in the night air. I could hear the laughter before they had even opened the door.

The passenger door opened. A massive figure unfolded itself from the front seat. I had met Colin Tuki a few times. He was hard man to forget. I'm 187cm and 99kg, plus or minus a pie, but he was a good head taller and could have used me as a toothpick. If he was trying to intimidate, it was working. He shrugged on a leather vest and walked towards me.

"Detective Kelly," he nodded. "You're early."

"Wasn't sure I had the right place."

"You sure now?"

"Nope, must have taken a wrong turn."

"Funny guy?"

"Depends."

"On?"

"Depends on whether funny gets me killed or not."

"Making no promises Detective." He stopped about 10 feet from me. "Put your hands in the air and step out from the car. One of the boys'll pat you down."

I took a step out from the car. Two guys stepped out from the light. I heard the unforgettable sound of a round being racked into the chamber of a pump action. One walked behind me, pushed my arms in the air and expertly felt me up. He stepped away and nodded to Horse. The other guy kept the pump on me the whole time.

"So what do you want?"

"I want to talk to you about your brother"

"What about him, he's dead"

"I know."

"About your brother," I tried to shrug some life back into my shoulders and arms. "Do you know what happened?"

He looked hard at me.

"If I did there'd be at least one dead honky, probably two, because you are really starting to piss me off."

"How do you know it's a honky?"

"No nigga is that stupid."

Hard to argue with that logic.

"What was he doing in Red Hills?"

"He was on business."

"What business?"

"My fucking business," he clenched his fists. I could hear the knuckles crack. He took a long breath, considered his options. "He was burying some cash. There was about half a million buried up there."

"Was?"

"Gone," he smiled. "You wouldn't know anything about that?"

I shook my head.

"We could make sure. How does that sound?"

"Uncomfortable." He smiled again. "Who else knew about the money?"

"A few of the bros. It wasn't anyone I know. They'd be dead already."

"Did you know Johnny Murphy?" I said.

He shook his head. "Should I?"

"How about Tony Murphy?"

Horse tried hard to hide his expression.

"The lawyer, what's that motherfucker got to do with anything?"

"You know him?"

"He's a slimy prick. Bought coke from us a couple of times, thought it made him a gangster."

"Did he know about the money?"

"How dumb do you think I am?"

That didn't seem like a safe question to answer.

I had an idea.

"Give me a day and I'll tell you who killed your brother."

"Why should I give you a day? Why don't I just fucking beat the answer out of you now?"

"Because I don't know the answer yet, and if you beat me up I'll just get blood on your boots."

"A day," he said. "And if I don't get an answer, the first white boy I kill will be you."

He nodded.

I heard the guy behind me take a step. I tried to turn, but not quick enough. I heard the crack of something hard and metallic strike the back of my head. And then there was darkness.

I woke, my mouth full of dust from the yard and my head throbbing. A blank business card lay on the ground, a handwritten cell number written on the back.

The sun was turning the horizon crimson by the time I picked myself up. I poked the card into my pocket and staggered to my car, driving out of the yard and onto the motorway before anyone decided to turn up to work early.

I got home and lay on the couch for a while, an ice pack pressed to my head and a cold flannel over my eyes.

I thought about everything I'd learned. It took a bit of putting together. Most of the day was gone before I thought I had it figured out.

It was time to pay another visit to Tony Murphy.

I arrived at the same time as Kylie was leaving. She slammed the door and stormed down the path to the yellow convertible parked in the driveway. I stopped and leant down to the open driver side window. Streaks of mascara smudged her cheeks. There was some fresh bruising beneath her eye that would become a pretty good shiner by tomorrow morning.

"You ok?"

"Fuck you."

Obviously not.

She slammed the car into reverse and stepped on the gas, reversing in a shriek of tyres on concrete. I had to jump to preserve my toes and almost fell on my arse.

I dusted myself off and walked up the driveway to the door. Tony opened it before my fist had hit the door.

"What do you want?" he said. He had scratch marks on his face and one of his eyes was bloodshot.

"You should find yourself a new cat, that one doesn't seem to like you much," I said, pointing to the scratches.

His knuckles were white on the doorframe, his face the colour of a ripe plum.

"Thought we should chat," I said, elbowing my way past him into the house.

For a second he was stunned but then he spun, reaching out to grab me.

My head still hurt from the previous evening and I was in no mood to be manhandled twice in twenty four hours. I caught the palm of his hand and turned it back against itself, straightening his arm, and twisting the shoulder. He struggled, and I put a little more torque on the elbow, 'til I felt the tendons in his shoulder stretch.

"Calm down Tony," I said. "Stress will kill you."

I pushed him away and he stumbled a few steps.

He turned and I saw him weighing his options. He wasn't going to fight, but there was no way he was going to be beat up in his own house without a show.

"Get the fuck out of my house." The cords in his neck stretched against the skin, his voice a bellow of rage. "I'll call the cops."

"Suit yourself," I said. "I can't wait to talk to them about a half million dollars of lost drug money and dead drug dealers."

The colour left his face and he balled his hands into fists. He took a step forward, forgetting himself for a moment.

"That's right. I figured it out. How long do you think it will take for his big brother to figure it out?"

"I have no idea what you're talking about. Get out of my house." The power in his voice had gone.

"I don't think so."

"What do you want, money?" he said.

"I'll make this really simple for you, mate. All I want is some answers."

I could almost hear the clockwork ticking in his head. Calculating an angle.

"What's in it for me?"

"If you don't piss me off too much, I can lose Colin Tuki's phone number." I rubbed my chin. "He isn't sure yet, but you might be able to get out of dodge before he decides to kill you on general principles. Fair deal?"

He didn't say anything.

"I'll keep an eye out for your obituary." I stepped backwards towards the door.

He held up his hands. "Stop."

"All right. I'll tell you what, you won't even have to speak. I'll tell you what happened and you just nod?"

He glared at me.

"You found out about the money buried in the hills." His face never changed. "My guess is Mark Tuki was on the scam. He was going to take the cash and use you as a cut out. What did he suggest, steal the cash, beat him up a bit, make it look like he'd been ambushed and then split the money between you?"

"You don't know shit," he said.

"I don't know. I think I'm getting warm." I looked at my watch. "Time's ticking, my bet is Horse is already asking himself some questions about you. So what happened, you get greedy, you wait 'til he turned his back and tap the back of his head with that rock?"

"Prove it."

"You're thinking like a lawyer, Tony. I don't need to prove it. I just need to share this story with Colin Tuki and he'll kill you just to make sure." I smiled.

"Ok, fine, you're right, now get out."

"I haven't finished yet. I bet you didn't think about how much five hundred thousand dollars in 10's and 20's was going to weigh. And I guarantee you have no idea how to get rid of a body. You decided to get Johnny to do the heavy work for you, eh?"

He folded his arms over his chest, trying to look hard.

"What happened? Johnny refused?" I said. "How did he die?"

"Didn't you hear, he shot himself."

I took a quick half step forwards and slapped him, hard. He stumbled, his hand on his injured face. He looked up at me, unsure what to do next. He was used to being the bully, not the victim. I could see fear and confusion in his eyes. I swear, I am not a bad guy, but that look made me happy.

"So, how'd it happen?"

He straightened himself up.

"The dumb fuck said he'd do it," he said. "I gave him $300 as a kicker, and he went out and got drunk. He called me from his car, crying, bawling like a little girl. By the time I got down to the marina he was asleep in a pool of his own piss. I shook him around a bit to wake him up but he was fucked up. I left him there, he was alive when I left."

A trickle of blood leaked from his lip. He pulled a handkerchief from his trouser pocket and dabbed at it. Wincing.

"So, how'd he die?"

"How should I know?" He shrugged.

"He was your brother?"

"He was a two-bit drunk with mummy issues."

I took another step forward. I hadn't been paying enough attention, he'd backed up to a coffee table. He swung a brass lamp at my head. He was quick. I leant backwards, felt the shade graze my chin. The weight of the lamp dragged his arm around, almost turning him. I stepped to the outside and jabbed a fist into his kidney. He gasped with pain and tried to turn towards me, using his momentum to swing the lamp in a backhand. It was slow. I bent away at the waist, let it pass me in slow motion before coming up and driving my fist into his gut. He went down hard, retching.

I kicked him once, but my heart wasn't in it.

I left him on the floor and walked out.

I called Colin Tuki later that day. I told him about my suspicions. He didn't seem surprised. I sent a text message to Kylie, told her to make herself scarce for a bit. I didn't get a reply.

I thought about visiting the grave, but there didn't seem to be much point. I tried to push the whole mess out of my mind. There are some questions to which you never find answers and some debts you can never repay.

I tried not to think too much more about any of them until I saw a newspaper article about a month later.

Body of Auckland Lawyer Found
The body of prominent Auckland lawyer Anthony Murphy was found yesterday in a disused quarry near Waihi Beach. He appeared to have been the victim of a gangland style execution.

I bet he was. I didn't want to think too hard about what happened to Tony Murphy when Colin Tuki caught up with him. I doubted it would have been quick or painless.

A couple of days later I got a postcard from Kylie. It was blank, but postmarked Rarotonga.

I guess she got the message.

We all dream of escaping sometimes—but there's more than one way to get away.

Man On The Run
by Laird Long

THE BIG CAB was pushing forty when he slammed on the brakes. The car skidded to an icy stop in front of her, its mammoth bumper nodding gently against her knees. He pulled his foot out of the floorboards and cursed. She walked alongside the car, tugged open the rear door, and slid in.

"Lady, I'm off-duty. You gotta ... get out." He wasn't steeped in subtleties.

"Light's on, bub."

"What?" He checked the dashboard and saw that she was right. His heavy face wrinkled in anger. "Dammit!" He had forgotten to switch his sign off. He switched it off. He draped a thick arm over the back of the bench seat and craned his neck around. He looked at her and tried to smile; but smiling gave him a headache so he gave it up. "Okay, my mistake. You still gotta leave, lady. I'm off-duty whether the sign says so or not." He waited for her to move. She didn't have the looks to be a hooker—unless she was the coin-operated kind.

"Light was on, bub."

"Yeah, it was. We signed the treaty on that one, already. Now it's off, so pack up your charm and beat it. I got somewhere I gotta be."

"1750 Cleveland Avenue. And punch it. Save the excuses for the old lady." She pulled her shabby coat together.

"Lady—"

"Look, driver! I've got to get home, and the only bus running at three in the morning is yours. So, point your face at the windshield and weigh anchor."

His eyes narrowed to gunslits. "I'll haul you as far as the pay phone on the corner. Then you're gonna call a friend. My garbage detail's over for the night."

"Friend." She snorted. "Do your duty, cabbie. Get it in gear."

"You ain't gonna beat it?"

"I don't even know you."

He frowned. "You gonna get out or I gotta strap on the rubber gloves and toss you out?"

"I'm not leaving this metal mansion until you bump the curb at 1750 Cleveland Avenue." She stared into his face. "Clear 'nuff?" She wiped her runny nose with the back of her hand.

He turned around to the windshield. He glared at her pasty reflection in the huge rear-view mirror. "You wanna go someplace?"

"Now you're getting it—slowly but surely." She laughed. "You must make a fortune, cabbie—the passengers have to coax you into driving. Thank God you got your figure."

He peered through the cracked glass and into the ice-fogged Twin Cities night. He didn't get very far. He hesitated, thinking about something. But thinking was something that gave him little comfort. "I bet you're gonna blow without payin'," he said.

She grinned at his angry eyes. "I got money, bub—don't think I don't. You start using your hands and feet instead of your mouth and maybe you'll see some of it."

Her voice was a pain in the ass. Her tired face was thin and sharp—a face to cut your lips on—and her hair was lank and dirt-blonde. She had a thin, blue coat wrapped around herself like a blanket, a pair of faded blue jeans, and the over-all look of a smart-ass teenager teetering on the jagged edge of an ugly adulthood. He made up his mind and threw the car in gear; the vehicle surged forward.

"There you go—like riding a tricycle," she sneered.

He tramped his boot down on the accelerator and the car jumped, then slowly gathered speed. "We're goin' for a ride," he muttered under his bad breath. "Me and the bitch are goin' for a ride." His face settled into grim, uncompromising lines and his knuckles glowed on the steering wheel.

She glanced around at the spacious back seat and her thin lips framed a scowl. "You need to own an oil company to drive this pig?"

"It's a Checker," he said tonelessly.

"Huh?"

"Checker cab! Checker Motors Corporation—Kalamazoo, Michigan, '23 to '82." His shoulders relaxed a bit, his hands stopped choking the huge, black steering wheel. "Built 'specially as a taxi—lots of room."

"Yeah? You could rent this back seat out as a motel room. You probably started your family back here."

He replied by hanging a hard right off of Washington Avenue onto Fifth. She held tight to the armrest on the door. A chill wind knifed through the thin crack between his window and the door frame and raked the side of his head. He cranked the window shut, wishing it was that easy with women. It was twenty degrees and dropping like a snowball outside, but inside the cab it was warm—a mobile refuge from the frozen dirt of the street, 'til someone opened the passenger door.

"Hey, cabbie, where the hell are you going?" She blew on the frosted window, wiped some of the ice away with her sleeve. "Falcon Heights is across the river. East. Your visa just expire, or what?"

"I ain't goin' east!"

She rubbed the window with her bare hand. "What'd you mean?" She glanced nervously at the twin rolls of fat hunkered on the back of his plug neck.

"Use those spitholders you call ears, sister," he said. "I told you I ain't goin' east—and I ain't goin' across the river. You can make it if you take a roll out the door and start swimmin'." His breath came hard and quick.

"What the hell are you talking about? Where're you taking me? You'll be one bean short of a sackload if you try anything! I'm warning you!"

"You wanna know where I'm goin'? That it?"

She shrunk slightly on the edges of his heavy anger. "Yeah. I want to know." Her voice grew distant. "1750 Cleveland Avenue is in Falcon Heights—across the river."

He grinned ominously. His red face shone ferociously in the glow of the dashboard lights. "I'm headed south, lady! South! Away from the goddamn cold and the goddamn snow. Away from the scramblin' day to day just to make enough money to pay the bills! Away from the f'in' grind of workin' for your car and your house and your goddamn ungrateful family! Workin' for what? For what!?"

He jerked the cab onto the 35W entrance ramp and gunned it. The car roared through the cold, early-April morning trailing noxious clouds of grey exhaust. Dirt-crusted snowpiles shunted along the sides of the interstate started flying by.

She stared at his coarse, grey-peppered hair. "You don't have to yell," she said to herself.

He drummed his cigar-thick fingers on the steering wheel as the cab shot through the gloom. He glanced at her in the mirror, but she looked away from his glistening eyes. "Listen careful, lady," he said. "I got a full tank of gas and a full auxiliary tank of gas—thirty-five gallons of go-juice. At, say twenty miles to the gallon, that's seven hundred miles from here to there. I'm gonna top it up one more time and then drive 'til the gas runs dry. Where the cab stops, so do I." He turned his block of a head around to look at her confused face. His neck cracked. His face was crusted with sweat.

She pointed at the road.

He turned back around with a grim look of satisfaction.

She kept quiet for awhile, then said: "When'd you figure all this out?"

"About five minutes before you jumped in front of me," he replied. "Been thinkin' about it probably my entire workin' life. And I ain't turnin' back now. Ain't stoppin' but twice—otherwise I won't make it."

She folded her arms together, watched blandly as Richfield, Bloomington, and then Burnsville drifted by.

They traveled in a tense silence, the car holding steady at sixty-five. The lights of the city ended and the frozen countryside opened its black mouth and swallowed the cab.

"You wanted by the cops?" she finally asked, when she saw the Iowa welcome sign. "Kidnapping, maybe?"

He shook his head, cleared his throat—his mouth was dry and cracked and begging for booze. "Nothin' like that," he said. "I'm just sick and tired of the way things been goin' and I'm gettin' out. There's gotta be somethin' better down the road somewhere." He sighed. "Look lady, I'm sorry about you—"

"Don't turn to jelly, driver!"

He stared at her ghostly reflection.

She looked out the window, at nothing. "Don't start blubbering to me," she said. "You're kidnapping me. That's what you're doing."

He shrugged his doughy shoulders. "I told you to get lost, you wouldn't. You wanted to go somewhere, you're goin' somewhere.

You're a stray I took in for awhile, that's all. You can blow when I stop for gas. Stay to the end of the line and you can keep the cab. I ain't gonna need it no more." He gave her a tight smile, the issue resolved in his own mind.

She laughed. "Yeah, just what I need—a thirty-year-old beater. Sounds like my last boyfriend." She wiped her nose. "You could've told me what you were up to and let me get out. You didn't, so it's kidnapping."

He frowned.

"Why're you stopping the once for gas, anyway?" she asked.

"I ain't throwin' everything away just to pick it up again in Council Bluffs." He stared into the lightening dark. "Why don't you stuff your mouth with sleep for awhile? You got a long ride ahead of you."

"It's not going to be that easy, cabbie. You kidnap me, drag me down your yellow-brick road to fantasyland, then you've got to pay the price. I'll speak my mind even if it means losing yours. You should be more careful about who you hijack."

He rubbed his face, then studied his shiny fingers. "What's your name, anyway? You look like somethin' that might have a name."

"None of your business."

He nodded. "You're a fun girl. You oughta be in a circus."

They drove on. He listened to the miles slowly clicking by. That's all he wanted to hear—the miles slowly clicking by. Foul-mouthed women like the one in the back were called family where he came from—as depressing as varicose veins and stretch marks. He settled into his seat and watched the road ahead. He had skipped town at the sagging end of a twelve-hour shift, but he wasn't feeling the least bit tired. Occasional trucks and cars sailed by on the other side of the interstate—rushing lights in a tunnel of inky nothingness. It was the end of the tunnel he was looking for.

She shifted around, grudgingly trying to get comfortable, her face sullen. She didn't want him thinking for a minute that he wasn't imposing a massive, undeserved hardship on her. "What's your route? Longest distance between two points?"

"I35 south. Kansas City, Oklahoma City, Forth Worth, and then ... we'll see. I'm not sure where—"

"Got that right!"

He turned a question loose on her. "What do you do to make ends meet—besides kiss your ass?"

"Ha, ha. It's funny that you're nothing more than a nut on the end of a wheel."

"C'mon, seriously, how do you pay the bills?"

"None of your business." She stared out the window, into the blackness, avoiding his eyes.

"C'mon. Your face says radio. Am I right?"

"I'm a goddamn waitress! Okay?"

"Okay." He jostled his head in a friendly manner. "That's—"

"Crap!"

He ran a nicotine-stained finger along the side of his large, broken-veined nose. "Maybe you 'n me ain't so different."

"Yeah, we're both talented mutts, all right. Make no mistake, cabbie—I'm not running."

"Sure you are," he said. "Everyone is from somethin'."

"The philosopher hack driver—step right up, folks! Just don't feed him."

The small towns of northern Iowa flowed by—Woolstock, Webster, Williams, Hubbard, Story City; left in the churning wake of the cab.

He gritted his teeth when she spoke again. "You aren't going to get away with it," she said.

Des Moines exit signs whistled by as the sun's weak rays revealed the aching emptiness that the night had only briefly hidden.

"Huh? Get away with takin' you? Who the hell's gonna miss you? I sure wish the cab hadn't."

"I'm not talking about me! I'm talking about trying to escape the past and start something new. Your old-life crisis."

"What about it?"

"It's not going to work, that's what. You aren't going to make it."

"Yeah, I thought you might say that."

"I'm telling it like it is, cabbie. Your past'll catch up with you." She pulled her hands out of her pockets—they were red and raw, the nails chewed down. "You're going to grind to a halt in Dirtsville, Texas, have a good time 'til all your money runs out, say a week, go hungry for awhile, say an hour, then start pushing a hack again. It's all you know how to do, right? So you drive so you can eat—you got that taken care of. Then you get lonely because you've probably never lived by yourself before. So you team up with some leathery cowgirl whose husband has disappeared like a Panhandle river come summer—so you got that taken care of." She snorted. "And you know what you got? You've got the same old life you left behind in Minneapolis moved to Texas. You put fourteen hundred miles under your can only to pick up where you left off. Same crap, different map."

"You don't know—"

"And you probably won't even know it, cabbie. That's the pathetic part. You probably won't even know it until it's way too late." She brushed some greasy hair out of her eyes. "Places change, people don't. You're wasting time and gas is all you're doing."

He frowned, hunched his shoulders. "Mind if I smoke?" he asked.

"Yeah, I mind."

He pulled a crumpled pack of Camels out of his breast pocket, shook one free, stuck it in his mouth and lit it. "What the hell do you know about people? You probably never even lived with any. How old are you, anyway? Thirty? Thirty-five? Try—"

"Twenty-one, wiseguy!"

He coughed on his smoke. "Old enough to drink and vote; in that order. Try drivin' hack for twenty years—then you can shoot your mouth about people. Until then, don't write any advice columns."

"Truth hurts, huh? You can't get away from yourself. That's the problem. You can drive halfway around the globe if you had the brains, but all you'll find is yourself waiting at the other end. You got to eat, you got to make money, and, from what I can see, you got to have someone to look after you. Your life is a dead, dull certainty." She smiled triumphantly.

He smiled back. "Let me hear your accomplishments, then maybe I'll unplug my ears."

"I'm young."

"I ain't hearin' anything I don't already know."

She didn't respond.

"I thought so." He checked the gas gauges—still a long way to go.

Wick, St. Charles, Osciola, Van Wert. They crossed the Missouri border around nine. The countryside rolled into hills and the trees and bushes grew tentative leaves. The sun was warmer.

He rolled his window half open and tasted the air—soft and mild.

"How many kids have you got?" Her voice cut through his calm.

"Enough."

"I bet you've got a whole big, fat family."

"Most of 'em are grown."

"Aren't they going to miss you?"

He considered that. "Maybe—some of 'em."

"You ever going to see them or talk to them again?"

"Maybe." He hadn't thought that far ahead. He knew that she knew that. "What the hell is this—twenty questions?"

"It sure as hell ain't twenty answers," she responded. "Just curious. You know, so I have some background information for the cops."

"You think I shouldn't've run out on—"

"Whoa! Back it up, cabbie. I don't know nothing about people, remember?"

He tightened his grip on the steering wheel, wishing it was her chicken-neck. His face glistened ugly in the sun's cutting rays. His stomach growled. She laughed—a coarse, irritating laugh, like a smoker's cough; more an opinion than a laugh. He caught her eyes and held them. "So what's your story? You waitin' tables the rest of your life or you expectin' a call from Prince Harry?"

"Watch where you're going," she said, gesturing at the road.

He eased the big car back into the right hand lane from where it had drifted, ignored, halfway into the left hand lane. A buzzcut teen-ager in a colossal pick-up zoomed by and gave him the finger. He could've plugged every dike in Holland with all the fingers he'd taken over the years. "So, how 'bout it?"

"Take the kid's advice, cabbie."

"Uh-huh! You make fun of me, but you can't even answer one little question about yourself! At least I'm—"

"Shut your goddamn mouth!"

"Okay, that's all—"

"I want to be a writer, okay? Make with the laughs and then shove 'em up your ass!"

"A writer? What'd you mean, like a reporter or somethin'?"

"A writer! You know, books, stories—fiction. You ever read a book?

Or do the blind read to you?"

He laughed, satisfied at having gotten her goat. "Yeah, I read this book once about an obnoxious, flat-chested, twenty-one-year-old—"

"It's all crap, anyway! The only writing I do is in library books. There's a big horse-laugh for you. I write my initials in library books." She stared at the back of his head, tears of rage and self-pity suddenly sparkling in her grey eyes. "Pretty impressive, huh?" She twisted her head back towards the dirty window and the wooded hills beyond, blinking rapidly, her cheeks flaming an unhealthy red.

He listened to her dry sobbing. It sounded like she was being sick. He didn't know what to do—never did. After a few minutes, he asked: "Why do you write your initials in library books?"

"Why the hell do you think? It's the only way I'm ever going to get my name in a book—with my talent. The only way I'm ever going to be remembered." She folded her arms together again. "Why the hell do you think?"

He pushed his hand through his hair and grunted. He couldn't figure women if he had the instruction manual.

They drove on; Eagleville, Ridgeway, and, finally, Kansas City. It was eleven in the morning when they motored past Kansas City.

He calculated that they could probably do another two hundred and twenty to two hundred and forty miles before they'd have to stop for gas. After that, the home stretch—when the tanks went empty a second time, that's where his new life began. It'd be warm at least, probably hot; because once they crossed into Kansas, summer was there to meet them.

They drove through Lawrence and Topeka and down the Kansas turnpike bound for Wichita. The terrain flattened out again—flatter than it had ever been before. The fields lay freshly plowed and planted. Fully-realized leaves stuck to the branches of the few trees and bushes that rimmed the almost-vacant highway. The noonday sun beat down hard on the big, yellow cab. He rolled his window all the way down, let the warm air rush in.

She kept her window sealed shut. "Aren't you going to miss your family?" she started in on him again.

A vague smile dried up on his face, leaving a white line. "Yeah, maybe. Sometimes. Why don't you give the family a rest, eh? They could use it."

She laughed harshly, stared into his mirrored brown eyes. "You're a pretty selfish sack of meat, aren't you? Well, maybe not pretty. But selfish."

Dust from the stripped fields blew into the cab. He rubbed a red-rimmed eye. "When I want your opinion, I won't ask for it, okay? You don't know—"

"You abandon your wife and kids in arctic Minneapolis while you take a joyride into the sun." She leaned forward as he threw up his hands in exasperation. "How's your family going to live without the so-called man of the house around?"

"You deaf as well as dumb? I told you already—most of the kids are grown; they can look after themselves. They don't need their old man. They've made that plenty clear." He sprayed water onto the windshield, turned on the wipers—succeeded in clouding the glass with streaks of dirt. "My wife's got a job. She'll get by. Maybe I'll send money, if I can."

She licked her lips. "You're a classic," she said. "You're running away to get away and now you're sending money back home. What's the point? You're your own square peg and square hole."

"Yeah, well, not all of us have our shit together like you, I guess. Lemme see if I got a book here for you to autograph."

"Shut up!"

He leaned over, fumbled around in the glove compartment. "Oh, yeah, here's one. The Bible. You wanna take credit for that?"

"Shut up."

He laughed, shoved the book back into the compartment. He glanced out the window at the fertile soil stretching endlessly to the horizon. He hadn't thought a lot about what he was going to do when he got to where he was going. Or what he was going to do about his family. That was the point—had he thought everything through he never would have done anything. His flight had been the first impulsive thing he had done in fifty hard years of living. Sweat gathered in the thick folds at the back of his neck and his head started to pound. He felt the heat for the first time.

El Dorado, Wichita—the Kansas towns and cities shimmered in the distant under a broiling sun.

By the time he drove over the Oklahoma border, his brain was boiling with memories—some good, some bad; all fighting for room inside of his splintered head. Memories of a young bride, a new-born child, a first car, some more kids, his tenth wedding anniversary, the guys at the garage, neighbors, family, friends, relatives. Milestones and landmarks littering a life slowly built and hastily discarded—a simple life grown to frustrating complexity with the many people and responsibilities it encompassed.

"You're probably getting low, driver," she said. "On gas."

He blinked a few times, then glanced down at the gauges. He would have to stop at the next town and re-fill the tanks—she was right.

The next town was Braman, Oklahoma; a small, work-deserted town in the middle of a hot, dusty nowhere. White clouds scudded aimlessly across a pale, blue sky, pushed around by a sharply rising and falling wind.

He steered the car into a decrepit, two-pump filling station a mile off of the interstate. The gas pumps were as old as the guy who emerged from the small, grey-weathered, wooden building. A faded windsock flopped around helplessly on a pole on the top of the building. The man wore a cowboy hat, a flannel shirt, and jeans. His face was brown and cracked like the topsoil that carpeted the surrounding fields, when it wasn't blowing around.

The man stared at the car for a long moment, then slowly ambled over to the driver-side window. "Woo-wee! That is some kinda old-time metal you is hauling around, son! You ain't come all the way down from New York City have you? I declare! Ain't seen nothin' like this since the Korean War ended and they turned all them Shermans back into nickels. Fill 'er up with the regular or does she drink the diesel like a real tank?"

"Yeah, regular," he replied. He undid a couple of more buttons on his shirt. The sweater his wife had knitted him and he had worn religiously the entire winter lay discarded on the seat next to him. "Hot, eh."

The man pushed back his cowboy hat with a bent thumb and chuckled. His laugh was warm and gentle and timeless, and came from deep in his throat. He spat into the dust and steadied his blade of a body against a sudden gust of wind. "Mister, this here is a cool spell compared to what we're gonna get." He shuffled off to the pump, chuckling to himself as the dust swirled all around.

"You gettin' out?" He turned around to look at her when she didn't answer. He hated to break her quiet. "I told you that you could beat it when I stopped for gas, and now I'm stopped."

She looked at him distrustfully. She spoke quietly: "What am I supposed to do—get Tex Ritter there to give me a ride back on his burro?"

"You can hitch a ride back with me if you can stand the company."

She frowned, her lightly glazed eyes firing back to life. "What?"

"Yeah, I'm headin' back to Minneapolis. The road to freedom is closed for repairs up ahead."

"Minneapolis!?" She leaned forward, grabbed the back of the front bench. "What'd you mean? I thought you were going to keep going south?"

"Yeah, so did I—for awhile, I guess." He shrugged. "But now I'm thinkin' better. Maybe the hot air's cleared my thick head. I dunno. I'm turnin' around and—"

"You gutless bastard!" Her lips trembled and her blanched face flushed a fevered scarlet. "You stupid, gutless bastard! You drive all this way only to turn around when your guts run out!"

His face hardened. "Yeah, maybe. I dunno. I guess you were right about—"

"I was right!?" Her clutching fingers blazed white on the scarred, black upholstery. She gulped for air like someone near to drowning. "What about your goddamn idea about starting over someplace new?" She choked on her words, tore her face away from his.

The old cowboy looked in at them through the dusty back window, his face serene and knowing.

"Hey, take it easy. It was just a pipe dream. You said so yourself. Things ain't really so bad back—"

"You gutless bastard!" she screamed a final time, then fumbled open the heavy door and stumbled out into the scorching afternoon.

"Howdy, ma'am," the old man said. He touched the blackened brim of his cowboy hat.

She shoved past his courtesy, her brutal, trailing laughter tinged with hysteria. She staggered through the brilliant sunshine, ran across the lot and out onto the service road.

The old man pulled the dripping nozzle out of the cab, hitched it back onto the pump, and strolled over and said: "Feisty little gal, huh? Married me one just like her—long time ago."

"Did you fill the auxiliary tank?" he asked, staring after her. She ran awkwardly down the road—tripping, falling, picking herself up, running again. Like a child. He couldn't figure her out. He'd thought she'd be happy about his going back.

The old man scratched the dry stubble on his beef jerky face. "You got one of those, too? I declare. Didn't know you had one of those."

He nodded impatiently, watched her retreating figure until she reached a curve in the road and her small body was lost behind a line of trees and brush.

When the tanks were finally filled, he paid off the old man and left him hanging in mid-sentence and a cloud of dust. He tore out of the station and shot the cab down the service road. Hot air thundered through his open window and his face dripped with sweat. He'd pick her up and haul the both of them back to Minnesota where they goddamn well belonged. It was too damn hot here anyway. The car rocketed forward and he grimly hung onto the wheel and shook his head. What the hell had he been thinking, running away like he had? There were plenty worse off than him. He saw them every day.

The big cab was pushing forty when he rounded the bend in the road and slammed on the brakes. Something had darted out of a clump of bushes directly into his path. He fought the steering wheel over hard to the left, but he wasn't nearly quick enough. A sickening thud resounded in his crimson ears.

He jammed the car to a stop, slammed the gear shift into park, and fell out the door. He was instantly crushed by the towering heat and smacked around by the angry wind. He ran jerkily down the cracked road to where her body lay mangled. Her legs were twisted grotesquely, and thick, black blood leaked out of the side of her head and onto the hot asphalt. She wasn't moving. He collapsed next to her, frantically dug into her thin neck with his shaking fingers—desperately searching for a pulse. He found nothing. He looked down at her staring, accusing eyes and her broken mouth. He retched over and over, his stomach heaving empty. His swelled head was lacerated with searing pain and scalding tears streamed down his burning face. He felt himself blacking out, then somehow pulled it together.

He glanced up and down the empty, windswept road. He swallowed hard, staggered upright, and then carefully dragged her body into the grassy ditch. She was amazingly light—easy to handle; and he did so tenderly. He walked quickly back to the big cab, climbed inside, and drove south—a man on the run.

The greatest detectives have always had their particular
methods and tools.

A Piece Of String
by Ahmed A. Khan

PERHAPS YOU, TOO, have heard of the legendary Arabian trackers and
detectives of the past. It was in 1952 that I happened to observe one
such detective in action with all the tools of his trade which, by the
way, were comprised of instinct, common sense, acute observation,
knowledge of people and places, and, oh yes, a piece of string.

It was my second year in Kuwait, working as a journalist. I lived
alone in a big house near an old market place, or 'souk' as it is known,
with roofed alleys, where you could buy almost anything you wanted,
from spices to the highest quality Persian rugs.

The souk was a busy place indeed, with all the shops opening at
seven in the morning and doing brisk business till eight in the night.
Then, one by one, the shops would close, the vendors pulling down
the shutters and locking them for the night, and silence would de-
scend and fill the dark alleys where for the last thirteen hours there
was light and all the sounds of life.

During my stay in that country, I had made friends with one Syed
Najem Al Khaleel, who was a police detective. Najem spoke good
English. He lived in the house beside mine, with his wife and six well-
behaved children. He was in his late forties, of medium height but
sturdily built. His bearded face with sleepy eyes was, if not handsome,
pleasant enough.

The old wooden tea-stall in the souk was one of my favourite
haunts in my free moments. It was here that I first heard about the
murder.

One Thursday, early in the morning, I was sitting at the tea-stall,
sipping a 'finjan' of 'qahwa' (a cup of black coffee, for you) when Najem walked in and sat at my table. I ordered another qahwa for him.
While we waited for his qahwa to arrive, I noticed that his mind
seemed pre-occupied.

"What's the matter?" I asked him. "Why so quiet today?"

"I am thinking," he said.

"Do you do that often?" I grinned.

"Don't joke. This is a serious matter."

"What is it?" His tone made me sit up.

"Murder."

"What?" I was taken aback.

Then he related the whole thing to me. Some time the previous night, a murder was committed in the souk. The victim was a young perfume-seller named Rafiq. His body was discovered that morning at five when people were out on the streets going to or coming from their morning prayers at the mosques. The case had been officially assigned to Najem and he was on his way to the scene of crime.

My journalistic instincts came fully awake. I had heard tales of the acutely trained senses of Arabian detectives. Here was my chance to find out about them first hand. I requested Najem to take me with him. He agreed.

It was now 7 AM, and as it was summertime, the morning was quite hot already. One by one, the shops in the souk were being opened and readied for business. The traffic on the roads was gradually increasing. Water sellers, some on foot and some on donkey-carts, were about. Bicycles were there too, and there were children prancing about in front of their houses.

We found the body of the victim lying in a dim and narrow alley of the souk. The cause of death was clear enough. His throat was cut. The alley had already been cordonned off by two policemen who saluted Najem and led him to the body.

Najem examined the body for some time, then stood up, his sleepy eyes looking sleepier than ever.

"There was a struggle before he died," he said.

I looked around for signs of struggle, and found them - broken buttons of the dishdasha (the common dress of the Arabs), torn sleeves of the same, and a puffed up left eye.

Najem then proceeded to inspect the surroundings. Bending low, he peered carefully at the ground. Then he whipped out of the pocket of his dishdasha a piece of string and started taking some measurements with it on the ground. Slightly surprised, I looked at him questioningly.

He called me near him.

"Footprints," he pointed to the ground. I looked. They were

barely visible, some moving towards the corpse and some going away from it.

"Murderer's?"

"Yes."

"How can you be so sure?" I asked. "So many people might have passed this way since morning. In fact the marks could as well have been made by us."

"Look around you. Don't you see a difference in the footprints made by us and this particular set of footprints?"

There was a difference. Our footprints were much more vivid and sharp.

"You remember there was a sandstorm last night?" Najem asked.

"Remember!" I exclaimed. "I can still taste the sand in my mouth."

Then I realised what he meant. Sand had covered the ground all around and it was this layer of sand which had made our footprints so vivid.

"That means these footprints of the murderer were made before the storm," I tried playing the detective.

"No," said Najem. "They were not made before the storm. They were made during the storm. If they had been made before the storm, they would have been totally obliterated." He paused. "In fact, judging the strength of the storm and knowing the time when the storm ended, I can place within a fifteen minutes bracket the time of the making of these footprints."

I was impressed, but immediately thought up another objection. "How do you know these are not the footprints of the victim?"

He seemed a bit surprised at my question. "Use your eyes, my friend, use your eyes," he said. "Look," he pointed to the victim's feet, "different size of feet, different kind of footwear."

"What were you measuring on the ground?" I quickly changed the tack.

"Steps."

"Steps?"

To demonstrate, Najem once again brought his string into play and measured the distance between two consecutive footprints. Then he proceeded to repeat the measurement randomly choosing another pair of footprints.

"Do you notice anything?" he asked after about four or five measurements.

"What?"

"All the measurements that I have taken are exactly the same."

"So?"

"So we can definitely say that the murderer had what you might call a measured gait."

"What's so extraordinary about that?" I really didn't see his point. Why was he giving importance to the gait of the murderer? "Many people have such a gait. In fact, even I have a measured gait."

"You are right. Many people have measured gait, but how many of those people could maintain it under these circumstances?"

"Under what circumstances?"

"Come here."

I went near him.

"Do you see any difference between the footprints which move towards the corpse and the footprints which move away from it?'

I examined both the sets. "The prints moving towards the corpse are sharper than the ones moving away from it," I said.

"Good. What does that suggest to you?"

I had an inspiration. "The murderer was carrying something heavy when he came here and he had dropped the weight before moving away."

"Very good. I will make a detective of you yet. Now tell me what heavy thing could he be carrying?"

I had another inspiration. "The corpse."

"Once again right on the head," said Najem.

"You mean to say that the murder was not done at this spot?"

"I am positive. Look at the evidence. First, there is the matter of the footprints. Second, even though the victim died due to his throat being cut, there is very small amount of blood on the ground. Third, even though the body shows signs of struggle with the murderer, the ground itself is devoid of such signs."

I thought over what Najem had said. "What has all this got to do with the gait of the murderer?" I asked.

"You said you have a measured gait but do you think you could keep up your measured gait while carrying a corpse on your back?"

I considered. "No, I don't think so."

"There you are."

"So what does the measured gait tell you?"

"It tells me that the murderer is a strong man and a man whose measured gait is the result of years of training."

"Who?"

"A military man," he stated positively.

My respect for this man was growing by the minute. Truly, this was the stuff that legends are made of. But then there were thousands of military men in the city. How was he going to pinpoint the right one among them?

"Now let us see where the murder was committed and why it was necessary to shift the corpse." Eyes to the ground, Najem started tracing back the footprints which came towards the corpse. After a while, the footprints vanished, being obliterated by the day's traffic. Najem took his bearings and moved off in the general direction from which the footprints seemed to have come. His eyes were still fixed on the ground. After about five minutes, he stopped and looked up. He was in front of a house with green doors. He stood there for some time, deep in thought. He took out his notebook and wrote the number of the house in it. Then he came away from there and motioned his assistants to remove the corpse.

"Well, that ends our investigation here," he said. "The next part of the investigation will take place at the police station." He turned to me. "Want to come?"

"Does a fish want water?"

As soon as we reached the police station, Najem called his young assistant, Hameed, to his office. He took out his notebook, flipped the pages until he reached the place where he had written the number of the house with green doors. "I want full details about the occupants of this house," he ordered, showing Hameed the house number. Hameed nodded and left.

Najem then got up and poured two cups of tea, one for me and one for himself, from the kettle that lay on his table. For the next twenty minutes, there was no mention of the murder. We just drank our tea and talked of this and that. Then the assistant came back and placed his report in front of Najem. Najem read the report, nodded as if the report had confirmed some theory that he had, and passed the report to me.

Briefly, the report indicated that the house was occupied by a cloth merchant named Zubair who owned a shop in the souk where the murder had taken place. He was a widower of about fifty. The only other occupant of the house was his eighteen-year-old daughter, Yasmeen. Probably the most significant fact in the report was that the daughter had been quite friendly with Rafiq, the murdered man.

"Describe the old man and his daughter," Najem ordered Hameed.

"The man looks older than his age, has deeply etched furrows in his forehead, as if he is accustomed to scowling. He is not a jolly fellow. On the other hand, according to the neighbours, the girl is extremely jolly. She is also quite pretty. She is also of the modern bent and does not wear the Islamic hijab. In fact, her dresses are as meagre as the present Arab society could allow. She has completed her high school education and helps her father in his shop."

"Get the girl and the father here."

Another half an hour passed before Hameed returned with the news that they were here.

"Send the girl in. Keep the father with you. Question him to see if he saw or heard anything last night."

Within moments, Yasmeen walked in and, at Najem's command, sat down on a chair. I looked at her carefully. She was quite attractive and would probably have been even more attractive if she was smiling instead of fidgeting nervously, looking tense and worried.

Najem just looked at her silently for some time and this made here even more nervous.

"Why have you called us here, inspector?" She broke the silence.

"The murder of your friend, Rafiq, must have come to you as a shock."

"Yes, oh yes!" She breathed hard and seemed on the verge of tears. "He had just proposed marriage to me a day ago."

"That makes it even sadder," Najem nodded, "and then circumstances heap tragedy upon tragedy." He paused. "You know, your other friend, the one who is in military ... what's his name..." He tapped his forehead as if he was thinking hard to remember the name.

Yasmeen sprang out of her chair. "Matar? What happened to Matar?"

"Matar, yes. Give me his full name."

"Matar Al-Mutawa. What happened to him?"

"Nothing happened yet but something is going to happen soon," Najem said calmly. "He is going to be arrested for the murder of Rafiq."

"Wha!" Yasmeen was looking at Najem open mouthed, her face pale, blood drained out of it.

"What are you talking about," she managed to say, in a small voice.

"Last night, when Matar heard about Rafiq's proposal, he was angry because he wanted to marry you himself. They had a confrontation right in front of your house and Matar, being so much stronger than Rafiq, managed to grab him, cover his mouth with one hand to prevent him from screaming, and cut his throat with the other."

He paused. "Am I right? Tell me, am I right?"

"I—I don't know."

"How could you not know when it happened right before your eyes?" Najem went on relentlessly.

"No," she almost screamed. "No. I don't know anything."

"There is absolutely no point in denying. How do you think I know all this? I have another eye-witness."

At this, Yasmeen's legs seemed to turn rubbery. She flopped back on the chair sobbing hysterically.

Najem called Hameed. When Hameed walked in, he pointed to the crying girl. "Take her to your office and get her statement."

After Hameed had left with Yasmeen, Najem leaned back on his chair, looking sad and tired.

We sat there for a long time, staring into the empty air, not talking, each of us thinking our own thoughts.

"For the sins of your fathers you, though guiltless, must suffer."—Horace

Mockingbird Rail Yard Blues
by Jim Downer

I DUG THE book I was reading out from under a stack of college paperwork that sat on my desk. After a week of celebrating my high school graduation I just didn't have the drive to dig in to all of that yet.

Just before lunch, I heard the doorbell ring. I walked to the top of the stairs to see who it was. My mother opened the door to see a man in a very nice suit, his black hair cropped close, almost military. He raised a pistol and shot her. She fell and I wanted to scream, go to her, yell for my dad, but I all I could do was stand there speechless. My feet were frozen to the floor and I thought briefly that these were my last moments on earth. The man at the door walked down the hallway toward the kitchen without even looking upstairs. Still frozen, I heard a lot of movement downstairs.

"Hello Dragan, it's been a long time," the gunman said. "If you want to beg you should start now, but I have to warn you that it won't do any good. Be a good *cetnik* and come on out."

My father said something that sounded like "*pico jedna*." Two shots followed and I ran downstairs to see the man in the suit lying in the hallway with half of his head gone. My father leaned back against a chair at the kitchen table, bleeding from the midsection, blood covering the floor around him, a pistol in his right hand. I started to cry. I tried to hold it in but couldn't. I kneeled beside him and took his hand.

"Listen, son," he said between labored breaths, "There are things from my past, things I should have told you.   There isn't time now. Men will be coming for you, and they won't care if you know what happened or not." He fished keys out of his pocket, held up one key, and handed it to me. "Go up to my office, look in the safe. There's a belt with money and our passports. Wear it under your shirt so no one can steal it." As my father closed his eyes his last breaths came painfully.   I squeezed his hand one last time and turned to leave.

My first idea was to just drive until I couldn't and then stop somewhere. I realized that if they could find my dad then they could probably find my car so I went with plan B. I had always been fascinated with railroads and had always wanted to hop a train. I had watched several YouTube videos on the subject and felt confident in my expertise. I parked my car about a mile from Mockingbird Rail Yard, took the pack I had thrown together, and walked the rest of the way. I managed to sneak through the fence and find some bushes to hide in near the tracks. My internet studying had told me that today's trains speed up a lot faster than they used to, so when you go you have to run as fast as possible. I saw a train that looked good, but as I got into a crouch to run toward it I felt a hand on my shoulder.

"Hey man, if you go out there now the bulls are going to catch you," a voice said from behind me. I turned and saw a dirty guy who looked like he might have been on the rough end of forty or so. He was wearing a black wool cap, jeans, and a sweatshirt. A bedroll hung diagonally over his shoulder. He pointed back toward the train I had been about to hop. I looked and saw the SUVs the railroad cops drive come past us.

"There won't be another one for about fifteen minutes, we can make it now," he said. We got up and ran towards the train. He jumped on a flat car and pulled me up after him.

"Stay down and don't get cozy until we're out of the rail yard," he motioned with his hand as he spoke. We rode for a bit before he pulled out his sleeping bag.

"You're gonna get cold with nothing between you and the metal," he said. He put a piece of egg crate foam that he had stowed in his sleeping bag on the floor of the car. "We can sleep back to back, but I'm not into dudes OK?"

"Yeah, me neither," I said. "It's summer time, I should be OK."

"Man you're green," he said, "the metal will suck the heat right out of you and we'll be in the breeze all night on this flat car. Trust me, you'll get cold."

"Okay, yeah, I've never done this before. I had some trouble at home and had to make a quick exit," I said, feeling vulnerable for the first time.

"I'm Cinci. Everyone on the rails calls me that cause I'm from

Cincinnati. I ain't been there since I was a teenager, but that's how it is out here, you get a nickname and it sticks." He shook my hand as he spoke and then we both hunkered down in our sleeping bags. Sometime during the night I started crying and couldn't stop. My parents were dead and my life would never be the same. I kept trying to rationalize things and think my way through, but in the end it became too exhausting and I slept. I hoped that Cinci hadn't heard me crying, but we were lying back to back so I'm sure he felt it if nothing else. I didn't know him at all and I didn't want him to think of me as weak.

We woke up just before dawn. The train was pulling in to Oklahoma City. Cinci shook my feet.

"Welcome to Okie City, kid. There are trains leaving today but they're all going east. If we wait until tomorrow we can catch one to Kansas City, or better yet, somewhere west." He started putting his things together. "And just so you know, out here we're all running from something, so whatever it is, I ain't gonna ask you about it cause I know you'll pay me the same respect. If you wanna talk then go ahead, but it don't matter to me one way or the other."

"I'm all right, just going through some tough times," I replied.

Cinci laughed. "There's nobody out here that ain't," he said.

We jumped a train that morning to Kansas City. Cinci told me that people on the rails called it KC-MO for Kansas City, Missouri, to differentiate it from KC-K or Kansas City, Kansas, just across the river. When we got to Kansas City we found a spot by the river and camped. I just slept until Cinci woke me up and said it was time to hop our next rail. I hadn't eaten in two days, but all I wanted to do was sleep. He was heading west so we hopped a train headed to Cheyenne, Wyoming. This time we got on the best rail car of them all, the big daddy, an old-fashioned box car. It was half full of bags of rice, which made great mattresses. I slept pretty well, all things considered. After I woke up there was a minute there where I felt okay, and then the events of the past few days hit me and I had trouble thinking straight. Cinci opened the door on the car a little and we watched the countryside go by.

I slept as much as I could to keep from having to deal with everything.

We got to Cheyenne around noon. I had been sleeping so much I didn't even know what day it was. We found a spot to camp and Cinci started gathering wood. I hadn't contributed anything since I met up with Cinci so I told him I'd go into town and get us some food. My stomach was making funny noises and I was ready to eat. I emptied my pack so that I'd be able to carry a lot of stuff and found a grocery store. I picked up a roasted chicken, some ribs, and mashed potatoes. I got some donuts, too. When I got back to our campsite, we feasted. It was one of the best meals I've ever had, before or since. It's funny how you can be at rock bottom and something little like a good meal can remind you why it's good to be alive.

After we ate we kept the fire going. I've never seen as many stars as I saw in the sky that night. After dinner, Cinci pulled out a deck of cards and began shuffling. He knew a few games but he had never played Texas Hold 'Em. My father was a poker fiend and he, my mother, and I used to play family games for whatever spare change we had lying around. Cinci and I played with pebbles and I felt a little normal for the first time since all this had happened. After we put the cards away, Cinci began to speak.

"All right, kid, it's time for Cinci's crash course on trains," Cinci said, looking animated. "Don't worry none, there won't be no crashing, that's just an expression. The first thing you should know about hopping trains is the cars. We've been on a flat car, the first night; the car that looked like it was carrying stood-up ice cream cones is called a hopper. They put stuff like dirt and gravel in the top and then empty them out the bottom. That cubby on the end we rode in is the only place to ride on those. Don't ever ride on anything hauling cars cause the bulls check those a lot."

"I feel like I should be taking notes," I said, smiling for the first time since all this started.

"You should be, but it's OK that you ain't, this information has been passed down by hobos for years. Used to be thousands of us riding the rails but now there ain't that many. When I first started the old guys told me about how it used to be. They had hobo jungles in most big rail towns where you could go and stay for a few days if you wanted. Word is they called 'em jungles for a reason, though. There wasn't any law or anything; I guess you could say it was just the law of the jungle."

Cinci fell asleep still pontificating on hobo culture and how September 11 had marked the end of it. I had been sleeping for two days and felt wide awake. I just sat by the fire and thought about trains and hobos and why people are willing to give up their freedom when they were scared, anything to keep my mind off the last few days or the next few. The cold Wyoming night didn't penetrate my sleeping bag and I kept the fire going for the rest of the night, alone with my thoughts.

When morning came I was hungry again and a hot breakfast was sounding good. The train Cinci wanted to catch didn't leave until that night. I asked Cinci if he wanted to go into town with me but he didn't. I found a diner and got us some eggs, sausage, and biscuits and gravy.

When I got back to our spot, three guys in tracksuits stood over Cinci. One of them had Cinci's arms pinned behind his back, another was punching him in the gut and slapping him, and the third was shouting questions I was pretty sure concerned me.

I ran and waved, shouting, "Here I am, here I am, please don't hurt him, he has nothing to do with this!" My yelling clearly got the attention of the man swinging his fists because the first thing he did was draw his gun, turn, and shoot. I felt the bullet hit me low in the gut and I hit the dirt. I heard one of the men cuss and then they were all gone. Cinci came running over and started to staunch the bleeding with his filthy shirtsleeve. He held my hand and told me to hang on. I felt myself getting sleepy so I slept.

When I woke up with tubes coming out of each arm, it took me a minute to figure out what was going on. I was still really tired. I blinked my eyes and slowly took a look around the room. A door opened to the hallway on my left and a wall locker sat next to that.

A TV from a bygone age hung over my bed and a rolling table with a pitcher of water stood to my right.   I looked past the crappy TV and saw an old man sitting and staring at me. When I saw the old man staring, I freaked out so bad that my heart monitor alerted the nurses.

"It is OK." The old man told them, "He just woke up and is

probably a little curious. I am a friend; I will let him know what happened." The nurse looked at me and I nodded, because whatever was going to happen I wanted to get clear of this.

"Where's Cinci?" I asked.

"I don't know the man named 'Cinci,'" the old man said, "but there is a wallet and passport on the nightstand there. The nurse said that was all they found with you."

"I guess he needed the cash more than I did," I said.

"You will not know me. I am a Bosnian but I live in Saint Louis now. Many of us do. As you know, your parents were Serbian. Your father is considered a war hero by most of the people he served with, but like many heroes, the other side thinks he was a monster." He handed me a manila envelope. I opened it and took out several pictures. My father was in all of them. I had never seen him with a beard, but it was him. There was a picture of him standing over what looked to be a mass grave as men in ski masks shoveled dirt over bodies. There was a picture of him and a group of men in the same masks standing with their AK-47s, posed to look tough. The last picture showed him with cuts on his face that would later become scars I recognized. He stood pointing a gun at kneeling man with bound hands. "Unfortunately, your father lost his ability to draw the line between warriors and civilians. It happened a lot in our war, on both sides, although mostly by the Serbs. Twenty years ago is a long time, but now the children of men we lost are getting involved."

"My father said something that sounded like 'pico jedna' to his killer before he died, can you tell me what that means?"

"Your father was calling his killer a pussy," the old man said, laughing. "It is important that you know that I did not order or condone your parents' murder. The men who made that decision did so without my approval. They are here," he said. He handed me a newspaper folded to the front page of the metro section. There was a small article about three eastern European immigrants from Dallas who had been murdered.

"If my father did all those things, then why didn't you want him dead?" I asked, starting to feel a little woozy. My voice cracked with cotton mouth and the man handed me a cup of water from a bedside table.

"Your father did do horrible things. Many of us had decided after the war to try to bring men like your father to justice instead of making revenge killings. We knew that if we killed them they would be viewed by both police and media as being victims. If we sent them to trial they would live, but the world would know what they did and others would know that there is no safe haven for killers like that. It has to end somewhere. And then there was your mother. There was no reason for her to die, and there was no reason for them to chase you. These men cannot see past their hate, but they have all lost family members to men like your father, so they thought your father's family should die too. This doesn't make them right. We took some action, but the men who killed your parents didn't start out as monsters. I'm sure your father didn't either."   The old man looked down at the floor and then back up at me.   He slowly patted my foot with his hand as if that would make things better, then walked out of the room.

I walked out of the hospital two days later with nothing but some donated clothes and a bag full of antibiotic pills.   The sun forced my eyes into a squint but as soon as I grew accustomed to the light I saw Cinci sitting on a bus stop bench across the street with my pack and his on the bench next to him.

"Man, it's good to see a friendly face," I said walking over to him.

"Well, I felt real bad about you gettin' shot and all, plus, a good rail buddy is hard to find." Cinci rose from the bench and clapped me on the shoulder.   "You know, it occurs to me that with all of this going on I never got your name."

"Well, it occurs to me that I thought I'd have some answers by the end of this and I'm more confused than when I started.   I'm Dallas." I smiled at Cinci and held out my right hand.   As he shook it, I said, "Let's hop a rail."

Things have a funny way of working out—for some people, anyway.

The Ring
by Aislinn Batstone

ELLIOTT DIDN'T KNOW what had made him stop in at the pawnbroker's on his way home from work that Tuesday evening. Perhaps simply the fact that it was so close to his apartment, just across the street behind his building. He certainly hadn't anticipated buying Olivia's engagement ring from a pawnbroker, but once the fellow in the shop had shown him the ring he simply had to have it.

Olivia wouldn't care where the ring came from. She loved him, and he wasn't from a rich family. He rearranged his accounts and on Saturday stepped out into the sweltering summer morning with a bank cheque for twenty thousand dollars in his wallet. He'd shoved the wallet in his back pocket, fearing to do anything out of the ordinary. Normally he didn't mind living in this slightly edgy part of town but not in these circumstances. Soon he was sweating freely and mopping his forehead with a handkerchief.

Midsummer in Sydney. The very bitumen had a life of its own. It heaved, warm and soft like a woman's breast, petrol and tar shimmering off it like perfume. Light speared his eyes from every angle, from car windscreens and shopfronts, but most of all from the glaring sun, high as noon. Elliot felt it burn the top of his head where the hair had receded. Thank God Olivia didn't seem to care about baldness, either.

He shielded his eyes from the sun and slipped into the pawnbroker's. The shop was dark and cluttered and it took a moment for his eyes to adjust. The same man was there, and this seemed a good sign. Imagine if he'd had to explain the whole transaction to some casual weekend salesperson!

The pawnbroker, seated behind his counter, greeted Elliot with a show of teeth. "A-ha! You're here for the ring?"

"Yes." Elliot suddenly felt anxious. The twenty thousand dollars in his back pocket represented the savings he'd made towards a house deposit. This was a huge moment, a momentous decision. But actually no decision at all. Olivia was worth it.

The pawnbroker had been eating a bacon sandwich. He put it

down on a plate, stood from his stool, held up a finger and walked into his back office. He emerged carrying an unusual ring-box, carved wood in the shape of a flattened ball, detailed with brass.

"Did I show you the box?"

Elliot shook his head. "No. Does it come with the ring?"

"I use these for all special pieces. There's a trick—like this—adds a layer of protection from thieves."

Elliot watched as the pawnbroker moved his fingers over the brass elements and pressed. The box sprang open to reveal the large diamond set on an elegant ring of rich gold. To Elliot's untutored eye it was the most stunning solitaire he'd ever seen, and the pawnbroker's valuation papers had confirmed its exceptional worth. All in all, it was perfect for Olivia.

"I have a bank cheque." He fumbled for his wallet, hands damp, struggling with the heavy denim. He opened the wallet and pulled out the cheque.

"Marvellous," the pawnbroker said with a grin. "I'll get those papers."

Elliot accepted the ring box and waited for the papers. He toyed with the brass buttons, imitating the other man, pressing here and there until—*click*. The box opened. He looked at the ring and smiled. It was perfect. Just like his bride-to-be.

Tonight, he'd show her this magnificent ring and ask her to be his wife. There wasn't any question, really, but the ring was important, essential that it not only mirror Olivia's beauty, but also her value. Limitless.

Elliot walked home with the ring shoved into one pocket and the papers in the other. He contemplated the emptiness of his savings account with a giddy feeling. He knew he'd done the right thing. In fact, he couldn't stop smiling. Back home, he put the ring and the papers on his kitchen table and went to iron his suit for dinner with Olivia.

Claus, the pawnbroker, finished his bacon sandwich and licked the crumbs from his fingers. He stood and took the plate into his back room. On top of some papers on his desk, alongside a couple of new acquisitions, sat a puzzle box identical to the one he'd given the customer. This box contained the real diamond ring.

What a brilliant scheme! The diamond ring had been the ultimate investment, and in fact had cost him close to thirty thousand dollars. The copies he'd had made had cost him twelve hundred each. The gold was real, of course, though less valuable, but the stone was a complete sham. A zirconia, sparkling enough to fool the unknowing, particularly when viewed alongside the valuation papers. Claus had made multiple copies of the originals on the excellent colour printer at the office shop three blocks down. He didn't feel bad about the deception. Some people even thought a zirconia, with its rainbow flashes, more beautiful than a real diamond anyway.

Elliot was in his bedroom, ironing his mid-grey suit. Tonight he was taking Olivia to Doyle's at Watson's bay, an extravagance that would have to be put on his seldom-used credit card. He hoped the weather wouldn't turn stormy. While a summer thunderstorm brought drama and excitement, it wasn't quite the backdrop he preferred for the night of his engagement. Elliot heard his dog Jimmie barking but ignored him. It was probably only a cat at the kitchen window, or a bird.

In fact, Elliot had left the kitchen window open. With his owner safely out of the room, Jimmie the Jack Russell leapt up onto the table to investigate the smell of bacon on a small brown box. He picked up the box in his mouth. Was it edible? It was hard, but then, so were bones. He gave it an experimental lick. Delicious. He sank his teeth into the box. Just then, a marmalade cat appeared at the window.

When it came to cats, Jimmy was a traditionalist. He charged at the window and skidded to a halt at the edge of the table. Too clever to jump out the window, he couldn't let the cat continue up the fire escape without a warning. He opened his mouth and barked. *RO-RO-RO-RO-RO!*

The puzzle box fell out of Jimmie's mouth and clanged down the fire escape where it bounced off a step and fell into an air-conditioning unit. It rattled through a gap in the machine before the sound of its movement stopped. The air-conditioner also stopped, and when its hum started up again it was decidedly deeper, the sound of a motor working hard against an obstruction.

Ethel Trott, retiree, was the only person who heard the change in the air-conditioner's pitch. She'd always had sensitive hearing, which was at times a blessing, at others a curse. Crossing the street behind Elliot's building, she heard the air-conditioner change its tune and she paused momentarily, not consciously interested, but alert to the auditory.

A driver coming too fast had expected Ethel to have moved out of the way by the time he reached that point. She had not. He braked hard and swerved with a screech of tyres. His car slammed into the front of the pawnbroker's shop, smashing the window and coming to a halt with its nose buried in the jewellery cases, guitars and bicycles. The shop alarm went off, piercing the air with a siren that made Ethel Trott, who'd run back to where she'd started, drop her string bag and put her hands up over her ears.

Eighteen-year-old Vince Flint saw the whole thing on his way to the gym. He watched the driver climb out of the car. The pawnbroker had come out of the shop and the two began to talk with loud hand movements. Vince continued on his way. The gym shared a back alley with the pawnbroker and Vince went this way, a short cut from his bus stop.

Vince couldn't help but notice that the back door of the pawnbroker's stood open, perhaps to let a breeze through. He went closer and peeked in. There was a small back office and past that, the shop. Further still, beyond the broken mess of merchandise and the car, the pawnbroker talked on the footpath with the driver.

Vince never seemed to earn enough at his casual job to pay for rent and food and all the other things he needed. With the damage to the front of the shop, the pawnbroker wouldn't notice a few things missing. Possibly his insurance would cover the entire stock. Vince ducked into the office for a squiz. There wasn't a lot here in the back room, just a few bits of jewellery on a shamble of papers on the desk. He picked up a necklace, a watch and a small carved wooden box, shoving them in his pocket. Checking to make sure there was no-one around, he ducked into the alley and continued on to the gym.

A wail of sirens approached. Vince sped up, trying to remain non-chalant. Doubts began to assail him. He wasn't a criminal. How on earth was he going to sell this stuff? He'd need a 'fence', but didn't even know where to find one. He supposed he could take the jewels to a pawnbroker on the other side of town, but what if there was a network, and they knew where he'd got them from? God, he'd made a big mistake.

He used his card to swipe into the gym and climbed the staircase at the back. In the change rooms, he found himself alone and quickly emptied his pockets into a random locker. He pushed the door half-closed and, further down the bench, chose another locker to stow his backpack. Much relieved, he changed into his gym gear and set off in good spirits for his workout.

At the gym, Fergus, the off-duty fireman, found the jewels in the locker when he came back from his weights session. He'd left his clothes on a bench and caught a glint of metal from a nearby locker. Curious, he opened the door and found the necklace, watch, and the small wooden box. He considered handing the stuff in at the office but didn't trust the casual receptionist. He'd rather take the whole lot to the cops. He packed his gear and tucked the abandoned necklace and watch in a zip pocket of his duffel.

The wooden box intrigued him. It should open, but he couldn't figure out how. He held it, absently fingering the bumps of brass.

Fergus had left his car parked around the corner from the gym, opposite the pawnbroker. Police cars had gathered but Fergus was the only one to notice smoke coming from an air-conditioning unit on the second floor of the building opposite.

"Oy!" he yelled, pointing up to the building. A policeman grabbed his radio. Fergus dashed across the street and began to climb the fire escape. Reaching the second floor, he realised he still had the wooden box in his hand. He stowed it on the iron landing near his head before banging on the window beside the air-conditioner.

A head of long blonde hair came into view and Fergus gestured wildly to the air conditioner, which was billowing smoke.

"Switch off the power!" he yelled.

The girl disappeared. She came back within moments and opened the window. She seemed to be around twenty years old and was the most beautiful creature Fergus had ever seen.

"Is there anybody else inside?"

She shook her head. Her eyes were as blue as a tropical ocean and wide with alarm.

Fergus said, "Come on out by the window. The fire engine's on its way."

He helped her climb through the window and down the stairs to the street. Together they stood and watched as the fire crew arrived and unravelled the hoses. Fergus noticed the girl was shaking and, after some mental debate, he wrapped an arm around her shoulders to make her feel better.

Elliot heard the sirens from the street but ignored them. There were always sirens in this area. He'd pressed his suit and tried it on and was looking at himself in the mirror, turning this way and that to make sure it was good enough. He jumped when he heard a banging at the door. Jimmie the Jack Russell barked joyously as Elliot went to open it.

"Bernard. What are you doing here?" Elliot was completely stumped. Bernard was a real estate agent they'd met during the week when they'd inspected a lovely cottage near the school where Olivia worked. They'd even met the old lady selling the place, but it had been out of their price-range. Elliot had given Bernard his card, expecting the usual kind of phone calls when similar properties came up for sale. He certainly hadn't expected a home visit.

Bernard was also wearing a suit and his face was red and sweaty. "Mate, I've rushed over here because the old duck's decided she wants to sell you her house. 'That nice young couple who came on Wednesday,' she said. 'I like the thought of them living here.'"

"Well, I'm sorry, Bernard. We'd love to buy the place, but we simply can't afford it. Our budget's more in the five hundred thousand dollar range. And that's stretching it. Wasn't she asking five eighty?"

Bernard grabbed both his arms and shook. "That's what I'm trying to tell you. She wants you to buy it. If five hundred's what you can pay, that's the price she'll take. It's mad! I shouldn't allow it. My boss would *kill* me if he found out. So, your loan's sorted?"

"Not quite." Elliot stood stock still. Even if he hadn't just spent twenty thousand dollars on the ring, he would not have been able to raise enough for a five per cent deposit. Twenty thousand dollars was all he'd had. But the ring was supposedly worth twenty-five thousand, the equivalent of five per cent on a five hundred thousand dollar loan. Could he conceivably use the ring as a surety? "I'll go to the bank right now."

"Call me." Bernard disappeared down the stairs and Elliot shut the door. He went to put on his shoes and socks.

Elliot looked himself up and down. He was certainly dressed for an approach to the bank manager. He strode into the kitchen, eyes trained on the table, ready to grab the ring and the envelope of papers and leave. There was the white rectangle of envelope, but where was the ring? Elliot's eyes darted this way and that. He'd left it near the fruit bowl, he was sure of it!

Just then a spray of water shot in through the window.

"Hey!" Elliot shouted in surprise. The water stopped and he stuck his head out to see what was going on. A fire engine was parked behind his building with the hose trained on the apartment below.

As Elliot moved to draw his head back inside the window, he spotted the ring box on the fire escape landing.

"Oh my God." He couldn't believe he'd nearly lost it. How the hell had it fallen out the window? Jimmie. Jimmie must have knocked it out. Elliot reached out the window and grabbed the box, brought it in carefully and opened it. The ring was still there. Phew!

He shoved it deep in his pocket, picked up the papers and his wallet and keys, closed the kitchen window and headed out.

Elliot waited nervously while the ring was valued by a local jeweller. Boris the bank manager had been sympathetic and was willing to use the gem as security on a no-deposit loan but had insisted on an independent valuation. Boris came back into the room, beaming.

"All good," he said. "If fact, the jeweller would even have put it a few thousand dollars higher. Now, we've got a bit of paperwork to do, if you'll just bear with me."

An hour later, Elliot walked homewards with a bounce in his step. First he'd ring the real estate agent and then Olivia. He couldn't wait to tell her the good news.

On his way back to his building he spotted the damage to the pawnbroker and stopped to express his sympathy. What a shocking event! Perhaps his good news would cheer the poor fellow up.

"I must thank you for this wonderful ring," he said. "It's helped me and my fiancé secure the most wonderful little house." Elliot pulled the ring box out of his pocket and opened it to admire the ring once more. He turned it so the pawnbroker could see it. It really was the most magnificent solitaire.

The pawnbroker knew with a glance that the ring Elliot held was genuine, a real diamond on a pure gold ring. In fact, it looked just like the one he'd kept in the back office for future transactions. How had this come about?

"Well done." He almost choked on the words before staggering back through his broken shop to the back room. He lifted paperwork, throwing it here and there in a frenzy, but to no avail. He could not find the ring. The ring was gone.

The pawnbroker slumped into his office chair. It was clear to him that Elliot hadn't stolen the ring. The man was an innocent. The pawnbroker thought and thought, but he just couldn't figure out what had happened.

Wouldn't you be surprised if he could?

Author's note: with thanks to two great stories, "The Necklace"
by Guy de Maupassant, and "Who's Got the Apple?" by Jan Loof.

True love is hard to find.

Sirens
by Gary Cahill

THE STROLL FROM sidewalk to shoreline was longer than ever, formidable on a given day, crossing the rare beach in Jersey getting wider every year, erosion from the north dumping more white powder to the south and pushing water's edge further into the Atlantic. But his trek was languorous, lilting, a relief after what he'd left by the street, in the motel shadows.

He'd been sprayed back on the pavement—*must have been the beer, right?*, nothing more—warm, salty, like the water here in dead summer, but tinged with a whiff of metal, like chewing a penny, got the nose twitching. It showed black on him in the waxing autumn moon, its light a narrowing pathway back across the breakers and the rollers and the swells and up to the border of the night blue sky. Clearly inviting; still had time to freshen up for later; wise to take a cleansing roll in the surf.

He'd developed an overly untidy personal history along the eastern seaboard, from south of the Mason-Dixon up through New England. Myrtle Beach, Virginia Beach, Rehoboth off the bay in Delaware, the quaintly Victorian Cape May, up to Crane in Cape Ann and Orleans in Cape Cod, all had served his purpose until the women's failings, over and over again, dashed his needs ashore and left wreckage in his wake. Every last, damned one; flashing potential as a partner for paradise. Every one, fallen. Not a single exalted angel among them.

And so he had prowled on, leaving no hint, no trace, avoiding any tell-tale pattern or behavioral arc. There was no flippantly discarded Jersey Transit ticket stub, no crumpled doughnut wrapper, nothing holding evidence of his touch or essence; no way a voodoo-fied black magic trifecta of a careless clue, a desperate coin flip and a lucky guess might lead some investigative brainiac to a crackling a-*ha* flash of genius and dropping a dozen cops and a dozen gun barrels in his face, leaning in above the morning newspaper, the dry wheat toast, and the eggs, over easy. What a sad gray day that would be.

He waited for a long while, the onshore breeze drying his clothes, pushing back his hair, holding his tears right where they shone by moonlight on lashes, and eyelids, and cheeks. Huh, he thought; no reason to cry. He was at ease with the natural elements here, alone and confident, and in no hurry to go anywhere. He had a date to-night.

They'd met over breakfast at one of the few places still open this far into October, she in no rush to leave town, lingering to help clean up and shut down a friend's twenty-room summer place until it would reopen for the season by Mother's Day, latest. Not at all beach-bleached with only lightly streaked dark hair pulled into a tail, athletic without being a kick boxer, skin with an outdoor glow in place of the usual baseball-glove-to-stressed-teak-wood patina most females sported as their complexion down the shore. Not a sun bunny, as in, "I'm workin' most days when I'm here, and I don't want to fry on the others." She laughed easily, conversed comfortably, welcomed getting together if they could work it out.

And he felt sure they could work it out after watching her routine, very closely, for three days, maybe more, noting her lunch breaks, her shopping trips, her loping sunset gambols through the small dunes and past the high tide line onto the water-packed sand, better footing for her oceanfront wanders in the starlit dark. He was an old hand at this, having studied and waited for the many others, and been frustrated, extremely, every time. This had to be, *would be,* the one, she'd be along soon enough, and until then he would contemplate the mystic, necromantic call of her name; Micki, diminutive of the French and Hebrew for "who resembles God."

Angling from the dark between the street and rustling reeds and grass on the dunes, she walked toward him through the wind-stirred swirl, beach ghosts they called them, like fingers running across the skin of the shore. Ambling, almost floating, quickly so near, feet obscured by the blowing sand, blue jeans, leather vest over a soft denim blouse, open to her belly. Her head down, she watched her own hands work the last few snaps on her shirt, slide it to the sides of each breast. He saw her creamy and night light golden, imagined a soft smile on her face, certain it was there, as she let her eyes drift down to his waist and lower. He felt the brush-kisses lighting back and forth along his jaw, butterflies and moths in the losing light flitting across his cry-dampened cheeks, whispering into his lips; the tingle, the aroma, like a sea breeze. Her jeans were off and gone, gorgeous, revealing even more cream and gold, Elysian milk and honey, and his jeans must have come off too because he had her with both hands up under her bottom and straddling him. He was hard and erect, she insistent and receptive; and together a reactive natural element on this, his beautiful beach, on his beautiful night. He rocked straight and steady, in rhythmic repeat, and his head rolled back as hers came down to him, face tucked in under his chin, and as they stayed together it was all warm, all wet, all over, and he turned to face the moon with her on him.

He was nearing the end, and drove quicker, and bucked once, and again, and again, and began to calm. His shoulders had been hunched up to his ears, and he relaxed and lowered her to the sand. His mind was loosed, he felt like he was breathing out without breathing in, about to let go of an old life to make room for another.

He knew she still had the soft smile as she retrieved her jeans, had them on in a flash, must be bell bottoms, he thought, to get them over shoes or sandals that easily, and she tossed the pony tail at him as she walked back the way she'd come, into the dark but toward the banging lights and hell-raising racket of the police and emergency medical vehicles that had gathered on the street. He'd been right up there earlier in the evening. He couldn't imagine what had gone wrong. Better go see what's doing. And reaching down to get dressed realized his jeans were on him, zipped and buckled, when'd that happen?

Pushing his way up and over the hilly soft, dry sand toward the street, moving in on a crafted set piece conjuring the so many times before, he felt it—slick, viscid, along the inside of his right thigh—took a look and saw the dark staining down the pant leg, leeching from the inside out, smelling sweet, astringent, ammoniated, rich, of sex. He yanked his pullover way down and hoped the seaside air would waft the odor away, keep the cops and crowd from noticing.

They were all busying themselves at a crime scene, note taking, photographing, hadn't gotten to stretching the yellow tape yet, right where he'd argued with Micki before they'd made up and hooked up on the beach. Yelling at him, she'd spit out the usual bile, he'd heard this same-old before, so many times, "... what do you *mean* you're following me ... yes I don't mind talking and hanging out but I barely know your name much less ... you need me to *complete* you *how*? ... *this* is so different for you from *how many others*? ... *what are you doing*?"

What he was doing was spinning on his toes, a beer bottle in each hand, figured they'd share a drink before they put themselves together now that destiny had taken its course, but the suds were flying everywhere, all over them, and he was livid, this whole scene, not again, not this time, and winged them at the stone bench and over-stuffed trash barrel and sandy sidewalk where they cracked open, and the shards, glowing embers in the street light, tinkled like high emerald chimes, and he breathed in, and in, just drew air in, and forgot who and where he was, God, just stop yelling, and yelling, on this quiet seaside evening.

He'd walked away, and her squalling had faded. Or had hard quick silence come first? He'd lingered at the shoreline, and she'd come to him. Glorious. And somebody must have nailed her good on the way back up the beach; had some maniac been watching them? Hunting?

As two cops and two ambulance guys stepped back from Micki on the ground, beer and blood and other stuff drooling down either side of her, half a bottle, a tool with a green neck and jagged teeth, jabbed and jutting out of where it'd opened her, he wondered why he wasn't crying, wailing, shuddering to the ground, soaked in sadness, shoulders heaving and pulling his forehead to the concrete walk, oh my lost love. And then he found clarity and figured why.

He was sated, for now. Transiently self-satisfied, because he'd done it, hadn't he? Laid her out and shut her the fuck up when her irrational rejection of their eternal pairing brought back that old feeling all the others had engendered, the need to cut bait and move on.

And do move on, right now.

Get to your room, before uniforms and plainclothes detect more than just a passing interest in this mess. Shake your head, keep going, no sir, didn't notice or see or hear anything, and he'd be long gone before anyone in town recalled the round-faced, Beatle-cut, shambling, starchily awkward breakfast companion—not at all how he'd look or dress by tomorrow afternoon anyway, when he got off the bus in Philly, where he now newly planned to keep searching.

These saltwater environs were not working out, much as he loved them and that open water wading. He longed to join the origin, the sea, the crux of life, where it all began, as part of a loving tandem. But things might get too tight along the coast, and so better to move west, use the rivers, the Delaware, even the Hudson up past the city was majestic north of the GW Bridge, cleaner than it's been in decades ... or the inland waterway. The Intracoastal. It ran from New England to Florida, always landfall on either side, a lot of it fresh river but plenty of it brackish and wild, it was like hiking a water trail, secluded, whole stretches nearly barren. But could those places serve and brim him over, finish it? He didn't think so. He'd always been a seashore guy.

Back to the motel, right across the street from the slop on the sidewalk, bottles of red and white in the fridge, the pizza guy over on the bay side open 'til at least one in the morning. He locked the door, poured some chardonnay into a glass, more like a jelly jar, and realized she was the closest he'd ever come to a sharer, a partner in the last journey, the vision and the action at the water's edge now embedding in memory. They should have traveled together, one step and another and into dark water. The power of connection, the huge blue arc circuitry, dwarfed his thoughts, and what sense he had left. He was too close to pull up and shove off, too close to let her go. The beach Micki was alive, unlike whatever was on the sidewalk.

He could not have killed this one. He couldn't have. It was nuts to think he did. She'd been with him, after their fight, he'd seen and touched, smelled the blue jeans, tasted the blue denim, his fingers tangled in her hair tie, the flesh in the moonlight, the sex, the longing, her, in and out, liquid, sticky, heavy, temporal, physical and real as blown sand roughing your skin, their lovers' cooled soothing sweat like the whipped mist from offshore, and the last flash of her hands like wind over waves, a breezy ruffling in your hair, drying your eyes.

His mind had nearly refreshed, struggled to reboot, right below his motel window, on the concrete, where she'd left him the first time. But a gaining madness and his starving need called it certainly only a body down there. Not the rest of her, the immortal coil of her.

Down by the water, after he'd dropped her on the walk, *she'd* found *him*. Something more remained, bigger than life, and sought him out. Beckoned.

And the idea he was crazy showed itself, took a peek in the mirror to give him a glimpse, at least half-glimmered in his head.

He wouldn't dwell on any of it; the madness, the need. This was complicated. Transcendental.

He wasn't drunk. He wanted to be, and finished off the bottle of white, set sail from the moorings, drifted and floated a little more, saved the red for the food.

Wait. Where were her shoes?

Not on her, not near her, the deep sky blue canvas deck shoes with the royal blue stitching, the white trim and soles. He hadn't swung her around by the ears, drop kicked her, leg swept her, dislodged them. He'd put her down, and she'd stayed down, and they hadn't come flying off; didn't mean they were there. On the sand he hadn't seen them, either; maybe she'd slipped through the fingers of the beach ghosts without them, must have left them on land to come to the waterline, and you leave your shoes behind when you know you're going to take the plunge. Why hadn't he pulled her in? She was committed, ready, why hadn't he taken her, ended it?

He had been distracted; enchanted. Enraptured. Then she'd slipped away, why had she left him, gone back? To finish up what he'd started, was that it? To go die on the broken glass?

Or was it something else, bigger than all this, some mythical marshaled tragedy, luring him, back to the horror, to make him *her* partner on some eternal road? Who was fishing now? Who was hooked? Where were her shoes?

The devil is in the details. Lurking.

And behind his eyes he took off, one way out of town, never looked back, and his crazy blew way past half-glimmering.

The cops were prepping to take the body away, and soon enough they'd be canvassing any building with lights on, witness hunting, interviewing, sniffing around. Nothing to tie him to anything right now. He breathed, and plucked from the aery ether one last semi-sane moment, and opened the merlot, knocked a little down. Nice.

His window view opened up to the sky, and the rising moon etched a path to the south and east, the shimmering light across the water now off to the right, two scallop boats straight ahead a few miles off, steady red lights tracing their tracks to the beds. The ambulance, body in the back, departed, the mournful sound whining and dropping off while three guys from the clean-up crew decontaminated, denatured and flushed away what was left of the corporeal Micki.

His mind and eyes hooded from the wine, at a loss once again, he pulled open the door and stepped out onto the common balcony walk to clear his head and get a better look out to sea. The scallopers' lights were flickering now, so rhythmically, in and out of view somehow, even on calm, easy seas, even with the tide receding, and no boat traffic between them and the shore. Something hiding, then showing. A cloak. A secret. Concealed. Revealed. What was that?

He glanced down and linked eyes with a detective, the cop recognizing him from the earlier street scene, no doubt. And now one and another shield turned toward the motel and scuffed over.

The inside of his skull began to burn. He slammed his eyes closed, open, closed, and then open to something new as he yanked back to face the sky, and reveled in the impossible wonder of terns and gulls, sea birds you never see flying at night, in measured meter, driving toward the beach, stroke, stroke, a long, lush tempo carrying them, the boats' mast lights still blinking, a soft pulsing beat of some unknown heart. See 'em, don't. See' em, don't. The heat in his head spoke in a buzz, a constant static sound, then hard and sharp, ringing. He looked over the railing, saw the two cops come out of the office and head toward the elevator, not many guests staying here, they'll be along any minute—it cannot end like this. Now that he'd seen the way.

He spun toward his door but around the corner the elevator rang and opened, shit, shit, shit, no, no, no, then he smelled spinach, garlic and ricotta in the big flat box and he told the pizza guy, "Sorry I made you come over so late, sorry, sorry, I gotta go, I gotta leave, look, here's twenty, thirty, and two more, keep it, and look, take this," handing over the bottle of red, "make a party of it, give it away, find somebody, but I just ... I gotta go." And after, "Well, OK, you bet, thanks a lot," the pizza guy took the only running elevator car back down, holding off the two badges a little longer.

Go.

He turned and ran along the walkway, down the outdoor stairs toward the pool, looped behind the motel, sensed even more birds improbably winging through the dark toward the beach, with the wind picking up and snaking through ropes on flagpoles, serrated plastic leaves on fake plastic palm trees faux planted on pre-fab plastic decks, upper floor railings of shuttered summer houses and hotels, whistling down corridors and through phone and cable wires and power lines.

And all of it began to sing, first a choir, then with one voice, not the shrieking you hear peeling off gale-battered fishing boats when sailors' widows hear the cries of their dead, but a thick rich blend, swimmingly decadent, riding a rail into his head and enveloping the white noise inside him with sublimity and allure. A song apart. The birds were hearing it, flying to find it, drawn to the beach. He needed to see.

Everything he'd wanted, so very near. He hurried along the side of the building, looked carefully around the corner for the cops, got down low, and dodged their streetlight silhouettes one block up at the front of the motel, and jogged onto the sand, through the dunes Micki had navigated.

And as more terns and gulls and sanderlings milled about in fervent reverence, his body and mind turned to see, to witness in awe and welcome discovery, her great wings, over the water, undulating in erotic sync with her breathing, up and down, obscuring and revealing the presence of the scallopers so far offshore, pushing air into the music in the wind and the wires, calling, to the wayward. And, more than anything, he wanted to, so he dashed ahead and got salty and wet and ocean warm once more. Religious converts say when the damaged see the light, God comes into you through the wound. Maybe sometimes God comes out of the wound, and sings a song.

He slogged through and past the surf, his face a giant split-cheeked grin, ascending to her face pale and golden like the moon, the great and mighty wings frilled and ephemeral like clouds in a nighttime sky, welcoming, and yes, now surely beckoning, in a gilded streak across the white caps, and when his foot caught he stumbled under and scuttled out along the bottom and tried to rise as the sea floor deepened and dropped off sharply beyond the second sandbar. When he lost his breath his body reacted and pulled for the surface, but he was no swimmer.

Struggling to stay atop, gasping, trying to time the rollers, the wind knocked over a climbing rogue wave and it broke right into his gaping face and down his throat to fill stomach and lungs, and with his body fighting to survive his insanity, so briefly lucid and practical at the end of the line, he thought, I won't be on that bus to Philly, as he slipped behind the sandbar and began to lose his arms and legs.

And facing the surface, sight fading through the last seconds, with lustre and lunar backlight, up and out of his reach ... her wings, passing over and back above him, like waves and swells, ebb and flow. Now the song was over, that high-pitched buzzing back again; not harsh, not a warning, more a lament, like he'd heard on the beach when other sirens had come for her. And if the sea or something in it didn't lay claim to what was left, those sirens would come for him.

Hanging out a couple hundred yards north, a happy couple has it all, all they need, with surf and sky. They'd be out here, or anywhere land ends, anytime they could; their butts on the sand, backs to the bulkhead that holds storm surges off the streets, eyes to the stars, ears to the breakers' rumble and hiss, the scent of a crisp autumn ocean. And while a few under-achieving sea birds still picked at crab carcasses to fill their gull bellies after another off-season day of humans not leaving enough French fries behind, these two were wolfing down a manna-from-heaven spinach, garlic, and ricotta pie and a bottle of not bad merlot, all on the arm, courtesy of some customer too busy to enjoy himself, at least according to the pizza guy who offered and left it. "Thank you sir, and a very Happy Halloween," or whatever holiday comes next, and he was gone.

"Wow," through the food, in a fake-gruff shuck-jiving blues man voice, "yeah, dinner *and* baby's got a new pair of shoes."

"I know," she said to him, thrilled, "they're beautiful, what a ritzy blue, raised stitching, slip-on ... perfect. He went by, that man before, kinda grubby, homeless or something, you think he dropped them?"

"What would that guy ever have them for," he said, "why would he even pick 'em up? Maybe it was that girl dropped 'em, remember? I didn't get a good look. Hanging around down the way there, jogging or something with the ponytail waving? But she'd have come looking for these booties for sure. They're just the thing for down here, the shore. She wouldn't leave 'em."

Hugging his arm, she corrected him. "These *beauties*. Yeah," she said, "unless she was heading to the water."

They heard the sirens, not too far off. They were used to them from years in the city, and tuned them out.

They leaned back, each with a good pull off the merlot, let their faces and hair catch that ruffling night wind and watched the light play, do funny things on the waves, and lived well, the way you can in the magic dark at the beach, beloveds' toes just touching the cool deep, right at the edge, down their beloved Jersey shore.

It's magical when kids help out around the house.

House Cleaning
by Ian Creasey

THERE WAS A dead mouse in Mum's bedroom.

Simon gently pushed the door open and crept in. He smelled his mother's perfume, almost overwhelmed by the odour of sweat and cigarettes and sour alcohol. A ray of morning sunlight shone through the curtains like a spotlight, illuminating a snoring shape under the covers. Simon was always surprised by how small Matt looked when he wasn't shouting. His feet didn't even reach the end of the bed, but fell short by—well, a foot.

Navigating the minefield of socks and cigarette papers and empty glasses, Simon stole round the bed to the other side. The cat always presented her gifts to Mum. This side of the bed lay in shadow and Simon had to peer hard at the carpet, but there was less debris here, and he soon spotted the mouse.

Simon put on the yellow rubber gloves he had brought. They were too big for him, and he had to splay his fingers to pull them on. The left glove snagged, then gave with a *pop*. Simon froze, his heart jack-hammering. Matt mustn't wake up. If he did, he would yell at Simon for creeping round the bedroom, then he'd shout for Mum to find his clothes and make his breakfast and bring him the paper and clear up the room because it was a damned mess. Normally Matt slept in 'til about eleven or twelve, and the quiet morning hours were the best part of the day.

He should have put the gloves on in the hall. Ninety per cent of magic—of anything—is preparation.

The snores continued their slow rhythm. Relieved, Simon scooped up the broken scrap of fur and needle-thin bones. He carefully retraced his steps, walking silently as Squeak the mouse-killer. When he reached the safety of the door, he turned towards Matt's sleeping body and stuck out his tongue. It was all Matt's fault. If he hadn't left the door ajar when he finally went to bed, the cat's night-time harvest wouldn't have given Mum such a fright when she woke up.

Simon closed the bedroom door behind him as he left, shutting in the snores and Matt, leaving the rest of the house free—for the next couple of hours.

He went out by the front door, so that Mum wouldn't have to see the dead mouse again. A warm breeze caressed his skin: summer was coming. Simon dropped the mouse in the outside bin and covered it with yesterday's tea-bags. The bin's aroma attracted a fly, and Simon put the lid back on, trapping it inside.

The sun shone over the tall hedges that surrounded the garden. In its light the roses glowed yellow and orange and red, saturated with colour. The grass needed cutting. Out by the pool a long-haired tortoise-shell cat rested on a sun-lounger. Simon envied Squeak's easy life, her ability to walk away at will and come back when she liked.

He walked through the back door into the kitchen, where Mum sat eating grapefruit. She didn't even put any sugar on. He rinsed the gloves under the tap, then left them dangling over the edge of the sink to dry.

His mother got up and held out her hands. She shifted slightly as if about to hug him, and he braced himself. But instead a coin appeared in her palm. Misdirection! He hadn't seen the move—he wasn't good enough yet.

A pound coin was the going rate for disposing of a dead mouse. Simon wished it had been a rat, not a mouse. He found it harder to manipulate the big two-pound coins, but last winter's slug problem had helped him master fifty-pence pieces, which were nearly as large.

Simon accepted the coin with his right hand, then ostentatiously transferred it to his left. He opened his right hand to show that it no longer held the coin. After a dramatic pause—which he timed as an imaginary drum roll—he opened his left, which was empty too. All the while he watched his mother's reactions, knowing she knew where the coin had gone.

Her eyes widened in pretend amazement, and he knew that this time he had passed. He put his hands in his pockets and deposited the coin, which he had clasped between his fingers so that it protruded unseen behind his left hand.

"How do you do that?" he asked. "Misdirect without even moving."

She raised her eyebrows.

He knew the answer anyway. "Practice."

"And?"

"Confidence."

"Body language is like any other language—you can lie with it. Now, eat your breakfast."

She always said that. Simon got himself a bowl of corn flakes and said, "Why don't you ever eat breakfast?"

"I've had half a grapefruit—the other half's in the fridge if you want it."

"I mean real food," he said. Grapefruit was more punishment than food.

She laughed. "If I ate too much I'd get fat, wouldn't I? But you're a growing lad—you need a proper breakfast."

"I suppose if you got too fat, you wouldn't be able to get into your outfit," he said.

Mum had been a magician's assistant once, with a spangly red costume that looked good under spotlights. Every few months she'd wait until Matt wasn't around, then get it out and put it on again. It looked a lot sadder now—many of the sequins had fallen off, and the rest were dulled, but Simon had seen pictures of his mother in her touring days. She looked like a tiny fairy that had stepped off the top of a Christmas tree. All the best magician's assistants were small, because that helped with the illusions. She was even smaller than Matt. Simon's height stood between the two.

After breakfast, Simon went into the living room to watch the morning cartoons, but the smell put him off. How many cigarettes and joints and cigars had been smoked last night? The ashtrays overflowed with butts and roaches. The floor was full of pizza boxes and foil trays with scummy residues—curry rather than Chinese, judging by the whiff. A sharp stink of alcohol came from the dozens of empty glasses and bottles and lager cans, and sprinklings of cigarette ash surrounded the cans used as supplementary ashtrays. The carpet felt sticky under his trainers. Playing cards lay scattered under the coffee table, many of them soaked with lager and stained red by the colouring in the spicy chicken.

It wouldn't take an archaeologist to figure that Matt and his mates had been playing poker last night, even if Simon hadn't heard them arguing over whether five of a kind beat a straight flush. They shouldn't play with two decks if they couldn't agree the rules, he thought, but then there were lots of things Matt shouldn't do.

He was surprised Mum hadn't cleared up yet, but she probably thought there was plenty of time before Matt woke up. She'd opened a window, which so far hadn't had much effect. The fug lay heavy upon the room, coiling about the furniture like dry ice shrouding a stage. It would take all day to dissipate, and in the evening it would regenerate again.

Simon walked back into the kitchen, which had a much nicer smell of peppermint tea and fresh air through the back door. Mum looked tired, he noticed.

"I got rid of the mouse. Why don't you go back to bed for a bit?" He paused. "I'll clear up down here."

His mother shook her head. "I'm all right. You go outside and play."

"Maybe later," said Simon. The cloudless sky promised fine weather all day. "I guess I need to put in some practice, though. Can I use the garage?"

She nodded, and touched his arm as he passed her on the way out.

Matt occasionally complained about the junk in the garage, but since he'd lost his licence Mum did the driving, and she always just left the car in the drive. The garage held all sorts of stuff. Simon's old toys and teddy bears rested here, and when things were really bad in the house he used to come and sit in the boxes, hugging Big Koala, heedless of the cracked yellow patches where the fur had long since fallen off. Some ugly furniture—wardrobes, cabinets, a table—had been exiled to the garage when Mum redid the whole house a couple of years ago. And, right at the back, there was the equipment from Mum's magic days.

Simon had long since transferred the portable items to his own room. He had the hoops, he had the handcuffs, he had the hats and the cards and the multi-coloured scarves. The garage held only the bigger apparatus, such as the long trolley, the trunk for escape tricks, and the Severed Lady kit. Simon had wondered how they managed with it all on tour, until Mum said that they didn't do every illusion in every show. The first tricks would be simple—hoops and cards and the like—and the show would build to one big illusion at the end.

"We didn't have any of this bigger stuff early on—we had to work our way up to that. The escape trunk was first, and we had to buy a van to put it in. Before that we just had an old Ford Escort with all the kit on the back seat, Gareth's suit and my red outfit hanging up in the windows to stop them creasing. We'd sit in the front in our T-shirts, driving to the next show, me with the map on my knee...."

Whenever she spoke of the touring days, his mother always had a wistful smile. She loved travelling, loved being in show-business. But it had all ended one night in Blackpool, while she was being sawn in half.

The trick relied on her squeezing into a narrow compartment in the apparatus, hidden from the audience by cunning angles and shadows blending with the black lining of the innards. That night she found invaders in the secret compartment: spiders crawling over her flesh, moths fluttering in her face and hair. And she heard a buzzing.... She couldn't move in the narrow prison. She couldn't scream, or Gareth would be angry with her for spoiling the trick. She could hardly breathe for fear of swallowing something. She could only endure the aeons of Gareth's patter.

She emerged to the usual applause, and tried to stand without trembling or being sick. Seeing her pallor, Gareth signalled for the curtain. He helped her back to the dressing room—

—Where his girlfriend smiled sweetly and said, "Good show?"

Mum collapsed on a chair, while Gareth opened the window and got her a glass of water, fussing about until she said she felt better. Then he and Sylvia went down to the bar.

She knew Sylvia must have been behind it. Gareth's girlfriend had always hated her, and she knew Mum was squeamish. She was sick of Gareth's touring, his long absences with Mum. Sylvia wanted him to settle down and stay at home with her.

The sabotage was perfect. No matter how often Mum checked the apparatus and scoured it beforehand, she couldn't bring herself to climb inside. They didn't have a closing spectacular for the show. Gareth suggested that he drive home and pick up one of the other kits, but Mum didn't want him to go—she thought Sylvia wouldn't let him come back.

"She put those bugs in the box, you know. She hates me. She hates the show."

Gareth shook his head. "Sylvia wouldn't do anything like that. One moth probably got in accidentally, and you imagined there were more. I don't blame you, it must have been horrible—"

"It *was* horrible! That's why Sylvia did it! You know she wants you to stop touring, so she's trying to kill the show. What will she do next?"

"Nothing," Gareth soothed. Yet he wouldn't look her in the eye.

"She's got to you, hasn't she? What has she said?"

"I was going to wait till the end of the run to tell you.... But Sylvia's right. I can't keep travelling the length of the country to these flea-pit venues, not when the money's so bad. Not when we're starting a family—"

Mum screamed. The scream had been building up since the spiders, and it came out loud enough to shake spotlights off the gantry.

Gareth stepped back. "I know it's a shock. We'll do the final shows, and I'll pay you for a month afterward—"

"What with? What are you and Sylvia going to do when you're not *making babies?*"

"I'm going to manage that place in Margate. It's a lot more secure booking the acts than being one of them."

"Well, go to bloody Margate and rot, then! Fester in that shit-hole for the rest of your life and see if I care. You won't be needing the kit, so I'll have that off you. I'll finish the run myself. Pay me for a month, will you? No need, I'll carry on and play every theatre in the country—*except for Margate.*"

That was one of the few times Mum ever stood up for herself. And it didn't work out. She knew all the tricks, but couldn't carry the show. "Magic is a man's world," she told Simon. "A woman's place is to fetch and carry and be sawn in half. The audiences heckled me. They wouldn't accept a woman running the act."

But Simon knew it wasn't just that. Mum couldn't project authority: she wasn't assertive at all. She was like those girls at school who panicked over their maths homework and blushed whenever a boy looked at them.

Simon wasn't like that. He knew the importance of showmanship. He knew it was vital to have a commanding presence, to master the audience, to dominate them.

Still, whenever he looked inside the big apparatus, he couldn't help checking for moths.

The garage had no windows. Simon liked that. It gave the space the enclosed feel of a theatre, and he could pretend that the fluorescent strips were stage lights. He'd asked Mum to get them wired up for remote control. When he was ready to perform to the public—well, to friends at school—he would bring them here. Magic needs the right setting. When the audience sits in the dark, watching the spotlit performer, that's half the atmosphere already.

He wondered which of the big tricks to practise. Some needed an assistant, so he couldn't do those properly, but he could still rehearse the moves.

But first, preparation. And half of preparation is maintenance. Simon oiled all the hinges and sliders in every piece of equipment. Then he got a rag and wiped down the surfaces, cleaning off the dust and checking for moisture damage. Before his performance, he'd have to get furniture polish and buff the apparatus to a deep gleaming shine. No-one respects a magician with mildewed kit and a dirty wand. He needed a costume, too—he could rely on Mum for that.

The sound of voices interrupted his thoughts. Tension wafted out of the back door and polluted the morning. Simon could hear it from inside the garage. Even when the words were muffled, he could always hear the tone of it, the rhythm of it, the long harangue punctuated by protests, or worse, by silence. What was it this time? Simon checked his watch: it was only a quarter past ten. Matt was up earlier than usual, and Mum probably didn't have the house ready.

If it wasn't one thing, it was another.

Heels clattered on the concrete, and Simon heard the car door opening. Were they both going out, or—?

Matt's voice was loud outside the garage. "Get the money from Frankie first. Then go to Joe's: he'll have it ready for you. Don't let him pull one of his last-minute price hikes—we agreed on five. He's a devious bastard, but if he mucks you about, tell him it's off."

Mum said something from inside the car.

"Whatever. Just don't spend it on bloody useless tat this time. We're practically out of beer."

The engine started, and the car purred down the drive. He heard his mother get out to open the gate. Then she drove into the street and away.

Simon waited. There was no sound outside. Oh, he heard a crow on the roof and an ice-cream van two streets away, but nothing useful. Matt's trainers were much quieter than Mum's heels. Simon couldn't pick out what Matt was doing, and he was left with the same old guessing game. Should he dare the back door, or go round to the front? Or should he remain here where it was safe?

It would be easiest to stay in the garage, but Simon didn't want to cede the whole house to Matt. It was his house too. Besides, he needed the bathroom.

He opened the garage door, looked around, and saw Matt walking down the lawn to the pool. In one hand he held a plastic ring dangling three cans; the other hand dropped a Twix wrapper. Matt left a mess wherever he went, like a slug oozing a trail of slime. He put the cans down by the poolside, dislodged the cat, and flopped onto the sun-lounger.

Simon had the house to himself. He raced inside, enjoying the freedom. It was even better than when Matt hadn't got up yet, because he didn't have to worry about making too much noise and waking him up.

The living room still smelled—it hadn't been cleaned yet. Simon knew it would be a long time before his mother returned. Matt's errands might sound simple but they always involved delays and complications. She'd probably phone in the afternoon, and Matt would shout as if it were her fault. So Simon dealt with the worst of the mess: he took all the bottles and foil trays and pizza boxes to the outside bin, and he put the glasses in the dishwasher. That was enough. Simon didn't mind cleaning up mice and slugs for Mum—he'd do it even if she didn't pay him—but he hated clearing up after Matt.

At first he ignored the cards under the table. If Matt wanted them, he could pick them up himself. But then Simon noticed that there were two decks of cards: one advertised whiskey, and the other had a blue checkerboard pattern. The promotional pack was Matt's, but the other.... Simon examined the cards, which were very slightly narrower at one end.

He scowled. This was his special deck. It made the old "pick a card, any card" trick easy—he rotated the pack before the punter returned his card, which was then easily found by its protruding edge. Another trick had the punter sorting the pack into black and red, which rarely took less than a minute; but by turning the reds opposite to the blacks before shuffling them back together, Simon could separate the colours in five seconds, blindfold.

Matt always jeered at his magic, saying he should be out playing with girls, not playing with cards. Well, Simon wouldn't be playing with these cards any more, not after they'd been covered with gunk from last night's take-away. Magic needs a slick deck—Matt had stolen this pack, and ruined it.

Simon ran upstairs to see if anything else had vanished. His room still contained his other equipment: the hats, the cuffs, the hoops and wands. But no doubt if Matt wanted any of this, he'd take it and break it, just like he ruined everything.

Through the bedroom window Simon could see Matt on the sun-lounger, surrounded by cans and cigarette butts. An empty can rattled on the tiles, as Squeak batted it with her paws. Matt was asleep. He'd stripped down to his shorts, his body an unhealthy-looking splodge on the lounger's white mattress. How was it possible for someone so small and wasted to have such a blobby belly? If Mum were here, she'd have to go out and slather sun-screen on the red face and hairy torso. But Simon took a secret pleasure in the thought of Matt waking up with sunburn, the more painful the better.

Of course, they'd all suffer for it. He knew how it would go, tonight as always. There had once been a time—he hardly remembered it—when Matt was kind to Mum and even friendly to Simon. But over the years the shouting had grown louder, the storms of rage breaking ever more often until they became the normal climate of the house.

Matt had been growing worse for years, and surely he would keep on doing so. New torments would arrive tomorrow, next month, next year, each more dreadful than the last... unless he was stopped. And as Mum would do nothing, it was up to Simon to stop him.

Again he stared at Matt, who was still asleep. Simon selected the necessary equipment, then left the house and walked down to the end of the garden, where the sun cast ephemeral jewels of light on the pool's breeze-ruffled water. Squeak slipped away through the hedge. Matt was asleep, his mouth open, a dribble of saliva smearing the chocolate stains at the corner of his bottom lip.

His left arm lay on the arm of the sun-lounger, almost begging to be cuffed. The right arm was harder, as it lay across his belly. Simon didn't want to touch Matt's flesh, but he had no choice. With delicate care, he picked up the slack limb and placed it on the sun-lounger's armrest. Quickly, he applied the other handcuff. With each set of cuffs he left one dangling and wrapped the other around both the armrest and Matt's thin pockmarked wrist. The sun-lounger's arms curved back into the metal frame, so the shackles couldn't slide off.

Matt muttered in his sleep. "Oh baby, yeah."

Reflexively, Simon stepped back, almost tripping over one of the discarded cans. But Matt didn't wake up.

Simon backed up further. He looked around and saw no-one. It took him a few seconds to steel himself, a few seconds in which a starling landed on the lawn and eyed him warily. It flew away when Simon ran down the garden and launched himself at the sun-lounger.

It slid across the tiles and fell into the pool with a huge, slurping splash. A few drops of backwash caught him and Simon ducked back, but then he stepped forward again to get a good look. The sun-lounger rested on its side at the bottom of the pool. Simon could only see Matt's legs, frantically kicking without breaking the surface. He walked round the pool for a better view of Matt's bulging eyes and panicky writhing. Matt frantically tugged at the restraining cuffs, but he didn't know the trick of undoing them.

"Not so scornful now, eh?" said Simon, smiling. It gave him an idea for a stunt: maybe he could escape from the bottom of the swimming pool as part of his first show. Mum would disapprove, but he didn't need to tell her in advance.

Simon contemplated the details, while watching Matt's contorted face suck in a final, fatal gasp of water. Matt's pale body twisted and kicked once, twitched for a few moments, then fell still. The pool's surface waves slumped into calm.

The garden sounded eerily quiet, as if with Matt gone the world was at peace. He'd left a faint smell of alcohol and cigarettes. Simon picked up the cigarette butts and put them into one of the empty cans, then carried all the cans to the bin. He went back for Matt's shirt and took it up to the laundry basket. All these tasks were necessary, but they were also just a way of putting off the next, most distasteful, job.

He removed his trainers, and stripped down to his underpants. Then he went back out to the pool. It took him longer to nerve himself for this task than it had for the initial shove. After a minute or so Simon dived into the pool and swam down to the sun-lounger. He unlocked one cuff and surged down, wanting to undo both on the same dive. But the left armrest lay on the bottom of the pool, and it took him long moments to release the cuff. He floated to the surface and gasped for breath. As he turned to swim to the side, he recoiled when he saw Matt's body drifting next to him. The swollen tongue, the agonised face—

Matt shouldn't have dished it out if he couldn't take it.

It was harder to drag the body out than he'd anticipated. In the end Simon got the garden hose and topped up the pool so that the body floated up to the level of the tiles. Then he pulled Matt out onto the side. The corpse's skin was wrinkly. Well, it was probably the longest bath he'd ever had.

As Simon already had the hose out, he used it as a rope to pull up the sun-lounger. Then he put the hose back in the shed and contemplated the final task—clearing away the vermin. If he just left the body by the pool, Mum would get a dreadful fright when she came back. No, it was Simon's job to dispose of it, just as he got rid of slugs and spiders and mice. He went into the garage and brought out the appropriate apparatus.

This time, Simon didn't bother checking the secret compartment for moths. He hoped there were spiders in there. He heaved Matt's body into the Severed Lady kit. Water dripped off the corpse and puddled on the black lining. It was hard to manoeuvre the body into the narrow compartment, and Simon had to shove and shove to get the beer-gut in. But at last Matt disappeared.

Simon wheeled the apparatus back to the garage and put it in a corner out of the way. He wiped down the surfaces with a dry cloth. Then he found a dust-sheet and draped it over the kit.

Back in the garden, the sun-lounger was already beginning to dry out. Now everything was clean and quiet. Simon smiled and went inside to wait for his mother.

If the going rate for disposing of dead mice was a pound, this had to be worth at least a fiver.

Sometimes, there's no plan at all. Only improvisation.

Murderous Lies
by Peter DiChellis

I REMEMBER EVERYTHING about that night: the truth, the terror, the luck, and the lies. Someday I want to forget.

As always, Larry's Tavern was dark and dank as a moldy cellar. A woman sitting at one end of the bar had hiccups. A leathery, trailer park grandma in a frizzy red sweater, she kept herself company with big gulps of bourbon and ginger ale. A stocky boomer guy slumped at the other end of the bar, wearing a gaudy blue golf shirt with a shiny brown sport coat. He burped and chuckled through a nasty grin. Six hours of cheap draft beer.

And I dawdled behind the bar, figuring how bad my tips would be if the night stayed like this. It didn't, and then one thing led to another.

At first, the bourbon and ginger woman's hiccups seemed like good news. When people at Larry's got hiccups, I got more tips. Because there are about a million dumb ways to try curing hiccups, but one cure works every time. And I knew it cold.

I stepped up to the bourbon and ginger woman. She swayed on her barstool, squinting to see me.

"Heek-hupb," she squeaked.

"Sounds like you got hiccups?"

"Heek-hupb."

"I can cure those right now. Here's what you do ..."

Her hiccups vanished in half a minute. She pealed a delighted drunken laugh and handed me a nice tip. Works every time.

It was a slow night, so I planned for the burping golf shirt guy to get hiccups too. I grabbed a bottle of crappy, mint-flavored schnapps and poured him a shot. This rotgut always got me two tips, one for the free drink and another when I cured the hiccups it caused. But that night, one shot of schnapps would change everything.

"On the house," I told golf shirt guy. He gave me a small tip. I knew I'd get another soon enough. Wouldn't take long.

He downed the shot. And that's when they walked in.

The tall one came straight to me and pointed a huge black revolver at my face. The short little rat-faced one stood to the side, bare hands in front of him, light hair drooping long and limp under a filthy baseball cap. They both looked dirty, jumpy, stupid, and stoned. Both were skinny as needles, with pasty skin as white as prison sandwich bread.

"The money," the tall one said. He waved the revolver back and forth.

Jumpy.

"Yours," I told him.

The bourbon and ginger woman had covered her eyes with her hands, head down. Golf shirt guy stared into his beer mug, eyes like harvest moons.

Larry kept several thousand dollars in the rattling old cash register, more than anyone might expect at a lonesome tavern.

"Righteous place to stash it," he always told me. "No paper trail, no questions."

I put the money, all of it, into a small, cash deposit bag Larry pilfered from a local bank but hardly used. I turned around to hand it over.

That's when it happened.

"Heek-hupb."

BLAM!

Golf shirt guy got hiccups. And the jumpy robber's bullet got golf shirt guy, bad.

"Go, go, go!" the tall shooter yelled.

He and rat-face sprinted out the door, swallowed by vacant darkness.

I tossed the bank bag onto the beaten stainless steel beer cooler beneath the bar. Staggering a little, I headed toward golf shirt guy. From where I stood behind the bar, I couldn't see where he fell, only a spreading pool of blood, thick and wet on the grimy floor.

The bourbon and ginger woman still covered her eyes. She was shaking. I was too. When I gasped for air my mouth filled with a taste like rotting meat. In that moment, the bourbon and ginger woman passed out.

The cops came, asked questions, took golf shirt guy's body away.

The cop in charge looked at the open cash register, empty.

"You did the right thing," he told me. "Always give them the money."

Still wobbly, I glanced at the beer cooler. No bank bag. And it wasn't anywhere on the floor, either. I already looked, before the cops got here.

The local newspaper ran the story two days later. "Man Killed in Robbery-Murder" the headline read. Golf shirt guy was a salesman named Marvin, traveling on business from Cleveland. Survived by a sister, Maylene, living in Seattle.

And based on my description, the newspaper wrote, police were looking for two robbers. Two tall men with short, dark hair, olive skin, and muscular builds. Exactly what I told the cops.

I told Larry I couldn't work at his tavern any more, after everything that happened. He said he understood. But, of course, he didn't. Mostly he didn't understand how the bank bag fell into the open gap behind the beer cooler, where the bar and cooler weren't flush against each other. How it got stuck down there, but I found it. Then, after the cops were done, how I reached and strained and pulled to get it. How I opened it and counted the money ... $5,251.

Maybe not enough for some people, at least not enough to do what I did. But for somebody like me, born to live a hard life, it meant everything. Because Larry also didn't understand what it was like to work in a place like his tavern, night after night, where even a good night really wasn't good and on a bad night somebody got killed and you felt grateful it wasn't you and ashamed you felt that. Dark, sad places with a faint odor you can best describe as desperation. Desperation to escape to anywhere, to be anywhere except wherever you were. $5,251 gave me a ticket. Escape.

But right now I wasn't going anywhere except the police station.

On the phone, the cops said they just needed to ask me a few more questions. Routine, they said. I'm not what you call highly educated, but I'm not stupid either. When they put me in an interrogation room, I knew they meant business.

Police interrogation rooms are cramped, mean little places where cops lie to people they think lied to them first. I believe this not because I lied to the cops about the robbery, which I did of course, but because I've read every Harry Bosch crime novel ever published. I planned to stick to my story anyway, because everything I remembered about that night whispered to me. Every detail.

The room smelled like sweat. The cops were the same two detectives that came to the tavern after the robbery, a lean older man and an attractive younger woman. Now intent on exposing my lies by lying to me, they wore savage smiles. Suspicious and distant, they seemed to despise me.

The older cop's raspy voice was somewhere between a hoarse growl and a raw scrape. He told me another witness gave a different description of the robbers. Mine was way off, too far off. And wasn't it funny that I quit my job right after the robbery? Like maybe I just came into some money. I guess cops think like that.

Then he got right in my face with his raspy voice, his spit spraying me. They knew I was part of the robbery, he screamed. Remember, they both told me, you didn't shoot the gun but the murder's still on you. The murder is on you, it's on you, just like if you pulled the trigger. They kept repeating it, screaming it. They knew all about it, knew everything, they said.

The older cop got frenzied, uncontrollable, screeching and spitting at me. "Tell us the names of your partners," he shrieked. "Is a three-way split from a chicken-shit bar heist worth a felony murder charge?" They knew all about it, the cops kept saying. The murder is on me. But if I would just sign a statement, they confided, maybe I could get a lighter sentence.

Five hours later, they let me go. There was no other witness. No partners. No three-way split. Almost nothing but lies.

The cops didn't apologize for the deceit.

"You were a suspect," the woman detective said. "We always check somebody like you."

Four days later, the cops arrested a short little rat-faced man after he robbed a liquor store. The prosecuting attorney told me about it. He said the detectives put the rat-faced man in an interrogation room, where they told him they had a witness to the robbery-murder at Larry's Tavern and they knew rat-face did it. They knew all about it, knew everything, the cops told rat-face, because their witness saw rat-face and another man take the money, and saw rat-face do the murder. It's on you, they told him, the murder is on you. But if he would just sign a statement, they said, maybe he could get a lighter sentence.

So rat-face figured cooperating made sense. He confessed to robbing Larry's, taking the money, exactly the way the cops told it. Except to get a lighter sentence he put the murder on another guy, a tall, skinny man with a pasty white face. The tall, skinny man told a completely different story, of course. Said the cops and rat-face got it wrong. Said it didn't happen like that.

Then ballistics matched the murder bullet to a gun the tall man was arrested with. That was the end of it. The robbers gave guilty pleas, went to prison. And I made plans. To take the $5,251, leave the lies, and be anywhere but there.

Case closed. The prosecutor said witnesses like me make mistakes because we're traumatized from getting robbed, seeing someone murdered. But confessions and bullet matches don't lie, at least not the way guilty killers do.

"God moves in a mysterious way
His wonders to perform;"—William Cowper

Doing God's Work
by Wayne Scheer

ELI AND VERNON Browbridge rolled The Fat Man's bloated body from the trunk of their 1987 Pontiac Grand Prix into the hole in the ground they had just dug.

Eli spoke first. "I wonder if a dead fat guy smells worse than a thin broad that's been roasting in a hot car trunk?" He grabbed a dirty handkerchief from his back pocket, blew his nose and wiped the sweat from his face. Dirt and snot streaked his cheek.

"You got me," Vernon replied. "Ain't never had no dead broad in my trunk. But The Fat Man sure stinks."

Eli put a hand to his chin. "Makes you think."

Vernon nodded, but he paid little attention to his brother. He was enjoying the cool breeze drifting down from the North Georgia Mountains. As a child, he'd spent nights in the hammock on the back porch falling asleep to the sound of chirping insects. Even with the skeeters, Vernon preferred the view of Mount Yonah to the room he shared with his brother, who would spend half the night asking him questions he had no idea how to answer.

"Vern," Eli asked. "How we gonna get The Fat Man into this little hole?"

Vernon circled the overstuffed grave. He tried bending Fat Man's legs, hoping the stiffening limbs might snap off. No luck.

"We gotta dig more. That's all there is to it. We gotta push The Fat Man on his side and dig this hole deeper."

It was hard work digging through the roots and hard Georgia clay that passed for soil in the mountains. When they finally pushed the body towards the deeper side, Eli wondered if that was enough.

"No," Vernon said, the body still stuck up on one side. "We gotta fit him in and cover him up good or we won't get paid."

Eli spit a mouthful of dirt. "Why's Georgia dirt get so hard in the sun?"

"Iron," Vernon said. "Georgia soil's got a lotta iron in it." He felt proud when he had an answer to one of Eli's stupid ass questions.

"That's why it's so red. The iron rusts when it mixes with rain and that turns it hard." He paused to let Eli appreciate his smarts.

While Eli dug some more, Vernon took a breather. "I sure like the way these woods smell when there ain't no Fat Man stinking it up."

"Yeah. Me, too. Remember how when we was kids we'd run through the woods nekkid after a rain? Give Mama a fit."

They continued digging. The midday sun took no pity on them. Their T-shirts stuck to their bodies; their jeans felt like they'd have to be scraped off.

An hour later they had dug The Fat Man's grave about three feet deep. There was still a little hump along the middle of the hole where they had dug around a big rock, but the brothers decided it would do. They laid out The Fat Man's body until he looked almost comfortable and began shoveling dirt and leaves over him. A mound, formed by his belly, remained visible, but they covered it with more leaves until it evened out.

"You think we should say a prayer or something, Vern?"

Eli was back with his damned questions. "Wouldn't do no good," Vernon said after a few seconds. "Only prayer I know is 'Now-I-Lay-Me-Down-to-Sleep.' I reckon it's too late for that one."

"Vern," Eli had on his serious face, the one where his forehead wrinkled and his eyebrows met. "Are we bad people for doing this?"

Vernon answered immediately. "No, sir. The man deserves a grave, don't he? We're giving it to him. We didn't kill him. Now that'd be wrong. We just doing a honest day's work for a honest day's pay, just like Mama always says." He leaned on his shovel. "When we get the money, we'll give her some and she'll give part of it to Reverend Atwater. So the way I see it, we doing God's work."

Proud of himself, Vernon topped off the grave with more leaves and tree branches. "I reckon this here's as fine a grave as The Fat Man deserves."

The two brothers stepped back to admire their work, threw their shovels into the back of their car and drove off to collect their pay.

In less than two hours, a pack of dogs happened on the shallow grave and uncovered most of the body. Soon after that, a young couple searching for wild blackberries saw the mangled corpse and called 9-1-

1. An hour later, Sheriff Erskine Calloway identified what was left of the body as Horace Latimer, aka The Fat Man, a local loan shark. He specialized in loans of twenty to one hundred dollars to illegals and gamblers, demanding twice that if the loan wasn't repaid within twenty-four hours.

"At least we won't have a problem finding folks who wanted him dead," the sheriff told his deputy. He sniffed at the body like a bitch in heat. "Sure is getting ripe out here in the sun. Don't reckon he's been dead too long, though. Can't see no gunshot or stab wounds, but it's hard to tell with all these dog bites. The man's so fat he just might have ate hisself to death. But I doubt seriously he buried his damn self." Sheriff Calloway looked at his deputy who was writing furiously in his ever-present notebook. "You getting all this down, son?"

"Yes, sir."

"We won't know nothing for sure till Doc Robbins has himself a look-see. Probably won't know much then, if Doc already drank his lunch." He turned to his deputy. "It sure ain't like that CSI show on television."

Eli and Vernon collected their five hundred dollars for a good day's work and visited their mother. LuAnne Browbridge had the sturdy, no nonsense look of a woman who raised two boys by herself after beating her drunkard of a husband nearly to death with a frying pan. Nothing surprised her, least of all Eli and Vernon. When they handed her one hundred dollars in twenties, she asked no questions. She just reached under the top of her faded house dress and stashed the money safely into her bra.

"You boys gimme that kind of money, you got plenty more. Hand over another hundred."

The boys complied without a word.

She separated twenty dollars from the money. "This here's for Reverend Atwater. I'll ask him to pray for your sorry asses. Now y'all wash up good. Supper's almost ready."

The next day, Dr. Robbins said he couldn't determine cause of death for sure until the autopsy, but it seemed natural enough. The dog bites, at least, were post mortem. "From what I can tell it looks like his heart gave way," the doctor concluded.

"Well," Sheriff Calloway said to his deputy, "we got ourselves a dilemma. If The Fat Man here died of natural causes, why'd someone go to the trouble of burying him in the woods?"

The deputy wrote the question in his notebook, adding three question marks.

Sheriff Calloway waited for an answer. When none was offered, he spoke. "My guess is someone didn't want us to know they was with him."

The deputy nodded.

"Off-hand, I don't know anyone who'd want it known they was with this sad sack of human feces. So we got ourselves a whole mess of folks to question. Or we could look at it another way." He paused for the deputy to turn the page in his notebook.

"If you had a dirty job you wanted done, like burying a body, who'd you get to do it?"

The deputy looked up, his eyes flashing wide. "The Browbridge brothers."

"And who would do the job so half-assed, the body'd be discovered before the devil had time to cart it off to hell?"

"Eli and Vern."

Sheriff Calloway smiled. "What say we have ourselves a little chat with the brothers Browbridge?"

Mrs. Browbridge wasn't the least surprised when she saw the sheriff's car pull up in front of her house. "Eli! Vernon!" she shouted to her sons who were watching stunt bowling on ESPN. "The po-lice is here. I don't know what y'all did this time, just keep me out of it."

Sheriff Calloway and his deputy removed their hats as they entered the surprisingly cozy Browbridge abode. "Ma'am," the sheriff nodded. "Your boys home?"

Eli and Vernon were trying to figure out how to record their show, but operating their mother's TiVO system might as well have been rocket science. They were pushing buttons and cursing when the sheriff walked in.

"What you boys up to?"

Vernon and Eli looked up from the remote. "Nothin'," Vernon said.

His brother added. "This danged recorder don't work."

"You boys trying to record this here bowling show?" the sheriff asked. When the brothers nodded, he took the remote and pressed the red record button.

"There. Now y'all do something for me. I got The Fat Man's body in the morgue. Found it out in the woods." He looked Eli and Vernon in the eye. "You boys know anything about it?"

"No, sir," said Vernon, speaking fast So Eli didn't say something dumb.

Eli still managed to get in a few words. "We don't know nothin' 'bout buryin' no body."

"Who said the body was buried?" He turned to his deputy. "You taking this down? We'll need this when we go before the judge."

"Judge?" Eli asked. "Why we need a judge?"

"Because murder and kidnapping and burying a body without a permit are crimes, that's why." The sheriff went silent, giving Eli and Vernon time to understand.

In less time than it would take a hungry fox to devour a chicken, the boys told him how Missy Taggert had hired them to put The Fat Man's body in the trunk of their car and bury him. "He was already dead," Eli explained. "We was just doing Miss Missy a favor."

"How much she pay you for this favor?"

"A hundred-and-fifty dollars," Vernon said. "We already give it to mama."

The deputy wrote furiously.

Sheriff Calloway took one look at the death stare LuAnne was shooting at her boys and figured they'd be punished enough. "Don't go spending that money or leaving town," he said, as he and the deputy walked out the door.

Missy Taggert had been good-looking enough in her youth to have made a comfortable living as the town prostitute. When her looks went south along with her other assets, she married Darnell Grimes. Still, everyone in town knew her as Missy Taggert, especially the men. Darnell worked construction when he could get on with a road crew and fixed cars when someone felt sorry for him or Missy. He wasn't home when the sheriff knocked on Missy's door. Since Sheriff Calloway had a personal relationship with Missy dating back to her former line of work, he had arranged for his deputy to meet him at the stationhouse.

Missy knew by the expression on the sheriff's face that this wasn't a friendly call, but she tried stalling. "Erskine, I haven't seen you since Tina Mae had her baby. How old is your granddaughter now?"

"She'll be two this coming winter, Missy. But I ain't here to talk family or old times." He wished he hadn't mentioned old times. "It seems we have ourselves a di-lemma. The Browbridge boys tell me you hired them for a certain job not long ago."

Getting Eli and Vernon to confess took more time than it took Missy to explain how she had been doing sexual favors for The Fat Man to hold her over while Darnell found work. This time his heart couldn't take the excitement. She didn't want her husband to know, so she did what everyone in town did when they had a cesspool that needed unclogging or snakes under the porch that needed killing. She called the Browbridge boys and paid them with half of the money The Fat Man had in his wallet. She kept the rest.

"A hundred and fifty dollars?" Sheriff Calloway asked.

"Is that what they told you? The boys may be smarter than they look."

After coffee with a shot of rum, he agreed to keep the incident on the hush and hush if the final coroner's report confirmed it was a heart attack. After all, The Fat Man had no family and no friends who'd miss him.

Sheriff Calloway had one more point of business to take care of before this whole mess could be wrapped up.

"Vern. Eli," he said, wrinkling his forehead to look as paternal as possible. "Missy told me the truth, so it looks like you boys are in the clear this time. There won't be no murder charges against you."

In unison, the boys blew air out of their puffed up cheeks. Eli wanted to shout "Yehaw!" but he thought better of it.

"But we still got ourselves a di-lemma." The sheriff rolled his tongue inside his mouth for a moment. "It seems Missy says she paid you five hundred dollars and you say one-fifty. Since I believe her, that makes your statement to me—that my deputy had wrote down for the judge—what we call lying to a officer of the law. Now that can get you jail time."

Eli and Vernon just stared at the Sheriff. Even Eli couldn't think of anything to say.

"But we can work something out. Say you give me two hundred. You boys keep the rest and we won't talk no more about this."

The Browbridge brothers readily agreed. Vernon reached into his boot and took out a wad of wet, smelly twenties. He counted out two hundred and handed it to the sheriff.

Sheriff Calloway took the money. Before walking away, he said, "You boys stay out of trouble now, y'hear? I can't always be bailing you out."

As he slipped into his car, he smiled and put nine twenties in his wallet. The other one he placed in an envelope on which he scrawled, "Rev. Atwater."

Feeling the spirit, he mumbled, "Aw, what the hell," and added another twenty to the envelope. "Somebody got to do God's work."

"Lie thou there; for here comes the trout that must be caught with tickling."
—William Shakespeare

Um Peixe Grande
by Patti Abbott

THOUGH HIS EYES were squeezed tight, Gas could *hear* Loretta standing in their bedroom doorway, his lunch bag crinkling in her hand. He also knew from a variety of signs and smells what the day outside was like: cloudy, damp, cold. He had no desire to do what his wife had in mind, though he'd been a fisherman all his life like his father and grandfather before him. But the money earned from throwing a line in the water no longer put much food on the table, and Loretta was after him to get a job at one of the tilapia farms if he was determined to stay in the fish business.

"Just take a good look, Gaspar," she'd said, stretching her arms out. "This place is fallin' down 'round us, case you hadn't noticed. Fish from a Dish pays a livin' wage. Nobody earns a livin' sittin' in a chewed-up boat anymore. Termites own more of it than you. If you'd stuck with one of the big operations—like that Buster Bragg crew—maybe then...."

Even the name of the tilapia farm made Gas cringe. He belonged out on real water, not in one of those huge aquarium-like structures where his job would be hauling out fish, or delivering them to a slaughterhouse or treatment facility. That wasn't fishing at all. He liked to imagine that every fish he caught had enjoyed a full, free life before he landed it in a fair fight. There was mutual dignity in this time-honored contest. Taking part in the butchery of trapped fish—that had never known a minute of liberty in an actual body of water—was disgusting.

"You're turning into a sentimental old fool," his wife said. "What do fish know about freedom? You know how big their brain is?"

About the size of yours, he felt like saying.

But instead—"The domestication of fish through farming is an environmental disaster." The pamphlet was in his pocket, and he patted it. "It's no better than how chickens are raised."

"Fancy words for a man with a leaky boat and a leaky house."

"You'd better get cracking," she said now, shaking the paper bag harder. "The ice-out's nearly over. You might even make a decent haul if you get out there early."

Loretta rolled her eyes as she said this—making it clear there was no chance of such a thing. She'd lost all respect for him years ago when he quit going out on the Atlantic with Buster Bragg and his crew. Their noisy camaraderie and rough behavior had not been his style either. What kind of fishermen drink beer all day and lunch on the pier's fast food, pock-marking the ocean with aluminum and paper trash?

"No breakfast?" he said. Eyes open now, he looked out the window glumly. What was that poem about November? No sun was one of the lines. No comfortable feel in any member, another, he remembered. He didn't know what that meant exactly—by member did they really mean.... And anyway it was May, wasn't it?

"In here," she said, shaking the bag yet again. His Sam's Club breakfast bar was probably in pieces by now. "Your thermos is on the table, and there's a beef pasty for your lunch—should you need one."

This was a slap at his early departure from the river yesterday. How long could you sit waiting for what wasn't going to come? He grimaced at the thought of the coffee—probably from yesterday's pot if a drop remained. She'd been known to hold the used grounds under the hot water tap in a pinch. He'd give anything for just instant.

Tossing the bag on the bed, Loretta left the room, her feet heavy on the bare wood. She'd become stocky in the last few years. Of course, who was he to talk with his face wizened from the years on the water? On the day they married, people sighed at her beauty when she came down the aisle on her Dad's arm. But thirty years had passed, hadn't they? Loretta never was able to have the children they both wanted, her job at the jeans factory had gone overseas, and all of her brothers left Maine long ago for better opportunities. She held all that against him too.

"If Gil and Jaime had the gumption to move across the country, why can't we? California has an ocean. You can stick a pole in the Pacific if that's what you have to do."

But California was another country. With its movie stars, orange trees, and surfers. He'd sooner take off for the Azores.

Fifteen minutes later, Gas headed for the St. Croix River and hopefully some salmon. Maybe some bass too. He'd never been much of a saltwater fisherman, even before Buster and his antics, always preferring the inland waterways. The Atlantic was too vast—you could get lost in it—in your head at least. Instead he usually headed for a lake, other times a river. He could fish there in solitude—a condition he preferred.

Half-drowsing, half-puttering along in one of the little alcoves he favored, Gas was thinking about the Red Sox's chances when the water suddenly grew choppy. A larger motorboat approached. The wake was sizeable because of the larger boat's speed, and Gas slowed to a standstill to compensate, pointing his boat toward the wake to save it from overturning. Clearly, the man at the helm hadn't even noticed the small boat on its port side in the weeds. The name, *The Clytemnestra*, was painted on the boat in large blood red letters. What sort of name was that for a boat? A far cry from the typical *Lady Luck* you usually saw around here.

Seconds later, as the boat sped around a bend in the water, Gas heard an enormous splash. Perhaps a large catch fell overboard? Or even one huge fish. This happened occasionally. Inexperienced fishermen—like the idiots likely to be on that boat—didn't always secure their catches adequately, and the fish skidded back into the water. But the inland waterways Gas knew boasted no fish big enough to sound like that. Sturgeon—fish who might splash that way—were only in places like the Kennebec River.

He spotted the object. Whatever it was—and it looked like a single fish as he drew closer—was undulating madly, thrashing about. What sort of fish swam like that? He pulled closer still, wondering if he could possibly catch the fish without capsizing his own boat. The thing had to weigh two hundred pounds. On closer inspection, whatever it was, seemed to be wrapped in a dirty tarp and tightly duct-taped every eight inches or so. Huh? Then he heard screaming, and it became obvious there was a man inside the bundle. Holy Mother of God!

Gas grabbed at the canvas, succeeding in grasping an edge on his second try, and yanked it as hard as he could. After considerable effort, the squirming body was in his boat along with several gallons of river water. The boat rocked violently, then shuddered to a more controllable sway. Catching his breath, Gas slit the tarp open cautiously. The man inside was unconscious now. Water streamed from his mouth: a gaping hole in a gray face that appeared lifeless. It was hard to decide whether to expel the water or supply him with more oxygen first. Gas flipped him over, put his head to one side, and began forcing water from the man's lungs. After a minute or two, the man's left eye popped open.

Minutes later, he was still wheezing, and occasional pieces of tarp and seaweed as well as brackish water continued to seep from his mouth. Gas pressed on his back until the flow stopped. Then he turned the man over, did a minute or two of old-fashioned mouth-to-mouth, and helped him to sit up against the bench. The guy's color began to return; his panting slowed. Gas grabbed a towel, a bottle of water, and a heavy blanket from his dry box. The water temperature of a Maine river in May was in the forties. The guy could still go into shock—he was plenty old enough to have a heart attack, even. Gas dried his head, wrapped the blanket around him, and offered him the water.

"Drink." It was more a command than an invitation.

Looking at Gas skeptically, the man finally obeyed, still shivering so intensely that his teeth chattered. Gas looked around for another blanket, finally coming up with a piece of dry canvas. Then he waited—his hands and feet under attack by pins and needles—for the man to recover. In all his years at sea, nothing had equaled this.

"Someone trying to murder you?"

It sounded like a joke when he said it aloud, but what else could it be? The man continued to pant and shiver, and Gas waited some more.

"So it would seem," the man finally said, rubbing his head with the towel. He coughed up some more debris. "If you hadn't come along I'd be swimming with the fishes."

Neither man laughed. In fact, Gas had no inclination to discuss the event beyond this brief exchange, and neither, it seemed, did his passenger.

"Where should I take you?" Gas said, starting up the motor again. "Need to get out of those wet clothes pronto." The man's shivering had not abated.

"Anywhere on shore. Have a cell?"

Even a poor fisherman didn't travel without one, and Gas tossed it to him.

"Not much of a signal," the man said, looking at the phone.

"We'll be ashore in five minutes."

"Hey, thanks." The man paused as if considering his words. "A thank you isn't enough, of course. What *could* be enough after something like that?"

Gus and the man looked out onto the lake; the other boat was gone for now.

"Give me your address and I'll send you a check. A check big enough for a long vacation." The man shrugged. "Or whatever you want. Something anyway."

"I don't want your money." And Gas certainly didn't want to hand this man—someone who would've been dead if he hadn't come along—his address. He was anxious to put a wide berth between them. And an even wider berth between himself and that boat—whatever its crazy name was. Men like that would have guns onboard.

"Well, what then?" The man stared at the phone as if an idea would come from it. "You have to take something." He coughed and shook his head. "I can't be in your debt. It's too much like unfinished business."

"Nothing. Nothing at all." All Gus could think about now was that speedboat reappearing on the horizon. What would happen to a witness of an attempted murder? "And you're not in my debt. Anyone would've done the same."

The man shook his head. "Not the men I know."

"Then you know the wrong men."

The man said nothing but from the look on his face, Gas knew what he said was the truth.

Dockside, a few minutes later, Gas helped him climb out of the boat.

"Look, take my card at least," the man said, reaching for his pocket. But he'd been stripped of any identification. In fact, to both of their horror, his pockets were filled with stones.

Gus thought once again of the boat that sped away. Had they

spotted him? If they had, they certainly would've returned to see to him. The weeds and water plants in the boggy alcove must have hidden his boat. Did they believe this man was at the bottom of the river? They must.

"Make your call," Gas said, nodding toward the phone.

After a brief discussion—and Gas couldn't help but overhear the name "Pinto" said twice—he was back. "Look, my name's Pasquale Trota. I'm putting my number in your contacts." He punched it in. "If I can ever do anything for you, give me a call. I mean it," he said. "Something might come to you later." He paused. "I have friends in lots of places."

And enemies in others, Gus thought. But he said nothing.

"I won't even ask your name. It's probably better for me not to know it."

Gas watched as the man headed for the blacktop. A dark SUV soon picked him up. The man turned back and nodded before he climbed inside. Gas held up a hand. He was glad he'd never given the man his name, glad Trota (he'd immediately looked at the new name on his phone) hadn't asked for it. This affair, strange and worrisome, would end right here.

Back home after another disappointing day fish-wise, he thought about telling Loretta about Mr. Trota. But she had a way of making even a good deed or something entirely innocent seem foolish. And the more he ran over the story in his head, the more he could imagine her saying that he was dim-witted not to ask for a reward. It'd be hard to make her understand the terror with which that enormous splash and the quick departure of that boat had filled him. He'd done nothing brave—hadn't even really known what it was he was pulling out of the water.

Instead, he got a tongue-lashing for coming home with only enough fish to make a dinner. And the next day, when it poured rain, Loretta insisted on him going down to Fish in a Dish and filling out an application. As he sat in the HR room with several other fellows, all younger than he and twice as muscular, he was full of despair. Why would anyone hire him when clearly these younger and stronger fellows would make better employees? So even here—at this terrible place—he would fail. And predictably, the man behind the desk hardly bothered to read his application once he took a quick look at Gas.

"My father did commercial fishing when I was a kid," he told Gas. "Takes the stuffing out of you," he added, looking Gas up and down. "And look Mr...." he looked down at the application, "Rios. You wouldn't like it here. It's not like fishing at all. It's back-breaking work even for a young man."

"But it pays a wage, right," Gas said, feeling he had nothing to lose.

"Probably not much more than you can earn on your own."

Gas nodded, and the two men parted.

"Any luck," Loretta asked before his foot was inside the door. She was darning his wool socks, an activity she only engaged in when she wanted sympathy for the hard life Gaspar had dealt her.

"The guy who interviewed me said I'd have to wait and see," Gas said, not wanting to go into it with her now. She'd blame him for not convincing the powers-that-be that he was a man who could haul a half a ton of fish out of a tank. "Looked good though," he added, trying to get a few hours peace. "I got the feeling...."

She smiled, but he could tell she wasn't convinced. "You did go down there, didn't you?"

He reached into his jacket and threw his copy of the paperwork he'd filled in on the table, then strode off, trying to look like a man who could pull half a ton of fish out of a tank. But having no experience with what that looked like, he probably wasn't persuasive.

"Mr. Trota," he found himself saying into his cell phone a few weeks later. He hadn't planned the call at all—but somehow ended up making it, bringing up the contact and pushing the button.

"Who wants to know?"

It was the lowest pitched voice he'd ever heard and not Mr. Trota's. "He won't know my name."

"He knows everyone's name," the man said.

"Yeah, but I...."

"Look, if you want to talk to him, you gotta tell me your name. Go ahead. I'm not gonna tell anyone your name but the boss."

"Okay, well, it's Gaspar Rios."

"What kinda name is Gaspar?" the man asked. He didn't sound curious as much as he seemed to be preparing the information for Mr. Trota.

"Portuguese. I fish in the St. Croix. That's where we...."

"Oh, sure. Probably you're the guy that pulled him out of the lake. Right."

"River."

"Right, river. Told me all about it. Okay, then. He'll be right here."

"Gaspar Rios, huh?" Mr. Trota said a few seconds later. "Is that Spanish?"

"Portuguese," Gas said again.

"Sure, sure, I shoulda figured." He paused. "Things okay with you? Didn't hurt your boat, did I?"

"My boat's good."

"Well, how can I help you, Gaspar?"

"Gas," he said. "My friends call me Gas,"

"And I'm gonna be your friend, huh." Mr. Trota paused. "Well, you deserve it. I wouldn't be sitting here drinking this beer or smoking this Robusto if it wasn't for you. Pulling me out of the water like you did. Like the biggest fish you ever caught, huh? So, how can I be your friend, Gas?"

Gas took a deep breath and plunged in, still not knowing exactly what he wanted.

"I wondered if you might have a job for me. Doesn't have to be anything fancy..." Gas felt as awkward as he had at Dish of Fish or whatever it was called. What in the world would a man like Mr. Trota have for him to do? Why hadn't he had an idea in mind before calling?"

"A job for a fisherman?" Mr. Trota laughed. "I don't even eat fish, Gus."

"Gas."

"Gas, right. You wanna sell me fish. Is that what you're saying? Maybe you think I have a restaurant. Louie, do I have a restaurant?" Both men at the other end of the line laughed.

"No restaurant, I'm afraid, Gas."

"Maybe I can watch the river for you."

"Watch the river?" Mr. Trota paused. "You mean the St. Croix?

Like watch the current move the water?" He laughed again. Gas had never known a man to laugh so much. Especially one nearly murdered a few weeks before. Before he could answer, Mr. Trota answered his own question.

"Of course, that's not what you mean. Just yanking your chain. You mean watch the river in case someone tosses me off a boat again? Hey, I got Louie here to do that. And a couple other amici. Look, that's not the way it works, Gas. If they come after me again—which they will—it'll be in some other way. Unless they're dumber than I think."

Gas heard him say to Louie, "We can only hope." Both men laughed. Gas got the feeling they used laughter in some other way than he did. He couldn't remember the last time he'd laughed. No one he knew laughed.

"Look, how much do you earn a year hauling fish out of that lake, Gas?"

Gas told him.

Mr. Trota whistled. "You actually live on that? What's your wife, some corporate bigwig?"

"Nah, she takes care of me and the house," Gas thought of the lunch waiting in his paper bag. He'd bet anything it was last night's leftover meatloaf. Loretta put pickle relish on it when she made a sandwich—like it was an added treat. Thirty years on, and he still hated sweet pickles on his meatloaf sandwich. But that didn't stop her.

"At church, they rave about my meatloaf sandwiches," she told him.

Mr. Trota sighed now. "Hold on a sec, Gas." Gas heard him talking to someone else—probably Louie—again. "Look, Gas, tell you what. I'll match your earnings for a year. So you can go out on the lake and fish, and I will equal what they pay you for that fish down on the docks. Maybe by the time the year is up, something else will come along for you. Or maybe we'll come up with an idea."

Gas thought about it. "So you're gonna pay me just to do what I've always done? Just sit on the water and fish?"

"Sure. You can keep an eye out for that other boat in case it comes along again. You might save my ass twice. Never know. Right, Louie?"

Louie murmured his assent.

Gas could tell Mr. Trota didn't believe such a thing would happen and neither did he, really. He thought he'd recognize the boat, but he couldn't remember the name anymore. Mr. Trota must've read his mind because he said, "*The Clytemnestra*, Gas. Must be a Greek, that cattivo who wants my ass in a sling hired. Everything's global now, isn't it? Want a hitman today, call Serbia or Cambodia." He was laughing again, but the laugh still had no mirth in it. "So keep an eye out. Not that I think Pinto's boys are still out cruising the waterways of Maine. But you never know."

Weeks went by. Every time Gas sold fish to the wholesalers, he sent a scanned receipt to Mr. Trota's number and Mr. Trota deposited money in Gas' account. As summer came, the daily haul picked up. He finally broke down and showed the numbers to Loretta, thinking to improve her opinion of him.

"Guess you were right to stick with the old way of doin' things," she said, staring at the figures. "Sure the bank didn't goof it up?"

"You think a bank ever makes a mistake in my favor?"

She kept nodding but he felt like she was really shaking her head, convinced he was pulling something over on her.

The St. Croix River runs 71 miles in length and forms part of the Canadian-U.S. border and Gas usually fished either the river itself or one of the lakes that lay along its path. He was usually just a few miles from the ocean and yet it never drew him.

"It's like you're afraid of it," Loretta once theorized. "The big bad ocean. Ooh."

"No, but I give it the respect it deserves," he told her. "I'm comfortable where I am."

"Comfortable," she'd said. "Well, I'm not comfortable where I am."

He had grown slack and lazy over the winter, telling himself he was too old for the sort of jobs he could find. He even turned down the church's offer to plow their lot, an easy couple of grand.

But now, for the first time since his arrangement with Mr. Trota, a month had passed without a bank deposit. He feared he was at the end of the soup line and began to look at the pecuniary of a forced retirement.

Seven bridges crossed the St. Croix, but Gus wasn't near one of them in May when he saw the boat again. *The Clytemnestra*. It was slowly making its way up the river, hugging the Canadian bank. Gas, on his boat, was sitting inside a marshy alcove half a mile south of the larger boat's entry point from a canal. It was a good place to fish and a good place to spy, although truthfully he'd long ago given up any idea of spotting the boat. If the name hadn't caught his eye that day, he'd never have given it any thought. He'd long ago concluded that Mr. Trota only gave him this assignment to justify paying him off for his good deed.

After a few minutes, Gas watched the boat drop anchor at a point where a rusty old truck with a beat-up trailer was waiting. He couldn't even tell the color of either one. It was certainly not a normal place to either load or unload cargo. There was no beach at all, and the incline was such that the nose of the truck was nearly in the water. In fact, the man who got out of the cab had his hands full not sliding into the river. Clearly something was wrong with this operation. Before Gas could think about what exactly seemed wrong, another man climbed out the other side of the truck, and together the two men opened the trailer and dragged five women—no, make that girls—out. All of them were bound at the hands, blindfolded, and gagged. Each wore a very short skirt, was preternaturally thin, and staggered in high heels. From their uniformly dark, straight hair, Gus thought they were probably Asian although they could have been wearing wigs.

Within a minute or two, they'd been loaded onto the boat. The next-to-last girl fell, losing her shoe. The man holding her arm seemed ready to strike her. Then he grabbed the heel that was stuck in the mud, pushed her down, and put it back on her foot. Although Gas couldn't hear, he knew she was sobbing from her shaking shoulders. Even from this distance, he could tell they were very young girls—perhaps under fourteen. It could have easily been his niece, Theresa, getting loaded onto the boat to hell.

His stomach in his throat, he picked up his cell and called 911, telling the dispatcher what he'd seen. The words tangled as they poured out of his mouth. He realized he was sobbing a bit. His heart hammered away.

"And where was this?" the officer asked.

Gus gave him the coordinates, the name of the boat, and information about the truck and trailer that made the delivery. The boat was practically out of his range already and the truck had pulled out of the drop spot, the trailer moving in a jerky fashion as the driver tried to back up.

Gas also gave his name and number.

"Do you want me to wait here?" he asked.

"Is the boat still in sight?"

It wasn't. So the dispatcher said he might as well go home and wait there for an officer to take down his story.

"Might have saved four lives today," the fellow said. "Who knows what those men had in mind for those girls. They probably picked them up in Toronto or Montreal. They could end up anywhere in the States." He paused. "Leave it to us, Mr. Rios. We'll get the guys who did this."

"Five," Gas corrected him. "There were five girls."

"Right. You saved five lives today."

Gas debated going home to tell Loretta. But that would take more than an hour so he called his friend instead. He'd called him once or twice over the last few months, mostly to thank him for a few deposits he made when the river was frozen and there were no fish to be had. When Gas had let the man's money put food on their table.

"That was real nice. You didn't have to do that."

"What do you usually do for cash in the winter?" Mr. Trota has asked him.

"Plow snow for some people I know. Chop wood for some shut-ins. Doesn't pay much but it covers my oil deliveries." Except this year when I got lazy, he thought but didn't say.

He'd resisted calling Mr. Trota last month when no deposit turned up. How long could he expect such an arrangement to last? How could he hold his hand out again?

Today he expected it would be him who was warmly thanked. Surely this would put the crew of that boat behind bars for some time. Mr. Pinto's goose would be cooked. His friend would not have to worry about taking a dive off that boat ever again.

"Hello," he said, recognizing Louie's voice but not wanting to hazard using his name. Maybe he wasn't supposed to know any of these guys. "It's Gaspar Rios. Is Mr. Trota in?" Then his excitement broke through. "Guess what? I saw that boat today. You know, *The Clytemn-estra?*" He wasn't certain if he'd pronounced it correctly. "You know the one I mean."

"Yeah, sure," Louis said. "Funny thing you should call. I think he forgot all about how you were out there looking for it. Looking for the boat. But it's okay 'cause he's out on that boat himself. Weird, huh?"

"What?"

"Yeah, he bought the boat about a month ago from Mario Pinto. Decided a nice little boat with a crackerjack boss might come in handy. He decided to turn his enemies into friends for some deal he had goin'." When Gas didn't respond, Louie added. "His business sometimes works like that." He laughed. "But more often, its vice-versa. Friends turn into enemies."

Gas'd never felt worse in his life. More than anything, he wanted to ask Louie not to tell Mr. Trota he'd called. But instead, he hung up and sat thinking quietly for a minute, then got some of the California brochures his wife kept forcing on him out of the hold. As he slipped the rubber band off, he wondered if the car was too old to make a cross country trip. Or if he and Loretta were. He guessed they'd find out.

Some people are so nice, it just seems too good to be true.

Loveable Alan Atcliffe
by S.R. Mastrantone

LOVEABLE ALAN ATCLIFFE: that's what they call him.

Like Mrs. Montgomery, who waited for the breakdown people for nearly an hour in the dark of winter 2001, before Alan pulled over in his taxi and changed her tyre in just five minutes. Or Father Chase, who knows Alan was the secret donor of the final £2000 that the church needed to pay for a new roof.

Loveable Alan Atcliffe, who lives in the cottage out on the plain, behind the school and the duck pond. Some people in Blythe would go further; they would use words like virtuous, or perhaps even saintly. People like Mrs. Donovan, whose mother timed her heart attack to coincide with the big snow of 2006.

Mrs. Donovan's car became stuck, and when she tried to dig it out her snow shovel snapped in two. She tried fruitlessly to dig with her hands, and was on the cusp of giving up when Alan's taxi lit up her drive and the man himself stepped out.

"It must be my lucky day," she said.

"God doesn't do luck," he replied and gave her a snowy-white grin. "Morris Danner told me he saw you struggling out here."

He began to dig but soon realised the true extent of Mrs. Donovan's plight. Throwing down his shovel, he said, "I'm taking you to the hospital myself."

"Alan, you can't take me to Shrewsbury. That's nearly sixty miles. You can't."

But he could and he did, and when she tried to pay him the fare that racked up on his meter, he refused to take it.

Loveable Alan Atcliffe.

Of all the people in the village that really love Alan, Mr. and Mrs. Baines would be the ones to talk to if you had only a little time. In the rainy summer of 2005 their only daughter, Verity, went missing after her piano lesson. She was a beautiful girl, with bright green eyes and long yellow hair: assets that made everyone in the village secretly fear for the worst.

Of course, it was Alan who helped organise the first local search party. Dressed in his Wellingtons and his brown Mackintosh, he banged on every door to drum up numbers. Then he led a team of nearly forty men and women from one end of the village to the other in the last hours of daylight. Mr. and Mrs. Baines had never expected such a response when they first knocked on his door to ask if he might have spotted Verity on his travels.

As if these efforts had not been enough, he took a central role in making sure that Verity's name stayed in the general public's minds once the national media grew bored of the story. He helped the Baineses build a campaign website to keep her memory alive and even donated the first funds to aid a private investigation into Verity's disappearance.

On Christmas Day 2006, not long after the big snowstorm, the Baineses invited Alan to dinner. As the pudding and brandy burned in the centre of the table, Mrs. Baines turned to Alan and asked, "Be honest with me. I know you will. Do you think she's still alive?"

The others assembled were silent. Alan placed a tender hand on Mrs. Baines' shoulder and looked into her hopeful eyes. "I believe she's alive more than I believe in the Lord Jesus Christ himself," he said.

Mrs. Baines tried to smile but cried instead. Mr. Baines came to hold her but she was already in Alan's arms, which, although she would never tell Mr. Baines such a thing, was her preference.

Loveable Alan Atcliffe, that's what they call him. Every man, woman and child in the village: Loveable Alan Atcliffe.

Of course Alan is a humble man, and he would never think of himself as loveable or saintly. But he understood why some thought of him that way. It was because they had not seen what Alan had done in the rainy summer of 2005. The thing that only the Lord Jesus Christ had been a witness to.

Alan had been lazy that day. He had not turned on the back wipers of the taxi. A harmless enough evil, and one born of a righteous belief that summer owed him a rear-window view. As he backed out of the drive—a thoughtless, automatic act—he assumed the way was clear, because it was always clear, and it was only in the daytime that the children came past on their way to school.

It was a fact of the everyday: the girl should not have been there.

But she had been and the Lord Jesus Christ bore witness silently as the car first knocked Verity Baines to the ground, and then ran over her head as she lay unconscious. Alan remained silent as he pulled at his hair and tried not to scream as he first caught sight of the awful mess dribbling down his drive from beneath the car.

"What were you doing there?" Alan asked the girl as he placed her in the boot on a pile of old newspapers and black bin bags.

The Lord Jesus Christ had no need to reply. Alan knew, God doesn't do luck.

Loveable Alan Atcliffe.

Who cried as he cleaned his drive with a snow shovel and a hose-pipe.

Who dwelled upon his reputation and his standing in Blythe for far too long, and then had to buy a large steel container from the DIY shop.

Loveable Alan Atcliffe.

Who once a year says a prayer in his cellar, and sets down a bouquet of flowers by the old entrance to the crawlspace that he filled with concrete as the rainy summer of 2005 came to an end.

Golf sometimes spoils more than just a good walk.

Slice
by Tom Barlow

HE WAS SEATED on the floor, snoring softly, outside my office door when I arrived that morning. He had no appointment.

The man appeared to have at least a decade on me, mid-50's, built like a stump with a saturnine face and hair that had no intention of obeying a comb. The tuxedo he wore had a mustard stain on the lapel, his bow tie listed to the left, and his pants were wrinkled.

Having been up until 3 a.m. myself bleeding money at a poker table in the local casino, I wasn't in the mood for uninvited company. However, I needed work; some of the poker stakes had been earmarked for rent.

I woke him with a toe to his rump. He opened his eyes, looked around blankly for a moment before figuring out where he was, and sheepishly rose to his feet. "You Morris? The private investigator?"

"Yeah," I said. "What can I do for you?"

"A minute of your time."

"I've heard that before, and it's never a minute," I said, unlocking the door. He followed me into the office, took a seat across the desk from me, and introduced himself as Jock DePaul.

"It's my wife," he said, not bothering to ease his way into the subject of his visit. "I haven't seen her in two days, since I dropped her off at the club to meet some girlfriends for a round of golf."

"Any reason she'd run away?" I said. "Your marriage hit a rough spot?"

"By no means. We just celebrated our 20th anniversary a month ago."

"You report it to the cops?" I didn't like working cases where the cops had a head start.

"They say they're looking for her, but the only thing I've seen them do is search our house and walk our woods with a corpse dog."

That they would react so quickly struck me as odd. Normally with a missing wife cops pussyfoot around for a few days to see if she turns up with a new lover.

"But you haven't been quarreling?"

He leaned forward, resting his chin on a fist. "No. We haven't spoken three cross words to one another in all the years we've been married."

"She carry much cash on her? Have access to some?" I was covering the big three reasons that marriages end; love, money, and pride.

"She usually keeps a few hundred dollars on her for shopping and emergencies. We share a bank account, and I checked online yesterday afternoon to see if she's made any withdrawals; she hasn't."

"She have her own car?"

"Oh," he said, "I should have told you. She's blind."

He caught me off-guard with that one. Now I understood the cops' quick reaction.

"She have a dog?" I said, struggling for something to say.

"Like a guide dog? No, she's deathly afraid of dogs. She gets by with the white cane."

"She's totally blind? Not just legally blind?"

"Right," he said. "Since birth."

I wrote *BLIND* in big letters on my pad, not that I was likely to forget it. "Where do you live?"

"Urbana."

I sat back. "You drove all the way here from Urbana? That's what? Two hours?"

"It's only ninety minutes. And my career is here in Columbus."

Something else was nagging me. "She's blind," I said. "I thought you said she went to play golf."

"Right. Oh, I see; how does she play? Many blind people play golf. They have a coach that accompanies them, lining them up with the ball, tracking where it goes, helping them with club selection and distances, that sort of thing."

"And she has a coach?"

"Yes, a young man that just graduated from OSU in Physical Education. Zane Taylor. They play three times a week."

"What's with the getup?" I asked, pointing to his tux.

"I'm a partner in a law firm. We had a client appreciation night last night. A missing wife is not a good enough excuse to skip it. It's a cutthroat business."

My guess? She'd contact DePaul for a divorce within 48 hours. I figured I could put a little time into the search without having to worry about ultimately solving the case.

"I charge $1,000 a day," I said, my special price for clients who wear tuxes and belong to country clubs. "I cover my own expenses. For that, you get a daily report. If I think I'm spinning my wheels, I'll let you know and you can decide whether to proceed."

To an attorney it was chump change, and he agreed without hesitation.

Since I had no other work on the hook, I followed him home.

He lived in a three-story monstrosity a couple of miles east of Urbana, on the crest of a glacial moraine overlooking an ocean of corn fields. Harvesters were busy bringing in the crop before the first freeze.

At my request, DePaul gave me a tour of the place, so I could familiarize myself with the layout. It wasn't immediately evident that a blind person lived there, except for a lack of clutter and low tables, and Braille tape on the controls of the appliances.

We looked in her closet; there were no obvious gaps in her wardrobe. Her medicines and makeup were in the master bathroom cabinet. All her suitcases were accounted for. I didn't like that.

He handed me a photo of his wife, a casual poolside shot from a barbecue the previous month. Her name was Deidra. She was a redhead, complete with pale complexion and freckles. Sunglasses hid her eyes, but her pert nose, cleft chin and high cheekbones were pleasantly arranged.

From DePaul's house I phoned Deidra's BFF and golfing buddy Tracey Wells, hoping I could visit with her first. By a stroke of luck, the three women who had played golf with her the day she disappeared were at the club together enjoying pre-round cocktails. Tracey invited me to join them.

The club was more upscale than I'd expected from such a small town, an old brick mansion with a wide veranda surrounded by 18 well-manicured golf holes. I found the threesome on the veranda drinking peach daiquiris from a pitcher on ice in the center of the table.

Tracey introduced herself first. She was a short, wiry woman with blond hair cut short in the back, gradually growing longer until it framed her face. Sunken cheeks and narrow-set eyes stood between her and beauty.

She pointed to the plump woman with a sallow complexion and tightly curled burgundy hair, introducing her as another friend, Ami Francis. Ami nodded, but didn't grace me with a smile.

The third at the table, Eloise McKinley, had long, lustrous black hair, an olive complexion that could have passed for Hispanic, and delicate features. She gave me a nice smile, exposing perfect teeth.

I took a seat at the table, enjoying for a moment the view of the course. They looked at me expectantly.

"You said over the phone that Jock had hired you to find Deidra," Tracey said. "What makes you think you'll do a better job than the cops?"

I shrugged. "Maybe I'm just arrogant. Or deluded. They've interviewed you, no doubt."

They all nodded.

"Would you mind going through it again with me? The three of you were probably the last ones to see her. What do you remember about that afternoon?"

"She had two birdies on the back nine and won the only skins of the day," Eloise said, pouring herself another daiquiri.

"A blind woman outplayed you?" I watched to see if any of them harbored a grudge.

"It's not so surprising," Eloise said without apparent rancor, "considering how Zane seems to find her ball dead center of the fairway no matter how far left or right it headed off the tee."

"So they cheated?" I said.

"Cheating's a harsh word," Tracey said. "The woman's blind, after all, so we cut her a little slack."

"Some of us mind more than others," Ami said, still not smiling. "It doesn't mean we did anything to her."

"I didn't mean to suggest you did," I said. "How was she planning to get home?"

Ami raised her hand. "It was my turn to give her a ride, but she told me Zane was going to come back to the club for her after we were done with our drinks. The last time I saw her she was sitting in the lobby waiting for him."

"What about you two?" I said, turning to Tracey and Eloise.

"The same," Tracey said, and Eloise nodded.

"Anything up between Zane and Deidra?" I said.

I caught a look of bemusement cross Eloise's face. "Have you met Zane?" she said. "Yum."

"So he's a good looking guy. Are you just guessing, or do you know for sure that they're getting it on?"

"He's not that good looking," Ami said, "and we're just speculating."

"Don't believe everything Ami says," Eloise said, grinning lopsidedly. "She's got a crush on Deidra."

Ami said, "So I'm gay. Is that any reason to treat me like a suspect?"

"We don't know if anything has happened to her yet," I said. "Hopefully, she's off on some adventure."

"You don't know her, mister," Eloise said. "She's not one to embrace change."

"She get along with her husband?"

"I thought you were working for him," Tracey said. "That sounds like you consider him a suspect."

"I'm just asking."

"There's a weird dynamic between them," Tracey said. "She's so dependent that it's hard to tell how much love is there. I never heard her bitch about him, but she wasn't eager to get home in time to welcome him home every evening. She'd stay here and drink us under the table if we let her."

"Was she drunk on Tuesday?"

"We have a standing 2 p.m. tee time three days a week," Eloise said, "so it's a bit embarrassing to admit that yes, we get a little tanked just about every time; sometimes before, sometimes after. It's how we tolerate our bad golf."

"So if you were to look for her, where would you start?"

"Zane," Ami said. The others nodded. "I think he's still living with his mother."

There were half a dozen Taylors in the phone book, and I had to call them all before I found the parents of Zane. When he came to the phone, he agreed to meet me at his home.

These Taylors lived in the valley formed by the Mad River, outside the village of West Liberty. The house was a modern ranch with a two car garage. There were three additional cars on the grass to the left of the garage.

Zane answered the door. The women weren't kidding when they described him as a hunk; he had a build just short of steroidal. His features were faintly Asian, with a small nose and deep brown, almond-shaped eyes. His short black hair was moussed into spikes.

He showed me into the living room, a shrine built for the worship of the 90" television perched in the farthest corner.

He licked his lips a couple of times as he took a seat on the couch. I sat next to him.

"So what's the latest with Mrs. DePaul?" he said.

"That's what I'm trying to find out."

"The cops have already asked me about her."

"And they'll be back," I said. "You gave her a ride home last Tuesday from the club?"

"Tuesday?" he said. "No, I came home right after we finished the round, around 5 p.m. I think she stayed to hang out with the women in her foursome. They usually have a few drinks afterwards."

"You ever give her a ride home?"

"I have, when she needed to get home to fix dinner and the others wanted to stay. But not Tuesday. I couldn't then anyway; some of us were having a pickup basketball game that evening over at the Y."

"And some of those players would testify to your participation?"

"Absolutely. You can ask my brother Paul if you want; he's downstairs. He and I are always on the same team; Mr. Inside and Mr. Outside. I'm Mr. Inside." He tried out a smile on me.

I didn't react. "You have any idea where she might have gone Tuesday evening?"

"I imagine one of the ladies gave her a ride home. She sure couldn't drive herself."

"Speaking of driving," I said, "rumor has it that you improve her lies, even when they're betting a skins game."

He hesitated for a moment. "Maybe I use a foot wedge sometimes, but it isn't like she is going to break any course records anyhow. It was just a stroke of luck on Tuesday that some of her approach shots ended up near the pin."

"Which cost the others some money," I pointed out.

"Not my problem," he said. "I don't believe in betting on golf; it's a hard enough game as it is. Why complicate it?"

"You ever sleep with Mrs. DePaul?" I asked, hoping to catch him off-guard.

"Jesus," he said, shaking his head. "Of course not. That would be unprofessional."

"If you had to guess, who would you figure had a reason to kill her?"

He rubbed his neck. "I don't know. I guess Ami, maybe; Diedra has complained about her to me more than once. Or maybe the creep that runs the club, he keeps copping feels when he thinks she doesn't know it's him. He practically bathes in Axe, so she can recognize him at 100 yards."

"And?"

He shrugged. "She's a beautiful woman, man; check every pervert in the county."

I gave him my card, told him to call me if he thought of anything more substantial, and headed back to the club.

Fortunately, the club member services director, Andy DeWitt, was still on duty. I explained what I was up to. Before he'd answer any questions, he called DePaul, who gave him the OK.

Andy looked like the type of guy that would excel at glad-handing the moneyed; tall and thin, dark hair combed straight back, chin like a fist and blue eyes. Zane was right; he smelled like he'd dumped a bottle of cologne down his pants.

He escorted me into his office, off the lobby. He fiddled with his name tag as he explained to me that in a club this size he did everything from parking cars to cleaning the restrooms.

"Do you remember Mrs. DePaul waiting in the lobby for a ride on Tuesday evening?" I said.

"Sure," Andy said. "I asked her if she wanted me to call the cab guy in Urbana; she uses him sometimes when she can't cadge a ride. She said someone was coming for her."

"Who?"

"She didn't say. Sometimes it's her husband, sometimes one of her lady friends, sometimes the Taylor kid."

"But you didn't see who this time?"

"No, I was cleaning a tray of chicken cordon bleu off the kitchen floor that evening."

"Anybody that can confirm that?"

He gave me pursed lips, probably the worst reaction he was allowed to have at the club. "The cook. I made her stay with me until the kitchen was spic and span. We were scrubbing the tiles until midnight."

"Mind if I walk the course?" I said.

"Any friend of the DePaul's is welcome," he said in a way to imply he was only cooperating because it was his job. "Just don't interrupt play."

I wasn't sure what I expected to accomplish on my walk, but it was a good way to meditate on what I'd learned. The course was beautifully manicured, with Bermuda grass fairways and white sand traps. I wished I'd brought my clubs; I doubted anyone would have caught me once I was clear of the first tee.

Like most country clubs, the course was lightly used; in fact, there was no one playing in the late afternoon heat. The ladies must have blown off playing their round after all.

I looked up at the veranda as I circled the ninth green, but they were no longer there either.

I checked the traps as I walked the course, in the off-chance that someone might have buried her body there. An absurd idea, I knew; most traps only held a scant foot of sand.

There was a pond on the 16th hole, forcing the fairway to dogleg around it. It was half-choked with cattails. I circled it. On the far side, abutting deep rough, I caught a glimpse of something white six feet from the shore.

I was wearing a pair of wool slacks that had set me back $100, and I wasn't about to sacrifice them. I climbed the small hill separating the pond from the 17th fairway. There were still no other golfers in sight, and the clubhouse was hidden by a stand of oaks. I returned to the pond, and, cursing a blue streak, stripped off my shoes, socks and slacks.

There was swamp gas trapped in the ooze on the bottom of the pond, which burst forth as I stepped in and gave me the sensation of walking in a sewer. The water came up to my calves, then my knees as I took a couple of steps toward the flash of white.

I pulled the cattails apart to find Diedra, her head floating a couple of inches above the surface. The white I'd seen was her forehead. The strap of her golf bag was wrapped around her waist, holding the bottom half of her body down in the water. Gaily-colored carp were nibbling on her arms.

I retreated to shore, managing to hold down my lunch.

You might think that the cops would be happy to have a body with which to start their investigation, but you'd be wrong. These were small-town peace officers whose only recent experience with murder was a trailer shooting where the perp was too drunk to flee in his pickup.

One of them suggested I could take off, since my job was done; I'd found the missing woman. I hung around, though, so that I could give a full report to my client.

It took them over an hour for the photo guy to get there and shoot pictures of Diedra in place before they brought her to shore. The sun had set, and they ended up working by flashlight.

She was fully clothed, with a whopper of a dent in the back of her head, about the size of a five wood. The coroner's assistant and one of the cops carefully lifted her body and placed it on the stretcher. I was the only one in a position to notice when her head fell to one side, and, along with a rush of water, a golf ball came rolling out of her mouth.

While the others followed the body to the ambulance, I knelt to check the ball. A Titleist Pro V1 with a wide slice on it, like the grin on an idiot's face.

I pointed out the ball to the coroner, explaining where it had come from. He picked it up and bagged it. He was more talkative than a big city coroner, probably due to the infrequency of his duties. "The blow to the head looks fatal to me. The golf ball... that was overkill."

After the body left the scene I called DePaul, figuring he should hear about it from me, since he was footing the bill. I was proud of myself for not once bemoaning the fact that I'd found his wife in one day while he was paying me $1,000 per.

"We located your wife," I said when he answered. "I'm sorry to say, not alive." I've found that it does no good to play coy with bad news.

"Oh, shit," he said. "Where?"

I explained the situation, including the expectation that the cops would be contacting him any minute. He didn't reply for a long minute, and I thought I could hear a sniffle.

"I should have asked you earlier," I finally said. "Do you have an alibi for Tuesday evening?"

"I was here in the office, until about 10 p.m." he said.

"Anybody to testify to that?"

"Phone records," he said. "For billing purposes, we log all calls. You think I'm a suspect?"

"Afraid so," I said. My foot itched, and I wondered if I'd picked up a fungus from the pond. "Who else has had corpse dogs on their property?"

"Then you better find out who really did it," he said. Now he sounded angry.

"You want me to keep investigating?"

"You've done OK so far. So yeah, keep digging."

I took a break for dinner at the Airport Café and grabbed a room at the fleabag hotel south of town. At 9 p.m. I headed back out to DePaul's house, taking a chance that he would be home and not down at the police station. He was, but not in very good shape.

The cops had been there and questioned him for a good hour, during which he'd refreshed his glass of scotch one too many times. He didn't seem to quite understand when I asked to see his golf bag, but he nodded and pointed to the garage.

He had a nice set of sticks, by Ping. His balls were Nike, not Titleist. I asked him what Diedra played, and he said she also shot Nikes.

He agreed to allow me to borrow his clubs, and at my request wrote a note to DeWitt naming me as his guest for a round of golf. He was too drunk to ask me why.

I showed up at the course half an hour before the 2 p.m. standing tee time of Deidra's foursome the next afternoon. I showed DeWitt the letter from my client; he was still peeved about my questioning the day before, and he said, "Replace your divots, and don't litter," as though he was certain I'd never played a civilized round of golf in my life.

The three all pulled into the parking lot at the same time, about 1:50 p.m. Tracey was the first to pass me on the putting green, and gave me a puzzled look.

I put a good stroke on a ten-footer, watched it drop and said, "Mind if I tag along this afternoon?"

She pursed her lips. "It's usually a girl thing. But I suppose we could make an exception."

I'm not so vain as to think myself a babe magnet, but I'm not dog meat, either. I gave her my best smile. "I promise I'll be agreeable."

"Well, why not?" she said.

I followed her over to the first tee, where we were joined by Ami and Eloise. Both of them unenthusiastically agreed to allow me to play with them.

It took me three holes before I knew who'd killed Deidra.

Ami had obviously taken lessons. She had it all; the full turn, the stationary head, the wrist break, and she hit the snot of out the ball. She admitted to a 10 handicap.

Although the youngest-looking of the women, Eloise played an old person's game; short backswing and follow through, slow club head speed. The payoff was accuracy. Her ball didn't go far, but she managed to keep it in the short grass each time, taking the straight line from tee to green.

Tracey was a hacker, with a hitch in her backswing that would break the elbow of an older golfer. She swung with all her might. When she connected, the ball flew, but more often than not, she hit worm burners that never ascended more than a few feet off the turf.

Over the course of the first couple of holes, I was able to check what balls each of them used. Eloise played a Ram, while Ami and Tracey played Titleist. It's only the most popular ball in the world, so I didn't take that as solid evidence.

On the third hole, a 405-yard par four with a sharp dogleg to the left, all four of us ended up lying two a wedge shot from the green. I watched the form of my fellow players. Ami plopped a sweet lob wedge into the center of the green. Eloise hit hers thin and it scampered onto the apron of the green.

Tracey hit down on her ball like she was trying to behead a snake. The ball popped up and fell to the ground only 20 yards further down the fairway.

I finished the round because, hey, I was hitting the ball well and had a chance to break 90, which I would have done if I hadn't duck-hooked my tee shot on 11. Besides, I needed to know why, now that I knew who, if I was to clear my client.

The ladies, now comfortable with me, invited me to join them for drinks after the round was over.

They were disappointed when I ordered ginger ale. I explained that I had to do some driving yet that evening. I intended to end the day at home.

I waited for them to broach the topic we'd assiduously avoided during the round. Finally, after downing half her gin and tonic in one long slurp, Tracey said, "So now that you found Deidra, why are you still here?"

I explained about my assignment. "What I can't figure out is who might have hated her enough to kill her. It smells like an act of passion, not a murder for profit."

"Well," Eloise said, "She wasn't exactly hard to dislike." The other two gave her a disgusted look, but she wasn't paying attention to them.

"How so?" I asked.

Eloise leaned forward and dropped her voice. "She had a pretty sharp tongue for someone so dependent on other people. We used to joke that we spent time with her so that she wouldn't have the opportunity to talk about us behind our backs." She took another sip of her drink. "And she could be a braggart to those who didn't have a big house or a power husband."

Ami nodded when I looked her way.

"If she was having an affair, would she be the kind of person that kept quiet about it or bragged about it?"

"She'd hint," Tracey said, her eyes like beads. "She'd play coy but you'd know that if she was banging somebody other than her husband, it was some absolute stud."

"And was she hinting lately?" I said.

"No," Tracey said at the same time that Ami said, "Maybe."

I asked Ami to elaborate.

"She's been wearing more makeup and perfume lately, and she's bought a couple of cute new golf outfits."

"So she was meeting Mr. Whomever here at the club?"

"Yeah, I assumed that if there was a man in the picture, she saw him here," Ami said.

Beyond that, none of them were willing to speculate. But I had already drawn my conclusion.

Zane and his brother were shooting hoops in the driveway when I arrived at his house. When he saw who it was, he asked his brother to give him a minute and joined me at my car. I took a seat on the hood.

"You find out anything yet?" he asked, wiping his palms against his thighs.

"Yeah," I said. "How long have you been sleeping with Tracey Wells?"

He didn't change expression, but the blush on his face told the tale. I pointed it out to him. It was enough to deflate any lie he was considering.

"How did you know?" he said.

"She's the worst golfer among the three," I said.

"I don't get that," he said. "But I'm not feeling guilty, if that's what you think; I'm just a little embarrassed. She's not exactly a beauty, right? And Jesus, she's twice my age. But I'm between girlfriends and stuck out here in the country, so that changes a man's standards. Don't tell me you never picked low-hanging fruit when you were young."

"How about Deidra? That fruit was hanging so low it was touching the ground. I mean, a blind woman?"

He rolled up on his toes and I prepared to block his swing, but it was just a nervous tic. "Jesus; how'd you find out about that? She was begging me, man. For a couple of months. Her husband was ignoring her and, well, you can imagine how lonely you can get locked up at home with no way out. It wasn't anything serious."

"Did her husband know?"

"Of course not," he said, heatedly. "It was only a couple of times, and we were careful."

"How about Tuesday?"

"She was going to call me if her husband spent the night in Columbus; he did that from time to time, when his business ran late. She did eventually call, but I was already at the game and we were going out for beers later, so I didn't answer."

"Did Tracey know about Deidra?"

"I hope not, but when those four get tanked, they lose inhibitions, so I guess anything's possible."

I had what I needed, and turned to leave when he grabbed my sleeve. "Could you do me a favor?" he said.

"Probably not," I said.

"Keep my sleeping with Mrs. Wells out of the newspaper? My brother will never let me live it down."

"That's the price," I said, "you pay for picking the wrong fruit."

I was waiting for DePaul when he arrived home that evening. He pulled into the garage, and I followed him in, placing his clubs in the corner where they belonged.

"What's up?" he said, waving me to follow him into the house.

He headed to the bar and poured himself a scotch while I waited for his attention. He finally turned to me with a raised eyebrow.

"I know what happened," I said. "You're paying me, so I thought I'd tell you before I go to the cops."

"Shoot."

"Tracey Wells has been having an affair with Zane Taylor all summer," I said. "Now this might be hard to hear. Your wife seduced him a couple of weeks ago. Tracey found out."

"How'd you figure that out?" he said, his face ashen.

I told him about the ball in his wife's mouth. "Wells is the only one with such a poor swing that she'd slice a ball like that. And Zack is the only man she met at the club that she got to know well enough to develop a crush on."

"Jesus," he said. "That's horrible. I never thought Deidra would run around on me. That was one of the attractions of her blindness, to tell the truth; I figured she'd always be loyal."

"Anyway," I said, "Zane was supposed to come back to the course and give her a ride home, if you were going to spend the night in Columbus. However, when she called Zane he didn't answer.

"Deidra was still sitting there when they all left. She must have called Tracey for a ride when Zane didn't answer, and she circled back to the club. Deidra followed her out to her car. It was dark by then.

"I figure Tracey grabbed one of her clubs and hit Deidra on the head. Once she was out cold, she put the ball in her mouth and held it and her nose closed.

"Once Deidra was dead, she dragged the body out to the trap on the 16th and dropped her in the pond."

DePaul shook his head. "That's horrible." He drained his glass. "What's with the golf ball?"

"That was her mistake," I said. "I'm guessing Diedra said something about sleeping with Zane, and that set Tracey off. She probably saw something symbolic in using the ball, since Deidra cheated her at golf and now was cheating with her boyfriend. Maybe the slice on it reminded her of Deidra's open mouth, mocking her. Or maybe it was just handy in her pocket."

"Jesus," he said, wiping a rogue tear from his cheek. "I guess we'll have to tell the police. God, I hate this."

Just about every case I work ends up with those three words.

Even in a sport as genteel as golf.

It's the familiar things you never notice that sometimes matter most.

How Green Was My Valet
by John H. Dromey

ALTHOUGH PERHAPS NOT young enough or tall enough to become a top model, and decidedly not svelte enough to squeeze her ample charms into the impossibly-small confines of size zero haute couture gowns, the smartly-dressed woman nonetheless moved with the feline grace and confidence of a runway model. She appeared to treat the sidewalk as though it were an unending extension of a Parisian catwalk lined on both sides by shutter-happy fashion photographers.

Her accessories, at least, were the real thing. Her designer purse in particular was a real eye-catcher.

The woman's approach did not go unnoticed by the uniformed doorman who was standing at attention near the entrance to a posh apartment building.

She was watching him as well, although not in an obvious way. She detected the subtle shift in his posture indicating he was preparing to open the door without challenging her right to enter.

Molly Sullivan glided into the lobby of the building without missing a step and went directly to the bank of elevators.

Fifteen minutes later, Molly was back on the sidewalk in front of the building. She dabbed at her eyes with a fine linen handkerchief as she stood shoulder to shoulder beside the doorman.

Without turning her head she started talking.

"What a fiasco. Every morning at this time Mrs. Henderson lets Prince play in the corridor for an hour. I thought I could safely visit her while her wee canine companion was outside of the apartment, but I was mistaken."

"Attacked you, did he?" the doorman asked.

"No, absolutely not. Some little dogs are vicious, but not Prince. He's a sweetheart; he wouldn't hurt a flea. Not that he has fleas, of course, though I must say he might be at risk since that diamond studded collar of his certainly wouldn't keep them away. I could buy three or four of these purses for what Mrs. Henderson paid for that one little doggie necklace."

Molly shifted her weight from one foot to the other. The doorman turned his head slightly in her direction. She tapped the index finger of her right hand on the clasp of the handbag. The man's eyes were attracted to the movement.

"What happened?" he asked.

"Prince walked right up to me in the hallway as I knew he would. He never sees a stranger. I held my breath as I walked by him and Mrs. Henderson let me in immediately. Once inside, I inhaled deeply and my allergies kicked in almost at once. Prince had deposited enough dog dander in the apartment to pollute a domed stadium."

Molly blew her nose.

"Would you like me to call you a cab?"

"No, thank you. It's a nice day; I'll walk. The fresh air will help clear my sinuses."

When the prospect of a tip vanished, the doorman appeared to lose interest.

Molly pulled an empty water bottle out of her purse.

"Is there somewhere nearby I can get rid of this? It's ruining the contour of my purse."

The doorman held out a gloved hand. He accepted the bottle without comment, spun on his heel, and then quickly entered the building.

Molly stepped to one side and then turned around before leaning slightly and tilting her head so she could watch the man's movements through the glass door.

The doorman didn't look back. Taking big steps and bypassing a trash receptacle on the way, he strode across the lobby. At the same time he removed the bottle cap and slipped it into his pocket. He deposited the empty plastic container in a recycling bin located beside a soft drink machine.

Her stratagem had succeeded in diverting the doorman's attention, but Molly was unsure whether or not it was a significant breach of protocol. Although he'd temporarily abandoned his post, the guardian of the portal had moved so quickly there would not have been time for an outsider to slip through the entrance unnoticed.

Molly took off before the doorman could return to his accustomed spot in front of the building. She was clear-eyed and her respiratory system was free of congestion.

The doorman habitually spent part of his day off in a nearby park. The following Sunday he showed up as usual. Molly Sullivan had arrived there ahead of him.

With her everyday handbag the size of a picnic hamper snug at her side, Molly took up two spaces on a park bench. Her face was scrubbed clean of makeup and she was wearing a plain dress and sensible shoes. In that restrained guise she bore little or no resemblance to the fashion plate who'd stormed the high-rise apartment building a couple of days earlier. She had no fear about being recognized.

She likewise had no fear of contact with the animal companions that were roaming around freely. Molly petted a couple of friendly dogs when they approached her on the bench and she suffered no ill effects whatsoever. That was the extent of her physical activity while she waited, but her mind was fully engaged as she reviewed the specifics of a baffling series of seemingly unconnected felonious activities.

The high-rise building she'd visited earlier in the week was home to an unusually high number of crime victims.

There had been several muggings that targeted residents who were either going to or coming home from fancy parties. Apparently, the thief knew exactly where they'd be and when. In each instance only seldom-worn expensive trinkets were taken—the sort of fashion accessories that were only removed from a secure bank vault on very special occasions. Guests wearing costume jewelry at those same events were ignored.

Valuable items sometimes disappeared from apartments with no evidence of a break-in.

At least two occupants were victims of attempted blackmail for youthful indiscretions.

The unoccupied vacation home of another was burglarized during a very brief window of vulnerability when the owner was switching from one private security firm to another.

And the list went on.

Taking into consideration the fact that many crooks and con men are creatures of habit with their preferred modus operandi, the highly concentrated area of the crime wave plus the diversity of the offenses—when considered from a statistical viewpoint—simply did not add up.

Then there was a significant variation in the pattern when a prominent businessman living in the penthouse was accused of committing a serious crime, namely illegal insider trading. In his defense he, too, claimed to be a victim.

Faced with a hefty fine and possible jail time, the alleged insider trader was determined to clear his name no matter what it cost.

Fortunately for him, Angus Steward had the resources and connections to contest the allegations of the Securities and Exchange Commission. He had deep pockets and he also had friends in high places.

Angus Steward was adamant in denying any impropriety in the conduct of his business affairs. Although he routinely was privy to confidential information that could have been exploited by unscrupulous trading in the stock of publicly-owned companies, he had not done so. Whenever he was "in the know," he restricted his conversations to trusted colleagues. He most certainly had never deliberately "tipped" anyone.

Despite his caution, Angus was found to have had access to privileged information that was presumably used by several traders to make a killing in the market.

Angus denied ever having had direct contact with the profiteers, but how could he prove a negative?

Perhaps he would not be able to do so, but he could try. He hired a private investigator who grilled him about his recent activities.

While mining his client's memory for buried clues, the PI unearthed a plethora of meaningless minutia and *one* potential gem of information.

Angus was willing to stake his reputation on his recollection that while standing on the sidewalk within hearing distance of the doorman of his apartment building he had used his cell phone to discuss the troublesome stock with his business partner.

Was it possible the doorman was somehow to blame for the spate of wrongdoings?

The local police cooperated in the investigation.

Preliminary results seemed promising. The doorman had a criminal record which he had not revealed on his job application. Additionally, he sometimes provided valet service for the apartment dwellers which gave him temporary access to their keys. Could he have had duplicates made? In particular, did he have possession of a key to the unmonitored private entrance located on the opposite side of the building?

Was the possible suspect somehow privy to intimate details of the private lives of the residents? An informal survey of the tenants revealed they frequently took the doorman for granted—or ignored him completely—and often spoke freely in his presence.

Further investigation proved frustrating. While the doorman might have had the means to carry out some of the crimes, he lacked the opportunity. In most cases he was either on the job, where he was plainly visible, or at home. In addition, there was no evidence that he had fenced any stolen property and there was no suspicious activity in his bank account. Did he have accomplices? If so, how did he communicate with them? Wire taps and surveillance produced negative results.

With no better suspect available, Angus was unwilling to give up on his attempts to prove a connection. With the help of the PI he organized a sting operation.

That was where Molly Sullivan came in.

The person who recommended Molly for the undercover assignment described her as "a freelance busybody."

"That's exactly what we need," the PI said, "just so long as she also looks the part."

Molly may not have enjoyed the extravagant fashion makeover financed by Angus Steward, but she endured it.

The undercover dog was already in place when Molly arrived on the scene. Prince casually explored the hallway outside of Mrs. Henderson's apartment while wearing his diamond-studded collar with its built-in tracking device. Was his canine ego bruised by Molly's apparent snub in passing him by with her nose in the air—not once, but twice? Prince gave no indication one way or the other.

As a sensible precaution in case the doorman later saw the

security footage, Molly faked a couple of sneezes, being careful to blink each time, and then dabbed at her eyes intermittently during her descent in the elevator.

Outside the building she verbally laid the foundation for the sting as previously described.

Only one big question remained. Would the doorman take the bait?

Although he was wearing a jogging outfit, the doorman was walking when he came into Molly's view.

She had a ringside seat as she surreptitiously observed his every move. There was not much to see. He appeared to wander around aimlessly for the most part. He did not approach any of the other park visitors, either of the bipedal or the four-legged variety.

Molly was disappointed.

Catching someone in the act of stealing Prince's collar would not be enough.

It was crucial to prove a connection between the doorman and the thief.

After a short while the doorman appeared to lose interest in the great outdoors. He tightened the cap before dropping a water bottle into a trash receptacle and then strolled out of the park.

Molly easily picked out the undercover cop who was tailing the suspect. She hoped the doorman had not done the same. She watched the two of them move out of sight, but remained right where she was afterwards, continuing her vigil.

Fifteen minutes later, still seated on the park bench, Molly called in her report.

"I've solved the mystery for you," she said, before relaying specific details of what she'd observed. "I'll let you handle the case from here, but I'd like for you to keep me informed about how it goes."

Shortly thereafter, a man was arrested for stealing Prince's collar. As part of a plea bargain for a lighter sentence, the thief implicated the doorman. The doorman, who had acted as a lookout, was charged with conspiracy. Other arrests followed.

Molly was invited to a debriefing in the DA's office.

"What tipped you to the doorman's system for sharing ill-gotten information?" an assistant district attorney asked her.

"He's green," Molly said.

"You're wrong about that, Mrs. Sullivan. That man's been in and out of prison numerous times. He's a highly experienced crook."

"A message in a bottle was his method of communicating with his co-conspirators," Molly said, "I saw him go out of his way to recycle a plastic bottle. There was no way he'd have thrown one in the trash without a very good reason. He's *green*."

Diplomacy is to do and say
the nastiest thing in the nicest way
—Isaac Goldberg

The Least Of These
by BV Lawson

SHE WAS A single mother from a micro-town in southwest Virginia who'd never had a single lucky break until she landed a job as secretary at the French Embassy in D.C. At least, she believed it was her lucky break. That was Leanne Coonts's greatest mistake.

Now, her little daughter was an orphan and Leanne's body was lying in a morgue awaiting an autopsy, while the Embassy staff remained tight-lipped, waving their diplomatic passports in the faces of police. It had only been two days since Leanne's death, but the show—or the party—apparently must go on. Scott Drayco surveyed the room full of Armani tuxes and designer evening gowns, as the Château Lafite Rothschild flowed as freely as the fountains of Versailles.

Drayco hadn't promised his clients he'd be able to uncover anything useful about the murder, but they thought a discreet civilian might be their best bet, and so here he was, in his own hated tux, minus the red cummerbund. The last time he'd worn the thing, it had been at a party much like this one, only the guest of honor had been shot. Maybe Drayco should have gone out and rented something else. Not that he was superstitious.

What he also hadn't told the clients was this was the type of case he'd be willing to do pro bono after talking with Leanne's ten-year-old daughter, Heather. Her brave little soldier act hadn't fooled him. As she'd told him the travel plans she and her mother began making only hours before her mother was killed, there was no light in her hazel eyes. Now, there was no place she could travel to escape, because Heather had lost her entire world.

Drayco flipped his mental folder of principal suspects, bios, and photos and grabbed a flute of red wine off a passing tray—when in Paris, *n'est-ce pas*? He'd chatted up some of the lesser possibles for the past hour, working his way up to the big fish. Tackle the bottom feeders first, the ones who were happy to nibble on crudités, with a side helping of fresh gossip.

But what had he learned so far, other than the fact he was developing a headache from the clash of colognes—jasmine, grapefruit, cedarwood, musk, sage—radiating off warm skin? There was the usual litany of employee affairs, drug use, and shrinks. The only interesting tidbits were hints of conflict between the French government and the Russian Embassy one mile up on Wisconsin Avenue. But then, who didn't have conflicts with the Russians these days?

He headed toward his first major target, the Press Liaison, Pierre Lamenteau, who sported a diamond-studded earring matching his sparkling tie pin. He was a foot shorter than Drayco, which made it harder to look him in the eye. But look Drayco did, with the realization that the man's picture should be added to the dictionary beside the definition for "shifty eyes." After a minute or so of banal chatter, Drayco learned one thing fairly quickly. For a man who was ostensibly a press expert, Lamenteau was remarkably unguarded. Drayco silently cheered, "*Vive le vin.*"

Lamenteau prefaced his comments with a belch. "So there I was, *que c'est embêtant,* in the middle of this press conference, when someone shouted, 'What about the woman who was murdered?' An appalling lack of manners and protocol. Americans can be such boors." He looked at Drayco. "Present company excepted, of course. Er, what did you say you do, Monsieur Drayco?"

"I'm a consultant."

"Oh." Lamenteau stifled a hiccup. "Who do you consult for?"

"Anyone who will pay me."

"Ha ha, *très bon.* As I was saying, there I was in the thick of the press and this lout has the gall to throw me off balance. What did he expect me to do, yell out the murderer's name, address, phone number? Perhaps his favorite color?"

If that lout had been an FBI plant, quite possibly. Drayco took a tiny sip from his own glass of wine. "That young woman's death must have caused a stir around here. Such an inconvenience."

"*Oui, oui,* that was my point exactly. She was a mousy little nobody and yet in swarm the police and *là*! We cannot get a bit of work done." Lamenteau leaned forward and lowered his voice. "And I think I was followed home."

"Is that a fact? *Zut alors.*" Drayco took a sip of his wine, hoping it would encourage Lamenteau to do the same, and he was happily rewarded. The man's eyes were beginning to match his ruddy cheeks. Red cheeks, white shirt and blue tux—a walking, or stumbling—human French flag.

"Tell me, Monsieur Lamenteau, what exactly did that mousy little nobody do around here, anyway? It couldn't have been all that important."

"The usual things I suppose. Letters, manning the phone."

"And files? There are always files."

"Ah *oui*, files."

Drayco goaded him. "In the movies, they'd say she saw something she shouldn't have. Or perhaps slept with her boss. Not a Truffaut movie, of course."

"*Mais non*, that would be beneath Truffaut, such clichés. As for sleeping with the boss? Her face was too plain. And what she should have had here," Lamenteau patted his chest. "She had here instead," he patted his ass. "Not like Geneviève."

Drayco followed Lamenteau's leering gaze to a woman with flaxen hair in a purple dress sculpted on her body. From the name, Drayco guessed the object of Lamenteau's lust must be Geneviève L'Abbée, cultural liaison. Another name from his mental folder and another Big Fish.

"Okay, so no sleeping with the boss for our mousy little nobody, Monsieur Lamenteau. But the files—now there's a cliché that might fly. Perhaps she saw something she shouldn't."

"No one would have trusted her with anything important. But all embassies do have their dirty little secrets." When Lamenteau smiled, he almost looked human. "Perhaps Babin's secrets. He's the political attaché. That Coonts woman did a project for him last week."

Lamenteau held his wine glass up to the light."You must excuse me, Monsieur Drayco, as my glass is empty and that will never do."

From his research on the staff, Drayco knew a lot about Raymond Babin. In his mid-50s, formerly French intelligence followed by foreign service. And now, a glorified diplomatic sycophant. At least he was well-paid—the blinding necklace on his wife Marie's neck must have emptied out a few ruby and emerald mines.

Perhaps the necklace was marital bribery? Drayco's research also discovered Babin had a stable of mistresses around the globe. A messy divorce would cost him at least half his estate. As Drayco approached the pair, Marie's thin nasal voice cut through the din of wounded civility around her with surgical precision. "I did not agree to change the draperies from mauve to puce and I will simply not pay for them. They're ghastly, like something out of *Better Homes and Garden*."

Drayco began to understand why Babin had strayed from his wedding vows. Marie's face might not be enough to sink a thousand ships, but that voice had a fighting chance.

"Ah, Monsieur Babin, Pierre Lamenteau was singing your praises and I must meet the man who single-handedly keeps the Embassy together." Drayco could play sycophant, too. He reached out to shake the man's hand, then turned to Marie. "And this must be your lovely wife. *Enchantée*," Drayco also wasn't above kissing the woman's hand—whatever it took to bring a spark of light back into the pair of empty young hazel eyes that had been haunting him all evening.

Babin shook Drayco's hand, then used his same hand to rub through his thin, unnaturally black hair. Rather unfortunate, since Babin's comb-over had now moved a little too far to the right. "I don't believe I caught your name, Monsieur—"

"Drayco. Scott Drayco. Consultant." Drayco looked around the room. "It's a surprisingly dull party, wouldn't you say?"

Marie beamed up at Drayco. "I said the very same thing to Raymond, did I not? But surely you are not here by yourself, Monsieur Drayco—do you mind if I call you Scott? Such a handsome young stallion all alone? Surely not."

Her husband shifted his feet, although Drayco didn't think the man was jealous. More like embarrassed. "That's very kind of you, Madame Babin, but yes, I'm alone."

"Please. It's Marie. *Quel dommage*, Scott. I'm sure there is someone around here we can fix you up with." She glanced half-heartedly at a group of twenty-somethings in a corner, all texting on their phones. "But with a such a dull party, it probably wouldn't be worth it. I suppose it's all that woman's fault. The one who was murdered."

"Yes, I did hear something about that. A secretary or clerk of some sort?"

"Secretary. Raymond worked with her, didn't you, dear? I think I met her once. Rather forgettable, but pleasant enough. For that type of job."

'Pleasant enough' was equivalent to a compliment for the likes of a Marie Babin. Drayco guessed that meant Marie didn't suspect Leanne Coonts of being one of the fillies in her husband's stable.

Babin tilted his head in a brief nod, looking uncomfortable expressing even that much emotion, and Drayco looked around for a wine tray. This man was far too sober.

"My wife is correct, Monsieur Drayco. I did work with that unfortunate woman. She was … competent."

"Yes, that's what Lamenteau said. She'd done some project for you last week, I believe. Competently. As your personal secretary, you must feel her loss deeply."

"She wasn't my personal secretary, Drayco. She worked for all the staff. But yes, we feel her loss. She will be … missed."

That was certainly diplomatic. But even a diplomat skilled at word choices wasn't always aware how much his body language was giving away. Babin's body was saying he couldn't care less about the secretary's demise. Drayco was beginning to wonder if anyone in the embassy cared for Leanne Coonts. Of the dozen or so staff he'd chatted up earlier, not a one seemed to know anything about Leanne except her name.

Drayco tried to rein in his anger at the disregard for a human life. These people were far more worried about their jobs than justice. Typical inside-the-Beltway pissing contests without which the city would implode. Maybe it was hard to care about one life when faced with global struggles of survival. But it was individuals, one by one, who made up that globe. Individuals like Leanne Coonts, lover of turquoise, hummingbird figurines and strawberry shortcake.

Feeling the need for a quick breath of fresh air, he excused himself from the Babins and beelined it toward an exit door, but paused just shy of the door, catching sight of a room that was surprisingly empty. It was the auditorium, doing its impression of a mausoleum as his footsteps echoed on the wooden floor. He sat down at the piano, tried a few keys and grimaced. Out of tune.

But he started playing anyway, feeling more alive than at any point since he'd set foot inside the building. He saw a flash of something out of the corner of his eye and took his hands from the keyboard as a woman entered the room.

She said, "You don't have to stop. It sounded like you were calling me."

Drayco raised an eyebrow. "I was?"

"The song you were playing. Debussy's 'Girl with the Flaxen Hair.'" She pointed to her golden tresses, elegantly pulled back with curls falling onto her forehead.

He smiled. "I'm not sure why I picked that tune."

"I was hoping it was because you were trying to seduce me. I've been watching you all evening. Quite the socialite, flitting from one person to another. But no partner." She looked at his hands. "And no ring."

"I'm not sure I'd want to subject anyone I like to death-by-party."

She laughed. "It is deadly dull, isn't it?"

"Marie Babin blames it on the secretary who was murdered. I guess the deceased showed poor manners with her timing. It's so much more thoughtful to get oneself murdered when there's nothing on the calendar."

Geneviève leaned on the piano. "It does seem no one cares. Rather heartless."

"Can you really care about someone when you don't bother to get to know them?"

"It's not that the French staff don't socialize with the locals, but these are temporary jobs, mostly. And that secretary was a little hard to understand at times."

"How so??"

"I believe it's called a southern accent."

Drayco started playing the Debussy again. "Did you get to know her, Leanne Coonts?"

"A little. I know she had a daughter, although I never met her."

Geneviève sat down beside him on the bench as the last notes of the song faded away. "Do you do that for a living? Play the piano?"

"I dabble."

"That is more than dabbling. You are very good. Sviatoslav Richter good."

"Coming from a cultural attaché, that's a compliment."

"I really have been watching you, you know. You've got the most amazing eyes. I can see that they're an intense blue, but in certain light, they look purple."

Drayco scooted down to make more room for her on the bench, all the while gazing approvingly at the movement of her tight purple dress. "Is that the only reason you've been watching me, Mademoiselle L'Abbée?"

"Please—call me Gennie. But no, I helped put together the guest list and I couldn't put a name with your face."

"Scott Drayco, at your service."

"Still doesn't ring any bells. When I realized I didn't know you, I wondered if you were one of those alphabet-soup people."

"Alphabet soup? Like Campbells?"

She smiled and shook her head. "FBI. CIA. TSA. ATF. I can't keep track of them all."

"No, not alphabet soup." That wasn't entirely a lie. He wasn't *currently* an alphabet-soup man. "It's a shame about the secretary's daughter. It's hard to lose a mother at that age."

"At any age. I'm sorry they won't be able to take that trip they'd planned."

"Yes, so am I." Drayco started playing Debussy's "Reverie," as Geneviève leaned in closer. Drayco found it easy to play and talk at the same time, one reason a former teacher called him schizophrenic. "So, Gennie. Who do you think's the most likely candidate for the murderer of Mrs. Coonts? Babin, perhaps? Lamenteau?"

Geneviève had a musical laugh, almost bird-like, less like one of Leanne's hummingbirds, more like a nightingale. "Lamenteau could have done it. If Mrs. Coonts had stolen something valuable from him. Like his prized bottle of 1990 Château Petrus Bordeaux."

"And Babin?"

"I can see him as a murderer, if Mrs. Coonts pointed out what other women have been afraid to."

"And that is?"

"His manhood resembles what you Americans might call an inchworm." She smiled and Drayco couldn't help smiling back. Geneviève was the kind of woman he could fall hard for, if he wasn't careful.

He played several more measures of the Debussy, trying to ignore the out-of-tune notes. "I am curious about one thing, Gennie."

"Just one? Do tell."

She was so close now he could smell the tiniest hints of something lilac-ish. Without missing a beat of the Debussy, he said, "I'm wondering why you killed Leanne Coonts. My guess is, she found out something you wanted kept hidden. Being a Russian spy, for instance."

Drayco stopped playing as Geneviève pulled back and stared at him with wide eyes he now noticed were also hazel. Coincidence, yes, but it gave him much-needed resolve.

"What makes you think I killed her?"

"You said you've never met Leanne's daughter and yet you knew of the travel plans she and her mother started making only a few hours before Leanne's death. Which was on a Saturday, when ordinarily you wouldn't have been around to hear her talk of such plans."

Drayco started playing again. He loved this piece, one of his favorites. "As for the Russian spy part—a wild guess. You said I reminded you of Richter. Odd comparison for a French cultural ambassador, to name a Russian pianist. And one who's not even a contemporary. I'd have expected Thibaudet, perhaps. Or Lortie."

"So you *are* in the alphabet soup."

"Just trying to help a little girl find justice. And closure."

Geneviève sat very still, listening or thinking—or scheming, Drayco couldn't tell. Finally she said, "If I am a murderer and spy, like you say, what's to keep me from killing you right here and now?"

"The hidden microphone I'm wearing, probably." He stopped talking long enough to finish the song, then turned to her. "I find it fascinating the person responsible for taking Leanne's life seems to have cared more about her than anyone else here."

Genevieve scooted toward him, and he didn't stop her. She gently pushed aside a lock of his hair that was falling over his forehead, and to his surprise, leaned over to kiss him. "That's to give your microphone friends some entertainment. And because you really do have amazing eyes."

She put her head onto his shoulder, and he decided to start playing again while they waited for his "microphone friends" to make their way inside. But nothing French or Russian this time. Neutral territory. Perhaps Edvard Grieg, the piece called "Little Bird." Grieg, the diplomat—Drayco liked the sound of that. And if you listened to the piece carefully, you could almost hear the flapping of a humming-bird's wings.

Not much ever happens in those little out of the way stores. Except when it does.

Miscellany
by Eryk Pruitt

THERE'S A FILLING station just south of Durham, North Carolina, that raised a ruckus a while back because the owner refused to take down a Confederate flag he'd hoisted above the building. Imagine how folks from miles around flocked to see what would happen when the National Guard came out to tell him to take it down. How for years and years after, old timers would bend your ear with the details of the Klan, the protests. The cheers and jeers.

Not since that day way-back-when had anyone paid any mind to Gerry Tompkins' place or what he said or did. The old-timers still hung out around there, but for the most part, people got their gas and goods a little closer into town. Tobacco dried up around there long ago and there wasn't much travel on those roads any longer. Just folks lost on their way out of town. Neighbors that came day after day for years and years until one day they didn't. Until one day they were gone.

But when those two came into Huck's Country Express and robbed Gerry Tompkins blind, they got folks started. Breathed new life into them, you could say. Now they had something to talk about again. Something besides how hot it was this year or what Duke or North Carolina did during the off-season or what may or may not be the reason why so-and-so's barbecue don't taste like it used to.

You had to go no further than Tompkins himself to hear how dramatic things were or weren't. For more than a year after, folks would get held up in line while trying to buy eggs or Lotto tickets or what have you while he told one guy or another the same damn story he'd been telling since it happened. How the kid acted suspicious when he first walked in. How he wasn't much to think about, but something seemed odd about him, all the same. How Tompkins had looked away, went back to stocking cigarettes.

"I mean, he wasn't black or nothing," Tompkins would say for years, as if the surprise were still fresh. "Here he come, looking at this or that, picking stuff up and setting it down. He's looking in this corner and along the doors and every which way, when finally he gets him a bottle of coke and tries to pay me with a fifty dollar bill."

"That's how they scope you out," Grit Beecher would often add. Grit, on that day and many, many afterward, would sit in one of the lunch booths and read a paper, smoke on a cigar, and jaw with damn near anyone who gave him a minute or two. Grit and Huck's Country Express went hand-in-hand. "They give you a big bill so they can see what's in the register. That's what the kid did. I saw him peek over the counter and look in the register while Gerry made change and I thought something was a little fishy."

"But like I said, he wasn't black," Tompkins would always explain.

There weren't many places like his left. Most of them got bought up by developers or fellas in cahoots with big oil companies. Used to be, there was a Jimmy's Mini-Mart, a Ronny's Highway Shop and even a Ronny's Too on the other side of town. But soon the sign saying "Jimmy's" got smaller and smaller until one day it was gone, replaced by a bulky neon "Exxon" or "Mobil."

Tompkins usually offered that as a reason why he didn't have drop safes or video cameras. Actually, he did have a video camera. It just didn't record anything. He quit buying tapes for it years ago and when it went on the fritz, he never bothered to replace it. Don't ask him why, but he fixed damn near everything in that gas station when it broke. Never bothered one minute with the video camera.

So the kid takes his change, then goes and stands by the door a bit. He looks out the window and nobody can ever agree if it was a little wave or a big wave or what, but most everybody believes it was a signal. Then he stops at the magazine rack and picks out one of those Hollywood magazines and starts reading.

Another thing most folks never agree on is what the man looked like that came in next. Tompkins said he had salt-and-pepper hair, put him at about five-ten. Grit said he was taller, had brown hair. Sandy Hightower, who'd been in the back aisle choosing between potato chips, agreed that he had brown hair, but for some reason gave him a beard, which didn't anyone else bother to do. Hell, they couldn't even agree on what kind of gun the man pulled or whether it came out of his pocket or the front or back waistband of his pants.

But they all agreed there was a gun. And they all agreed the man put it in Tompkins' face and shouted "Give me all the money." He saw the others and moved the gun to each of their faces. Then back to Tompkins. He said didn't need nobody to be a hero. He said nobody has to get hurt.

Didn't any of them think about the kid at that moment, but he stayed over by the magazine rack. He flipped through the pages. Grit always thought it plenty strange when the boy called over to Tompkins and asked him if this was the most recent issue of the Hollywood magazine they had. Said it was at least a month old and has he got the new one in yet.

"I told him I didn't and he didn't say no more about it," Tompkins would always say. "He set the issue back on the magazine rack where he got it then turned his attention to the stack of newspapers down at his feet."

The man with the gun, on the other hand, was all business. He motioned with the barrel, steered Tompkins to hurry, slow down, take it easy. Pointed it toward a carton of filtered cigarettes and told him to throw those in with the cash too. Tompkins did what he was told. He hunched his shoulders as he rifled through the drawer, unable to get the money out of the till and into the sack fast enough.

What happened next, everybody agrees on.

"In comes Officer Sherrill," as Sandy Hightower would tell it. "And it ain't just him, but this is a day that he's hosting one of the Explorer Scouts. The ride-along program brought kids up from the high school and taught them what it was like to work as a policeman. That particular Sunday, Mr. Sherrill had the Kessler boy with him."

The Kessler boy was Jimmy Kessler, a sophomore who had no shot of ever working with a police department, on account of his weight. Jimmy Kessler never met a candy bar he didn't like and when he walked into the Huck's Country Express that Sunday afternoon, his Explorer uniform stretched at the buttons. In fact, Grit Beecher seemed to remember him with a Snickers in his mouth.

"First thing I heard was the bell I keep over the door," Tompkins would say. "It rang just like it had any other time somebody walked in. So I looked up at the door, just like I would any other time. And first thing I thought was, *I'm so glad the police have come.* I thought that for about a split second, then didn't think it no more."

"I remember Sherry saying something about how hot it was and then it all got started," Grit would say. "I remember wanting to jump up and down and tell him to look out, the guy's got a gun, but things happened too damn fast. Before you know it, they was shooting."

One of the bullets hit the door frame. They dug out the bullet later, but Tompkins never had the frame fixed. He'll take anyone and everyone over to the door and point it out. Show them where the first bullet went.

"Missed Sherrill's head by yay-much," he would always say, holding his hands about a foot apart. "Sherry had just as much time to get a good look at him before that man squeezed off a shot. Didn't even have time to get his gun. He grabbed the fat kid he brung with him and dove into the whatnot aisle."

The "whatnot aisle" was the aisle closest to the door. This is where Gerry Tompkins kept automotive supplies and other things he'd found folks needed over the years. Sometimes folks needed cat food. He kept it in the whatnot aisle. Maybe you needed to grab a toy on your way to visit with a youngster. Those were also kept in the whatnot aisle.

"If it ain't food or drink, more than likely it ends up in the whatnot aisle," Tompkins often said.

The whatnot aisle is where Officer Sherrill and fat little Jimmy Kessler landed, Sherrill shielding the kid with his body while trying to fetch out his own sidearm. Tompkins went down behind the counter, Grit and Sandy Hightower hit the floor. But that didn't mean they couldn't see everything that unfolded.

"Gerry had one of those bent mirrors up in the corner," Grit said, "so that he could catch kids trying to take shit off the candy aisle. You can see the whole store off those mirrors and the fella with the gun, he's right in front of me and Sandy Hightower, but Sherry, he's a few rows back. I look up at the mirror and you can see him crawl on his belly toward the end of the aisle, gun in hand. He was looking to get a shot at that fella with the gun."

"I liked to shit my britches," Tompkins would say. "I ain't afraid to say it. I've had a colored boy in a time or two who talked rough but ain't never been gunfire in the store. The fella already shot once, and I saw him inching down the aisle, I saw Sherry inching down the aisle...

Like I said, ain't nobody ever fired a gun in my shop, and it looked like there was about to be somebody killed there. And if the fella got the drop on Sherry, more than likely he'd have to kill us all so there wouldn't be no witnesses."

This has always been a great spot to pause for dramatic effect. If Grit told the story in a bar somewhere, he found it advisable to suddenly empty his beer, knowing folks would buy him another so he would stick about and tell what happens next. Tompkins would take the opportunity to ring up another customer or two, let folks get antsy. Sandy Hightower, on the other hand, never had a problem launching into it.

"That kid... We'd all forgotten about that kid," was how she'd tell it. Sandy Hightower talked with her hands a lot. Right here, she'd get a workout. "That kid, he must have been watching the whole thing on the shoplifter's mirror and maybe he was worried that Officer Sherrill would shoot his buddy. Anyway, the kid isn't going to take it. He's up and running and next thing you know, he's got a gun in the back of Sherrill's neck."

Tompkins always shakes his head. He'll walk around the counter and take folks by the arm to the whatnot aisle and point to a spot on the shelf that's empty. He'll wait until you look at the spot before saying, "This is where I used to keep them. I don't keep them there no more. Not since that day. No sir."

Them are the plastic toy cap guns he'd sold on the whatnot aisle since the Eighties, back when toy guns were more socially acceptable. Back in the old days, toy guns looked like real guns. But a few black kids got shot by well-intentioned policemen and, come to find out, the gun was fake the whole time, just some toy. People—mostly Northerners—picketed and petitioned and all of a sudden, fake guns needed to look more fake. The company that made the gun Tompkins sold on his whatnot aisle compromised by sticking a red tip at the end of the barrel. Problem solved.

"But that little red tip don't do nothing for you when it's buried in the back of your neck, I don't reckon." Grit slapped his palms against each other, like dusting chalk off erasers. "That kid, he jams that gun into Sherry's head and tells him he'll blow it off if he so much as moves another inch."

"Don't Sherry or the fat boy he brung—don't *nobody*—move an-other inch."

About this time, if you're hearing about it at Huck's, Tompkins will take you around the end of the whatnot aisle and show you just where Officer Sherrill lay. He'll point up along the row of ice-cold coolers and draw his finger up alongside where you both stand.

"Around comes the older fella," Tompkins will say. "He ain't none too pleased with Sherry at this point. I reckon he'd have put a couple rounds in both him and that little fat fella if it weren't for the kid standing there with the little cap gun, saying don't worry, I got it un-der control."

Sandy Hightower will shake her head and furrow her brow. "He didn't have to kick him. Officer Sherrill was just doing his job."

"He kicked him once, good in the ribs," Grit tells it. "Fella wore size eleven Ariat boots and he put the tip of one right into Sherry's side, then told him to get up. Told us all to get up."

Officer Sherrill has never liked to talk about it. Rarely will he. However, there are occasions—usually regarding alcohol—where his side of the story is readily available.

"The suspect ordered myself and the other patrons of the store to line up by the cooler door," Sherrill said one night at a wedding recep-tion. His cousin Bob had just got married to a little girl from Greens-boro and he felt a bit festive. There wasn't a single person in atten-dance who hadn't heard the story at least a dozen times already, but none of them had ever heard it from Sherrill.

That night, he said: "The older suspect had already relieved me of my sidearm, or else I probably would have opened fire the second he told us to line up. They called Gerry around from behind the counter and told him to join up with us, asked him if the beer cooler could be locked from the outside. At this point, I felt the most important thing was to keep everyone calm, since we were outgunned."

Someone made a joke about the kid's cap gun and Sherrill stopped talking. A few beers later, he had to be restrained and taken home after he fired three rounds into the wedding cake. Folks figured it best not to talk to Sherrill about it after that.

The kid is the one who thought to remember to ask after their phones. While the older man held the gun on them, he came around with one of the station's go-bags and had each person drop in their phone. He pulled out Sandy Hightower's phone and thumbed around at the screen, asked Tompkins if they had wi-fi. Tompkins told him no, he didn't have wi-fi and then the older man got a bit fussy.

"He told the kid to quit jacking with the phone and the kid answers he was just checking the news." Tompkins shook his head. "They put that sack of phones over on the counter, well out of our reach and shoved us on inside the beer cooler."

"This is getting to be old hat for us," the kid told the older man.

Grit will tell you they were all in that cooler, freezing off their asses for the better part of an hour. Finally, in walked a couple black kids and, once they heard everybody hooting and hollering inside the cooler, they let them out.

"It's the first time I seen ole Gerry happy to have colored kids in his store," Grit said. "Let me tell you."

Around about this time, most folks will ask Gerry Tompkins has he bothered to fix up that old camera system yet. He's got two answers, depending on how well he knows you. If he don't know you well, he'll laugh and say hell yes, he's fixed the camera. What do you think he is, stupid?

But if he does... if he knows you pretty well, he'll look first this way and then the other, then lean in real close and tell you, "Hell no. There's just something not right about me sitting under a camera all day. I don't care what year it is." Then he'll take you by the hand and lead you all the way to the back of the store, then open up the cooler and point his finger inside. Follow his finger and he'll show you the brand new coat rack hanging on the wall above the twelve-packs. He's got four fur-lined coats hanging off it.

"But that don't mean I didn't learn nothing."

Sometimes with a shakedown you get more bang for your
buck than expected.

Stars & Stripes
by Jed Power

I'D BEEN LUCKY for a change; I'd opened my little fireworks shop just
at the right time—about three weeks after New Hampshire legalized
the things. I was right in on the ground floor. Perfect location too—
within spitting distance of the beach and right smack dab on Route
1A. All the crazy Massachusetts kids and the vacationers (who
couldn't even buy a sparkler in their own state) had to pass right by
my place to get to party city—Hampton Beach.

And man, was it a sweet operation at first. I had a ten-year lease
and I was making money hand over fist. It was pouring in and it was
legit. I hadn't had to do anything with the .38 revolver I kept under
the counter, except clean it, since I'd given up my old ways and
opened this place. I was selling anything and everything, I didn't give
a crap. I had all the old standards: M-80's, Cherry Bombs, Roman
Candles and 80 pack bricks of fire crackers. Yeah, all that old stuff,
but new things too. Like Saturn Battery Missiles, Sonic Jacks, Whistling Jupiters and little tanks that moved around on the ground and
shot out fire balls as they went.

And the amount of product I was moving? It was unbelievable.
Each year, for about a month before the 4th of July, I'd get a tractor
trailer load delivered every other night. And believe me, that's a lot of
stuff.

Of course, I had my problems too. Like the time some tough guys
(or at least they thought they were tough guys) came around to have a
little talk with me. Seemed they didn't like the idea I was buying my
fireworks direct from an out of state source. They wanted to set up
their own wholesale operation and sell to all the dealers on the sea-
coast, if not the whole state. I told them that was a nice idea, but if
they came back to see me again I'd shove a Blockbuster down their
throats. Oh yeah, I forgot—I had used the .38 once—when I flashed
it at those punks. They left; they didn't come back. And it probably
wasn't just the sight of the gun either. Christ, if you saw me you'd
probably wonder why they tried to muscle me in the first place. Plus

that, I've been around. Man, through the years I've been involved in everything from...well, maybe I'd better get back on track. I don't really know you too good, after all, and I don't want to get into more trouble than I've already got.

And what trouble's that, you want to know? The trouble that started the day that little squirt walked into my store. He was a nervy little bastard and I knew right away something was up as I watched him paw through my merchandise like it was the contents of someone's trash bag. He poked around through everything, as if he could tell the difference between Black Cat firecrackers (yeah, they still make them) and Wolf Packs. Right.

I kept an eye on him while I rang up an Iwo Jima Assortment box for some kids from Boston. The factory stamps a $179.00 on it, so I let the kids think they're getting over on me by giving it to them for a hundred bucks. Course I only pay thirty-five for them. On the other hand, they're probably doubling their money on them down in Beantown. Nice business, huh?

Soon as the kids are out the door, the squirt walks up to me, bouncing a little bit as he comes, like some short guys do, trying to look taller, I guess. It didn't work. Besides being a peanut, he had a bald head, a round face and nerd type clothes. A real dink. And his voiced sounded just like he looked.

"Business is good," he said. A statement, not a question.

"It's all right," I said, holding my hand up and making it shimmy. Even if I wasn't a little leery of this character I still wouldn't have gotten too chatty. I don't like getting to friendly with my customers. After all, selling fireworks is like selling cars—they all want to dicker with you on the price. So it doesn't pay to get too chummy with someone who in five minutes might be trying to gaff you on the price of a Toot and Twirl.

"Nice location too," said the squirt, "right on 1A here." He waved his soft hand in the direction of the road in front of my store. It was a nice Saturday afternoon and the traffic was bumper-to-bumper trying to get over the bridge to the beach. "Matter of fact, this is the only fireworks joint on 1A. Isn't it?"

For some reason, I didn't like the way the conversation was going one bit, so I stood up from my stool behind the register. That's usually enough to shut up most pests. But not this one; he didn't even blink. And that worried me. Like I said, I been around and I can smell trouble as fast as a strong fart.

"You ever think of selling this place?" he asked. He looked into my eyes like maybe he thought he could kick my ass. I didn't sense crazy; so I wondered what he knew that I didn't.

"Never," I said, real hard-like, even for me.

"Maybe you oughta consider it," he said, with a little smirk on his face like a real punk. "I'll make you a nice offer."

"Not interested, pal." And I wasn't. Why the hell should I have been? This was my little gold mine. After all the dues I'd paid through the years I damn well deserved it. And I sure wasn't about to sell while it was still paying off like it was.

"You better get interested," he shot back.

Now talk like that really threw me. I had to shake my head to make sure I wasn't dreaming and that the little twit actually said what I thought he'd said. Him threatening me? What's wrong with this picture? I was debating in my head whether the jerk had a magnum tucked under that stupid flowered shirt he was wearing when I was distracted by Iver coming out of the back room carrying a box of Jumping Jacks.

Iver's my helper and he's an old townie. Lived his whole life here and he knows if someone blows their nose the wrong way around town. He's retired, except for the part-time work he does for me stocking the merchandise, cleaning up, and helping the customers. He does everything except the register. No one touches the register but me. Like I said, I been around.

Well anyhow, Iver comes out of the back with the case of Jacks and I see him take one look at the squirt, his eyes bug, and he does a complete 180 and disappears back into the storage room.

I don't like the look of that one little bit; maybe the squirt *is* packing. Still, I got my pride. "Hit the road, fruitcake," I growled down at him. "I ain't sellin' nothin' to you."

"You'll change your mind," he said with that smug punk look still plastered on his face. "I'll give you a week to come around. No more." With that he pulls a piece of paper out of the pocket of that god-awful shirt he's wearing and drops it on the counter.

By now I'm ready to come around the counter and drill him into the floor, but in the back of my mind I could still see Iver's pop-eyes, so I stifled myself and instead just said, "Beat it," and showed him how a thumb looks pointing at a door.

He made a little snorting noise, turned and headed for the door. Just before he reached it he shifted his face back toward me, pulled some kind of rolled up poster out of his pants back pocket and said, "You don't mind if I put this in your window, do ya?" He didn't wait for an answer, which I was too stunned to give anyway. He even had the nerve to pick up a roll of my tape from one of the tables and use it to stick his poster to the inside of my front window facing out.

He's no sooner gone then I drag old Iver out of the back room. "Who the hell's that?" I asked.

"Rymer Swanson," Iver answered, and I noticed his voice was actually shaking.

"So?"

"He's a big politician in town."

"So again. What's that make him, a tough guy or something?"

"I guess it does," Iver answered, his voice still shaking. "His family is one of the oldest in town. They been here longer than the sand."

"And what the hell does that mean, exactly?" After all, I was from Boston. What's the big deal with a local-yokel politician?

"That means that his family and a few others been involved in business and politics since way back when. Now they run just about everything in town that's worth running." Iver lowered his voice and leaned in a little closer to me. I could smell his breath; it wasn't good. "They're all related. They intermarried. And some look a little odd. What'd he want with you, anyway." His voice was still shaky.

"He wants to buy the store," I answered. "He left his number; gave me a week." I picked up the piece of paper he'd dropped on the counter and looked at the phone number.

"That's bad," Iver said gravely, shaking his head. "You better sell."

"You're kidding, right?" I said, really pissed now. "Why should I? I'm not lettin' some local yokel muscle me. Especially with July four comin' up."

"He can cause you a lot of trouble," Iver said ominously.

"Like what?"

"I dunno, but if you don't call him in a week, you'll probably find out."

And man, was old Iver right. As soon as that week was up trouble started marching in the door like it was on parade.

The first to drop by for a visit was the fire inspector. And damn, if he didn't look an awful lot like the squirt. "Ya ain't got enough extinguishers," he said.

"I got the legal amount," I said, knowing I did.

"Not for a fire hazard area like this," he shot back, letting his hand flutter around in front of his face. "Get two more or I'll shut ya down."

Next up was the building inspector. He appeared the next day. He could have been the fire inspector's brother; they looked that much alike. "Your storeroom's too small for all these explosives," he said. "Get half of them outta here."

"Where the hell am I gonna put 'em?" I asked, not really expecting an answer.

But I got one. "Anywhere but in this town, pal," he said before leaving.

Next on the roster was...guess who? That's close, but no. It was the plumbing inspector. And you're bright enough so I know I don't have to tell you who he looked like. "This toilet's outdated," he said. "You're using too much water. Get a new one in here fast."

I thought I had him. "Hey, that toilet's grandfathered in," I said.

But like Iver said, these characters have been doing this for a long time. "Maybe," he said, jiggling the toilet handle, "but it ain't flushing right. So it still gotta go. If it isn't replaced, I'll have to let the department know."

I was afraid to ask, but I did. "What department?" I asked warily.

He gave me one of those punk smirks that I already told you I hate and said, "Water Department."

I won't tell you about the rest of them; my blood pressure's spiking already.

My first step was a meet with my Boston lawyer and he was a big help like they always are. "Look," he said, rubbing his face hard up and down, from forehead to chin. "I can come up there, we can fight it, take 'em to court. But I'm tellin' you, a city like that, they got it sewed up. They'll just nickel and dime you to death. Plus my bill won't be small. You want my advice? Seriously? Hey, you made some good money. Had a good run. Sell to the drip. Take what you can get and bail out. You aren't going to beat them; it's their playground."

"Thanks much," I shouted, as I slammed his door on my way out. I was hot and I pushed a couple of suits out of my way as I headed down the hall to the elevator. Man, I hate lawyers.

Anyway, when I got back to the store I was still steaming. I knew that wouldn't do me any good; still, it was a struggle to calm down. Eventually I did though, as I leaned on the counter, beside the register, staring out the window, trying to come up with an angle. Just thinking, coming up with nothing. Until...my gaze dropped down to the poster the ballsy, little bastard had taped to my window when he'd been here with his ultimatum. The sun was shining on it and I could see the letters clearly, but they were backwards and all scrambled up and I couldn't make heads or tails out of them. But some part of my brain must have been able to decipher it because even as I ran around the counter and out the door I knew what it was and what it meant. And man, was I right. That red, white, and blue poster read:

CITY COUNCIL'S FOURTH OF JULY SPECTACULAR!

Plus a bunch of other stuff about when and where, that I didn't care about right then because I was running with the idea. A good one too; I could feel it. I remembered hearing something once, so I checked with Iver in the back. And sure enough—the display wasn't only sponsored by the city council, but the fireworks were actually set off individually by the council members running up and down the line and igniting them with small flares. And best of all, the head of the council always set off the finale. And that was my buddy, the little squirt—Rymer Swanson. So that was it; it fell together real nice like. Screw around with me will you, you little bastard. Like I said, I been around.

Now don't get the idea it was a breeze after that; it wasn't. I worked on the damn thing for an easy week. Down in the store's cellar, alone, at night. The powder was easy; I had plenty of that upstairs. I just emptied more M-80's than even I knew I had.

The rocket though was tougher. I got hold of a bunch of aerial rockets (the kind they use in commercial fireworks displays) from my supplier and started playing around with them real careful like because I didn't want to get hurt. That's all I would have needed. And it didn't take me long to figure out what made them tick either. But still, trying to make one do what I wanted, that was a different story. I tinkered with the shape of the thing, the amount of powder it'd need, and the weight of the contraption. I tried everything. I even went down the dunes late at night a few times and fired off a few of them as trials. But no luck; they wouldn't do what I wanted. I felt like giving up, but I didn't. Instead, I kept fooling around with the damn things until I almost drove myself crazy. Then, suddenly—Yes!—I had it. I took one without a charge in it down the dunes, and baby, it did just what I told it to. Looking back now I don't know why I had so much trouble trying to figure it out because it was easy. All it took was a...well, I can't tell you that right now. But don't worry; I'll tell you later.

Anyway, all this time the squirt and his buddies were still trying to get me to sell, but I had my lawyer stalling them; at least the shyster was good for something.

I knew the squirt'd be back sooner or later to see if I was ready to yell uncle, so I wasn't surprised when he waltzed in a few days before the 4th. He walked right up to the counter, put his pudgy hands on it, looked up at me and said, "How much you want?"

And man, he had that smug, punk look that I hate on his face again. I could have gone over the counter and killed him right then, but that would have spoiled everything. "$100,000," I said, my voice shaking with rage I hoped he'd think was fear. "And I'll throw in all the fireworks you want for your 4th of July display."

"50,000," he shot back. "And we got all the fireworks we need."

"Not like that," I said, holding my breath.

The squirt glanced at what I was pointing at and then walked over to it. It stood taller than his waist and was half as round, with red, white and blue stripes and the words *Stars & Stripes* painted in Day-Glo letters down its side. It was a unique looking rocket.

"What the hell's that?" he said, as he sidestepped around it checking it out. He had his hands on his hips, below the white, patent leather belt he wore high on his protruding belly.

"Something new," I said, not lying. "Supposed to go up right after the finale rockets; fills the sky with a big American flag."

"No way," he said, bobbing his bald, glistening head. "That might be nice. Real patriotic-like. I'll send a couple of guys around later to pick it up."

"Yeah, sure," I said meekly, like I was intimidated.

The squirt was still talking as he headed for the door. "Oh, kid," he said, "my lawyer'll get all the papers drawn up for us to sign. And it'll be for 50, like I said. Any problem?"

"No," I answered, hanging my head like I was beat, but inside, man, I was anything but. And imagine that punk calling me kid. Well my turn was coming and it was going to be fun. I was going to enjoy it a lot. A real lot.

But he still wasn't finished. Just as he was ready to close the door behind him he turned, and said real sarcastic like, "Oh yeah. I forgot. You don't have to throw that big rocket in for free; I'll pay ya for it." With that he took a coin from his pocket, and with his thumb flipped it across the room just missing my head. I almost snapped right then and there. But again, I just grinned and held my fury in. He gave me that smug, punk look again and walked out slamming the door behind him.

Well, of course, I wasn't there the big night (I've always thought fireworks are dangerous in the hands of amateurs), but I heard the *Stars & Stripes* rocket went up and out and curved around over the water before it came right back and slammed into the ground not more than five feet from where the little squirt launched it. Not bad, huh? I guess the explosion was pretty deafening. Believe it or not, some people actually thought the nuclear power plant blew up. Ha! They had to call in emergency equipment from as far away as Portsmouth and Salisbury. It was that bad. But I won't make you sick with all the gory details; let's just say he got what he deserved.

Since then the state's made a lot of the good fireworks illegal again, but it doesn't matter to me. How the hell could I make any dough on them anyhow, sitting here in the county jail? My lawyer says it doesn't look too good (ain't he a big help again); still, they have to prove intent. Which they'll try to do. On the other hand, all their physical evidence went poof. That's good. No matter how it turns out, it's going to cost me every dime I made these past years hustling those crackers, plus more, all for the shyster.

And by the way, that brings us back to why I didn't want to tell you right up front the little secret to my invention. How I fixed the rocket to come right back on top of him like that. You see, I'm gonna need dough, and lots of it. So if you know anybody who's getting their toes stepped on, and they need a little help...well, I'm open to offers on how to make your own *Stars & Stripes*. It's a sweet little invention and worth every dime someone would pay for it. Just imagine what you could do!

Hey, don't look at me like that. After all, what choice did I have? It's a tough world out there and you got to do what you got to do. Take my word on it; I been around.

All's fair in love and war.

Alten Kameraden
by Ed Ahern

THE WATER-SPATTERED store window in front of Walter Peake held richly tooled leather desk sets and overweight filigreed pens, the kind given as retirement gifts but rarely used. The reflected image of the rain blown cobblestones behind him was empty. The sodden wind measured a few degrees above zero Celsius. His legs, hands and head were already soaked and every gust of wind drove wet chill through the wool to skin.

He'd arrived well within the meeting procedure of five minutes before and after the arranged time. A two hour train ride, an U-Bahn ride, a short walk, another U-Bahn hop and a 10 minute walk. Nothing unusual had been observed. In more than a decade, even with occasional support counter surveillance, there had been nothing noticeable.

The reflection of 327 slowly rose into view on Martin Strasse. His gray shape was a bandy legged bug crabbling up the dark cobblestones. Peake turned, keeping both hands in his coat pockets. 327 pulled his right hand out of his coat pocket, and put his left hand into its pocket instead. Peake took both hands out, walked up and shook 327's unpocketed hand. Had Peake noticed a problem his hands would have stayed in his pockets.

"*Hallo Harald.*"

"*Hallo Walter. Scheisses Wetter.*" Hello Walter. Shitty weather.

"*Wie immer für uns.*" Like always for us.

As they had for twelve years they both spoke German. English was Peake's native tongue, and Harald Brunner was nearly fluent in it. But in Hamburg English was noticeable and softly spoken German wasn't.

Peake wore clothing purchased from German department stores. He topped his nondescript ensemble with a Mutze cap which covered his bald spot. Brunner also wore a Mutze. They were a matched pair of middle-aged men.

Peake controlled their movements. "*Hier rechts und unten n'bißchen.*

Was zum essen?" Right here and down a bit. Something to eat?

"Nein danke Walter. N'a Maltezer und Bier wäre besser Heute Abend." No thanks, Walter. A Maltezer and beer would be better tonight.

The deserted business district in which they had met quickly mutated into neighborhood bars, restaurants and little shops before dropping downhill into the Reeperbahn, the raucous sex center. Peake and Brunner walked to the middle of a long block and into the Bruns Eck bar.

Hamburg was dominating Bochum in a Bundesliga soccer match on the television at the end of the bar. The seven occupants and bartender were absorbed in the game. Peake used the time it took to order drinks to sort through them. One woman, heavy, middle-aged, with two men of similar heft and vintage, both ignoring her advertised cleavage; bartender in his late sixties who squinted rather than wear glasses; four loud men in cheap suits and ties, in their thirties, with about sixteen empty shot glasses clumped into the table center.

The bar was overheated but still damp. It smelled of smoldering tobacco, stale beer and body odors that had spent at least a full day developing.

They ordered two rounds of Maltezer Kreuz aquavit and draft beer, and sat at a table toward the back. The beer would take five minutes of foam settlings and top ups before it was ready.

Funerals, Peake thought, are rarely fun. He had bet himself that as awkward as this would be it would go reasonably well. He and Harald were old comrades with few illusions.

"Gehts gut?" Peake asked.

"Good enough. The shoulder turns out to be arthritis rather than a rotator cuff. What a blessing, huh?"

"Sometimes it's okay to settle for a lesser evil. Still on your own, Harald?"

"Same arrangement with the woman downstairs. A couple times a month I buy her dinner and she lets me screw her. I keep my eyes shut and think about Irmgard."

Peake ignored the tacit invitation to talk about her again. Wallowing in emotional mud would only make this harder. He shifted the envelope in the inside chest pocket of his coat so that it bulged a little less. The pass had been made between the outside door of the bar and the heavy black rubber curtain that acted as a seal to keep the warmth in. No one could have clearly seen the transfer from inside or outside of the bar.

Once the beer and Maltezer were positioned in front of them they picked up the shot glasses of aquavit.

"*Zum woll.*"

"*Prosit.*"

They sucked in half of the aquavit. The Maltezer would have been frozen solid were it water. It slid down with the consistency of liquid butter and the after taste of caraway and anise. On the television Hamburg narrowly missed scoring a goal and ragged noise erupted and subsided from the suited tableful.

This would be the last time Harald met with Walter Peake, a cover name backstopped by a passport, driver's license, business cards, family pictures, credit cards, a couple of memberships and a social security card. The identity would hold up under thirty minutes of casual questioning, but probably less than two hours of interrogation and back checking.

John Swafford had grown fond of his Walter Peake avatar, part of the reason he had argued with Peter Alanson, his section chief, about maintaining the operation. Peter had been merciless.

"Look John, I know we've had 327 for a long part of the Cold War. I understand he's provided good intel over the years. I appreciate what we did to him and that woman. We both also know that when the wall came down he lost his usefulness. We have ex-Stasi walk-ins giving us better stuff than he does. It's time. If you can't terminate him I will, but he's getting pensioned off. Our glory years of coddling the Huns are over."

"Peter, he can still provide good commercial intelligence. "

"Horse crap, John and you know it. Summer interns from IBM could do as well. The power curve is passing us by. We're experts in the passé. If you don't want to get moth balled in Langley reviewing contact reports you have to roll up this operation and move on. I know you're close with 327, but that's become a handicap. In any case, we'll be giving him separation payments contingent on his keeping his mouth shut."

Alanson was pompous, but his logic was unflawed. 327 was of very little further use. And others as well. Peake's stable of intelligence stallions had turned into gossip nags. And Peake suffered by association. The organization's squinty focus had shifted east, to China and the Arab countries.

He and Alanson worked in a windowless and alarmed building on an Army base in southern Germany. The base provided security, a cover story, documentation, housing and cheap booze. Most of the case officers were married, lived on base, sent their children to the base school and socialized at the officer's club.

But Peake lived alone off base and socialized with Germans on the weekends. In order to explain his fluency in German he was titled a community liaison officer, but liaised with no one. In Cold War Germany the natives were generally polite enough to not point out this absurdity. All except one middle-aged neighbor and friend, a former officer in a Waffen SS tank brigade. "You speak German with an East Frisian accent that almost hides the American. And the only other American I ever met who could speak my language well enough to hold an intelligent conversation was a spy. Not you, of course, John."

The man, who had survived the Eastern Front and a Russian prison, faintly smiled. He had earned the right to gently needle a fraud.

Peake realized he had been blankly staring at Harald.

Brunner, sensing the unusual in Peake's stare, sat a little straighter.

"You seem preoccupied Walter. Your health is good?"

"Still healthy, just fatter, thanks. *Tscha*, Harald. Here it is. We've been doing this work together for twelve years, and you've been doing it for seven or eight years before then. That's a long time in any business. But everything changes, and we need to change as well. It's been a good, long run, but the conflict we were engaged in has passed us by. It's time for us to close up shop and move ahead."

Harald sippingly finished the shot of Maltezer and studied Walter's face.

"So the shoe drops. I doubt this was your idea, which means there is no way you can change it even if I begged. How does it end, Walter?"

"We pay into your account as before, until the end of the year. Then a smaller stipend for three years, paid monthly. There won't be any more tasking, so you effectively have almost four year's severance. We'll collect your equipment and have you sign an agreement. "

Harald smiled. "And you will have thought out the consequences of my going public or switching sides."

"There no longer is another side to switch to, Harald, and you'd be trying to compete with hundreds of East European and Russian operatives already peddling every secret they have or can make up for a few dollars."

Both men took a sip of their beers. It was, as always, fresh and complex and satisfying. The head on the beer would survive to the bottom of the glass.

"I've always assumed that Walter Peake isn't your real name."

Walter paused. "It isn't."

"Is your first name at least Walter?"

"No."

"Perhaps before we separate you could tell me your real first name. It would be a shame to have a fiction as my memory."

Peake nodded. "Perhaps Harald. But then again our stock in trade for all these years has been creating fictions. Maybe you should re-member me as Walter Peake."

They finished their drinks in near silence, knowing each other well enough to answer their own unvoiced questions. Walter broke his own rules and ordered another round.

"What about Heinrich and Wolfgang?" Harald finally asked.

"You advise them that things have come to an end, and pay them off from the usual funding."

"The office?"

"We have no interest. Close it or keep it open on your own."

Between questions and answers about how to bury a twenty-year-old operation the moments of silence expanded, not strained, but anticipatory. They knew that the beginning of the last silence would mark the end of their long, once-a-month life together.

Hamburg won the televised soccer match and the four well-soused men left. The noise level dropped with their departure and Harald and Walter lowered their voices. Harald raised an eyebrow and a shot glass toward Peake and got a confirming nod. He ordered a third round. As the bartender was preparing their beers Harald touched Walter's hand.

"Walter, I need to ask a favor of you."

"If I can."

"We won't have an operation to jeopardize anymore. When we've closed it down could you check with your new Stasi friends and try and find out what happened to her?"

There it was. He meant Irmgard of course. The young woman he had proposed to Peake eight years ago. They had sat in Bremen, in a bar much like this one.

Harald had pitched Irmgard to Peake hesitantly, but with conviction. He recommended Irmgard for extraction from East Germany and debriefing, citing her valuable familiarity with police security procedures and operations. He described a teaser list of information she could provide. He mentioned that he had approached Irmgard rather than the other way around, making it less likely that she was a plant. He mentioned that she seemed amenable to making a new life for herself in the west. He asked for quick action. He was an emotionally ruled idiot.

Harald was an intelligent work dog with bad teeth and the shape of a flop house pillow. The concept that Harald had proactively recruited a much younger and apparently attractive woman was mildly absurd. Under Peake's prodding questions, Harald admitted that he and Irmgard had become lovers three months previously, and that he had intimated to her that he had contacts who could facilitate her departure. Bingo.

Walter Peake, real name John Swafford, brought the problem back to Alanson, his section chief. A black op pro in Berlin before the wall, Alanson was never guilty of wishful thinking. He and Walter gnawed through several sessions of the what-ifs in late spring.

"You realize John, that 327 is almost certainly blown?"

"I know. I'm thinking we can flip 327 into a stalking horse and keep three or four Stasi looking into dead ends. If they formally recruit him we have him accept and we give 327 enough to keep them looking in wrong directions."

"And if he's put in jail?"

"His information is tactical, anything more than a few weeks old is valueless to them, and no threat to us. We trade him for a player to be named."

"And what the hell do we do with this woman?"

"She should have at least minimal information value. My sugges-
tion would be to try and send her back in with some bait and see
what we flush out. Brief stay, with the promise of a bunch of goodies
when she comes back out."

Alanson was doubtful. "327 won't go along with that. Now that
he's got steady sex he's going to want to keep her close."

"327 needs to be protected from himself. We're the ones who've
already been screwed. Harald is arguably blown but of limited value
to our friends in the east. Let's give this woman something tempting
that might coax a few roaches out of the walls. I'd like to be able to
do some screwing of my own."

"What's your bait?"

"Maybe a bite at me. I'm probably already tagged anyway."

"And on the outside chance she's legitimate?"

"We put her at some risk. I can live with that."

And that's the way it went down. Harald was told that Irmgard
would be extracted and debriefed. On his next trip in he pitched
Irmgard, who accepted with little hesitation. She made arrangements
for a three week summer holiday in Hungary, left Dresden by train
and while underway used the documents and ticketing provided by
Harald to switch trains and cross into Austria.

Harald met Irmgard at Güssing , near the Austrian border with
Hungary, and escorted her to a hotel restaurant. Walter was waiting.
Cloth table cover. Real flower in the bud vase. Better than Walter and
Harald were used to.

Irmgard was firmly rounded and narrow waisted. No angularities.
Skin like softly weathered snow with faint blue veining that coated
almost defined muscle. Heavy breasts that emphasized her points as
she excitedly talked. Light brown hair, hazel eyes, mouth that split all
the way across her face. Irmgard lived so much in the moment that
Walter wondered if she could follow directions for tomorrow. She was
about 20 years younger than Harald.

Irmgard was fully aware of her effect on both men. Not manipu-
lative, not coy, just pleased with her impact.

And Harald. Harald sat, saying little, occasionally making unneeded motions while he waited for the meeting to be over so he could take Irmgard up to a room. Walter prolonged the meeting an unnecessary 15 minutes to watch Harald begin to deconstruct. Irmgard gave Walter a complicit smile and continued the conversation, supporting the teasing.

"So Irmgard, what do you want to do now that you've come over?"

"All the television shows and movies that we never could watch. I'll leave the television always on even when I'm in the bathroom or kitchen. Go to political rallies, any party, it doesn't matter, so I can scream slogans and no one will stop me. Confront policemen, knowing they won't arrest me."

"You don't believe it now, but within a few months you'll become indifferent to politics and focus on your next vacation."

"So many possibilities, so few rules. I feel like I could run naked down the Elbe Chausse in Hamburg and no one else would care."

"Oh, there are rules. You have to be able to afford what you want."

As she spoke, her face, hands and body moved semi-independently of each other, as though the excitement had taken her body orchestra off tune in a still melodic way.

Walter grudgingly let them go, visualizing Irmgard undressed but unable to add Harald into that vision.

The next morning Irmgard and Walter went by train to a debriefing facility in Augsburg. After six days she was again moved, this time to a hotel in Frankfurt.

Walter was with Irmgard for the entire process, the good guy helping her through the intense interrogations and testing. During the process he painstakingly reviewed his action plan—the set up, pitch and return trip of Irmgard the presumed double agent. Walter scheduled a lunch with her the day after Harald's next departure into East Germany on business. She wore loose open clothing that showed Walter her bare arms and legs.

"Are you okay without Harald here?"

"I like Harald, but he's too old. You're younger than Harald, aren't you?"

"By a few years."

"No so beat up either. Do you have a German girlfriend?"

"Not right now."

The lunch meeting never evolved into dessert and coffee. Before their butter fried schnitzels were completely eaten Irmgard had invited him up to her room. Between the restaurant and her hotel room Walter jettisoned much of his action plan. Once in the room Irmgard was immediately physical.

Through the two hour bed wallowing neither mentioned Harald. As he meandered over her still sweaty body, Walter guessed that she was fond of but not emotionally attached to either Harald or him. She shaved her armpits but not her legs, and the hair on her calves was gossamer. Her breasts pendulumed left and right to make room for Walter's head.

Harald had known that Walter was with Irmgard through her debriefing and polygraphing (she passed, marginally). He did not know that the format was debriefing, dinner, and sex .

Irmgard began her post-coital conversations while Walter was still wandering through her body, examining moles and smallpox vaccinations and unpolished nails.

"How long have you been working like this Walter? Do you handle many men like Harald? Do you ever come east yourself?" (Come, Walter noted, not go.) "Is it always civilians or do you also work with military people?"

Walter told the truth when generalities were innocuous, and used pre-cleared lies to inflate his importance to the intelligence effort. Might as well make himself an attractive target.

Despite his hints and prompts, Irmgard never let flicker any illumination that she was a Stasi plant, so Walter played it on its face, a necessary trip for her to obtain additional and confirming information.

"*Liebchen*, why do I need to go back, I've told you everything I can remember, I don't want to get caught."

"You're just coming back from vacation a little early, no one should be suspicious. I have to show our people that you're worth the expense of keeping here, and that means your getting targeted information. Being unemployed here is worse than being unemployed in Dresden. Harald makes a modest living but could not afford to keep you."

At their third dinner, while eating another butter saturated schnitzel, Irmgard rephrased her objections from if to how.

"How would I be able to get back in and out? What happens if I'm delayed in Dresden?"

Walter cringed. Too easy, and much too soon. He had hoped that she would hold out another week, not so much for the prolonged sex, but to give him the faint hope that she was as she seemed, a bluntly erotic woman looking out for main chance. He was becoming fond of her.

"It's a three day trip, using documents for entry and exit that will be better than most real West German papers. We'll be watching for you the whole time. You'll never get caught, but if you do we'll trade you for someone they want back."

Irmgard capitulated, again too easily. The next step was Harald, who would not consider sending her back until he was clearly told by both Irmgard and Walter that he had no power of refusal. Harald succumbed, realizing that his tenuous chance to keep Irmgard next to him was based on her being comfortable.

Irmgard patted, then stroked Harald's hand. "Harald, I have to do this. It lets us both afford to be together. I can't stay in a hotel room for the rest of my life."

Harald had sex with Irmgard for the last time the night before she boarded a train from Austria back through Hungary to East Germany. But Walter was with them on the platform before the train departed. It was the last time either man saw her.

When she failed to show at the border crossing five days later the usual passive monitoring was intensified. Harald panicked immediately. Walter had practice keeping the fear churn hidden, but after another day let Harald see that he too was worried.

"Walter, I have to go east and check on her."

"Harald, you can't, not until your next scheduled trip. You can't change your pattern, especially now."

Harald held back for a week before making a scheduled business trip over the border. Irmgard had left no trace of a return to Dresden. Harald's questions to neighbors and acquaintances were answered with suspicion and ignorance. Walter added more names and topics to the passive monitoring of press, radio, television and police and military transmissions. Nothing.

Neither Harald nor Walter were approached with recruitment offers or threats. No surveillance was noted. Nothing. Walter, with no traces or clues, kept asking himself the same questions in an endless loop.

Were 327 and I so inconsequential that they had her switch to a better target? Did she just move in with another man? Was she disposed of? Or maybe, just maybe, she'd turned around in Hungary, come back out and dumped both of us as bad bets.

Seven months later the monitoring department reported a brief death notice for an Irmgard Thoden. The name matched but the biographical details were skewed. Walter told Harald only about his suspicions that Irmgard had made a u-turn with the bogus documents, and not about the obituary. Better for Harald to think that she's alive and missing than maybe dead.

Walter considered himself immune from emotional entanglements, but felt surprising guilt about Irmgard. He missed her cheerfully blunt acceptance of what life presented to her, and her equally blunt enjoyment in sex.

After the wall came down Walter had made vigorous inquiries. As anal as the East German intelligence service was about record keeping there was no mention of Irmgard being interrogated or punished. There was, of course, no record of her being an operative, that file would have been among those purged. The Stasi had noted her as missing from her work and apartment, but came up with no leads. Equally interestingly, there was no record of Irmgard Thoden's burial or cremation. Just a death notice.

Walter still had no answers to feed Harald's hungry memories. *We're both brooding about a woman who would have quickly told us to go to hell.*

He patted Harald's arm. For no discernible reason he recalled the music of a patriotic German march from the First World War—*Alte Kameraden*, old comrades.

"Harald, I know you still care for her. I've been searching. There's no record of her, good or bad. She just disappeared. We'll keep investigating, but at this point I can't offer much hope. I'll get back in touch if anything comes up."

They had spent three hours at the bar, far too long, and the processed beer and aquavit was pressing to exit. They took turns in the toilet, first Walter, then Harald. Like most German toilets it had a flat dry platform on which excretion rested before being flushed away. Walter sometimes joked that is was a final health check on the digestive process. This night he wondered if it could also be used for divination, to poke a stick into one's own feces and foretell the way forward.

They paused just outside the bar. The rain also had paused.

"Walter, *Spiel ist aus.* The game is over. The need for all the rules is over too. Let me show you what I do sometimes after our meetings. It's not far."

"Why not, as you say, the game's been played."

For the first time in their long association Harald led the way, shifting from one downhill street to another until the last narrow side street opened up onto the bright neon lights of the Reeperbahn, the sex center for Hamburg. They walked past tawdry souvenir stores and fast food restaurants and strip bars until they reached the entrance to the Eros Centrum.

There was no door, just an alleyway sized opening. Harald entered without hesitation and Walter followed. The large open space inside was unheated but covered. It was faintly lit and populated with about twenty roving women and another male twosome evaluating the prospects. Walter thought of a leper colony.

Harald waved away a pair of approaching women with a shoo fly motion, and turned to Walter. "I come here sometimes. I never buy sex from these women, but I look at all of them. I think maybe Irmgard is here. She loved sex, loved being with men. She had no real profession or aptitude. Maybe she's here. But she's never here, and I go back home. Pathetic isn't it."

The women were circling closer, sensing fresh meat. As they emerged from the dusk Walter saw that they had all left forty behind, and wore plastered makeup and forced smiles.

"Harald, Irmgard would still be better looking and younger. She would make love for enjoyment, not really just for money. She wouldn't have to work this desperately to find another man."

"*Jah*, maybe so. But all these years with no contact, no knowledge of her. I never changed my address or telephone number, just in case she found me."

"She's better off than this Harald. Irmgard is doing fine. Let's get out of here before these women whore us to death."

The two men pushed their way past women whose smiles sharply inverted as they passed, and stepped back out, blinking, into the glare of the Reeperbahn"s street and neon lighting. The almost freezing rain had resumed.

"I'll miss our times together Harald. I almost wish the Cold War resumed."

Harald's lip corners twitched upward. "I suppose there won't be a twenty-fifth reunion?"

"No, we end here. *Leb woll.*"

They shook hands as they had after every meeting and separated. Walter stopped and turned. "My name is John, Harald, John." He turned away. The wind and rain blustered down the street, pushing one man away, and slowing the steps of the other.

Sometimes a place takes on a life—or a death—of its own.

The Farm
by Kevin R. Doyle

FROM THE DISTANCE, the farm looked almost invisible. Just a slightly uneven line of lighter tan against the earth tones of the mountains. Only as I approached it, my rental car bumping and lurching over the rough ground, did the details become apparent, and then I began to feel kind of jumpy. I'd decided earlier to keep as positive a frame of mind as I could, but as I got closer that resolve began to melt away.

Up close, the place looked just about as desolate and Godforsaken as I'd expected. Set at the bottom of a range of mountains, the farm consisted of a grand total of three buildings, all with several gaping spots and the paint nearly flaked off. Up front, near the rusted-out metal gates, stood a small house that looked from the outside like it may have held three bedrooms. A ways back and to the right sat a small shed, no more than twenty by twenty, and even farther back was the largest structure of the whole setup, a barn, looming, paint-flaked and eaten through in parts, that looked, to my city-raised eyes, much larger than most of its kind.

The rest of the farm complex, a miscellany of fences, wells, and antique, rusted-out agricultural implements, didn't register all that much at the time. I did notice the large tree, standing gigantic and solitary, hovering over a once-red picnic table.

Seeing as how I was a bit earlier than we'd agreed on, I didn't worry a whole lot about not seeing any other vehicles around. To kill time more than anything else, I walked up to the iron gates and gave them an experimental shove. The one on my left side stayed stationary, but the right-hand one creaked its way inward for about a foot or so before it also ground to a halt.

"What a shithole," I told the surrounding desert.

My reaction, of course, wasn't just to the physical demeanor of the place. I was responding as much, if not more, to the history of the area, to what had happened here nearly forty years before. Someone else coming along the site, someone who either had never heard the story or didn't recognize this as the place, would probably look around and see only a decrepit, abandoned farmstead.

But anyone in the know, who had all the facts and memories, would no doubt recognize the front door to hell.

Standing alone out there, I began to feel a little odd, the skin at my nape crawling and quivering. I'd just about decided to go back and wait in my car, when I saw another vehicle coming down the road.

It was a big, shiny, bright blue Ford F-150, although covered with quite a bit of dust from traveling in the desert. Just what he'd told me to look for, so I took a deep breath and leaned against the gate.

It was about to start.

The Ford came up alongside of my rental and pulled to a halt. A minute later, a gangly old man, complete with the requisite checkered shirt, boots and cowboy hat, climbed out.

"Jessie Perkins?" he called out to me.

"That's right. You must be Sheriff Locher."

"Is so." He stopped to hitch up the waistband of his jeans before coming over to me.

He turned and looked out over the farm site, his hands on his hips as he contemplated the spread.

"Don't look like much, does it?" he asked.

"No, sir." I said, wondering if he had the same creeply-crawly sensation as me. Probably not because this was my first time to view the place; whereas, he'd lived in this area most of his life. On the other hand, continued proximity to the site could conceivably make a person's reaction even worse.

Kind of like living next door to a reminder of the Apocalypse.

"Say again just what is it that you intend doing out here?"

Although his face and demeanor seemed pleasant enough, I caught a slight, and totally understandable, hostility in his tone.

"Basically," I said, "right now I just need to look the place over. Get a feeling for it, so to speak."

"Pretty easy to guess what the feeling of this place is," the sheriff interrupted me. He reached up and rubbed the back of his neck as he spoke. As a city boy my whole life, all sorts of lame jokes about rednecks flashed through my mind.

I decided to keep them to myself.

"I understand what you mean, sir," I said, "but what I'm after..."

"No, son," he interrupted again. "I don't think you do quite understand."

He turned partially away from me and looked out over the sprawling, broken-down buildings. He lowered his hand from his neck and, even on this fairly cloudy day, shielded his eyes, as if trying to focus in on some distant point that only he could see.

"Sometimes," he said, "if you're quiet enough and you place yourself just right, you can almost hear them."

I knew what he meant, of course. The sheriff may have been a hard-headed realist in his way, but even an old duffer like him couldn't be entirely immune to the vibes the place gave off.

Hear the victims, he meant. Hear the moans and screams that must have echoed out from this place on that one really bad night forty years back. Outside of the participants, outside of the goddamned "family," only two people had actually witnessed the sounds and sights emanating from the farm on that night. Two of the victims, who'd somehow managed to survive until rescue arrived. In the years since the trials, they'd done their best to stay undercover and away from the press. They'd had to go public in the days and months immediately after, of course, but all these years later I doubted if more than a handful of people remembered their names.

Even so, imagination is a powerful tool, and most people with any experience at all could somewhat guess what the place must have sounded like back then.

Those who lived in the immediate area could probably gauge it even better.

In fact, for a second there my own imagination went into overdrive, and I could almost hear the "family's" victims crying out their last just before the end. I blinked rapidly to dispel the vision.

All this without having actually set foot onto the grounds yet.

"So what all is your employer planning to do with this place?" the sheriff asked.

"Not sure yet. Keep in mind I just work for Hodgkins and Crandall, the firm handling the estate work. The actual owner, like I said over the phone, is a distant cousin of the Kendalls. She lives in Boston and honestly has no interest in the place at all. But she's getting up there in age and just wants to get it off her books."

"So you're just out here to look it over and see what use could be made of it? Like how to pitch it to prospective buyers?"

"Something like that. More than anything, though, I'm supposed to do a rough appraisal of the estimated value."

Without looking at me, staring back at the farm again, Sheriff Locher said, "The Kendalls had nothing to do with it."

He said the words by rote, in a monotone, as if he'd said that same phrase over and over throughout the years.

"I know," I said.

The Kendall family had originally founded the small farm back during the turn of the twentieth century. Four generations had lived and worked on it until the mid-sixties, when Charlie Kendall, a widower with no kids, had cashed out his savings and moved to an L.A. retirement home. He kept the deed to the farm, and for a while somewhat desultorily kept an eye on it, until a stroke laid him low and he ended up pretty much vegetative. The farm was, at the time, so far away from any civilized haunts and so unknown that after Charlie's stroke it was pretty much left to go fallow. Other than a few initial notices of overdue property taxes, delivered to Charlie care of the nursing home and usually trashed by the staff, no one really knew or cared about the farm.

No one, that is, until a few years later when a total psycho wandered in from somewhere out in the desert and discovered the place, all deserted and welcoming.

"So you want to go inside?" the lawman asked me.

I nodded, feeling suddenly queasy at the idea of actually stepping onto the grounds. Standing outside the gate and looking in had been one thing, and that took nearly everything I had, but actually going inside ...

"Okay," Locher said, "let's go."

He reached out and, old as he was, easily swung open the rusted gates that I'd barely budged. I followed him, and we headed up the unpaved trail that led to the main house.

I had to work at it to keep from grinding my teeth together. As soon as we moved towards the house, the sensations of the place, what the strung-out losers who made it so notorious back in the sixties would call the "vibes," began really hitting me.

"You wouldn't think of it to look at the place," Locher said. "Wouldn't think all that stuff happened here."

My skin began crawling, and as I looked around at the flat, dusty spaces between the scattered buildings, I could almost see, like a fuzzy photograph from the old days, the scattered, mutilated bodies lying around the place, motionless in pools of cooling blood seeping into the parched dust.

"You okay, son?"

Only when he called out to me did I realize that Locher had progressed about fifty feet ahead while I'd stayed rooted in place, my head swarming with images of a past I'd never experienced outside of news stories and "tell-all" books.

I began rubbing my forehead, hoping for the sensations to pass, as the sheriff came up alongside. He took me by the elbow and led me over to the picnic table. As we sat down, I began to feel a bit better.

"What the hell was that?" I asked.

Locher shook his head.

"Not sure, but don't feel bad. 'Most everyone who comes out here the first time goes through it. What's that phrase? That Oriental word?"

I puzzled it over a minute before I got it.

"You mean Feng Shui?" I asked.

"Yeah, that stuff. Something about the moods and feelings of a place, isn't it?"

"Not exactly," I said. "But I think I get your meaning."

"I'm about as sensible as they come," the sheriff said, "but even I've noticed that this place has a powerful effect on people who come out here. Few years back, a documentary team from some cable channel showed up. They were here for a couple of weeks filming some sort of special, and for practically the first week they couldn't hardly get any work done. Practically all of them being hit with whatever it is that's got you right now."

Even though I'd calmed down a bit, the strange feelings the farm had aroused in me were stronger than ever. Any minute now, I figured I'd start hearing the screams of the victims.

What the hell was happening to me?

"Almost makes sense in its way," Sheriff Locher continued, "no matter how realistic and practical you look at the world, you can't quite conceive of that much hell and torment being visited on this small of a place without some sort of leftovers."

His followers called him John Smith, aka Preacher John. Almost certainly an alias, but afterwards some people thought it showed such a staggering lack of imagination that it almost had to be the man's real name. Because back in the sixties it was a lot easier for someone to stay under the radar than nowadays, practically nothing was known about the man until law enforcement raided the farm on Monday, the eleventh of August, 1969.

As far as could be told, Smith had been living on the abandoned farm, scratching a living from the surrounding desert, for about six months before, through some method which no one had ever quite figured out, a group of young transients began slowly coalescing around him. At the end of his first year on the farm, about the time old man Kendall had suffered that stroke, Preacher John felt strong enough, in control of his "family" enough, to begin branching out.

All of this, of course, was pieced together much later by law enforcement.

After the name of Preacher John Smith became a household word.

A sudden breeze popped up out of nowhere and lashed across us. Only when I felt the sudden cooling on my face did I realize I'd been sweating.

"Were you here?" I asked Sheriff Locher. "Were you part of the raid?"

For a moment it looked as if he'd taken offense at my question, then his lined face relaxed into a grin.

"Hell, boy. Just how old do you think I am?"

Feeling a sudden flush at how stupid I'd sounded, I croaked out a quick apology, which the old man waved off.

"Knew about it, though," he said. "I'm one of your actual natives around here. Lived in this area my whole life."

"Yeah?"

"Yeah. And heard about it second hand. I was only a kid of course, but my dad was a deputy back in those days." He tilted his hat back an inch or two on his head. "Guess you could say the law runs in the family. My dad was in the group that made the initial raid out here."

A distant look came into his eyes for a minute.

"As bad as all the reports?" I asked.

Locher shook his head briefly, then looked back at me.

"He wouldn't talk about it for some time. Wouldn't ever go into details. When I got older, I eventually pieced enough together to know that dad had found one of the young women still alive, somehow, and she died in his arms just as the ambulance pulled up."

I looked down at the stained, flaked-off picnic table.

It was a summer weekend in '69, one seemingly no more special than any other, when the police departments of the communities surrounding the farm were suddenly besieged with reports of missing people. From late teens to mid-thirties, within a hundred-mile radius it appeared that somewhere around thirty people had vanished between Friday night and Sunday morning. It had been a fairly equal mix of both male and female, but the reports were so scattered among the various small communities that it took until Sunday evening before the various departments involved began to suspect some connection.

It took another day or so before some eagle eye in one of the jurisdictions happened to notice that the area of the disappearances formed a rough circle, with the old Kendall farm smack dab in the middle.

This was back in the sixties, remember, and although the Miranda ruling had come along, out west things were still handled a little less formally than in most places. Within six hours, a coordinated force had formed together and descended on the farm.

According to anecdotal reports, most of the men who took part in that initial raid had to undergo psychological counseling for some time after.

"You seem to want to know a lot about this," Locher remarked. "More than a lawyer's rep should need to know."

I worked to keep my poker face on. No matter what, it wouldn't do for the lawman to get an inkling of my true intentions.

"You're right," I said. "Just idle curiosity, I guess. But you've probably got better things to do than hang around here all day holding my hand. Why don't we get on with it?"

I did my best not to look too closely at Locher as we stood up and began our tour of the farm.

It didn't take long. As I said, there wasn't a whole lot to the place. The sheriff mentioned a couple of times that he couldn't quite see anyone wanting to do anything with this plot of land, and he had a point. Notwithstanding the history of the place, there just wasn't that much of value there.

Forty years later, the story of Preacher John Smith, his "family" and the weekend of horror in '69, had become part of pop culture. Over the years, movies, books, songs, and even video games had featured the preacher. And even though all those fictional venues did their best, to one degree or another, to present the truth, there was no way to even really come close.

That afternoon at the farm, I came as close as possible.

On purpose.

Under the guise of looking the property over, I managed to draw Sheriff Locher out some more. First, we went inside the small shed, which took only a minute or two to examine. The shed floor was dirt, dried and cracked, with some of the cracks running several inches deep. Looking closely, I thought I could detect the faint traces of excavation, retamping and excavation again.

Imagination, of course. After four decades there'd surely be no trace left.

"Three of 'em in here alone," the sheriff said. He was staring downwards, kicking at the hardened earth with his toe.

"Buried or out in the open?" I asked.

"Two of them fully buried, the other partially so. Probably got tired after all that work and intended to get to it later."

"Which they never did," I said.

"Right. They never did."

He wasn't telling me anything I didn't know. Over the years, I'd studied, digested and memorized everything I could find about Preacher John and his followers. Odds were that, at least academically, I knew more even than most of the locals.

I also knew that this was the easy part. I could look in and walk around in this shed without it getting to me too much.

She hadn't been one of the three found there.

Leaving the shed, we turned and went back to the barn. I made some noise about wanting at least a superficial inspection of the barn structure, to see if it was at all salvageable after the years. Seeing as how the farm buildings had been built nearly a century before, it was probably safe to say that the structures were sound.

But after coming all this way, going to this much trouble, I needed to see the infamous barn for myself. Even though she hadn't been found in the barn either.

It took both of us to throw open the old, cumbersome doors. When we did so, a couple of birds whirled and rustled around a bit before settling down on the rafters up above.

"Good thing it's the wrong time of year. In the right season, this place would be chock full of bats."

I shuddered at the mental picture, but at least that was all there was to shudder at.

The barn was empty, of course, as I'd known it would be. It matched perfectly with the rest of the setup. Old, abandoned, a relic of a past time that had served a purpose once but now stood only as a physical symbol of unholy evil.

All these years later, there remained behind no evidence of the nearly twenty bodies that had been mutilated, then stacked one on top of the other in the rafters above. No signs of the hay stacks stained red. No trace of the overwhelming terror that simply must have resonated between the four wooden walls. No trace, except for that crawling unease, that skin-tightening tension, growing only worse, that I'd felt since first entering the grounds. Then the sheriff's voice broke in on my thoughts, and I knew that the time had finally come.

"I guess you'll want to look over the house, huh?"

※

The exact number of the Preacher's victims was never known, mainly because while they found a total of thirty-three bodies scattered around the site, a few more than that had been reported missing during that hellish weekend in the desert. The Preacher and his family, a scrawny, scrungy collection of misfits, castoffs and dope heads, never did have anything constructive to say. When questioned by authorities in the weeks after the raid, they merely spouted all kinds of the usual deranged, Apocalyptic nonsense. Stuff about how the Preacher was the Lamb of God, how they'd been doing his bidding in an attempt to cleanse the earth and bring paradise down here, and how everyone who dared defy them was going to get theirs in the end.

A total of thirty-three bodies, with no rhyme or reason as to how they'd been treated. Some clubbed, some strangled, others knifed, with others, mainly the slightly older ones, deliberately tortured. It turned out later that, while Preacher John had dictated the number and type of victims to be taken, he'd let his individual followers decide exactly how to go about finishing them off. So in one orgiastic weekend of bloodletting, over thirty people had been slaughtered at the farm, while the man who directed it all had, according to most accounts, stayed in one of the upstairs bedrooms, gazing out the windows at the ongoing hell he'd set up.

They'd intended the whole thing to send some kind of signal or other about the end of the world coming. None of it made much sense, and after an awkward, months-long trial, Preacher John and his various acolytes had been locked away to rot for the rest of their lives. And that had been about the last heard of them.

Until about a month ago.

The house gave me the biggest problem, as I'd known it would. They'd found her in the cellar, and although I knew the main story, when I was younger no one had ever told me any of the details. It had only been years later, when I'd done all that studying on my own, that I found out exactly what and how many atrocities had been committed on the grandmother I'd never known.

So we went through the two stories, the various rooms now basically empty. Over the years, wandering drifters had looted what furniture had remained, so that we came across barely a stick of furniture in the whole place. The windows, smeared and dirt-laden, admitted only feeble light, and I actually began to think I was going to get through it okay until Locher asked the question.

"You want to see the cellar?"

I froze, suddenly unsure of myself. In a way, the cellar would be the culmination of this trip, the final proof that I'd stuck it out as long as I could. However, there were more practical considerations.

I had, after all, one final step to take on this odyssey, and I had to make sure that I kept up my nerve. I realized that actually seeing the place where they'd found my grandmother would quite possibly do me in.

She hadn't been my grandmother at the time, of course. But Tammy Reubens, twenty-nine years old in 1969, was the mother of twin boys at the time the Preacher's people had snatched her up. And one of those sons had grown up to be my father.

I realized at that moment that this entire excursion had, in its way, been a pretty serious folly. I had only one thing to do here at the farm, and taking this magical mystery tour now struck me as completely unnecessary. So it was time to wrap things up.

The sheriff was staring at me, waiting for an answer to his question and probably wondering why I was taking so long.

"Not really," I said with a shake of my head. "Actually, I think I've seen about all I need to make a report back to the office. And this place really does give you the creeps. So if it's all right with you ..."

I didn't need to finish. I could tell by the relief washing over his face that he was as ready to get off the place as I was. Or at least, he probably thought so.

He opened the door and we headed back out into the sunlight. When we reached the gate, I paused for one last look around at the farm.

"Kind of coincidental you're showing up around now," the sheriff said.

I nodded, not really having anything to say to that.

A little over three weeks before my visit to the farm, Preacher John Smith passed away in prison. In his late seventies, one day he hadn't responded to the guards and, when they went into his cell, they discovered that he'd died in his sleep. It caused a big stir in the media for a day or so, but his heyday was long past, and despite the counter-culture hero status he'd once held, most people didn't seem to notice his passing. Forty years is a long time, after all, and it seemed that nobody much cared about what had happened during one really bad weekend back in '69.

I cared. Seeing the story on the nightly news, I immediately set about making plans. If Preacher John was really dead, then only one last thing remained to erase the stain completely. To my mind, the various helpers and assistants from his "family," the hangers on who'd done the actual killings, didn't really count. My entire life, since first learning my grandmother's story, I'd held Preacher John solely responsible.

Well, almost solely.

It took several phone calls, a few days off from my job at the store, and one last serious study of my books and newspaper articles.

I would have preferred not contacting the law, of course, but there was the chance that they'd be on the alert, waiting to nab any stray souvenir hunters or attention-seekers. So upon arriving from the East Coast, I contacted the sheriff's office with my carefully-constructed cover story.

And besides, I felt I owed it to myself to examine the place, up close and during the daylight, at least one time.

I shook Locher's hand and thanked him for his time. He stared at me for a minute, his eyes boring into me, and for a moment I thought he'd somehow managed to figure me out. But after a moment he simply nodded his head, wished me a good day, and climbed into his pickup.

It may have been my imagination, most likely was, but I thought he gave one extra close look at my car before he took off.

If he had any suspicions, I didn't do anything to aggravate them. I drove away from the farm just a few minutes after he did, not even bothering to look back.

That creepy, sickening feeling I'd had during my tour of the place didn't go away, but I'd rather figured it wouldn't. I did, however, have a pretty clear idea of when I would feel better.

Not when I got back to my motel, a short ten miles into town.

Not even a few hours later when I had a nice, leisurely dinner at a local steakhouse.

But later that night, when I returned to the farm and made use of the gasoline, incendiaries and blasting caps currently in the trunk of my car, the feeling, and all the emotions I'd carried around for so many years, should ease away.

Just as soon as I gave a proper cleansing to the farm.

There's nothing quite like a friend dropping in unexpectedly.

Old Friends
by Frank Byrns

THE BOYS LOOKED a lot different since the last time I saw them. They should have; it'd been almost ten years. Reed was twelve now, sandy-haired, the first hint of his old man's barrel chest beginning to show. Leo, eleven months younger, Irish twins, tall and rangy, his mother's son in every way.

They took turns pushing each other on the swing set, then got a little more ballsy, jumping off of the swing at the top of its arc, crash-landing on their knees, laughing, doing it again. Fearless. Young. I must have been that way, once. I can't remember.

I sat on a park bench, out in the open, watching, no fear of being spotted, nothing to hide. No dark glasses or hat, no newspaper to hide behind.

It's not like anyone would ever mistake me for a pederast. Guys like that have a certain look, a stink about them. I celled for a bit with a guy like that my last trip downstate. I killed him in the shower with a spoon I palmed after dinner one night. Nobody blinked an eye.

Gwen showed up around five, a sweaty mess after a two mile jog around the park. Unlike her boys, she still looked the same. For her, the ten years had passed in a blink of an eye. Still tall, still athletic. Still beautiful, even with that long brown hair pulled up beneath a white ball cap.

She stood hunched over, hands on her knees, catching her breath. She stretched, then straightened to her full height. She reached up to her ears, yanked out her white earbuds, scanned the park the way a good mother does, searching for predators.

She turned her shoulders as she scanned a protective circle around the park, then stopped cold when she saw me sitting on the bench. She pushed her sunglasses down the bridge of her nose, giving those dark green eyes a better look at me.

I wasn't sure she'd know who I was. Gwen may have looked almost exactly the same as that day a decade ago at Artie's funeral, but I didn't. 29 to 39 had been a long ten years for me. A little softer in the middle; a little bigger, maybe. I had grown my buzzcut out into something requiring a comb. Added a beard.

Across the park, Gwen's eyes narrowed as her brain worked hard to place my face. I decided to help her out. I reached up to my right cheek, and traced the long white scar that my new beard couldn't hide. I nodded.

Her eyes went a little tighter, then opened wide.

I gave her a small wave, lifting just the fingers of my left hand from the bench.

She raised a hand to her mouth. Quickly, but too slow to stop the scream.

Other folks in the park noticed me then, Gwen's scream creating a scene. I took that as my cue to leave.

It was Reed who answered when I knocked a couple hours later.

"How ya doing, Reed," I said, laying the Southern charm on thick. "I'm an old friend of your daddy."

Reed tilted his head to the right, sizing me up. Without taking his eyes off me, he folded his beefy arms across his chest and leaned shoulder first into the doorframe. Nothing between us but the flimsy netting of a screen door, and the kid wasn't afraid. Arthur would be proud.

"You were in the park," he said finally.

"That's right," I said, no need to lie. "I was hoping to bump into your mom—any chance she's here now?" I gave Reed my best smile.

He shrugged, using the movement in his shoulders to push off the doorframe. "Mom," he called into the house. "That guy from the park is at the door—"

Gwen must have been in the kitchen—a dropped dish shattered on a hardwood floor somewhere inside. She recovered quickly. "Reed," she called, her voice steady, betraying nothing. "Honey, come in here and stir this sauce."

Reed disappeared down the hallway. I stood on the porch waiting for Gwen, taking a look around. Plantation-style home on a half-acre lot, front porch held up by thick white columns, tree-lined circular gravel drive. Gwen had done well for herself with Artie's money.

"What the hell do you want, Ray?"

Like I said, Gwen recovered quickly. I turned around to see her in the open doorframe, the screen door flung wide open, daring me to come inside. Her face was as cold as steel, and twice as hard. A wild look, feral, a mother who would do *anything* to protect her children.

Even in that flour-caked apron, she took my breath away.

"Howdy, Gwendy."

"What the hell do you want, Ray?"

The intensity in her voice surprised me. "Real nice place you got here, Gwen. A real nice—"

"The hell you want, *Ray*?" she repeated, the country girl she used to be slipping back into her words. She was in no mood for small talk.

"A *real* nice place, Gwendy. The new hubby know how you paid for all this?"

"He knows that—"

"—'cause I was kinda wondering myself. The whole thing has me wondering if Artie was doing that much better than the rest of us."

"Ray—"

"—'cause just looking around your place here, you'd think he might have been holding out on us."

My flurry of interruptions left Gwen wary. She waited to see if I was done. I said nothing.

"Ray—"

"—unless you got something going on the side, Gwendy. That would explain it, too, maybe. You always had a good head for—"

"*Ray*." She said it with finality. Too bad. I could have done that all night. Time to shift gears.

"You *know* what I want, Gwen."

"I don't know what you're—"

"Did you sell it? That would certainly explain all this." I waved my hand in a giant circle.

"I didn't sell anyth—"

"Was it Lucas? You sell it to him? He found you first? Beat me here?"

"I—I thought Lucas was dead."

So did I—I was just fishing. Keeping her off-guard. "You thought *I* was dead, too."

Her face told me my guess was right. She *had* thought that I was dead. That's why she settled down, tried to put it all behind her.

"I haven't seen Lucas," she said quietly.

"So you still have it, then."

"Jesus Christ, Ray! I don't even know what you're talking about."

I've known Gwen a long time. Longer than Artie did, even. I introduced them. She was lying.

I traced a finger down the white scar that ran the length of my right cheek, a gift from my old man thirty years ago. I turned my face slightly in that direction, so that the scar was in the center of her line of vision. I lowered my voice, forcing her to lean in a bit, closer to the scar, if she wanted to hear what I was saying. That move has worked wonders in the past on a whole lot of folks.

"That's bullshit, Gwen. We both know it."

Her mouth opened slightly, the beginnings of an answer. I reached in quickly and placed a finger across her lips to silence it.

"Let me tell you how this is going to work. I understand that you might not be able to put your hands on it right this second, so I'll give you a couple of days. At which point there will be a transfer of ownership."

She raised her eyebrows, like she was asking permission to speak. I removed my finger. Her voice was as soft as mine, but still strong.

"Why can't you understand that—"

"—and if there is no transfer of ownership, then I'm sure that your respectable new husband would be very interested to know just how the pretty widow paid for the bed he's sleeping in."

"You don't even know him," she said, no conviction in the words, hoping she was wrong.

"A respectable citizen like that? The kind of guy that leaves his house each day at eight, heads downtown to work, that kind of guy? Works in Suite 681, something like that? A precious old thing— Myrna, maybe?—working the desk out front? That kind of guy? Brown bags a lunch, maybe, walks it across the street to that little park every—"

"All right," she said, broken. "Stop it."

I wasn't finished. "Just seems to me that a respectable guy like that—and I think your husband just might be one of those guys— seems to me that a guy like that might have a real problem with the true nature of his new wife's rather generous inheritance."

I smiled, and let my voice rise to its normal volume. "If he knew."

Gwen eyed me. I stared right back, not wanting to be the one who broke the stalemate. A full minute passed.

It was Reed that finally spoke. "Mom," he yelled from the kitchen. "The sauce is ready."

Gwen's eyes never left mine. "Be there in a minute, honey," she called over her shoulder. "Go ahead and turn the burner off."

I gave Gwen the toothiest bumpkin smile I could manage, pouring all the thick drawl of my childhood into my words. "G'on and take care of your family, sweetheart. They gotta be mighty hungry, what with that long afternoon in the park and all."

I showed her my back and moved down the steps, off the porch, hands shoved deep into the front pockets of my jeans. When I reached the driveway, I turned back to Gwen, who still hadn't moved. "Take care of your family, Gwen," I repeated. "Give me what's mine."

"Hey, Ray?" she said finally. "Go fuck yourself."

I left her standing there, arms folded across her chest, and walked down the drive towards the street, smiling. This was going to be fun.

I figured I'd give Gwen a couple of days to come to her senses. I holed up in a run-down motel on the frontage road out by the interstate and spent my time watching game shows and Braves games.

Nine years. A long time that gets even longer when you only have one thought the entire time. But that one thought was the one thing that got me through my time downstate. For nine years, my every moment was consumed with what I was going to do when I got out, and what I was going to have to do to reclaim what was mine.

It's easy to lose track of things when you're inside. I got picked up the day after Artie's funeral. I knew it was a probably a bad idea to go to the service, after the way things had gone down the week before, but I went anyway. I stayed on the outer edges of the gathering, far from the graveside, thinking I was being pretty discreet, but I guess the Feds were better. I never saw them, but they saw me. One plea bargain later, I was on The Farm, sharing a cell with a pederast.

Most of what you hear when you're in the cut is of a second-hand nature. My first year inside, I heard that Lucas died. I got that playing basketball in the yard with some guy who had run a long con with him a while back in Oklahoma.

Not long after that, I got wind from the outside that people were saying that *I* was dead. I let that go, figuring it would do more to help than to hurt once I got out.

Then, about three years ago, a guy working in the library told me that Gwen had remarried—he had seen it in the paper. I had him clip the article for me, and that's where I saw that she had married this insurance sales *schlub* named Larry.

The article also mentioned where the happy couple would be residing after the wedding, a pretty swank address on the east side of town. They weren't paying the bills there on Larry's salary, that much seemed pretty sure. It stood to reason that Gwen had not kept up Artie's end of the deal.

If Gwen knew Lucas was dead and thought I was, too, there was nothing to fear from cashing out Artie's share and moving on up. Unless, like I said, Artie had been holding out on the rest of us all this time. Either way, she owed me.

And that was the thought that consumed me, the one thing that kept me going those last couple years. Gwen owed me. And whatever it took, as soon as I walked off The Farm, I was going to get what was mine.

I told Gwen I'd give her a couple of days. I'm nothing if not a man of my word. But this time, I waited until Larry was home.

It was a little after 8:30 when I knocked, and the man himself answered the door.

"Can I help you?" he asked, rubbing his hands together to dry them, a small white dishrag slung over the shoulder of his off-the-rack collared white shirt. He didn't seem distressed in the least, which meant Gwen hadn't told him about our earlier conversation.

Good.

"I was hoping I could speak to the lady of the house for a moment."

Larry stopped rubbing his hands, and tilted his head at me quizzically. "And you are. . ."

I closed my eyes and exhaled, feigning embarrassment. "I'm sorry, where are my manners? I'm an old friend of Gwen and... Wow, this is awkward..." I shrugged apologetically. "Gwen and her first husband Arthur."

"I see," Larry said, sizing me up. As if he had a chance. "I don't think I caught your name."

"Ray," I said, smiling with all my teeth. "Ray Dooley."

"Well," he said. "Let me see if she's available."

Larry's artificial manners let me know for sure that Gwen hadn't said anything about my first visit. The way he firmly shut the door in my face before he went back in the house let me know he wasn't a dummy. I filed both those bits of information away, each useful in its own way.

When the front door opened again, Gwen stood there alone. "Walk with me," she said, shutting the door behind her.

I followed Gwen as she walked silently down the driveway. She stopped near the mailbox, just short of the street, and pulled a lone cigarette and match out of the pocket of her yoga pants.

I held up my finger, made a circular motion. "I would have thought that with all this," I said, "you would have given that up."

She gave me a pointed look as she struck the match against the mailbox. "I did quit," she said. "Started back a couple days ago."

I chuckled as she blew a puff of smoke right into my face, an attempt at letting me know she wasn't scared of me.

But I knew better.

"Thought about our conversation the other day, Gwendy?" I looked back towards the house, Larry's shadow lurking in the front window.

"Yeah, I did, and the answer's still the same. Go fuck yourself, Ray."

"Wow. You kiss the boys good night with that mouth?"

Gwen dropped the cigarette on the asphalt, ground it out under the heel of her sneaker.

"Don't talk about my children," she said quietly. "Ever again."

I held my palms up, took a step back. "Be glad to," I said. "Once I get what's mine, you'll never see me again."

Gwen sighed heavily. "There's nothing to give you, Ray. I don't even know what you're talking about. But even if I did?"

She waited, wanting me to finish.

"I could go fuck myself?" I said.

"You're learning."

"Soooo... I guess the next step is to walk up the driveway here and have a nice chat with good ol' Larry."

Gwen crossed her arms, shifted her feet so that she stood between me and the house. "Larry knows all about Artie," she said. "He doesn't like it, but he knows. *Everything.*"

"And he married you anyway."

"Go fu—"

"Yeah, yeah, yeah." I scratched my beard, waited a beat. "He knows what *you* did for us, too?"

She looked away, just a quick second. I had her. "Some of it," she said.

"So I'll just fill him on the rest of it, then? That's how you want to play this?"

"Just tell him what you want—he knows enough. The rest won't surprise him."

I made another circle with my finger. "You willing to bet *all* this on that?"

Gwen rubbed her fingers together, jonesing for another cigarette. I had a hardpack in my jacket pocket, but I didn't offer. "I don't know what else I can really do," she said. "Whatever it is you think you're looking for—I don't have it."

"'Cause you sold it—to help pay for all this."

"Jesus Christ, Ray. For the last fucking time—I don't know what you're talking about."

I shook my head, gave Gwen my best *I guess I've done all I can do here* look. "So I'll be seeing you, then," I said. "Real soon."

See, here's the thing about the whole situation: I knew Gwen was lying. One hundred percent, without a doubt, lying through her perfectly-capped teeth.

How'd I know? Follow my logic.

Eleven years ago, me and Artie and Lucas knocked over a high-end auction house in Asheville. We hit it the night before a big auction and cleared some real big-ticket items.

Me, I wasn't so sure just what we got our hands on that night, but Lucas had us convinced that we were into something good. It wasn't jewelry, paintings, rare books, or anything like that—we left the auction house that night with a big pile of baseball cards.

For the most part, Artie and I just took Lucas' word for it on the cards; after all, he was the super fan. Even though we all played JV together back in high school, Lucas was the only one of us who thought of himself as a baseball fan. Artie played to get girls. I played because I liked to hit things, at least until I got kicked off the team for helping myself to a hundred bucks out of the wallet our coach left in the locker room every day.

The auction house was hosting a near-perfect item for our purposes, Lucas said: a rare, uncut sheet of cards from the 1911 T206 series. Too rare, actually—any attempt to move the sheet would definitely draw the kind of attention we didn't want or need.

But—and Lucas said this was the real beauty of the job—we could cut the sheet into individual cards, rub up the corners with a damp rag and some dirt to 'age' them a bit, then sell them off piecemeal, a few at a time. Steal one thing, sell off another. Still suspicious, but not near as much.

The job itself was pretty smooth, in and out in a little under six minutes. Lucas grabbed the sheet of cards, Artie and I grabbed a sack each full of other things we found interesting, and we beat it out of there well ahead of the cops.

At the time, Lucas was staying with some gal whose husband was over in Iraq, some place out in the county somewhere, so we went back to his place where it was nice and quiet to divvy up the score. Artie and I worked on a bottle of Early Times while Lucas worked on the cards with an exacto knife; before long he had turned the sheet into over a hundred individual cards.

We all agreed ahead of time that once the score was split, no one would make a move to sell any of it for at least five years. A rare sheet turns up stolen, and a few weeks later those individual cards were for sale? We weren't *that* stupid. Better to let the heat die down first—we were viewing this job as a long-term investment.

Lucas pulled some sort of pricing sheet off the computer, and we let him sort the cards into three more or less equal piles. The piles didn't have the same number of cards, but they all had roughly the same value, according to Lucas' sheet.

My pile is still safe, wrapped and stuffed in a hole in the mattress in the back bedroom at my mama's house back home. The same mattress my grandma died on when she came to live with us when I was nine; the same mattress I hid my porn in when I was twelve.

Lucas' pile? God only knows at this point. The plan was to tackle that one next, since I didn't even know where to start.

But Artie's pile? Gwen knew. Gwen always knew everything about Artie's scores. She was usually the one that did the hiding, if hiding's what was needed. She either knew where the cards were, or she had already moved them.

Either way, she was going to pay.

It took me two minutes on that bench in the park to figure out where to hit Gwen to make it hurt the most. It surprised me, really: I would have thought for sure that tipping off the new husband and the new social circle to her background would have been the play. But she didn't seem to care about that at all.

The only thing she seemed to care about was the boys.

When I went away, you'd have been hard-pressed to find a worse mother than Gwen. She and my baby sister were best friends going all the way back to the Sunday School class they were in together. Hell, Heather's probably the one that introduced Gwen to her first taste of the shit they both got hooked on. Gwen was right there in the room when Heather OD'd, too fucked up herself to do anything about it.

Nine years ago, the nicest thing you could get Gwen to call the boys was an inconvenience. Now, though... You could see it in her eyes at the park. Fierce. This was a woman who'd do anything to protect her children. She'd even got clean to protect them, and that was no small task given where she was when Artie got killed.

It was surprising, but I didn't doubt it was real.

So if I needed to get to her, I'd have to do it through the kids.

I gave it another couple days to hopefully have Gwen let her guard down just a little bit. I watched the boys walk home from school a couple times, learned the route they took, cutting through the park for a short cut. Then I went back to the motel and had a beer and a hooker for dinner.

On the third day, I drove my car down to the park and sat down on a bench that Reed and Leo walked past every day on their way home. They walked up at 3:15, right on schedule.

I waved as they approached. "Whatcha say, boys?"

Reed, the oldest, made as if to keep walking, but Leo stopped. Reed grabbed his brother by the arm, trying to pull him along. "Let's go," Reed said, ignoring me.

"Hey, Leo," I said as the kid shook Reed's hand loose. "Long time no see. You were barely walking the last time I saw you."

"I don't know you," Leo said.

Reed exhaled deeply, his face darkening the same way Artie's used to. "Yeah, you do," he said to Leo. "This is the asshole's been bothering Mom."

I gave a little laugh, hoping it seemed genuine. "Is that what she said?" I kept smiling, shook my head. "Look, I'm gonna be honest here. Your mama and I ain't always gotten along that great. I was more your daddy's friend."

"You knew my daddy?" Leo said.

"C'mon, you little shit, let's go," Reed said.

"Oh, yeah, Leo, I knew your daddy," I said. "Me and him was best friends since... hell, since we were your age. What are you, ten? Younger than you, even."

"I'm eleven," Leo said.

"Well, there you go," I said. "Your mama talk about your daddy much?"

"Just that he was some no-count white trash that did a lot of stupid shit and got himself killed," Reed said.

I tried to study Leo's face before I answered, but he wouldn't look up, his eyes down on the sidewalk. Based on that, I figured he might have a little better opinion of Artie than Reed did, and wondered how to play that to my advantage. "Yeah, Reed, all of that is probably true," I allowed. "We were both no account, and we both did a lot of stupid shit."

I scratched my beard, playing at being deep in thought. "I tell you this, though. Everything your daddy did, he did for his family. Everything so you and your mama could have a better life. She probably don't always remember that part of it."

That wasn't exactly true, but it was true enough for what I was selling. "Look, can I let you in on a little secret? I got a couple things back at my motel that your daddy wanted you to have. I tried to get your mama to take 'em and give to you, but she didn't want nothing to do with it."

"That's why she's been yelling at you?" Leo asked.

I nodded, then moved in for the kill.

"What if—" I cut myself off. "Nah, forget it. Wouldn't want anybody to get in any trouble."

"What?" Leo asked. I could barely hear him, what with the giant hook in his mouth. Metaphorically speaking, of course.

"No, I was just thinking I could just give the stuff straight to you guys, and that way we don't have to bother your mama with it."

"That sounds like a bad idea," Reed said.

"You go home if you want, Reed," Leo said. "I'm going to get Dad's stuff."

I kept my mouth shut and let the boys play it out.

"You don't even remember him," Reed. "C'mon—we're going home."

"No. I'm going with... " Leo looked up at me. Stupid kid didn't even know my name.

"Ray," I said. "My name's Ray."

Leo shot his older brother a 'fuck you' look that rivaled Gwen's best from the old days. "I'm going with Ray, Reed," he said. "You go on home if you want to."

Reed's eyes flashed with anger. I could tell, though, that is was directed at me, not Leo. "Not by yourself, you're not. Let's go, I guess, if you're not going to listen to me."

"Great!" I said, clapping my hands together with fake enthusiasm. "If it'd make you feel better, Reed, I can call your Mom and let her know where you are."

Reed thought about it. "Nah, I better do it myself."

"Let me—that way when she gets mad, it'll seem like it's my fault."

"Whatever." Reed shrugged and handed me the phone from his backpack as the three of us walked towards the parking lot and my car. I found "Mom" on his recent call screen and punched the redial button.

"Hey Gwen, it's Ray... now wait, calm down a minute." Reed and Leo were watching, so I looked down and gave them a wink—*we're in this together now, boys.*

"Yeah, the boys are right here with me—we're headed back to my motel... You don't have to pick them up, I'd be glad to drop them back by the house when we're through... Yeah, sure, whatever you want."

I gave her the motel address as we climbed into the car and pulled away. "Don't forget your seatbelts, boys," saying it like I gave a fuck, for Gwen's benefit. "Room 113—it's on the back side, away from the highway noise... Bring me something when you come, would ya? I don't know, surprise me."

I barely had time to zip-tie the boys to the toilet before there was a loud pounding at the door. "Goddamit, Ray, you open this fucking door right now!"

I opened it, and Gwen barged into the room, a heavy tote bag in her hands. "Ooh, is that my surprise?"

"Where are the boys?"

"The boys are fine, Gwen. I looked towards the bathroom and raised my voice. "Aren't you, boys?"

"Is that you, Mom?" Reed called. He didn't sound so tough now, the little shit.

"I'm right here, baby," Gwen said. "We'll be out of here in just a second."

Gwen turned back to me, stared right in my eyes. "I'm going to fucking kill you," she said in a quiet voice.

"Thought you might say that—let's make sure you're not carrying anything to do it with."

She dropped the bag on the ground and held her arms out to the sides. I patted her down, letting my hands linger a little bit in all the right places. She bristled under my touch, but no gun.

"You know I had to do that, right?" I said.

"Fucker," she said. "Let's just get this over with."

Gwen dumped the duffel bag out on the bed—and there they were. Lying in the middle of a pile of old signed balls and bats and gloves and old wool jerseys was a carefully bubble-wrapped stack of vintage 1911 baseball cards.

"So you did have it," I said.

"Whatever it is," she said. "I brought all of Artie's shit I still have since I still don't know what the hell you're looking for."

I brushed past Gwen and moved to the bed. I sat on the edge and focused my attention directly on the cards, ignoring everything else. I wasn't sure if I should touch them, or even undo the bubble wrap—shouldn't I have been wearing some kind of white gloves or something? Lucas would know, but he wasn't there.

"I brought your shit, Ray—give me the boys."

"In a minute," I said, trying to remember the name of the fence we all used in the old days. He'd know what to do with these cards—all of it, really. Might have to take fifteen cents on the dollar, but it would still be a nice little nut to get some things going again.

"Ray."

There was a rustling behind me, as Gwen rooted around in the empty duffel bag. "In a minute," I said again, really starting to get annoyed with her.

"Hey, Ray?"

"What!" I yelled, then looked up just as Gwen blasted me in the face with the same two and a half pound bat the Babe used to club a homer in the 1926 World Series.

When I came to, I was handcuffed to a hospital bed with a broken jaw. I also had a broken nose, two black eyes, three missing teeth, and a grade three concussion.

Clearly, Gwen had hit me more than once.

The beat cop stationed in the room read me my rights a couple minutes later.

"Whazz de charge?" I said, every syllable of every word shooting explosive pain throughout my body.

"You were found unconscious in a motel room with the door wide open, lying on a big pile of shit that was reported stolen ten years ago. Not to mention the parole violation. You tell me what the charge is."

"Alone?"

"When the maid found you, yeah. But somebody knocked your

ass out, so not really. Must've pissed your partners off royally."

I closed my eyes—even that hurt. "Cardzh?" I asked.

"Say again?"

"Bazhballlll cardzh...."

"No, man, you had gloves and balls, old jerseys. A couple of hats. Little bit of everything—no baseball cards, though."

I tried to smile, but couldn't.

Gwendy. Artie'd be so proud.

It's never too late to catch a dream.

Write Your Epitaph
by Laird Long

THE JUDGE WAS banging down hard on his gavel, but the angry hammering was lost in the babble of furious voices—shouting, swearing, screaming, howling. Someone stole a purse, busted into a store, scored some drugs, turned some tricks, fell down drunk—who knew? Who cared? The scum of the earth came here for their five minutes of assembly-line justice: step forward, plead your case, get sentenced. Next! Keep it moving! Too many criminals, too little justice. The gavel would bang all night long. And the next night, and the next night.

Leonard Easton was supposed to be taking notes, taking pictures, taking sides, taking time off the clock. He was supposed to be packaging something together for his uncredited newspaper column: Court Beat. Dish out the muck from the courthouse—order up! So the readers could shove some more breakfast toast in their mouths and laugh at others more pathetic than themselves. It didn't come any lower than night court, and Leonard's job was to scrape something interesting off the bottom and write it up as news.

But not right now. Right now, Leonard Easton was having none of it. He was drifting; drifting back to the day fifteen years ago when he sold his first song. That was a time, he thought. You and your buddies had just graduated from high school, and the summer stretched ahead like a sun-baked highway to infinity. You hung around the used record stores, the second-hand instrument stores, the all-night coffee shops, and the dingy nightclubs - where anyone with a tune rattling around in his head and a piece to blow it through could get up on stage and sprinkle some notes over a drunken audience. You were going to be singers, songwriters, musicians—good ones; the kind people remembered long after you slept with a tombstone for a pillow. It was only a matter of time, and time was taking your side. All you had to do was follow the rhythm of your dream—the music would take you to the top. Money, food, clothing - they weren't important. They were the prey of the soulless hunters who scrounged around their entire lives for material trophies, while their hearts rotted from the inside out. The music was the thing. The music was important. It was everything and the only thing; you ate it, slept it, drank it, and, most importantly, listened to and played it. You were on a quest for the perfect melody—something you could string across the stars and make the heavens take notice.

The bailiffs cleared away some of the drunks and the judge called a recess. Red bumped Leonard's arm. "Sorry, Len, didn't see you there."

"Sure, no problem." Leonard glanced down at the blank pad of paper, fallen on the dirty tile floor. He tried to think what he was going to write; what combination of truth and fiction he was going to scrawl on that blank, white tablet, and spoon-feed to the readers. Bang out some point-blank prose long on hyperbole and short on thoughtfulness—newspaper-style. Something that would get them jawing with their cronies as they chugged coffee in the lunchroom, or sat crammed together on a bus, desperately trying to slow down the time until they had to return to work.

But you weren't writing down a damn thing, were you?, Leonard thought. No, you were drifting away again - to the days after graduation. Fall had come, the air had grown cold and grey, and all around you things had started to die. Larry took off for college, to become a pharmacist like his old man—the path most taken. Heather got married. Crystal started full-time at the department store. But that was okay, not everyone could follow their dream—that's what made the dream so special. There was you and Jerry and April and Pete. You'd sold your first song just a few months ago and—

Leonard's watch buzzed shrilly in the temporary quiet.

"Deadline comin', eh news-hawk," Red said, laughing.

"Yeah."

Leonard pushed himself off the hard wooden bench, stretched, walked stiffly down the aisle, and yanked open the heavy courtroom doors. He would phone it in tonight, he decided. Dream something up in the dingy basement cafeteria and phone it in. No need to go back to the office. There was nothing for him there, anyway. There weren't many jobs lower than the court beat reporter at the newspaper, and he had heard all their jokes a thousand times before. Phone it in. He could do without their contempt, or, worse yet, their sympathy.

He grabbed a table and a coffee in the smoke-filled dungeon which masqueraded as a cafeteria and jotted down the highlights of the night in point-form. He shoved a quarter in a pay phone and dictated the story to the girl at the end of the line—some bright-eyed, bright-voiced, recent journalism grad who would be leapfrogging over Leonard Easton's tired thirty-three year-old body in the time it took to hammer out an obituary. His dusty memories were the only thing keeping him on the rails. That, and the booze.

He shucked on a faded, green parka and pushed through the front doors of the courthouse and out into the night. A raw wind blew off the river and knifed through his body as he trudged down Front Street. Beads of frozen rain battered his face. A block of pawnshops and Chinese restaurants gave way to a three-storey dilapidated apartment building. Home.

"Shut the door! You're lettin' the heat out!"

"Sorry."

"And don't track any dirt on the floor! Take your shoes off!"

He did.

His wife looked up from the TV briefly, and then back down. "Supper's in the fridge," she said tonelessly. She took a drag from her cigarette. The room was packed with smoke.

Paulette Easton was a fat, sour-faced woman a year older than Leonard. She had bottle-blonde hair cut very short, blue, red-rimmed eyes, and a double chin. She smoked constantly. She worked as a parking lot attendant and made more money than Leonard.

Leonard dragged himself across the living room and into the kitchen. Paulette waved a pudgy hand impatiently when his body blocked her view of the TV for a split-second. Leonard grimly tugged the fridge door open. The bulb was burnt out, so he picked up the cracked plate inside and examined it under the kitchen light. Meatloaf. He tossed the plate back into the fridge.

Paulette yelled: "If you ain't goin' to eat it, I will!"

"Sure."

"Huh!?"

"I'm going out," he said softly.

The couch springs groaned as Paulette shoved herself up. She stomped into the kitchen. "You're goin' out!?" She brushed some ash off her faded sweatshirt. She pulled the cigarette out of her mouth. "You're goin' boozin' is more like it!" Her mashed-potato face flushed red. She looked him up and down and let loose with a horse laugh. "You ain't nothin' but skin and bones, for Christ's sake!"

"I—"

"And where the hell you gettin' the money for booze!?" She waddled closer, stuck her face in his. "Huh!?"

Leonard sucked in a ragged breath. He coughed as acrid smoke filled his nose. Easy, he thought. Take it easy. She's looking for a fight. Itching for one. A real knockdown, drag 'em out brawl. She's been waiting up all night for it; looking forward to it. And you know who's coming out on the short end, win or lose. That's what landed you in this mess in the first place - you were tanked to the gills and a broad got lippy and you smacked her around a bit. She ended up in a hospital for three months and you ended up in a jail for three years. And that was when you were riding high. You ain't riding so high now. You got paroled and ended up here, where you belonged all along. You started with nothing and you'll end it with nothing. Sure, you had it good once, but you couldn't hold it. You cracked up and broke into little pieces—pieces so small that they could never be fitted together again. But don't cry too hard.

"I've got some money."

"You got money!?" Paulette stabbed out her cigarette in the ashtray she always carried around—an empty coffee can half-filled with sand. She fired up another one immediately. "You ain't gettin' paid 'til the end of the week, chum!" She positioned her bulk squarely in the doorway. "I know when you get paid."

"Okay. Let's watch some TV," Leonard suggested quietly. "Okay?"

"That's better!" She turned back into the living room and hunkered down on the ratty couch.

He walked quickly through the apartment and out the front door. The building exploded with profanity as he shoved his way back into the cold night air.

Sarah was sitting in a corner booth. She was nursing a Long Island iced tea. Leonard slid in across from her. She looked up, smiled. He told the waitress: "Double scotch, no rocks."

"Do you have any money, Leonard?" Sarah asked softly.

He stared at her. "Yeah, I've got money."

"She giving you trouble, again," she stated sympathetically. She patted his pale hand.

He jerked his hand away. He nodded. "Sorry. I'm kind of jumpy, I guess." He studied her face briefly, then looked down at the scarred table separating them.

She was twenty-two, willowy thin, with big, brown eyes, and long, black hair. She was cheerful, enthusiastic, and blissfully idealistic. She cradled a lot of the old dreams Leonard used to cherish, about music and life; before he had snuffed out the fire of a promising career with gallons and gallons of booze. The three year stretch in the government hotel was his final curtain.

Sarah had a good singing voice, if slightly untrained. She sang in lounges and clubs, and the local bars that littered the streets of the Richland section of town. Sometimes she would take one of her more ardent fans into a back room or an empty parking lot. Male or female. She was a part-time student and it helped pay the rent. Come summer, she jumped on the folkie bandwagon, picking up a few bucks on the road, drifting from festival to festival. A lot of the time, she only got paid in weed. She met a lot of washed-up bums like Leonard, and a lot of starry-eyed hopefuls like herself—kids who weren't old enough yet to be strewn on the rocky shores of obscurity.

"I was hoping that you'd show up tonight." She sounded sort of breathless.

"Yeah. I'm a regular. A fixture. Like that bar stool over there." He pointed. "The old joint wouldn't be the same without me." He tossed back his drink and banged his glass on the table for a refill. "You going to sing?"

She smiled gently. "Maybe later." She sucked some air into her lungs and held it. "I've got some great news, Leonard."

He looked up at her for a couple of beats, then glanced nervously around the near-empty bar. Her face was lit up like the cherry on a cop car. "Huh?"

"I took some of your songs to a music agent friend of one of my instructors. He liked them! He liked the way I sang them, too!" She grabbed hold of his cold, twitching fingers, rubbed them with her warm hands. "So he helped me cut a CD in his studio and he's going to shop it around - see if he can get anyone interested!"

Leonard pulled his hands free. The waitress dropped his refill on the table and he downed it. He felt something start to crawl to life inside of him, and he wanted to drown it. He had been down this wreck-strewn stretch of broken road before—getting excited about something big happening, and then never getting so much as a phone call or a letter back. Or, if they did have the courtesy to let you know, all they said was that your stuff didn't fit their needs. And that was it. "I didn't mean for anyone else to hear those songs."

"They're too good for just you and me!" Her excitement spilled all over the place; out of place in the dusky bar. "The agent recognized your name!"

Leonard shrugged indifferently. "Yeah?"

"Yeah! You better believe, yeah, mister!" She leaned across the table and kissed him. "Try to cheer up, will you?"

Leonard smiled wearily. "'Nother drink?" he asked.

The judge hammered the court into silence and then declared a half-hour break. Leonard pushed his way through the crowd of angry miscreants and went outside. He bummed a cigarette from Red. They flattened themselves against the grimy brick wall, sheltered from the howling north wind.

"Another blue ball special, eh?" Red chuckled. He shivered in his government-issue jacket.

Leonard huddled deeper into his parka. Snow was falling sideways, smacking him in the face. Another cold day in hell, he thought.

"We got a good one comin' up," Red said, blowing smoke back into his own face. He spat on the butt-strewn concrete. "Somethin' for you to write about, maybe."

"Yeah."

"Yeah. Biker case. Some righteous citizen filed a complaint against a guy who rides with one of those outlaw motorcycle gangs." Red pressed down on his right nostril and sent a stream of hot snot out of his left. "They all drive four-wheel drives this time of the year, I bet. Anyway, this citizen says that this biker stole his snow-blower. Can you believe that? Citizen lives right across the street from the gang's clubhouse, no less." Red shook his head. "That guy's got bowlin' balls between his legs. Or rocks in his head. We got three extra bailiffs on tonight to make sure there's no trouble. The bikers are righteously pissed-"

"Leonard!"

Leonard heard someone call his name, before the wind tore it apart. He glanced down the street and saw Sarah running towards him, trying not to slip on the icy sidewalk.

Red whistled, nudged Leonard with his elbow. "I'll leave you two alone," he said, grinning. He threw down his cigarette and slipped back inside the building.

Sarah ran up and hugged Leonard. He shrugged her off. "What are you doing here?" he asked angrily. "This isn't any place for you."

"Yeah, yeah! Try not to look too disappointed." She kissed him on the mouth. She quickly pulled her head back. "Yuck! I thought you hated cigarette smoke?"

"You can get used to anything after a while, I guess." He smiled at her.

She grinned back at him. She was wearing bright red earmuffs, a red coat with a fur collar, a short skirt, and long, black boots. She looked eighteen years old. "I come bearing glad tidings, oh worried one."

"Yeah?"

"Yeah. Are you ready?"

Leonard grimaced. "It isn't going to get any warmer."

"That agent I was telling you about wants to meet with you and me tomorrow afternoon." She paused dramatically, eyes sparkling. "He's got a recording label interested in our CD!" She did a little jig on the sidewalk, splashing around in the grey slush.

Leonard stared at her, numb with disbelief. A tiny flame burst to life inside of him—a flame he thought he had extinguished years ago.

A man walked up to them. "Excuse me," he said politely. He was trying to get into the courthouse and they were blocking the entrance. He was thin and wiry, with horn-rimmed glasses and a determined look on his grim, grey face.

"Hey, asshole!" someone shouted from across the street. A group of men were standing at the corner, waiting for the traffic to thin out so they could cross. They were dressed in leather jackets and blue jeans, and they were huge.

The man with the glasses turned and looked at the men; looked scared.

One of the big men pulled something out of his pocket.

"No, Darryl!" someone yelled.

The night exploded with gunfire.

"I told you before, and I'll tell you again: he ain't here! Quit phonin'!" Paulette slammed the phone down and waddled into the kitchen. She slumped into a chair, spilling over the sides. She stared at Leonard across the small table, a cigarette burning in her right fist. She banged the coffee can on the stained table face.

"Easy," Leonard said softly. Take it easy, he thought to himself. She's really cruising for trouble this time—burning for it. And if she knew the half of it, there really would be trouble. Big trouble. The kind of trouble that gets people hurt. So everyone just take it easy. Let it ride. There's no point in fighting; never was. Just sail along and enjoy the ride; no need to worry about the destination. And remember, there's a bottle of scotch waiting for you at a bar somewhere—just the thing to send you sailing.

"Don't tell me to take it easy, mister! Why the hell is that Jew phoning all the time!?"

Leonard shrugged. "What Jew?"

"You know damn well what Jew! That Morley Thorstein, or Thorsteinson, or somethin'! Says he's a talent agent and he wants to talk to you about some songs!" She angrily mashed out her cigarette, set fire to a new one. "Talent agent! And he wants to talk to you! Ha!"

Paulette eyed Leonard suspiciously. "What'd you know about writing songs, anyway?" Her fat face was red, slathered with a sticky sheen of sweat.

Leonard gently set down his coffee cup. "Must be a gag," he said. "Trying to sell me some records or something."

She nodded. "Good," she said, resolving the matter to her satisfaction. She grinned sadistically as another thought struck her dull mind. "So you gotta testify in court about that girl who got herself killed outside the courthouse a couple of weeks ago, eh?" She blew a cloud of blue smoke in his face. "That'll be a switch, I bet."

Leonard closed his eyes. He was desperately trying to listen to a sweet, young voice softly singing a corny love song; but it was already starting to fade from his memory.

An Unexpected Invitation
by Daniel Marshall Wood

"DO YOU THINK black tie?" Delia asked her husband late Sunday afternoon. Beyond the diamond-paned library window flagstones disappeared under white powder.

"What?" Adam stirred from dedicated concentration on the *Times*
crossword, upsetting a grey tabby from her corduroy perch. "The clue
is 'Barker of filmdom.' Should be Les, but that's three letters, not
four."

"Les is not less," Delia murmured. "Asta. That cute terrier in the
Thin Man movies. Myrna Loy and William Holden."

"William Powell, dear. Oh, now I get it. Barker—a dog barks. I
may write the puzzle editor again. What were you saying?"

"Do you think black tie?" Delia admired her now-white garden.
"It's snowing. Rhododendrons love cold feet. The angels are dusting
us with powdered sugar."

"Then let the angels shovel the damned stuff. Black tie for what?"
Adam uncrossed his legs and the cat immediately reappeared, circling
twice before settling down.

"For our next dinner party, of course. It's been ages…"

"We had a dinner party before Christmas. I wouldn't call that
ages. Sixty-three down. Garden implement. Five letters."

"Trowel? Spade? It's been ages since we had black tie. December
was tweedy and homey. You looked smashing in that jacket with the
currant overplaid."

"Black tie is fine. I have it, so might as well wear it." Adam shifted
slightly so as not to upset the purring Markle.

"The gardens are a hoary wonderland."

"Pimps and prostitutes will adore it." Adam's pen poked at the
crossword.

"Silly boy." The ice in Delia's highball glass rang softly against the
crystal. "Need another drink, darling?"

"Just a thimbleful," Adam responded, meaning 'fill 'er up.'

"Just a thimbleful for me, as well." In one deft stroke tongs flipped the hinged lid of the silver ice bucket and grasped an ice cube.

"Here we go." Delia perched on the arm of Adam's wing chair, mindful of the sleeping cat. "Thirty-three across is bogus."

"The clue or the answer?"

"The answer, silly. Whom should we invite? So many of our circle are no longer with us."

Adam looked up from the half-inked puzzle. "Is that your euphemism for death?"

"Sometimes."

"I know you dearly miss Phoebe."

"I had such high hopes for Phoebe." Delia rose and then settled onto a linen slipcovered loveseat. "Months went by with no word. I prayed she'd come through, like so many times in the past." Her voice trailed off.

"But she didn't. Not this time," Adam consoled.

Delia sighed. "We enjoyed many delightful evenings together—both here and at Phoebe's Riverbrink. Such a wonderful house—and the name, Riverbrink."

"Succinctly poetic, as the house is at the brink of a river."

"I love our house name. Crathorne. Delightfully English-sounding without stuffy connections to politics or furniture." Delia leaned forward and shifted a cushion to her liking. "But Phoebe and Riverbrink are in our lives no longer. I wish Jefferson were still around."

"Old Jeff. He went too quickly." Adam gazed absently at a gilt-framed late-Impressionist painting depicting a gilt-framed Renaissance portrait.

"The very day after our dinner party. Do you think the police really suspected us in his death?" Delia closed her eyes.

"Simply a routine inquiry. How could they possibly think anything untoward? We couldn't anticipate the unfortunate timing of Jefferson's demise."

Delia's fingers brushed through slightly-highlighted hair. "Are we old, Adam?"

"Chronologically, we're on our way, but don't we feel otherwise? I may climb an Alp any day."

"Of course, Adam—after you extend your walk to a mile. Most everyone feels younger than one's true years." Delia stood. "So many funerals lately. I'm weary of black, though it looks good on me."

"You were the best-dressed mourner at Jefferson's send-off. The grieving widow received less attention."

"It was the veiled hat, you flatterer. Maybe that's why I married you. One of the many whys."

"Almost forty-five years ago." Adam smiled. "I love you even more now, Cordelia Gardiner Weyforth Collier—if that's possible."

"And I love you forever, still. Just don't remind me of how long," Delia said wistfully. "You make me laugh. That's another why." Delia caressed Adam's shoulders. "Need any more help with the crossword?"

"It's going well. Markle and I are contented beasts, soothed with respective lap and word game." An upraised white-tipped chin demanded scratching.

Delia paused. "Whom should we invite? It's time for new faces and fresh, witty conversation at our dinner party, with so many friends gone."

"Gone for several reasons. Anyone in mind?" Skepticism tinged Adam's voice.

"No one, really. It would be nice to find someone we know nothing about. Provided they're charming, of course." Ice cubes clinked.

"Charming—that's understood." Adam and Markle both yawned.

Delia flipped through the *Times*. "Such a lovely couple."

"Whom, dear?"

"On the weddings page. They were married last month, though the announcement is made only today."

"And how do these heretofore unknown nuptials affect us?"

"They're an appealing pair. Mid-thirties it says, so time enough to have developed into the colorful, intriguing guests we seek."

"Even if we don't know them."

"That's the point, Adam. An infusion of new blood."

"Maybe they don't have black tie. Won't that rule them out?"

"Oh, but they do. Right here, in the photo. Frank's in black tie and kilt. That's serious dressing up. If Frank has a kilt, he's not renting."

"Scottish descent, no doubt."

"MacDougall. Do you think?" Delia laughed heartily. "Edwina is Frank's lovely bride. They were married in a castle. I like them even more."

"Hmm. Hanoverian ruler, seven letters. I'm listening, dear."

"George the first. Edwina and Frank. Lovely traditional names. Edwina is English, it says. Devon. That cream is to die for."

"As many doctors concur, but what's a scone without it? So Edwina's been imported to Staten Island?"

"I wouldn't phrase it that way. Makes her seem like a mail order bride. Frank grew up here." Delia squinted. "Attended St. Something's school. There's a blur."

"St. Swithen's? Elite boys' school. Great basketball team. League champions almost every year."

"Yes, that's probably it—I can make out the 'ith.' I should look up Swithen in my saint-a-day book. Saints lead such interesting lives, or used to. I wonder what saints do now, day-to-day?" Delia lost herself in saints.

"Can't really say." Adam responded diplomatically when no answer would suffice.

"Frank looks tall, so he may have played basketball. I'll get more ice. Freshen your drink?" Delia asked.

"Just a thimbleful." Markle stretched, but didn't claw.

Delia crossed to the desk. "Freshen your drink?"

"You're a godsend. Just a thimbleful."

"How's the new story going?"

"Rambling, but I'm amusing myself. Want to read it?" Adam handed Delia six pages before she could answer.

Delia read silently, standing at the window. "It's snowing."

"You've already made that observation in the story—and more eloquently."

"Oh, yes, I see. I like what I said. You're using our names."

"Do you mind? Write what you know is the dictum. Our names—I know them well."

"Silly boy. You can change them later."

"Why should I? Have we anything to hide?"

"You're including my gardening and your crossword puzzling. Very autobiographical."

"Start with what's familiar."

"You've made us older. I'm not ready for my sixties." Delia tugged at the corners of her eyes.

"Delia and Adam can be so much more worldly and wise if I put them in their prime," Adam said. "Traveled. Comfortably well off. Retired."

"Just as we dream. Okay, then, but age me well." Delia stretched her throat to remove any trace of a line or droop that might have crept in overnight.

"Like a vintage wine. Smooth and fragrant, with a surprisingly tart finish."

"Your winemaking hobby has languished, so I'm not sure that's a valid compliment." She paused. "Delia comes across as rather vacuous. Am I that lightheaded?"

"My bride is too complex to accurately portray, so she must be abridged."

"Oh, you are good. I'll fetch your drink and see about Markle. She's much too quiet. Ciao and meow for now." Delia blew a kiss.

"Here's your drink. All's right with the world. You and me and a cozy fire and soft snow blessing the garden landscape." Delia remained at the window.

"Is falling snow anything but soft?"

"Do you prefer icy pellets?" Delia turned toward Adam.

"But that's not snow. Snow is always soft, so what you said is redundant."

"I call it expressive. Saturday?"

"For what?"

"For the dinner party with Frank and Edwina. Two weeks from Saturday, perhaps."

"They may already have plans."

"No one has plans in February. It's so cold and bleak. It's too soon after all the holiday hubbub to have plans. That's a good crossword word, hubbub. Add it to your list, next to hurly-burly."

"But we'll have plans if we invite Frank and Edna."

"Edwina. So will they. That's the point. A blank square on the calendar transcends into a delicious, impetuous, decadent black tie dinner party. Thursday?"

"For what?"

"Would a Thursday be too rash? No, I think Saturday for the first occasion. Mid-week might be off-putting. Too much, too soon."

"If you say. The food will taste the same either evening." Adam's pen poised, mid-air.

"What about Bitsy and Charles?"

"At the dinner party?"

"Yes. Do you think they'll mix well with our new friends?"

"Why shouldn't they, since none of us know anything of Frank and Edwina. They're a blank slate."

"Waiting to be inscribed—in a proper, cursive hand like we learned in third grade." Delia traced capital D's in the air.

"Or waiting to be erased."

Delia frowned. "Give them a chance before you erase them. Frank and Edwina may come through and delight us to no end with reciprocity and thank-you notes. But what do you think about Bitsy and Charles?"

"Invite away, dear lady."

Delia's hands flew up. "An alphabet run. I love it!"

"Whatever do you mean?"

"Like that odd puzzle clue—alphabet run or alphabet trio, just a string of letters. With Bitsy and Charles, we're now an alphabet run. A—B—C—D—E—F. Adam, Bitsy, Charles, Delia, Edwina and Frank."

"So?"

"It's too wonderful! Edwina and Frank are so thoughtful to have the right initials. It's all falling into place, like it's meant to be. Prophecy fulfilled, don't you think?"

"Can't really say."

"Maybe I'll just ask B & C for drinks. On Saturdays they usually dine with Charles' mother at the club."

"A command performance to keep in the good graces and better will of his rich heritage and parentage."

"That's not nice." Delia assessed her nails.

"But it's true. You know it is."

"Well, yes, but one doesn't have to say it."

⚬⚬⚬

"Or write it." Delia read over Adam's shoulder. "What would they say if they read your story?"

"I've disguised their names. Betsy and Carl would never recognize themselves as Bitsy and Charles. Besides, when do they read? They're too busy golfing and drinking."

"Adam Collier, stop that. They're dear friends. They reciprocate, unlike so many others. That alone is irreproachable."

"B and C can be amusing, at times. We'll postpone judgment on E & F until we actually meet them." Adam discreetly cleaned under a thumbnail.

"Carl's so handsome. Such a distinguished gentleman—all that salt and pepper hair and craggy laugh lines. Men age so deliciously. It's not fair."

"Perhaps I'll have a transplant in twenty years and go from badly thinning mousy brown to a full black and white mane. Would you like that?"

"I'm teasing. I love you just as you are, thin and thinning. But you must admit Carl is quite easy on the eyes."

"Your eyes, perhaps. He does nothing for me. But Betsy? For her age, she's well put together."

"Then it's agreed. We'll keep them because they're beautiful and invite them to meet Frank and Edwina." Delia twirled.

"What if they can't make it?"

"They have to. There's no story if they don't."

"So it's settled. We'll invite everyone for two weeks from Saturday. I can't wait." Delia twirled twice.

"What if Frank and Edwina can't make it? Aha." Adam confidently entered letters into empty squares.

"They have to. It wouldn't be the same without them." Delia twirled again.

"That's true."

"What?" Delia's brow furrowed.

"The same. If they weren't here it wouldn't be the same." Adam's voice rang sharper.

"You are being silly again, Adam. You know what I mean."

"But what if they can't come?" Adam asked again.

"But what if they can? I'm always the optimist—half full to your half empty. Maybe that's another why, as to why I married you."

"What do you mean, dearest why-er?"

"We balance each other."

"Or cancel each other out."

"Either way, it works. Bitsy and Charles are a given. Keep your fingers crossed about Frank and Edwina. They just have to!"

Adam held up the finished puzzle. "All done. Not a bad afternoon's work."

"It's not work to you. What shall we serve? Bitsy and Charles know my repertoire by heart. I'll find something new. The last time I was in the basement I tripped over a stack of Gourmet magazines from the late '80s."

"Something chocolate for dessert?" Adam licked his lips.

"Isn't chocolate trite in February? Commercialization of Valentine's Day has soured my taste for chocolate that month only. We need to counteract—nutmeg and anise poached pears or angel food cake."

"Why not both?" Adam hesitated. "With a chocolate sauce."

"Oh, yes! Dessert is settled. I'm wondering about Dimple."

"What about her?"

"She'll have cross words for days if I ask her to stay late to serve and wash up."

"Dimple is getting on a bit. Maybe it's time to look for someone else. We could ask her daughter to start coming in."

"Oh, that would never do. Dimple is too proud. It would kill her not to work until she's dead."

"Such a way with words, my dear."

"No, I'll keep Dimple on just for drinks. That'll make a nice impression on Edwina and Frank. Dimple can leave after serving the soup. I'll handle the rest."

"All in good order." Adam's breathing signaled relief.

"And I'll do most of the dishes. Dimple can wash the crystal in the morning. She's so protective of the Waterford. That'll keep her happy."

"She'll be ecstatic if most of her work's been done by us."

❧

"So Delia and Adam have a maid." Delia leaned on Adam's shoulders and kissed his neck. "Dimple. Such an odd name, but it suits her."

"She's a housekeeper. One must be P. C." Adam cleared his throat.

"In Britain they're called cleaners. Sounds so clinical. Being politically correct takes the fun out of life." Delia grabbed Adam's apple and took a bite. "Where did you get the idea of inviting total strangers to dinner? Isn't that rather bizarre?"

"Not at all." Adam leaned back. "Remember that peculiar cocktail party in Stapleton last fall? The overstuffed Edwardian townhouse. Our twin hosts said they had done exactly that—invited strangers to a dinner party."

"I must have missed that conversation while flirting with the handsome Greek stockbroker," Delia said dreamily. "So you just made up the details?"

"No. It's all true. Weddings page, kilt, English castle, invitation from unknown hosts to unsuspecting guests for a black-tie dinner party."

"So you're a plagiarist?"

"Every writer tucks away odd bits in his head, like you tuck away recipes. This peculiar scenario was filed in my brain, waiting for the right time."

"Did the twins have a grand evening? Were Frank and Edwina everything we imagined?"

"Their story didn't end well. Frank and Edwina never responded to the unexpected invitation."

"Their lives may never have been the same." Delia mused.

"Would you have accepted?"

"Of course, dear. I'd have no qualms. If it's black tie, they couldn't possibly be axe murderers."

"What if they're axe murderers?" Adam tossed the business section aside. Compared to the crossword, it held little interest.

"Who, dear?" Delia's foot straightened the upturned corner of a threadbare Oriental rug as she crossed to the desk.

"Frank and Edwina. They could be axe murderers, for all we know."

"And they might think the same of us, once they receive our unexpected invitation penned in distinctive calligraphy." Delia picked up a green pearlized pen.

"We could all be axe murderers, Bitsy and Charles included. An impromptu convention of axe murderers. One never knows."

"Darling, if it's black tie it couldn't possibly involve axes. Too unwieldy. Too much blood. Ick!"

"That's comforting."

"Do they still make axes? It's all electric or gasoline now. Chain saws to hack away at will for easy disposal. Trees or people." Delia lettered the invitations. "There may still be metaphoric axes to grind."

"Surely a few old-fashioned lumberjacks use axes," Adam said. "What about that paper towel guy? He's been updated, yet the axe remains essential to his masculine persona."

"Poisons. That's the way to go if one should need to do away with dinner guests. Much neater. No blood. Lots of different symptoms and time frames." Delia paused. "From a sudden slump-in-your-soup, hands clutching a constricted and burning air passage..." Delia clutched her own throat and struggled. "... to days of lingering, brain-frying, stomach-churning, fever-wracked comatose torture. Definitely poisons."

"And how do you know so much about this subject?"

Delia looked up from the desk. "Poisoned pen, perhaps? I read. I watch crime shows. Fascinating concoctions, poisons. An endless variety to rid the world of unwanted pests."

"Or unresponsive guests?"

"Certainly an option." Delia waved her pen. "What about place cards?"

"Always a nice touch."

"No, not this time," Delia mused. "With B & C out of the way after cocktails, it'll just be the four of us. We know who we are and E & F will automatically take the other two seats."

"Unless you need them at certain places for specific reasons," Adam offered.

"That may be necessary, but I've got time to decide."

"A couple of weeks to answer the burning social question: to place card or not to place card?"

"Can 'place card' be a verb?" Delia capped the pen. "The invitations will be posted posthaste." Her voice hinted of satisfaction.

"Edwina's dress in the newspaper looks like dark velvet. Crimson would go well with our library rug during cocktails. Or emerald. I'll wear winter white silk taffeta, so as not to compete."

"Edwina is certain to appreciate such a thoughtful hostess." Adam stroked Markle's soft fur. "Every detail accounted for, down to coordinating with the rug."

"It reads like a play." Delia put down the pages. "Is that what you had in mind?"

"I visualized it somewhat as a play." Adam clasped hands behind his head.

"Then why not structure it that way?"

"I'm too lazy to type all the names. Adam. Delia. Adam. Delia. We're the only ones with lines, so far."

"I like it being just the two of us, so I don't have to share you." Delia kissed Adam. "The descriptive passages read like stage directions. And I quote: 'Delia's foot straightened the upturned corner of a threadbare Oriental rug as she crossed to the desk.' End quote." Delia crossed to the desk, mimicking the words she had just read aloud.

"So they're stage directions. It'll be easier to convert to a play."

"Oh do another play! Your last one was an SRO hit!" Delia bowed to her husband.

"Two evenings at the Sundog Theatre, underwritten by me and anonymously reviewed by you. Is that what's called a smash hit?"

"I found it smashing. So did B & C. Perhaps it's time for a revival so Frank and Edwina can also be astounded by your talent."

Adam bowed at the waist.

"A director would appreciate as few characters as possible. Keeps expenses down," Delia said, ever practical.

"It's a slim cast already." Adam sounded skeptical. "Whom could we cut?"

"Bitsy and Charles may be expendable." Delia pondered. "I know—just allude to them. We'll say goodnight at the door and wave as they trundle off to a command performance with his filthy rich mother. The audience would never see their faces. Stage hands could fill in if a backside or two helped the scene."

"That's a possibility. Now we're down to four."

"Don't forget Markle. We can cast about for a trained cat." Delia sighed. "Poor Bitsy and Charles. With their characters cut, those actors may never qualify for their Equity cards. They'll be waiters forever."

"We could hire them to serve at our dinner parties." Adam said tartly.

"That's a splendid idea, dear. Then Dimple won't have to stay late and be all crabby."

"What about Edwina and Frank?" Adam asked.

"What about them?"

"They aren't as superfluous as Bitsy and Charles. So far, the story..."

"Play," Delia interrupted.

"Or play. Anyway, the storyline hinges on them."

Delia moved to the window. "Now I'm having second thoughts about the story becoming a play."

"Just when you've begged me to turn it into a minimalist stage production?"

"But if it's a play, we won't have those delicious passages with the real Adam and Delia between the sections with the pretend us."

"Why not?" Adam crossed to the window and ran fingers through Delia's auburn hair.

"Well, those passages are just transitions—the real us talking about the story. Or play."

"Let's see." Adam paused. "Maybe we can use props to distinguish between the separate identities."

Delia turned, smiling.. "A headband for the older Delia and a pipe for the seasoned Adam. Small props easily put aside when not needed. Perfect."

"You are too clever, by half, to solve a problem we didn't know existed." Adam hugged her. "And may very well never exist."

Delia absentmindedly adjusted her black velvet headband. The subtle, woodsy aroma of Adam's pipe reassured her of his loving presence. Dimple entered the library and handed her mistress the morning post.

"Bill. Bill. Junk. A Neiman-Marcus catalog. Markle and I can curl up with that. What's this?" Delia turned over the envelope, not rec-ognizing the hand in which it had been addressed. "It's from them!"

"From whom?" Adam tamped fresh tobacco into the briar bowl.

[Headband and pipe are removed.]

"Wait a minute. How did we get their address?" Delia stamped her foot. "You have to consider every detail."

"We looked them up in the phone book. Remember, Frank grew up here."

"What if he's unlisted? Or moved?" Delia persisted.

"Then we called his parents and said we wanted to send a wedding gift. How's that?" Adam volleyed back.

"What if they're unlisted, too? We've got to think this through. The MacDougalls may be a very private family, shunning the public eye we've suddenly cast on them."

"Then we called St. Swithen's. Said our son went to school with Frank and he's lost the address."

"But we don't have a son."

"They don't know that."

"What if they ask his name?" Delia kept on.

"They won't."

"But what if they do?"

"Then we found an old yearbook at a tag sale and picked someone who looks like he could have been our son and friends with Frankie. Someone on the basketball team."

"What if our son died ten years ago in a fiery, multi-car pileup on Route 17?"

"Stop it, Delia. There are many ways we could have found Frank's address. Satisfied?"

"I guess so. I'm just teasing you. And testing you."

"And I passed with high marks, right?"

"The highest I've ever given. You set the curve. Did Frank and Edwina accept our unexpected invitation?"

[Headband and pipe are replaced.]

"Good night, Bitsy. Good night, Charles. It's been too much fun, as always. Thanks for joining us for cocktails. Sorry you can't stay for dinner." Delia slammed the door. "Dreadful people. I don't know why we've kept them around for fifteen years. He's a pompous ass who pontificates about golf. She was in her cups upon arrival and still knocked back three martinis. Good riddance!"

"But they reciprocate, dear."

"Their only redeeming quality. Let's get back to Frank and Edwina. A charming couple, don't you think? His kilt and her sapphire gown—perfect! At least they're socially adventurous enough to accept an invitation from total strangers who could be axe murderers, for all they know."

[Headband and pipe are removed.]

"Edwina and Frank accepted! A grand time for all at our fabulous dinner party."

"As the song says, 'tain't necessarily so," Adam said wryly.

The county coroner added to Crathorne's distinctive red front door another strip of fluorescent yellow tape reading 'CRIME SCENE. DO NOT ENTER.'

"Wha' shappened?" Bitsy slurred her words.

Charles feared his wife could be arrested for public intoxication. "We were headed home and noticed the hubbub and hurly-burly at our friends' home. We were here earlier for cocktails."

"So I smell," the coroner replied. "Sorry to tell you, but this is a crime scene. Possibly homicide. Four bodies found head down in their soup bowls."

"You're wrong!" Bitsy teetered on the lawn's brown grass patched with snow. "Soup plates. Delia said she was serving cream of cauliflower soup, so they had to be the Herend soup plates."

Several weeks later the coroner released his findings. Boiled down: Adam and Delia Collier died from tainted homemade red wine, a hostess gift from their guests, who did not partake. Frank and Edwina MacDougall succumbed to cream of cauliflower soup, a lethal dose of laudanum blended into the extra strong pesto garnish.

The MacDougalls had informed the Colliers they were moving to England the following week and would never have the opportunity to reciprocate.

"How funny! I love it, Adam!"

"Thanks to my best—my only—cheering section." Adam blushed.

"You've brought in Bitsy and Charles, after all."

"They brought themselves in, though I tried to stop them. The scene just didn't work any other way. Stories and characters often play unexpected tricks."

"And now Bitsy and Charles will get their Equity cards. This promises to be the start of distinguished stage careers." Delia kissed Adam on the cheek. "I love you—and happy endings."

"For Bitsy and Charles, at least. They're the only survivors."

Delia put her arms around Adam's shoulders. "You're the proud papa of a spanking new story that's soon to grow into a strapping play. Congratulations."

"Finishing is always a mixed grill." Adam turned to Delia.

"Whatever do you mean?"

"A combination of pride and regret. Pleasure in a satisfying conclusion as well as sadness that it's over—and soon to be examined and poked and subjected to God-only-knows-what by agents and editors everywhere for years to come."

"Silly boy. It's perfect. They'll love it." Delia massaged Adam's shoulders.

"That's wonderful. Don't stop."

"How did you ever come up with the notion that I—the faux Delia, I mean—was knocking off our dinner guests with poison? Preposterous!"

"Is it? Remember, writers write what we know."

"I've never done—or even said—anything remotely related to killing friends in our dining room."

"What about your annual January hit list?" Adam smiled wickedly.

"That's only purging the cretins who have not returned our kind invitations during the previous year. Simple and appropriate etiquette-approved cleansing, that's all." Delia smirked. "Certainly nothing relating to death."

"Don't you use the term 'social death,' dear one? Remember Phoebe? Alive and kicking, but dead to you because she didn't extend an invitation to afternoon tea one last time."

"That's not what I meant and you know it!"

"But that's the concept I worked from. Delia as social arbiter to the extreme. Miss Manners on steroids, run amok, eliminating purported friends yet to reciprocate in kind or with close-to-even numbers of invitations. Or those who—gasp!—fail to send prompt notes of thanks. Dainty crustless strychnine-laced cucumber sandwiches or pork tenderloin stuffed with prunes and dioxin will usher them to their proper places—six feet under."

"Any situation can be misconstrued. What about Betsy and Carl? They're still around." Delia put her hands on her hips.

"Currently exempt because they adhere to the strict rules of the reciprocity game."

"You are wicked and too, too clever. That's two more whys on my list."

"A never ending list?"

Delia kissed Adam's forehead and reached for the jingling telephone. "Hello?... Betsy! Adam and I were just speaking of you... Dinner? We'd love to!... Black tie? Wonderful!... A Thursday? Thrilling and too, too decadent... A new couple to meet? Could it be any better?"

Delia perched on the arm of the chair, patting Adam's hand and Markle's back. "Won't it be great fun? Let's surprise Betsy and Carl. Or is it Bitsy and Charles? After five years of aging in our musty basement, let's unveil your homemade Crathorne Reserve red wine at their party."

"Dare we?"

Edwina (in reality, Laurel Pierpont Fitzpatrick) again pondered the unexpected invitation received last fall, now tucked away in the drawer of her dressing table. The prospect of a dashing dinner party—black tie, no less—hosted by twin strangers had thrilled her. Her husband, though, had been reluctant. So they remained at home, not even sending their regrets. She still wondered if that had been the right decision.

Bad John
by Adam Howe

SADIE SHIVERED IN the falling snow, hands dug deep in the pockets of her mangy leopard print coat, hungrily eyeing the cars curb-crawling the Strip. Music boomed inside the titty bar behind her, the black tinted window quaking to the bass. She'd danced there herself when she first hit the Strip, before she was busted turning tricks between lap dances to feed her habit. Now she was lucky if they let her inside to slam back a shot to wash away the taste of her last john.

An ancient green station wagon tootled up to the curb, the exhaust farting fumes. It had wood-paneled sides and an I LOVE MY POODLE sticker in the rear window. A fluffy white cloud on legs scuttled back and forth, barking, inside the cage compartment at the back of the car. *Who goes out whoring with their dog in the car?* Sadie thought. *And a poodle, no less.* He was a mousy little guy with a mustache and a black frizz of hair swaddling the sides of his shiny bald skull. He wore a maroon parka over a knit Christmas sweater with a smiling snowman on the front. Sadie frowned. The guy's goofy sweater was reason alone to roll him.

He popped the central lock, pushed open the passenger door. "Come in out of the cold." His voice was shrill and whiny. She climbed inside quickly before he changed his mind. He rolled the window back up, made a shivery noise: *Brrr*! "Too darn cold to be standing around outside." Like she had any fucking choice. He pulled away like he was driving home from church. "Mind putting your seatbelt on?" he said. "We don't want to get pulled over, now do we?" The guy gave a little chortle that reminded her of Ned Flanders. *I'm about to fuck a* Simpsons *character*, Sadie thought. Wouldn't be the first time. Usually it was Barney the drunk, or Cletus the redneck. Hell, by now she'd screwed half of Springfield.

But the guy was right; the last thing she needed was another bust. And she had plans for this dope. After she rolled him, she'd knock off early; pay Sport what she owed, hit him up for more rock; head home to her flophouse and her pipe.

She buckled up and then thawed out her hands over the tepid air sputtering from the AC. She fished in her coat for her smokes, reassuring herself that her .38 Special was in there too. It still amazed her she'd never pawned the gun to feed her habit. "Mind if I smoke?" The guy sucked his teeth disapprovingly. "No offence," she said, "but it smells kind of doggy in here."

She looked in the rearview at the dog in its cage. Ugly fucking thing wouldn't stop yipping at her. Maybe it suspected what she had in mind for its owner? Its coat was an unruly white hedge; its muzzle streaked with nasty brown stains like the dog spent a lot of time tossing its own salad. Its lips were snaggled back in a yellow snarl. Beady eyes glared back at Sadie. The poodle yip-yip-yipped.

The man glanced at the dog in the rearview. "Oh now, Queenie, that's quite enough of that." Smiling sheepishly, he leaned towards Sadie, giving her a whiff of his Old Spice. "She gets jealous. Fetch one of her toys off the back seat there. She won't shut up otherwise and I find it difficult to, uh...*perform*." He grimaced apologetically, wetting his mustache with a nervous flick of his tongue.

With a sigh, Sadie leaned over the backseat, fingering through the chewed-up dog toys strewn across it. She picked up a slobbery rubber duck, holding it out towards the cage, giving it a few halfhearted squeaks. Queenie was barking furiously now, outraged that this stranger was taunting her with her own toys.

"Keep at it," the guy said, "she'll come around."

Squeak-squeak-squeak.

Yip-yip-yip.

"The name's Bob, by the way." And so it was; the name printed proudly (BOB!) on the key-fob dangling from the ignition. "Queenie, you've already met."

"Sadie," she said.

"Sexy Sadie," Bob chuckled, and hummed a few bars of the Beatles song.

"So listen, Bob, where'd you wanna do this?"

"Oh, I know a little out of the way place," he assured her. "Discretion's very important to me."

Fine by Sadie, thinking of the gun in her pocket.

The lights of the Strip blinked out in the rearview. Bob checked his mirrors and indicated—a real stickler for road safety—before making the turn off the highway. The station wagon puttered across a bridge above a white ribbon of frozen river, jouncing uphill along a rutted dirt track through woods. Queenie scuttled about her cage, trying to find her footing as the car rocked about, voicing her discomfort with yips and mewls. "It's all right, Queenie," Bob reassured her.

Driving through the woods, the guy hadn't stopped yapping like his yipping fucking dog. Telling Sadie how he was married. *Very happily married, thank you.* (Sadie had noticed the pale band of skin on his finger where his wedding ring usually was; that was good, a married man was unlikely to report a robbery.) And that he loved his wife, but since she got sick ("The Big C") Mrs. Bob was unable to fulfill certain wifely duties. And darn it, a man has *needs*—

"This is far enough, don'tcha think, Bob?" Sadie said, interrupting his nervous chatter.

He looked around the woods in surprise. "Oh! Listen to me, prattling away..." With another chortle, he eased his foot off the gas, pulling to the side of the road. The car crunched to a stop in the snow. "How are you and Queenie getting along?"

"Swell, Bob. We're getting along just swell." Sadie turned back to look at Queenie in her cage. She gave the squeaky toy one last honk, reaching with her other hand for the .38 inside her coat, and while her head was turned Bob struck her a bludgeoning blow to the base of the skull, and the world went black—

She was blind, her eyes gummed shut with blood and tears. An icy wind whipped inside the car through the open driver's-side door. Snow spattered the windshield. Sadie could hear the poodle skittering about its cage in the back of the car; and outside, the sound of a shovel biting into frozen earth.

She forced her eyes open, crust flaking from her lashes. She was slumped forward in the passenger seat, her blood-matted hair glued to the dash. The back of her head throbbed sickly where Bob had brained her. *What the hell had he hit her with?* Sagging back in the seat, her hair tore from the dash with a sound like Velcro. She cried out in pain as the lump on the back of her head prodded the headrest and seemed to catch fire. She thought she was seeing stars until she realized they were snowflakes, devilling inside through the open driver's door. A few swirling flakes landed on her shoulder. Melted. Skated down her bare torso. She wasn't wearing her leopard print coat anymore. Her shirt was ripped open—buttons scattered in the footwell—revealing her bra. When she tried to hug her shirt around her, cover herself, she found that she couldn't; something clanked on her wrist, jewelry she'd never seen before. Her left wrist was handcuffed to the steering wheel. Instinctively, she jerked her arm back, but the cuffs were locked tight, the bracelet scraping painfully against her wrist bone.

She looked outside the station wagon, where the sound of digging was coming from. The world seesawed as her vision blurred in and out of focus. The car was parked in a thicket of woods, propped on a grade, the hood angled up. Pine trees speared the night sky, trying to puncture the moon. Bob must have driven off-road while she was unconscious. *I know a little out of the way place...* She could see him through the windshield using a shovel to dig a hole beneath the outstretched branch of a pine tree. Bob's parka and her leopard print coat were hanging from the branch like decorations on a Christmas tree.

Despite Bob's mousy frame, he was wiry strong. His Christmas sweater was rolled up to the elbows. He stabbed the shovel into the frozen ground, grunting with effort as he flung snow and dirt back over his shoulder. Happy as a Disney dwarf, whistling while he worked. Completely at ease. He'd done this before.

Sadie turned in her seat, looking behind the car. The handcuffs jangled against the steering wheel, the bracelet gripping tighter to her wrist. Her panicked eyes darted about the lonely woods. Somewhere behind her, she heard the crackling flow of the iced-over river; and further downhill, the distant echo of traffic on the highway. If she honked the horn, screamed for help, would anyone hear her? Apart from Bob, that is. The last thing she wanted was to attract Bob's attention.

The car keys were gone from the ignition; she couldn't just drive out of here. She looked at her coat, hanging from the tree. Her cellphone was in the pocket. The same pocket where she'd kept her gun...the gun she saw was now stuffed in the front of Bob's chinos. Then he knew she'd meant to rob him. Not that she thought it made much difference to what he had in mind for her.

She opened the glove compartment, wincing as the hinged door squealed. A flashlight and a spray can of antifreeze rolled out and thudded into the footwell. She rooted inside the glove compartment. Maybe Bob kept a second set of car keys in here, or keys to the cuffs, or even something she could use as a weapon?

Maps, CDs, bungee cord, Kleenex—

Fighting panic, she forced herself to breathe...

Had anyone seen her leave the Strip with Bob? Another one of the working girls? They always *said* they had each other's back...but that was only to see where best to stick the knife; it was every bitch for herself out there.

How could I be so fucking stupid? She wasn't the same naïve runaway she'd been when she first started hooking. She'd learned the hard way there were guys out there who couldn't get hard without hurting, who'd rather fuck you up with their fists than with their dicks. And then there were the real Bad Johns. Sick tricks like Bob. She'd always thought she could spot them. But Bad Johns aren't always easy to spot. They don't wear hockey masks or razor-fingered gloves. They smile and wear Christmas sweaters and drive station wagons with poodles in the back.

It was that fucking poodle, Sadie thought. That's made what her lower her guard. She glared in the rearview at Bob's accomplice. Queenie was curled inside her cage, muzzle propped on her paws, watching Sadie with a snippy expression. "You fucking bitch," Sadie hissed at the dog. Queenie raised her head, snarling. Then she started to bark. Not the little yips she was making before. The kind of noise that belonged to a dog three times her size.

Bob heard the commotion and turned his head. "Hey there, Sleeping Beauty!" He planted the shovel in the ground and then hopped up out of the hole, wiping his hands on his chinos. "You about ready to have some fun? Sorry to keep you waiting, but there's nothing I hate more than digging the hole *afterwards*."

He started ambling towards the open driver's door.

Sadie pulled hard against the handcuffs, the steel bracelet cutting into her wrist, tearing the skin. "Stay the fuck away from me!"

Bob watched her struggle in quiet amusement. "How's that working out for you?"

Sadie sagged back against the passenger door, panting for breath, her hand still cuffed to the wheel, her arm outstretched like she was beckoning Bob in.

Queenie continued to bark inside her cage.

Bob raised a finger. "That's *enough* now, Queenie," he said, "Daddy's got the filthy slut."

The dog quieted.

Sadie glared at the poodle in the rearview. She'd never seen an animal look so fucking smug.

Bob continued towards the car.

Sadie hammered the horn. "Help! Someone help me! Please!"

Bob indulged her. He tilted his head back, cupping a hand to his mouth and hollering over the forest. "*Help me! Please! Heeeeelp!*" His mocking voice hung in the air, the echo fading into the distance.

Then he frowned theatrically, moving his hand, still cupped, to his ear.

"Would you hush up?" he said. "I think I hear something..."

Sadie listened intently.

"My mistake." Bob gave his goofy laugh. "Nope, we're way the heck out in the willywags. No knights in shining armor out here."

She thrashed her legs, kicking and screaming and yanking on the cuffs like a trap-snared critter. Exhausted, she huddled on the passenger seat, sobbing over the footwell, breathing in ragged whoops, and through her tears she saw the can of antifreeze that had fallen from the glove compartment. Glancing at Bob from the corner of her eye, she dangled her free arm into the footwell, closing her fingers around the spray can.

Bob didn't seem to notice; he was shaking his head like an exasperated parent.

"I swear, the way you girls carry on, you'd think it was the end of the world. Now let's not make this any harder than it has to be. I need this, okay? And honestly—what's waiting for you back there on the Strip? An overdose? AIDS? I'm *saving* you from that life, honey. I'm doing you a *favor* here. Best of all you'll have plenty of company.

There's little Patti and Kristen and Faye—"

He was pointing around at various trees; Sadie gave a low moan as she realized the tree where Bob had been digging was *her* tree.

"And...and I forget her name. Tall. Blonde. Butterfly tattoo on her butt." Bob frowned, looking at Sadie as if *she* might know. "Nope, it's gone. It'll come back to me." He swept an arm about the woods, like a game show host showing off tonight's prizes. "Hell, it's a regular sewing circle out here! Now let's get this road on the show, and then you gals can bitch about ole Bob when I'm gone."

He took a step towards her. Stopped suddenly. Following her gaze, he glanced down at the handle of the .38 stuffed in the front of his chinos, grunting in surprise. "I'd forgotten all about that." He pulled the gun from his waistband. "I bet you'd like this around about now?" He chuckled. "And no prizes for guessing what you planned to do with it, either. Tell me, Sexy Sadie, just how many fellers have you rolled with this cap-gun of yours?"

When she didn't answer, he said: "What I figured. You whores, you're all the same..." He raised the gun suddenly, thumbing back the hammer.

Sadie shrank back in the passenger seat. *"Please, no, don't—"*

Bob held the gun on her awhile, relishing her reaction. Then he lowered it. Gave a little snort of amusement. "Oh now, don't you worry none," he said, "I'm not gonna shoot you. Where's the fun in that?" He stuffed the gun back in his waistband. Then he reached behind him, unsheathing a hunting knife hidden beneath his sweater. The saw-backed blade was at least a foot long. He turned the knife slowly in his hand, admiring the steel, a falling snowflake shearing in two upon the guillotine blade.

"Me and Mr. Buck Skinner here—" Bob said, "Mr. *Doe* Skinner, I should say. We're gonna show you the time of your life. You ever been fucked by a Buck?"

He bent towards the open driver's door, reaching towards her—

She whipped up the can of antifreeze, sprayed him a burst in the face.

Bob screeched like a scalded cat. The knife jerked from his hand and landed with a thud in the driver's side footwell. He lurched back from the car, yanking up the front of his Christmas sweater and scouring his eyes. Queenie started barking frantically. Bob staggered blindly through the snow. Sadie prayed he'd fall into that hole he'd been digging and break his fucking neck. But no such luck. He let the sweater fall from his face, his eyes slitted in pain and fury, his mouth a bestial snarl, his hair spiking from the sides of his head. He charged at the car.

Sadie scrambled into the driver's seat, reaching outside the car through the open door, her arm at full-stretch, hand clawing for the handle...

...grabbing hold of the grip and dragging the door shut—

Bob bounced off the door with a surprised grunt.

His hand found the handle. Started to pull.

Sadie slammed down the central lock.

Bob clawed at the locked door. "Open the door."

She reached in the footwell and snatched the big hunting knife off the floor.

"Put...put that down!" Bob sputtered, a bratty kid who didn't like sharing his toys. He wrenched at the door, the car pitching and rocking. Then he prowled around it, testing the other doors, cursing and muttering to himself under his breath: "See, this is what happens when you get complacent, Robert. Was a hand-job really that important, you couldn't cuff *both* her hands?" As he tested the trunk—*locked*—Queenie whined and scratched her paws on the window. "Daddy's okay, baby. Everything's gonna be fine." He trudged back to the driver's-side door, wrestling the gun from his waistband and raising it to the window. "Open this goddamn door!" Then a smile lit his face. He tapped the barrel of the gun against the glass. "Don't you go anywhere now," he grinned.

He stuffed the gun back in his chinos, and went to the tree where he'd been digging. His parka was still hanging from the tree branch. He fished in the pockets, turning back towards Sadie like a triumphant magician, the keys with their personalized fob (BOB!) jangling in his hand. "Now we're gonna do this the hard way," he said, stomping back towards her. "It's gonna be worse for you than it was for Sherry. And she was squealing so hard she—" He stopped in his tracks. "Sherry! *That* was her name. Long-legged Sherry with the butterfly on her butt." He continued towards the car. "Well, she wasn't so high an' mighty after a little *ménage a trois* with ole Bob and Mr. Buck Skinner. No, sir! And that's nothing compared to what's coming to *you*, Sexy Sadie. I'm gonna peel you like a fucking orange, girl."

With a cry, Sadie hacked with the knife at the handcuff chain; tried to jimmy the lock on the bracelet with the tip of the blade, hardly able to see what she was doing through her tears. Bob appeared suddenly in the driver's-side window, jangling his car keys. The smiling snowman on his sweater seemed to be leering at her, as Bob stabbed the car key into the door slot. The central lock popped as he cranked the key.

Sadie lurched back from the door, barking her elbow on the upraised handbrake, hissing with pain as her funny-bone flared. The knife fell from her hand into the footwell. Before she could fetch it, the door swooped open with a rush of cold air. Sadie slammed down the handbrake.

The car shuddered violently, swooping down the grade like a boat being launched. The driver's-side tire crunched back over Bob's foot. He howled in pain and the car kept rolling, ripping the keys from his hands, the keys hanging from the door, the door slamming shut. Bob dropped on his ass in the snow. Clutching his foot, he watched helplessly as the car rolled away from him. He snatched the gun from his waistband, firing wildly, bullets whizzing past the moving car, grazing the hood with a flash of sparks. Sadie ducked as two shots punched holes through the windshield, splintering the Plexiglas, and embedded in the headrest behind her. Snow swirled inside through the bullet holes. The gun clicked empty and Bob tossed it away, teetering to his feet.

The car gathered speed. Sadie clung to the wheel, peering over the dash, eyes darting between Bob in the windshield, lurching after the car, and the looming pine trees in the rearview. She wrenched the wheel, left and right, the station wagon slaloming through the pine maze. A wing mirror exploded as the car clipped a tree. The rear tires hit a pothole that shook the car like airplane turbulence, tossing Queenie about her cage. Sadie's face slammed into the steering wheel, the horn giving a startled toot. Dazed, she snuffled blood and shook her head to clear her vision—

And saw Bob hurling himself at the car. He landed with a thud, clinging to the car like a nightmare hood ornament. "Let my Queenie go, you bitch!" Hearing her name, Queenie gave a frantic yowl. "Daddy's coming, baby!"

Sadie jiggled the wheel, trying to dislodge him from the hood. Bob ducked as an overhanging tree branch whipped above his head, showering him in snow and pine needles. Glaring at Sadie through the punctured windshield, he removed a hand from the hood, snaking it through one of the bullet holes, Plexiglas crumbling around his thrusting arm as he snatched at her throat. She clawed his hand, raking it with her nails. Hissing in pain, he grabbed the wheel, trying to steer the car into a sliding stop. She hammered her fist on his fingers, but the hand didn't budge—not until she bit his thumb, blood flooding her mouth, her teeth chipping on bone. Bob let out a screech and let go of the wheel, snatching his arm back through the windshield. Sadie spat out a mouthful of gristle that spattered the windshield. She stole a glance in the rearview—

And saw the frozen river behind them.

Bob saw it, too. His eyes widened in horror.

Sadie wrenched the wheel. The station wagon swerved sharply. The front end fishtailed. The car went into a wild spin, slamming sidelong into the stump of a fallen pine tree, jolting to a stop that catapulted Bob off the hood. Sadie's neck whipcracked, her teeth snapping shut on her tongue. Bob soared through the night, screaming and flailing, before he hit the ice with a meaty thud and then skated like a hockey puck to the middle of the river, skidding to a stop.

Again, she was blind. Sadie groped her way back into the cold world. The freezing wind whistled through the holes in the windshield, dusting her with snowflakes that settled in her hair and eyelashes. Twisted metal creaked and groaned. Queenie whined somewhere in the back of the car. Sadie mopped blood from her eyes, one-handed, her other hand still cuffed to the steering wheel. She pulled weakly at the cuffs, but they held tight. She reached to adjust the rearview. Ignoring her blood-streaked reflection, she peered past Queenie's crumpled cage—the dog's eyes glinting in the gloom—looking through the splintered rear window. She needed to see him; to know he was dead.

Bob was splayed on the ice like a bloody snow angel. Arms outstretched. Hands twitching like dying spiders. One leg twisted horribly beneath him. He was moaning feebly. Haloes of breath frosted above his tortured face. His eyes rolled in his skull, peering up at the wrecked station wagon upon the riverbank.

Sadie tried futilely to free her hand from the cuffs, her fingers numb, blood drizzling from her wrist. Her eyes found Bob's knife lying in the footwell. A mad thought flashed through her mind: to just cut off her hand at the wrist. She had to do *something*. If she stayed in the car she would surely freeze to death.

Then she thought of something else.

She unrolled the driver's-side window, reaching outside the car to remove Bob's keys from where they were still hanging in the door. Attached to the fob was a small key. Much smaller than any other key on the fob. It turned in the cuffs with a tiny click. The bracelet snapped off her wrist and she sobbed in relief, hugging her bruised hand to her chest like an injured bird, massaging life back into the numb fingers. With both hands free, she fumbled open the driver's-side door, staggering from the car, her feet crunching in the snow. She braced herself against the door until the world stopped spinning. An icy wind whipped the tails of her shirt, the sudden cold making her gasp. The right side of the station wagon was horseshoed around the tree stump. Shards of broken glass scattered the snow. Queenie peered fearfully from her crumpled cage. Seeing Sadie outside, she gave a hopeful wag of her tail.

"...help..."

Sadie blinked heavily.

For a moment, she thought it was the dog talking to her.

"...please..."

Hearing her master's voice, Queenie whined and propped her paws against the splintered rear window, cycling her legs, claws scratching the glass.

Sadie turned her head slowly towards the voice, saw Bob sprawled in the middle of the frozen river.

"...please help me..."

His face contorted in pain.

"...ice...won't hold..."

Sadie just stared at him, standing next to the station wagon with the I LOVE MY POODLE sticker in the window. A strange calm descended over her. A serenity she'd never known. A calm that not even the rock had granted her. She liked seeing Bob out there. Helpless on the ice.

She smiled at him, cupping a hand to her mouth. "*Heeeeelp!*"

A look of dread filled Bob's face.

"I think I hear something..." She cupped a hand to her ear.

"My bad," she said. "I don't think anyone's coming."

Bob started sobbing.

Queenie howled in sympathy.

Sadie rolled her eyes at Bob's theatrics.

"Let's not make this any harder than it has to be," she said, limping to the back of the station wagon. "I mean, it's not like you won't have any company out there..."

And then she opened the trunk, splintered glass raining down as she levered up the door.

"Go to daddy, bitch."

Queenie sprang from the car, down the bank and onto the river, claws clicking on the ice as she scuttled to her master, a jagged line of cracks splintering the ice in her wake. Bob's eyes widened in horror. "No! Queenie! *Stay!*"

Sadie turned her back, started limping towards the distant sound of traffic on the highway, smiling at the sharp crack of ice behind her, and then the heavy splash of water, and it was hard to separate Bob and Queenie's screams before the river swallowed them.

There's a blurred line between truth and fiction that you
don't want to cross.

Death by Fiction
by J. M. Vogel

ALEXANDER SAT AT his desk, his fingers pounding away on the keyboard. After days of trying to figure out this one particular passage of
his novel, he finally knew how he wanted to end it. The theme to
"The Twilight Zone" trilled from his left, startling him and effectively
ending his momentum on the story.

"Dammit," he cursed, shoving papers around the desk in his
search for his cell. He snatched it and clumsily hit talk just as the
phone finished its final pre-voicemail ring. "Franklin," he answered,
irritated.

"Mr. Alexander Franklin?" the male voice asked.

"Yes," he said, his finger twitching toward the off button. Tele-
marketer. Only telemarketers used his whole name. Ever since his detective series made the New York Times Best Seller list, the world
knew him as A.M. Franklin. Only those with access to his credit report called him Alexander.

"I'm Detective Richard Dunham with the St. Clairsville Police
Department."

Alexander's finger froze mere millimeters from the "end" button.
"How can I help you, Detective?" he asked.

"Sir, we need your help in identifying a homicide victim."

"Homicide victim?" It had been nearly five years since Alexander
lived in St. Clairsville. He hadn't spoken to anyone from that area
since he left and was doubtful anyone he knew was still there. Being a
college town, the population was transient to say the least.

"Sir, I'm sorry to inform you that we've found the body of woman
we believe to be your wife."

Alexander's heart stopped. His muscles tensed as his mind stumbled to make sense of the detective's last statement. "Detective
Dunham, I don't have a wife."

The police detective paused. Alexander could hear papers shuffling in the background and then computer keys clicking away. "This
is Alexander Franklin, formerly of 2525 Mount Pleasant Place?"

"Yes," Alexander confirmed.

"Date of birth January 15th, 1985?"

"Yes."

"Then I'm not sure where the disconnect is. We feel we've found the body of Marjory Mariposa Franklin -- the same woman you reported missing on July 5th, 2007."

Alexander's head began to pound. He grabbed a pen from his drawer and began tapping it against the desk as he tried to make sense of this information. In early 2007 he'd been in St. Clairsville, locked in a hovel of an apartment, slaving away over manuscript during his post-collegiate stab at literary fame. Sporting a mountain-man beard and unkempt hair, women were not exactly lining up to date him, let alone marry him. By July, with his novel completed and lease expired, St. Clairsville was a distant memory.

"Detective Dunham, I really have no idea what you're talking about."

"Perhaps this is something we need to address in person. Meet me at the St. Clairsville police station tomorrow morning at eight o'clock."

"That won't work." He pulled out his calendar. "I have a meeting tomorrow morning and a conference call in the afternoon. Maybe we can set up something for next week?" A six hour drive for an obvious mistake seemed ridiculous. If he could push it out a week, undoubtedly the mistake would rectify itself. Or maybe he could come up with an excuse to move the trip out even further. Already behind deadline for his next book, the disruption of his time was the last thing he needed.

"Good God, man!" the detective spat. "A woman is dead. The very woman you reported missing. If you are not here by eight tomorrow morning, I am issuing a warrant for your arrest." And with that, the detective hung up, leaving Alexander holding the phone.

After a heated discussion with his editor, Alexander rescheduled his meeting and left his plush apartment in the city for the rolling hills of St. Clairsville. After six hours and what probably amounted to a gallon of coffee, he arrived at the police station at five minutes to eight.

"Detective Dunham?" he asked the desk clerk. The clerk escorted him to a tiny office and gestured to a chair situated in front of a dilapidated, metal desk. The dented, rusty desk fit right in with the wood paneled walls straight from the seventies. Each paneled wall sported plaques of various dead fish and wildlife while the fourth wall, comprised completely of glass, overlooked the reception area. Overhead fluorescent lights cast a dismal, sallow tinge over the room. The office brought one word to Alexander's mind—despair.

After what seemed line an eternity, an overweight, balding, middle aged man entered the room, his clothing looking at home in the dated office.

"Mr. Franklin?" the detective asked, extending his hand.

Alexander nodded. "Detective Dunham," he said, returning his grip.

"Please have a seat." The detective gestured to the uncomfortable-looking chair directly in front of the dinged up desk.

Alexander sat and then dove into the problem at hand. "So as I was saying yesterday, I am not, nor have I ever been married."

The detective pushed a piece of paper toward Alexander and rested his chin on his hands, his lips pursed. "As you can see, this is the statement you gave, five years ago, describing the disappearance of your wife."

Alexander perused the document, trying to make sense of it. The details were simple enough to understand. Per the report, Alexander had reported Marjory Mariposa Franklin missing from his apartment on July 6th of 2007. She'd last been seen passed out on his couch after a party. Oddly enough, the report did indeed list her as his spouse.

"Ring a bell?" the detective asked.

Alexander read the page again. "No, I'm sorry but it doesn't."

The detective's ears caught fire as a sigh escaped his lips. With hard eyes and a furrowed brow he reclined slightly in his desk chair. "So you're telling me that you reported this woman missing—this woman who was reportedly your wife—signed the statement, and moved away, never to think of her again?"

"No, I'm telling you that I never had a wife and therefore never reported her missing. Why is this so hard to understand? You have the wrong man." Alexander shoved the paper back toward Detective Dunham and pointed to the signature. "This isn't even my signature."

The officer examined the signature. "It isn't?"

Alexander shook his head. "Whoever signed that is left-handed. I'm not."

The officer further scrutinized the signature. "Although interesting, that's hardly conclusive evidence, Mr. Franklin."

"Conclusive or not, that's not my writing. So, the question is, who signed my name and why?" He stroked his chin as he considered. The two gentlemen sat in pensive silence.

The whole situation eluded Alexander. Why would someone fill out a police report in his name and concoct a marriage he never had? And just who was this Marjory to whom he was supposed to be married? "Do you have a picture of this woman?" Alexander asked. The name certainly wasn't ringing a bell, but maybe if he could see her he might recognize her.

The detective nodded. "I can do you one better."

Alexander then followed the detective into the down to the morgue.

The detective pulled back the sheet on the gurney.

"A mummy?" Alexander asked, staring at the corpse.

"Yep."

"How in the... Wow," he exclaimed in awe. "Do you know the cause of death?"

The detective removed a pen from his shirt pocket. "Nearest we can tell," he began, pointing to the mummy's neck with the point of the pen. "It appears that she was strangled. We can't be sure until an autopsy is performed, but the striations on the neck suggest strangulation by a thin rope or twine. It will be a few days before we know for sure."

Alexander bent down to peer at the marks on corpse's neck. He had never been this close to a dead body before, let alone a mummy. But as strange and unexpected as this situation was, there was something familiar about it. "Where did you find her?" he asked?

"A few hikers found her near the river. We had some minor flooding recently and it caused just enough erosion that the hikers tripped over her arm. The grave must have been pretty shallow."

Alexander gulped. "Interesting. Do you have a photo of her when she was alive?"

The detective opened the manila folder and pulled out a blown up driver's license photo. "The deceased is Marjory Mariposa. Her license hadn't been changed yet to reflect her married name. Per the notes of the officer who took the missing person report, you...I mean the filer of the report said that you two were newlyweds." He handed the photo to Alexander who gasped when he saw it.

"Echo?" he asked, looking at the photo. The girl in the picture had long brown hair that hung freely around her shoulders. Her effervescent smile directly contrasted the mocking grin of the desiccated corpse lying on the table before him.

"I'm sorry?" the officer asked, looking confused.

"I knew her as Echo."

"Did Echo have a last name?"

"Maybe. I don't know. She was studying acting. I guess Echo was her stage name."

The detective set the file folder down on a table behind him and took a notepad from his pocket. "And how did you know Echo?"

"She dated the guy who lived across the hall from me."

"And the name of your neighbor?"

"Devin. Devin Cooper."

The officer wrote a few notes on the notepad before putting it back in his jacket pocket. He tugged the sheet over Echo's face and picked up her file. "You want some coffee?"

Alexander nodded and followed the detective back upstairs to the land of the living.

Alexander and Detective Dunham returned to the office and resumed their previous positions. Alexander leaned forward, resting his arms on the desk. He began rubbing his brow.

"We found her buried with a paint brush," Detective Dunham said, filling the silence.

Alexander sighed, hanging his head. "Are you still looking for the murder scene?"

"We are. Are you able to tell us anything about that?"

"Well, I would check the old mill—the boiler room to be exact. I think you'll find that at least the mummification happened there."

The detective leaned forward over his desk. "Are you confessing to the murder, son?"

Alexander shook his head. "No. But that's how I wrote it."

"Excuse me?"

"That was the way I wrote it in my first novel, *Love You to Death*. In the novel, the main character was strangled with rope, mummified in a building that I based on the old mill and buried in a shallow grave by the river. The murderer was an artist."

"I thought this whole scenario seemed familiar. You're A.M. Franklin. I've read that book."

Alexander nodded. "I was actually writing that book when I lived here."

"No kidding?"

"She was kind of my...well, muse I guess you'd say."

Detective Dunham leaned back in his chair. "Now wait a minute. You said she was your neighbor's girlfriend. But she was *your* muse?"

Alexander took a deep breath and stood up. He always thought better when moving. He walked over to the window and peered through the blind slats. "It's...complicated."

The officer opened a small drawer in his desk and removed a recording device. "Then why don't you explain it to me?" He pushed record.

Alexander let the slats snap back in place and began pacing around the room. "Echo was dating Devin, but we were all friends. I was an English major, Devin was a modern art major and Echo was a theater major. Artists can be kind of an eccentric lot and Devin definitely fit that stereotype. He was very... passionate... especially about Echo. He loved her but was so manic—up and down all the time—it started to wear on her. They fought all the time."

"So she left him for you?"

"Not exactly." Alexander continued walking back and forth, his arms crossed behind his back. "One night they had a major blow up. I could hear them yelling from across the hall. When she left she was a wreck and came over to my apartment. Well, one thing led to another and we... well... we slept together." The memories of that night flooded his mind. She was so upset that when they kissed, every kiss, every touch had a sense of urgency, need. The encounter was so real, so charged with emotion. Even now he could still smell the lavender perfume she'd worn and feel her soft, porcelain skin as if it just happened yesterday. A not-so-subtle cough from the detective awoke him from his reverie.

"How long did this go on for?"

"Just that once. She loved Devin and felt so guilty that she couldn't even look at me after that. It was a mistake. In the meantime, though, I began the novel. The main character, Alice, was based on Echo."

The detective massaged his temples as he thought. "Did Devin ever find out?"

Alexander shook his head. "I don't think so. At that time, we both decided not to tell him. He was a little... unpredictable... and there was no way to know how he'd react. A few months later, I moved to the city."

The detective turned off the tape recorder and stared off pensively. "So, here is my problem. Your book was published when?"

"Spring of 2008."

"The disappearance and murder occurred in 2007, but used details from the book which was of course not yet published. You see where I'm going here?"

"I do." Alexander plopped back down in the chair and leaned forward, his arms crossed on the desk. "But I didn't do it."

Detective Dunham nodded. "I don't think you did it either, but I'm having trouble coming up with an alternative scenario here." The room was silent for a long while as both mulled over the absurd situation. "Wait a second," the detective said, sitting bolt upright. "It has been a while since I read your novel, but I don't remember the paint brush."

"Well, that part was only in my first couple drafts. It was edited out later. The editors felt it made the murderer too obvious."

A cautious smile formed on the detective's face. "Now we're getting somewhere. Who had access to early drafts of your novel?"

Alexander's brow furrowed as he thought back. "No one really read my stuff back then."

"Professors? Fellow students?"

"No. I didn't start writing until after graduation. I guess just my mom. And Devin."

As soon as the words escaped Alexander's lips, everything clicked for both of them. "Devin," Alexander said, his voice so low that it was almost a whisper. He shook his head. "Wow." He knew Devin was a little unhinged, but a murderer?

"So now all we have to do is find the young man and see if we can put this to rest," Detective Dunham said, turning toward the computer. "Devin Cooper was it?"

The detective searched through various databases. Somehow, Devin Cooper ceased to exist beginning around August of 2007. It wasn't that he died, he just disappeared.

After a few hours of searching, the detective gave up. "Well, Mr. Franklin, I think we've done all we can do for today. I'll keep working it from my end, but why don't you head on out?"

"I'm free to go?"

Detective Dunham smiled. "For today. Don't leave town. I may need you. And, until I get more information, you're still a person of interest."

Alexander huffed in irritation. "I've been nothing if not forthcoming and I can't just put everything on hold. I already had to reschedule with my editor as it is."

"I have no choice. I'll check in with you tomorrow."

Alexander took off toward campus in search of a place to stay for the foreseeable future.

Alexander stood outside his old apartment building, reminiscing. A long afternoon with nothing to do left him curious about his old digs. "It hasn't changed a bit," he said to himself.

He looked up and down the street at the various shops and restaurants that now called Mount Pleasant Place home. Despite different names on every shop, the street appeared exactly the same. He'd been so busy with life that he'd forgotten just how much he loved this place. The artistic vibe permeated everything in the neighborhood, giving it an almost bohemian feel. It was like coming home after an extended trip.

He stepped up to the apartment listings and perused the names, just for the sake of curiosity. The name on his old apartment listing gave him pause. "D. Mariposa," he whispered to himself. It was a long shot, but Mariposa was not a common last name. And since Devin obviously had changed his name within the last decade, he found the coincidence too intriguing. Devin Mariposa?

He didn't want to buzz D. Mariposa because that would just be weird. Instead, Alexander leaned against the wall, and waited for someone to enter or exit the building. As it was a large building, it only took a few minutes. Once through the doors, he headed to the fourth floor.

On the fourth floor, Alexander slowly ambled his way toward D. Mariposa's apartment. He still wasn't quite sure what he was going to do when he reached the door. Would he knock? Would he just hang out and observe? Would he run to the police station and alert Detective Dunham? He resolved to make that decision once he learned something.

Alexander stood at his old apartment, his fist just inches from the door. His mind might not have decided what to do but his body seemed to have made up its mind. His fist knocked automatically as his muscles tensed, not sure what awaited him on the other side of the threshold. His heart drummed out a staccato beat as he heard footsteps approach. After a brief moment, the door creaked.

"Al Franklin," a man said as the door swung open.

"Devin?" Alexander asked, appraising the man who stood in the doorway. He looked an older, gaunter version of the Devin he'd known. The years had not been kind. Wild, dark eyes sunk into his face and a tall, jet black Mohawk sprouted from the top of his head. Shirtless and painfully thin, he wore low fitting jeans that highlighted his hip bones which jutted out over top of the waist band.

"I was wondering when you'd show up again," he said. "It's been a long time."

"It has. So, Devin Mariposa, huh?"

Devin sneered and chortled humorlessly. "Call it a pen name."

They stood on opposite sides of the threshold, staring at each other. "So what's new?" Alexander asked.

"Why don't you come in so we can catch up?" Devin motioned him inside. The odd smile on his face made Alexander wonder if that was the best idea. Devin seemed a little too smug and not nearly surprised enough to see Alexander on his doorstep. Apparently, he'd been expected.

Unease and discomfort seized Alexander as he walked into the small studio apartment. His stomach lurched. Paintings of all shapes and sizes hung on each wall, leaving only small lines between pieces where the black wall paint was even visible. Despite the differences in color and dimensions, each work had a unifying theme—mummified faces. In fact, they appeared to all be the same face.

Devin took no small amount of pleasure watching Alexander interpret his work. "You like what I've been working on?"

"I imagine you've been 'working on' this for about five years now," Alexander responded, not able to take his eyes off of the disturbing exhibit before him.

"Well, you always said your instructors told you to write what you know, so I figured the same probably applied to painting. Speaking of which, I'll bet Marjory would have loved to see that she made it into your book."

"Excuse me?"

"Well she told me about you two one day when we were having it out. Isn't it interesting that she ended up being both of our muses?" he asked as he gestured at his art.

Alexander turned toward Devin. "So you did do it," he accused, unable to hide his disdain for the monster in front of him. She'd been a vibrant and fascinating woman and Devin squandered her. Alexander's hands formed into fists at his side, waiting for the justification that would make Marjory's murder acceptable in Devin's mind.

"What do you care? She wasn't good enough for you to stick around. Then you killed her off for your art, just like I killed her off for mine."

"You son of a bitch," Alexander spat, his hands still clenched at his side. "I worried about her. Her death in my book is what I feared for her if she stayed with you." Alexander took a deep breath, trying to keep his anger in check. "Why did you do it? You could have just let her go."

Devin laughed. "What, you want to understand my reasoning? Do you think it'll make you feel better? Make it so you don't feel responsible? I can't do that for you, Al. I can't take away your feeling of responsibility because it is all your fault."

Alexander took out his cell phone and began to dial 9-1-1. "It doesn't matter. The police can sort it out."

Devin quickly stepped up to Alexander and jarred the phone from his hands. "Yeah, I can't let you do that."

Alexander stared at Devin, unsure of what to do. Looking into Devin's wild eyes left him doubtful that a fair fight was in the cards. "How do you see this working out, Devin? No matter how I look at this, it doesn't end well for you."

"I don't know. I have been waiting for this opportunity for years now. They finally found the grave, didn't they?"

Alexander nodded warily. How could a best-selling mystery novelist have made such a grievous error? He should have known better than to come here alone. His eyes swept the room for some kind of escape option.

"The question is, what do I do now? Do I disappear and let you take the rap for the murder as I always intended? Or do I write your ending the same way you wrote hers?" He ambled slowly toward Alexander.

Alexander said nothing. He just stared at Devin, trying hard to keep emotion from his face. If he could remain calm, cool, and collected, maybe he could keep this from blowing up around him. Way too emotional and manic, Devin couldn't keep his wits about him. When Alexander refused to engage him, Devin continued his musings.

"I could leave town, change my name—perhaps Devin Franklin?—and start over again. It would be so easy. Or, I could allow you to experience the pain you left her to experience. Decisions, decisions..." Devin walked to the door and locked it before heading towards the two tall windows and pulling down the shades. The horrified faces on the walls seemed to scream out in agony in the darkness, sending a shiver down Alexander's spine.

Alexander remained motionless as Devin continued his march around the room. When he reached the kitchen of the efficiency suite, he reached into the drawer, and pulled out a large butcher knife. He began stalking toward Alexander who was unconsciously easing backwards.

Alexander's pulse raced. His ears felt ablaze as the blood coursed through his body at a sprint. "You killed her. She chose you and you killed her."

Devin tossed the knife from one hand to the other. "You'd like it if it were like that, wouldn't you? If it was all *my* fault? The fact is, Al, it's not. You lured her from me, had your way with her, and then left. See? Not my fault."

Alexander continued his retreat away from Devin. "Then why not come after me? If I made her leave you, why kill *her* and not *me?*" Alexander's retreat came to a halt when his back slammed into the desk. He tried to step left, but Devin matched his movement. The same thing happened when he moved right. Cornered, his hand groped behind him for anything that could serve as a weapon. He came up empty. Nothing sharp or blunt. Only mail and a newspaper lay behind him.

Devin shrugged, still juggling the knife. "If I let her go and she took up with someone else, I couldn't have lived with it. But I also couldn't be with someone I couldn't trust. It was the only solution that made any sense." He took another step forward.

With the desk still at his back, Alexander began rifling through the drawers behind him. Paperclips, tape, stamps, sticky notes, tissue—nothing of any use. Devin peered around him at the desk and sneered. "What, are you going to tape me to death?" He snickered to himself. "Come on, you're a writer. Use some imagination!"

Alexander thrust his hand into the left drawer but again, nothing sharp. What he did find felt like twine. He'd have to get pretty close to use it as a weapon, but from the looks of it, that wouldn't be a problem. The question remained how to get the man to turn around. If he didn't want a knife plunged into his chest, the only way to garrote him would be from behind. As Devin's eyes darted around in an almost paranoid manner, inspiration struck. Whether drug induced or imbalance driven, Devin's obvious impaired mental state could be just the thing Alexander needed to get out of this situation.

"Devin, you have a problem, man," Alexander said as he stared over Devin's shoulder. "This really isn't going to end well for you." Alexander let his eyes dart intermittently from Devin's face to the wall behind him. It didn't take long before Devin began to show agitation.

"What are you doing?" he asked, obviously fighting the urge to turn around.

Alexander shrugged. He stared into Devin's face for a long moment, but then continued to glance back over his shoulder. "I think you should turn yourself in," he said, staring over his shoulder to the door. "You'd be able to get the help that you need." Alexander nodded towards the door and then shook his head. Unable to hide his curiosity, Devin turned his upper body toward the door, to see with whom Alexander was having this silent conversation. Alexander lunged.

He looped the twine around Devin's neck and held it tight. Devin thrashed about, haphazardly sending the knife through the air. His goal wasn't to kill Devin, just make him fall unconscious. Alexander waited for him to stop flailing to loosen the noose, but he just kept thrashing about—until all of a sudden he didn't. Devin's body relaxed, his face purple. Alexander stepped back as Devin's lifeless form fell to the floor. He leaned against the chair as he tried to catch his breath.

He stared at Devin for what seemed like an eternity, willing some part of him to move, but nothing happened. He crept forward and kicked the knife away before crouching over the body. Alexander outstretched his hand and felt for a pulse in his neck. Nothing. Alexander's hand began to shake as he reached for Devin's wrist. Once again, nothing. Alexander flopped down on the floor beside the body, his head in his hands. How had this happened? One day. It only took one day for his life to turn completely upside down.

Once he regained his composure he stood, his eyes fixed on the man he'd just murdered. As he looked at the body, he noticed the twine he'd just used to garrote his old friend. "Well I'll be damned," he whispered before bending over and picking it up. He examined the rope carefully, noticing its size, design and strength. His mind quickly flipped to the morgue where Marjory's mummified corpse lay lifeless on the slab. The marks around her neck mimicked the properties of the twine exactly. "How do you like that?" he said as he continued his inspection of the murder weapon. Just then, the door burst open. He straightened, only to see four uniformed officers, each with a semi-automatic trained on him.

"Devin Cooper, you're under ar..." the detective began as he stepped out from behind the officers. He stopped when he saw Alexander. His eyes moved from Alexander to Devin's corpse and back to Alexander again. "What the hell happened here?"

"I found Devin," Alexander said, the twine dangling from his hand.

"So it seems. Can you explain how you found him? And how he came to be murdered in the same fashion as your alleged wife?"

Alexander stared at the rope in his hand and then at the body below him. "I think I'm going to need my lawyer."

Even when you're just passing through, sometimes you can't help but notice when something's wrong.

The Chunk
by Michael McGlade

THE WEEKEND AFTER Halloween is when they have the annual *Punkin Chunkin* championship in Delaware, which is where a bunch of backyard engineers compete to turn pumpkins into projectiles. Folks wear hollowed-out pumpkins as war helmets and vendors pass out pumpkins in an open competition for you to catapult as far as possible by any and all mechanical means available in a regulated and officially governed event. These folks take decorative gourd season to a whole new level. It's local customs like that can make a traveler feel at home.

"Getting married on a dare in Delaware is grounds for annulment, Daddy."

Missy knew how to keep us entertained. She rarely had her head out of a book, and this one she had been consulting was the state legislature penal code.

"Pays to be well versed in the local laws," I said. "We ever get married here, and I change my mind, I've got a cast-iron get-out clause."

"Daddy, you really think I'd ever lower myself to marry a man like you?"

"I can be pretty persuasive."

"But I'm not the kind of gal can be bought."

Missy and me, a whole year we've been together with no last names, no fixed abode, no listed occupations, no tax returns, no traces of the past, nothing, but the two of us, together, forever, treading the blacktop.

The red Toyota I was driving had a hundred thousand miles on the clock because we weren't looking to stand out from the crowd. Our clothes were always pre-packed in a suitcase in the trunk and there was fifty thousand dollars cash money taped beneath the seat.

Our bumper sticker says, "Eve was framed."

We were driving through Delaware on our way to Sussex County and the urban sprawl became a repeating pattern of neighborhood, strip mall, home depot, neighborhood, strip mall, home depot, neighborhood, home depot, Christian mall.

"Daddy, you're driving like we've got somewhere to be. We're not late for an appointment. Slow down."

It hadn't taken her long to learn how to give orders and I've since discovered it's easier not to argue, so I eased off the gas.

My name's Jackson. I'm thirty-three years old. Missy is my wife-to-be, even if she doesn't know it yet. She calls me *Daddy* on account of the age difference, me being five years her senior.

I've been told I look older and not in the *distinguished* kind of way—just old. Used to be a captain in the First Cavalry Division, Second Brigade—the Blackjacks. I mustered-out when I won a jackpot after being caught in a roadside IED in Baghdad city and my prize included five cracked vertebrae and eighty-seven pieces of shrapnel removed from my body. I empathize with pin cushions, I truly do. I also won a new titanium hip that provides an unerring ability to forecast rain. Lady Luck spared me that day. But I wasn't saved till I met Missy. We've been together ever since and are equal-stakes partners, and if she wanted to win that Punkin Chunkin championship then I meant to see it happen.

We entered Georgetown at six o'clock on Thursday evening. We'd bed down for the weekend, have a crack at the Chunk, and leave out of town come Monday.

We hitched up at the inn and went to the local watering hole, The Irish Eyes.

The middle-aged barman wore a t-shirt: Warning, I do dumb things.

I ordered two Wild Turkeys, my favorite bourbon.

"You here for the Chunk?"

"Yup."

"Then the first drink's on me," he said. "What kinda hardware you bring?"

Missy took a notebook from her purse and showed him her design for a trailer-mounted catapult we'd been towing halfway across the country.

"That's a beaut of a catapult. Might just be a contender."

"Still need some supplies to finish off."

"How far it toss a pie?"

"I reckon it'll throw far enough."

"You need supplies, go to Felton's Hardware. Won't open till first light. Say Bigpeen sent you."

"That name get me any kinda discount, Bigpeen?"

"Used to," he said. "Not no more. New owner's name is Jim Duke. Just bought the place a week back. He's the ornery sort."

"Any tips for the Chunk?"

"Go for the La Estrella pumpkin. Got a thicker rind. Holds up better under pressure."

The next morning we went to Felton's Hardware store on Bedford Street but the store was cordoned off with yellow tape and two police cruisers were parked nearby. Missy and me got out of our Toyota and approached an officer.

"There's been a murder, folks."

"Who?"

"Jim Duke. The owner."

A crowd had begun to gather, mainly tourists in town for the championship. There'd be as many as twenty thousand by this evening.

"You catch who done it?"

"Have him arrested at the station. Bigpeen Halloran. Owns a bar—"

"I was there last night," I said. "The Irish Eyes. What was it over?"

"Money," the officer said. "Unpaid bill. The two of them had a big argument in the store yesterday."

Missy and me got back in the Toyota. About thirty people were crowded around the hardware store jostling to see inside. The body had already been removed, which I clocked straight off having heard the coroner's van leaving from the side alley. Smelled the gun smoke, too. The murder couldn't have happened more than a half hour ago.

"He didn't do it," Missy said.

"So now you're a medium? You can commune with the dead?"

"Bigpeen didn't have murder in his eyes. You can always tell someone fixing to kill."

"All I know is we've got a fifteen-mile round trip to gather supplies for the catapult..."

She stared out the side window at the hardware store. Silence was never a good sign with Missy.

"You fixing to get us in trouble every which where we go to?"

"I can't stand cowards," she said. "If someone was wrongfully arrested, and we can help, which we can, then it's our duty to see justice done."

There was no arguing with Missy.

I asked around and discovered the murder weapon was a Colt .45 and had been found at the murder scene. The weapon was registered to Bigpeen and contained his fingerprints.

"Can we go get them supplies now?" I asked Missy.

"Why would he leave the gun behind? The police picked Bigpeen up at his home. No blood on him. No trace evidence."

"Except for the murder weapon."

"Exactly."

I wasn't agreeing with her but she acted like I was.

"They have hard evidence," I said. "He's not getting off."

"When ever have you taken the *evidence* at first sight?"

"Then what?" I said. "You're gonna tell me the gun was planted?"

"I am."

"By who?"

"The murderer, obviously."

I took a deep breath. Fanned some air into my face with my Stetson.

"This isn't our fight."

Missy said, "Well, Daddy, I'm making it our fight."

The consensus around town from the dozen people I spoke to categorically stated the same thing: Bigpeen didn't do it. Not only that, but he wasn't the type to fly off the handle. He wasn't the murdering sort. Sure, Bigpeen and Jim Duke had an argument but that was on account of the state of affairs left behind by the previous owner, Harry Felton. Said it was nothing more than a mistake in the accounting books. Bigpeen was known as someone who paid his debts in a timely and orderly fashion. The more I spoke to folks, the more I started to side with Missy. Bigpeen didn't kill Jim Duke.

"How'd that Colt revolver get to the crime scene?"

Missy and me were in a diner having lunch.

"Bigpeen kept the gun locked away. So it was someone who knew him, knew where he kept it."

I cut into the cheese steak, and heaped a forkful with slaw, fries and pickle.

"Why'd Harry Felton sell up so quick?" I said. "He owed that store for a couple years, ever since his pa passed on."

We parked outside Harry Felton's red brick house on Market Street. I knocked on the door and a forty-year-old man with receding hair answered. This was still the kind of town where people opened their doors willingly. Probably still illegal to profane, too.

"Can I help you?" Felton said.

There was caution in his voice. I can sometimes make the wrong impression. I'm six-two and two hundred and fifty pounds.

"It's nothing to worry about, sir," I said. "I'm friends with Bigpeen."

"I've never seen you before."

"Can I come in and talk?"

Felton looked us over and let us into his living room.

"Bigpeen got his self in a whole heap of trouble," Felton said. "I would've lent him the money, had he asked."

Missy said, "Did he really owe the new owner all that money?"

"Course he did. The debt passed over when I sold the shop."

"How long have you and Bigpeen been friends?"

"We were in high school together. But I only moved back when my father died a couple of years ago. I guess you could say we've been friends since then."

"Good enough friends that you'd be in his home?"

"What other kind of friend is there?"

"You think he could do something like killing a man?"

Felton glanced around the room. For a rich man, the room seemed oddly bare, and there were large tracts of space where objects used to be. Like he'd been selling his things.

"Sometimes people just snap. Oftentimes over the simplest things—"

"Like money?"

"That would do it," he said.

"Why'd you sell the hardware store?"

"I was never the hardware store type. My father was, but not me. I kept it on as long as I could. But, you see, I'm a broker. Got my own business." He pointed to a laptop. "I buy and sell commodities. And I've been making a killing." He chewed his bottom lip. "I've been making so much money in brokerage I didn't need the store anymore."

It was nine o'clock in the evening. Missy had spent the afternoon on the phone and her laptop checking into Felton's brokerage company.

"His company has had impressive year-on-year growth," she said. "Too impressive. He's being investigated by the IRS for tax irregularities."

"He's cooking the books?"

"I believe that's what the IRS investigation will reveal. But by then Bigpeen will have been sentenced for that murder. We can't wait for the IRS investigation. Felton's too sneaky. He's already got the money from the sale of the hardware store. Two hundred thousand went into his bank this morning. As soon as this murder blows over, he'll disappear."

"What do we do?"

"Daddy, you need to teach Felton a valuable lesson. Where's the pliers?"

I lashed Felton to a hard chair in his kitchen. Breaking in was easy when the door was unlocked.

Missy told him everything we discovered, laid it all on the line.

"Bigpeen's innocent," she said. "You framed him. Even though I shouldn't, on account of you lying to me, I will give you this one opportunity to admit the truth."

"They've already charged Bigpeen," Felton said. "And I'm never going to confess."

"You're forgetting something," Missy said. "We're not the police.

And Daddy here is a trained military specialist. What specialism did they educate you in, Daddy?"

"Information extraction through the utilization of systematic torture techniques."

I clamped a pair of pliers onto the fingernail of Felton's index finger.

On Saturday morning I drove toward the World Championship Punkin Chunkin or *The Chunk,* as they call it, which is a field outside Georgetown at grid coordinates 38° 43′ 20″ North and 75° 32′ 08″ West. We wore our "Gonna Hurl" t-shirts. In Bridgeville I took the turnoff near the intersection of Seashore Highway and Chaplains Chapel Road. Over twenty thousand people were in attendance.

I parked in my designated area and set about fine-tuning our catapult.

People were staring. News travels fast. That's the thing about small towns: folks were always up in each other's business. A couple came to shake my hand, oily and greased as it was from work.

Felton had made a full and frank confession, which Missy recorded on her Dictaphone, then we delivered the memory card and the perp to the Georgetown police department. The "torture" was just a bit of karmic digression, something to scare the bejesus out of him. I didn't actually hurt Felton. Amazing what a prop (such as pliers) and the confidence of your convictions can do to a cowardly individual. It's a simple and effective technique.

It transpired that Felton ran the hardware store into the ground. He cooked the books, inflating its net worth, and sold the business to Jim Duke. Felton knew it would only be a matter of weeks until Duke discovered the fraud. But it didn't matter. Felton had already planned to frame Bigpeen for the murder. He waited for Duke to tell Bigpeen that ten thousand dollars was owed for unpaid bills, knowing Bigpeen always paid his debts and would be shamed into a public argument. Felton killed Duke with Bigpeen's gun. So much for friendship.

The championship was about to begin and we were first to shoot. I had a couple minutes to complete the build on our catapult. I'd be surprised if it worked at all.

"Looks ain't everything," Missy said.

"Don't expect it to beat *Big 10*."

Missy had been researching the best build techniques, finding the perfect device and *Big 10 Inch* had set the world record in Moab, Utah. It was a pneumatic cannon. But Missy was old school. She liked the idea of entering the catapult category because it was based on Roman technology, except taken to the extreme. The goal is simple: controlled mechanical explosion.

"But the Moab record doesn't count," she said. "It's only here in Bridgeville that counts. And last year's record breaker shattered the distance by..."

Didn't let her tell me anymore. Ignorance is bliss. Not knowing can free you up.

I tensioned the rubber bands, each as thick as a two-inch piece of PVC pipe, and traced the couplings to the throwing arm and the winched-down bucket. No obvious weaknesses. It very well might not kill everyone in a fifty-yard radius. Small mercies.

Missy finished spraying on its name. We were going to call it "Sir Chunks A Lot" but due to the clunky appearance from the rushed build we called it "Chunky."

The arm was cocked into the loaded position and Missy selected a green-gray La Estrella pumpkin and placed it in the bucket. I hit the quick-release mechanism. The arm snapped forward, bucket whipping overhead. Something crunched. The mechanism lurched and the pumpkin shattered to vapor.

"It's pie," a woman said.

Pie—short for pumpkin pie in the sky. It didn't count.

We moved to leave but the crowd called for another. Strictly speaking, you're only allowed a single shot per day but they made us take another. Such are the perils of being a temporary celebrity. Big-peen brought us a pumpkin this time. Officially, this throw wouldn't count, but we carried on regardless.

I struck the quick-release and the pumpkin hurled upwards. Intact. Landed seven hundred feet away. Not too shabby. Best of the day so far. Although we were the first to launch.

"I believe we have a winner," I said.

"Not exactly, Daddy. The record's five thousand feet."

Oh well, there's always next year. Might even dream of breaking the mile.

A girl needs to do what she can to stay safe.

The Basement
by MJ Gardner

SO IF I tell it to you all over again can I get out of this dress? Why do I have to tell it to you? They wrote it all down. But I suppose you're a shrink and you just want to get inside my head. Well, come on in, if you want to. Only it ain't pretty.

All right. I'll try to tell you everything, so you won't have to ask me any questions. I'm tired of all these questions. Let me start at the beginning, which was when I was born a Miller, I guess. If you're going to understand, you have to know how I was raised. It wasn't normal. It wasn't nice. You have to understand that.

What do I mean? You know how they say that it's sad when cousins marry? Well, it is. And after a few generations of it, it's worse than sad. My parents are cousins. Not first cousins, but related. And my Papa, some people say his Grandpa's his daddy, you know? I told you, it ain't pretty and it ain't nice.

My Mama drinks from sun up 'til she passes out sometime after lunch, and then she just nips a little until bedtime so Papa doesn't see how bad she is. Sundays she doesn't drink at all. Well, not much anyway.

But no matter how drunk she is, Mama can sew anything from nothing. My Mama can make the most beautiful dresses out of remnants, goodwill castoffs, hand-me-downs. She buys old clothes at garage sales just for the lace and buttons and trims. She even made this wedding gown.

We were poor but we always had pretty dresses. And we were not allowed to get our pretty dresses dirty. Even though Mama didn't seem to notice that we had no shoes or that our hair wasn't combed, she'd see a smudge or a tear from a mile away, and then we'd catch hell. She'd pull that dress off, right where we stood -- in the yard or the living room -- and often we were naked underneath 'cause Mama never sewed us any underwear. Then she'd scream at us about how she spent so much time sewing and how she'd scrimped and saved so we could have pretty things to wear and how we didn't care at all about her or her work. Sometimes she'd hit, depending on how drunk she was. Or sometimes she'd just wind down to a mutter and forget you were there, and then it was best to sneak off to the bedroom and hide for a while. When you figured it was safe to come out again you put on another pretty dress and hoped Mama had forgotten.

Now, Papa hit too, but mostly he locked us in the basement. I spent a lot of my early life locked in the basement. I believed it was because I was a bad girl. Sometimes I still have to tell myself that I'm not.

Papa would send us down there when he and Mama fought, which was three-four times a week, or when she got too drunk, or when he was too drunk, or when our brothers misbehaved. Papa whupped them with his belt, he never locked them up. One time Mama suggested it and he just sneered, "Can't lock up boys," like she was out of her mind.

I learned a lot being locked up down there. I learned not to argue or try to stall. When Papa said to go we had to drop whatever we were doing and go right away. I learned to be prepared. I kept my favorite toy in hand. I was always ready at dinner with a napkin or paper towel to scoop up my food. These are skills that served me later in life. When I got a job I knew how to be punctual and prepared and to do what the boss said without sassing back or rolling my eyes like some kids.

Sometimes they would forget us down there. There was a trunk full of old blankets and quilts and clothes. My sisters would sleep in the open trunk and I would wrap myself in blankets and sleep on top of some packing crates under the stairs. The next day when Mama or Papa remembered we were still down there they'd make us a good big breakfast, even if it was the middle of the afternoon. As long as we didn't make noise and hurt their heads we could eat whatever we liked: bacon, jam toast, even johnny cake with syrup.

See, I learned that patience and suffering are rewarded.

Being locked in the basement wasn't all bad. My sisters and I would take off our pretty dresses, so as not to get them dirty, and play down there more freely than we could outside, where we had to worry about mud and grass stains and sharp twigs. We played like boys, wrestling and running. And in the darkness, wrapped in blankets and sitting around an imaginary camp fire, we would tell ghost stories and talk about our future husbands and babies and how wonderful it would all be when we were grown up.

The basement was a refuge from what went on upstairs. From the yelling, the screaming, the snap of Papa's belt, things being broken. It was a safe haven from our brothers too.

See, Bobby and Daryl are older than me, and Cassie and Joleen are younger. They were stronger and bigger and meaner. Mama never sewed them good clothes. It was no use dressing up boys, she said, they're too rough and dirty.

They were proud of it too. Dirty ripped overalls and no shoes were signs of manhood to them. They spat and smoked and snuck away some of Papa's whiskey in a mason jar. They weren't mama's babies like us, they said, all dolled up. Sometimes I think they were jealous.

Most of the time they ignored us, but then sometimes they'd play games with us. Not games that we wanted to play. They knew that the worst trouble we could get into would be to get our dresses dirty. They'd wait and ambush us as we came home from school and push us down in the dirt and lay on us till we screamed. Sometimes they'd throw mud. Mama never listened when we told her that the boys had done it. Or she never heard 'cause she was too drunk.

Other times their games were more inventive. They'd make us do things under threat of mud puddles and dog shit. They'd make us kiss the cows that pastured in the field next to our yard, or suck out a raw egg. One time they made us pee in a bucket, and when they had all that Miller piss in it they went and dumped it on some other kid. Their games weren't reserved just for us.

But, see, I learned from that too. We learned to stick together, Cassie, Joleen and I. There was some safety in numbers. If Bobby and Daryl caught one of us alone they would try to stick things up our skirts. Sticks, screwdrivers, rake handles, empty gin bottles. If Mama or Papa caught them at this game he sent all of us girls to the basement. Papa would beat them, but it didn't stop them. It just made them craftier.

Sometimes it wasn't just things they stuck in us either. When she was fourteen Cassie had to have an abortion. Mama cried and cried.

She said she was a good Christian woman and she didn't believe in abortion. But Papa said he wasn't going to let his daughter have a baby got from her own brother. It was liable to have two heads or be a retard. He said it was Mama's fault for dressing Cassie in short frilly dresses still, even though she was a woman.

Papa beat the boys so bad they couldn't leave the house for a week. He beat them both because he didn't know which one did it. At first they denied it, but when he started using the buckle end of the belt, they started to blame each other. They were both big boys, but they never raised a hand against their Papa. They had been inseparable before, the Miller boys, the terrible twosome, but when they turned on each other, it broke that bond. It broke them.

After that Bobby and Daryl left us alone and only bothered other people's sisters. I don't know if it was the beating so much as the bastard.

Mama was quiet for a long time. She sipped whiskey and sewed. She sewed up a whole new wardrobe for me and Cassie, with longer grown-up skirts and long-sleeved blouses and old-fashioned pantaloons.

Cassie didn't talk about what happened. She doesn't talk hardly at all anymore. She never goes out, and she started carrying around one of Joleen's old dolls.

Soon after Bobby moved in with some other boys. They lived in an old wreck of a cottage, with junker cars in the yard and beer in the fridge. Daryl got a girl pregnant and had to marry her and move in with her folks.

Without the boys bothering us life started to get better, and it gave me hope, you see. We were almost happy.

When I was seventeen I got a job as a cashier at Stevenson's Groceries. Mama still made my clothes, but now I bought the material and the patterns and she made me whatever I wanted. She was pleased with that. She said I was a real fine young lady.

I went to the beauty parlor to get my hair cut. That's where I met Josie, who washed and cut and permed my hair. Josie's only two years older than me and she has a pretty little baby girl. She taught me about washing my hair with shampoo instead of Ivory soap and using a cream rinse and a curling iron. Sometimes after work on a Friday night, if she could get her mother to babysit, we'd go down to the Rose Bowl and sit in the bar together and drink beer. Well, she drank beer. I didn't do much drinking on account of Mama.

After I gave Mama some money for room and board I could still go to the show or have lunch at the Woolworth's lunch counter. I bought myself grown-up nylon panties and pantyhose and bras and slips and shoes and costume jewelry. I even got my ears pierced.

When I stood at my cash register I heard the old women muttering to each other how I was a nice girl and how I wasn't like the rest of the Millers. At first I was proud. I didn't want to be like my Mama with her bleary eyes and her dirty shapeless housedress. I didn't want to be like Daryl's little wife, with her pouchy baby belly and her black eyes and bruises. She was clumsy, she said. Ever since they moved out of her parent's house and into a trailer she had been falling into things. Door frames, chairs, coffee tables. They shouldn't have rented that trailer. They should have gotten a house with a basement. That's the only way to live with one of my brothers.

But then I started to feel ashamed for Cassie and Joleen. They were ragged and barefoot. I took them both to the beauty parlor and Josie did their hair for half price. I bought them pantyhose and slips. We did each others nails and on Sundays I curled Joleen's hair with my curling iron.

It didn't seem to have much effect on Cassie. She looked better, but only on the outside. When you look in her eyes you can see she's lost. One time I went down to the basement looking for her -- I hadn't been down there for a long time -- and she had a whole baby's room set up. There was a crib and a high chair and one of those baby swings and toys and everything. All for a doll. I didn't tell anybody.

Anyway, I had a job and I was making money. I looked like a normal girl now. My brothers were gone from the house and Papa didn't send us to the basement anymore 'cause we disappeared on our own before he could think to do it. Plus, with the boys gone there were less fights. I didn't think life could get any better.

And then I met Jimmy.

I met him at the grocery store when his mama sent him for a pound of butter. After that he kept coming in for little things. At first he'd say that his mama wanted something. Eggs, sugar, milk, a hot rod magazine. Every day on his lunch hour his mama sent him to the grocery store. Then he started coming for things for himself. A chocolate bar, an apple for his lunch, a can opener. Eventually he stopped buying things and just hung around the checkout to talk to me. My boss didn't like it, though, and Jimmy had to stop coming by. So he asked me out.

Our first date was to church. And we went to the movies too. I went to his house for dinner and met his mama and his little brother. His daddy was dead, which is why he stayed living at home, he told me.

Jimmy was a nice boy, or so I thought. He wasn't like my brothers. At work he had to wear mechanic's coveralls but after work he'd clean up and put on jeans and a button-up shirt and polished cowboy boots. His sandy hair was always trimmed and clean. He said no ma'am and yes ma'am and held doors for me and even bought me a heart-shaped box of chocolates for Valentine's Day. When I finally got up the nerve to bring him home to meet my Mama and Papa, he didn't criticize and he wasn't scared off. Cassie hid from him, but he joked with Joleen and never laid a finger on her.

When Jimmy asked me to marry him I nearly soared through the air with joy. We had to wait a year to save up money for the wedding, and then we'd have to live in his mama's house. He didn't want to leave her alone, but I didn't mind. I liked his mama, and their house was so much nicer and cleaner than ours. He treated me so good sometimes I cried for shame. I didn't think I deserved such a good man.

The truth is that I don't, 'cause I was just pretending, see? I know that now. No matter how nice my clothes are and my hair, no matter how normal I look, I'll always be a Miller. Daryl and Bobby will always be my brothers, and my Mama and Papa with always be no-good drunks and poor crazy Cassie will always be my sister. I don't deserve somebody like Jimmy, only Jimmy wasn't as good as I thought he was. He had just been pretending, fooling the world like I was.

We had a small wedding, just family mostly, and Josie and some of the guys Jimmy works with. And then for our reception we went to the Holiday Inn. It was so beautiful. There were flowers and champagne and candles on the tables and it was like a fairytale.

The guys from the garage, they'd all gone together and rented us a room as a wedding present, so we wouldn't have to spend our wedding night in his Mama's house, they said. I thought it was really great, 'cause I'd never stayed in a hotel before, especially one as nice as the Holiday Inn.

It was in that room that I found out about Jimmy. That was where I found out that he wasn't nice, really, after I was married to him and it was too late. He wanted to do the same thing my brothers had done to me. He was just as disgusting as they were.

That's why I had to kill him. I had to. That's how I got all this blood on my dress. I worked so hard to get away from all that, to be nice and normal. I had to do it because there wasn't any basement to go to and lock myself away.

Now can you loosen these restraints and get me a clean dress? They said my Mama's here and I can't let her see me like this.

Whoever said that there's honour among thieves must have worked alone.

The Bulldog Ant is Not a Team Player
by Dan Stout

SCIENTISTS BOTH CRUEL and curious have demonstrated that a Bulldog Ant cut in two will continue to lash out at anything nearby, including itself, the heads and bodies biting and stinging their missing halves until either death or their nest mates claim them. The crew that hit Wayne Jewellers was like that—solid planning, flawless execution, but three days in a cabin and they were at each other's throats.

Take, for example, the way Kit Rosland drowned Teddy Wilson in the toilet. Teddy had saved their lives, darting the getaway car down side streets and arranging for the second vehicle they swapped into. Now he lay slumped into the toilet, his forehead resting in the curve of the bowl while Kit stood over him, trying to listen over the sound of her own panting breath. The other two in the crew—Henry and Matt—should be asleep, but she couldn't be sure if they'd been drunk enough to slumber through her fight with Teddy.

She leaned on the vanity, waiting for her heart to calm and her limbs to stop shaking. When she was steadier, she washed her hands. It made her feel cleaner, even if it didn't do anything to combat the rank smell of sweat and urine. She wondered if she should bother doing anything with the body, or if that was only postponing the inevitable. Matt and Henry would surely notice that their happy little family had been reduced by a full fourth. She decided her best bet was to get dressed fast and prepare to bolt. She exited the bathroom cautiously. There was no noise from the bedroom, the one Matt and Henry shared. Kit had let Teddy take the other bedroom. She preferred the living room couch; it was easier to monitor the comings and goings of the others, and she didn't feel cornered the way she might in one of the bedrooms.

She didn't like being in this situation. She might have been content to stick with the plan, to wait it out in the woods drinking beer and shooting the cans full of holes with a BB gun, but Teddy had started giving her looks. Hard looks. When the conversation in the cabin lapsed, Kit swore she could feel him—hell, she could damn near *hear* him looking at her. The crow's feet around his eyes crackled like old leaves on pavement when he gave her that look, the one whose message was clear: "I want what you have."

She'd felt that look from belligerent drunks in bars, from her classmates in university, from the bums and whores who watched her walk out of a restaurant with a stomach full of food and a wallet full of cash. It was Envy, a desire to take her and the things that belonged to her. It made her tired to see it.

When Teddy had reached the point where he was clearly ready to move on her, Kit moved first. Pretending to sleep on her couch, she waited for him to take a leak. A five-count later she was up and to the door. She hadn't even needed to pop the lock, he'd left it not only un-locked but un-latched. Sloppy.

She could hear the tinkle of piss on porcelain, and as she slid past the door she found comfort in the heft of her makeshift blackjack: a sock full of BBs. The toilet faced outward, so Teddy's back was to her as he relieved himself. When she hit him, Teddy's head pitched forward and cracked into the wall. Reflexively, he covered his pecker with his hands, but that wasn't where she was aiming. She kicked the side of his knee. Kicked hard, and he dropped. On the way down she hit him again with the blackjack. Teddy landed across the toilet, head down, not looking at her, not looking at anything.

It was a small amount of wrestling to reposition him, but Teddy wasn't a big guy, and she got his head into the toilet without too much trouble. He'd started to kick, right at the end, but by then her back was wedged against the wall and the leverage was in her favor.

Back in the living room, she reached for her clothes, which lay across a gym bag tucked beneath the couch. There was a soft click as the other bedroom door opened. Silently she rolled onto the couch, lying still. Someone walked to the bathroom. She couldn't see if it was Henry or Matt's oversized frame. The light clicked on, streaming out from underneath the door. Kit tensed, ready for the yelling to start, but there was nothing. After a moment, the sink began to run.

She jumped up, considered making a break for it. Instead she stepped on the coffee table, and reached into the overhead light, loosening the bulbs. She just had time to regain her seat on the couch when the bathroom door opened, and Henry walked out. The bathroom light was still on, and he was back-lit, reducing him to just a silhouette.

"Hiya Kit." He walked towards her, very slowly, drying his hands on a towel. "You mind if I have a sit-down?"

She said nothing. She knew there was no stopping Henry, only making things enough of a pain in the rear that he'd give up and walk away of his own accord.

Henry stepped out of the shaft of the bathroom light, sliding into the darkness with her. "I notice that Teddy had a little accident. You know anything about that?" He moved slow in the dark, his eyes not yet adjusted from the bathroom light.

She wished to hell that she'd had time to put on clothes. Yoga pants and a t-shirt seemed an awful outfit to wear for this confrontation. And if things went poorly, it would be an awful outfit to die in.

Holding the towel in his left hand, Henry reached with his right to turn on the light. The loosened bulbs didn't respond, and he didn't bother trying it twice. He was moving towards the recliner now, next to the couch. "I think we need to talk about how that affects the take from this job."

He sat down in the la-z-boy, his slippered feet looking ridiculous on a dangerous man. He raised his hand, and Kit pulled away, ready to fight. But instead he reached for the lamp. *Aw Hell,* she thought, *I forgot to take the bulb out of—*

With a click the end table lamp came on. Henry looked at her, wearing that little smile that annoyed her so much. The one that looked like he practiced it in the mirror. He didn't move, one hand on the lamp, the other holding the towel on his lap, light blue with dark crimson stains on it. He didn't look away from her eyes. "It's a pretty healthy take, when split two ways, don't you think?"

"And Matt?" she asked. Her southern Ohio accent stretched the syllables like honey on a hot day.

"Yeah... Matt's not going to be playing with us anymore." He withdrew his hand from the lamp, slowly. He was trying not to spook her. "And I think the same's true of Teddy, right?"

"Pretty much."

"I s'pose he kinda had it coming. And Matt... well, Matt was always sort of the weakest link, don't you think?"

Henry always did that—end sentences with a question. It was something he'd picked up from some sales infomercial. But in this case he was right. Kit shrugged an assent. "He probably would've talked sooner or later."

"Well, then I'm glad that we could establish a base line for our negotiations."

She looked at Henry, studied his face, the line of his lips, tried to see past his friendly poker face to the shark beneath.

"Yeah, negotiations," he said. "We already agree that we're the two who should get the profits from this job. Now we just have to decide how we'll split them up."

"Isn't that a little cold?"

"You just drowned a man in his own piss."

"Fine. 50/50. We go our own ways."

"80/20 and I take the car."

"You can't leave me without a car. What am I supposed to do, hitch a ride with that old couple in their RV?" She pointed to the west, towards the only nearby cabin.

"It's a favor to you. Cops'll be looking for it."

"No, they won't."

"Yes, they will." His voice was grew sharper at being contradicted. "Any car lifted in the last week is going to be flagged once they find our ditched getaway." He shrugged in a what-can-you-do fashion. "That thing's a liability."

"The car we're in was picked up months ago and has clean plates. Teddy was smarter than that."

"If he was all that smart he'd still be alive, right?"

"He was smart about cars. Not about staying alive."

"You're smart about security." He didn't ask if she was smart enough to stay alive.

Kit was tensing, ready to run or pounce. She felt naked and wished again that she'd had time to get dressed. She wondered how much of Henry was fat and how much was muscle, wondered if she could wrap the cord of the table lamp around his thick throat.

Her nerves must have shown, because Henry softened his voice, took the edge out of it. Kit thought it made him seem even more like a snake about to strike. "I ran the show," he said, "and you took out the alarm system. You deserve a cut. The other two? Muscle and drivers we could have picked up anywhere."

She turned her head away, but kept him in the edge of her vision. "You going to do anything to clean up this place?"

"Nah, no point."

"We could take the bodies to the woods, give us a couple days, maybe."

"Why bother? We leave here two days before the rental is up, it's the same effect. You need to think further into the game, Kit." He was still covering the towel with his left hand, fingering the fringe at its end.

She nodded, trying to appear reasonable. "60/40. It was your plan, you deserve a majority cut."

"Yes, I do," he said. "75/25. You keep your full original share and walk out of here alive."

"Sure you could take me?" She cocked her jaw, just slightly, but it was a challenge.

"Sure enough that I didn't bother to stick you yet." Henry shifted his left hand, revealing the long and ugly knife wrapped in the towel.

Kit stared at it, at the coagulating blood which hadn't quite rinsed off the blade. When she spoke her voice was cold. "You planned this the whole time."

"You didn't?"

"Teddy was self-defense." Her voice rose.

"Looked to me like you hit him from behind while he was taking a whiz."

"He was getting squirrelly on me."

Now that the knife was out in the open, Henry played with it while they talked. He watched her eyes track it for a while, then set it down on the arm of the chair. She got the message: he was so confident, he didn't need the knife. He just didn't want her to forget he had it, either.

"25 percent of this take's a good cut."

"Make it 30."

He started to respond, but she cut him off. "The extra 5 is for taking care of Teddy."

Henry stared at her, round cheeks obscuring his dark eyes. She knew he was doing math, figuring just how much trouble she was worth. Going in her favor was the fact that Henry wasn't really a fighter. She'd been surprised that it had been him to come out of that bedroom. He must have gotten Matt drunker than she thought. Finally, just as she began to think that he was going to come after her anyway, he gave in.

"Fine," he said, "70/30. I'll take the car." He stood up, finished with her.

"It's a liability."

"You convinced me otherwise." He kept facing her as he walked to the closet where the stash was secured. He may have won, but he clearly wasn't going to turn his back to her. "And even if it is," he said, opening the closet, "don't you think—" He cut off, must have seen movement or heard the 'click' as the closet door opened, but still the shotgun blast caught him under the jaw and there wasn't much left of Henry after that. Kit had spent some time positioning the shotgun at just the right angle, its stock wedged into the corner with the luggage stand and a simple pulley switch connecting the trigger to the closet doorknob.

She reached under the couch and pulled out her travel bag. All evidence of a fourth person, and certainly any sign of a female, had already been picked clean from the cabin. The security tapes at the jewelry store showed two men, and the cops knew there was a driver, but no one had seen her. At the cabin she'd been especially careful not to be seen by their only neighbors, the elderly couple with the RV. She stepped lightly over Henry's body as she retrieved the satchel with its glittery, precious contents. The police would find two murdered crooks, and another caught in one of his dead partners' traps, their car sitting in the driveway. The cops would assume that no diamonds meant that they'd been stashed somewhere else before hiding out. Just another heist that would never be solved.

She was out the door, and across the field towards the older couple's cabin. She knew that there was a spot behind the AC roof unit on the RV where the couple had a tarped-over equipment bag, for bikes or backpacks or whatever. She could fit under there, long enough at least for them to get to another truck stop, another campground. From there she'd hitchhike, or carjack someone. Whatever it took to make it clear, Kit knew she could do it.

Because she was alive. And because nobody thought further into the game than she did.

When you're the only detective around, no case is too small.

The Mystery of the Missing Puskat
by Lavie Tidhar

DENSLEY TAKES ON A CASE

HE KNOWS AMERICA well; there are cars in Detroit, and gangsters in Chicago. New York has the Mob, and Man Jew, and Broadway, and Hollywood is called La-la land and it is magical: it is where movies come from.

Father Ben has the books, and he lets Densley read them. Thirty or so: it is a vast library of knowledge. Women are called dolls; men use their fist, or a gun. Densley too has a gun; he has carved it himself, of the burau tree.

It is *sava*, dusk, when he returns home across the football field. He is deep in thought; the gun is in the waistband of his trousers. When he glances left he can see the sea beyond the trees, and rising above it, the volcano, obscured by clouds. When he goes past Eliezer's house he sees a girl, playing alone by the side of the road. When he comes closer he sees that she is not playing: she is crying.

"Olsem wanem?" he says. *What's going on?* The girl doesn't stop crying. She says, "No gat"—but clearly, Densley thinks, something *is* wrong.

The girl's name is Isabel, and she is the daughter of his cousin Samson, not the one from Gaua but the one who once worked in the Public Works and had since disappeared, *sans* wife and daughter, into the bright lights of Luganville. He says, "Isabel..." and waits for her to look up. "*Si?*"

"What's going on?" He kneels down beside her.

Isabel says, "I can't find my *puskat.*"

Densley feels disappointment. Here, he had felt, was a client and here, he had felt, was a case. The moment he had seen Isabel cry (for she never cried) he knew that something was wrong, and his help would be needed. It was a promising encounter, but now... a missing cat?

"She probably went in the bush," he says. Isabel shakes her head. "She always waits for me when I come back from school," she says. "She doesn't like to go outside. The other children scare her."

"Did you ask your mummy?" Densley says, and Isabel shakes her head again and says, "Mummy's not home either," and starts to cry again but makes no noise, which somehow makes it worse.

Densley stands up. "*Gerrap*, doll," he says. When she does he takes her by the hand. "I'll find your cat."

They call the city Sola: for when the *waetman* came, he had asked in his language what the name of the place was, and the women roasting crabs by the sea had replied in their language: Sola, sola. Crab. Crab. To a visitor it is a sleepy coastal town, a village really. But for Densley, it is The City: it has two street-lights, and indeed there used to be electricity here, until the town's generator broke; it has a police station (the only one in the whole province, which covers over fourteen populated islands); it has a clinic, a secondary school Densley goes to (the only one in the province), many shops, and many dark and quiet bars selling kava, where men sit on wooden benches and speak in whispers in the light of a single hurricane lamp. It is The City, running from the one creek to the other, sprawling across the *solwota*, lying in the shade of the tall green hills, a city carved into the bush by men. But the bush is never far away.

He takes Isabel the short distance to his house. The house lies at the end of town, beyond the football field. There is a wide yard, a mango tree and eggplant shrubs and flowers, and a row of chilli bushes. They have a flush toilet. Densley's mother sits in the yard fixing his brother's Maxwell's trousers. "Isabel!" she cries, and she takes the little girl by the hand and takes her into the kitchen, where a fire is always burning, and bustles around her as if full of secret knowledge. Densley follows them inside. "Where is the *mami blong pikinini*?" he asks. The mother of the child. Names are to be avoided when discussing people. Densley's mother shoots him a glance like whipping out a pistol and says, "I don't know. She probably went into town."

"But her cat is missing," Densley protests, and his mother makes that guttural growl that serves as a warning to the kids, and says,

"Densley..."

Excitement, then; for he recognises it for what it is: a warning to stay off the case. He turns to leave. "Densley!"

"What?"

"Where are you going?"

"*No gat...*" he says, innocently, and walks out.

The sun had set, but the moon is half-full, and there is light, and anyway he knows the road well. He walks back the way he came. He could go to Carlo's house, and play. He could go find Maxwell, who is probably diving for fish. He could go up to the Anglican Diocese, where there is a working generator and his aunty lives and where he could most likely watch a movie. But now he is on a case, and he has a cat to find, and so he chooses none of the above, but makes his way beyond the creek that marks the border of the town, to Isabel's house.

DENSLEY INVESTIGATES THE SCENE OF THE CRIME

Isabel's house lies beyond the creek, on Densley's family's land, which extends all the way from the end of town, beyond the point, and over to the other side and the small island that lies beyond. A narrow path leads to the house; it sits in a clearing in the bush. It is dark here, despite the moon, and there are many mosquitoes. It is quiet, and no lights are on.

As he approaches the house he calls softly to the cat, but nothing stirs in the bushes beside the black lizards that live there, and they scuttle away from him unseen with a rustle of leaves. The door of the house is closed, and the door of the kitchen too.

He stops and looks around. There is a truck's tire lying on the ground, which might have once been a swing. The place feels abandoned, which makes Densley suddenly uncomfortable: homes, here, are to be lived at. They are rarely empty. He looks around again and notices that the wooden bench from the kitchen is outside. Guests, he thinks. Someone had been here—to see Esmeralda?

Esmeralda is Isabel's mother. She is pretty, a girl from the Torres Islands where people are a mix of Polynesian and Melanesian, and Densley likes her. He wonders who her visitor was. He notices that the mat has not been used, which suggests it was not a family visit: for doesn't family sit down with you on the mat? But perhaps it was an elderly person, who needed a bench in the absence of a plastic chair, like the ones Densley's parents have, which they bring out for the guests. He sits down on the bench. Why wasn't it returned to the kitchen before Esmeralda left? She must have been in a hurry, he thought. He looks down.

There is the butt of a cigarette lying on the ground. Densley is excited again; the case is going well. He carefully picks up the cigarette end. Esmeralda doesn't smoke. Women don't. So the visitor must be a man. He looks—the cigarette hasn't been smoked down to the stub, but left when it was not yet finished. He had assumed it was a Peter Jackson, the only brand sold in the shops in Sola, but no—the writing around the base says it is a Marlboro. So, he thinks. A visitor, someone from out of town. He must have come on the flight from Santo in the morning, there are only three flights a week and today was airport day. Someone wealthy—he smoked his cigarette like a *waetman.*

Could a *waetman* have come to see Esmeralda?

It seems unlikely. But now that he has surveyed the scene (finding no trace, it had to be said, of the cat) he was provided with plenty of leads. He decides he had learnt as much as he could: the answer won't be here, he thinks; and he decides to pursue the investigation into the town.

Down The Mean Street Densley Must Go

Down the mean street of Sola Densley goes; for the city, his city, has the one street *nomo*, a wide dirt track running from creek to creek. It is a dark road, and a long one, but Densley walks it like one who is its master; for he had grown up here, on this swathe of coast, and knows the road the way he would one day want to know a woman. He walks past the football field and there is a great silence around him. He walks past the wharf, and the moon glints off the dark water like a watching eye. He walks past the offices of the Province, and the empty police station, and the offices of Health and Education, and still he meets no one on his way. It is just another quiet night in Sola, and he can smell the smoke of many small kitchen-fires, and hear, as he draws nearer to the centre, the many small sounds of families at rest.

Yet one family at least is not amongst them. His cousin's daughter Isabel, who is now in Densley's house, crying for her missing *puskat*; and her mother, too, is not where she should be, in the house with her child, for she too is missing, in a town where it is impossible to disappear.

He reaches the town; a strip of stores and *nakamals*, and as he approaches there is the first light, and he can hear singing, and he thinks—*of course*, and feels disappointment again, for the solution is simple, and obvious.

He comes to the Market House. It is an open concrete floor, a high roof above it, and benches set down underneath the electric neon light from a generator. Sitting on the benches are rows and rows of women, clad in flowery island dresses, Mother Hubbards they were called, back when the missionaries came and brought them to the islands: and the women, aunts and cousins and neighbours to Densley, sit and sing with enthusiasm if not grace. They are the Choir, and they practice for their trip to the Solomon Islands in the summer, where they will represent the Diocese of the Banks and Torres in a great big gathering of the church.

He searches for Esmeralda. This is where she would be, of course: for she too is in the choir, and will be going to the Solomons later in the year.

Yet he cannot find her. Scanning the benches he can see no trace of her, and so he waits, until the conductor of this orchestra, the august Augustus, a wide and genial man who had only ever beaten his wife before their children came, approaches him in one of his circles around the hens. "Yes, Densley?" Augustus booms a whisper.

"Is Esmeralda here?"

Augustus turns to check and returns a puzzled face back to Densley. "No," he says. "I haven't seen her."

Densley turns back. She is not at the house, nor at his mother's. And she is not at Choir. It leaves him with little; and yet, knowing where she is *not* is a clue in itself, a way of eliminating the easy answers. Think, then; and he does, and of the visitor of Esmeralda's, with the expensive cigarette. Was he staying in one of the guest-houses? There are three, and he had already passed the first. But he thinks of that cigarette, and he thinks he knows where he should go: for it is long after *sava* now, and the kava-bars are open, and a man who smokes, women business or no, has only one place to go at this hour. And so Densley turns, feeling again the comforting butt of his gun against his hip, and though he is a boy, he decides to check the *nakamals*.

An Encounter in a Kava-Bar

The *nakamals* of Sola are many and varied; huts with wooden benches and small quiet yards, and a single dim light. Densley begins to go through them, but cautiously. He is not sure what he is looking for. He is going on a hunch. When he goes into Father Sol's *nakamal* the place is almost deserted, only the old priest sitting behind the counter, and two men from the village of Vetuboso, from the other side of the island, sitting quietly in a corner sharing a cigarette of *lif-tabak*. "Yes, Densley?" Father Sol says, "Are you looking for your father?"

Densley's father is a great drinker of kava; and at some times Densley or his brothers must carry him back from the *nakamals*, and particularly on second Fridays, for they are pay days here, in this Province town. But not tonight. "Have you seen Esmeralda?" he says, and sees Father Sol's surprised frown, and a shake of the head given, Densley suddenly thinks, a little too hastily. "This is a *nakamal*," Father Sol says, and implicit in that the gentle rebuke: it is not a place for women.

But Densley knows that sometimes women do come to the *naka-mals*. They sit on the benches outside, and they come accompanied by their men, and many get their kava to take-away, and drink in the privacy of their homes; and he hears that in Port Vila, the great capital city of Vanuatu, which has many trucks, men and women mingle freely in the *nakamals*. But this is not Vila; this is Sola, and some things here are simply not done.

Nevertheless, he persists. He goes to the Vice-Chairman's *naka-mal*, and to the Former Secretary-General's, and to the Chief Mechanic's, and it is there at last, right by Qiqi Store with its generator noise and electric light, that he makes a discovery.

"Densley..." says a voice he had half-expected to hear, and the way his name is pronounced, with half a growl and half amusement, makes him suddenly tense.

He says, "Samson?" and turns around to the dark figure sitting by its own on the bench outside.

"Come here!" His cousin rises and hugs him. The smoke of his cigarette curls behind Densley's back and reaches his face. Samson smells expensive: aftershave, and smoke, and just the hint of alcohol on his breath, which is the mark of a successful man, for beer is expensive here and hard to come by.

"What are you doing here?" Densley says when Samson at last releases him. His cousin's movements are slow and careful, and he sits back down on the bench with a sigh suggesting much kava. "Family visit," Samson says. "Let me buy you a shell."

"I don't drink kava," Densley says, and Samson laughs and says, "You are a man now, Densley. Come!" and he rises again and takes him and leads him inside, and says to the man behind the counter, "One shell for my friend here."

The man pours two measures of brown dank liquor into the polished coconut shell, and the same for Samson. "Drink!" Samson says. Densley takes the shell. But he doesn't yet drink.

"Where is the cat?" he says.

"The cat?" Samson says, eyes opening in comical surprise. "What cat?"

"Isabel's cat," Densley says.

"My cat," Samson says, and the humour leaves his eyes. "My girl. What's it to you?"

Densley shrugs, feeling clumsy and small beside his cousin. "Drink," Samson says, and he pushes the shell gently up until it reaches Densley's mouth.

He drinks. The kava tastes like earth and mud, and as he drinks it he almost gags, but doesn't. The kava makes his lips numb, and he feels a slowness spreading through him, a heaviness that wasn't there before.

"Good!" Samson says, and he claps him. "Give me your shell." He takes it from Densley's hands and returns both shells to the counter, and measures out two hundred vatu onto the counter. "And one for yourself," he says, and tosses another one hundred vatu coin onto the counter.

"Come!" he says, turning to Densley. Already he has a newly-lit cigarette in his hand. "Let's sit down and talk."

The word, in Bislama, is *storian*, which means to talk, to chat, to *story*. Yet Densley's tongue feels heavy and unresponsive, and his cousin, for his part, seems content to sit back, his shirt off, the cigarette casually dangling from his lips.

"Where is the cat?" Densley says again, at last, and his cousin laughs and lays a hand on his shoulder and says, "I have the pussy."

He makes Densley uncomfortable. "Why?" he says.

"Because I'm taking it with me," Samson says, and his smile is lazy, but his eyes are not. "What's mine is mine, Densley. And it stays mine."

"Where's Esmeralda?" Densley says. And then, "Are you taking her too?"

The smile remains. "But you left her."

"And now I'm back. So?"

"So does she want to go with you? And Isabel?"

"You drink kava, but you are not yet a man, Densley," Samson says, and the smile flickers and dies. "Go. Go back home to your mummy."

"Isabel wants her cat," Densley says.

"And she'll have it. And all the cats she wants, in Luganville."

"You're going to take her away? But she doesn't want to!" Anger makes him stand up, and clears the weariness of kava.

Samson flicks his cigarette away. The light arcs overhead and falls by the side of the road. Suddenly he rises, and before Densley can do anything to stop him he cuffs him, hard, on the back of the head, and then a slap, and another, and another: an assault Densley is helpless against.

Samson moves away. He is breathing hard. His teeth gleam in the dark. "Go home, boy," he says. And then, patiently, almost gentle: "When you're a man you'll understand."

He pushes Densley, not hard, towards the road. Densley goes, not looking back.

DENSLEY CRACKS THE CASE

When he gets home his mother is furious, but not at Samson. At him. "I told you -!" she says, and stops. Densley says, "What?"
"Why do you have to get into trouble? What did you *do*?"

"I found Isabel's *puskat*," Densley says, and then he smiles, even though it hurts.

"Isabel is asleep," his mother says, and she suddenly looks tired. "She has a long way to go tomorrow."

"But why?" Densley says.

"Because sometimes we don't do what we want," his mother says, and her eyes make him uncomfortable. "When Isabel grows up and becomes a woman, she will understand."

Densley doesn't argue with his mother. But he goes and looks for Isabel, who is sleeping on the mat in the next room, and he gently shakes her awake. "*Gerrap*, doll," he whispers.

"Densley?" she says, opening big round eyes full of sleep. "What is it?"

"Your cat," Densley says, and he extracts the small furry animal from its makeshift hammock inside his shirt, and gives her to Isabel.

"*Puskat!*" Isabel cries, and she hugs the sleepy animal and smiles at Densley and lies back down, and in a moment both her and the cat are asleep.

"Where did you find it?" his mother asks when he comes out again.

"*Olbaot*," Densley says, and he says no more, and his mother doesn't ask. For he did not go home after leaving the *nakamal*, but rather to the one place where he knew he would find Esmeralda now: Samson's mother's home, which lay beyond the creek towards the airport. He had gone, and he had found Esmeralda there, sitting alone with the old woman, both staring at the small fire in the kitchen. The cat was whining softly against the door.

Densley took the cat quietly and went home. It was only when he went to bed that night that he realised that, somewhere along the way, he had lost his gun.

Be careful what you wish for.

Other Wishes
by Richard Zwicker

CHRISTMAS WREATHS, TINSEL, and stars lined the smoky walls of the White Hart Pub. Memories of holidays, softened by distance, battled the harder edges of my current situation. The lack of possibilities in my dark flat once again sent me here, where I'd at least find a cast of characters. I pulled apart a wishbone from the remains of my chicken and chips dinner, the larger piece remaining in my left hand. 1902 had been disappointing. I wished to be a part of something positive in 1903. In hindsight, I advise not to bet the house on wishbones.

"Did you make a wish?"

I looked up and saw standing before me a young, dark-haired woman with a pleasing face and an expensive fur coat draped over her shoulders.

"Yes, I wished there was more meat on this chicken."

"Are you hungry? I could buy you something."

"No, I'm fine. To what do I owe this interest in my eating habits?

"Your name is Rodney Balsam?" I saw no reason to deny it.

She slid into a chair at my table. "The man behind the bar says you are a detective who might help me." Her voice had a low purr that made me want to bark. I glanced up at Frank, who smiled as he wiped down the bar counter.

"That depends on the kind of help you want."

"Do you believe in magic?"

I winced. "I believe in people who, by the quickness of their hands, are able to deceive others."

"That's not the kind of magic I mean. Perhaps you're not the right person for this job."

"Maybe not, but I doubt you'll find him this late, so why don't you tell me what's on your mind?"

She loosened her otter coat. "It's not an easy story to tell. I insist you listen to its entirety before judgment. If you can't do that, I will go elsewhere." I agreed to the terms. "My name is Rebecca Stewart. My father, William Stewart, was killed under suspicious circumstances. He was a librarian and died on the job." I tried to think of life-threatening aspects of a librarian's job but came up blank. A disagreement over an overdue book? Speaking too loud? Rebecca read my puzzlement. "A bookcase fell on top of him," she said. "He was 50 years old. It was rumoured that, despite being a librarian, he had a lot of money, but it was never found. His death was ruled accidental, but I know it wasn't."

"And you know this how?"

"A month ago a retired soldier named Morris came to me with a wild story. He said he had known my father and had received a strange gift from him: a mummified monkey's paw."

"I would have asked to be taken off his Christmas list."

She ignored my comment. "Actually, Morris had originally given the paw to my father and after a short time, my father returned it. This paw was fashioned by an Indian fakir who wanted to prove fate ruled our lives and those who tried to change their destiny did so at their peril. He put a curse on the paw, enabling it to grant three wishes to its owner. Inevitably, the wishes were granted, though they never pleased the wisher and appeared as deadly coincidences. According to Sgt. Major Morris, my father had his three wishes."

"What did he wish for?"

"I know only that the third one was for death. He specified that in his suicide note."

"He left a suicide note? Then why do the police think his death was accidental?"

She frowned. "Because they never saw it, and they don't know about the paw. I want to know why my father wished for death, and what his other two wishes were for. I am also very interested in finding out if the rumors about his money are true. If it exists, I would be most generous in sharing it with whoever helped me locate it."

I glanced at her outerwear and the otters that would never again body slide into a pool of water. "By the looks of your coat, you're not doing so bad right now."

She patted her fur-covered shoulder. "This is a gift from an admirer. That's not the same as having your own money. You have to do something to get gifts."

I imagined what someone like her might do to earn something

like that coat. She gave me a pouty, imploring look that would have made a beggar out of any man. "Will you help me?" she asked.

I could have said my rates were not cheap. I could have said the logistics of this case might very well stretch to the edges of the British Empire. I could have said I was busy. Instead, I said, "Yes."

She smiled like a Cheshire cat and pulled her father's suicide note out of her pocketbook. At twenty pages, suicide saga was more like it. I riffled through the folded sheets of paper and looked helplessly at Rebecca. "I take it you've read the whole thing."

Her eyes narrowed. "Of course."

"Maybe you could give me a quick summary of its most salient points."

"I'd prefer you read it yourself and come to your own conclusions."

I nodded. "That would be my preference too..." I made sure to finish the rest of the sentence only in my head..."if I had some kind of guarantee I'd live to be 130."

I retreated to the privacy of my office to study the longest suicide note in the history of the written word. The first thing I discovered, after only a few paragraphs, was William Stewart had not used one of his wishes to become a good writer. He favoured an unwieldy, passionate prose style that made this reader feel like an emotionally stunted attendee at a stranger's funeral. A typical sentence: "How could I have known, how could anyone have known, that in suddenly being presented the opportunity to sate three of my deepest heartfelt desires, to appease the hitherto unappeasable, that in doing so it would bring the crushing weight of the world down on my overburdened skull?" Clearly, I was dealing with what had been an overwrought man. But while navigating the non-essential phrases and adjective-infested waters of run-on sentences, my thoughts turned to self-preservation. The note being literally the biggest clue, however, I had no choice but to read and deconstruct.

I gleaned the following: Sergeant Major Howard Morris and William Stewart were mere acquaintances, brought together by a love of books. Perhaps to escape the realities of his work in the armed forces, Morris liked to read the novels and stories of Rudyard Kipling. Whenever he could spare the time, he did this in the reading room of the London Library where Stewart worked. The librarian eventually recognized Morris from his habitual appearances and the two talked about their favourite works. Stewart encouraged the Sergeant Major to expand his reading, recommending other works set in India. During one of their conversations, Morris mentioned dismissively that while stationed in Bombay he'd acquired a monkey's paw. Stewart showed such interest that the Sergeant Major gave it to him as a gift.

A lieutenant friend of mine gave me Morris's home address, a slightly rundown building of flats in Hendon. The night I went there, he wasn't home, but a neighbour informed me he was likely in the nearby Three Arrows Pub. I had only a vague description of what the man looked like, "a tall burly man, beady of eye and rubicund of visage." When pointed out to me, he was leading a discussion at a table with five sycophants hanging on his boisterous words. What his eyes lacked in beady-ness was compensated by his rubicund face. Before introducing myself, I listened to his story, a dramatic account of death-defying heroism he and his men had performed in the first Boer War. I allowed him to receive a few more oohs, ahhs, and jolly goods before I interjected myself into the conversation, introducing myself as a private investigator.

The beady-ness appeared in his bloodshot eyes. I asked if his friends could excuse him for a moment while we went to another table to discuss a private matter.

His fleshy hand swept through the air. "I have no secrets from my brother soldiers."

"Maybe not, but I do."

Sensing the Jovian gravity of my tone, he nodded, looked suspiciously around the table, then downed the remains of his pint of ale. "I'm always happy to do my part in upholding law and order," he muttered, raising his not inconsiderable bulk and accompanying me to an empty table at the far corner of the pub.

"What's this all about?" he asked, brushing some crumbs from the tablecloth to the floor.

"You have no idea?"

He scowled. "I have many ideas, all of them presently muddled. You, on the other hand, have one. Let's save time, shall we?"

"Fair enough. I have been hired by Rebecca Stewart." That got his attention. "She's interested in how a certain monkey's paw contributed to the recent death of her father. She told me he got that paw from you."

"Someone should have cut my hand off before I picked up that damned thing."

I told him what I knew about the paw, including its ability to grant its possessor three disastrous wishes. Hearing myself say this, I felt as if I'd attributed the British national mint's wealth to the benevolence of the Easter Bunny. "How much of this is true?" I asked finally.

"All of it," Morris said, soberly as possible.

"You'll pardon me if I say that's hard to believe."

"I'd question your sanity if you didn't. At first, I thought it was a joke. It cost next to nothing."

"You talked to the fakir that put the curse on it."

"I did. Scrawny, dirty Indian chap wrapped in a loincloth and turban, with a silver beard no self-respecting bird would nest in. He practically forced the paw on me."

"Yet he said disaster would befall anyone who made wishes with it? Not a great selling point."

"I didn't believe it, so it didn't matter."

"But you say it does work."

"Stewart found that out the hard way, didn't he?"

"So it would appear," I said. "He left a suicide note saying his third wish was for death." I waited for a reaction but got none. "Do you know what his first two wishes were for?"

"He never told me."

"Might one of them have been for money? His daughter is under the impression he had some hidden."

He eyed me sadly. "We didn't talk about money."

I looked to see if anyone was following our conversation, but the pub's customers ranted, stared, and drank in their own incurious worlds. "For the sake of argument, let's say the paw does work, and the fakir cursed it for the reasons he said. What good would it do him to give it to you? He must have known he'd never see you again. How's he going to know if the paw proves people can't intervene with fate?"

The burly shoulders shrugged. "I can't answer that."

"Where is the paw now?"

Morris looked disgusted. "A week ago I was visiting friends and, after many drinks, I did what I should have done in the first place. I tossed it into the fire, but Joseph White, that fool, yanked it out."

I asked for the address, which was in Basildon. "I have just one more question. Did you make any wishes with the paw?"

Morris met my gaze. "I've done stupid things in my life, but not that stupid."

The next day I hired a coach that took me to the hills of Basildon. Lakeshore Villa reminded me of a dinner jacket belonging to someone who'd given up eating. The Whites, an elderly couple, showed neither surprise nor interest when I introduced myself and told them I got their name from Sgt. Major Morris. Mr. White, instead of inviting me in, merely moved away from the front door so I could enter. The tasteful paintings adorning the walls and the abundance of furniture told me this had once been a comfortable home, but there were tell-tale signs of neglect. The sofa had a rip on one of the cushions, and the eighth step of their staircase jutted out of sync.

We sat down in the living room.

"Do you play chess?" I asked, noticing a table set up in the middle of the room.

Mr. White's eyes flickered. "I used to play with my son, before he died. He always beat me though." At the mention of the son, Mrs. White wept softly.

"Let me get to the reason I'm here. Sgt. Major Morris told me you had in your possession a monkey's paw."

That set off Mrs. White like a hole in a dam. "That paw was a cheat! It was supposed to grant three wishes, but all we got was one. We wished for Herbert to return and he didn't, he didn't, he didn't!" Her husband excused himself and led her out of the room. A full two minutes passed before he returned alone. He sat back down on the sofa and struggled to speak.

"She won't admit the paw did grant three wishes," he said finally. "The first was bad enough. I honestly didn't know what to wish for because I had all I wanted, but Herbert and my wife talked me into wishing for two hundred pounds."

"And the wish came true?"

"Yes! Herbert was killed in an accident at the factory. Our compensation was two hundred pounds. A week after his death my wife, desperate with grief, made me wish for Herbert to come alive again."

"You're not telling me that came true."

His eyes blazed. "I'm telling you it did. A week after our poor son was laid to rest, that devil paw raised him up and he was knocking on our very door."

"You saw him?"

"No. My first wish killed my son. My second wish turned him into a fiend." He took a wheezing breath. "My third wish freed his soul." He explained that before his wife could open the door, he commanded whatever was at the door to return from whence it came.

"So you still have it?"

His face grew ashen. "I do, and it's staying with me. Morris said it can grant only three sets of three wishes each. I have no desire to allow anyone else to go through what I have."

I wanted to see paw, but White was adamant. "The father of my client had three wishes, and you had three. Who had the other three?"

He looked at me as if I was stillborn yesterday. "Sgt. Major Morris, of course. I thought you said you talked to him."

"I did. He told me he didn't make any wishes."

White sniffed. "You must have misunderstood him. He told us that the paw was of no use to him because he'd had his three wishes. He wouldn't say what they were, but having had three of my own, I understand his reticence."

So the good Sgt. Major lied, either to me or the Whites. I'd have to find out which, and more importantly, why. So far I'd spoken to three people: Rebecca, Morris, and White, and all three of them were, to various degrees, convinced the paw possessed wish-granting powers. None of them had definitive proof of this, however. To my limited knowledge, the only people with that were William Stewart, Herbert White, and perhaps the fakir. The first two were dead. My chances of finding the fakir in Bombay were equivalent to finding a particular blade of grass in one of the stomachs of a sacred cow. But that mattered only if I believed the paw was magical, which I didn't.

If I could confirm neither Morris nor Stewart had his wishes granted, that would help prove to Rebecca the paw had done nothing for her father either.

"I need to ask a few more questions, Mr. White. Did Herbert have any enemies at work?"

"What difference does that make?"

"It's just a routine question."

He thought for a moment. "As a matter of fact, there was a gentleman Herbert had a disagreement with. Herbert liked to hunt, and someone named--Walker, I think it was—used to give him a hard time about it. Imagine a British citizen against hunting."

"Do you know if Herbert mentioned the monkey's paw to anyone?"

He shrugged. "He died the day after we got it. He thought it was all rubbish and was making jokes the whole time. But I suppose he could have told someone at work."

I made a mental note to check up on the animal lover. Perhaps the simian dismembering had driven him to extreme action. Maybe he killed the librarian in anger of all the trees chopped up to make books. First, however, I wanted to get to the bottom of Morris's three wishes.

I found Morris at his home. His hands shook as he opened the door. His eyes were fiery as if he'd just sat on a tenterhook. He was not surprised at my reappearance, however, and bid me follow him to his dark living room. I could barely make out the mementos of his army days adorning the wall space. On a tea table sat a glass and some bottles that definitely weren't tea.

"Drinking alone tonight, Sgt. Major?" I asked, sitting to the right of the incriminating table.

He refilled his glass with some scotch. "I wasn't in a storytelling mood," he said plaintively.

"That's good because neither am I." I mentioned the discrepancy between Mr. White's and his own version of who made wishes on the monkey's paw.

He sighed. "On that night I was in a storytelling mood."

"Morris, two people have died under very strange circumstances." My voice rose in frustration. "You're involved. Either you start telling me the truth or I can get the police involved."

"I just want this episode to be over with. The paw is cursed, just not the way some people believe." He told me another story, this one less imaginative but more veracious. William Stewart had come into some money, but not from the monkey's paw or his meagre librarian's salary. He was blackmailing a married baron who made his liaisons at the library. Stewart got greedy and raised his demands. The nobleman, a loose cannon, threatened him and Stewart feared for his life. During a conversation with Morris, the subject of the paw came up. Stewart got the idea to use it to fake his own death, hence the suicide note. The plan was foiled when the bookcase fell and killed him.

"I believe the baron sabotaged that bookcase," Morris said.

I remained skeptical. In my business I'd spent many years dealing with blackmailers. I'd seen them killed by unbalanced associates, unbalanced lovers, and unbalanced victims. This was the first time one had been killed by an unbalanced bookcase. At any rate, Morris retrieved the paw, allowing the family to believe it caused Stewart's death. He hoped the mystery of the paw would act as a smokescreen over Stewart's blackmail activity and Morris's knowledge of it. The Whites' involvement with the paw was an accident. During a visit Morris couldn't resist pulling out the paw, which he had kept on his person since the death of Stewart.

"So when you told White you'd made three wishes..."

"I lied."

"You are aware he made three wishes and, according to him, they came true."

Morris scowled contemptuously. "I guarantee it wasn't due to any magical properties of the paw."

I next went to the library. Though I like to read a good yarn as much as the next fellow, I hadn't been in this library in some time. They'd taken my card away, saying I'd never returned a copy of *Fanny Hill*. I told them I never returned it because I'd never taken it out, but they insisted I reimburse them. Out of principle, I refused, so we were at a standoff. Unfortunately, the person I ended up talking to about Stewart was the same evil old lady that had voided my card, and she remembered me. Between condescending sneers, she told me Mr. Stewart had worked for the library upwards of twenty years and was very meticulous. The decrease in funding for the library in recent years, resulting in fewer new books and a general run-down condition of the premises, was a source of disgruntlement for him. She believed the drop in funding was responsible for the drop of the rickety bookshelf that killed him. She scoffed when I asked if Stewart had any enemies, saying only someone who would steal a copy of *Fanny Hill* would ask such a question. With palpable insincerity, I thanked her for her time.

That night in my apartment I thought of what I would wish for, were the paw magical and mine. That I could bring back my wife, dead of consumption three years ago. That life was free and I could search for what interested me. That someone rich and beautiful as Rebecca Stewart wanted me for reasons other than unexplained death and hidden money.

The textile factory was a gray, frightening looking monstrosity, with tiny windows, roaring machines, and belching smokestacks. A crusty, cigar-smoking foreman led me past poorly lit rows of sad-eyed men and women anchored to their repetitive tasks, until we came to Amos Walker.

Walker looked to be in his early twenties. If he was a vegetarian, he'd managed to eat enough plants to amass an incipient potbelly. His curly hair reached shoulder level and he had a full beard. He was too busy to stop working, but as that meant he couldn't leave, it worked in my favour.

"Is your name Amos Walker?" I asked rhetorically.

"And if it is?" he asked, not looking up from the moving belt.

I introduced myself. "I'm investigating the death of Herbert White. What was your relationship with him like?"

"Similar to my relationship to you. My oppressive bosses have this belt moving so fast we barely have time to develop relationships."

"I heard you made the time to criticize his hunting."

"So? Can I help it if I don't think shooting down a fox in cold blood is sporting?"

"Maybe you did something about it that you could have helped. Like stop him from ever hunting again?"

Amos laughed. "Everyone knows White died by getting caught in a machine. I wouldn't wish that on anybody except the people that own the machine. That definitely wasn't Herbert White."

I asked if White had ever mentioned a monkey's paw. He didn't know what I was talking about. I then interviewed the foreman, who I found in his office drinking coffee and smoking another cigar. His name was Greavey and he seemed to have a low opinion of everything. That included the factory, me, himself, and especially Amos Walker.

"I don't know why that guy is working here."

"For a paycheque?" I asked.

Greavey shook his big head. "Everyone else counts the days until we get paid. Half the time Walker forgets to pick his up until after the weekend. He's got money, that one."

So Walker wasn't what he seemed. Welcome to the club. "I understand a collection was taken up for the family of Herbert White."

"That's right. Couldn't have been much of a collection though. Most of these blokes don't have a shilling to spare."

"It came to exactly two hundred pounds."

"Two hundred pounds, my eye. Two pounds is more likely."

I could think of no reason why Mr. White would lie about that. "Whose idea was it to make the collection?"

"Now that you mention it, I believe it was Walker's."

Another visit to the Whites confirmed that the nervous young man who brought them the money was indeed someone who looked exactly like Amos Walker. I confronted him as he ate lunch with the rest of the workers at a long, dingy table. He quickly ushered me back to his position at the temporarily stopped conveyer belt.

"What do you want to know?"

"How much of the collection for Herbert Walker came out of your pocket?"

He glanced nervously at the eating men and women. "Don't tell them, but almost all of it."

"So Herbert did tell you about the wish for two hundred pounds."

Walker nodded. "The idea of someone carrying around a monkey's paw was repulsive to me, so I decided to play a joke on the family."

"Rather a sick joke."

"I'm an environmentalist. I'm not supposed to have a sense of humour. I'd decided to give them the money on some pretext before Herbert had his accident. After he was killed, I wasn't sure, but I figured I might as well go through with it. The money would help his family and if I could scare a few more people from buying animal parts, then all the better."

"Why do you work here if you have money?" I asked.

"This is an experiment. I'm trying to get a better understanding of the working class." He frowned. "I'm not sure how much more I want to learn."

"OK, so your donation to the Whites explains the first wish, but not the last two."

"What were the last two?"

"His father wished he'd be alive again, then when he heard the knocks on the door, he wished him dead again."

Walker's eyes widened. "When did he hear the knocks?"

"A week after Herbert died. Late, maybe 10 o'clock."

Walker stared at the floor and sighed. "That was me."

"What do you mean?"

He explained that after leading the family to believe that the paw had magical powers, he was racked with guilt. Preserving nature was important, but so was educating the public. Playing with the minds of people such as the Whites went against his philosophy. So that night, not sure what he was going to say, he knocked on the Whites' door, but when they didn't answer, he gave up.

Surrounded by the familiar ambience of the White Hart, I had a drink with Rebecca Stewart, two weeks after we'd first met.

"This is what we know," I said. "Your father was blackmailing a baron for a monthly sum. He made quite a bit of money, but eventually the baron balked, and Stewart feared for his life. After planning to fake his death, he actually did die, in what was probably an accident. The monkey's paw was a diversion. Though it didn't have any special powers, in a way the fakir was right. A number of people tried to use the paw to change things, but all with unhappy results."

"But where is the money?" she asked.

I sized her up one last time. "You don't care about how your father died, or the monkey's paw, do you?"

"I was curious. I had to know if he was involved in something dangerous, that I needed to worry about. But those answers take me only so far."

"Well, his money could be in a bank under a false name. He could have buried it. If he didn't want people to find it..."

"Who is this baron?"

"I never found out that either, but if he hasn't contacted you by now, he's probably content to leave things as they are."

She opened her purse and handed me my fee. "I'll pay double for his name."

Again, I saw that pouty look that implied, only you can help me. Her beauty, cold as the London winter, was like the monkey's paw. One could easily think Rebecca Stewart granted wondrous wishes that turned out to be undesirable. Had she always been this way, or had she been hardened by men acting like fools in her presence? Like the paw, which had no power of its own, our irrational beliefs supplied something that could only result in disappointment.

"I'm not interested, but..." I reached into my pocket and placed the monkey's paw onto the table. After some doing, I convinced White to surrender it. "You could try this. It supposedly has three more chances." Rebecca looked at it, and then me, with revulsion.

I walked away.

We are what we wish.

They say you can't go home again, but you can't get away again, either.

Afterwards
by Jeff Poole

AFTER THE DIVORCE Fred Buckley used some of his frequent flyer miles to leave it all behind. It had been an acrimonious affair. He traveled a lot for his job, so he'd piled up enough mileage to travel anywhere on the planet he wanted to go, round trip. He chose the Croatian coast because it was June. That's when the weather was just turning nice and the Italian tourists hadn't overrun the place yet. Two days after the divorce was final Fred landed in Dubrovnik, rented a car and took the coastal highway to the Peljesac Peninsula and on to the town of Orebic where he caught the ferry to Korcula. It was a city on an island of the same name with the perfect mix of European mystery, age and modern amenities.

He and Marion had honeymooned in Korcula. They'd spent three days alternating between the bedroom and the restaurants located amongst the small city center's old ramparts.

It had been easy to find a room this time of year. People would approach you with offers, and small photo albums containing pictures of the interiors of their establishments. A young woman with hip huggers and heavy eye makeup approached him when he parked along the street near the docks.

"Look, kitchen with bath. You say me how long you stay." She said holding her photo album aloft.

Fred dickered about the price, more out of habit than concern for finances, and settled on the equivalent of 30 bucks a night. The price would double by August, but he'd be long gone by then. He followed the woman up labyrinthine stairs; the Croatian coast was all about the stairs, until they entered a small courtyard filled with yellow and blue flowers surrounded by tan brick walls. He threw his suitcase into his new quarters, and started wandering around town.

Not much had changed since he'd last been here. It was still bright and beautiful with the same orange and blue colors, water, old brick, and large white cobblestones. The Adriatic was nearby every-where you went. You could smell the water on the warm air. Boats were plentiful, as were the early tourists, backpackers and young lovers. The lovers depressed him so he went looking for the Café Bar Massimo. It was in one of the old castle towers of the city center. You had to climb a steep narrow ladder before stepping onto an open air platform overlooking the water. You could order a drink, which was hauled up on a manually operated dumbwaiter, and enjoy the best views in the city.

Fred found the Massimo, and since it was only seven in the evening, getting a seat wasn't difficult. He entered the lower floor and clambered up the ladder, looking up at the wood framed sky as he ascended. He stepped up onto the platform and made his way to a table near the bartender. Everything looked the same. Same young crowd, hell, it even looked like the same bartender, but he knew that couldn't be the case. He ordered a rum and coke, without the lime, and watched the people wandering the ancient street below.

Men had once stood guard here. Probably the last place you wanted to be back in the day. Now it was exactly where you wanted to be. Unless it brought back memories you no longer enjoyed.

The waiter delivered his drink, which he slammed down in one gulp. After dropping a Croatian twenty kuna note on the table, Fred gingerly backed down the ladder and made his way to his rented room.

How long would it take them to find him if he meandered purposelessly from destination to destination? He'd exchanged a lot of money before he'd left home. Normally it's always smart to use ATMs, you get the best exchange rate, but they only allowed you to take out a limited amount, and it wouldn't be long before his account was locked anyway. Besides, they could trace his location by his withdrawals. He could take the ferries, the buses or walk. There'd be no credit card to trace, and in Croatia it could be weeks before they were able to locate him by his passport. He could wander towns, sleeping in hostels or parks for weeks.

After returning to his room Fred realized he'd been wearing the same clothes for days. He showered and changed into jeans and his old school sweatshirt then walked down to a convenience store and bought two four-packs of Croatian beer and potato chips.

They'd find his car, and they'd assume he'd boarded the catamaran to Hvar Island, but they wouldn't be sure. He could have taken the short ferry ride back to Orebic, rented a scooter with cash, and went back towards Dubrovnik. It was the only purpose in life left to him now, seeing how long he could elude the authorities.

On the way to his room he stopped by the ticket office and bought his ticket for Hvar. Fred knew tickets for the six a.m. departure could go quickly, and he wanted to be one of the first passengers. It was always nice to be early and get a comfortable seat.

He and Marion had spent weeks going up and down this coast. They'd hop onto a ferry and go wherever it took them. If that meant backtracking they didn't care. She'd been a flirt even then, but he was younger and more certain of himself in those days. But he'd gotten older and as her flirtations became more pronounced he'd become less comfortable and more irritated by it. Marion had seemed unaware of his slow, quiet wrath. She'd become more blatant in her philandering. Marion started coming home later, and then sometimes not at all, saying she'd been with a friend all night.

When he entered the room he became aware of its furnishings for the first time or rather, the lack of them; a chair, a bed, and a small TV. The tiny adjacent 'kitchen' had a microwave, and a toaster oven. He didn't care. He'd just wanted to be near the city center and the departure docks.

He'd come home early to get ready for the office party and there she was, rolling around on the floor with Mel Dyer, his boss. They hadn't even bothered to get to the bedroom. Mel had seemed embarrassed, but Marion had just laughed while shooing him out the door. "Come back in an hour." At the party later that night he'd endured his co-workers' knowing looks as Mel and Marion spent most of the evening talking by the punch bowl.

Fred drank beer while he watched American reality shows, the only thing broadcast in English, until he dozed off. The sound of the city's tower bell woke him. Fred showered again, put on the same clothes, and headed towards the dock. It was still dark, and wet and cold enough to be comfortable in the sweatshirt. He'd left his suitcase behind, and was carrying a plastic bag with the potato chips and the few beers he had left.

He relished the idea of having no possessions except the clothes on his back. He felt almost weightless, and carefree. Nothing he did mattered anymore. The end was a foregone conclusion, what little happiness or piece of mind he was searching for would have to be gotten in the next few days or weeks. That was all he had.

As he made his way towards the departure point, people were starting to fill the streets. Not all for the ferry or the catamaran. Some wanted to get to the fish market before the later morning throngs swarmed the vendors. They wanted first pick of this morning's catch.

When he came home after the divorce Marion was waiting for him with a suitcase. He said nothing as he walked in the door, and she set the case in front of him with a bored expression on her face. It was time to move on she said. He grabbed Marion's arm and started dragging her towards the basement. At first she was amused. Marion laughed and she started to struggle, disdainfully at first, then with more urgency as he seemed oblivious to her efforts. As he started to drag her down the stairs she panicked, his emotionless blank stare, and absolute silence finally scaring her into action. Marion fought but it was useless. Fred been a wrestler in high school, a good one. He manhandled her with ease.

Fred was nearing the dock. The catamaran already had its engines running. People were milling on the wharf waiting for the ticket booth to open. He wandered along the edge of the dock, looking at the brightly colored little boats bobbing on the small morning waves.

Marion fought as he tied her up. When she started scratching at his eyes he rained blows on her until she put her hands down. She screamed that Mel would be arriving soon. That was the only time he smiled. He gagged her, bounded up the stairs and went through the cutlery looking for the knife they used for the Thanksgiving turkey. Making his way back, he tapped the blade against the wall and strolled leisurely down the steps. It took only a few minutes with the knife to make Marion realize what the rest of the night held in store for her. He made certain she was still securely trussed and went back up the stairs to wait for Mel.

"Sir?" A small boy with an Australian accent awoke him from his reverie. He was standing by the boarding walk. He must have gone into auto pilot.

"You here for the catamaran to Hvar? They're getting ready to leave."

Fred shook his head. He'd changed his mind. He tore up his ticket, and walked the half mile to the dock on the other side of the city center.

Marion must have given Mel a key. Fred allowed him to take a few steps into the house, and grabbed him from behind in a choke hold. It had been so easy. When Mel awoke he was momentarily annoyed. What kind of ridiculous game was weak old Freddy trying to play? His eyes registered concern when he realized he was bound securely. Fred watched with a satisfaction he hadn't felt in years as Mel turned his head and saw what was left of Marion's face and her terrified expression. Fred knelt down between them and looked into Marion's frightened eyes. She was still alive, and she'd have a front row seat while Fred "worked" on her lover. He stood back up, leaned over Mel, and smiling down at him said, "Well now, Melvin. Let's get started."

The ferry back to Dubrovnik had just arrived when he reached the dock. People were already forming a line for tickets. Fred stood behind an elderly couple, and made small talk while the line slowly inched forward. After getting his ticket he waited by one of the old walls of the city for the call to board. He could see small, dark forms moving along the bottom of the ancient brick ramparts. Cats.

He remembered now. The city had feral cats living in some of the old alleys. He was like them now—alone, separated from normal civilization, completely removed from his previous life.

There weren't many people on this particular crossing. It was an early Sunday morning so the heathens not at church had the ferry to themselves. Once on board, he made his way to the coffee shop and ordered a latte. It cost too much, but he ordered it anyway. He sipped his overpriced beverage while watching Korcula recede into the distance. There was a young couple sitting on a bench, holding each other, giggling and kissing. Fred paused in front of them and smiled. They smiled back. He reached into his back pocket, and pulled out his wallet. Fred looked at the Croatian notes within; purple, yellow, red.

So much more colorful than our U.S. notes. European money has such a festive appearance.

He closed the wallet, handed it to the puzzled young man, and made his way to the back of the boat.

Later, when questioned by the police, the young man said he could swear he saw the strange man smile before he jumped into the waiting propellers below.

One half-caf demitasse skim vanilla crime latte, please.

The World's Best Coffee
by C. D. Reimer

THE COFFEE SHOP overflowed with people drinking coffee and eating pastries when Mark walked through the doors to step in front of the pastry display case, where the separate lines for paying and picking up orders at the opposite ends of the counter mingled together. Looking at the pastries with undecided interest, he listened to the new orders being given by the customers and the finished orders being shouted out by one of the Goth girls with multiple nose and ear-piercings.

The world's best coffee is a simple affair.

An order for a medium mocha with whip cream by a woman named Georgia caught his attention. Looking over his shoulder when she walked by, he noticed that she was an average-looking woman in trendy workout clothes. If she had a toy dog in hand, she would've blend in well at this European-style shopping center and upscale community. He glanced at the monitor above the espresso machines where the Goth girls kept track of the orders. Georgia's order was number five, which meant a five-minute wait. He continued looking at the pastries as people jostled around in the lines behind him.

"Medium mocha with whip cream for Georgia," announced one of the Goth girls, placing the drink on the counter before moving on to the next order. "Your drink is ready."

Mark stepped in front of Georgia to sweep the counter in one perfect motion to pick up the drink, a heat sleeve, and some napkins. He was out the door before anyone noticed that something was amiss. Once around the corner, he slowed down his pace to blend into the crowd and sip his drink for the first time.

The world's best coffee is free.

"Hey, you!"

Mark looked over his shoulder to see Georgia at the corner, waving at him. He frowned. When an order disappears from a crowded coffee shop, the Goth girls get pissed off that they have to make another drink for an already impatient customer. That's it. Never in all his years of coffee diving has anyone bothered to follow him out.

Turning left into a covered alleyway that served as the outdoor dining area for a seafood restaurant and led to a parking lot on the other side, Mark stepped over the rope fence to enter the restaurant from the side. Walking past the hostess like a customer coming back from the restroom, he sat down in the waiting area with his back against the window and holding the coffee cup between his legs. When Georgia jogged through the alleyway into the parking lot, he went out the front door. He crossed the southbound street, hop-scotched around the large chess pieces on the brown-and-tan flag-stone chessboard as the players cursed him for interrupting their game, and crossed the northbound street to blend back into the crowd.

The world's best coffee lets you enjoy the neighborhood.

"Hey, you!"

No further than the next intersection down did he find Georgia following him again. This time she was across the street as she waited for traffic to clear through the intersection before coming over to him. He pretended not to see her by looking straight ahead. Noticing the bookstore entrance at the corner, he danced through the slow traffic with the coffee held up high on his fingertips like a French waiter with a serving tray, and swung open the door to go inside. He hurried past the cashiers into the magazine section as if he was dying to see the swimsuit issue of *Sports Illustrated*, ducked through the greeting card section, and made his way over to the metaphysical section with the tarot cards and reading-the-future books. His immediate future looked dicey if this persistent woman didn't get off his case. Coffee diving shouldn't take this much effort. With the corner of a bookshelf and the drink raised to his lips to hide his presence, he watched her come through the front doors.

The world's best coffee lets you appreciate the deeper meaning of life.

Georgia came in breathless. She had one hand hanging on to something inside the front pocket of her sweatshirt that Mark hadn't noticed before. He frowned. *Cell phone?*

When she talked to the cashiers, one of them pointed towards the metaphysical section. He slipped into the manga section where some teenagers—and some adults who never quite grew up—were sitting on the floor to read their favorite manga. With a watchful eye on where she was among the bookshelves, he passed through the history section to find the elevator hidden away at the back of the literature section. Exiting the elevator at the second floor, he walked over to the crowded cafe to pick up *The Wall Street Journal* from a table, sat down with his back against the wall with the coffee placed between his legs again, and waited with the paper raised up in front of him.

Georgia came up the escalator as expected, made one circuit around the floor without glancing at the cafe, and went back down the escalator. He read an article on how more people are drinking specialty coffees than plain old regular coffee these days.

When he finished off his drink, he threw both the coffee cup and the newspaper into the trash, and stepped out on to the balcony over the bookstore entrance that had an excellent view of the shopping center. On the street below was a parked police cruiser, a police officer and Georgia. She pulled something out of the front of her sweatshirt to hand over to the officer. He froze.

A black leather tri-fold wallet.

Mark's hand crept to the back pocket where he kept his wallet to find the usual bulge gone. That was *his* wallet down there. No wonder she'd been persistent. Maybe it wasn't about the coffee after all.

"Hey, you!" Georgia pointed up at him. The officer looked up. "You dropped your wallet at the coffee shop." She then turned to the officer, still pointing at him. "This is the creep who stole my coffee."

Perhaps this wasn't the world's best coffee after all.

He'd do anything for her. No, really. Anything.

Zero Sum Game
by Doug J. Black

BARSTOW WAS MY paradise.

Not something you hear very often about a Mojave town with triple the violent crime of the average U.S. city.

Barstow, the idiot offspring of the gold rush and the continental railroad, is surrounded by registered sex offenders living in plywood shacks and one of the Wal-Mart greeters is a leathery two-dollar whore named Bamby.

Slanders aside, my knack for forgery and Sally's uncanny expertise in growing the finest strains of bud, left alone and barely noticed out there in San Bernardino County, made this my own empire nestled within Desert Town, U.S.A. Neat packaging, like the occasional welding gig and regular donations to Toys for Tots, kept me below IRS radar.

The only thing missing was a cure for Sally.

Then, some guy named Joe Franco descended into my life and hooked me up with that sick son-of-a-bitch in Vegas. Son-of-a-bitch being Homer Skelton.

So my first meeting with Homer culminated with poor Joe Franco's heels hanging over the edge of a crater of fire the size of an indoor swimming pool. All duct tape and tears.

And me on the hot seat.

The local desert vagrants called that place the "Gates of Hell."

Don't I know it.

Not sure I would have done it any different, though.

Twenty years ago Sally was the hottest stripper in Los Angeles, working the classiest joints. Heart-shaped ass and copper-colored hair. Slinking like a big, sexy cat across that stage. Five hundred dollar lap dances. She gave it up to wander the desert southwest with me, a broken-down veteran, after Uncle Sam bent me over, fucked me with no lube, and sent me away with a minuscule disability check.

Then inflammatory breast cancer struck like a viper and reduced her physique to concentration camp levels. IBC usually struck woman over fifty—Sally hadn't even hit forty yet. Purple chemo sores covered her once-smooth skin—and the treatment wasn't working. Next step was invasive surgery or a trip to a special treatment center.

That morning, she wore the same flowing red scarf she always wore to hide her baldness, even when staying in. Even when she'd taken down all the mirrors in the place.

She sat at the kitchen table in front of the candle infuser, filling in the blanks of a page of Mad Libs. A minty cloud of eucalyptus floated off the dish and wafted through the trailer. Some kind of eastern music flowed from her iPod speaker, something like a wind chime and ocean waves.

The percolating dark roast beans in the kitchen beat out the pine aromatherapy scent. I walked around her to the cabinets and rummaged for my favorite chipped mug, stolen from an IHOP in Toluca Lake.

"Good morning," she said. Her soft voice had gained a rough tinge through sickness and exhaustion.

"Mornin'. You turned my alarm off." I poured my coffee and walked over to her, smiling. I'd forecasted the attempted sabotage. "I'm about to roll out."

She continued filling in the nouns, verbs, and adjectives of a puzzle called "Moving to a New Town." Since her diagnosis, she'd been picking the most bland, obvious words to complete the story. For a noun, she'd pick "sofa" instead of "douchebag" or "platypus." For verbs, she'd use "drive" or "love" instead of "jerk off" or "freebase."

Alternative medicine, I figured.

As for the silence, two decades with that fiery angel and I knew what was coming—she was priming one last salvo of an idea to keep me from going to Vegas and meeting Homer.

"That warehouse downtown is still for sale. Nice place for a fabrication shop." She didn't look up from her scribbling. Halfway through a word, she dropped the pen and winced, squeezing the fingers of her hand tight with the other.

Peripheral neuropathy from the chemo. She'd say it felt like she was holding her fingertips on top of a red-hot stovetop.

A few seconds and it'd subside. She continued writing.

I stood behind her and rubbed her neck. Her collarbone and shoulder were hard edges and lumps threatening to break through her dry skin. "Can you pass me my smokes?"

"This'll be hilarious when we both have cancer, huh?" She looked up and handed me the opened soft-pack of Camels. Her eyes, sensual orbs of bright blue, were the only features left untouched by the scourge. "Look, this Joe character just rubbed me the wrong way and I've got a bad feeling, Danny." She laid her thin hand on top of mine. "Like it's time to cash in and disappear."

"I know." I leaned down and kissed her forehead. "I gotta go. Long drive."

The screen door screeched and slapped shut behind me like a giant mousetrap. Through the sheer white curtains, I took one more look back at Sally. Her shoulders quivered and she covered her face with her hands.

According to Joe Franco, I'd be coming back through the door with some hope for her. It'll be easy, he said.

Joe Franco was a cousin of a friend's roommate. Or something like that. I think.

I come home one night, about a week earlier, after working a project down in Victorville, and there's some Italian guy with slick, black hair sipping Chai tea with Sally at the kitchen bar. He was just a fresh-faced kid in a form-fitting suit, looking like he should be modeling underwear on a Rodeo Drive billboard instead of hanging out with middle-aged folk in a doublewide.

Sally had that look on her face like her bullshit detector had gone off the scale, yet was trying to be a polite hostess. She'd opened her mouth to make the introduction, but Joe popped up from the stool and grabbed my hand in a firm, sweaty shake.

Joe rattled off a list of names of people he'd gone through to get referred to me, while he pumped away, cheesy grin showing fine car-salesman teeth.

I looked over his shoulder to Sally. She was doing that thing where she rubbed the back of her neck, hard, with her eyes closed.

"I need some help," he said. "Everyone in the county says you're the man." He finally let go of my hand. "Could be a win-win for both of us." He jerked his head back toward Sally. "Is there anywhere we can chat? I've got a business opportunity for you."

"We're fine out here," I told him.

We sat back at the bar and he outlined a plan to oust some up-and-comer in Vegas, a guy named Homer Skelton. Said Homer had hurt some people he was close to and that he was working to bring him down, off the clock from his day job at the ATF.

He flashed his laminated ID card. If it was a fake, it was done by one of the best. I was impressed—it was either the best fake credentials I'd ever seen, or there really was a fed sitting at my bar, drinking tea.

"Homer's looking to expand across SoCal and eventually wedge Ramon Juarez out of LA," said Joe. He took a sip of tea. He actually stuck a pinkie out while he lifted the cup. "He's amassing as much talent as he can for his grand push."

"And this has what to do with me?" I asked.

"I just want you to meet him and offer your services. You'll have a tiny, hand-made recorder with you." He put his thumb and forefinger together with a gap about the size of a dime. "All I need is for you to confirm his plans. He won't know it was you that helped me out." He looked at me and stopped his goofy smile. "One meeting with Homer, and anything you get in the process is yours to keep. It'll be easy."

He stood and thanked Sally for the tea.

She returned the pleasantries without looking at him or standing.

Joe didn't wait for an answer. He just said he'd be back in a day or two to talk details and logistics. "You've got a fine lady there, too. You're a lucky man." He leaned forward and spoke lower. "Too bad about the...well, you know."

He was good.

Joe let himself out of the trailer and we sat in silence until the sound of his car had faded.

"He smells like shit," said Sally.

"Probably just spilled his bottle of Hugo Boss on himself this morning. My eyes were watering."

We didn't laugh.

I lay awake that night, thinking about the fresh, papery smell and crisp feel of the stacks of cash that would bring Sally back from the edge of death.

A string of brass bells jingled when I opened the door to Homer's custom chopper workshop. The familiar metallic ozone scent of arc welding filled the air inside the steel Quonset hut.

Two men played cards at a desk, both wearing light jackets that revealed the butts of automatic pistols. One of them, tipped back in his chair with his boots kicked up, said, "Have a seat, Mister Hendricks."

The gunman across from him, a younger kid with acne and a cowboy hat, slapped his cards on the table. "Eat shit!" he yelled, smiling, and then shuffled the cards.

I sat down behind a worn coffee table layered with issues of *People Magazine* and *Guns & Ammo*. Led Zeppelin II had just started blaring through the speakers placed around the workshop, angry guitar riffs of "Whole Lotta Love" buzzing through the workspace and rattling my brain into the seismic beginnings of a small headache.

In the back corner, three men knelt over a motorcycle frame, wearing welding shields and working over a sparking area. The sound of the welding was like frying bacon broadcast over a megaphone.

A scream ripped through the workspace from another corner. More sparks and the orange licks of an oxyfuel torch flame shone through a brick-enclosed welding station. Through the dingy rubber flaps that covered the entry, I could see the shapes of at least three men.

There would be a few minutes of quiet in that corner and then the torch would light up again, accompanied by the agonized screaming.

I couldn't focus on who the Kardashians were screwing or the performance statistics of the Remington Versa Max.

The gunmen continued their card game, never once looking toward the shrieking and crying taking place within spitting distance of where they sat.

I rubbed my sweaty palms on my thighs and wondered what Sally was doing.

By the end of the flip side of Led Zeppelin II my bad back was tightening like an invisible fist clenched my spine. The two goons playing cards had been trading insults as hands were won and lost.

A short man walked out of the curtained area, flipped his mask up and poked his head back into the enclosure. "Patch him up and send him back up to Reno." He took off his gloves and shield and walked toward me. "Danny, right? C'mon back," he said. He put on a pair of horn-rimmed glasses from his breast pocket, at least half a century out of vogue, and wrapped in medical tape across the bridge.

Two men walked out of the curtained workspace, dragging a fat, sweaty man with a towel wrapped around his hand. He sobbed and muttered to himself with his eyes closed. "I'm sorry, Mister Skelton. It won't happen again!"

"I know, Bobby." Homer watched his goons drag the fat man out a back door.

I walked behind the card players, my back stiff twisting with each step. The man in the glasses held his hand out. "Homer Skelton. Nice to meetcha."

A barrage of screeching chairs, thumps, and insults erupted behind me. The two goons stood locked in a Greco-Roman wrestling pose, the taller, balding man swinging the kid around like an empty suit of clothes. Homer peered around my shoulder, a full head shorter than me. "Shut the fuck up! We've got a guest."

"Sure thing, Mister Skelton," said the older guy. They continued their argument in a whisper.

A pinch from one of my lumbar nerves shot up through my back and I winced.

"Ouch. You got a bad back, too, huh?" said Homer. "How'd ya get yours?"

"A helicopter accident in Desert Storm," I said.

"Oh, yeah? Who were you with?" He beckoned for me to follow him and he walked to the water cooler.

"Second Marine Division."

He poured water into a cone shaped paper cup. "Is that right?" He downed the water, crumpled the cup, and tossed it over his shoulder. "I was with the 82nd Airborne over there. I guess a jarhead like you probably thinks us Army dogs were all fucked up, huh, Danny?" He stared up at me, his thin lips just a slash across his face, dark eyes waiting on my answer.

I had nothing. My heart just pounded while I tried to think of something neutral to say to extricate myself from the topic.

He lunged forward and punched me in the shoulder. "Lighten up, man. I'm just fucking with you!" He pushed the glasses up his nose and loosed a braying laugh, like he was hyperventilating. "Oh, man. You should've seen your face."

One of the card players, the one in the cowboy hat, piped up behind me. "I heard him shit his pants from here, Mister Skelton."

Homer's smile disappeared. "I didn't ask you, dipshit." He directed his gaze back to me. "I hear we both have welding in common, Danny." He stepped closer. "You know what I love about it?" Glasses pushed back up his nose and he stared straight ahead, eyes glazed. "Holding six thousand degrees in the palm of your hand, almost as much heat and power as the surface of the sun. Molding something as solid and unyielding as steel into anything you want." His eyes focused back into mine. "Ya know?"

Welding for me was just a paycheck, but I nodded.

"I like to think of myself as a modern day Hephaestus. Armorer of the gods." He chuckled and clapped me on the shoulder. "I started off in arms. Anyway, enough banter. Look, with me in Vegas and you in Southern California, I wanna punch a hole across southern California and pry old Ramon Juarez right out of LA." He highlighted the *punch* with a jab from his sweaty fist. "I could use a man with talents as diverse as yours. An equal partnership once we drive those wetbacks out." He put his hand on my shoulder and walked alongside as he led me to the front door. "We just have one loose end I want to tie up before we can begin." He stopped next to the desk and looked over at the card-playing cronies. "Tony, call up Mort and tell him we're on the way. And you, dipshit..." Homer slapped the younger kid in the back of the head, knocking the cowboy hat into his eyes. "Bring the truck around." He looked back at me. "I got something to show you. You're gonna get a kick out of this, my man."

The same dread that slithered through me on the way to Vegas that morning squeezed tight.

A gunmetal Suburban pulled up to the door. I sat between Homer and Dipshit in the back seat. Tony, the older, balding gunman, drove. A Hispanic tough in a leather jacket rode shotgun.

I patted my pack of smokes in my breast pocket, wanting to assure myself it was still there. Or maybe I wished it wasn't. I already had what I needed for Joe. Homer was quick and to the point. I'd hoped to leave with a generous sum of cash by then—not driving off to an unknown destination.

I hate surprises.

Homer leaned his head back and was snoring before we'd pulled out of the gravel parking lot of the fabrication shop. Tony pulled an old cassette tape out of the center console and popped it in.

Michael Jackson.

Thriller.

Volume up to the max, pop synth crackling through the worn speakers. Not a peep from Homer.

Fuck me.

Dipshit sang the entire time we drove through Death Valley. Every word.

Michael Jackson was finishing up side B when we approached a fence that curved away on both sides into the tan and sienna landscape. Rusted, twisted links about the height of a basketball hoop. A white sign in bold red letters informed us of the penalties for trespassing on government property. A gaping hole had been pulled back in the chain-link barrier, big enough for the vehicle to drive through. Homer stirred, murmured, and wiped a line of drool from the corner of his mouth. "Ah, here we are."

Ahead was another Suburban, parked with a group of people standing outside. As the distance closed, the outlines solidified into the forms of men puffing on cigarettes. Just past where they mingled appeared to be a crater or depression.

Homer was watching me lean forward to look ahead at our destination. "What'll you see this shit, Danny."

We pulled up next to the identical SUV and parked. Upon stepping out, I could feel heat emanating from the enormous hole in the desert floor, a prickly blast on my cheeks and forehead. Homer walked over to the men who had already arrived. I walked to the edge of the crater, wary, like a kid, afraid I'd get sucked in or something.

What I looked down into was a seething lake of burning ash and slag. Small flames littered the surface, about six feet down from where I stood. Twisted steel beams jutted like broken bones tearing through skin. Parts of the crater seemed to crawl, like some type of lava. Standing that close it felt like being too close to enormous bonfire—my face was burning and itching from the immense, drying heat.

Homer's two gunmen stood further down from me along the edge. Tony grabbed Dipshit's jacket like he was gonna shove him in and laughed when the kid jumped back and cussed.

"Beautiful, isn't it?" Homer had walked up behind me. "Back in the seventies, an oil rig inadvertently hit a deposit of natural gas here, causing the structure to collapse into a toxic sinkhole. In order to avert a major environmental catastrophe, they had to burn the rig. They thought the fire would be out in a matter of days. But it's been burnin' ever since." His smile grew. "The local white trash call it the Gates of Hell." He looked back at the group who'd arrived before us. "Bring him!" He looked back at me and rubbed his hands together. "I tossed and turned all night, waiting for this. Like a kid before Christmas."

The SUV door opened and two goons pulled out a man, mouth duct taped. I knew the fancy suit and curly black hair.

Joe Franco.

They dragged him to the edge of the crater next to Homer.

Joe was crying through the gray tape. His eyes darted. His sobs gained a frantic pitch when he saw the lake of fire.

Homer's smile was gone, replaced by a cold slab. "He's one of Ramon's." He slapped Joe's cheek and squeezed his face like he was a long lost nephew. "Joe's ambitious. Been trying to gather up intel for his boss." He slapped Joe again, harder. "Probably wanted this piece of the pie once he got rid of me."

Joe shook his head and sobbed through the gagged mouth.

Homer walked up and stood shoulder to shoulder with me. "Push him in."

"Into there?" I said, pointing in to the burning hole.

He nodded.

"You're fucking kidding me."

Homer took off his leather welding jacket and threw it to Tony.

He held up his forearms. They were completely covered, from shirt-sleeve to wrist, in tattoos of skulls, each about the size of a silver dollar. "You know what each of these means?" He pointed into the crater. Homer smirked. "I like to hold tryouts before I start a new partnership."

"No way, man."

He kicked at a rock on the ground. "Gee, that sucks. Especially with Sally and all." His eyes darted up at me to catch my reaction.

It shouldn't have been a surprise, a guy with connections like Homer's, knowing about my life. It still sent a freezing bolt up my spine when he said her name, though.

Homer laughed, loud, head tilted back and looking up at the sky. "I know what you're thinking," he said. "But if you say no, I'm *not* gonna tell you you're both gonna get tossed in, like some TV bad guy."

Dipshit and Tony both chuckled, low, like it was some private joke.

"What'll happen is you'll walk back to Barstow empty-handed. You see," he pointed at Joe. "This guy's goin' in, either way."

Joe fell to his knees and shook his head, mumbling through the gray strips of tape.

My stomach clenched and bile rose, but not for Joe. It wasn't my fault Joe got pinched. It was that moment of selfish clarity, where I blamed everything in my life for that situation I found myself in. From shitty parents to the helicopter accident that got me booted from the Marines.

And everything in between.

Even Sally. It makes me sick to even think badly about her, but I was mad at the world that the most important thing in my life needed six figures of cash to even have a shot of getting better.

"It doesn't make good business sense to toss *you* in there." Homer walked up to the edge of the crater and looked in. "I may need a man of your talents soon. Your cuts will be just be substantially reduced." He turned back toward me. "And if you do say no to me now, if I find out you're working for those spics in LA, both you and Sally are gonna barbecue together."

His threat to Sally caused me to calculate that about ten running paces separated me and Homer, who stood at the lip of the crater with his back to it.

Seven gunmen. All armed, but relaxed and far from vigilant.

He should fry just for bringing her name up.

But then I saw Sally and her sad blue eyes, telling me all the ways I could have avoided this.

And I pictured her sitting in that trailer, alone, wasting away. Me, shot up and tossed into that hole, turning into a charred piece of charcoal.

Sally's really why I came to Vegas. Every time she pukes from the chemo or cries herself to sleep from pain, it chips off another piece of my heart.

I walked toward Joe. His eyes widened and he tried to talk, reasoning through his gagged mouth, like he wanted me to remember we were supposed to be on the same team.

Joe's last mumbles under that tape were what made up my mind.

ahn-ne. ahn-ne. Like he was trying to say my name.

Homer leaned toward his mouth, interested at the muffled syllables Joe mumbled.

I had to write off Joe as a sunk cost.

So I pushed him.

It's better to rip the band-aid off quick, then to take all day peeling it back.

Right when he passed that point where gravity took over, I already wished I could reach out and pull him back.

But then, to do what? Beg Homer to be a humanitarian?

Joe tumbled back and landed with a dull splat onto the lava. There was a second of shocked silence, where his body registered the intense pain eating away at him, and then he thrashed like he was having a grand mal seizure. His screams grew higher in pitch. Smoke rose from his back and flames licked at his coat and jeans. The molten surface slowly covered him, like burning quicksand. The stink of scorched flesh wafted up to us. The whole time, Joe shook and twisted and flopped.

Homer watched with his hands clasped behind his back.

Someone retched behind me.

Dipshit was peeking down at Joe, giggling.

Joe had flipped over and red-hot slag sizzled the skin on his face.

"Look, Tony, he's doin' The Worm," said the kid.

Joe's clothes burst into a full flame. Smoke obscured the spectacle and burned my eyes.

Homer put his arm around my shoulders. "Come on." He led me away from the crater and his goons.

He looked back and gestured to one of his men in the van. The man brought a briefcase and handed it to Homer. He snapped his fingers in my face. "Hey? Danny?"

For a minute I thought the whole thing was a daydream. But then I could smell the scorched flesh.

"Here's a retainer for future services." He laid the briefcase flat in his arms and lifted the lid. Stacks of Ben Franklin, about ten disapproving glances staring up at me. "Fifty thousand. And more once we hammer out the details of our new enterprise."

He slammed the case shut and handed it to me. He yelled at his men to get ready to depart. "Hey, Danny, how 'bout a smoke?" He patted his trouser pockets. "I'm all out."

My stomach dropped into my feet. "Huh?"

"Yeah, a smoke. What's the matter, you that squeamish?" He snatched the pack of Camels out of my pocket. "Got a light?"

I snapped open my zippo and held it under the cigarette while it dangled from the corner of his mouth. He took a monster drag that killed a third of the cigarette.

Homer pulled out a slip of paper. "Call this guy when you get home and he'll start putting things in motion." The trucks started up behind us. "Now let's get out of here, huh?"

He got in the back seat and I told him I just needed a minute.

"Sure thing, Danny."

I walked to the edge of the crater. The only sign that a human had been there minutes earlier was the patch of fresh ash in the rough shape of a person.

I placed a cigarette in the corner of my mouth and looked at the pack of smokes. Joe had hidden the small voice recorder inside the package. No bigger than a dime.

My half of the deal with Joe.

I threw the whole pack into the lava, still half full of smokes and the damning piece of surveillance equipment. It popped and then melted. I tossed in the cigarette in my mouth, too. The thing tasted like cat shit.

"What'd you do that for?" yelled Homer from the truck.

I told him it was time to quit.

"Yeah, I know what you mean." He flicked his cigarette butt out the window and pulled his head back into the truck.

I walked over to the SUV. The suitcase felt like it was full of bricks, pulling me down to the ground so the desert could swallow me up. The cash would go straight to an account that wouldn't raise any red flags when I used it to pay the first instalment of Sally's treatment. I told myself I wouldn't even go home first—that way she wouldn't be able to argue with me, because it'll be a done deal.

It didn't really matter if Joe was ATF or enterprising criminal, or both. Driving away from there that day, I figured, better Joe than Sally.

But that was the wrong equation. It was my soul I'd traded.

A Derringer Award winning author, more than 100 of **Patti Abbott**'s stories have appeared in various print and online venues. She is the author of two ebooks through Snubnose Press, *Monkey Justice* and *Home Invasion*. You can find links to some of her online stories at http://pattinase.blogspot.com.

Ed Ahern resumed writing after forty odd years in foreign intelligence and international sales. He has his original wife, but advises that after forty-six years they are both out of warranty. He has had forty-six stories published thus far, with a novella, *The Witches' Bane* due out this fall.

Nick Andreychuk is a Derringer Award-winning mystery writer. His stories have appeared in magazines such as Austin Layman's *Crimestalker Casebook, Over My Dead Body!* and *Sherlock Holmes Mystery Magazine*, and anthologies such as *Techno Noir* and *Who Died in Here?*

Tom Barlow is an Ohio, USA writer. He is the author of the short story collection *Welcome to the Goat Rodeo* and the science fiction novel *I'll Meet You Yesterday*. His work has been featured in anthologies including *Best American Mystery Stories 2013* and *Best New Writing 2011*, as well as many magazines including *Hobart, The William and Mary Review, The Apalachee Review, Temenos, SQ Magazine, Needle, Thrice Fiction* and *Redivider*.

Aislinn Batstone is an eclectic reader whose tastes range from the 19th century classics to 21st century mysteries. Since having children, she most enjoys light-hearted fiction where the bad guys get what they deserve—or turn out to be not so bad after all. Aislinn writes across genres and her short stories can be found in anthologies and magazines including *Stringybark Stories Australia, Every Day Fiction, Timeless Tales* and upcoming in *Nature Futures*. Aislinn lives in Sydney with her three favourite people and the world's best dog.

Doug Black is serving in the United States Marines and recently completed his second deployment to Afghanistan. His fiction can be read in *Blue Lake Review*, *Literary Orphans*, *The Quotable*, and *Smokebox* and is upcoming in *Pantheon Magazine*, *Bete Noir*, and James Ward Kirk's *Demonic Possession* anthology.

Craig Faustus Buck is an L.A.-based journalist, nonfiction book author, TV writer-producer, screenwriter, short-story writer and novelist. Among his six nonfiction books, two were #1 NYT bestsellers. He wrote the Oscar-nominated short film *Overnight Sensation*. He was one of the writers on the seminal miniseries *V: The Final Battle*. His first noir novel, *Go Down Hard*, which his agent is currently shopping, was First Runner Up for Killer Nashville's Claymore Award. His indie feature, *Smuggling for Gandhi*, is in preproduction. Stark Raving Group published his novella, *Psycho Logic* in 2014, the novella's prequel, his short story "Dead End," is an Anthony Award nominee, and his short story "Honeymoon Sweet" was selected for inclusion in the Bouchercon 2014 anthology.

Frank Byrns has published over three dozen short stories in a variety of genres; his crime stories have been or will be featured in *Shotgun Honey*, *Powder Burn Flash*, *Everyday Fiction*, and *The Rusty Nail*.

Gary Cahill is a member of Mystery Writers of America New York, International Thriller Writers, and the NYC-based Irish American Writers and Artists. His first short story, "That Kind of Guy", ran as a *Black Mask*-style homage in *Ellery Queen's Mystery Magazine*. Other work has appeared in print and e-formats with *Short Story Me Genre Fiction*, *Pulp Empire*, *The First Line Literary Journal*, the *Big Pulp Magazine* speculative fiction anthology *The Kennedy Curse* and *Shotgun Honey*. He worked in Hell's Kitchen for nearly twenty-five years, and is now a staff member across the Hudson at the Weehawken NJ Public Library. He thinks *noir*-ist David Goodis got it right when he wrote pretty much anything.

Sally Carpenter is native Hoosier now living in Moorpark, Calif. She has a master's degree in theater from Indiana State University. Her plays *Star Collector* and *Common Ground* were finalists in the American College Theater Festival One-Act Playwrighting Competition. She also has a master's degree in theology and a black belt in tae kwon do. She's worked as an actress, college writing instructor, theater critic, jail chaplain and tour guide for Paramount Pictures. She's employed at a community newspaper. Her books in the Sandy Fairfax Teen Idol mystery series are: *The Baffled Beatlemaniac Caper*, 2012 Eureka! Award finalist for best first mystery novel; *The Sinister Sitcom Caper* (Cozy Cat Press) and *The Cunning Cruise Ship Caper* (in progress). Her short stories include "Dark Nights at the Deluxe Drive-in" in *Last Exit to Murder* anthology and "The Pie-eyed Spy" in *Kings River Life* ezine. Her blog is at http://sandyfairfaxauthor.com

Sarah M. Chen has worked a variety of odd jobs ranging from script reader to bartender and is now an indie bookseller and private investigator assistant. Sarah's crime fiction short stories have appeared in the *Deadly Ink 2007 Short Story Collection*, Shannon Road Press's *Little Sisters, Volume 1*, *Plan B: Volume 1*, and Elm Book's *Death and the Detective*. Sarah is contracted with Stark Raving Press to publish her noir novella *Cleaning Up Finn*. Visit Sarah at www.sarahmchen.com.

Ian Creasey lives in Yorkshire, England. He began writing when rock & roll stardom failed to return his calls; since then he has sold fifty-odd short stories, mainly science fiction and fantasy. His debut collection, *Maps of the Edge*, was published in 2011. Ian's spare time interests include hiking and gardening — anything to get him outdoors and away from the computer screen. For more information, please visit his website at http://www.iancreasey.com.

Peter DiChellis is a new mystery-suspense writer. His sinister tales appear in a handful of publications, most recently at *Shotgun Honey*, *Over My Dead Body!*, and in *The Shamus Sampler* private eye anthology. For links to his published stories, visit his site, *Murder and Fries*.

Jim Downer has loved mystery novels since his youth. He started with The Hardy Boys and Sherlock Holmes and later graduated to Elmore Leonard and James Ellroy. He makes his home in Denton, Texas.

A high school teacher and fiction writer living in central Missouri, **Kevin R. Doyle** has seen his short stories, mainly in the horror and suspense fields, published in over twenty small press magazines, both print and online. In 2012 his first e-book, a mainstream novelette titled *One Helluva Gig*, was released by Vagabondage Press. In January of 2014 Barbarian Books released his first full-length mystery novel, *The Group*. Doyle teaches English and public speaking at a high school in rural Missouri and has taught English, journalism and Spanish at a number of community colleges in both Kansas and Missouri. He's currently shopping for a publisher for his newest novel, *The Litter*. More information can be found at www.kevindoylefiction.com or at www.facebook.com/kevindoylefiction.

John H. Dromey was born in northeast Missouri. He's had short fiction published in *Alfred Hitchcock's Mystery Magazine*, *Gumshoe Review*, *The Literary Hatchet*, *Mysterical-E*, *Woman's World* (a minimystery), and elsewhere.

MJ Gardner's writing credits include a handful of student and local writing awards from the 80s and 90s, including two Golden Fang awards from the Vampyres listserv. In 2008, her short story "Juliette: A Cautionary Tale" was optioned for a low-budget film in Britain.

Robert Guffey's first book of nonfiction, *Cryptoscatology: Conspiracy Theory as Art Form*, was published by TrineDay in 2012. His first book of fiction, a collection of novellas entitled *Spies & Saucers*, is forthcoming from PS Publishing in 2014. His short stories have appeared in such publications as *Catastrophia*, *Flurb*, *The Mailer Review*, *Pearl*, *Phantom Drift*, and *The Third Alternative*. Forthcoming short stories include "The Advertising Man" in *Nameless Magazine*, "The Wedding Photographer" in *Postscripts #32/33*, and "What Is a Cloud?" in *Chiron Review #97*. He's currently a lecturer in the Department of English at California State University—Long Beach.

Michael Haynes has recently sold stories to *Intergalactic Medicine Show*, *Beneath Ceaseless Skies*, *Daily Science Fiction*, and Otto Penzler's upcoming anthology *Kwik Krimes*.

Martin Roy Hill is a former newspaper and magazine journalist, now working for the Navy as a military analyst. His nonfiction work has appeared in *Reader's Digest*, *LIFE*, *Newsweek* and *Omni*, among others. His fiction work has appeared in the *Alfred Hitchcock Mystery Magazine* and *San Diego Magazine* among others. He is also the author of two books, *Duty: Suspense and Mystery Stories from the Cold War and Beyond* and *The Killing Depths*, a military mystery thriller.

Adam Howe is a British writer. Writing as Garrett Addams, his short story "Jumper" was chosen by Stephen King as the winner of the On Writing contest. His fiction has appeared or is forthcoming in *Nightmare Magazine*, *Horror Library 5*, *FEARnet*, *Of Devils & Deviants*, *One Buck Horror*, *Beware the Dark*, and *Bete Noire*. He has recently completed a trio of bizarro noir novellas, "Of Badgers & Porn Dwarfs," "Frank, The Snake, & The Snake," and "Jesus In A Dog's Ass." Tweet him @Adam_G_Howe.

Ahmed A. Khan is a Canadian writer whose works have appeared in several venues including *Interzone*, *Strange Horizons*, and *Anotherealm*. He has also edited the anthologies *A Mosque Among the Stars* and *Dandelions of Mars: A tribute to Ray Bradbury*.

Author, poet, blogger and journalist **BV Lawson**'s award-winning work has appeared in dozens of national and regional publications and anthologies. A three-time Derringer Award finalist and 2012 winner for her short fiction, BV was also honored by the American Independent Writers and Maryland Writers Association for her Scott Drayco series. A novel featuring Scott Drayco, *Played to Death*, was published via Crimetime Press in July 2014. BV currently lives in Virginia with her husband and enjoys flying above the Chesapeake Bay in a little Cessna. Visit her website at bvlawson.com. No ticket required.

Mary Ann B. Lee is a former government worker, now retired and living in Florida. Her crime and mystery stories have appeared in the on-line magazines *Mysterical-e*, *Cynic Magazine* and *Everyday Fiction*.

Laird Long pounds out fiction in all genres. Big guy, sense of humour. Writing credits include the magazines: *Blue Murder Magazine, Hardboiled, Damnation Books, Bullet, Robot, Albedo One, Baen's Universe, Sherlock Holmes Mystery Magazine*, and *Plan B*; stories in the anthologies *The Mammoth Book of New Comic Fantasy, The Mammoth Book of Jacobean Whodunits, The Mammoth Book of Perfect Crimes and Impossible Mysteries*, and *Action: Pulse-Pounding Tales*; and the standalone book *No Accounting For Danger*.

Josh MacLeod has been writing for going on ten years (and seriously for the past year or so), working on novels and short stories. He would like you to know that being put on a reality TV show was the worst witness protection plan ever, but writing fiction is perhaps not much better. This is his first published story, and writing the story was perhaps easier than deciding on this bio. Make of it what you will.

S R Mastrantone writes and watches too many documentaries about dinosaurs in Oxford, UK. He's working on his first novel, and his short fiction has appeared or is forthcoming in places like *The Fiction Desk, Shock Totem, Lamplight, Vignettes from the End of the World* and *carte blanche*. He also plays in a band, though you probably didn't need to know that.

Michael McGlade has had 35 short fiction stories appear in journals such as *Spinetingler, Ambit, Grain, J Journal, Green Door*, and *r.kv.r.y.* He holds a master's degree in Creative Writing from Queen's University, Ireland. You can find out the latest news and views from him on McGladeWriting.com.

Tekla Dennison Miller is a former Michigan warden of a men's maximum security and a women's multi level prisons. She is also the author of two novels: *Life Sentences* and *Inevitable Sentences* and three memoirs: *The Warden Wore Pink, A Bowl of Cherries* and *Mother Rabbit*. She is a national speaker on criminal justice and women's issues.

Mike Miner lives and writes in Connecticut. He is the author of *Prodigal Sons* (Full Dark City Press), *The Immortal Game* (Gutter Books) and *Everything She Knows* (SolsticeLit Books). His fiction can be found in the anthologies, *Protectors: Stories to Benefit PROTECT* and *Pulp Ink 2* as well as in places like *Thuglit, All Due Respect, Beat to a Pulp, Burnt Bridge, Narrative, PANK, The Flash Fiction Offensive, Shotgun Honey* and others. His story, "The Little Outlaw" in *Plan B Magazine* was a finalist for a 2013 Derringer Award.

Kou K. Nelson is a writer, animal trainer and former teacher. Her short story *Safe Upon the Shore* was published in the anthology *Specter Spectacular: Thirteen Ghostly Tales* and made Tangent Online's Must Read List in 2013. She won Honorable Mention in the Bethlehem Writer's Roundtable Short Story Award 2013 contest and has also published in *The Again* and *Tales of Blood and Roses*.

Mike O'Reilly spends his working hours as an emergency medicine doctor in Christchurch Hospital, New Zealand. He writes crime and horror fiction for light relief. Between bouts of darwinian observation and criminal exploration he is a husband, and father to a little boy. He has previously published stories in *Criminal Class Press, Dark River Press* and *Night to Dawn*. He also hates writing in the third person.

Jeff Poole writes sporadically and has had stories accepted in the anthology *Tales of the Undead, The Undead in Pictures, Horror on the Installment Plan, Bards and Sages, The Santa Fe Reporter, Downstate Story*, and roughly a dozen other publications. His upcoming story, "Paradise for Purgatory," will be included in the anthology *To Hell With Dante*. He's a member of The Horror Writers Association.

Jed Power is a Hampton Beach, NH based writer and an "Active" member of Mystery Writers of America. His three novels in the Dan Marlowe crime series, *The Boss of Hampton Beach, Hampton Beach Homicide* and *Blood on Hampton Beach*, are now out in both e-versions and trade paper. The fourth book in the Dan Marlowe/Hampton Beach crime series is nearing completion. He also has a completed crime novel, *The Combat Zone*, about a PI who hangs his hat in 1970's

Harvard Square and spends time in the Combat Zone, Boston's red light district. He is now working on the second novel in this series and is looking for an agent/publisher.

Eryk Pruitt is a screenwriter, author and filmmaker living in Durham, NC with his wife Lana and cat Busey. His short film FOODIE won several awards at film festivals across the US. His fiction appears in *The Avalon Literary Review, Pulp Modern, Thuglit, Swill,* and *Pantheon Magazine,* to name a few. In 2013, he was a finalist for Best Short Fiction in *Short Story America.* His novel *Dirtbags* was published in April 2014 and is available in both print and e-formats. A full list of credits can be found at erykpruitt.com.

C.D. Reimer writes about the everyday reality that he finds weird, twisted and absurd for which most people accept as being perfectly normal. He lives and works in Silicon Valley, consoling hurt computers and fixing broken users.

Stephen D. Rogers is the award-winning author of *Shot to Death, Three-Minute Mysteries,* and more than 800 shorter works. His website http://www.stephendrogers.com/ includes a list of new and upcoming titles as well as other timely information.

Wayne Scheer has been nominated for four Pushcart Prizes and a Best of the Net. He's published numerous stories, poems and essays in print and online, including *Revealing Moments,* a collection of flash stories. Wayne can be contacted at wvscheer@aol.com.

Tom Swoffer's stories have appeared in print in *The Storyteller* and *Detective Mystery Stories,* online at *Mysterical-e* and *Pine Tree Mysteries,* podcast on *Nil Desperandum* and in the anthology *Pulp 2011/Twit Pub.*

Dan Stout lives in Columbus, Ohio where he writes about the things which terrify and inspire him. His fiction draws on his travels throughout Europe, Asia, and the Pacific Rim, as well as an employment history which spans everything from subpoena server to assistant well driller. In his free time, he tries to convince himself that time spent playing match-3 games is somehow educational.

Lavie Tidhar is the World Fantasy Award winning author of *Osama* (2011), and of *The Violent Century* (2013) in addition to many other works and several awards. He works across genres, combining detective and thriller modes with poetry, science fiction and historical and autobiographical material. His work has been compared to that of Philip K. Dick by the *Guardian* and the *Financial Times*, and to Kurt Vonnegut's by *Locus*.

Elaine Togneri is a member of Mystery Writers of America and Sisters in Crime. She has sold over 30 short stories, most recently to *Woman's World* and the MWA Anthology *The Rich and the Dead*.

J. M. Vogel is from Columbus, OH and is setting out to show the world that a degree in English does not predestine you to life in the unemployment line. For more information about her work, check out her blog at http://jmvogel.blogspot.com/.

Tom Ward is a British writer who was recently named the recipient of the GQ Norman Mailer Student Writing Award 2012. His winning piece will be published in the June issue of *British GQ*, and he is a contributor to *Vice* and *Sabotage Times*. His first novel, *A Departure*, was published by Crooked Cat in spring 2013.

Daniel Marshall Wood leads a double life (legally) as an identical twin and as an innkeeper and executive assistant in New York. He cranks out short stories (mostly mysteries) on the side, published on several online sites and in *Woman's World* magazine. Dan has also written a mystery play.

Richard Zwicker is an English teacher living with his wife in Vermont, USA. His short stories have appeared recently in *Penumbra*, *Fantasy Scroll Mag*, *Perihelion Science Fiction* and other semi-pro markets.

Copyrights

Made in the USA
Middletown, DE
26 March 2021

36258698R00321